the girl from the sea

MOLLY KNOX OSTERTAG

COLOR BY MAARTA LAIHO

graphix

An Imprint of
■ SCHOLASTIC

For my parents and the home they
made on Wilneff Island.

And for Noelle, who came into my life
like a storm from the sea.

All rights reserved. Published by Graphix, an imprint of Scholastic Inc.,
Publishers since 1920. SCHOLASTIC, GRAPHIX, and associated logos
are trademarks and/or registered trademarks of Scholastic Inc.

The publisher does not have any control over and does not assume any
responsibility for author or third-party websites or their content.

Library of Congress Control Number Available

ISBN 978-1-338-54058-1 (hardcover)
ISBN 978-1-338-54057-4 (paperback)

10 9 8 7 6 5 4 3   22 23 24 25

Printed in China   62
First edition, June 2021
Edited by Amanda Maciel
Lettering by Molly Knox Ostertag
Color by Maarta Laiho
Book design by Molly Knox Ostertag and Shivana Sookdeo
Creative Director: Phil Falco
Publisher: David Saylor

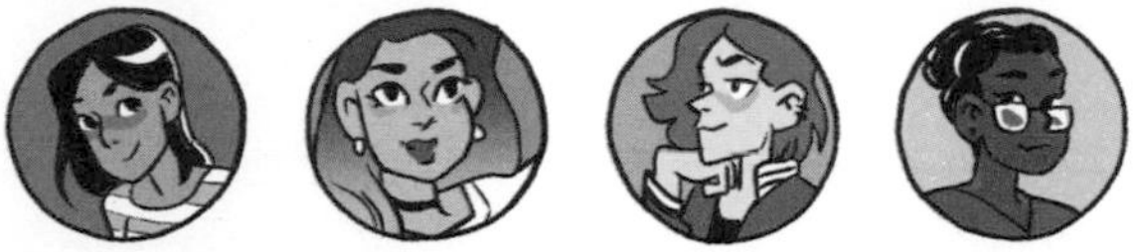

Morgan Serena Jules Lizzie

Tue, June 11, 9:04 PM

ok ladies

now that summer vacation has officially begun...meet me in town tomorrow

it's a ✨surprise✨

i'm THERE

we have been cleaning grandma's house for a week and

i'm

so

I have to work 😿

bored

when?

LIZ NO

12-8

ok so meet at like 10! at figgys

morgan you in?

MORGANNN

creepy ghost whisper morgan...

Morgan Serena Jules Lizzie

9:34 PM

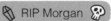 that's it she's dead

🪦 RIP Morgan 💀

 NO don't be horrible!!

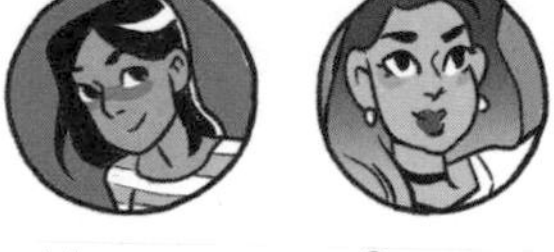

Morgan Serena

Tue, June 11, 9:42 PM

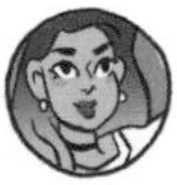

we're meeting at figgys tomorrow at 10!

you okay?

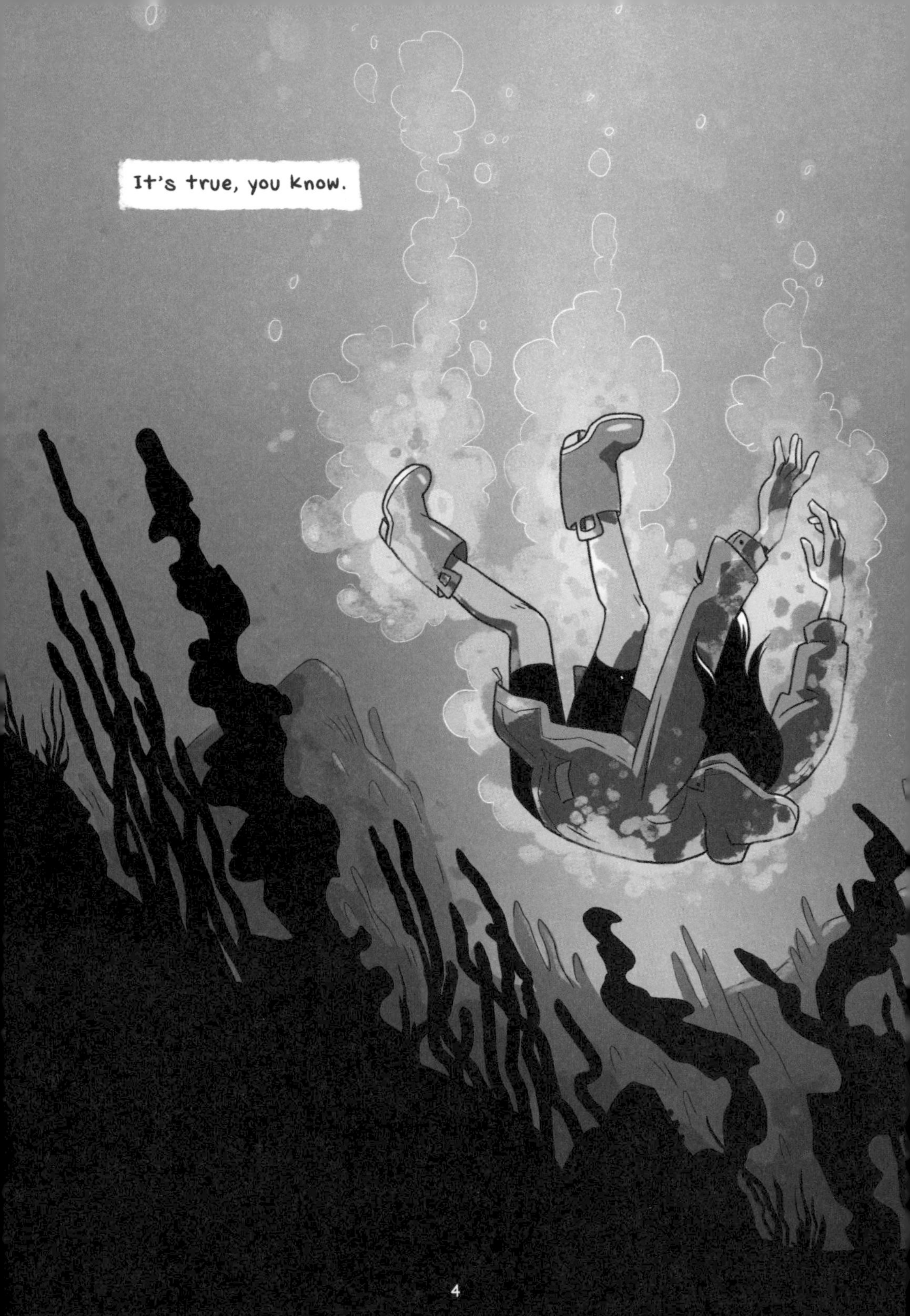
It's true, you know.

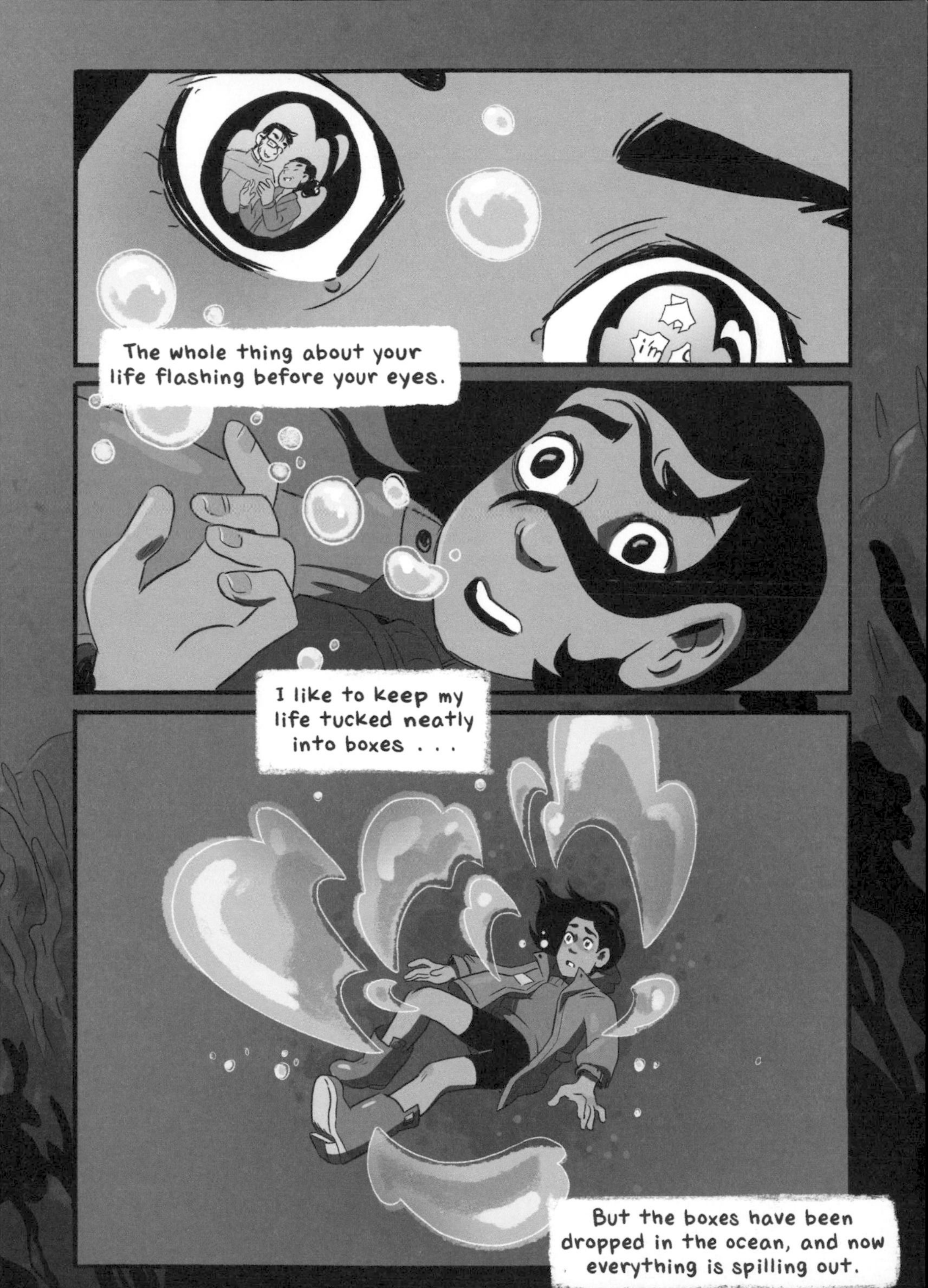
The whole thing about your life flashing before your eyes.
I like to keep my life tucked neatly into boxes . . .
But the boxes have been dropped in the ocean, and now everything is spilling out.

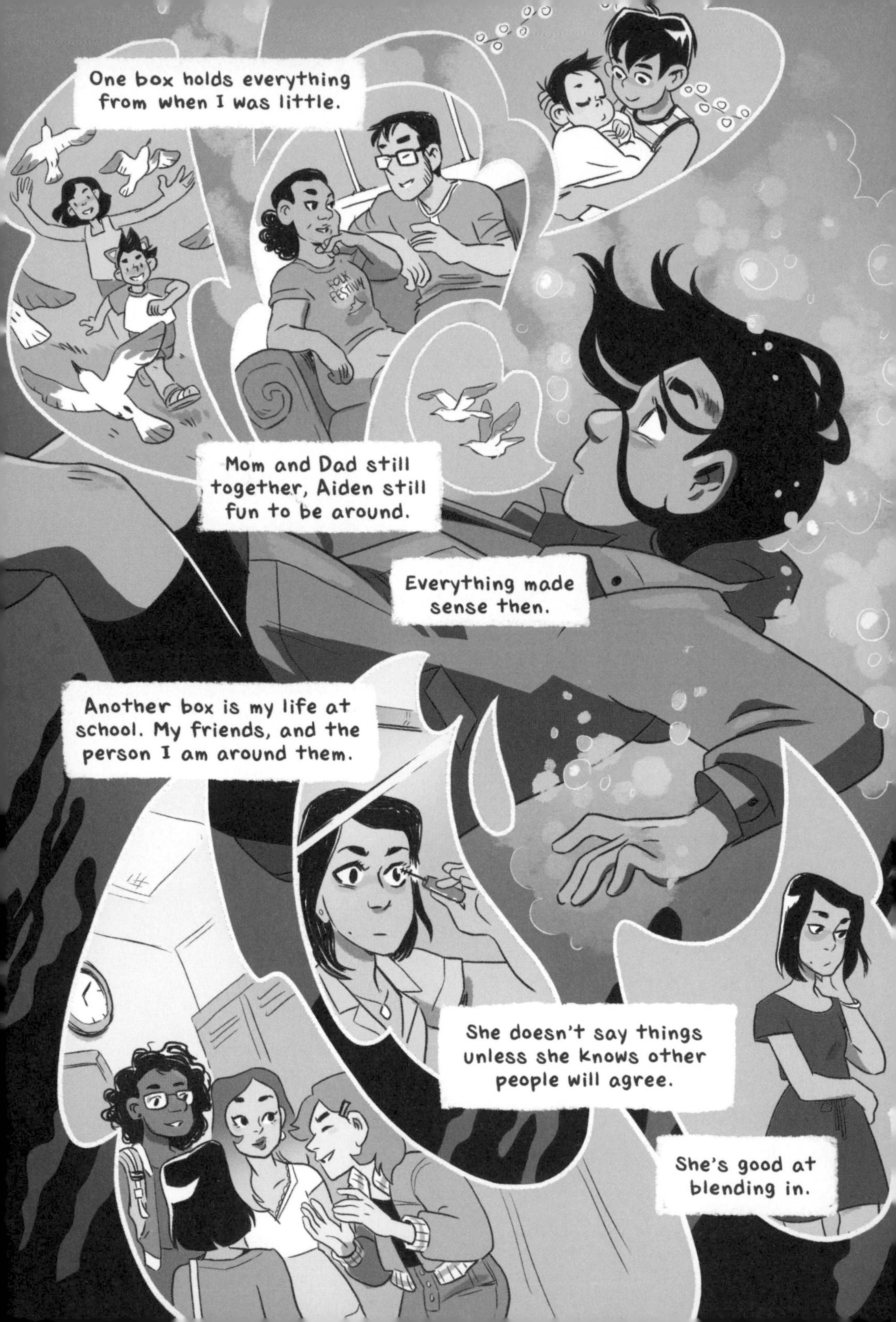
One box holds everything from when I was little.
FOLK FESTIVAL
Mom and Dad still together, Aiden still fun to be around.
Everything made sense then.
Another box is my life at school. My friends, and the person I am around them.
She doesn't say things unless she knows other people will agree.
She's good at blending in.

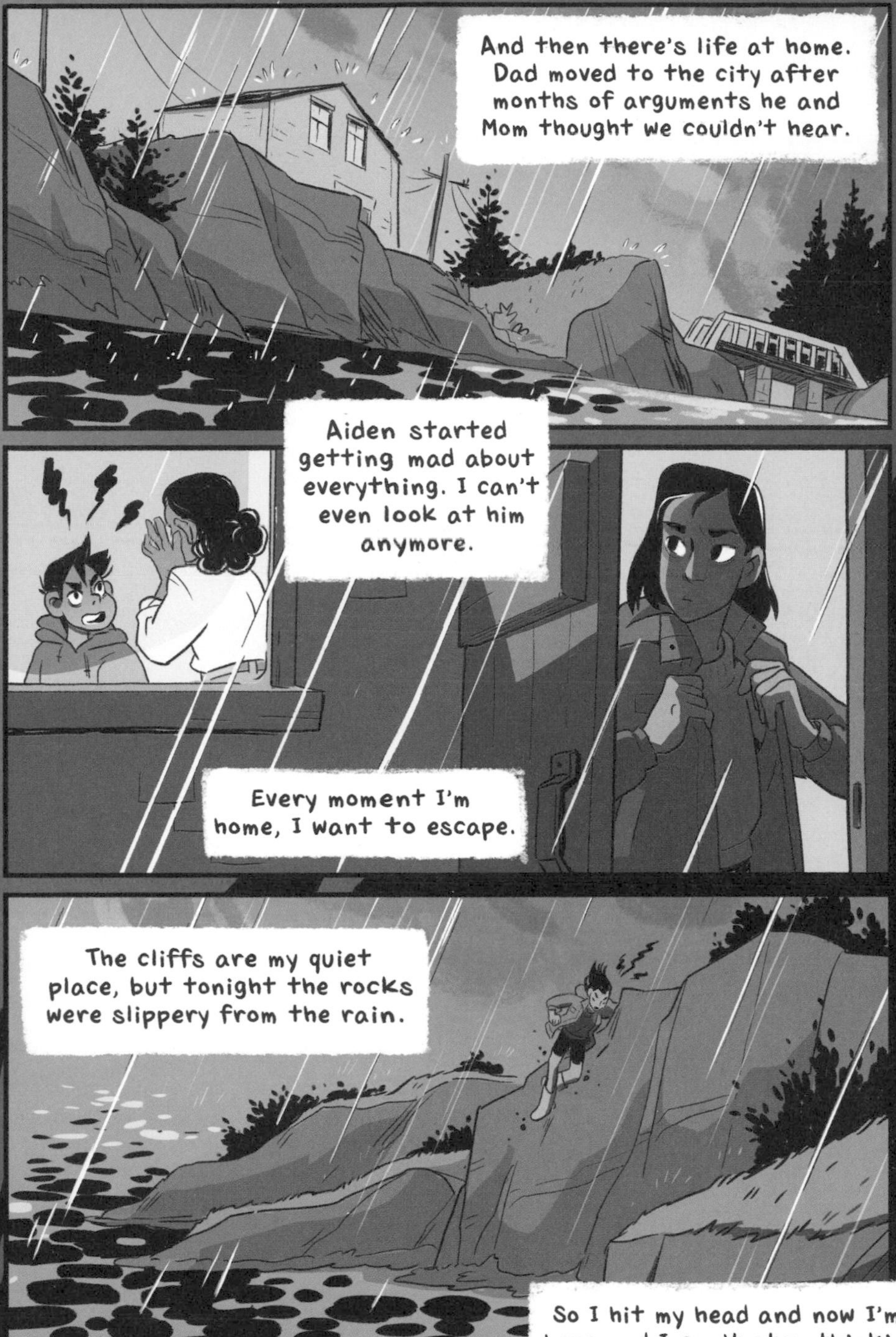
And then there's life at home. Dad moved to the city after months of arguments he and Mom thought we couldn't hear.
Aiden started getting mad about everything. I can't even look at him anymore.
Every moment I'm home, I want to escape.
The cliffs are my quiet place, but tonight the rocks were slippery from the rain.
So I hit my head and now I'm here and I can't stop thinking of the last, secret box . . .

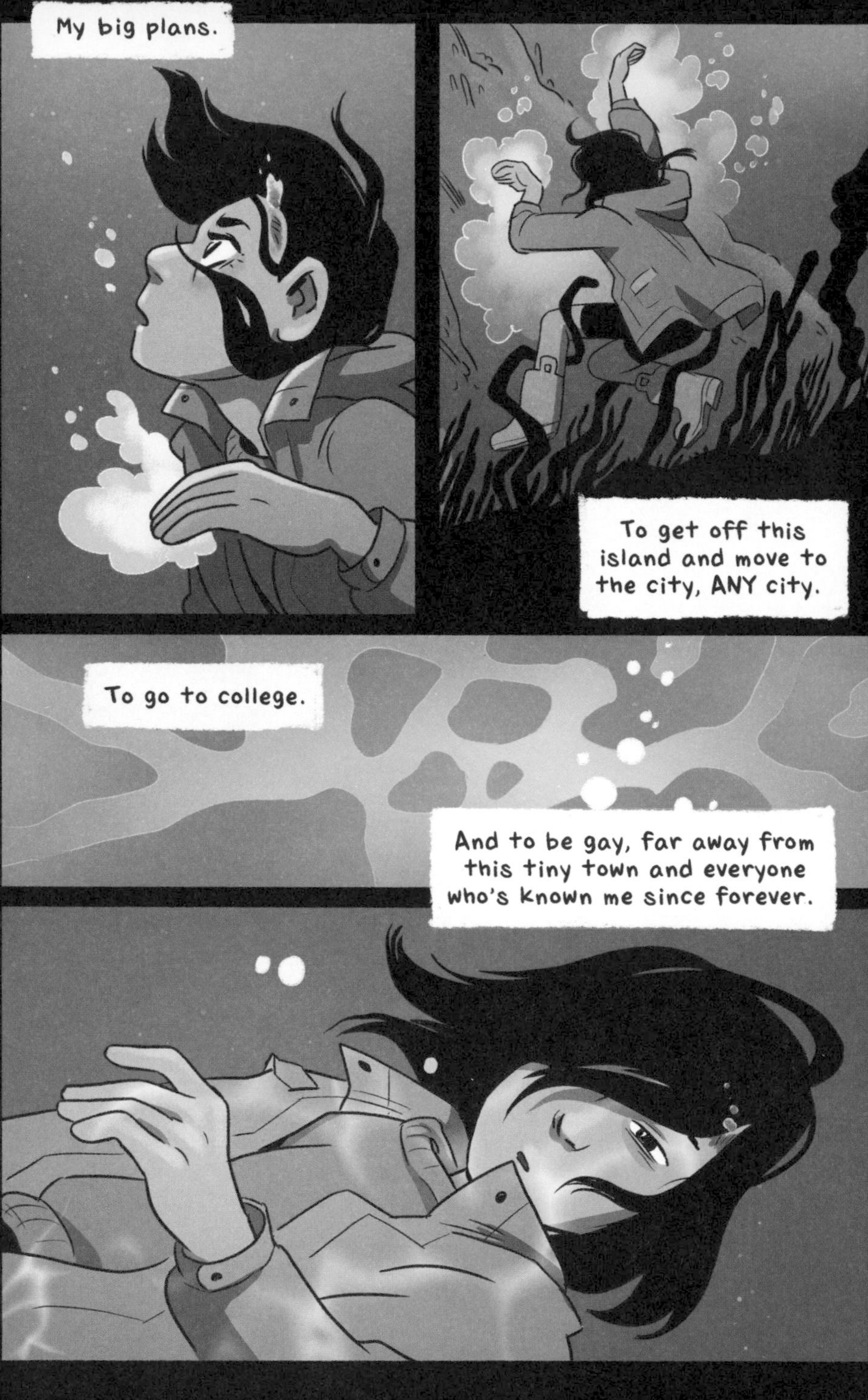
My big plans.
To get off this island and move to the city, ANY city.
To go to college.
And to be gay, far away from this tiny town and everyone who's known me since forever.

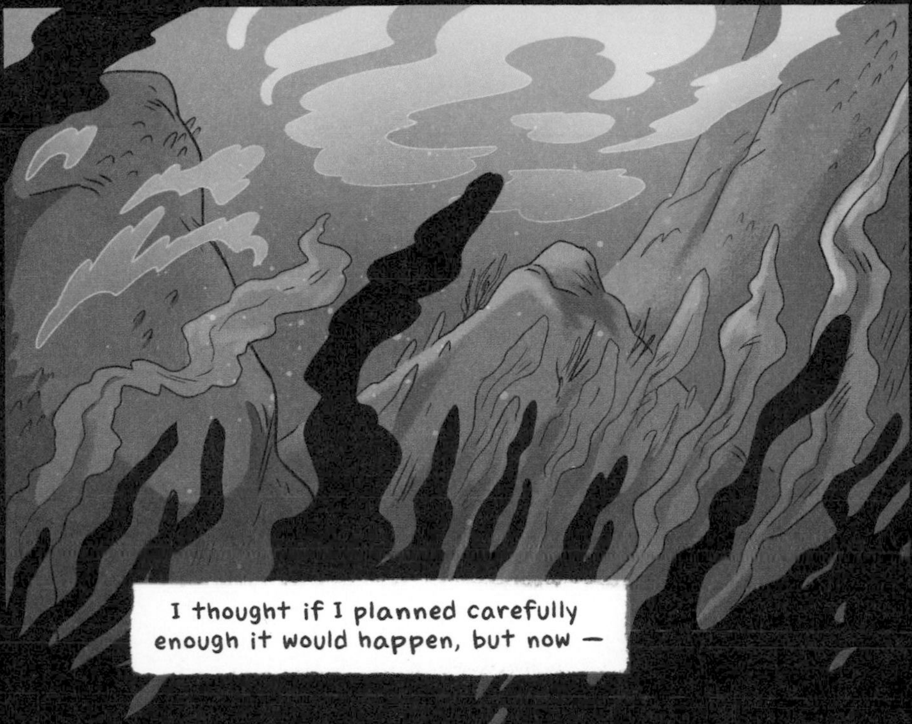
I thought if I planned carefully enough it would happen, but now —

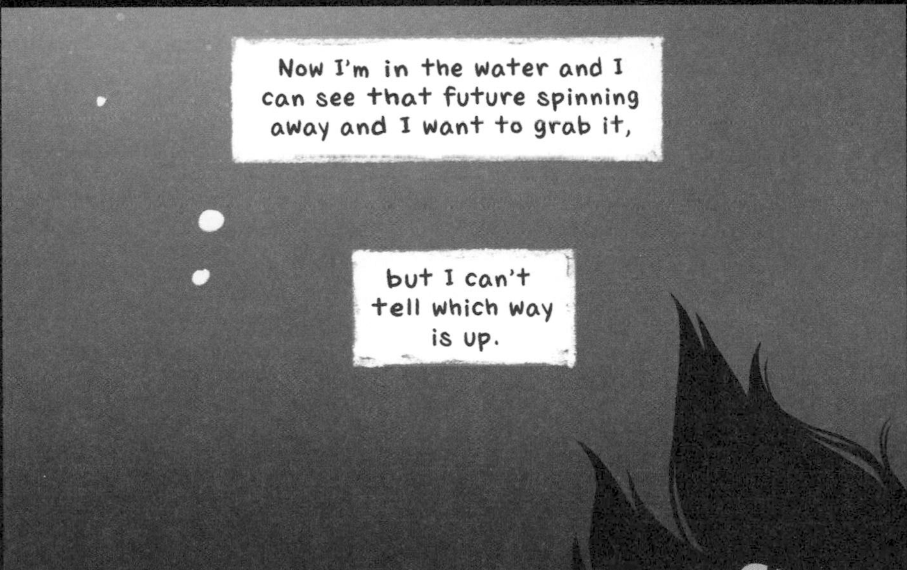
Now I'm in the water and I can see that future spinning away and I want to grab it,
but I can't tell which way is up.

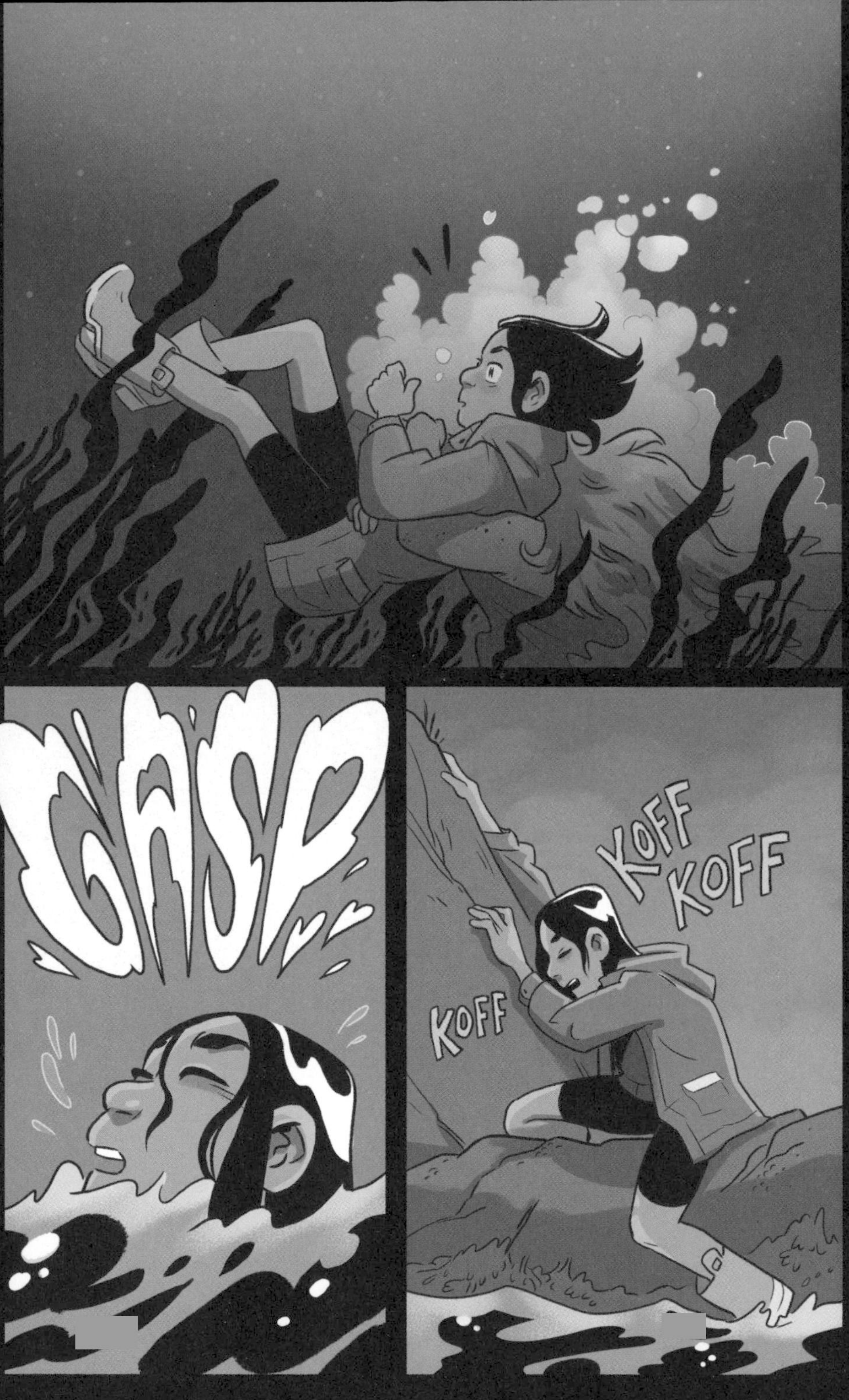
GASP
KOFF
KOFF
KOFF

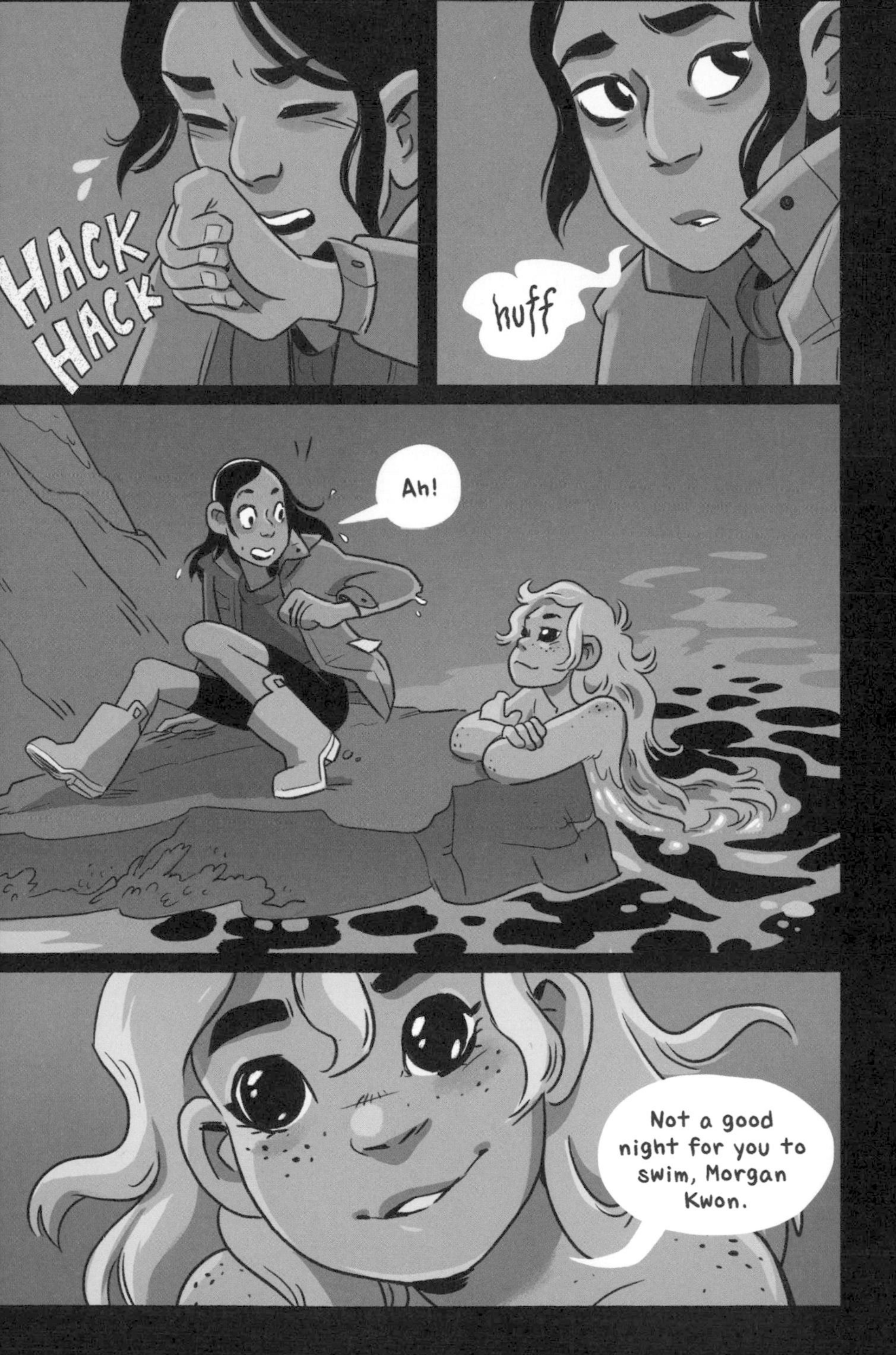
HACK HACK
huff
Ah!
Not a good night for you to swim, Morgan Kwon.

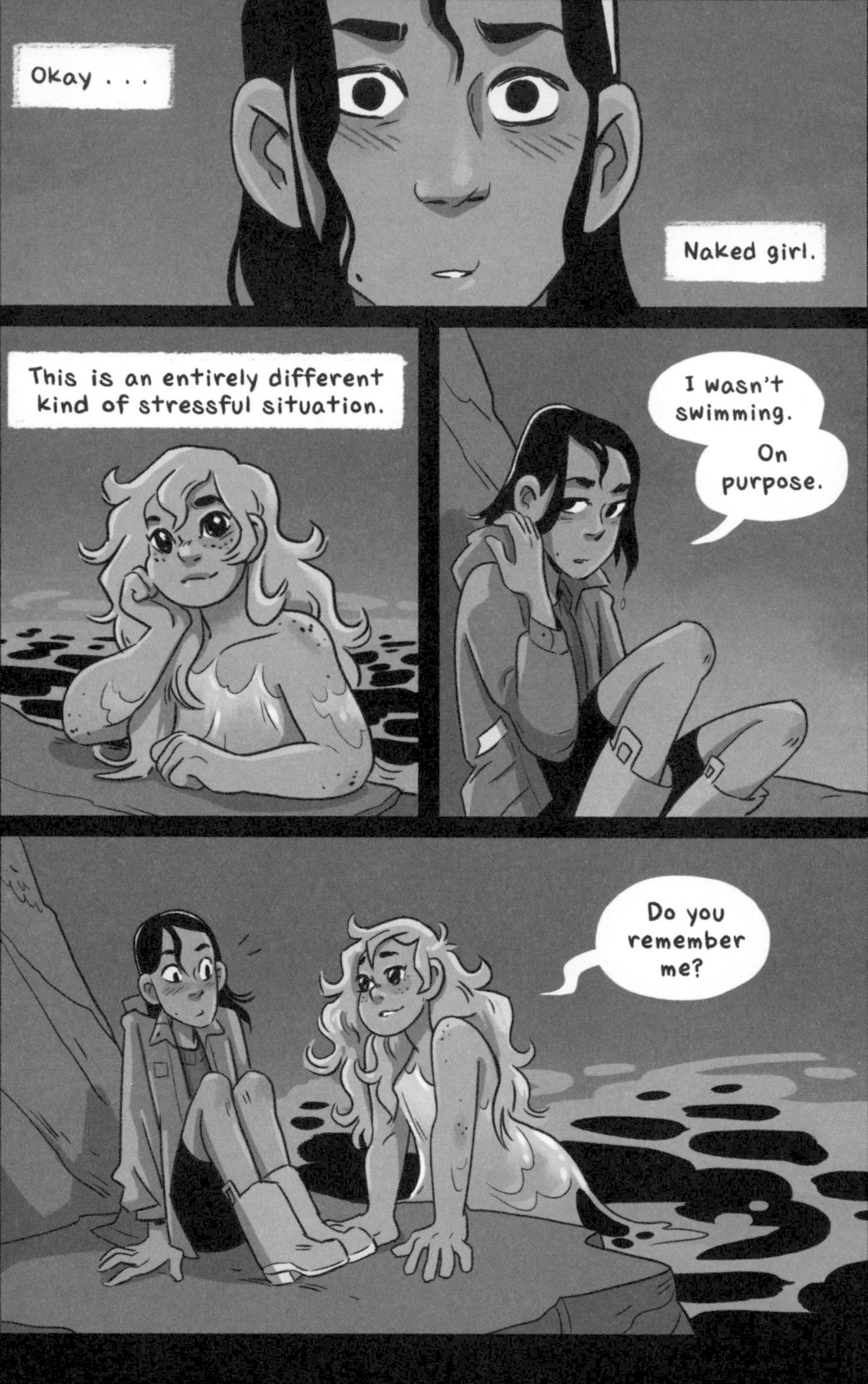
Okay . . .
Naked girl.
This is an entirely different kind of stressful situation.
I wasn't swimming.
On purpose.
Do you remember me?

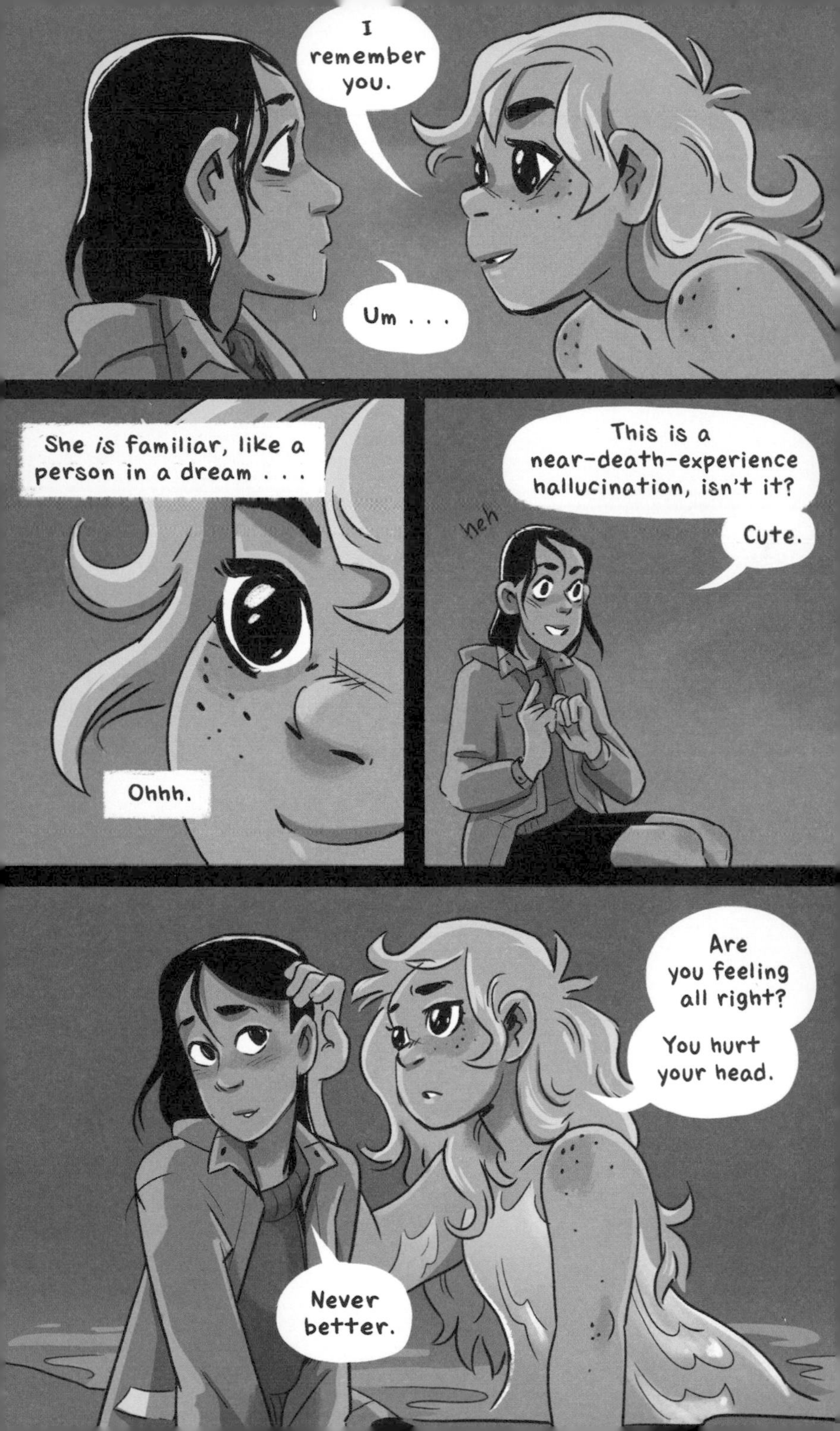

I remember you.
Um . . .
She *is* familiar, like a person in a dream . . .
Ohhh.
This is a near-death-experience hallucination, isn't it?
heh
Cute.
Are you feeling all right?
You hurt your head.
Never better.

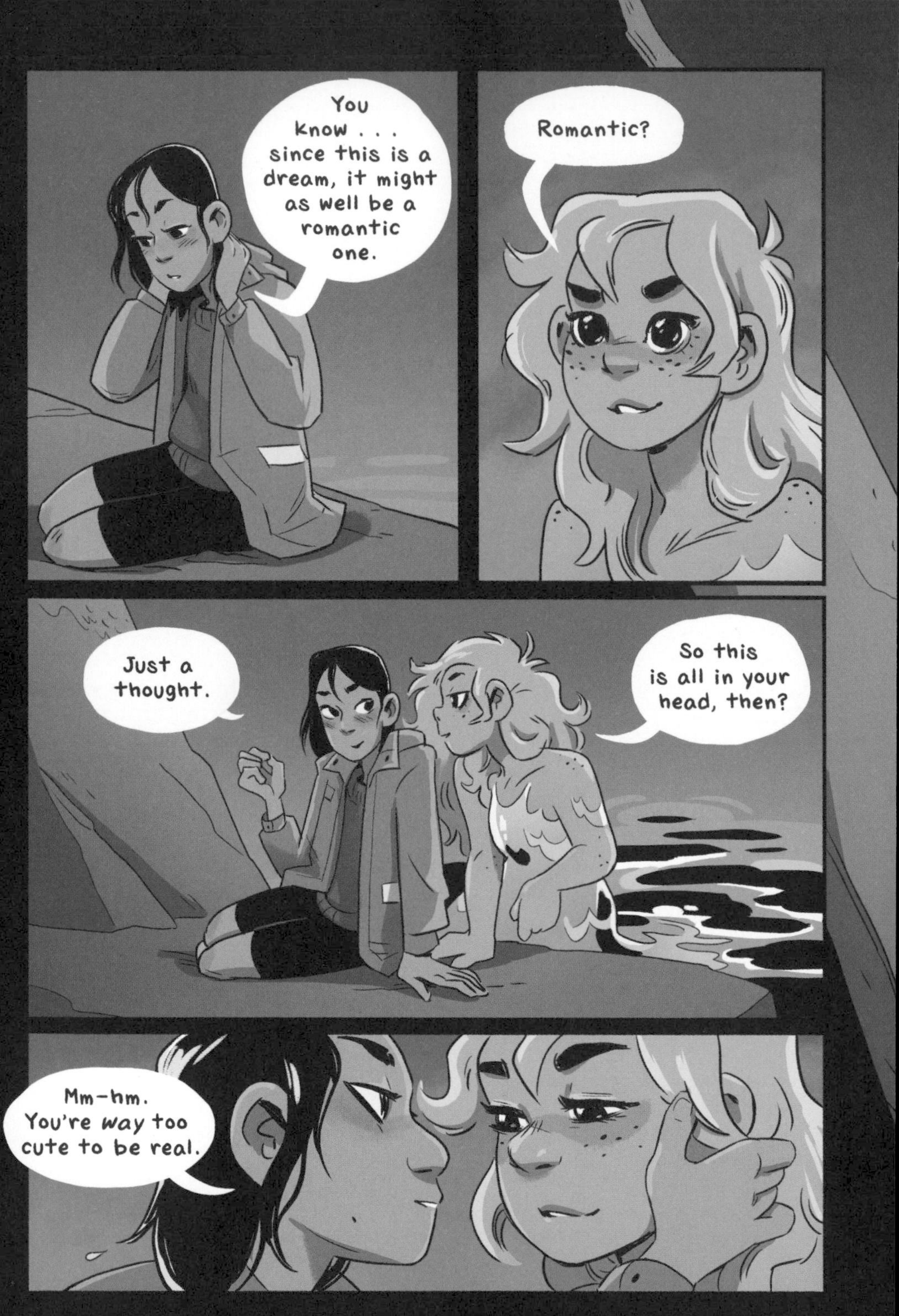
You know . . . since this is a dream, it might as well be a romantic one.
Romantic?
Just a thought.
So this is all in your head, then?
Mm-hm. You're *way* too cute to be real.

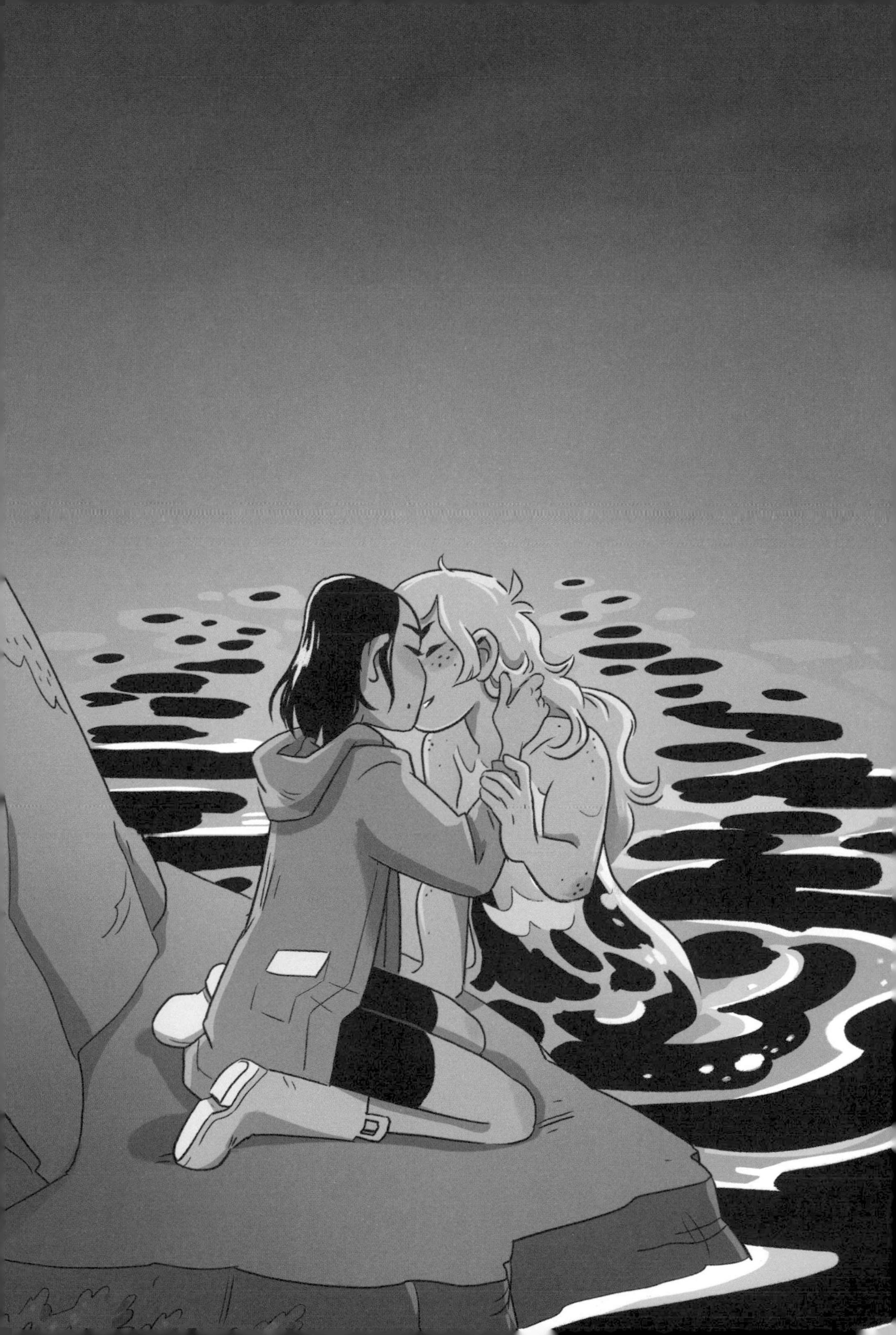

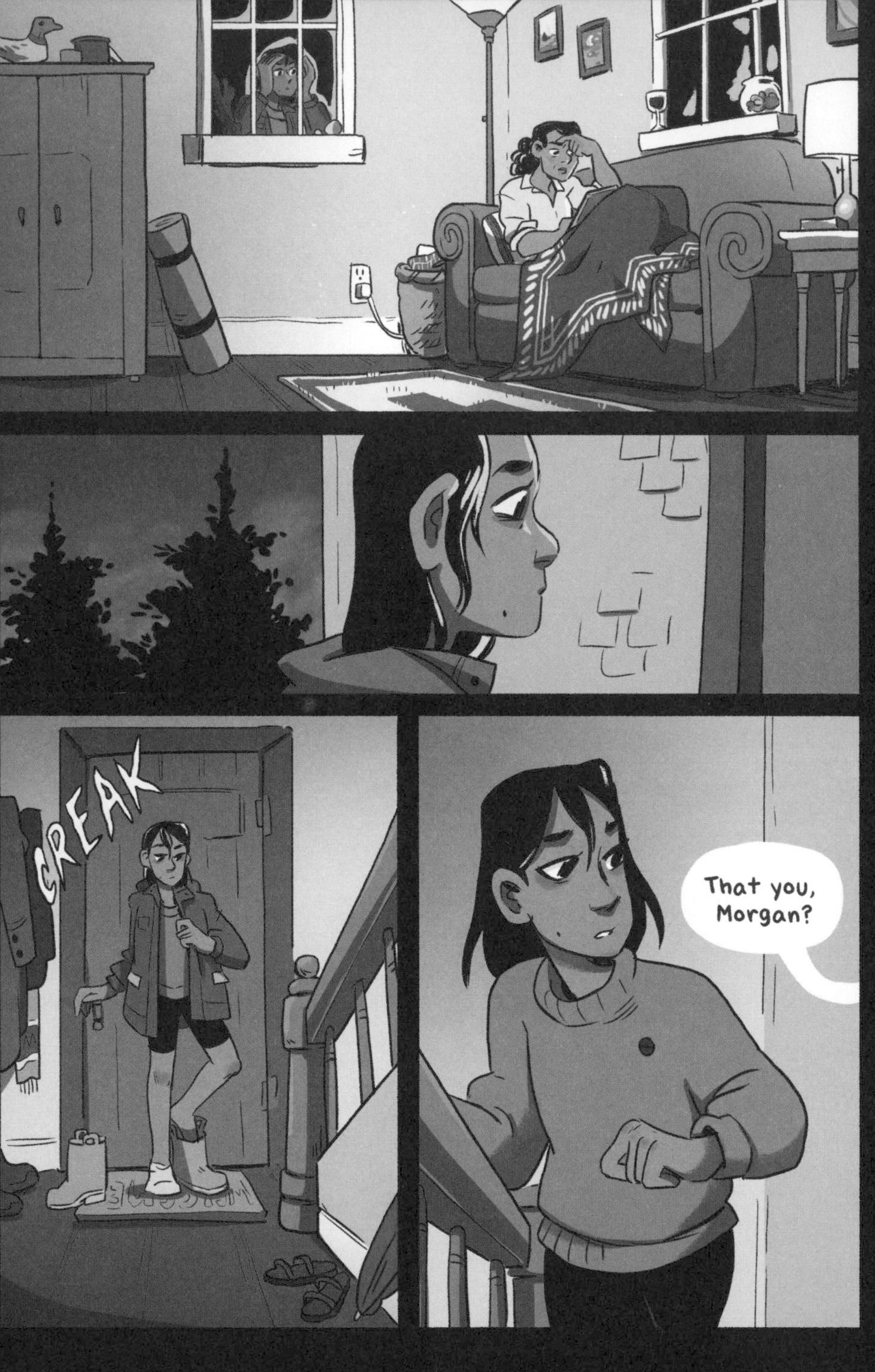
CREAK
That you, Morgan?

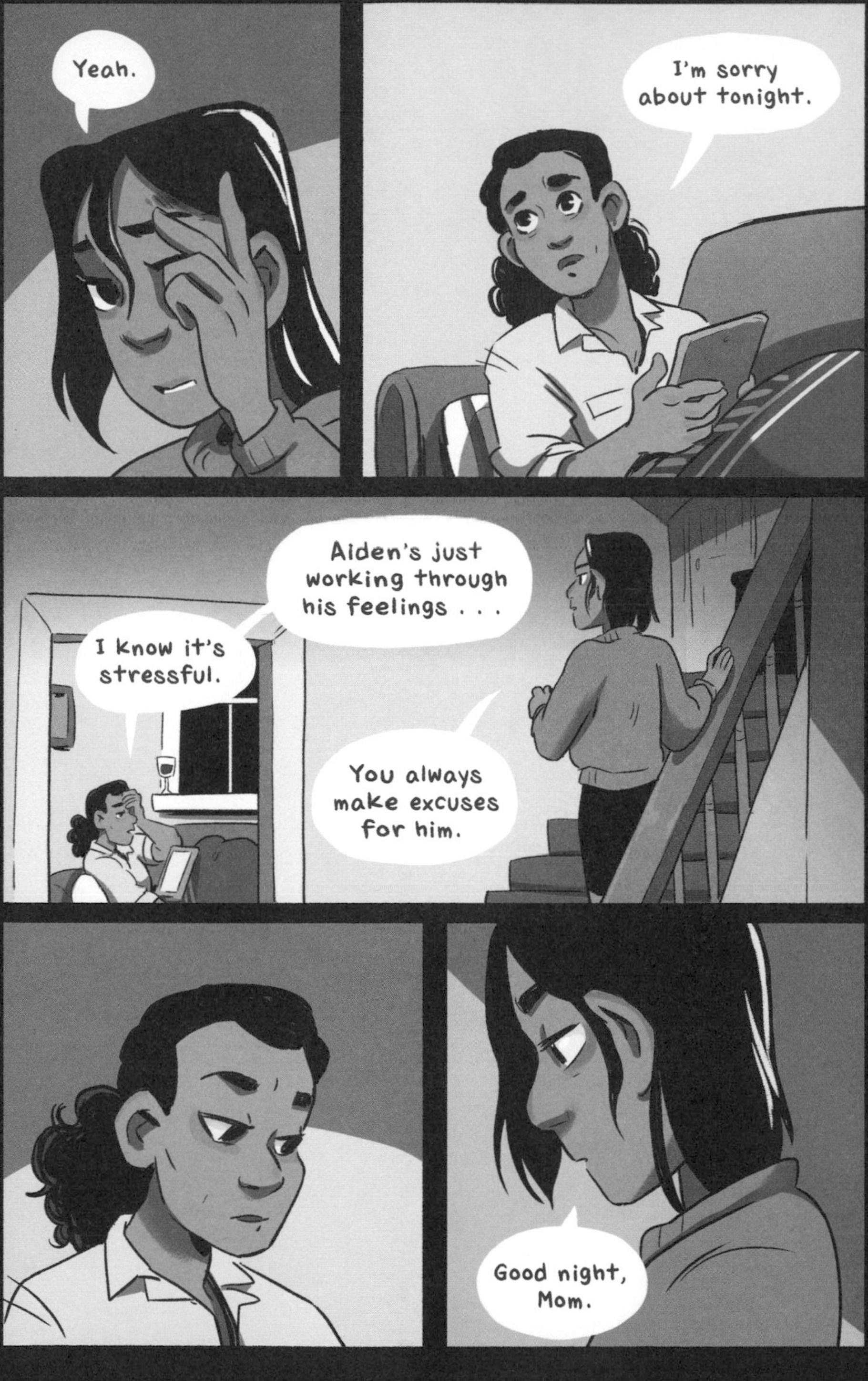
Yeah.
I'm sorry about tonight.
Aiden's just working through his feelings . . .
I know it's stressful.
You always make excuses for him.
Good night, Mom.

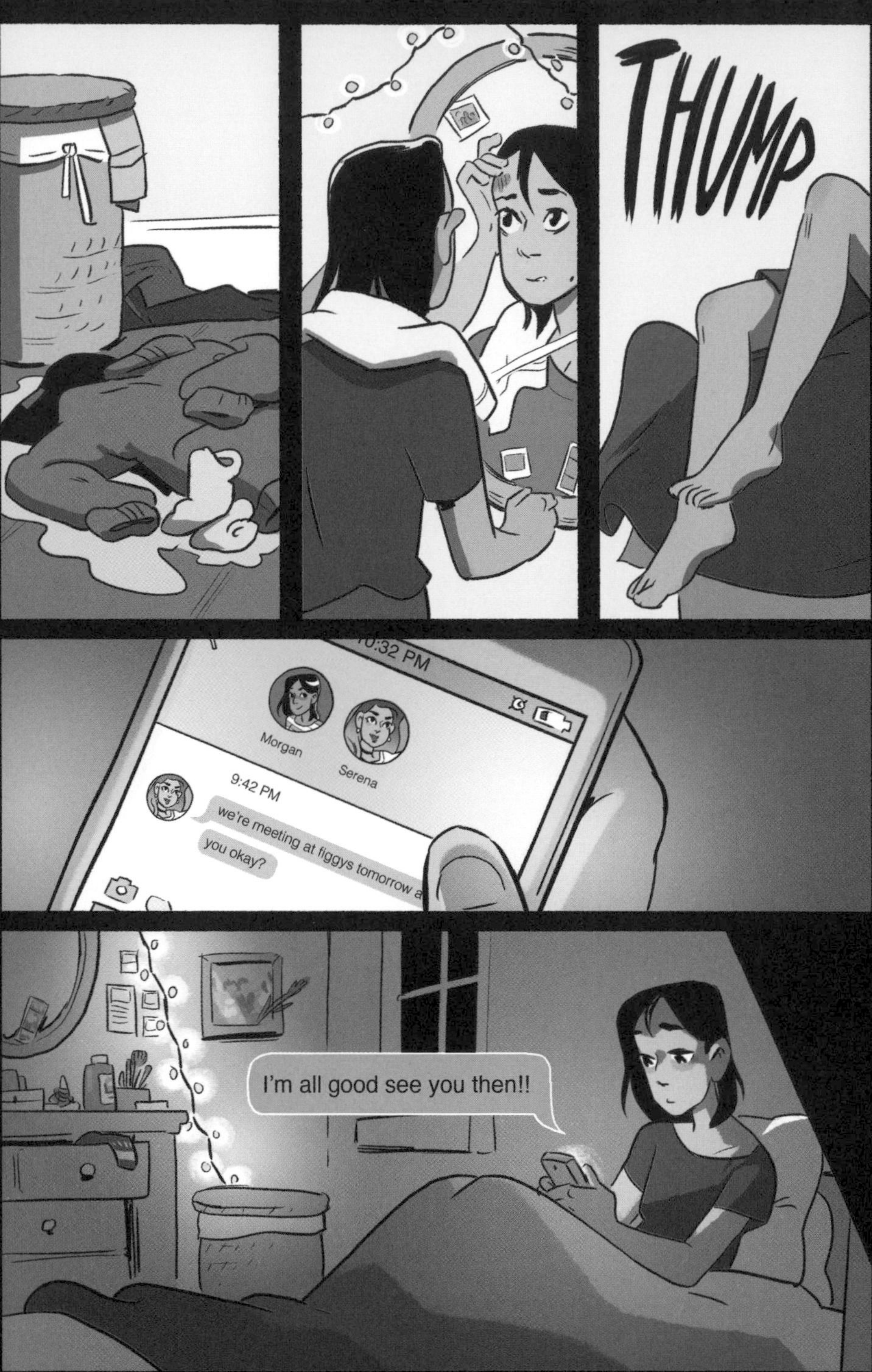
THUMP
0:32 PM
Morgan
Serena
9:42 PM
we're meeting at figgys tomorrow a
you okay?
I'm all good see you then!!

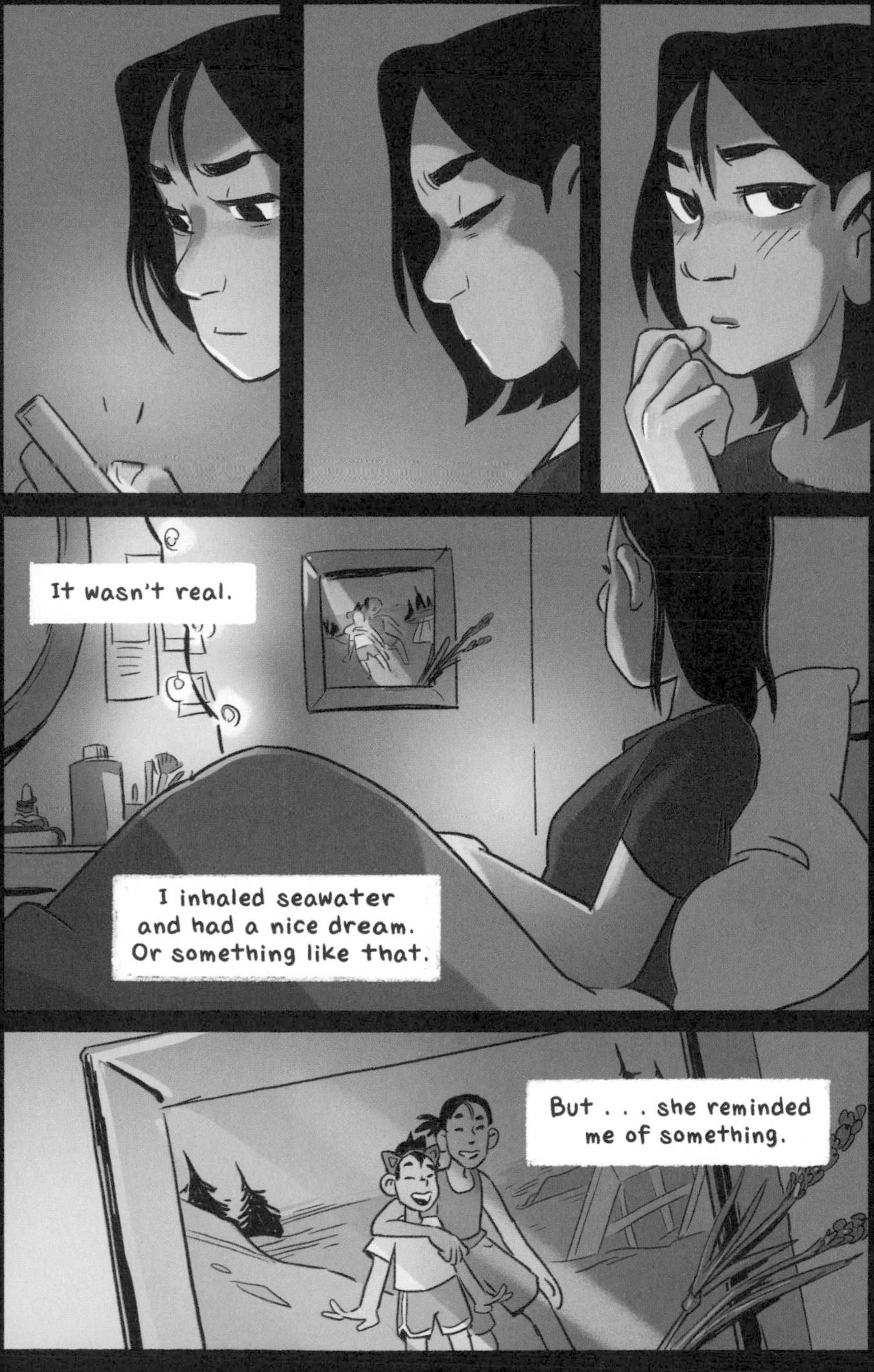

It wasn't real.
I inhaled seawater and had a nice dream. Or something like that.
But . . . she reminded me of something.

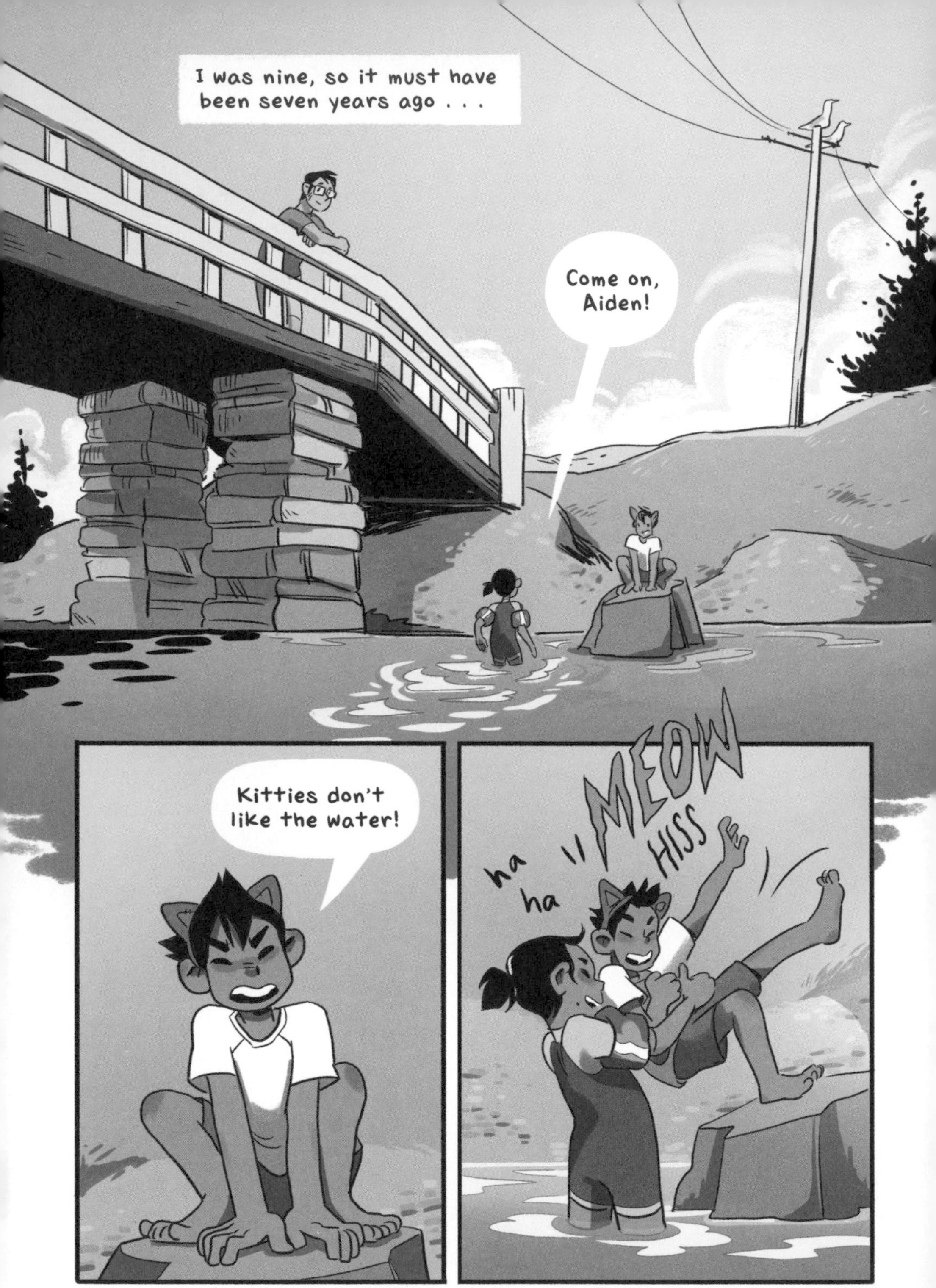
I was nine, so it must have been seven years ago . . .
Come on, Aiden!
Kitties don't like the water!
MEOW
HISS
ha ha

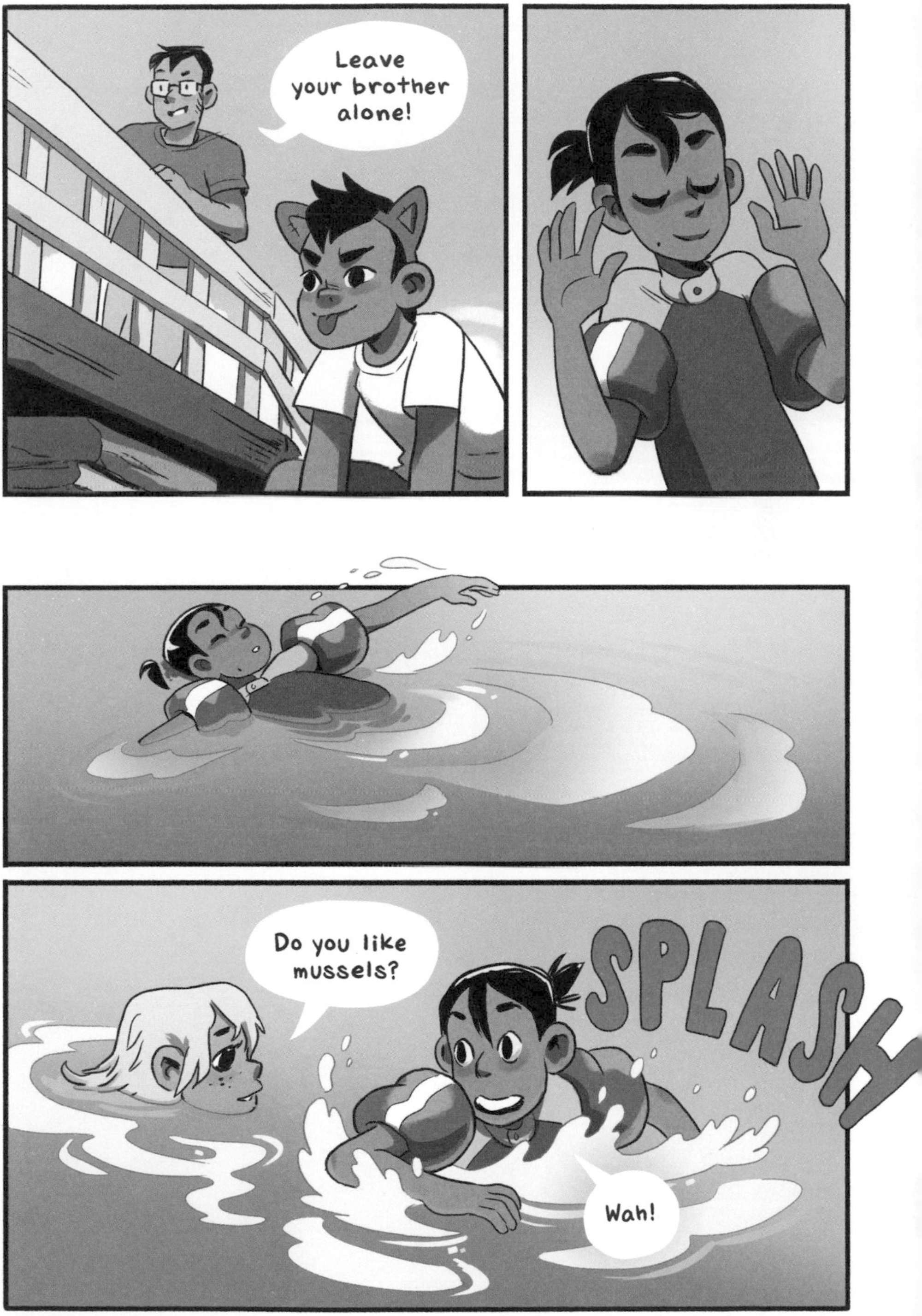
Leave your brother alone!
Do you like mussels?
SPLASH
Wah!

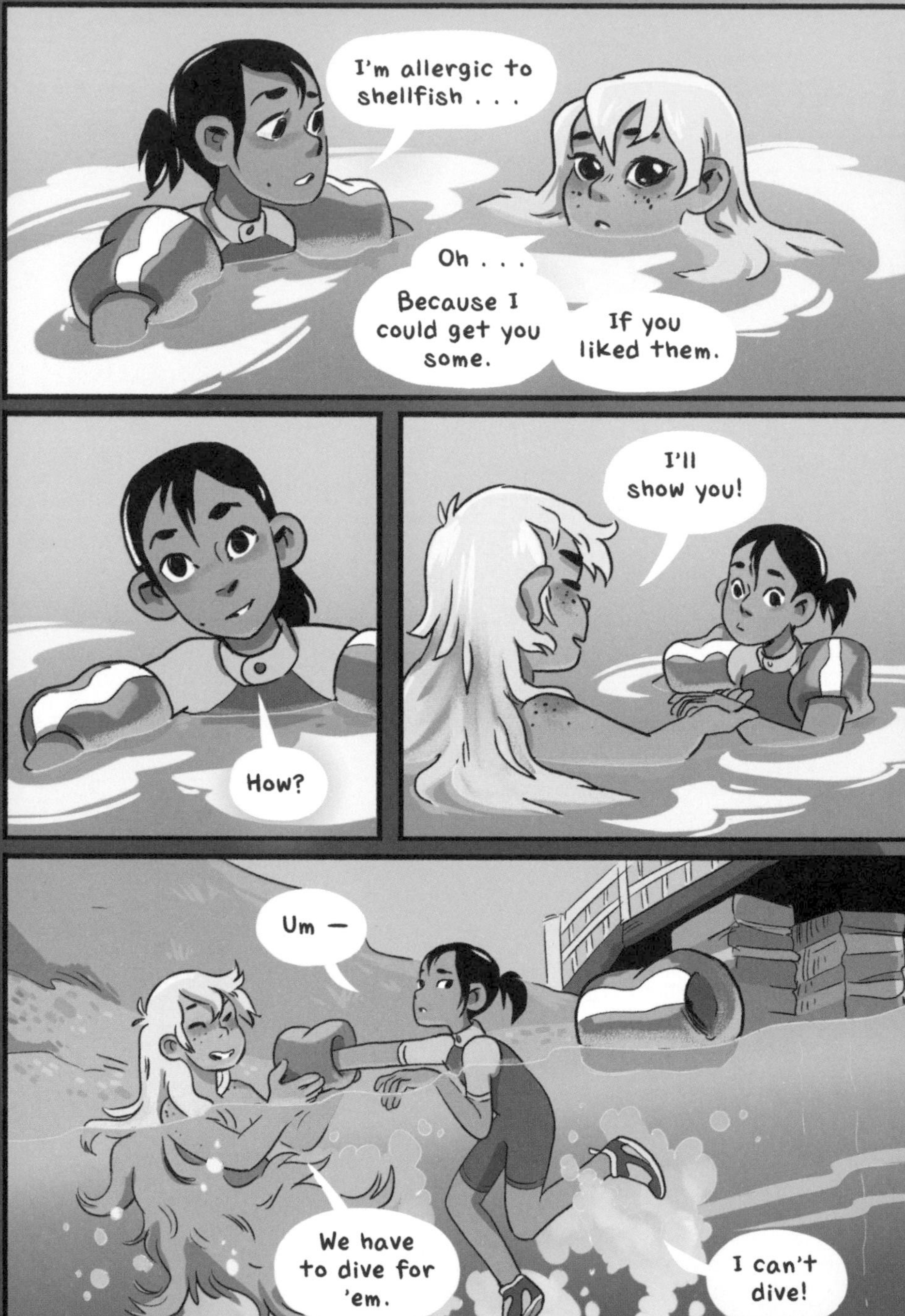
I'm allergic to shellfish . . .
Oh . . .
Because I could get you some.
If you liked them.
How?
I'll show you!
Um —
We have to dive for 'em.
I can't dive!

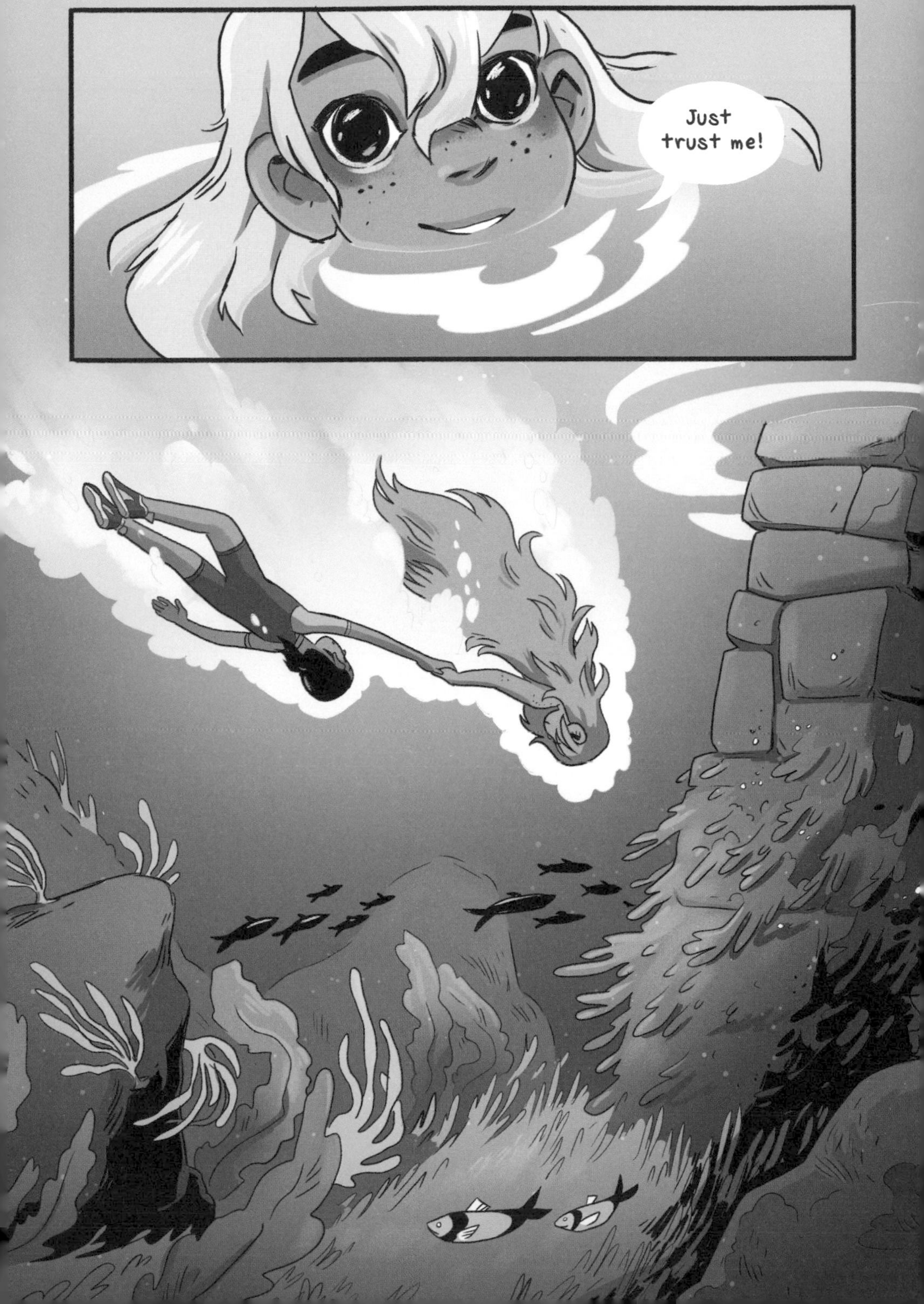
Just trust me!

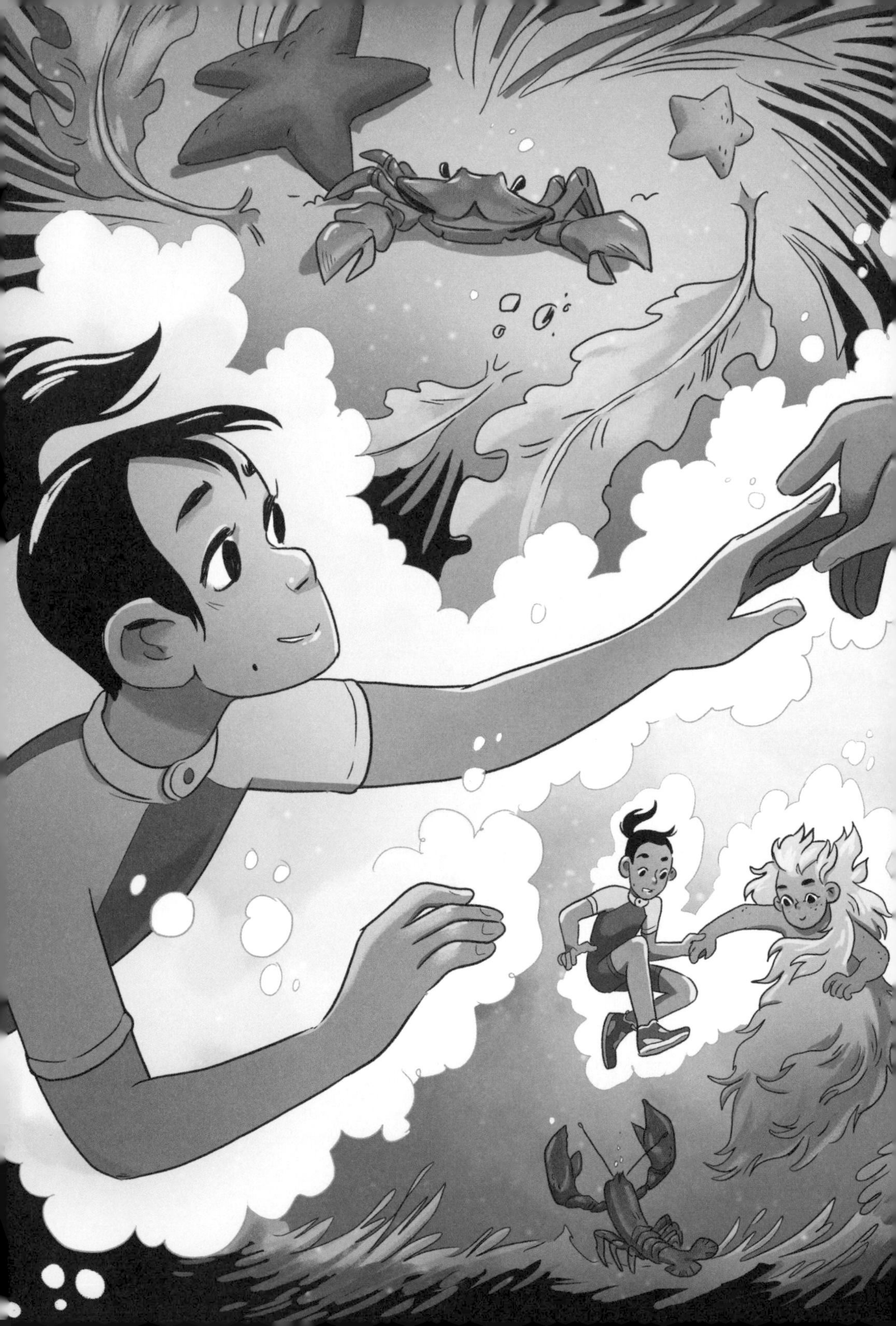

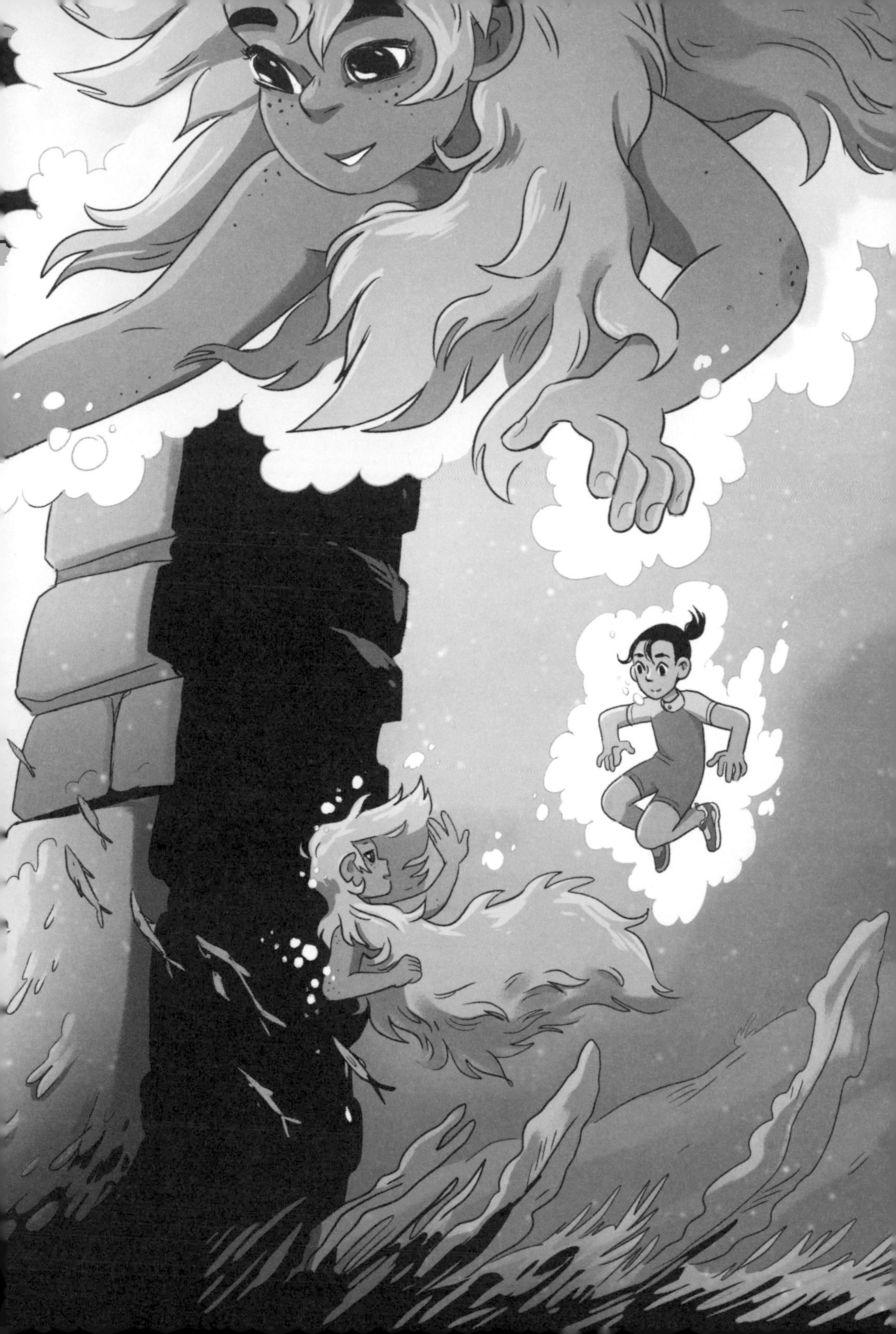

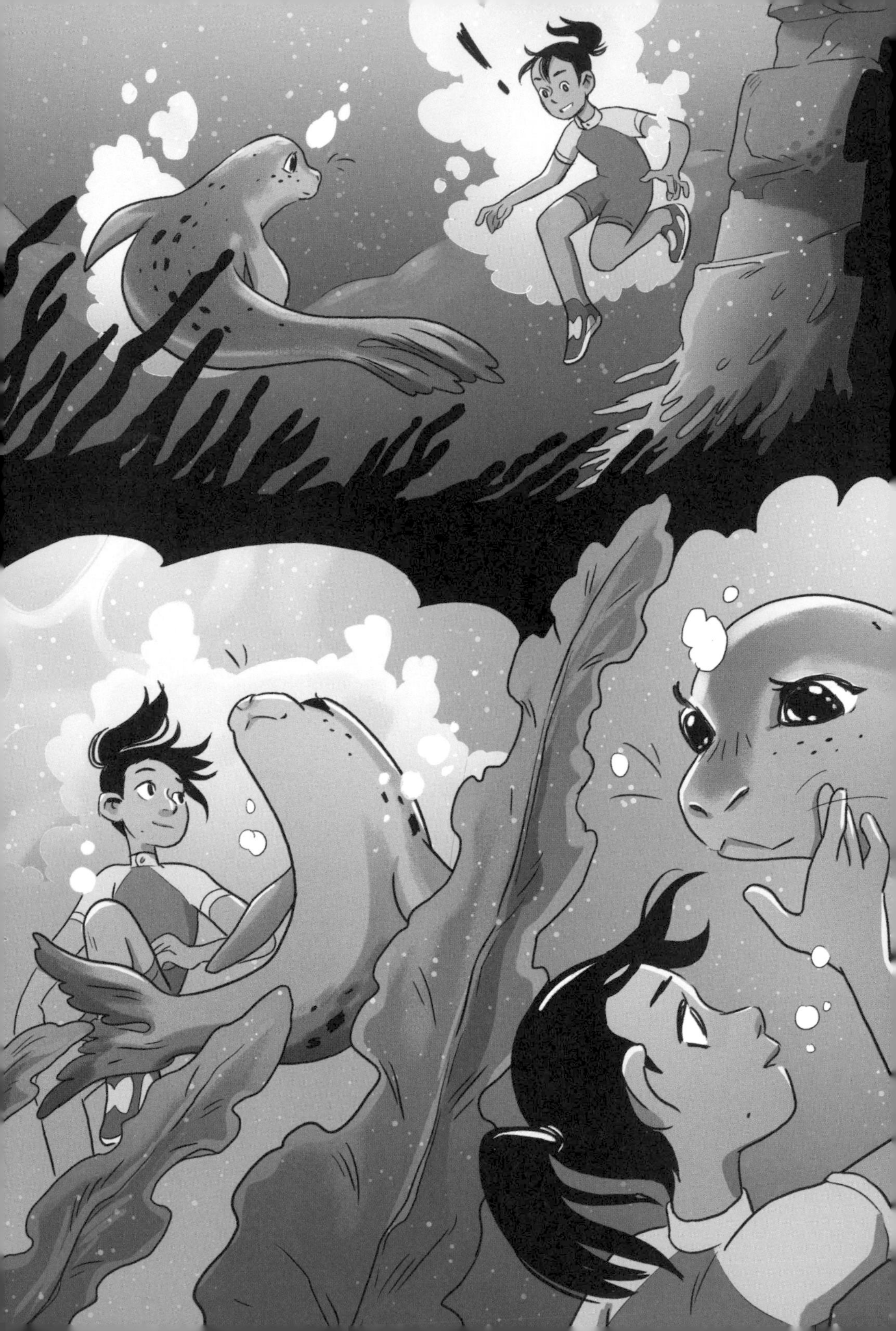
!

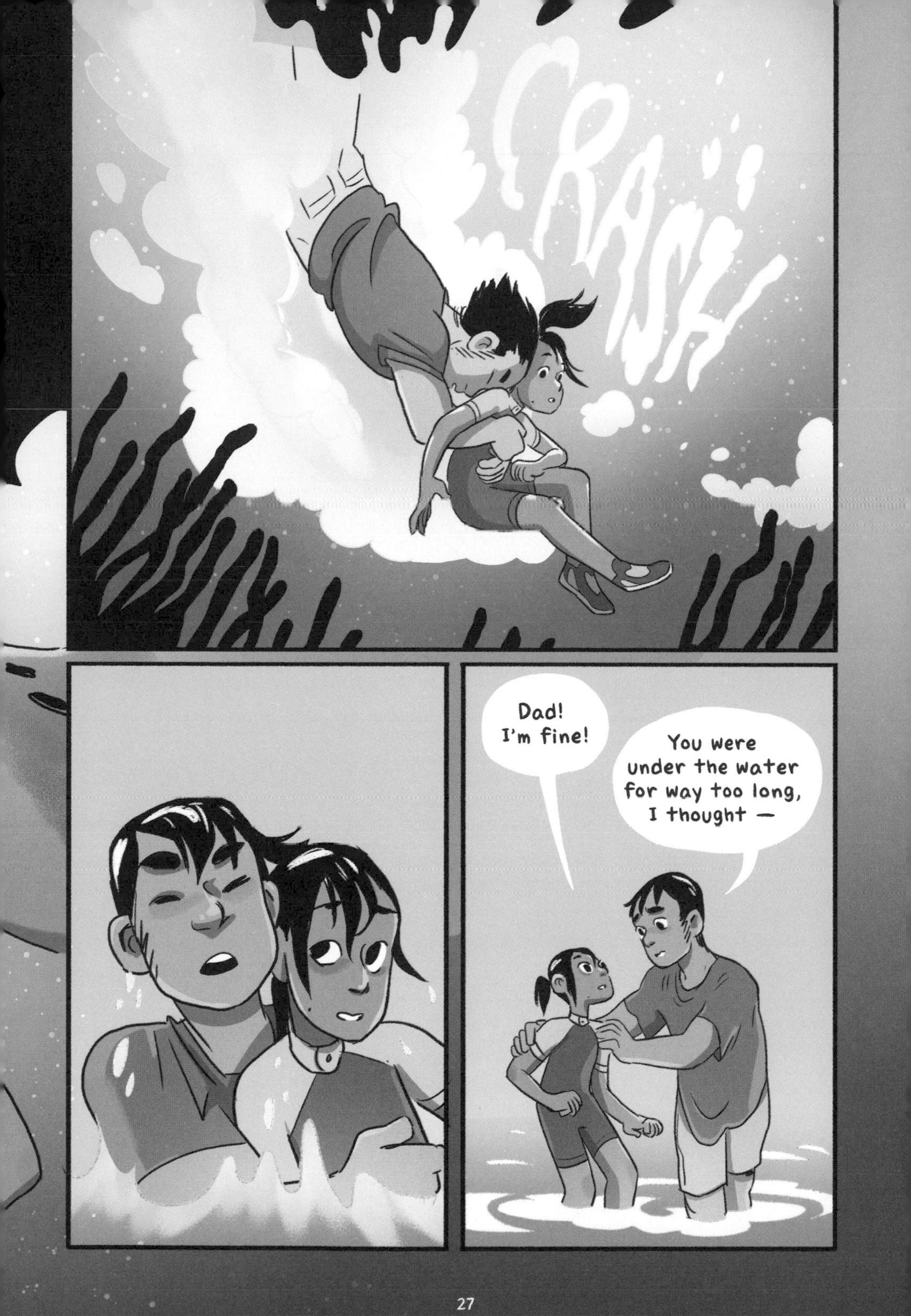
CRASH
Dad! I'm fine!
You were under the water for way too long, I thought —

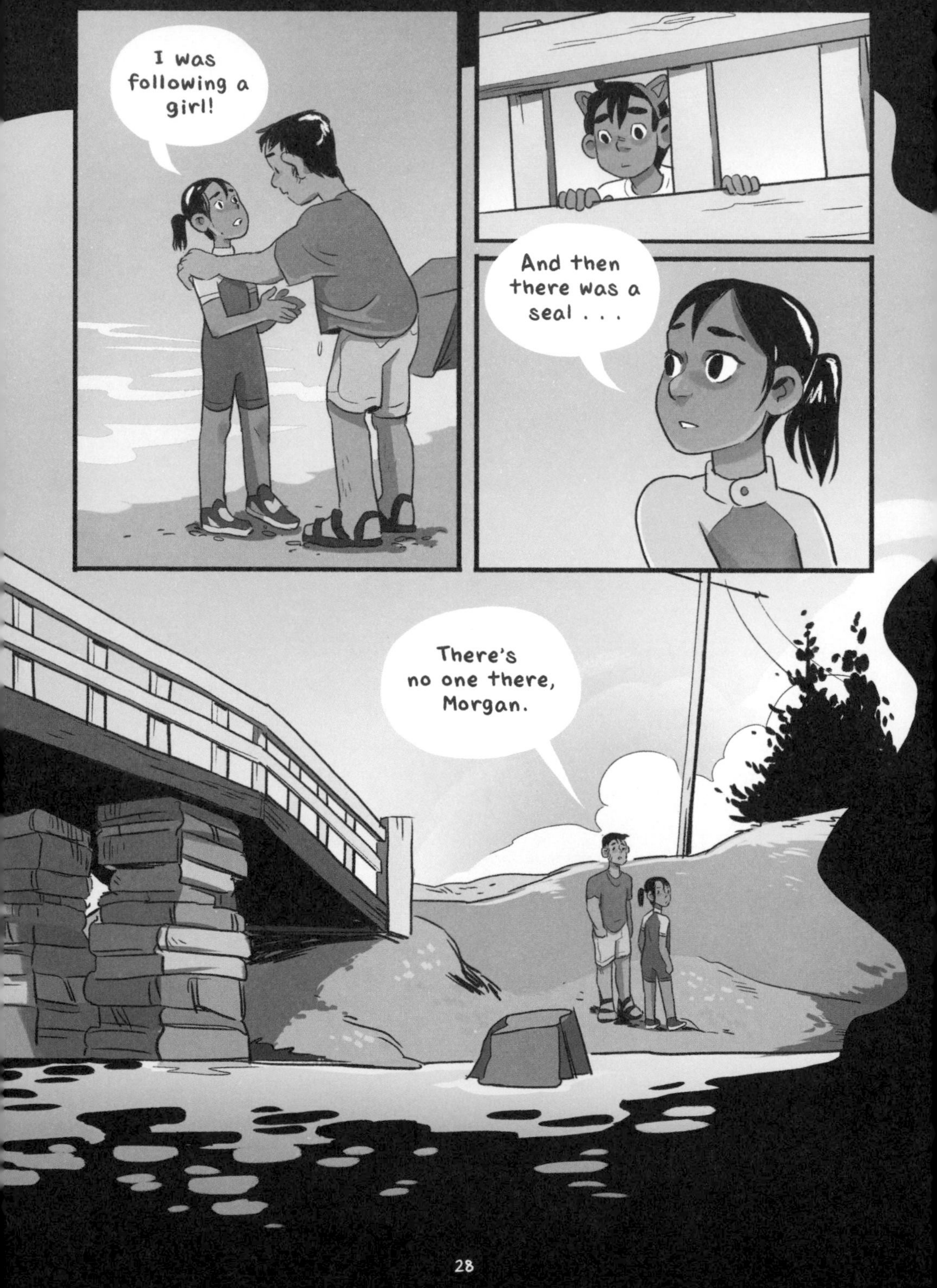
I was following a girl!
And then there was a seal . . .
There's no one there, Morgan.

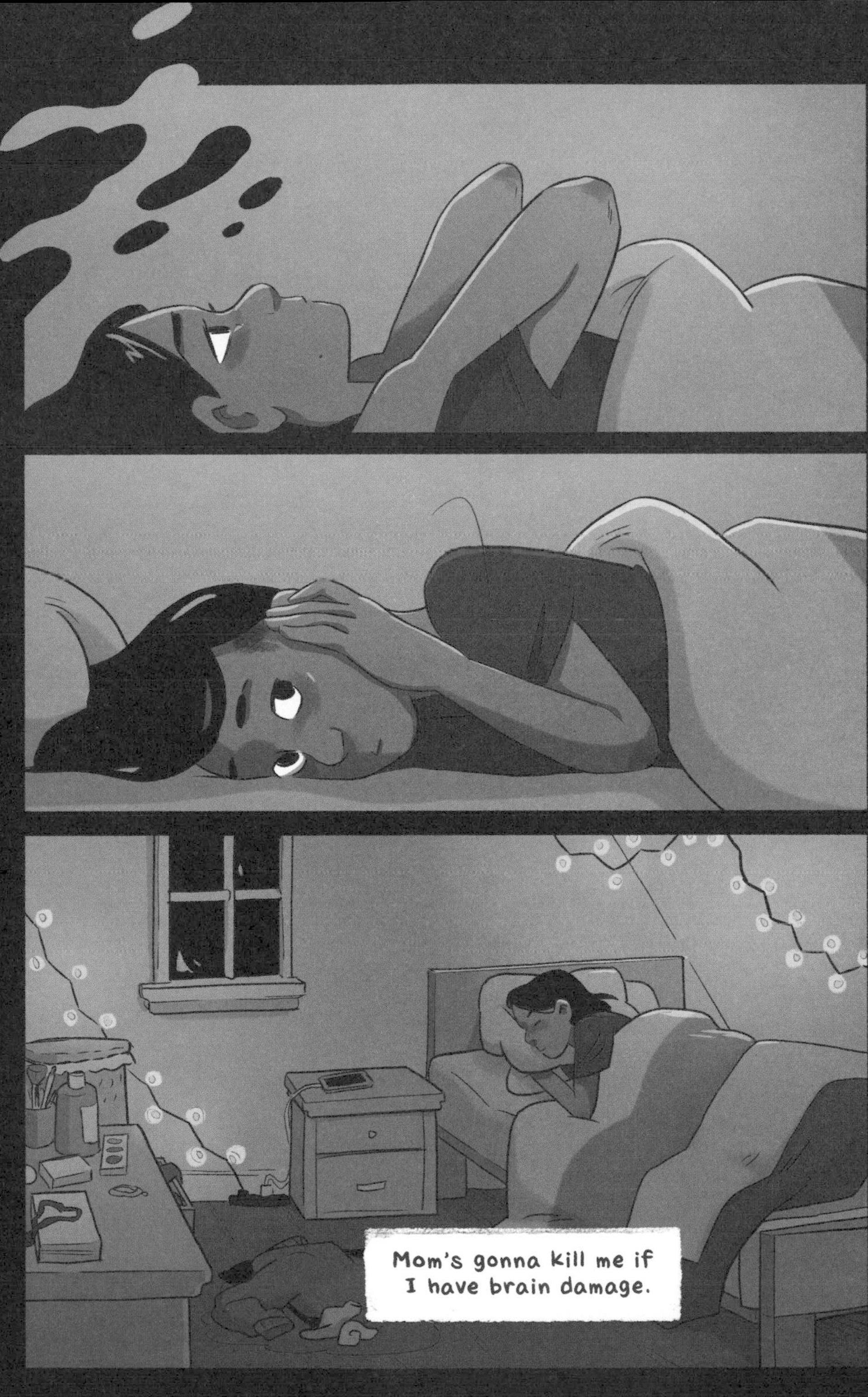
Mom's gonna kill me if I have brain damage.

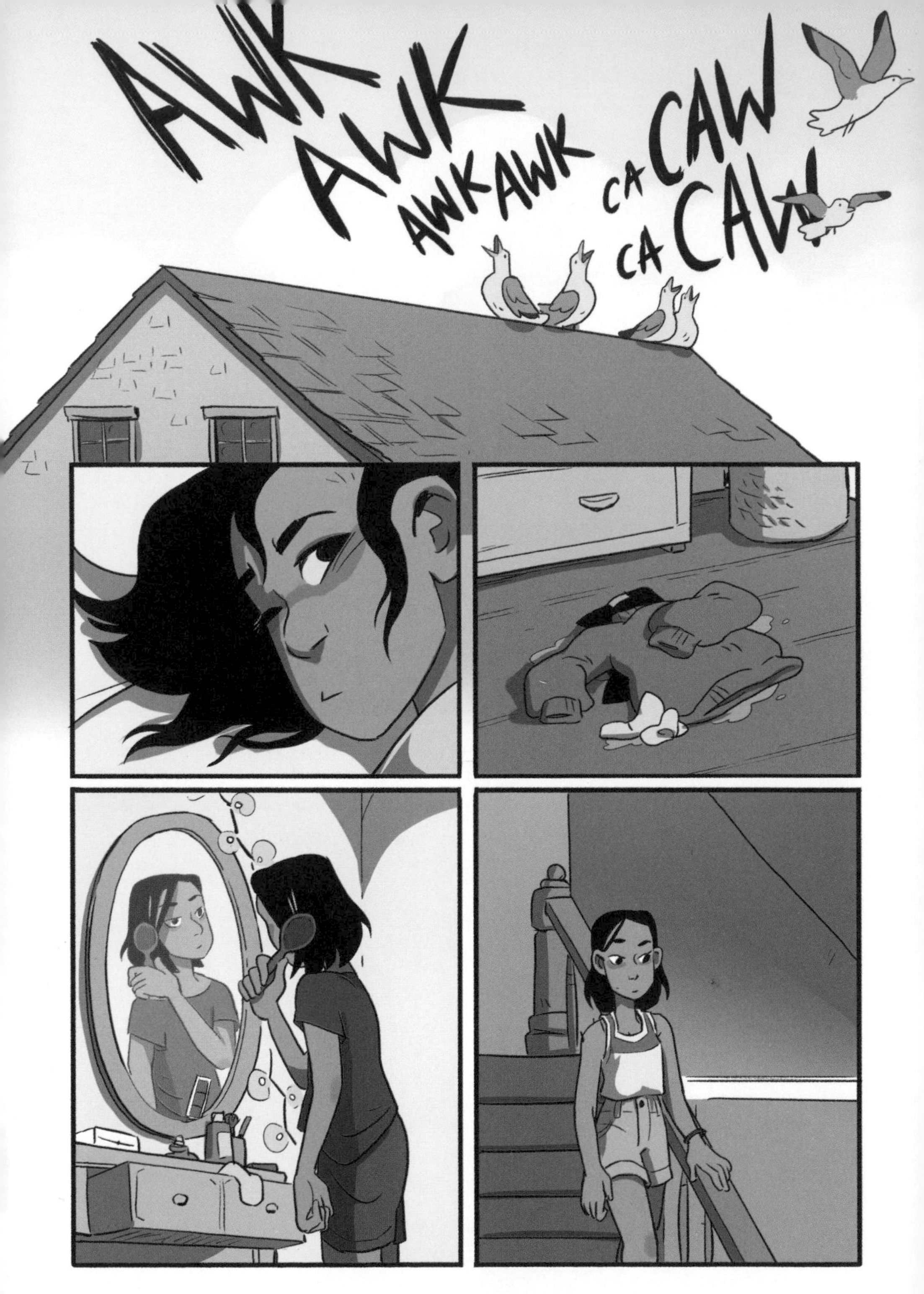
AWK
AWK
AWKAWK
CA CAW
CA CAW

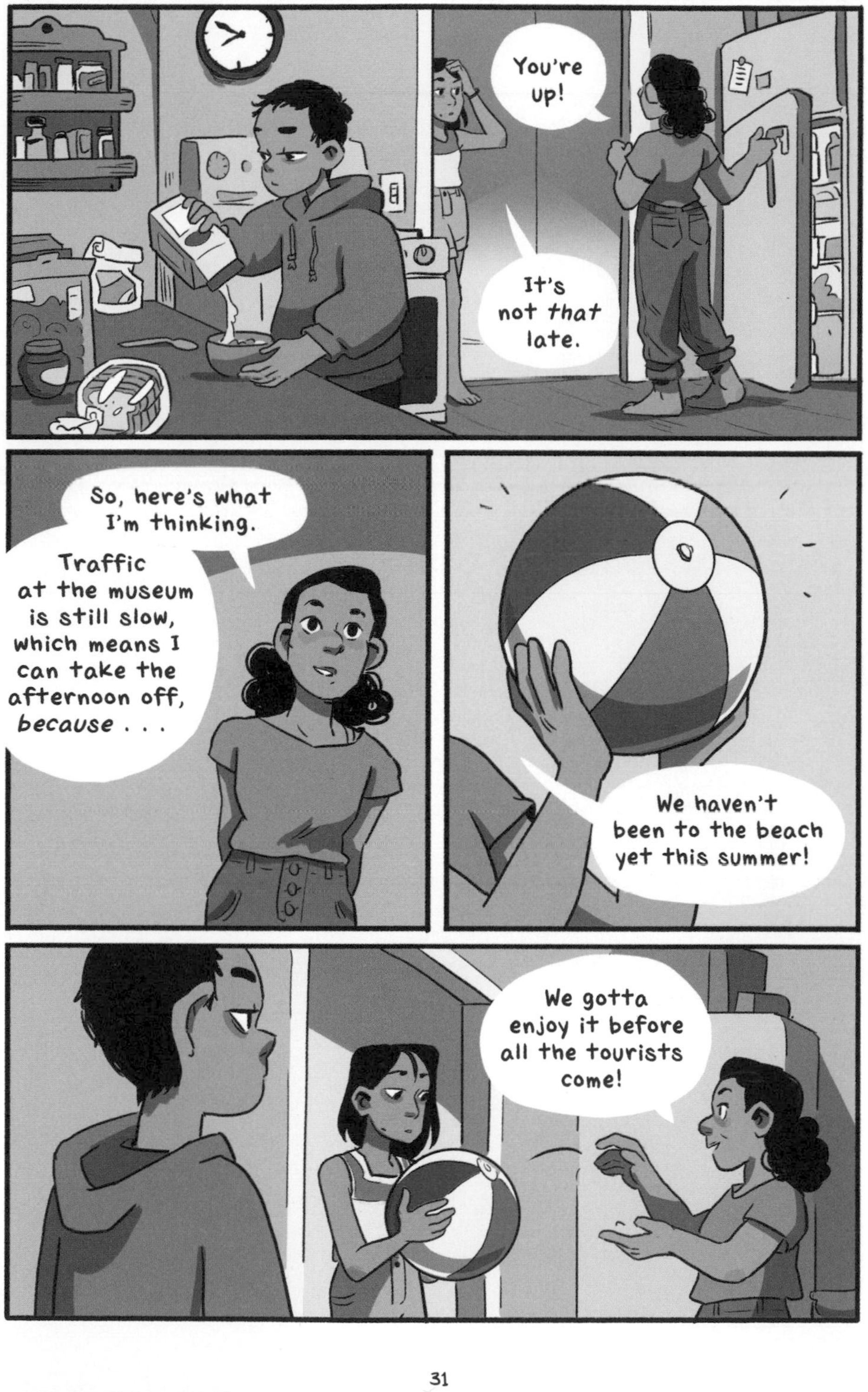
You're up!
It's not *that* late.
So, here's what I'm thinking.
Traffic at the museum is still slow, which means I can take the afternoon off, *because* . . .
We haven't been to the beach yet this summer!
We gotta enjoy it before all the tourists come!

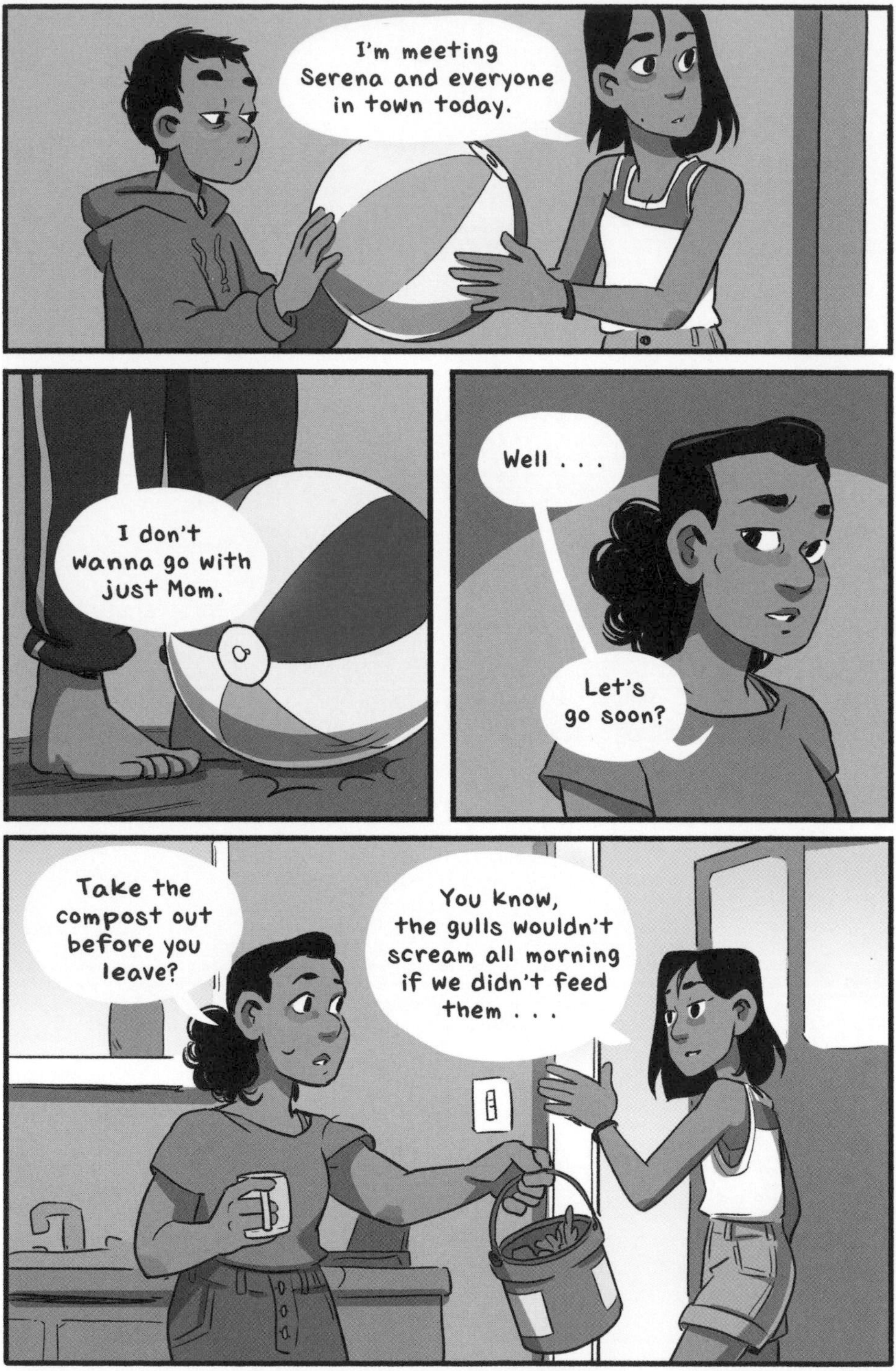
I'm meeting Serena and everyone in town today.
I don't wanna go with just Mom.
Well . . .
Let's go soon?
Take the compost out before you leave?
You know, the gulls wouldn't scream all morning if we didn't feed them . . .

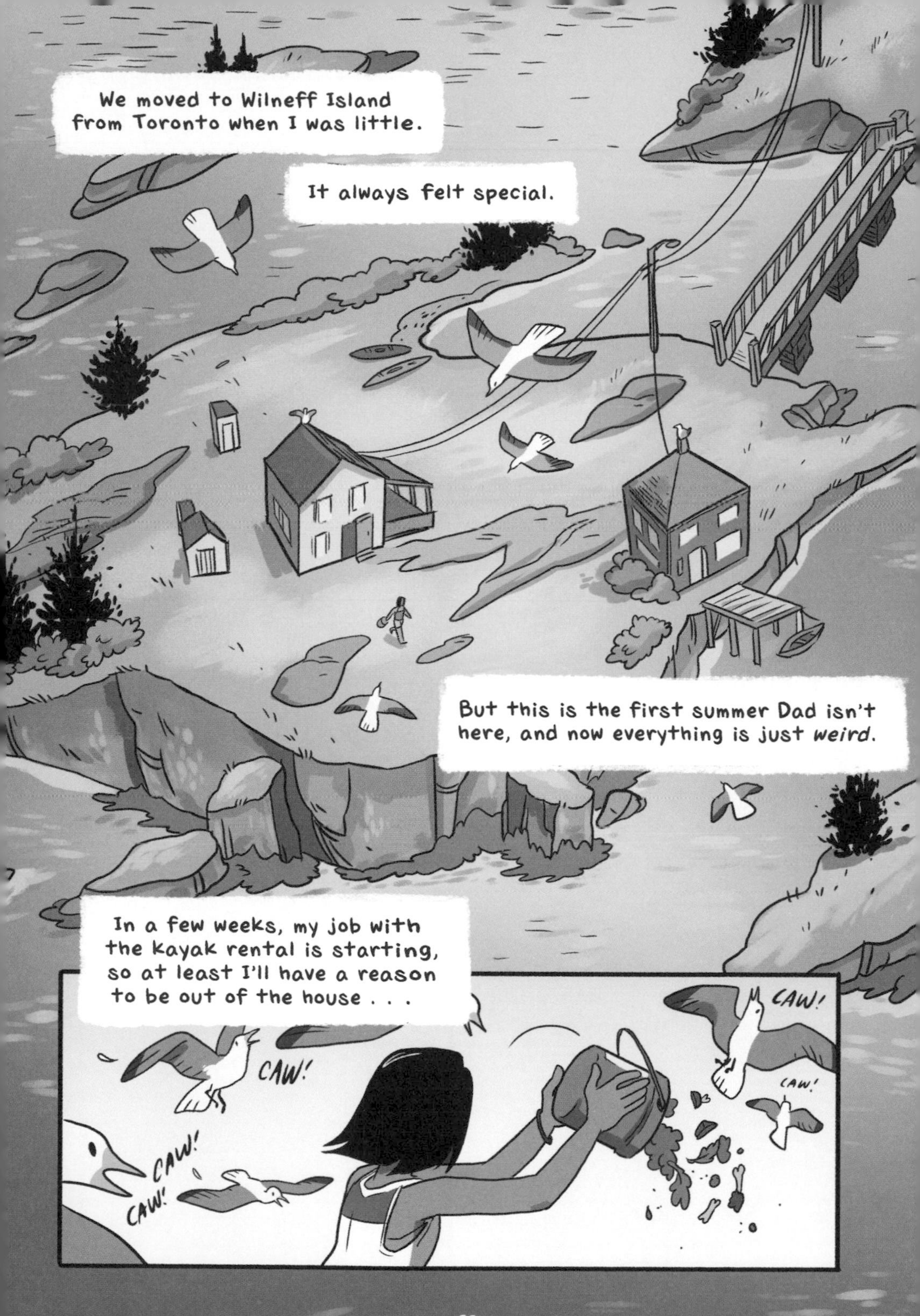

We moved to Wilneff Island from Toronto when I was little.
It always felt special.
But this is the first summer Dad isn't here, and now everything is just *weird*.
In a few weeks, my job with the kayak rental is starting, so at least I'll have a reason to be out of the house . . .
CAW!
CAW!
CAW!
CAW!
CAW!
CAW!

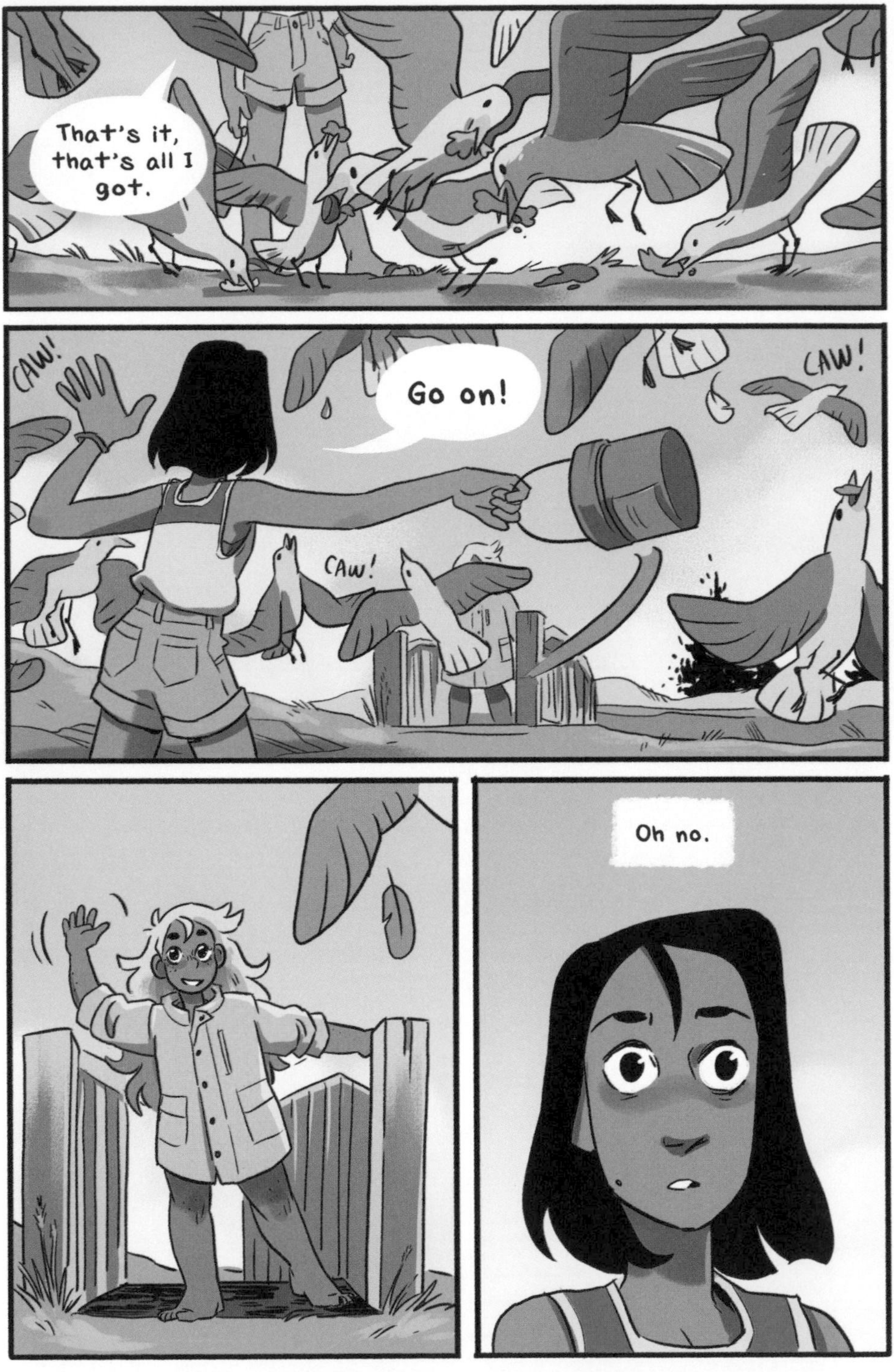
That's it, that's all I got.
CAW!
Go on!
CAW!
CAW!
Oh no.

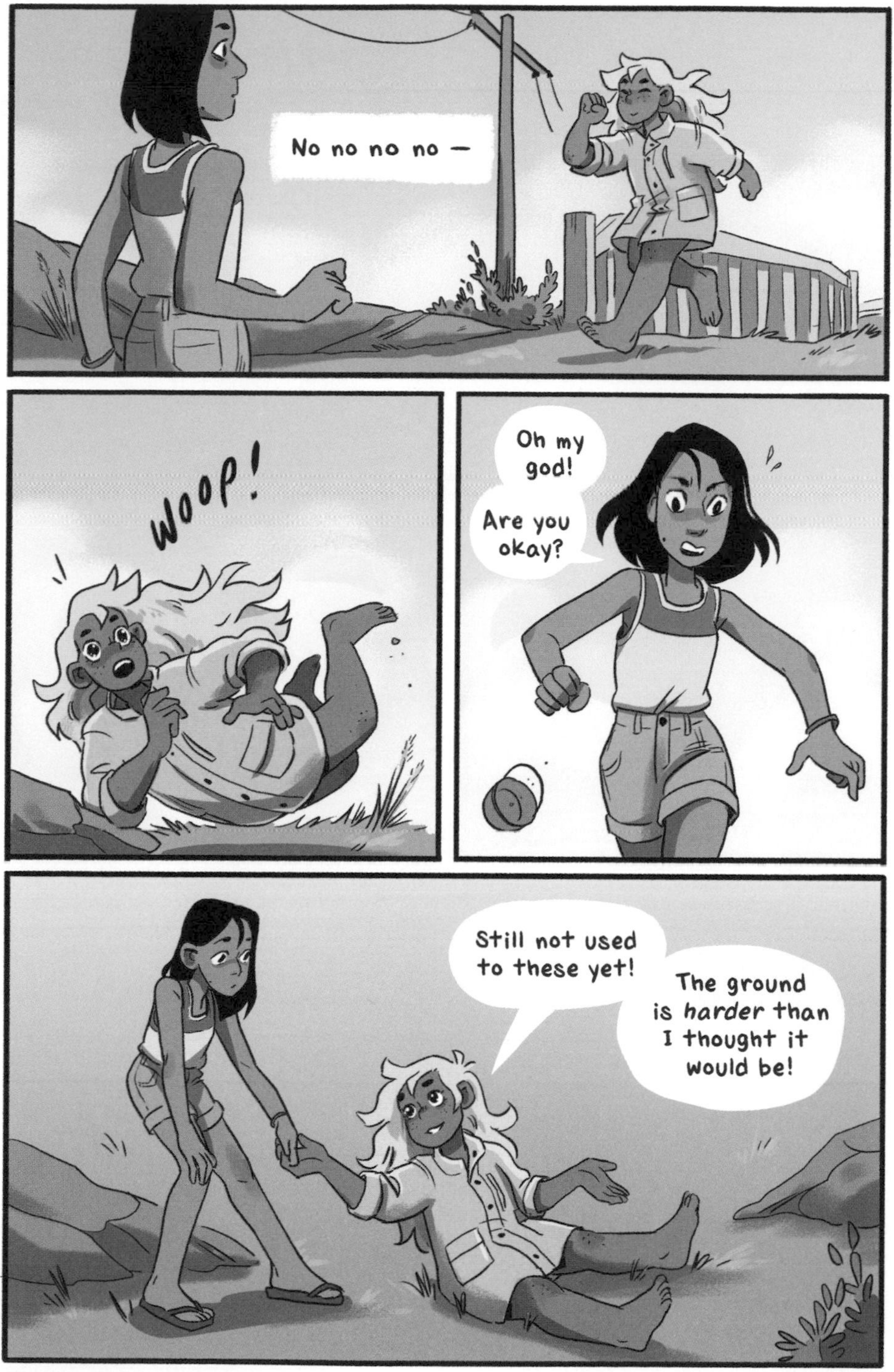
No no no no —
WOOP!
Oh my god!
Are you okay?
Still not used to these yet!
The ground is *harder* than I thought it would be!

What do you — Um —

Who are you?

It's me, Keltie!

. . . I'm Morgan.

I know!

Morgan!

I am a selkie, and you are my true love, and your kiss has allowed me to transform from a seal into a human and walk on land.

Now we can find our fortunes together!

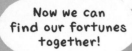

Yeah, no, nope, we're not doing that.

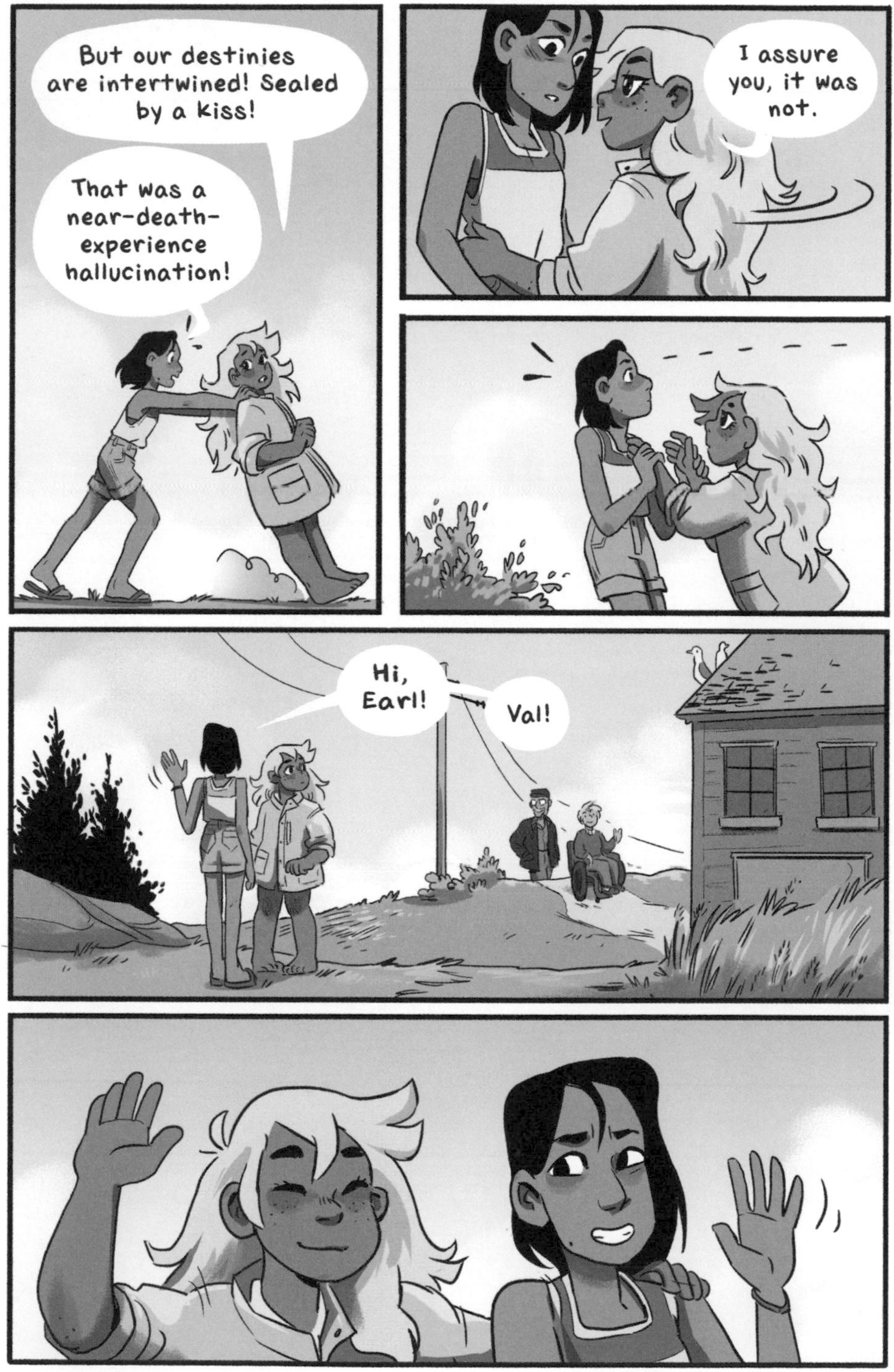
But our destinies are intertwined! Sealed by a kiss!
That was a near-death-experience hallucination!
I assure you, it was not.
Hi, Earl!
Val!

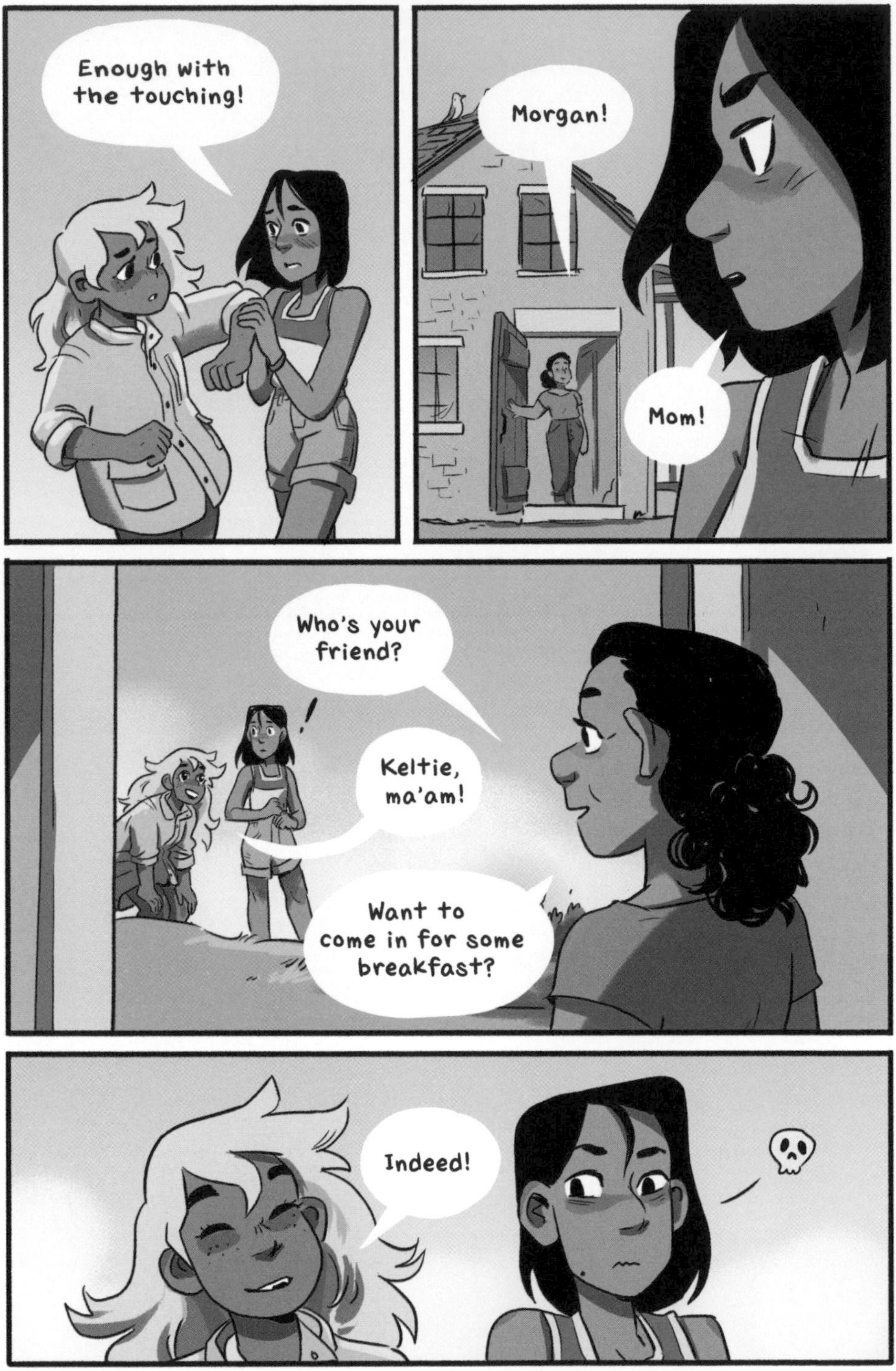
Enough with the touching!
Morgan!
Mom!
Who's your friend?
Keltie, ma'am!
Want to come in for some breakfast?
Indeed!

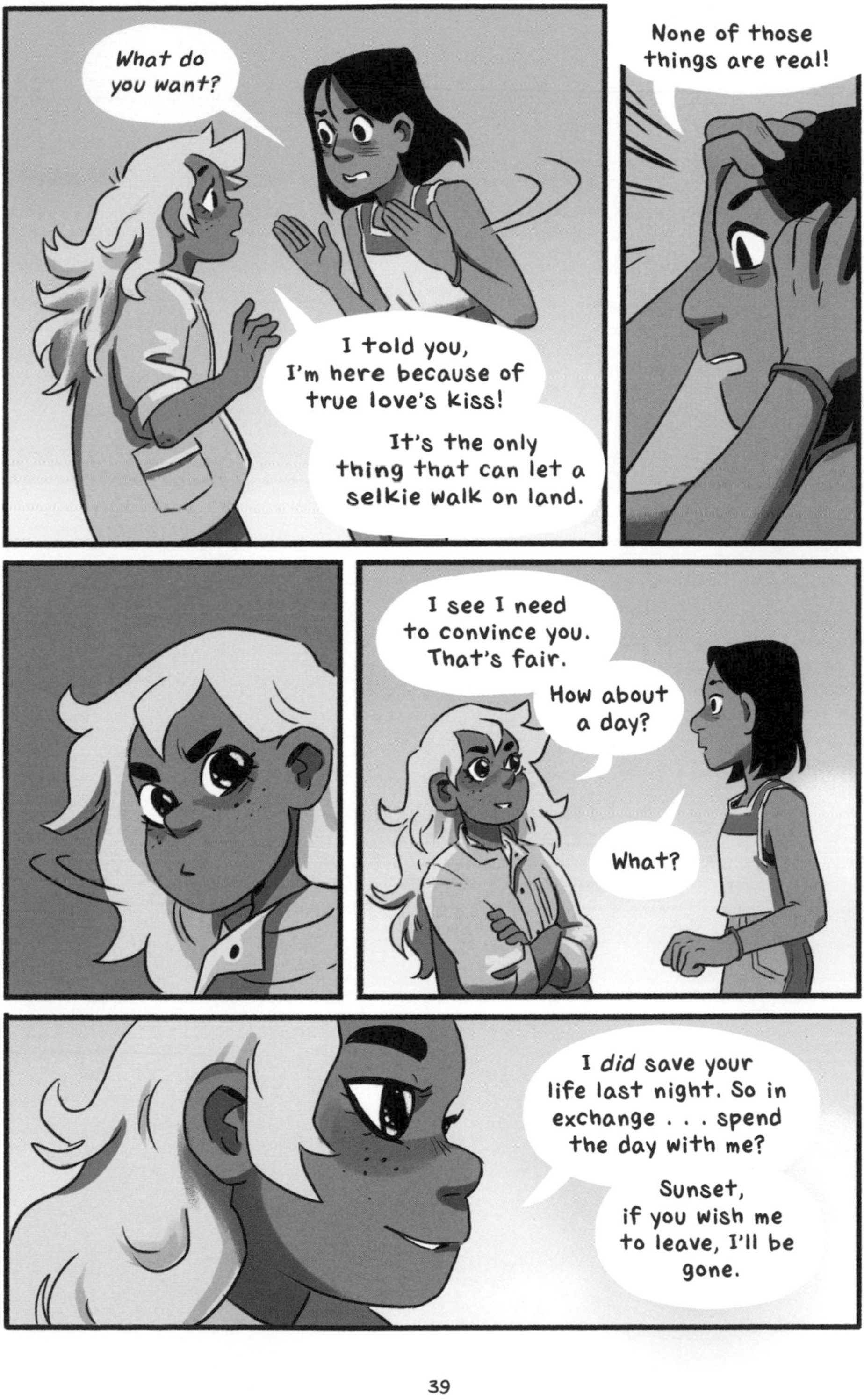
What do you want?
I told you, I'm here because of true love's kiss!
It's the only thing that can let a selkie walk on land.
None of those things are real!
I see I need to convince you. That's fair.
How about a day?
What?
I *did* save your life last night. So in exchange . . . spend the day with me?
Sunset, if you wish me to leave, I'll be gone.

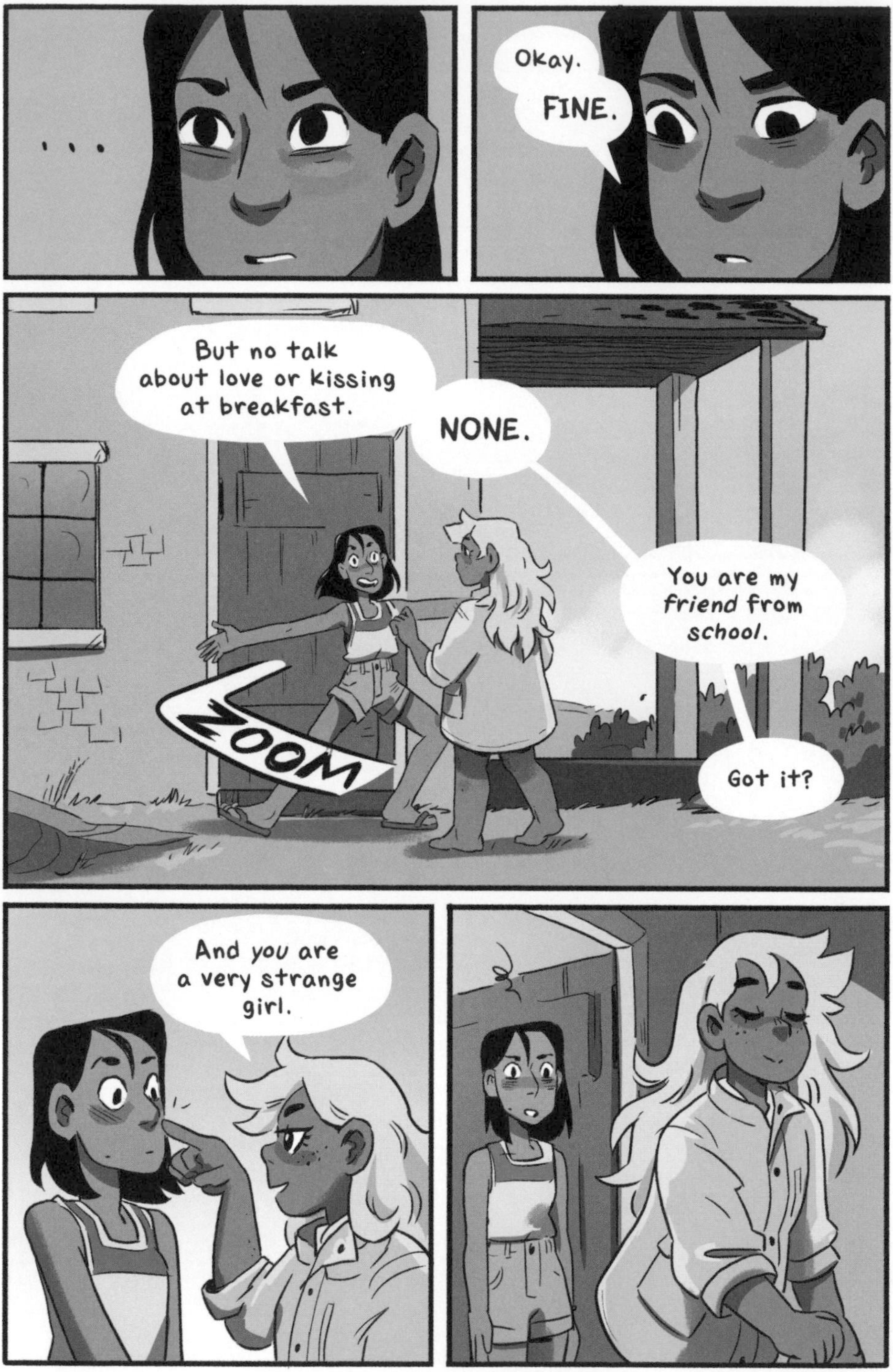
...
Okay.
FINE.
But no talk about love or kissing at breakfast.
NONE.
You are my *friend* from *school*.
Got it?
ZOOM
And *you* are a very strange girl.

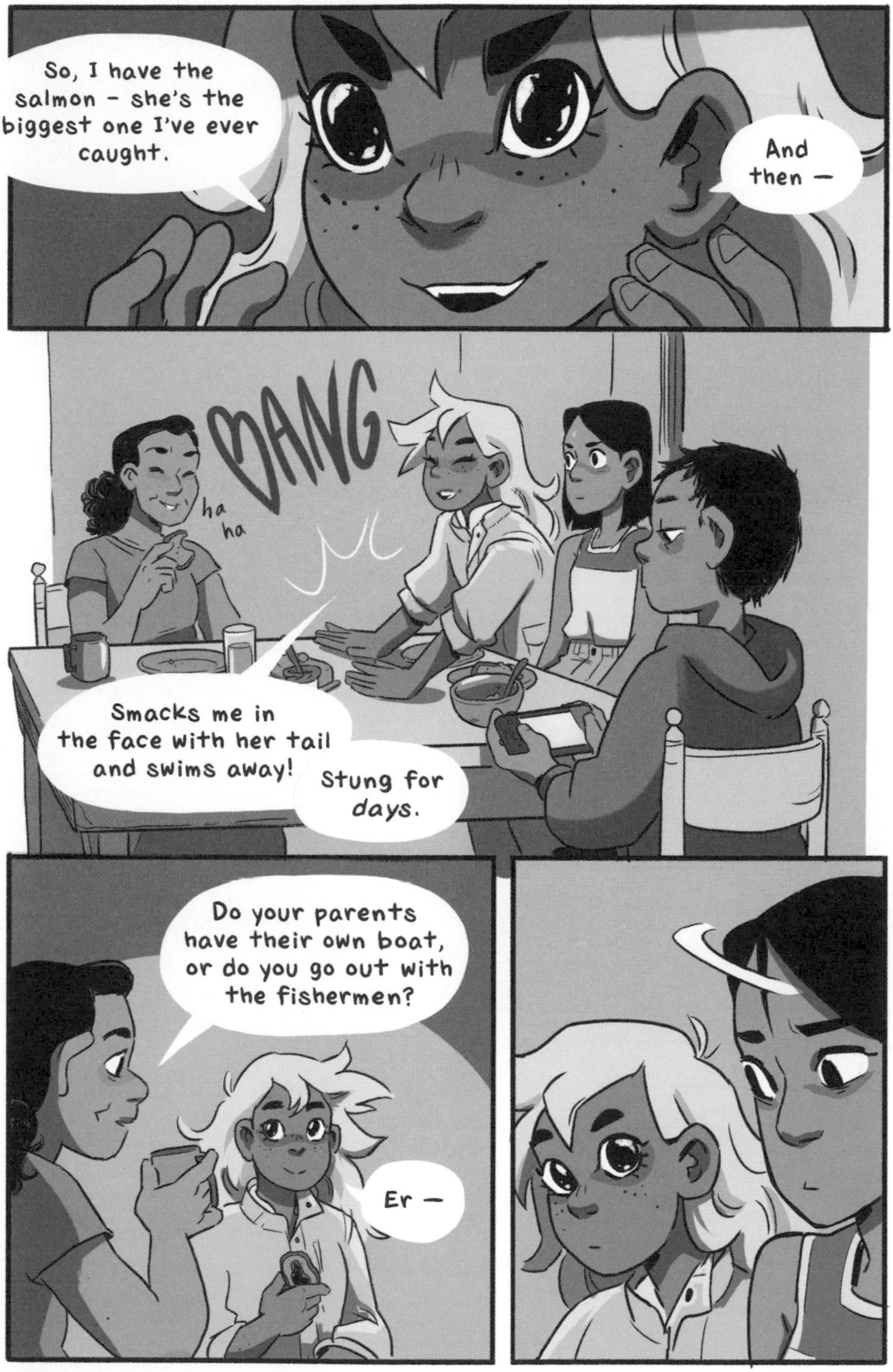
So, I have the salmon – she's the biggest one I've ever caught.
And then –
ha ha
DANG
Smacks me in the face with her tail and swims away!
Stung for *days*.
Do your parents have their own boat, or do you go out with the fishermen?
Er –

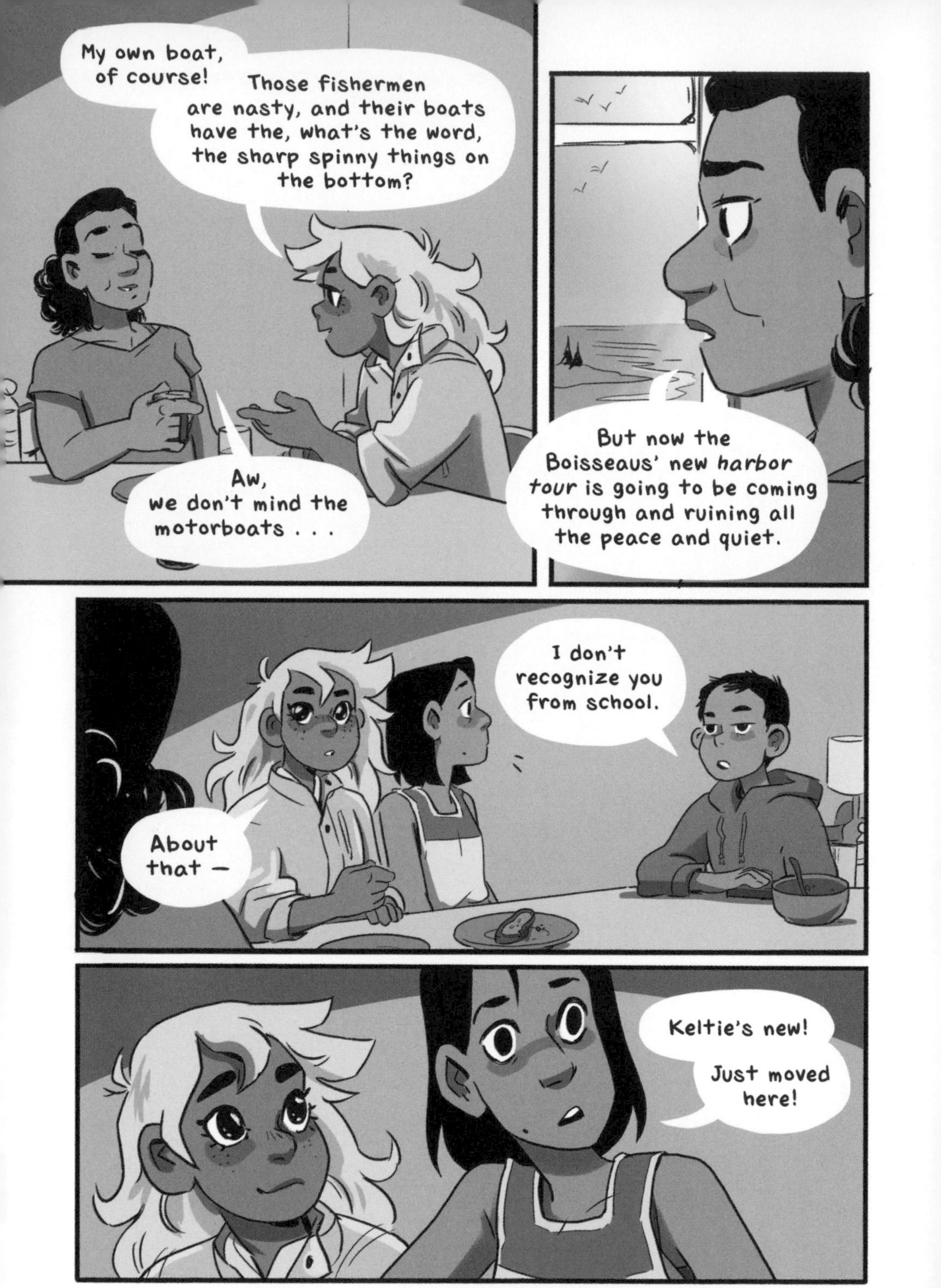
My own boat, of course!
Those fishermen are nasty, and their boats have the, what's the word, the sharp spinny things on the bottom?
Aw, we don't mind the motorboats . . .
But now the Boisseaus' new *harbor tour* is going to be coming through and ruining all the peace and quiet.
I don't recognize you from school.
About that —
Keltie's new!
Just moved here!

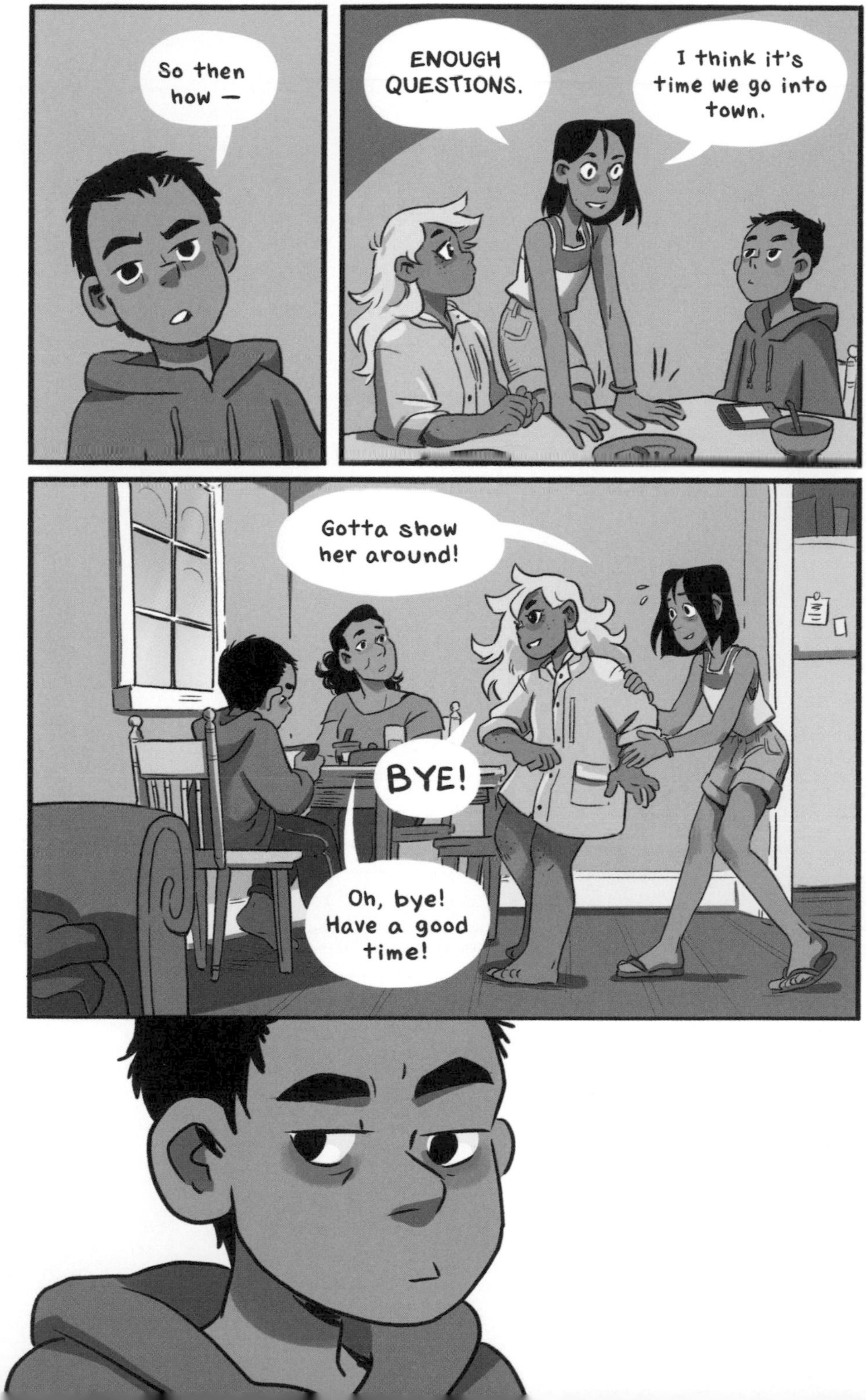

So then how —
ENOUGH QUESTIONS.
I think it's time we go into town.
Gotta show her around!
BYE!
Oh, bye! Have a good time!

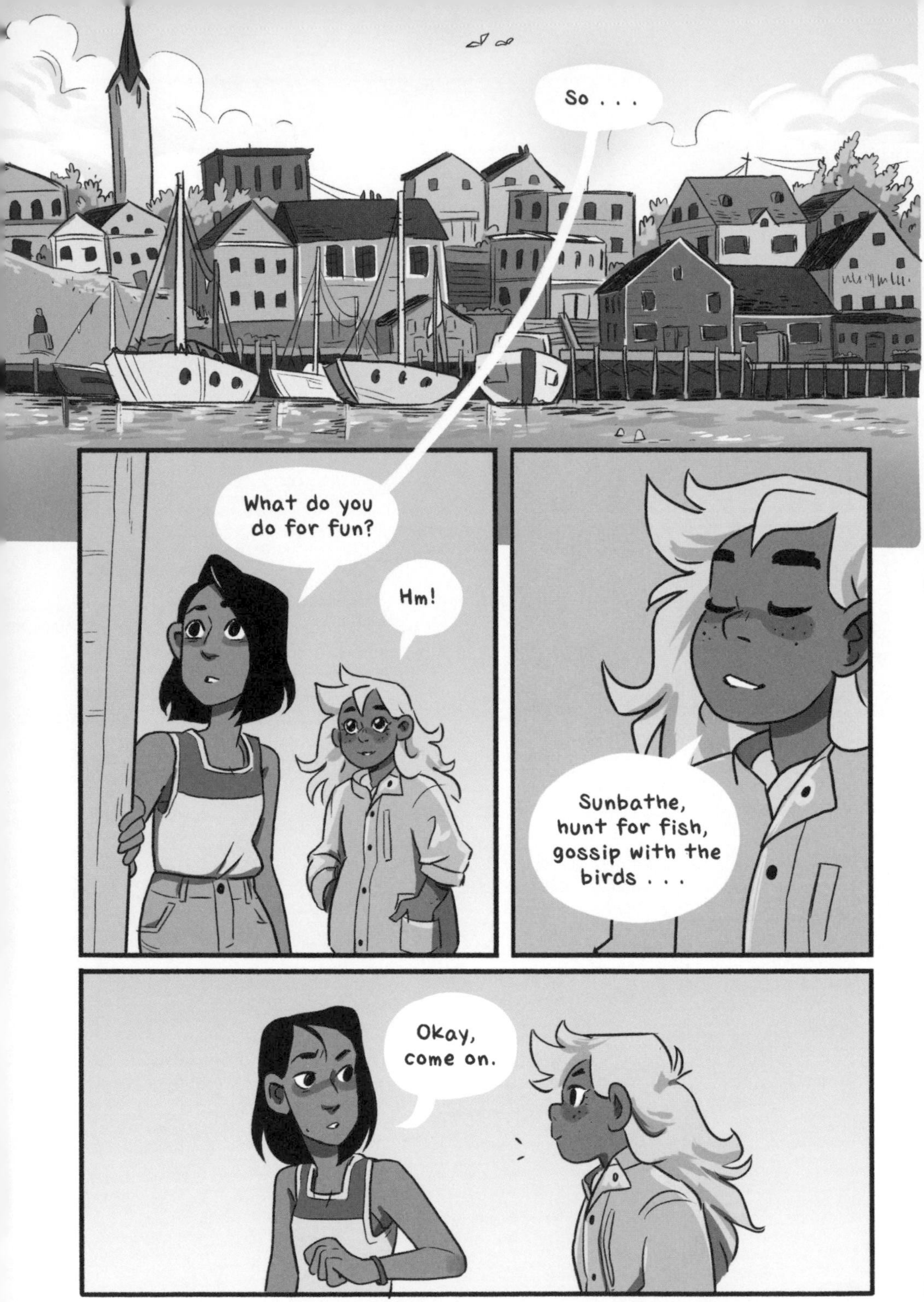
So . . .
What do you do for fun?
Hm!
Sunbathe, hunt for fish, gossip with the birds . . .
Okay, come on.

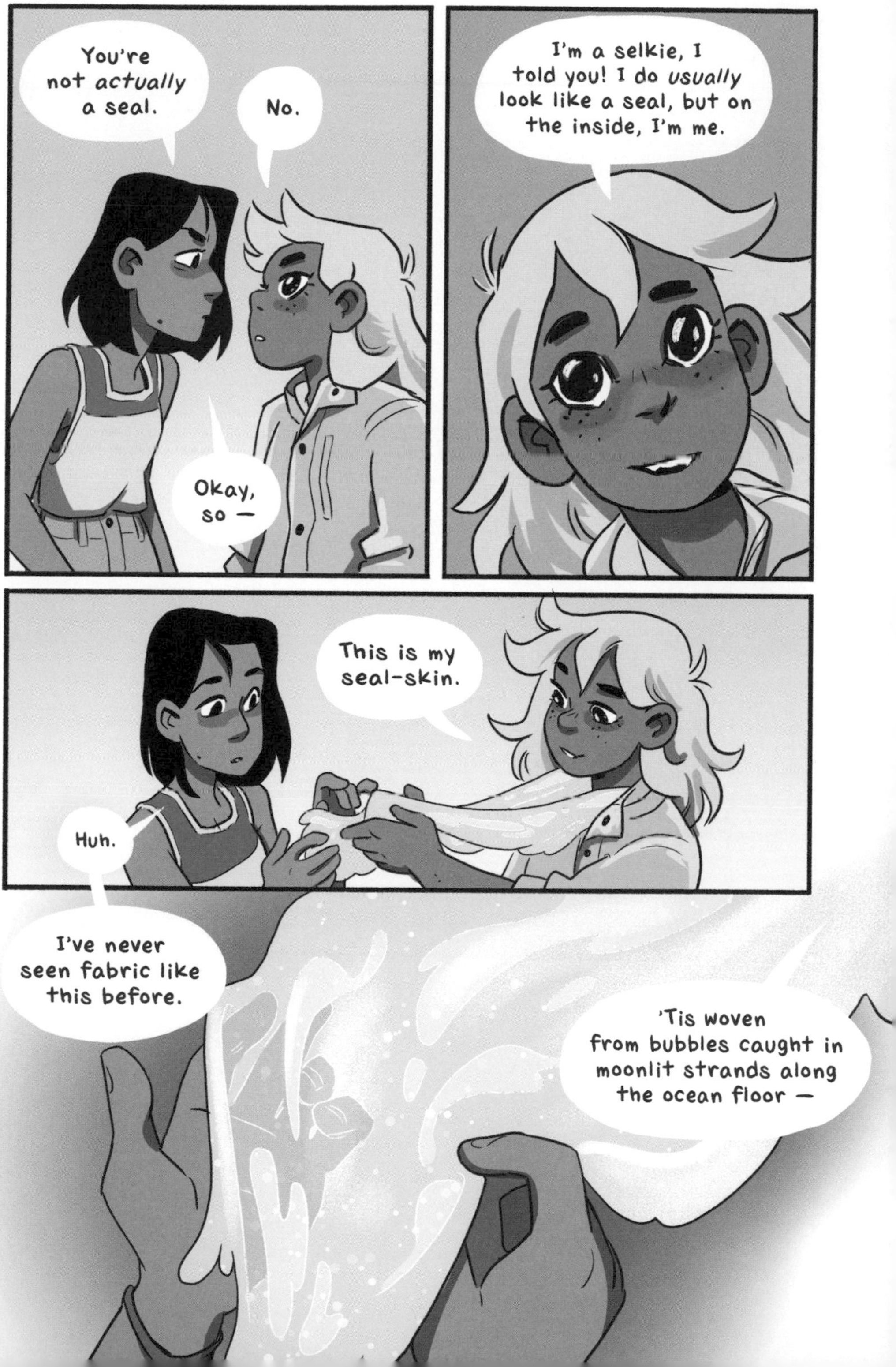
You're not *actually* a seal.
No.
Okay, so —
I'm a selkie, I told you! I do *usually* look like a seal, but on the inside, I'm me.
This is my seal-skin.
Huh.
I've never seen fabric like this before.
'Tis woven from bubbles caught in moonlit strands along the ocean floor —

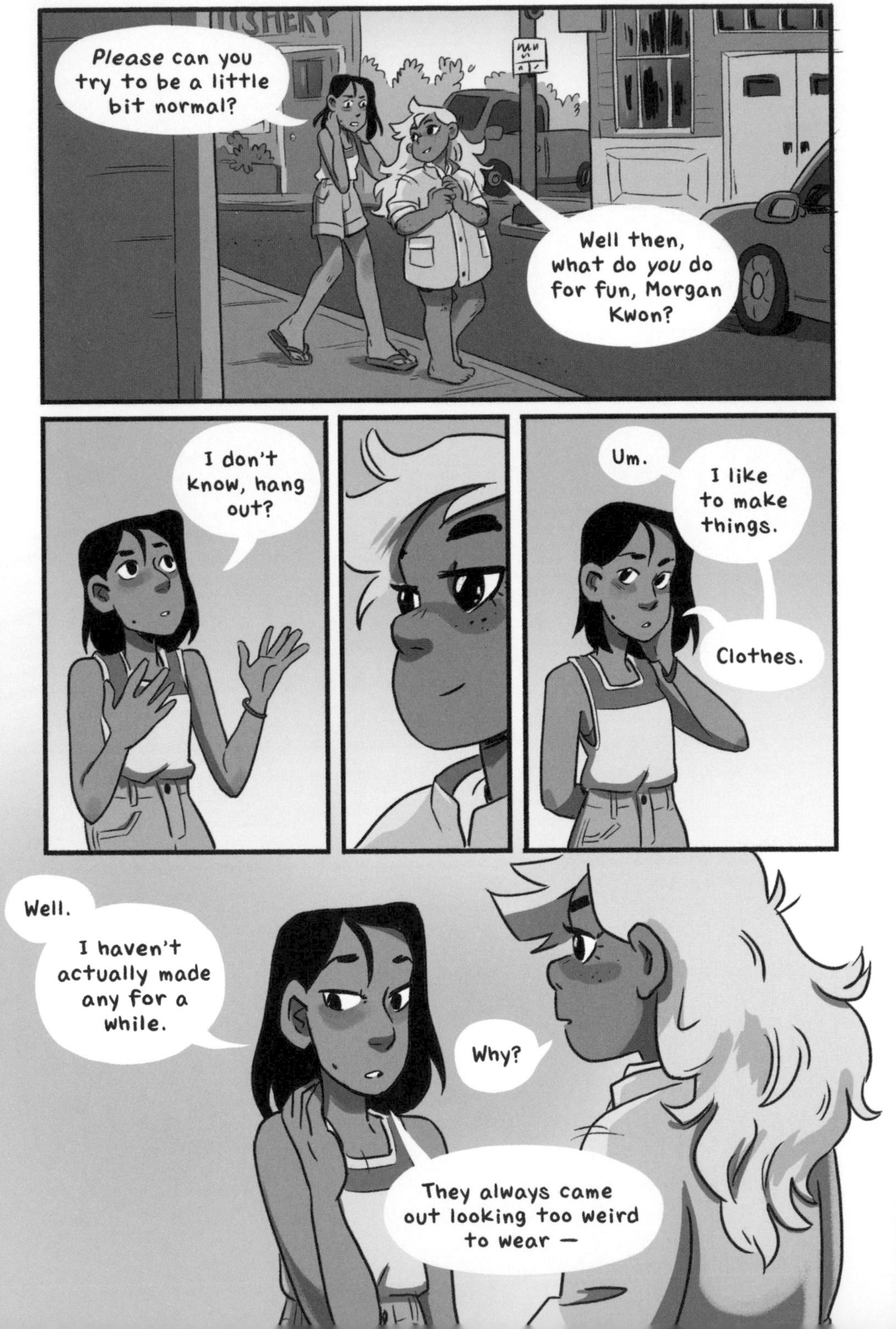
Please can you try to be a little bit normal?
Well then, what do *you* do for fun, Morgan Kwon?
I don't know, hang out?
Um.
I like to make things.
Clothes.
Well.
I haven't actually made any for a while.
Why?
They always came out looking too weird to wear —

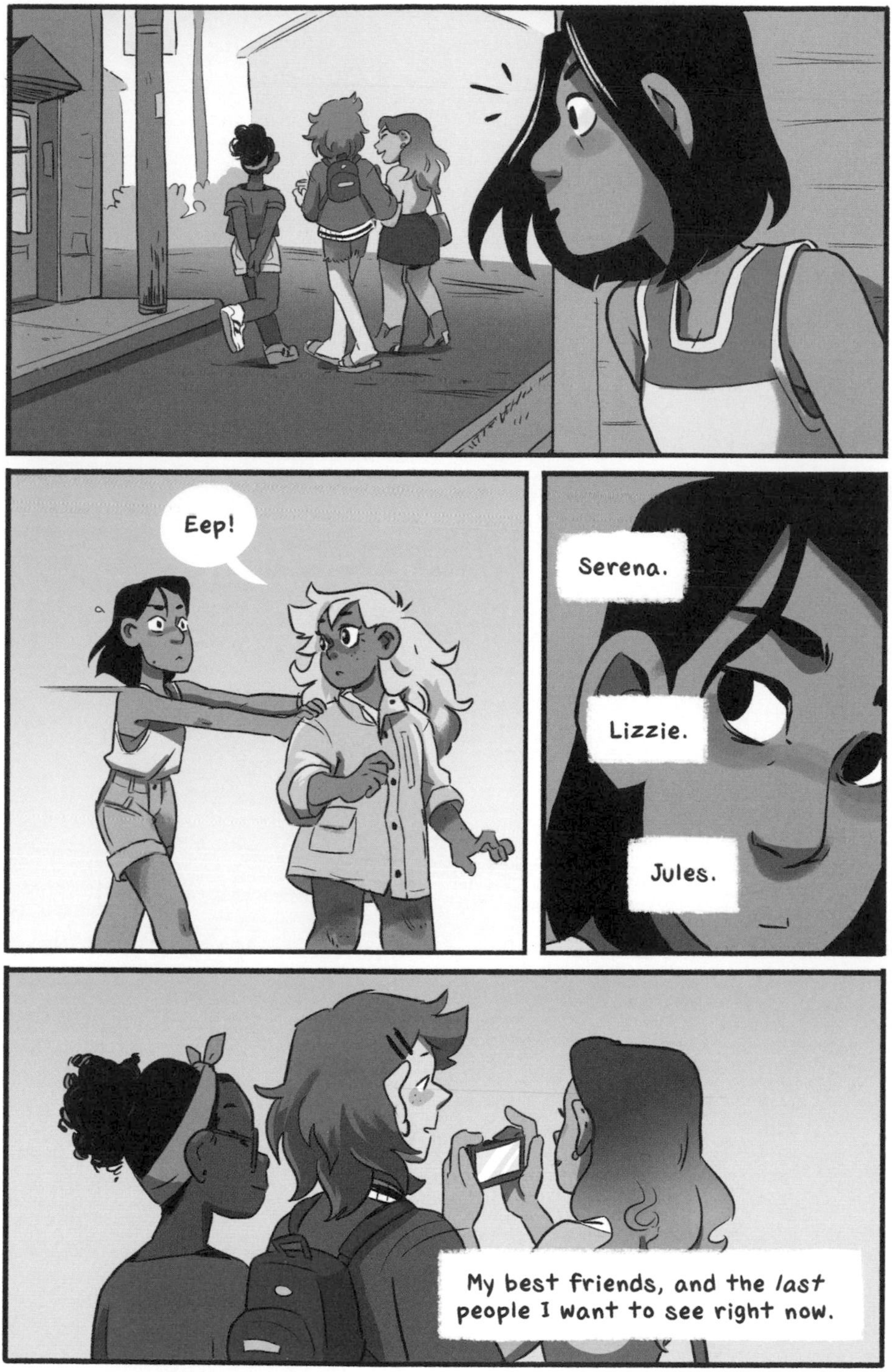

Eep!
Serena.
Lizzie.
Jules.
My best friends, and the *last* people I want to see right now.

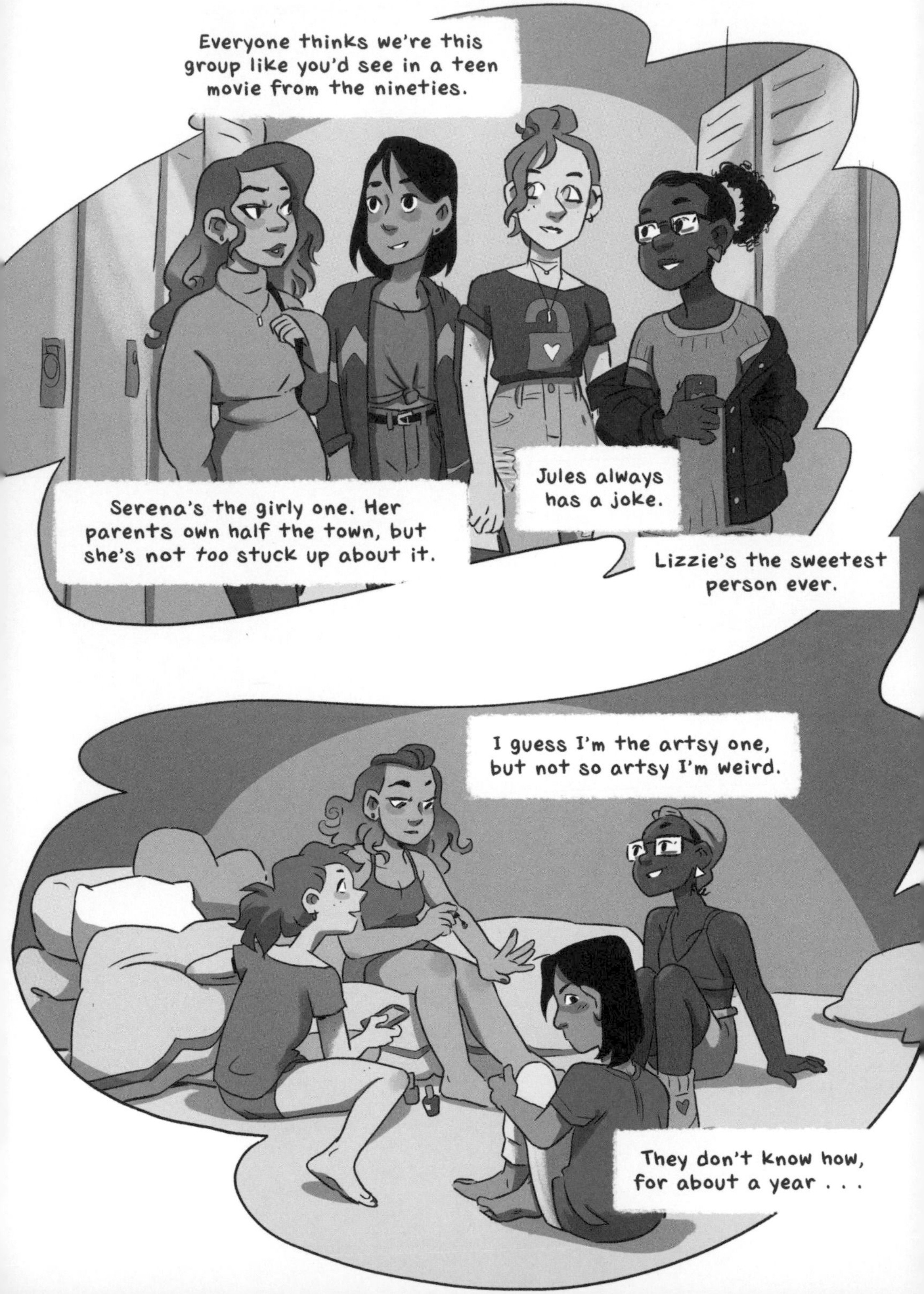

Everyone thinks we're this group like you'd see in a teen movie from the nineties.
Serena's the girly one. Her parents own half the town, but she's not *too* stuck up about it.
Jules always has a joke.
Lizzie's the sweetest person ever.
I guess I'm the artsy one, but not so artsy I'm weird.
They don't know how, for about a year . . .

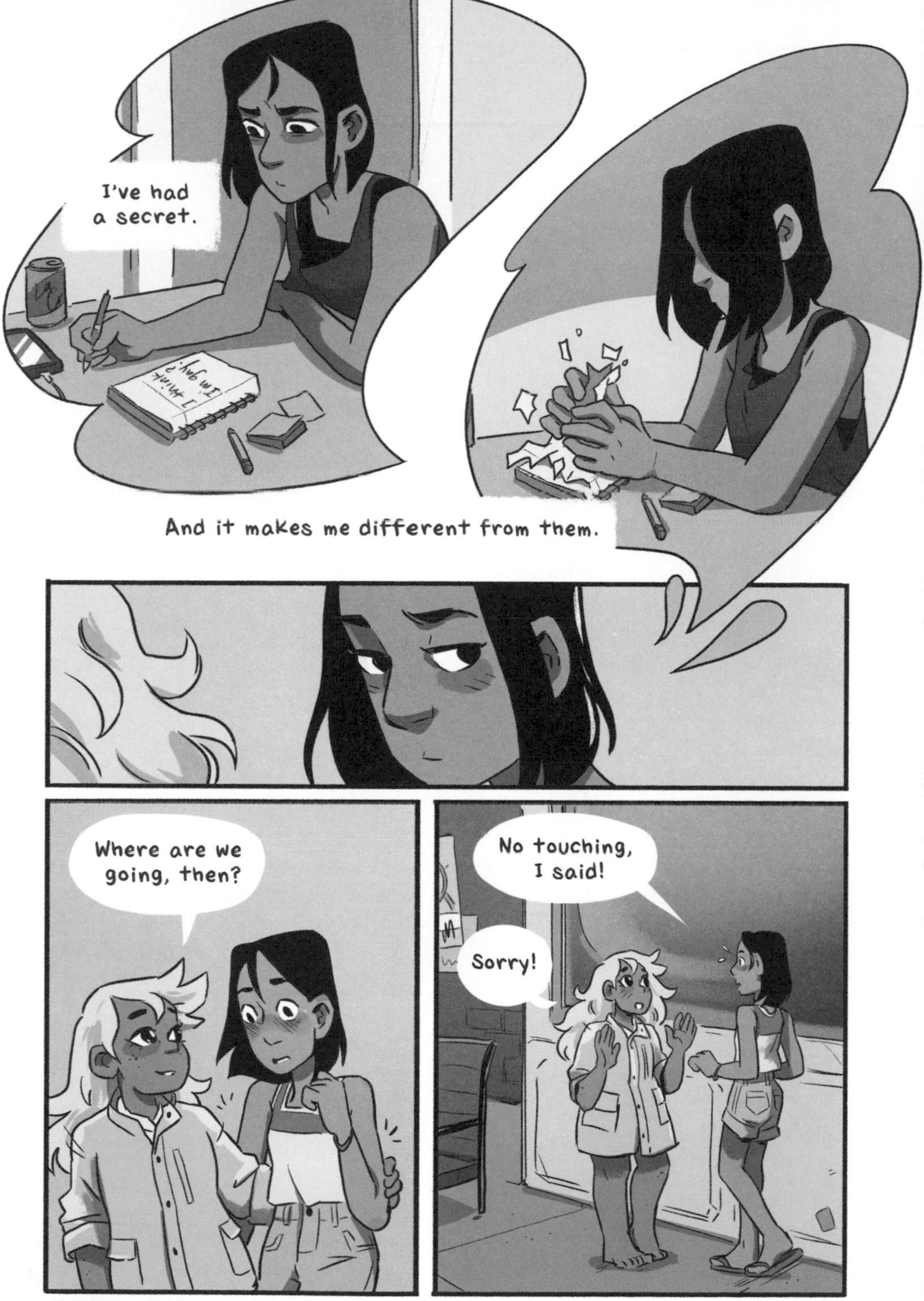
I've had a secret.
And it makes me different from them.
Where are we going, then?
No touching, I said!
Sorry!

THEY'RE touching!

It's different.

As a reminder, you kissed me.

Ah, it's amazing how red you become!

AAAAAH

We have to get you some normal clothes.

And SHOES.

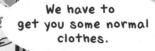

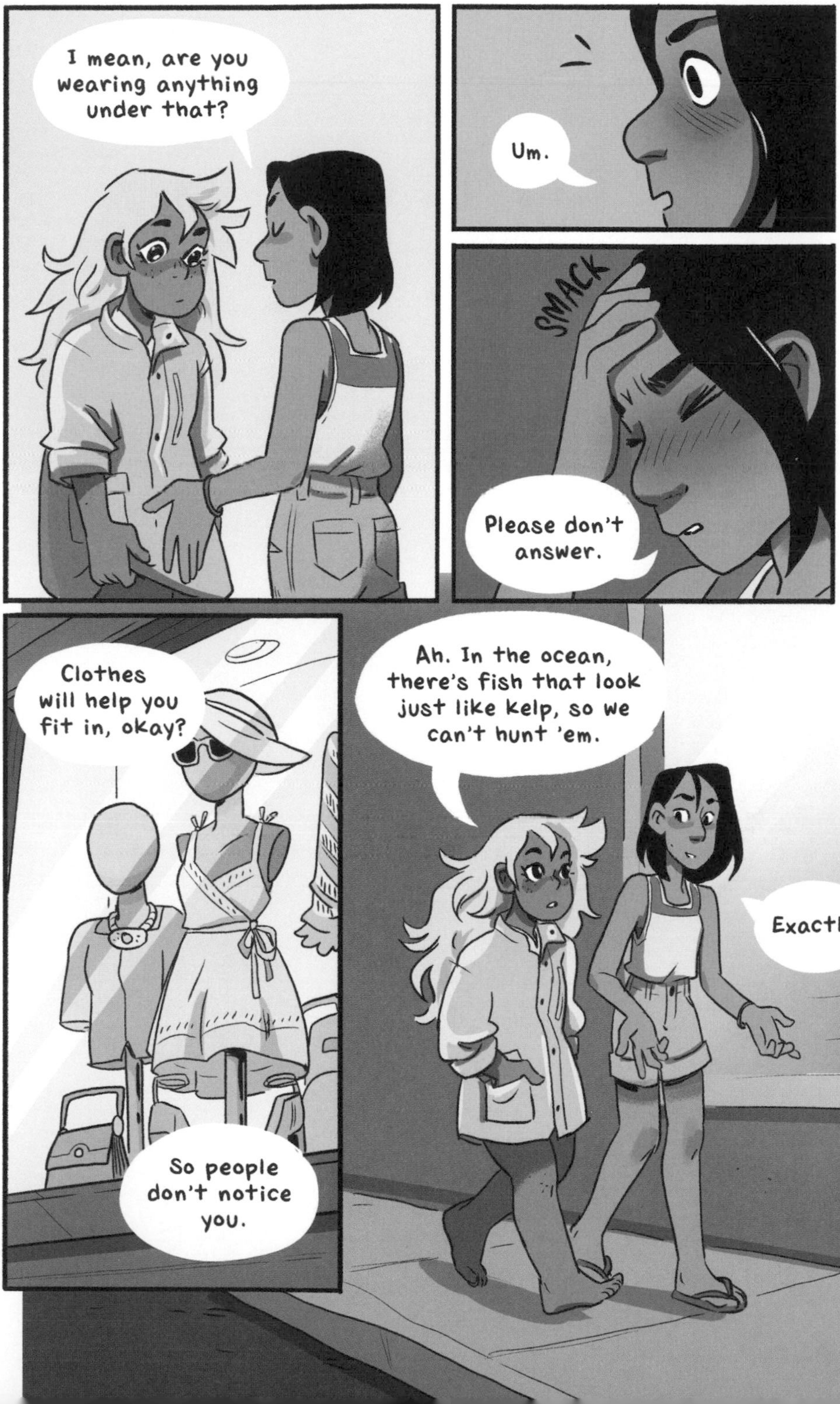
I mean, are you wearing anything under that?
Um.
SMACK
Please don't answer.
Clothes will help you fit in, okay?
So people don't notice you.
Ah. In the ocean, there's fish that look just like kelp, so we can't hunt 'em.
Exactly.

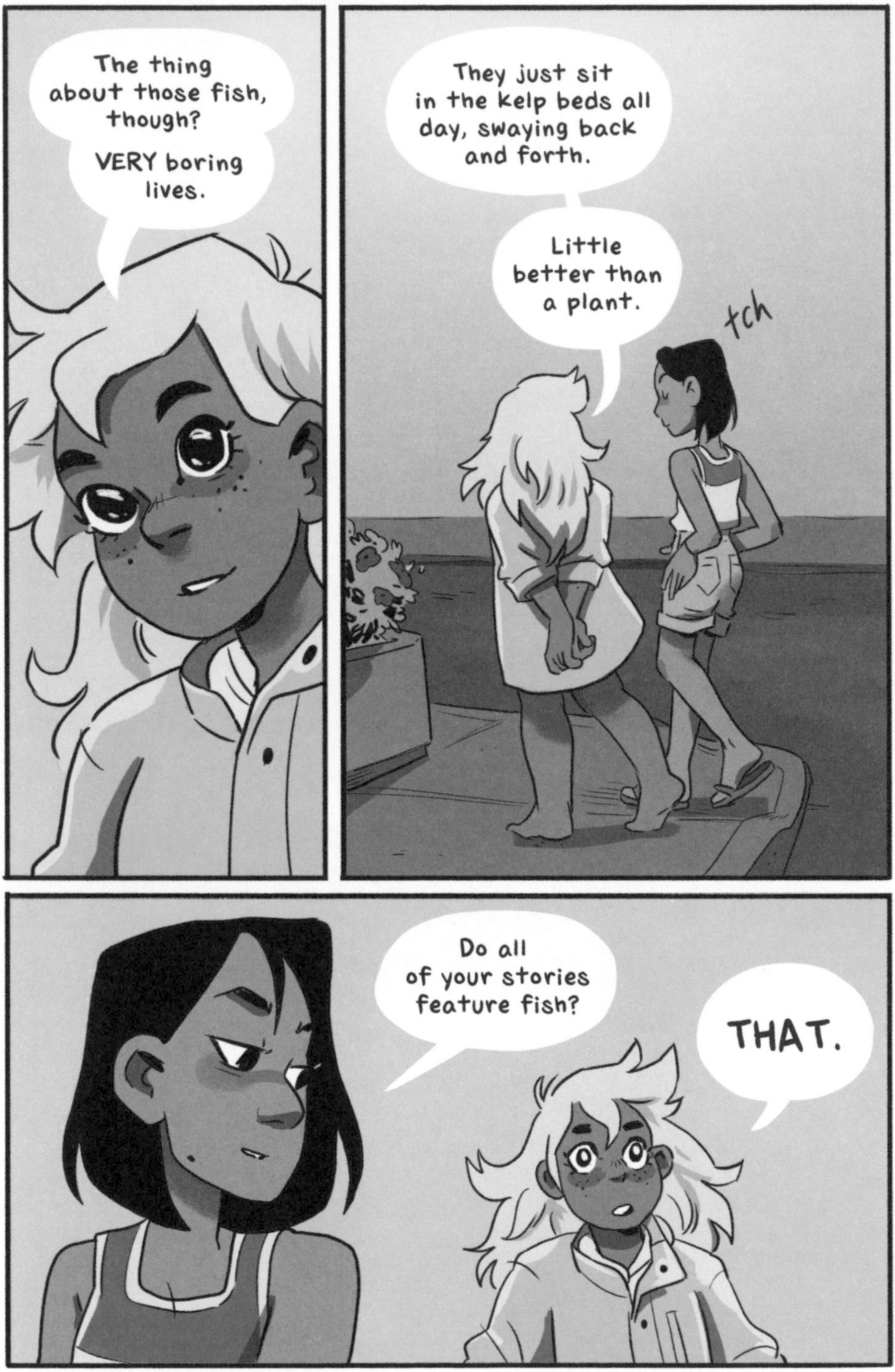
The thing about those fish, though?
VERY boring lives.
They just sit in the kelp beds all day, swaying back and forth.
Little better than a plant.
tch
Do all of your stories feature fish?
THAT.

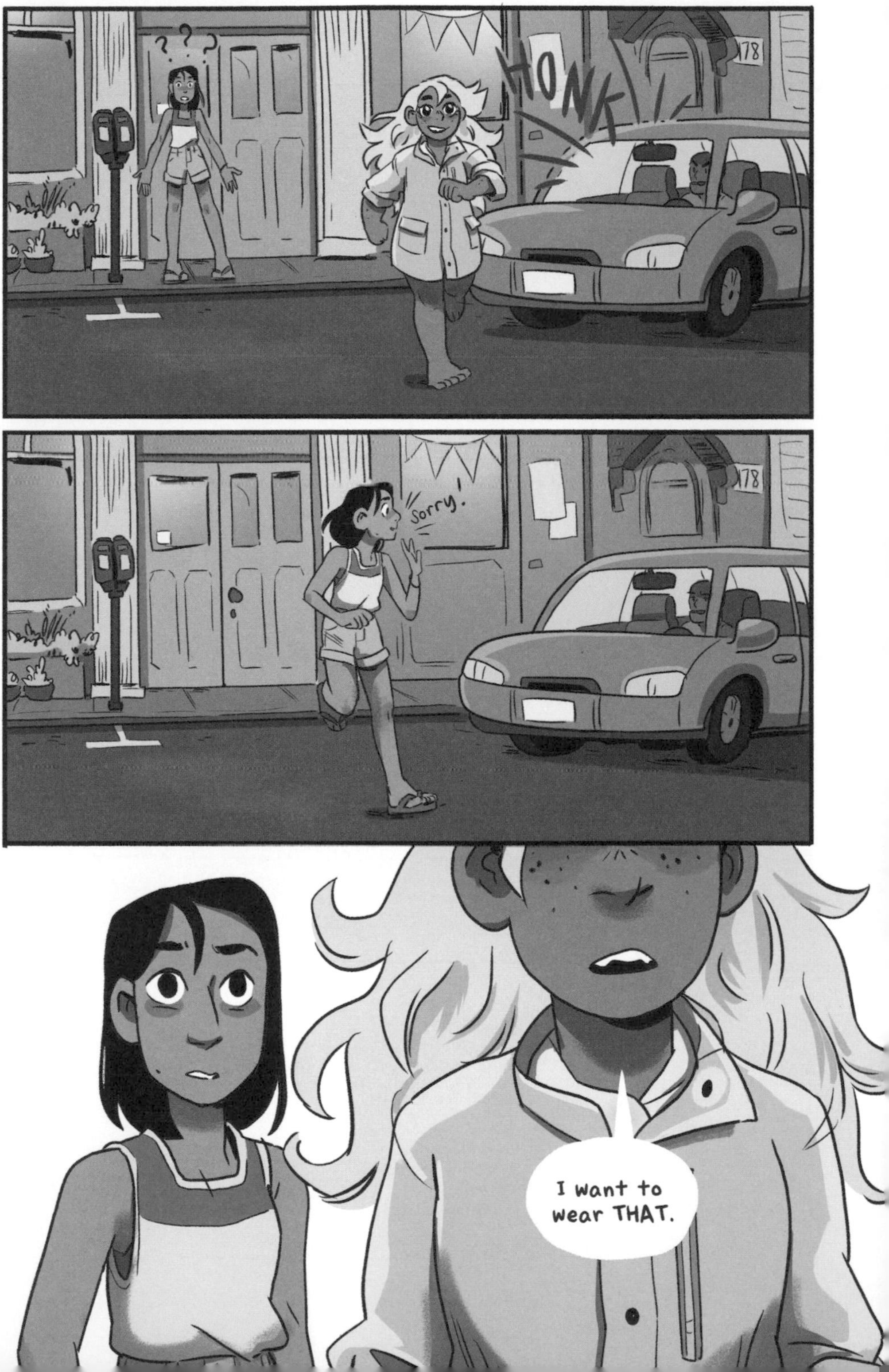
? ? ?
HONK
178
Sorry!
I want to wear THAT.

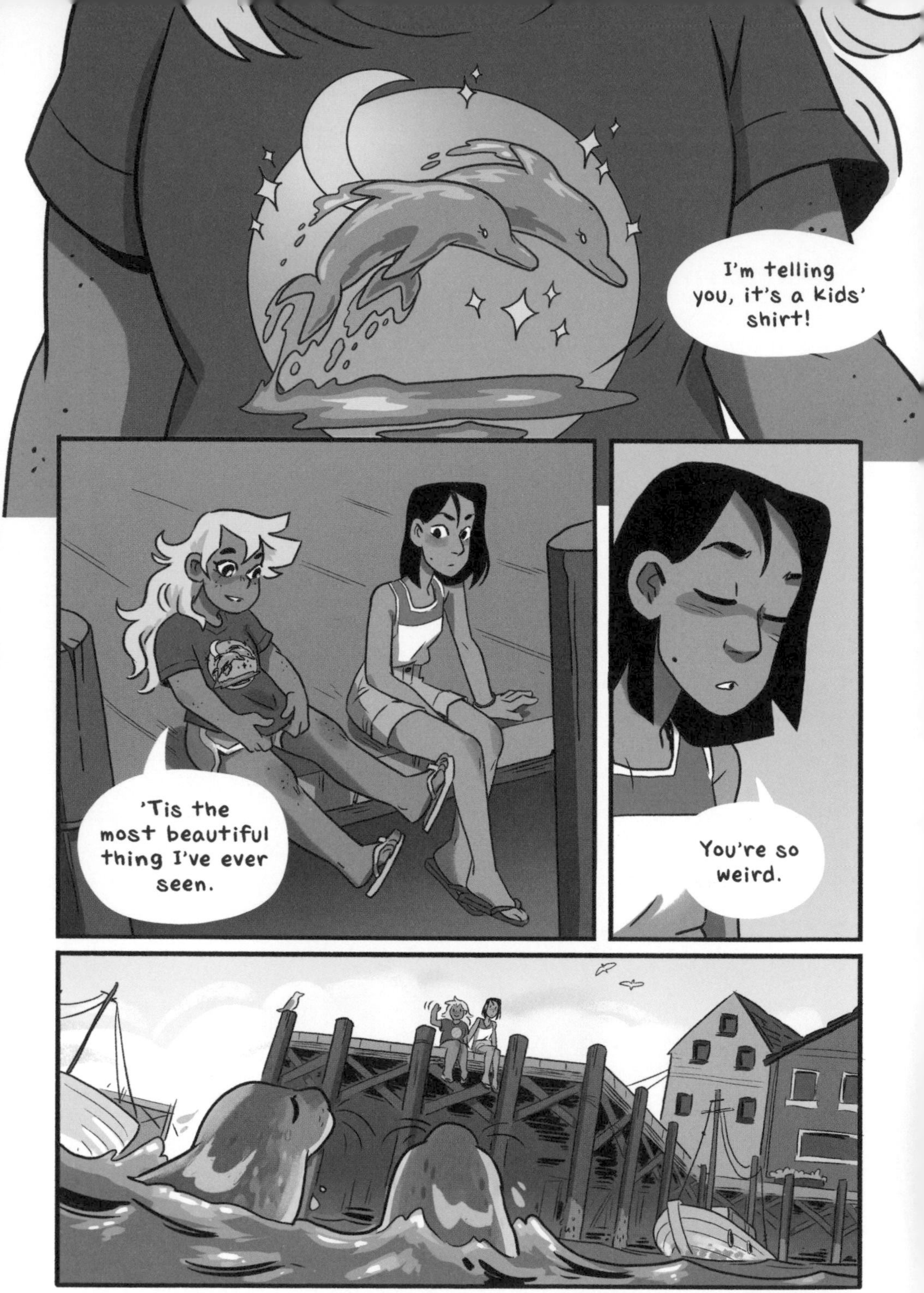
I'm telling you, it's a kids' shirt!
'Tis the most beautiful thing I've ever seen.
You're so weird.

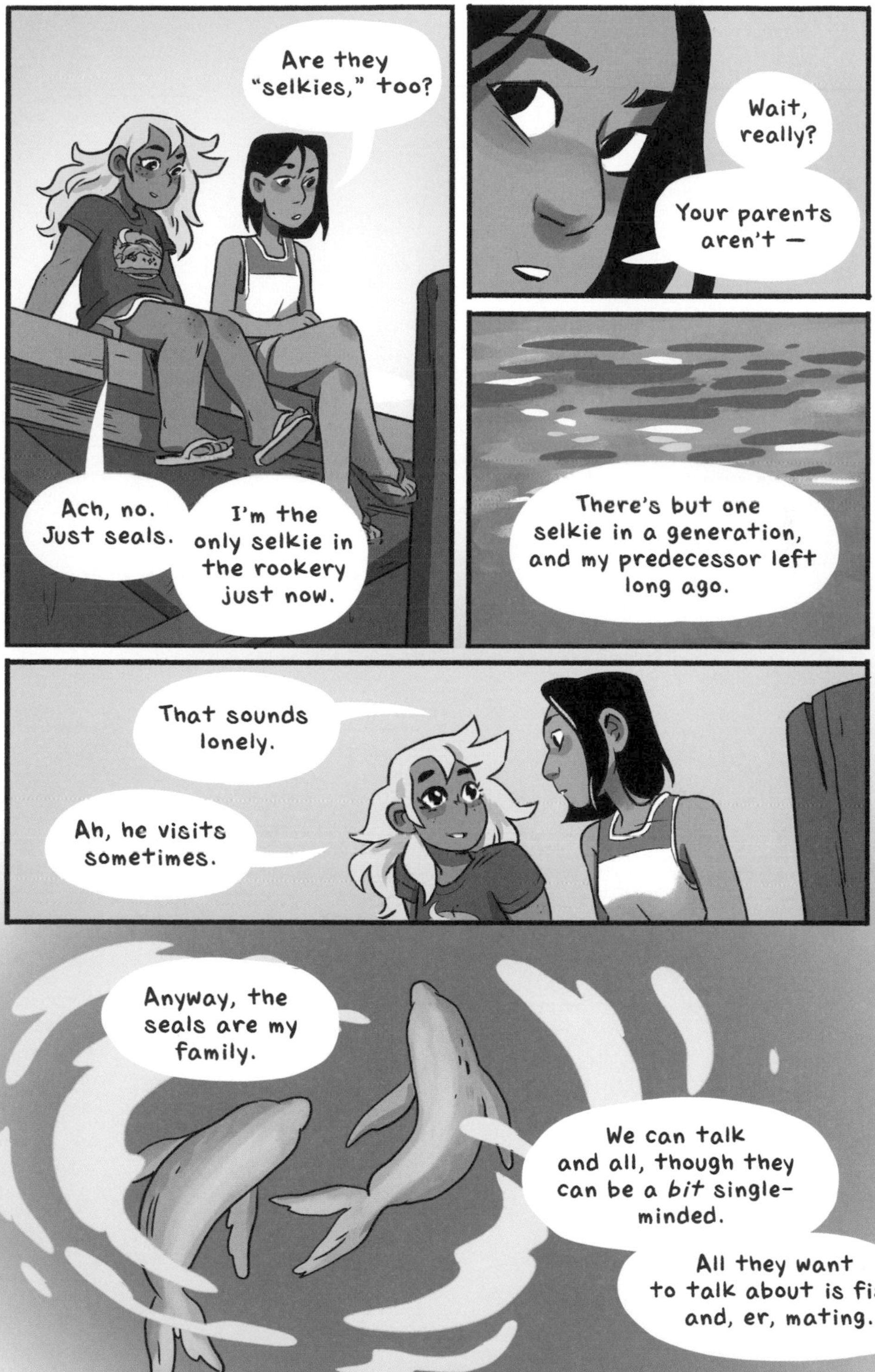
Are they "selkies," too?
Ach, no. Just seals.
I'm the only selkie in the rookery just now.
Wait, really?
Your parents aren't —
There's but one selkie in a generation, and my predecessor left long ago.
That sounds lonely.
Ah, he visits sometimes.
Anyway, the seals are my family.
We can talk and all, though they can be a *bit* single-minded.
All they want to talk about is fish and, er, mating.

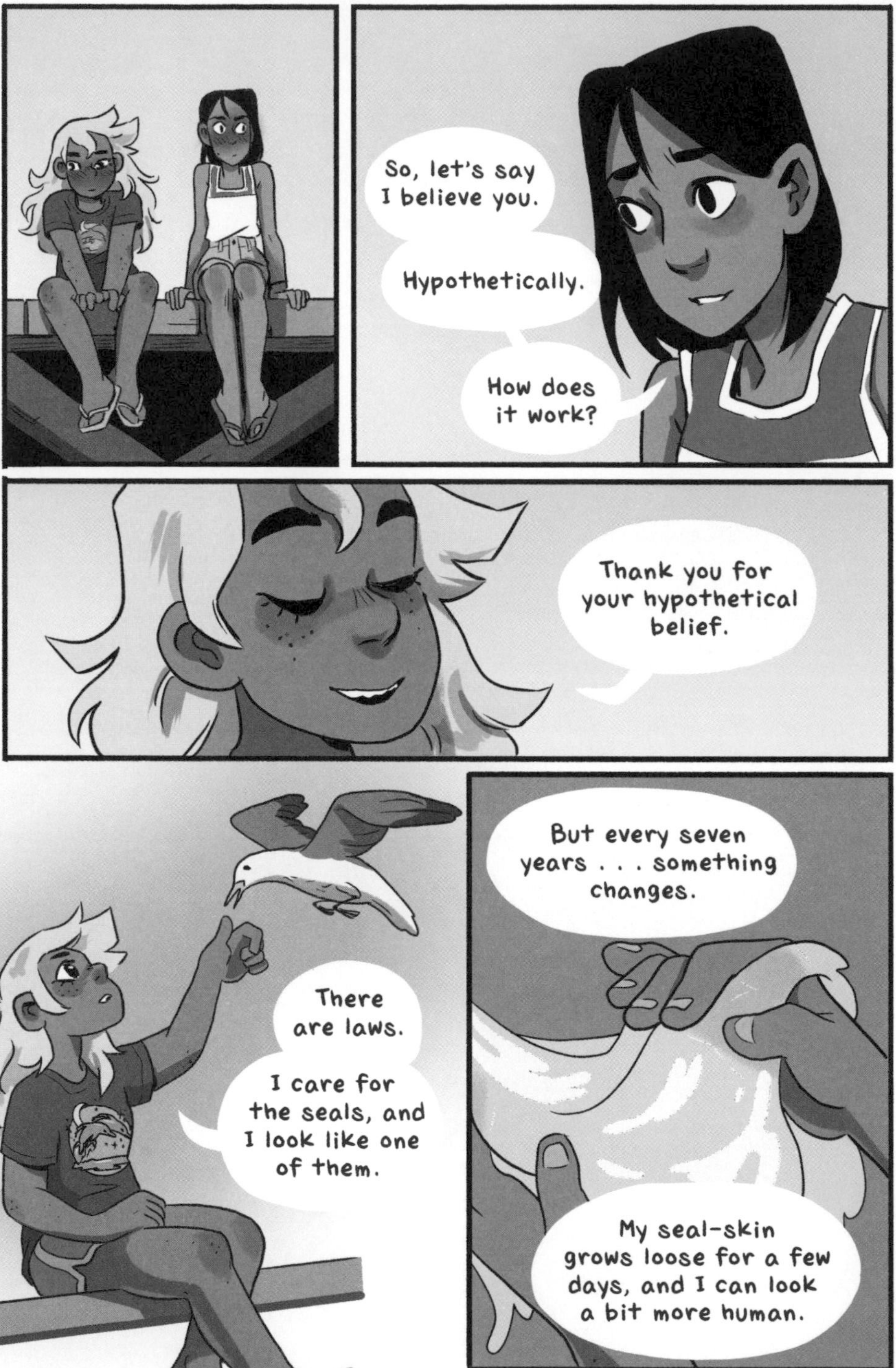
So, let's say I believe you.
Hypothetically.
How does it work?
Thank you for your hypothetical belief.
There are laws.
I care for the seals, and I look like one of them.
But every seven years . . . something changes.
My seal-skin grows loose for a few days, and I can look a bit more human.

The last time that happened, I met you!

But to be like I am now, with legs and all . . .

I need something to tie me to the land.

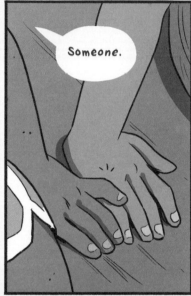

Someone.

This would be a lot easier if she weren't cute.

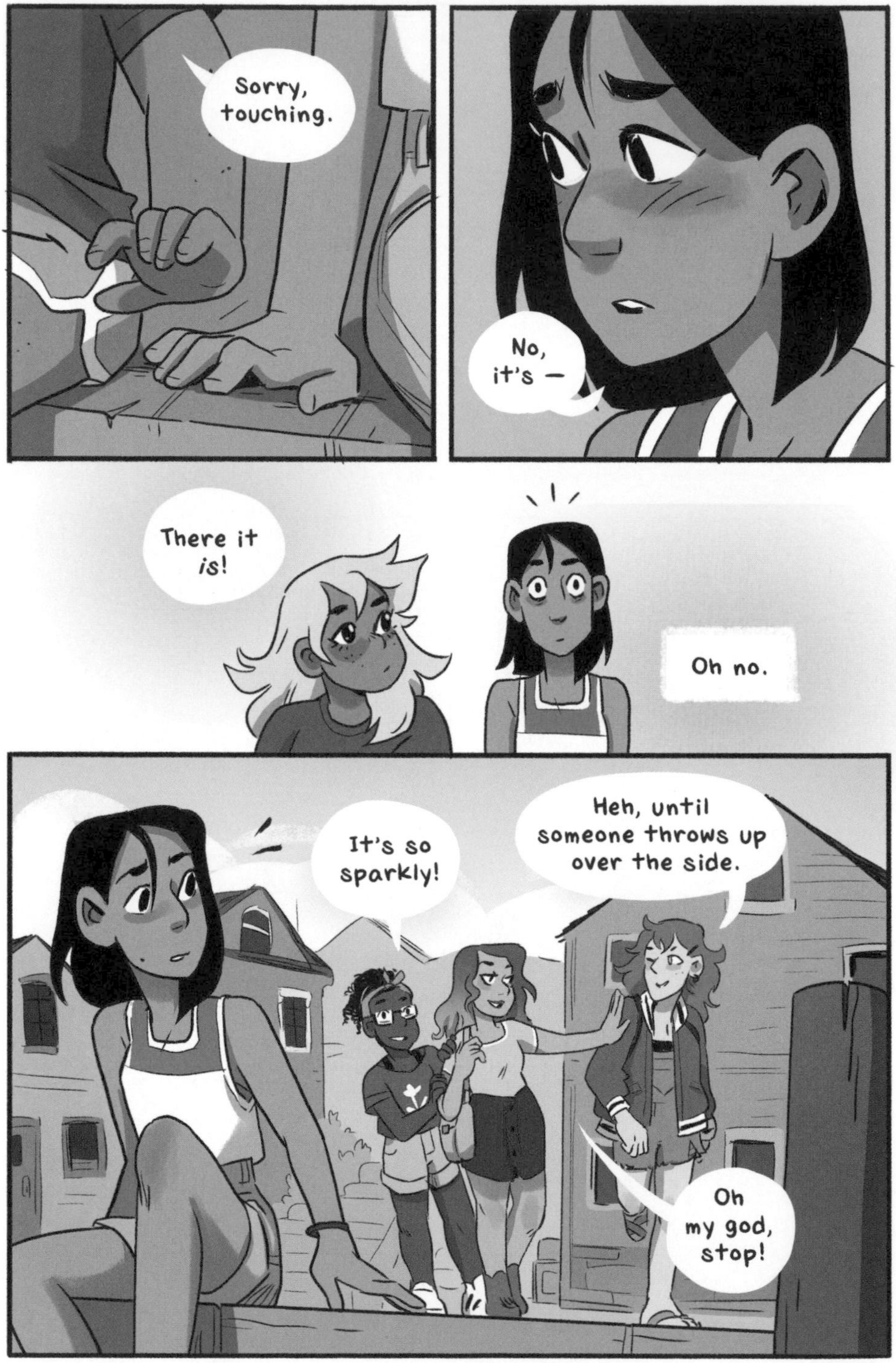

Sorry, touching.
No, it's —
There it is!
Oh no.
It's so sparkly!
Heh, until someone throws up over the side.
Oh my god, stop!

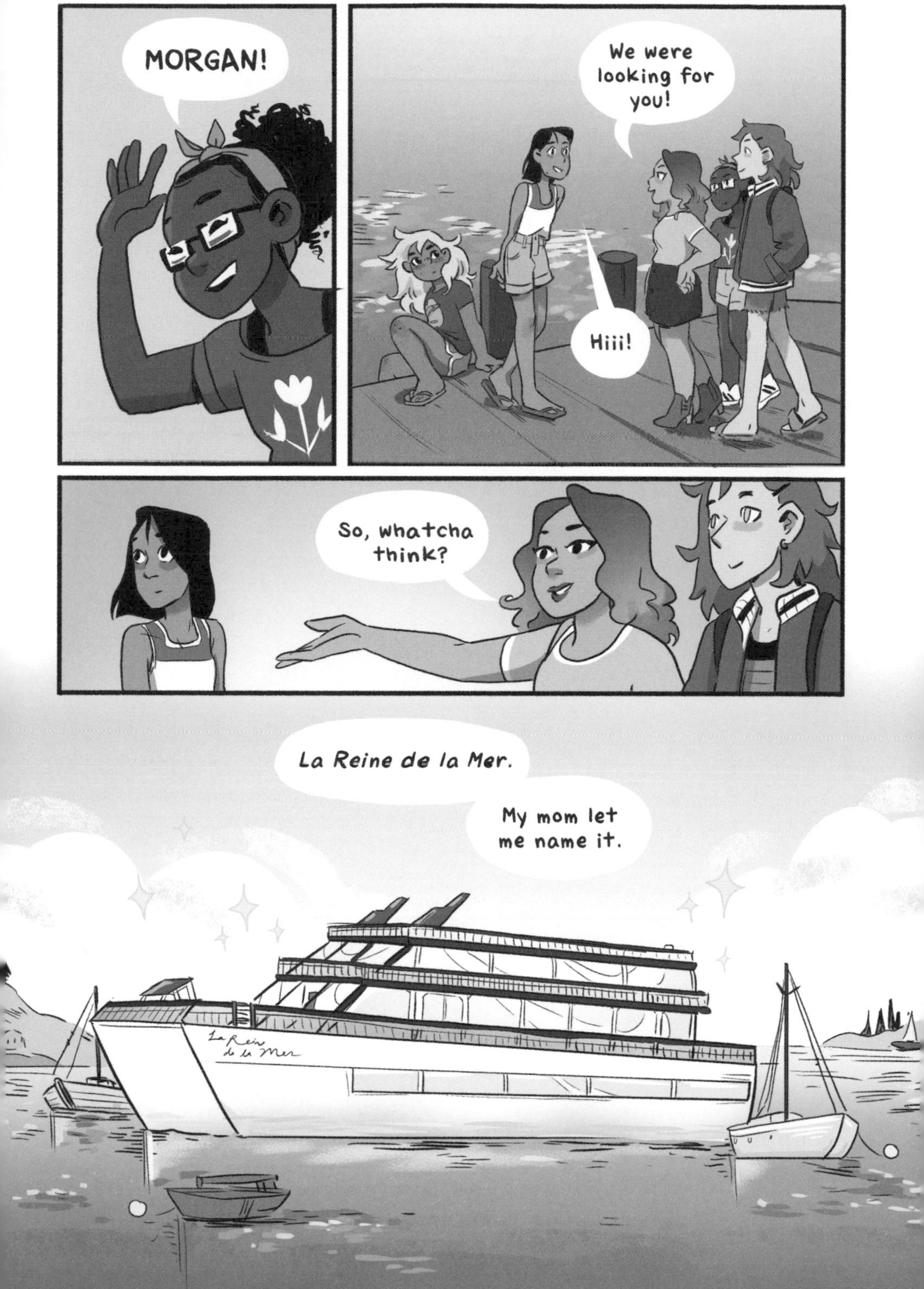
MORGAN!
We were looking for you!
Hiii!
So, whatcha think?
La Reine de la Mer.
My mom let me name it.

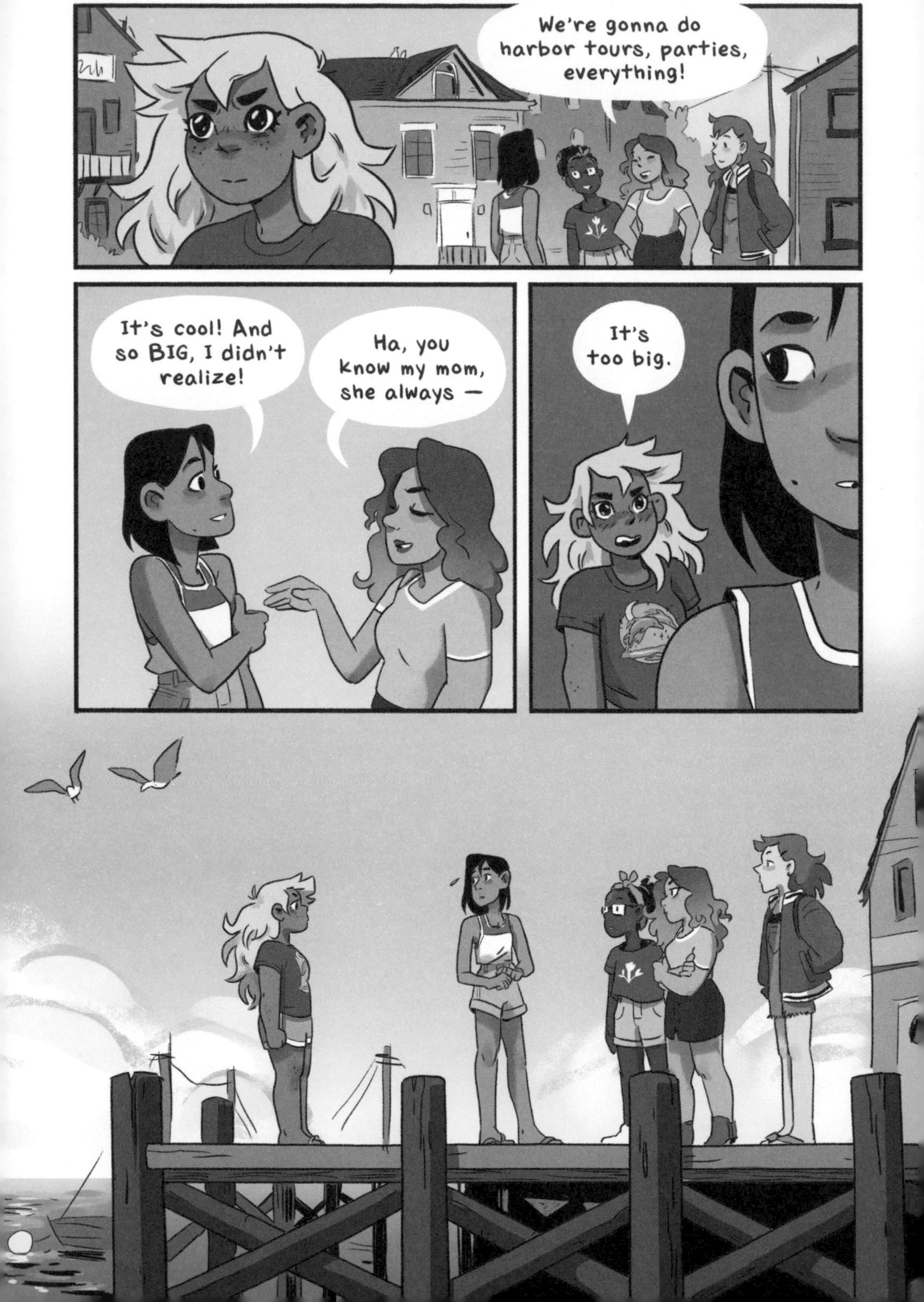
We're gonna do harbor tours, parties, everything!
It's cool! And so BIG, I didn't realize!
Ha, you know my mom, she always —
It's too big.

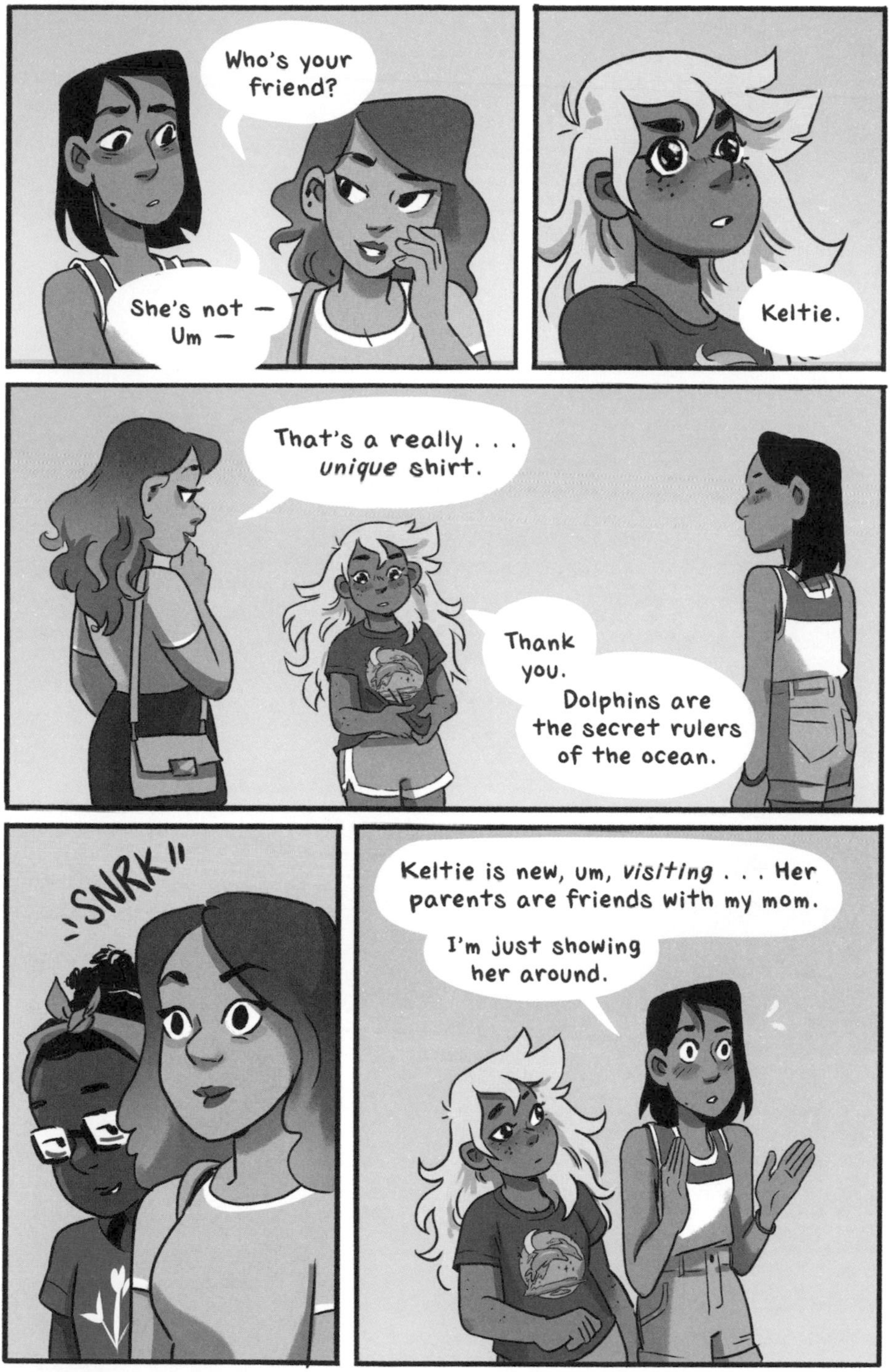
Who's your friend?
She's not — Um —
Keltie.
That's a really . . . *unique* shirt.
Thank you.
Dolphins are the secret rulers of the ocean.
SNRK!!
Keltie is new, um, *visiting* . . . Her parents are friends with my mom.
I'm just showing her around.

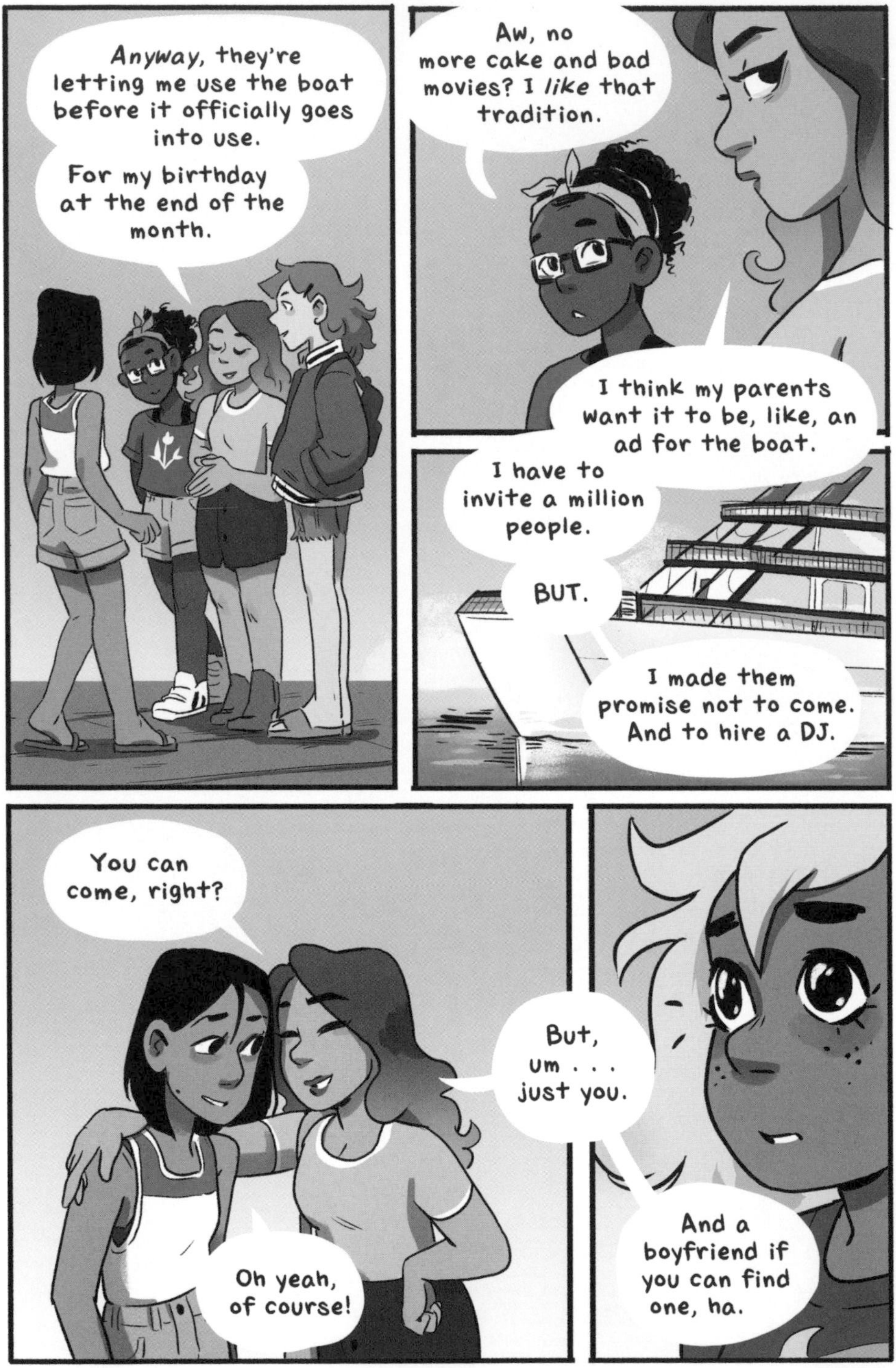

Anyway, they're letting me use the boat before it officially goes into use.
For my birthday at the end of the month.
Aw, no more cake and bad movies? I *like* that tradition.
I think my parents want it to be, like, an ad for the boat.
I have to invite a million people.
BUT.
I made them promise not to come. And to hire a DJ.
You can come, right?
Oh yeah, of course!
But, um . . . just you.
And a boyfriend if you can find one, ha.

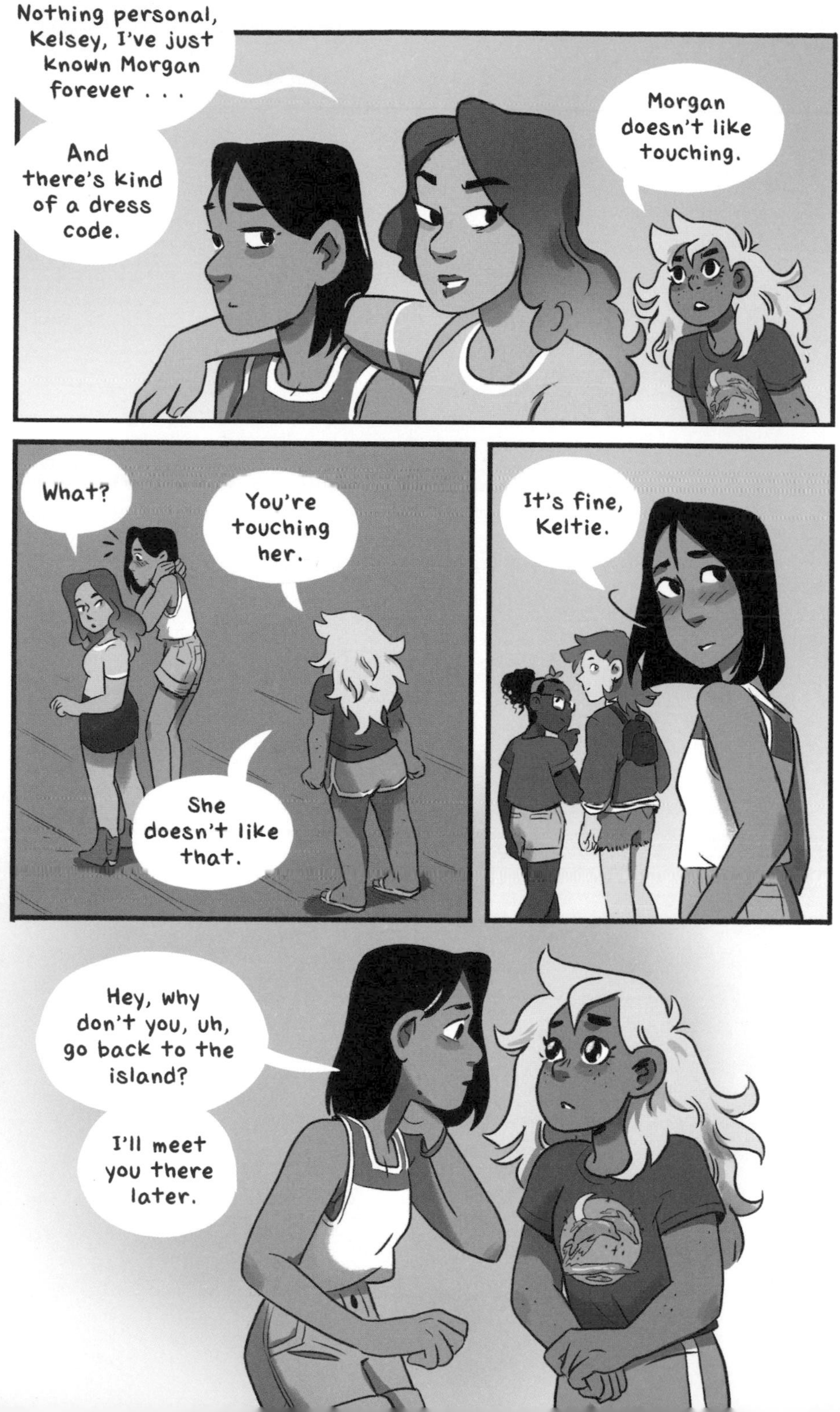

Nothing personal, Kelsey, I've just known Morgan forever . . .
And there's kind of a dress code.
Morgan doesn't like touching.
What?
You're touching her.
She doesn't like that.
It's fine, Keltie.
Hey, why don't you, uh, go back to the island?
I'll meet you there later.

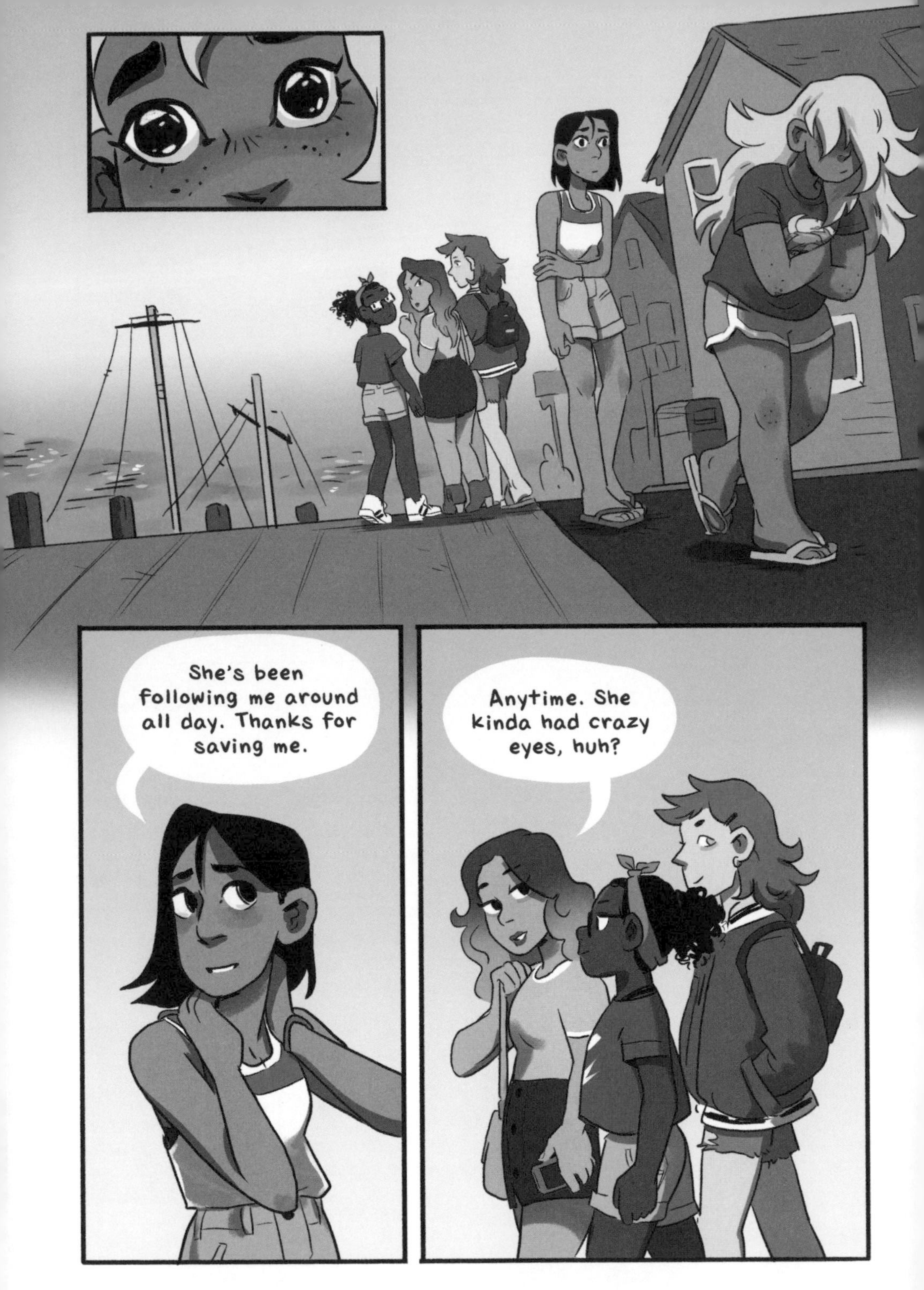
She's been following me around all day. Thanks for saving me.
Anytime. She kinda had crazy eyes, huh?

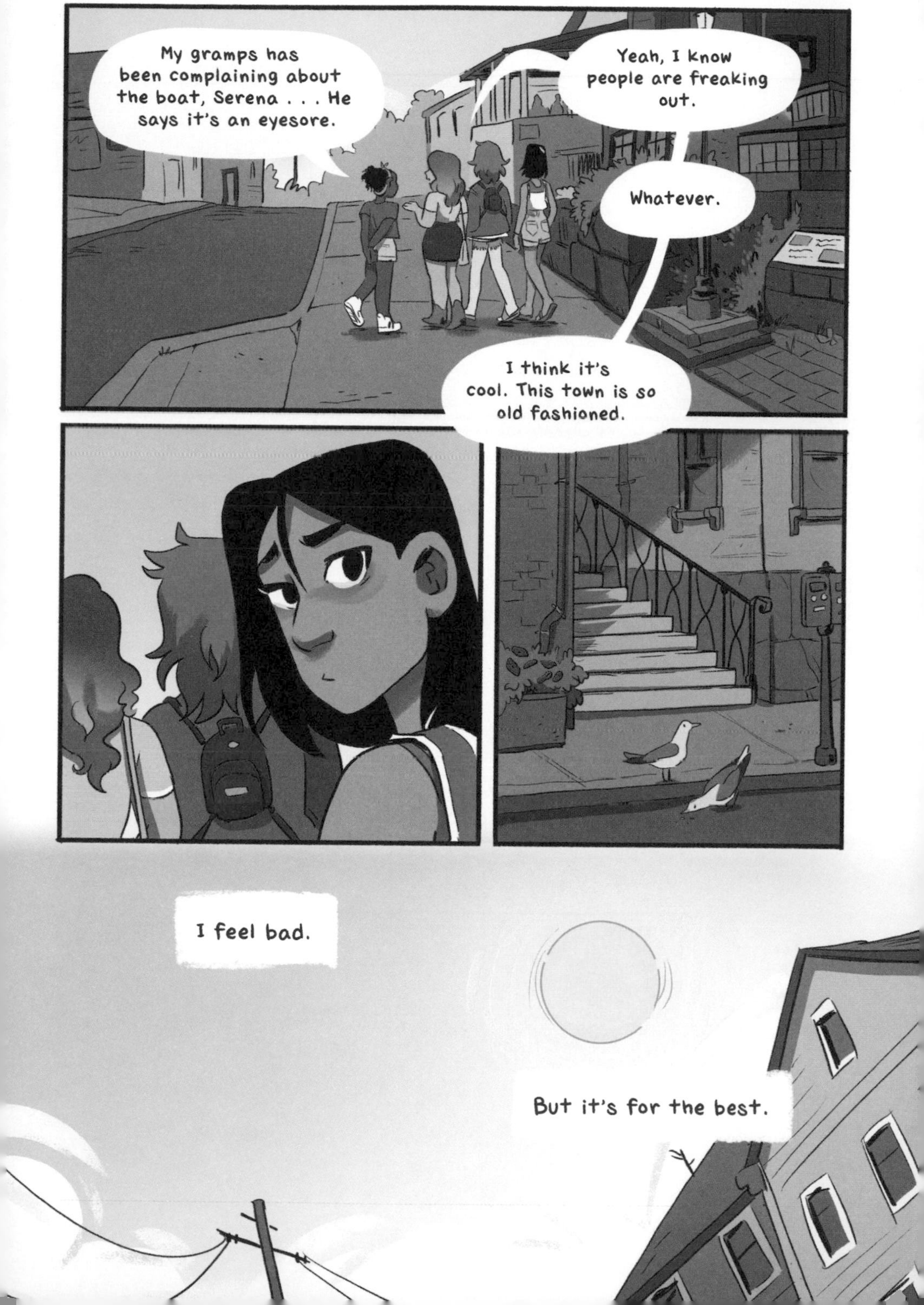
My gramps has been complaining about the boat, Serena . . . He says it's an eyesore.
Yeah, I know people are freaking out.
Whatever.
I think it's cool. This town is so old fashioned.
I feel bad.
But it's for the best.

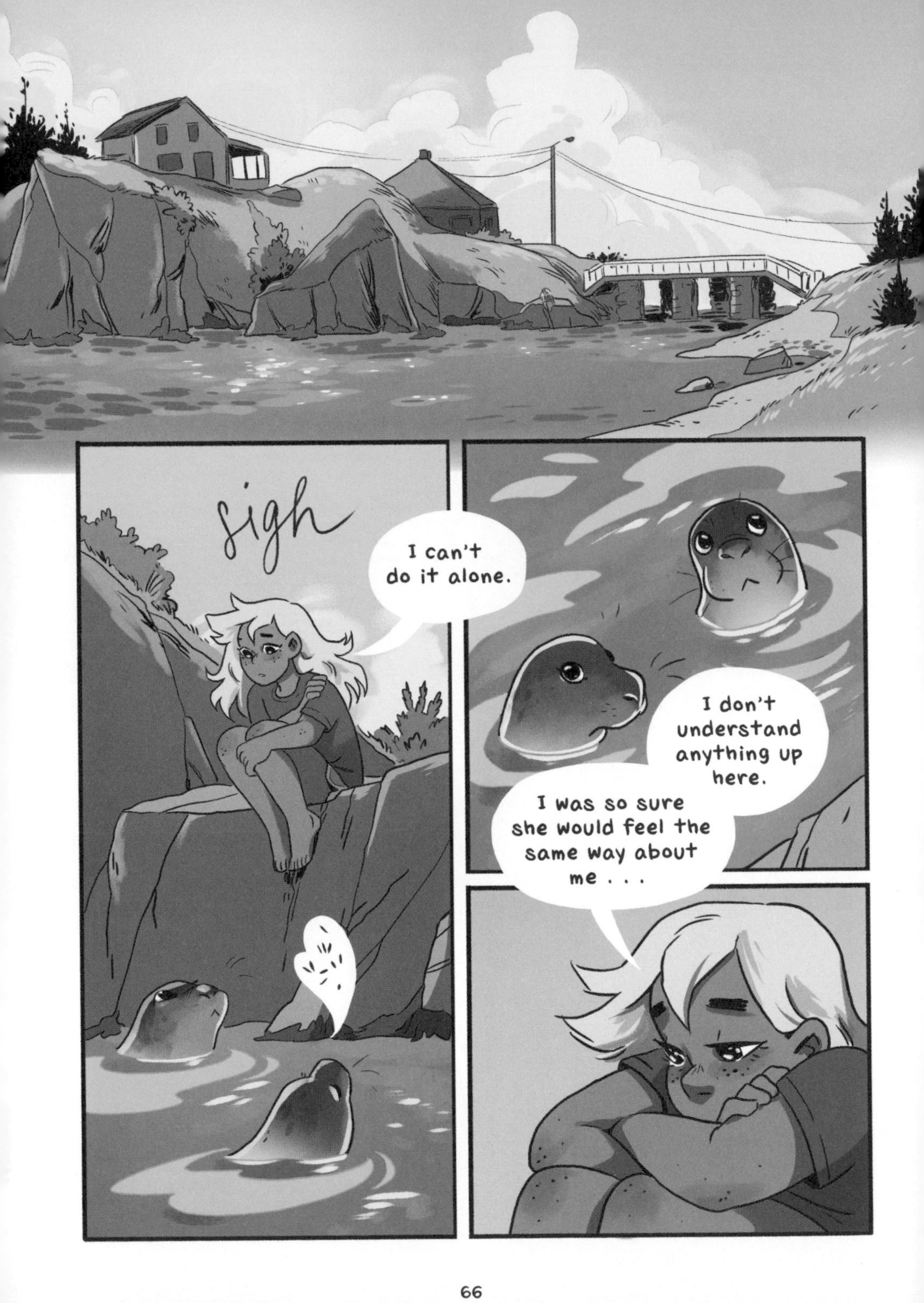
sigh
I can't do it alone.
I don't understand anything up here.
I was so sure she would feel the same way about me . . .

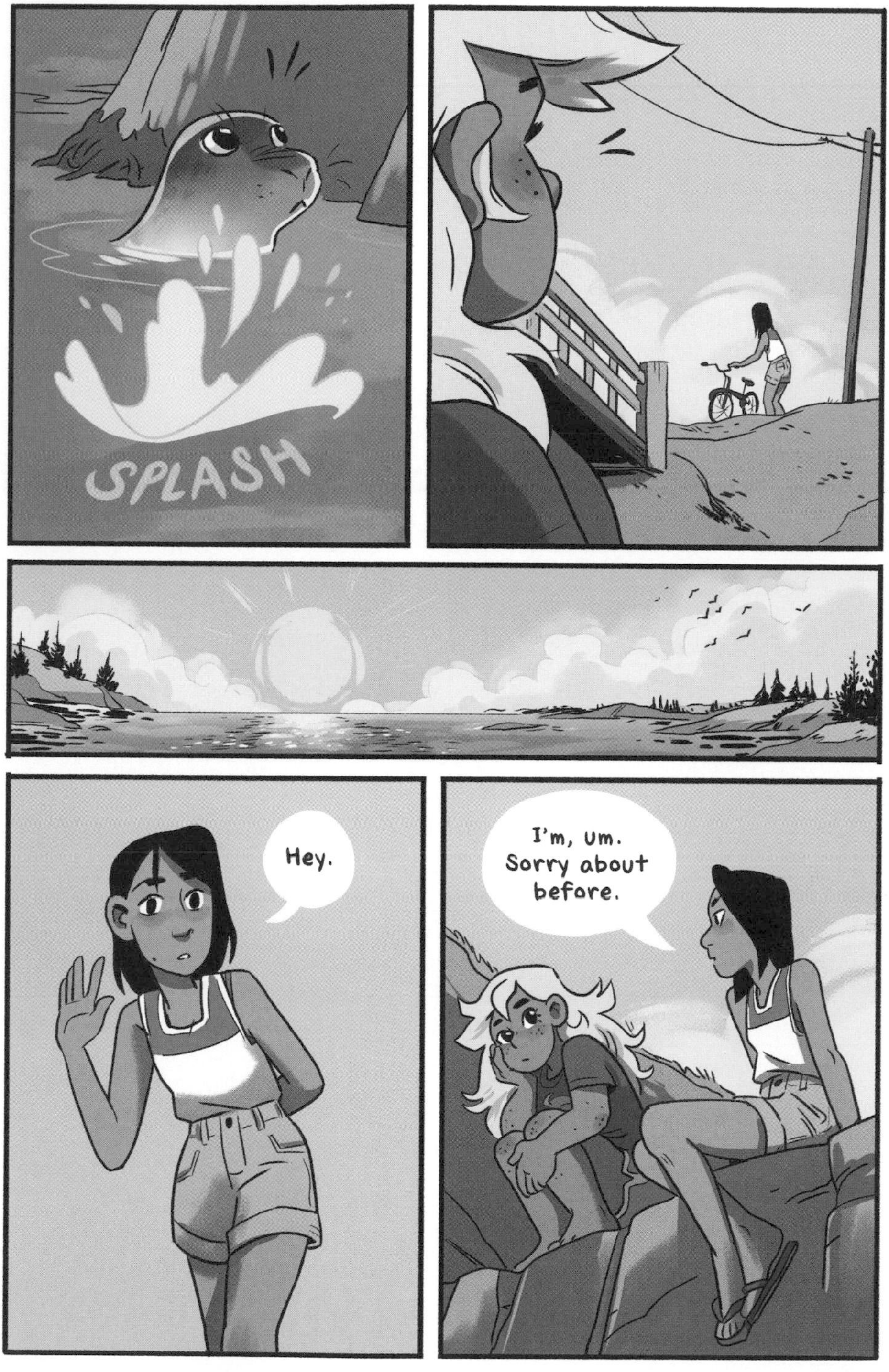
SPLASH
Hey.
I'm, um. Sorry about before.

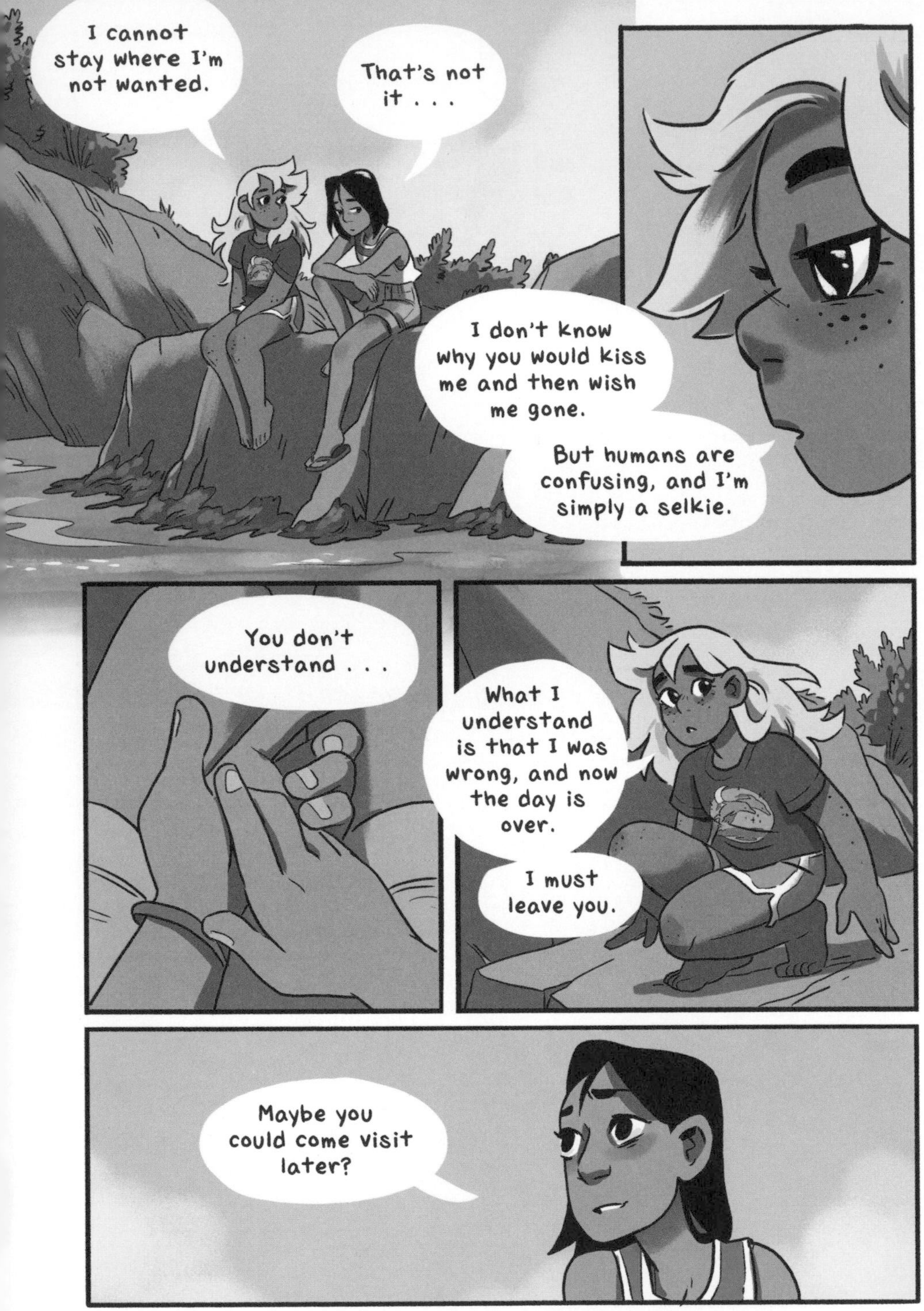
I cannot stay where I'm not wanted.
That's not it . . .
I don't know why you would kiss me and then wish me gone.
But humans are confusing, and I'm simply a selkie.
You don't understand . . .
What I understand is that I was wrong, and now the day is over.
I must leave you.
Maybe you could come visit later?

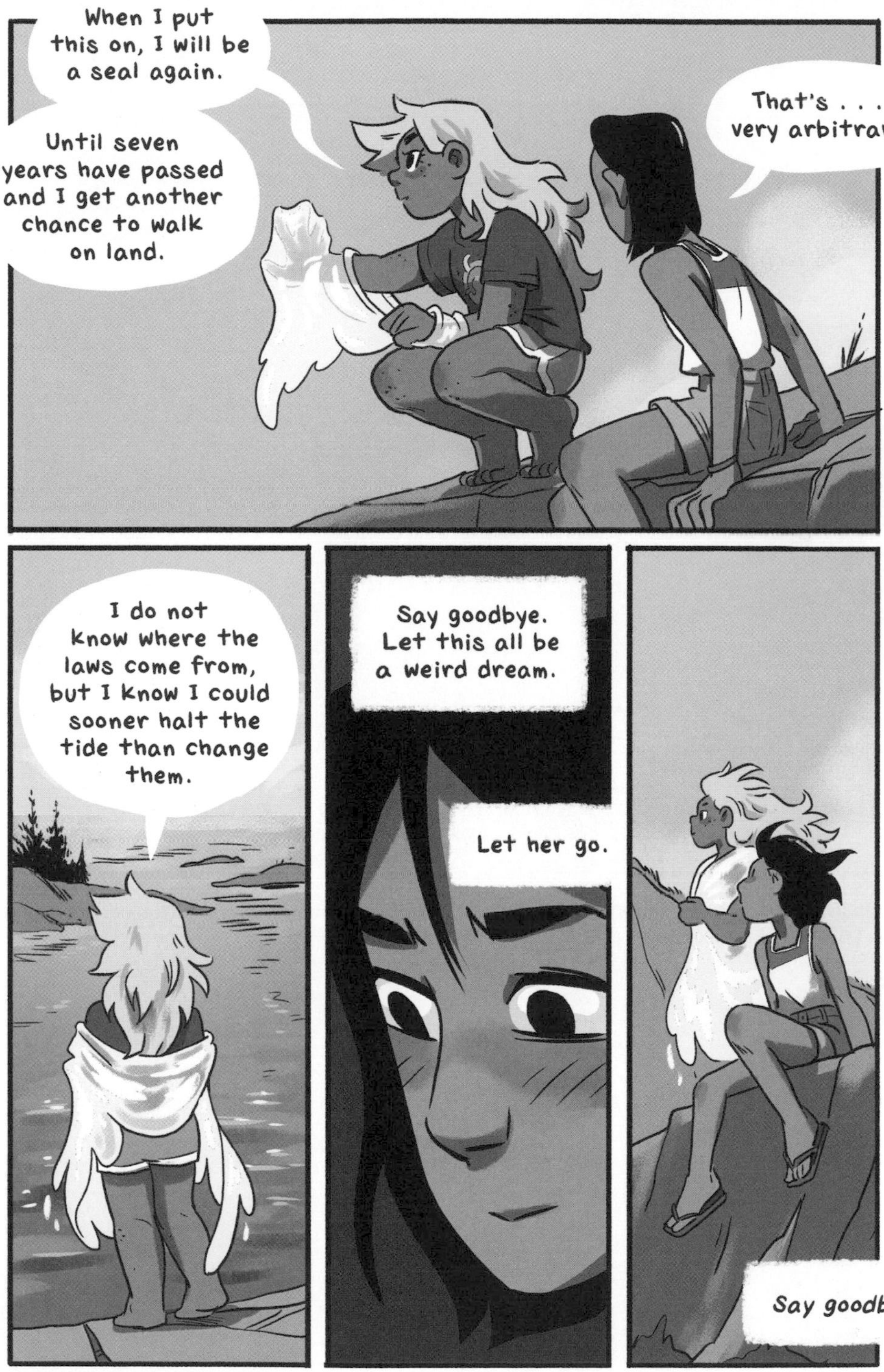
When I put this on, I will be a seal again.
Until seven years have passed and I get another chance to walk on land.
That's . . . very arbitrary.
I do not know where the laws come from, but I know I could sooner halt the tide than change them.
Say goodbye. Let this all be a weird dream.
Let her go.
Say goodbye.

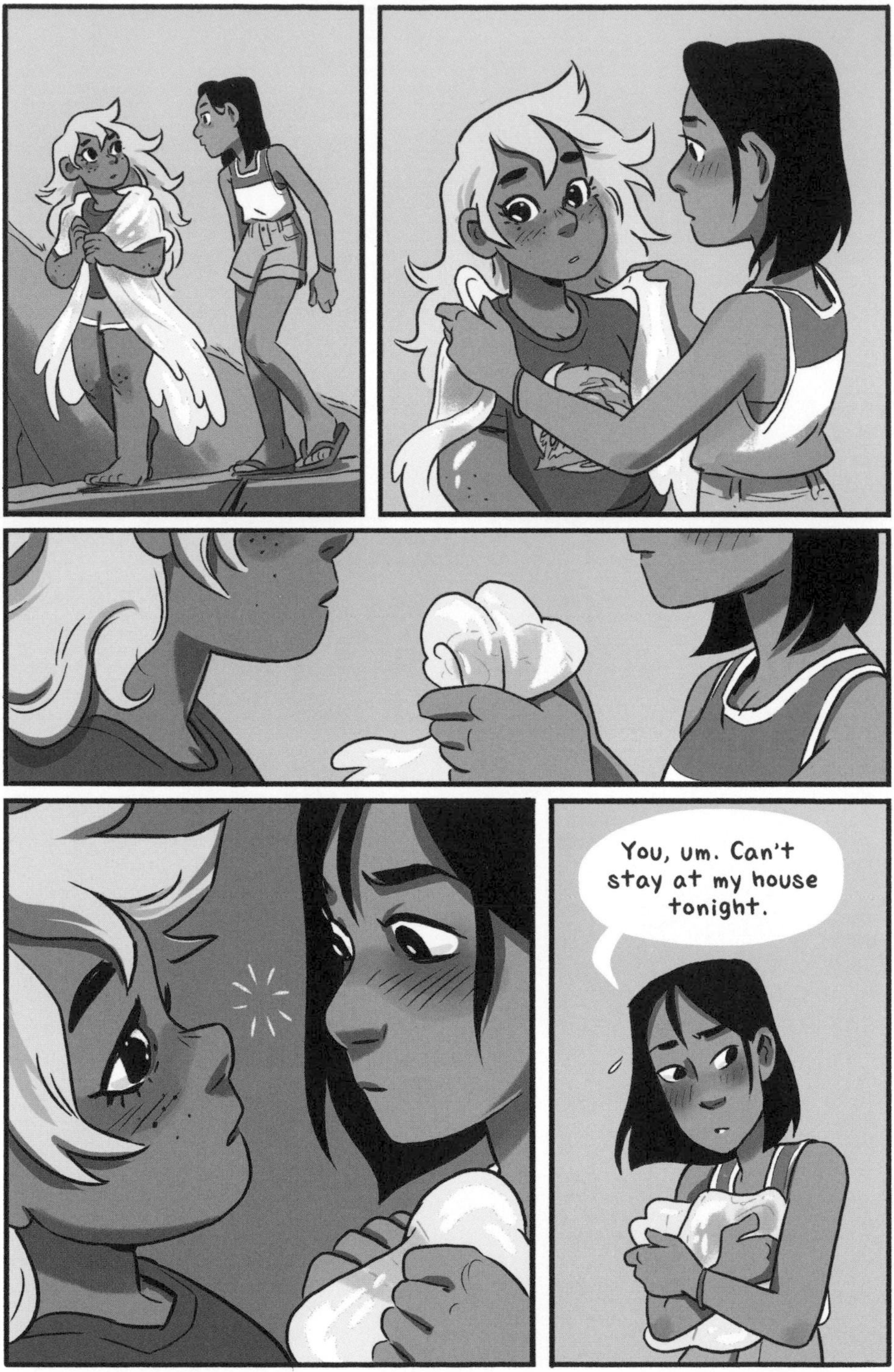
You, um. Can't stay at my house tonight.

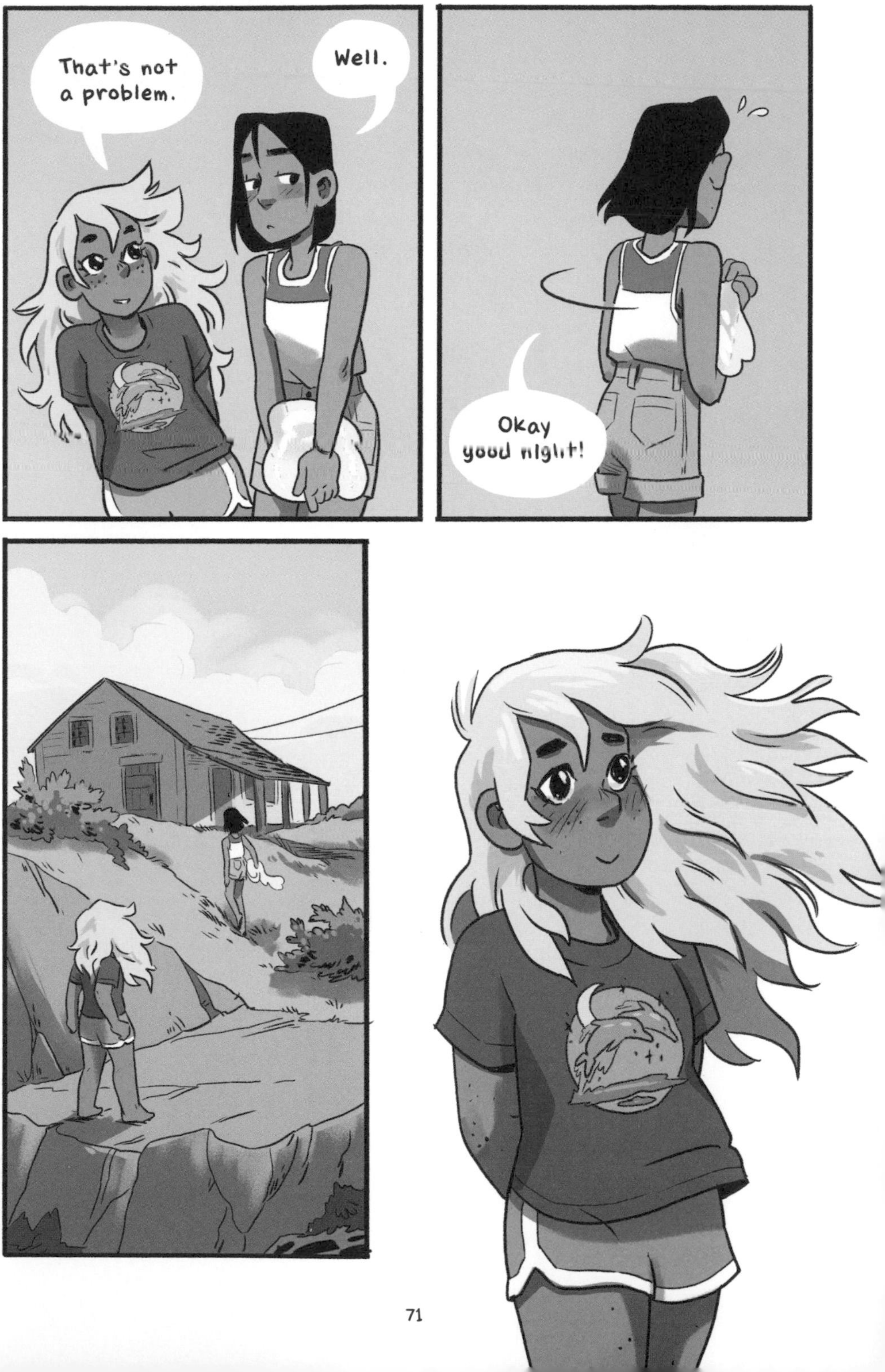
That's not a problem.
Well.
Okay good night!

Morgan   Serena   Jules   Lizzie

Wed, June 12, 10:14 PM

 Have you guys ever done something really dumb

 literally never

Morgan.....what did u do

 did you eat shellfish again. sweet foolish morgan, we tried to warn you. so, so many times

 What's up, Morgan?

 nevermind

 ???

 why the mystery

 nvm sorry i'm being stupid!!! ignore me!

 did you get a bad haircut

because if so you are legally obligated to show us

 the worst

goodnight guys <3 <3

72

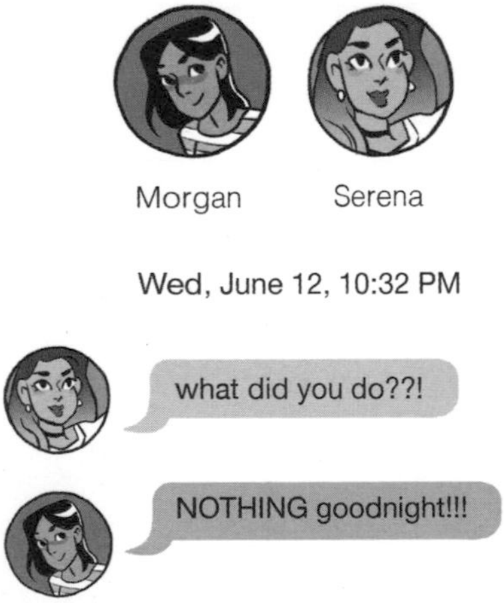
Morgan
Serena
Wed, June 12, 10:32 PM
what did you do??!
NOTHING goodnight!!!

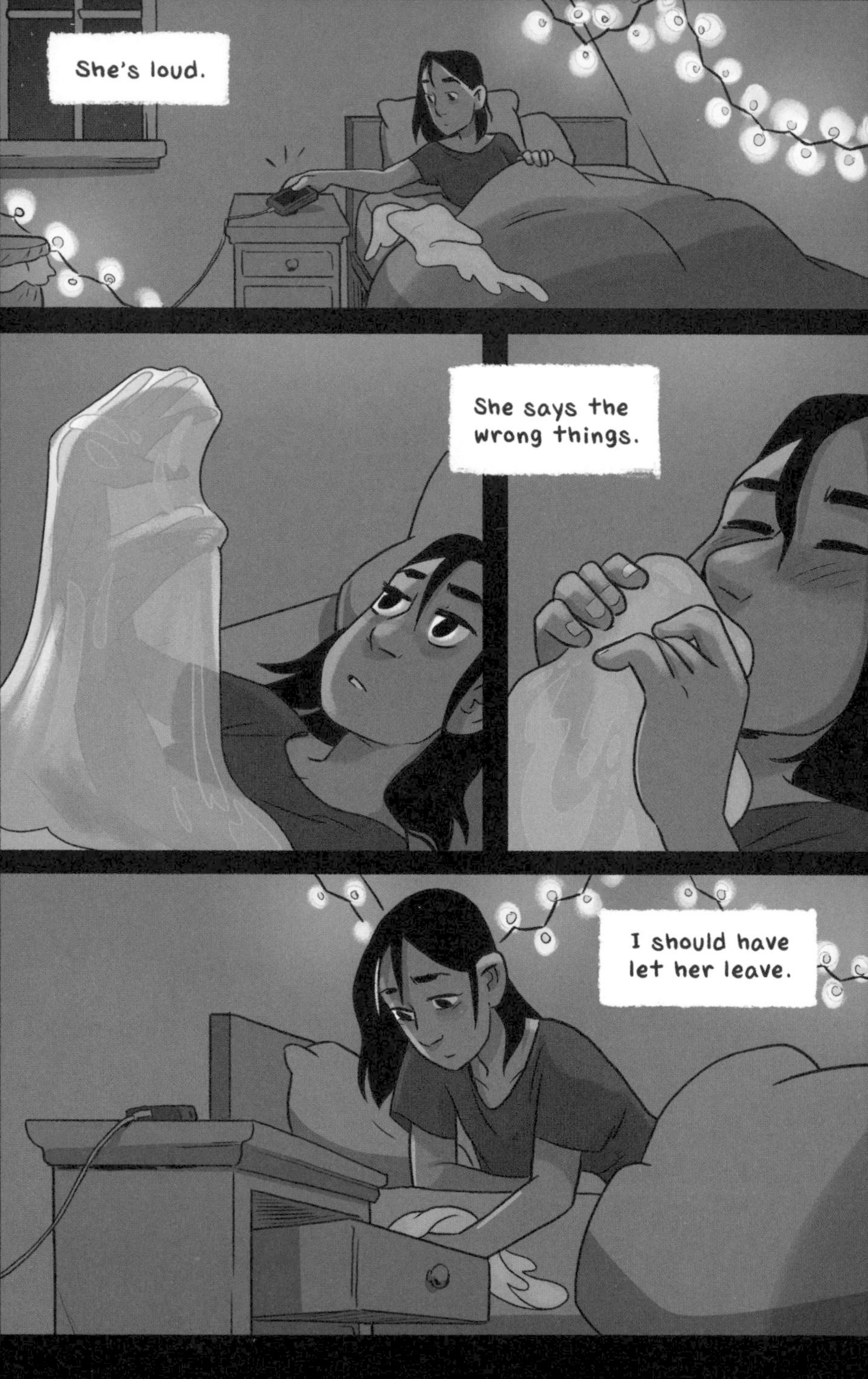
She's loud.
She says the wrong things.
I should have let her leave.

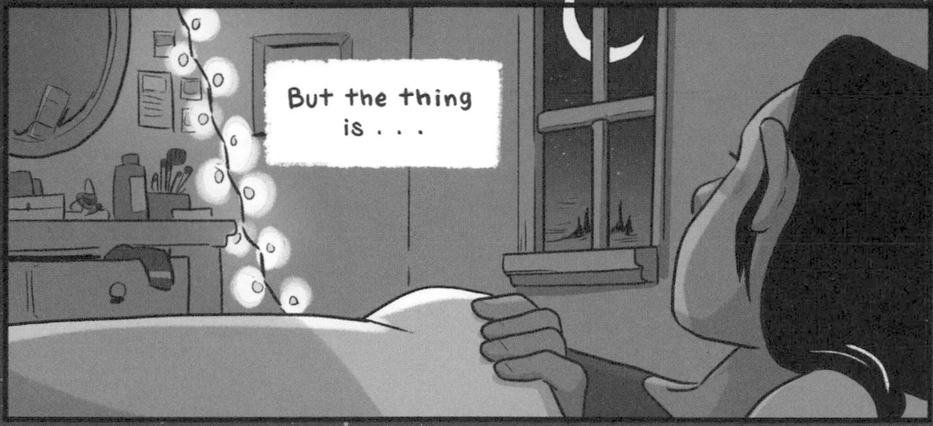
But the thing is . . .

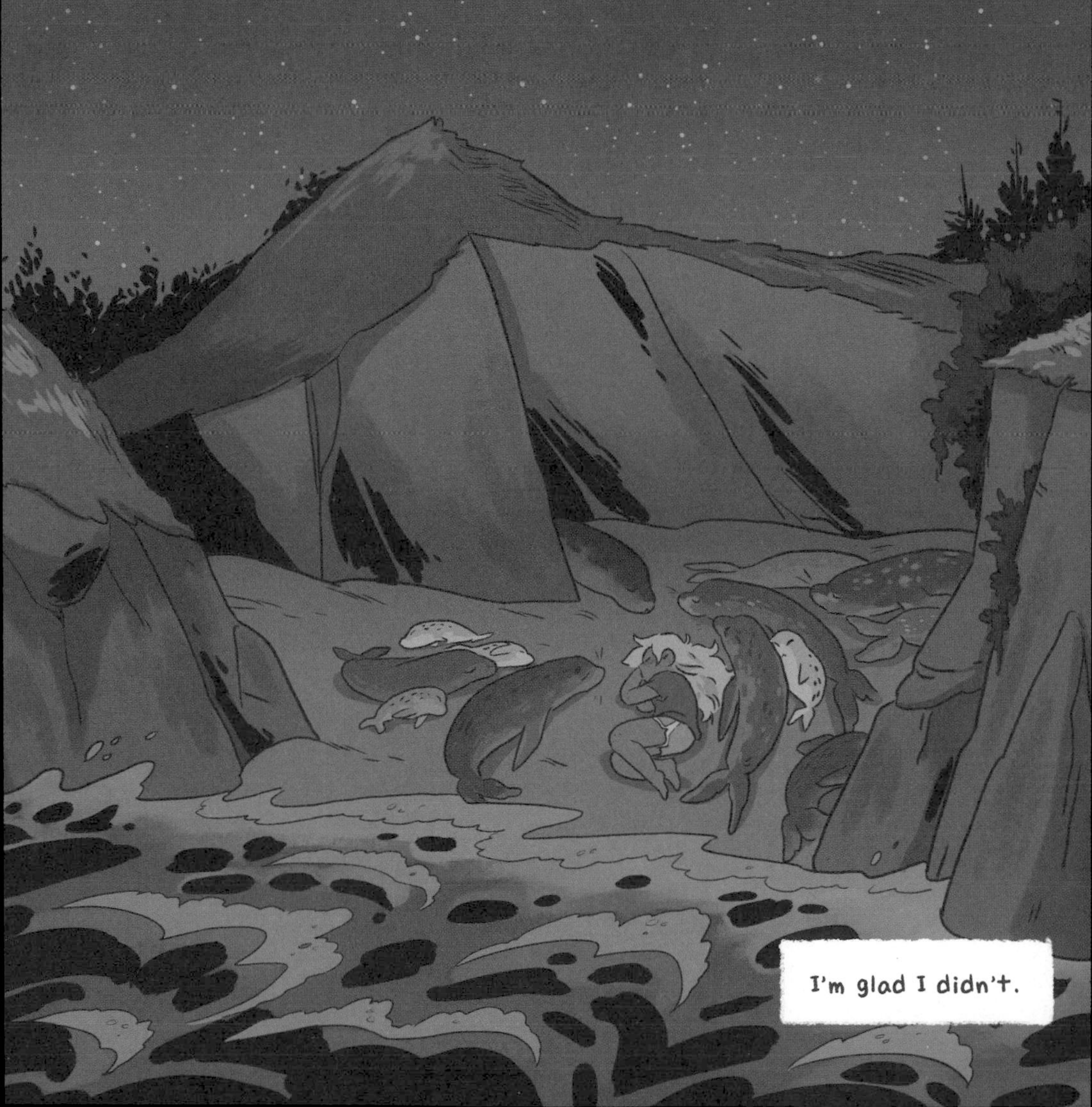
I'm glad I didn't.

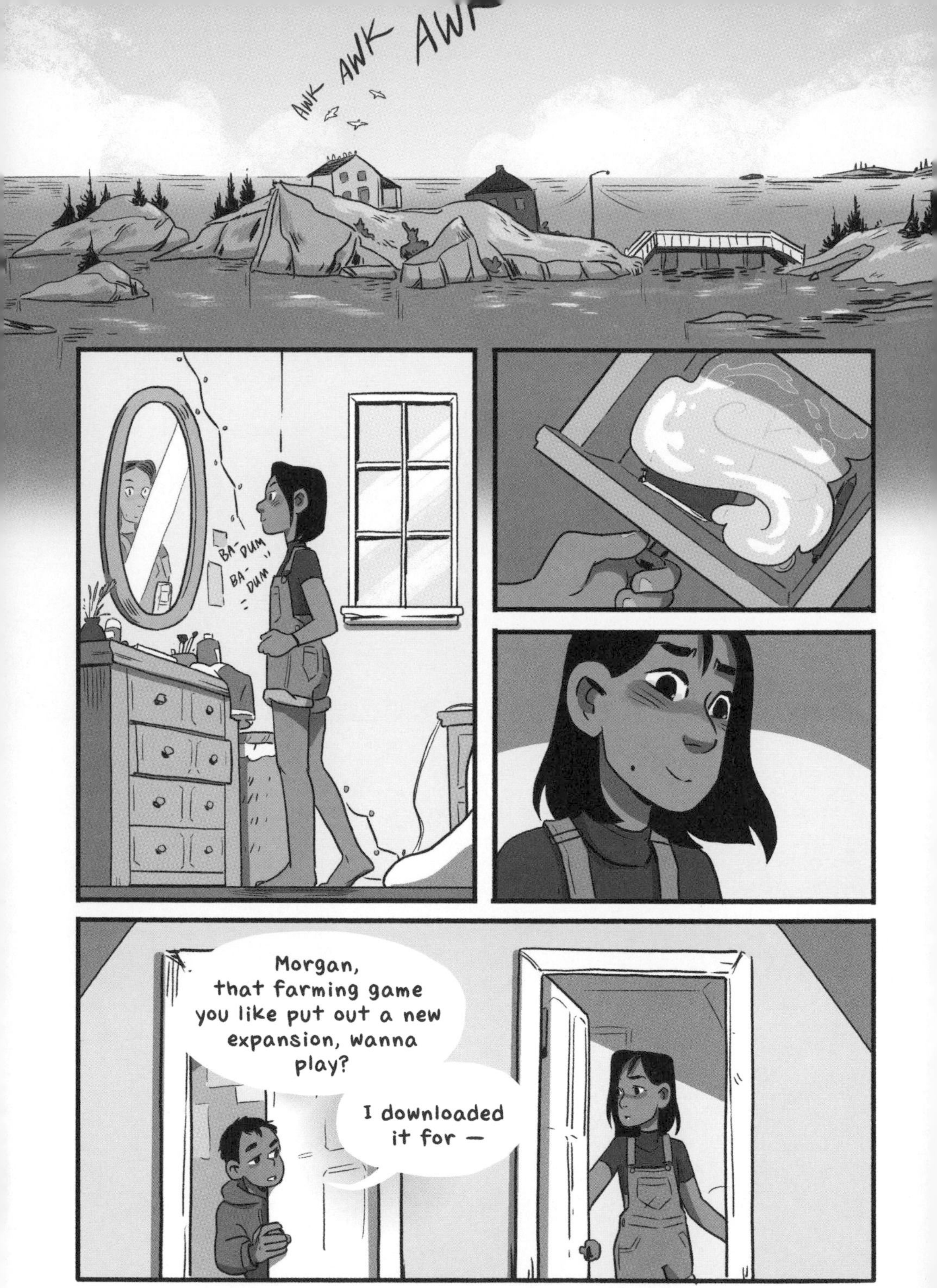
AWK AWK AWK
BA-DUM
BA-DUM
Morgan, that farming game you like put out a new expansion, wanna play?
I downloaded it for —

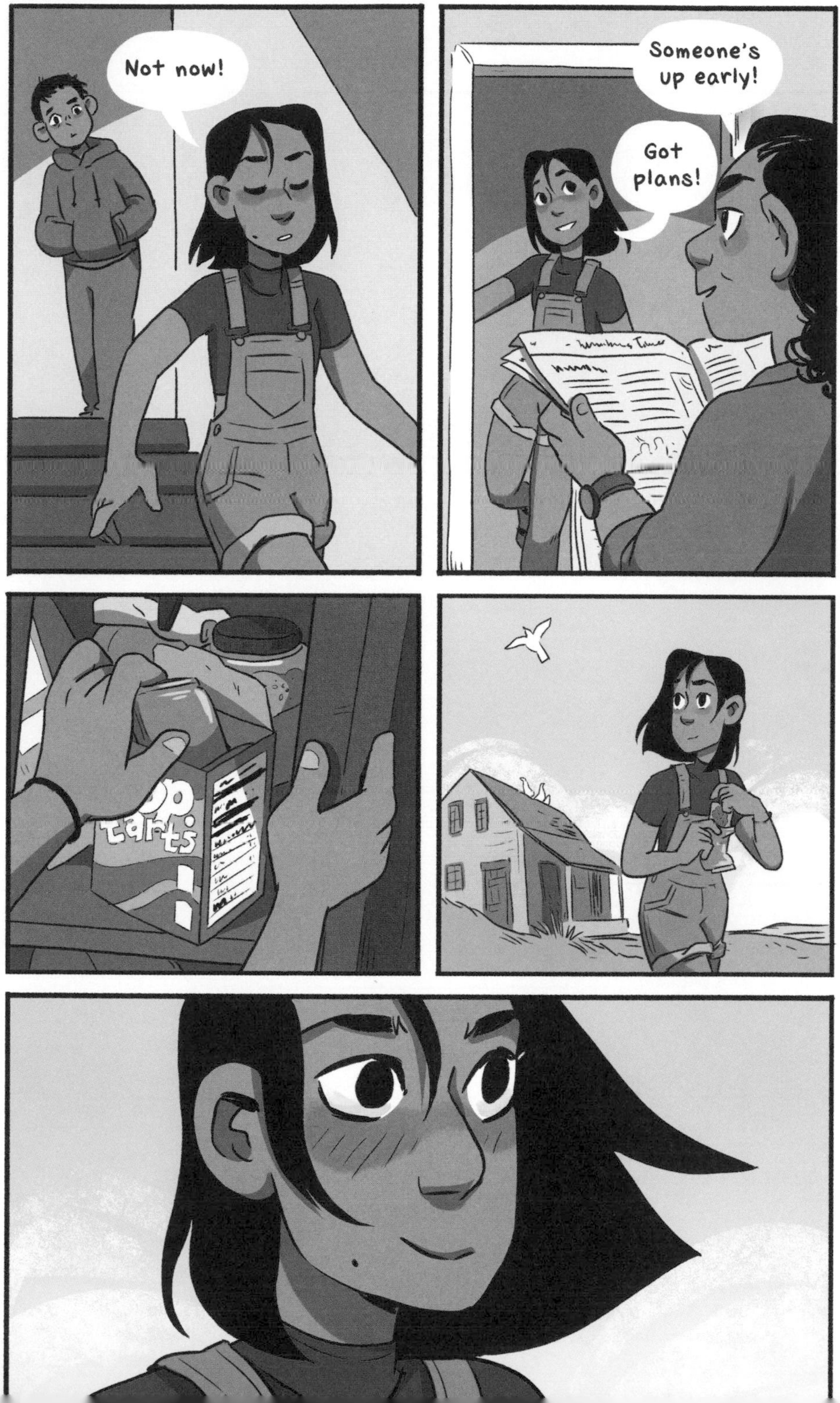
Not now!
Someone's up early!
Got plans!
Pop tarts

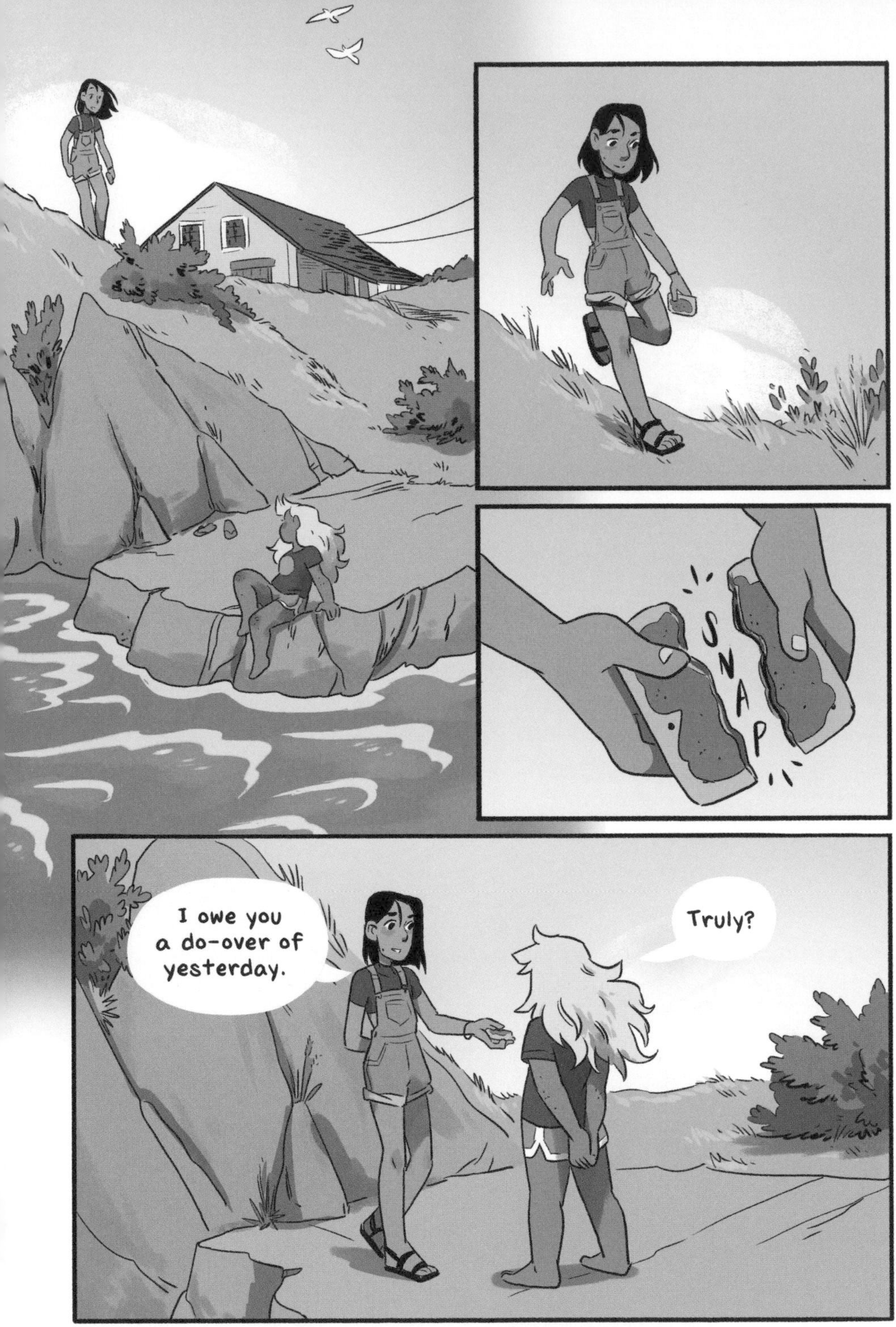
SNAP
I owe you a do-over of yesterday.
Truly?

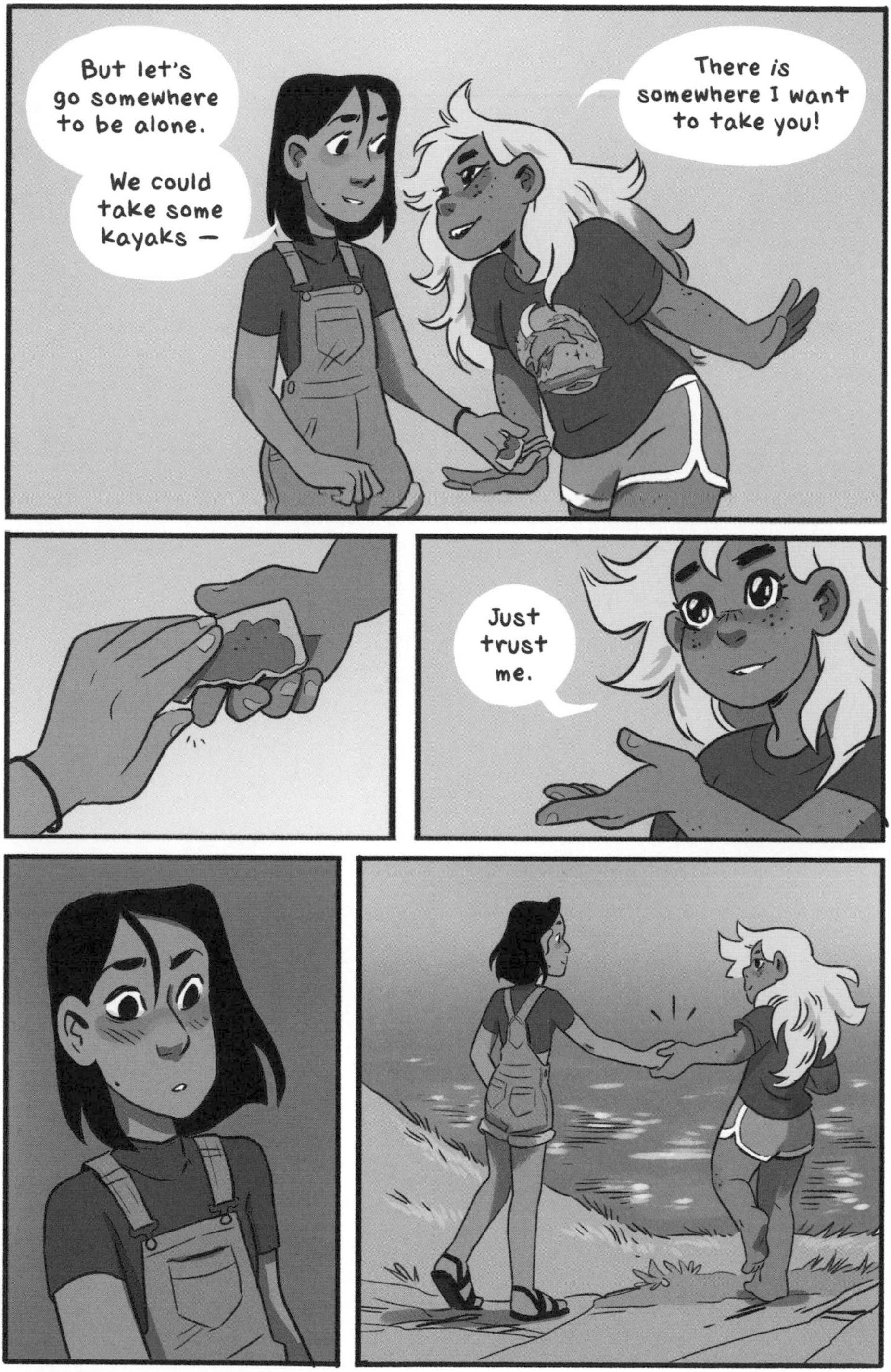
But let's go somewhere to be alone.
We could take some kayaks —
There *is* somewhere I want to take you!
Just trust me.

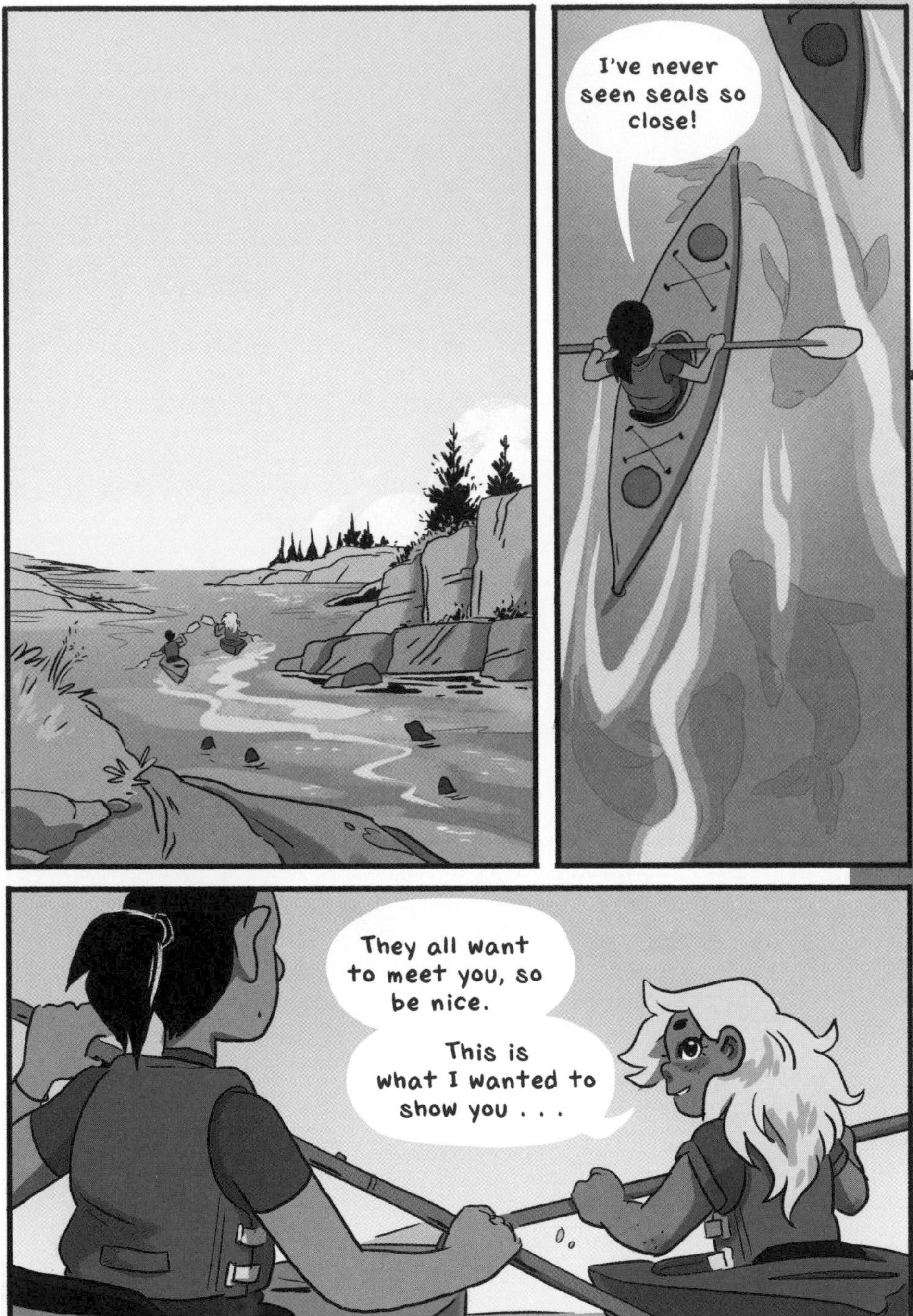
I've never seen seals so close!
They all want to meet you, so be nice.
This is what I wanted to show you . . .

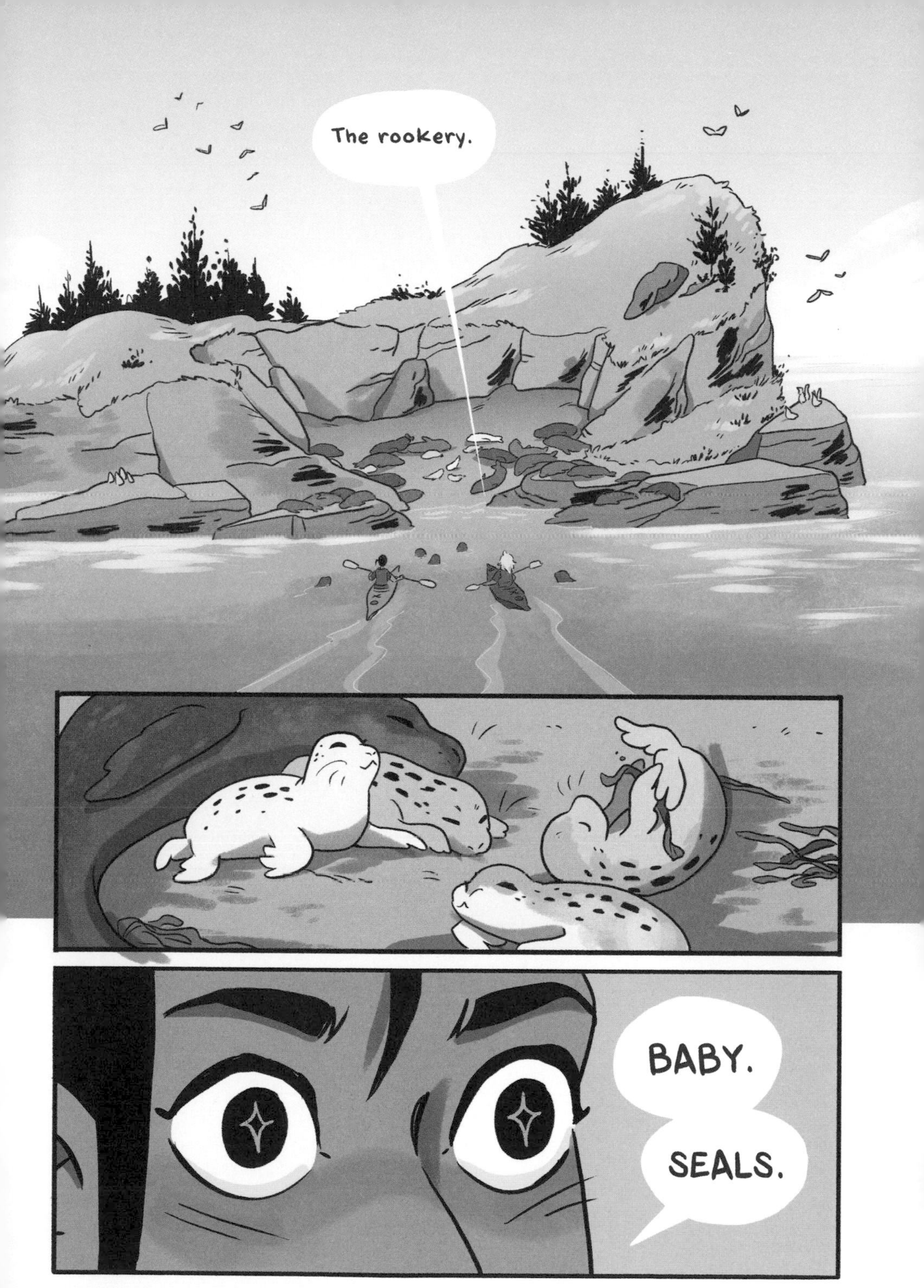
The rookery.
BABY.
SEALS.

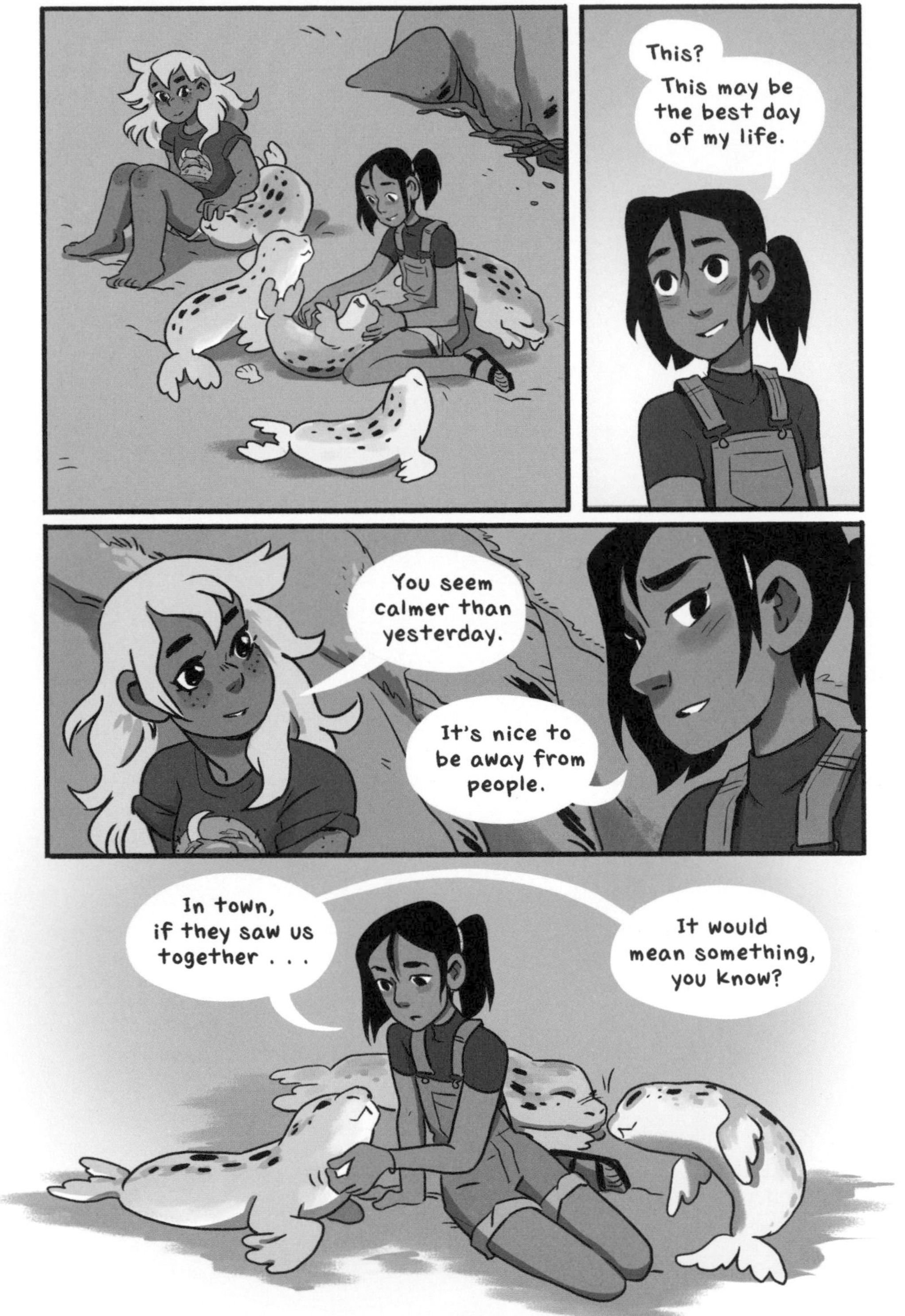
This?
This may be the best day of my life.
You seem calmer than yesterday.
It's nice to be away from people.
In town, if they saw us together . . .
It would mean something, you know?

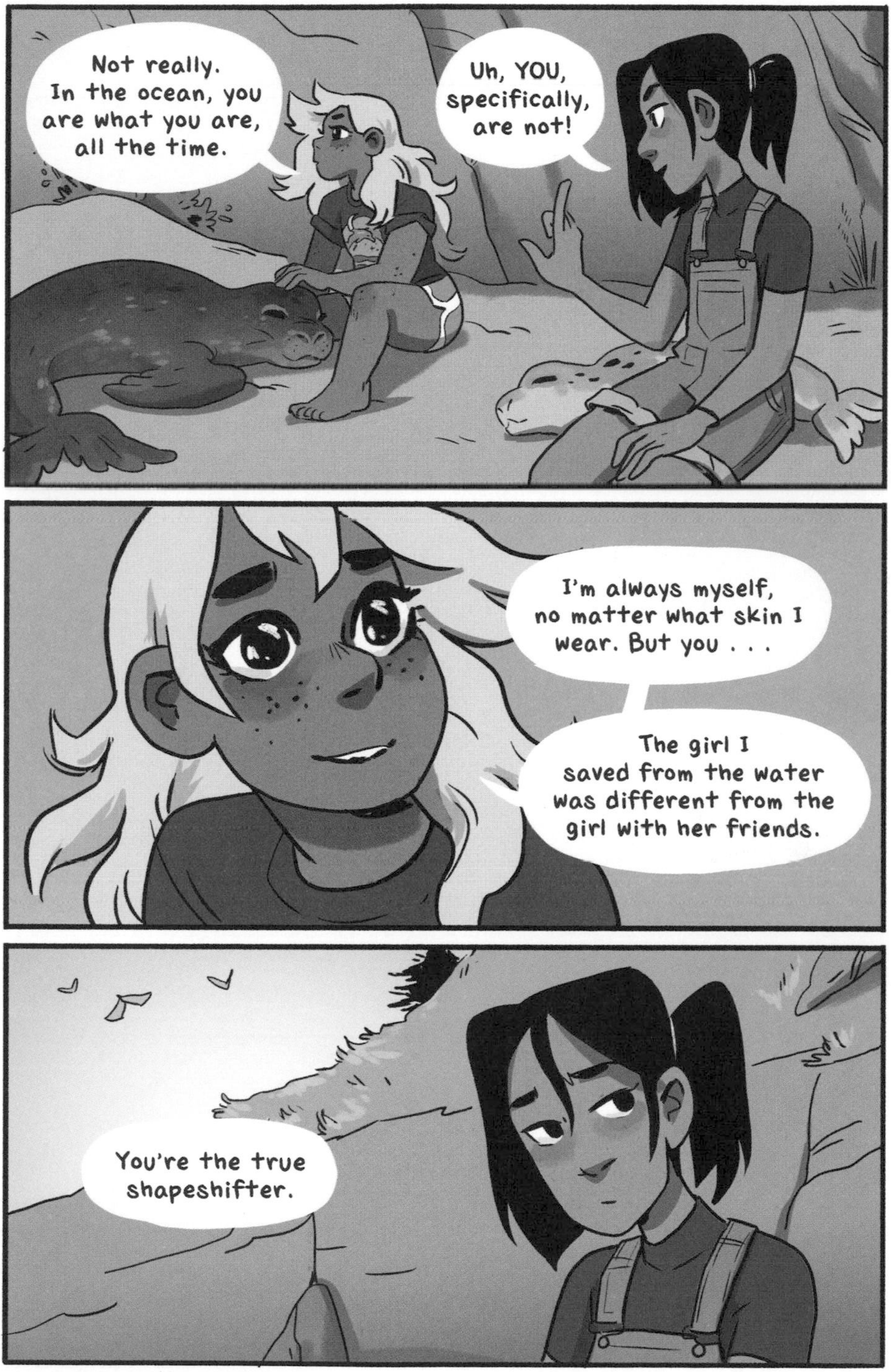
Not really. In the ocean, you are what you are, all the time.
Uh, YOU, specifically, are not!
I'm always myself, no matter what skin I wear. But you . . .
The girl I saved from the water was different from the girl with her friends.
You're the true shapeshifter.

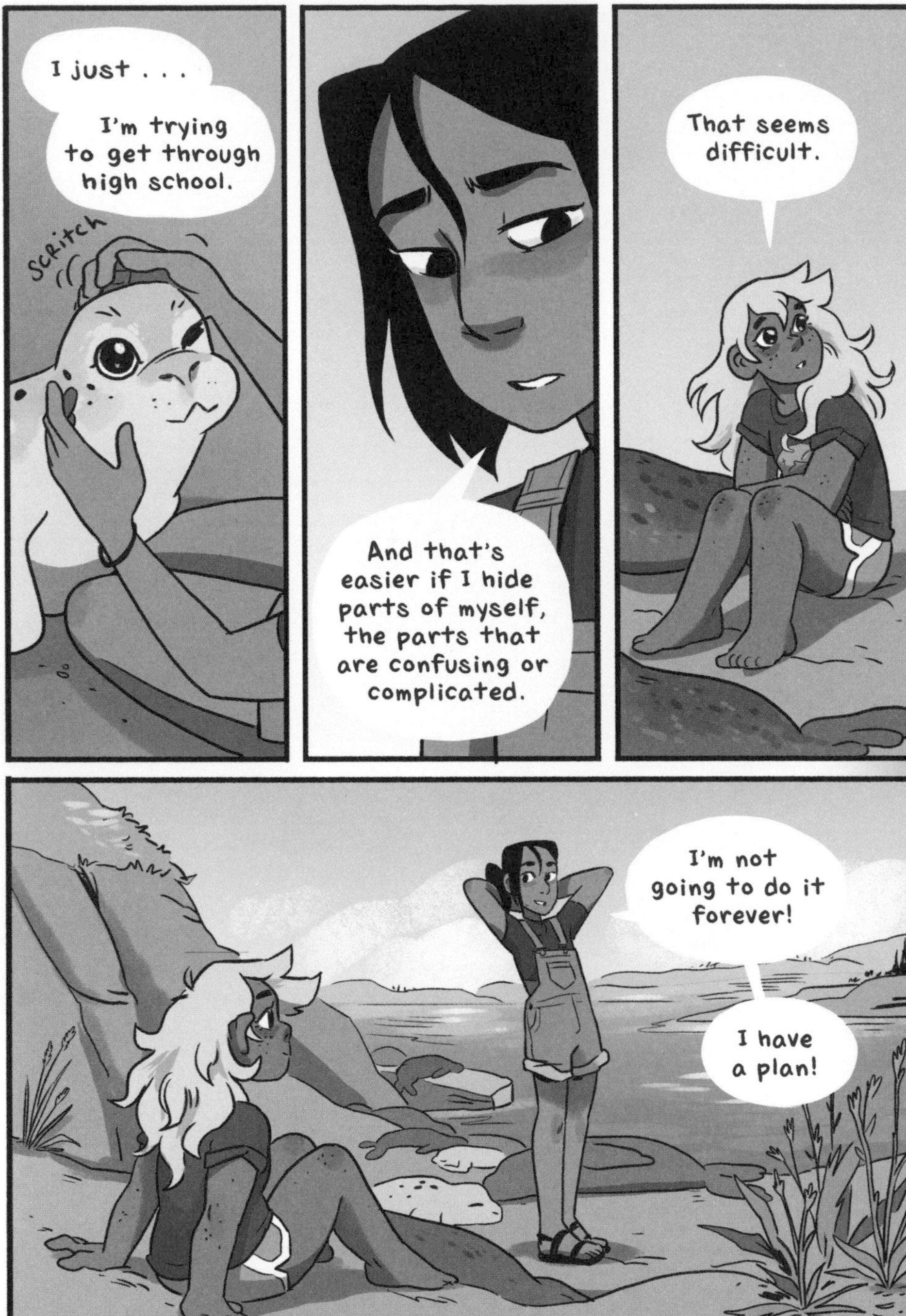
I just . . .
I'm trying to get through high school.
SCRITCH
And that's easier if I hide parts of myself, the parts that are confusing or complicated.
That seems difficult.
I'm not going to do it forever!
I have a plan!

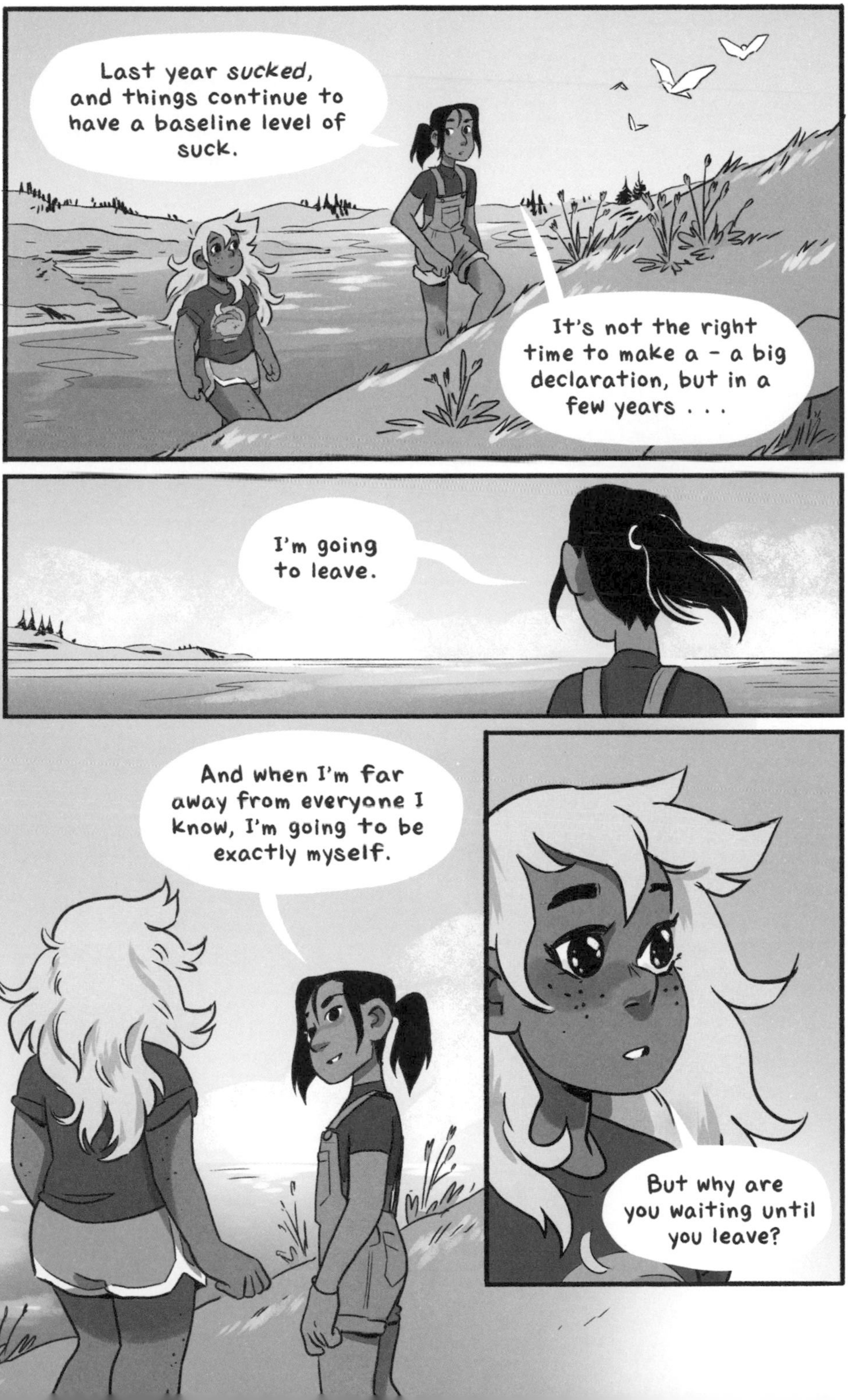
Last year *sucked*, and things continue to have a baseline level of suck.
It's not the right time to make a - a big declaration, but in a few years . . .
I'm going to leave.
And when I'm far away from everyone I know, I'm going to be exactly myself.
But why are you waiting until you leave?

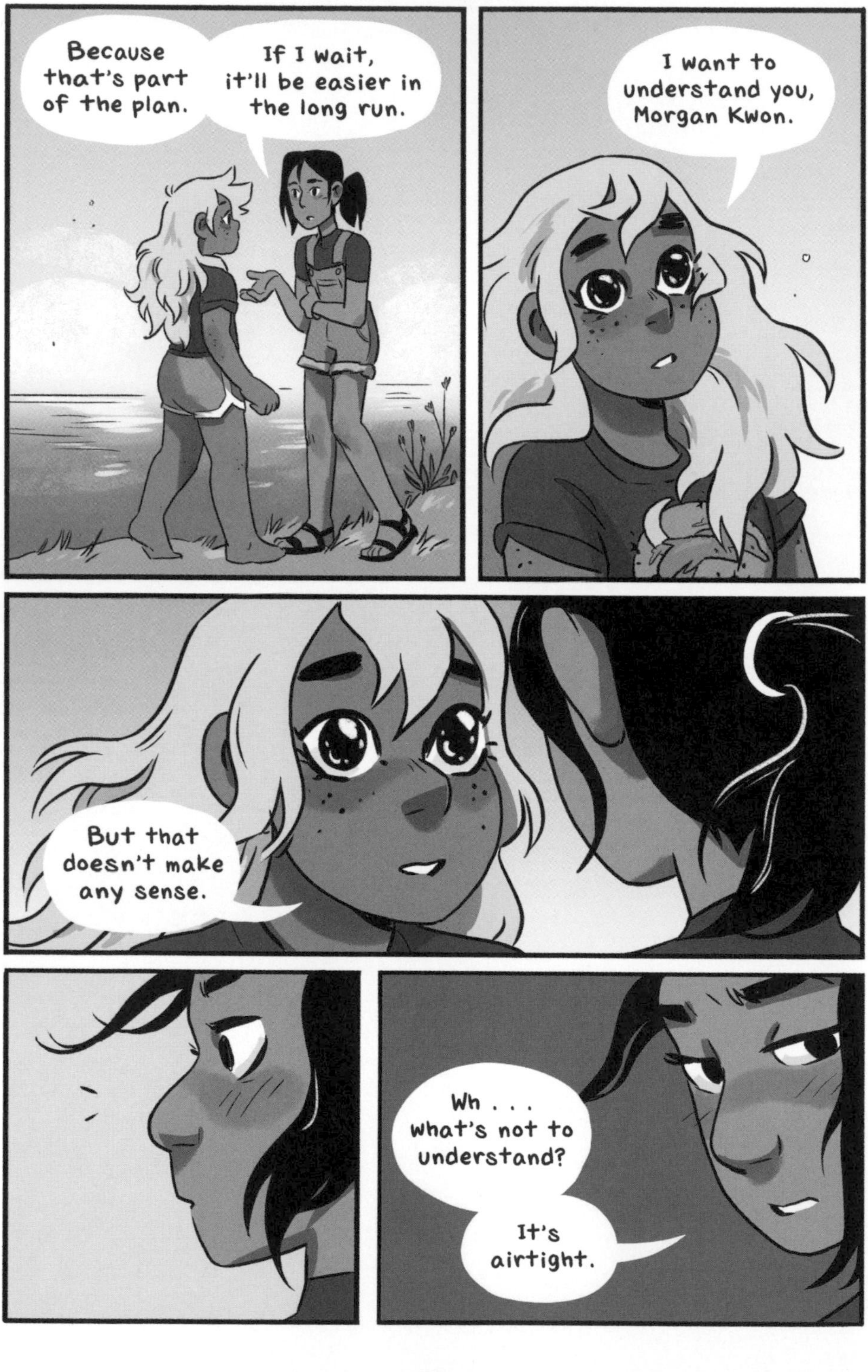

Because that's part of the plan.
If I wait, it'll be easier in the long run.
I want to understand you, Morgan Kwon.
But that doesn't make any sense.
Wh . . . what's not to understand?
It's airtight.

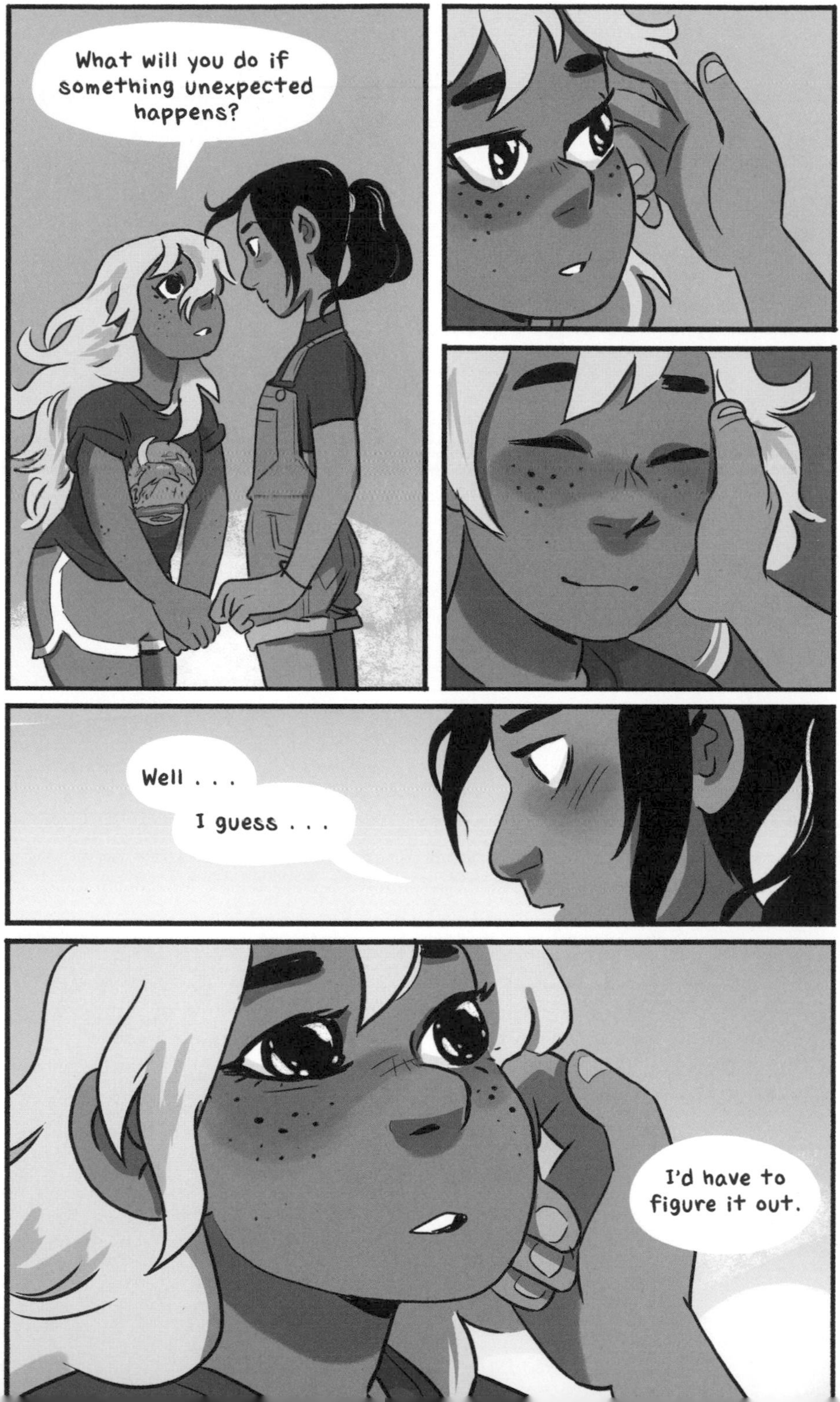
What will you do if something unexpected happens?
Well . . .
I guess . . .
I'd have to figure it out.

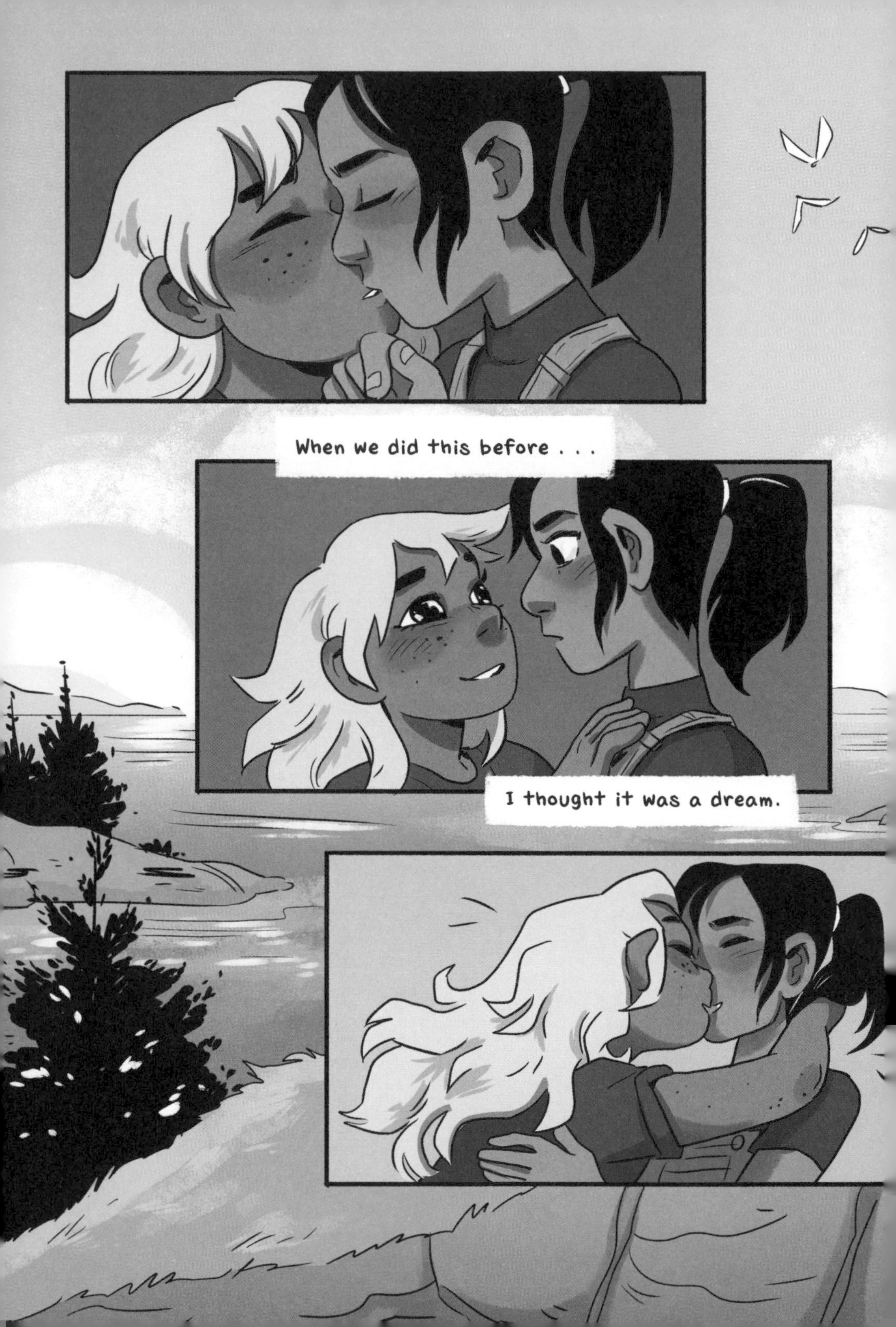
When we did this before . . .
I thought it was a dream.

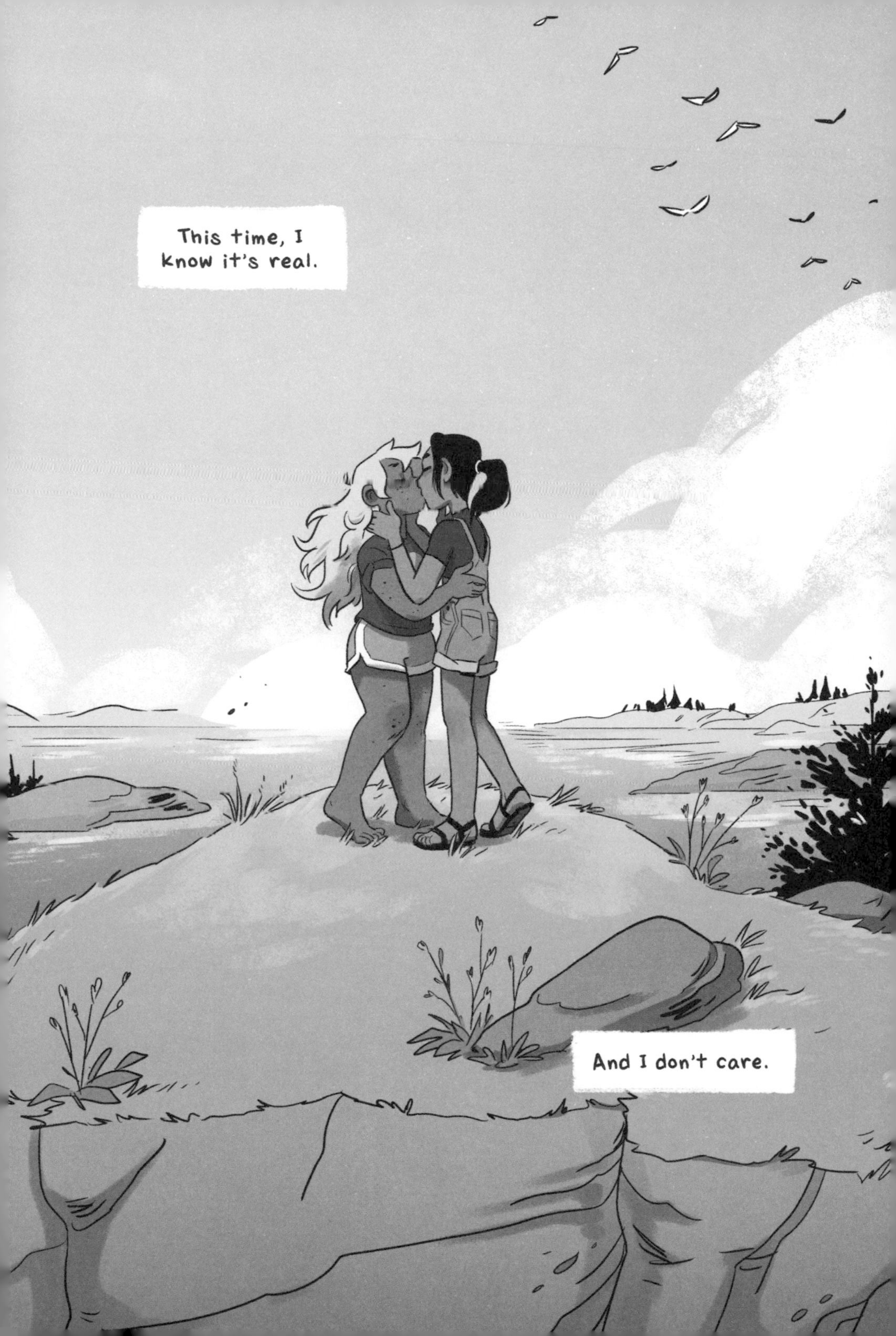
This time, I know it's real.
And I don't care.

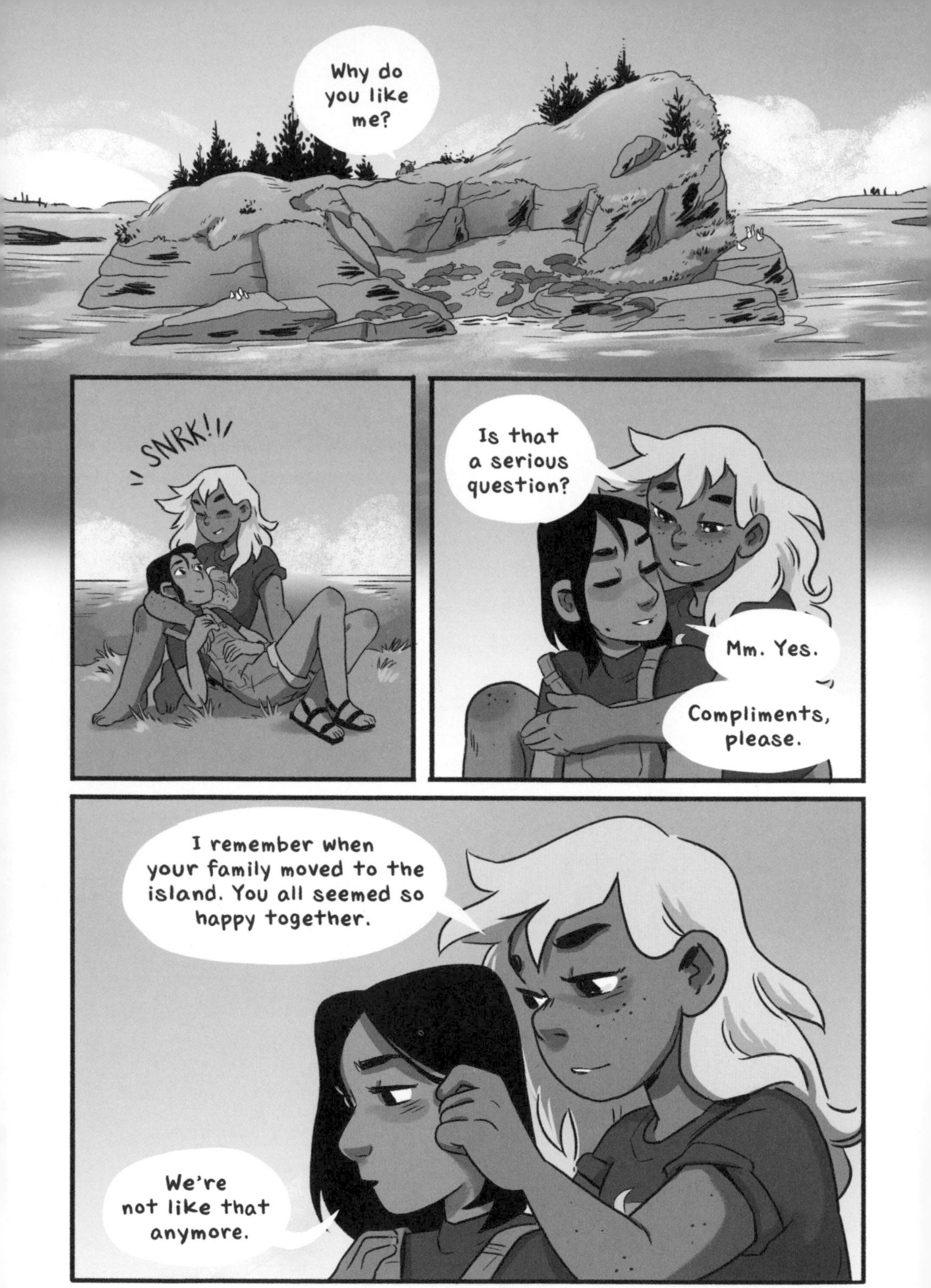
Why do you like me?
SNRK!
Is that a serious question?
Mm. Yes.
Compliments, please.
I remember when your family moved to the island. You all seemed so happy together.
We're not like that anymore.

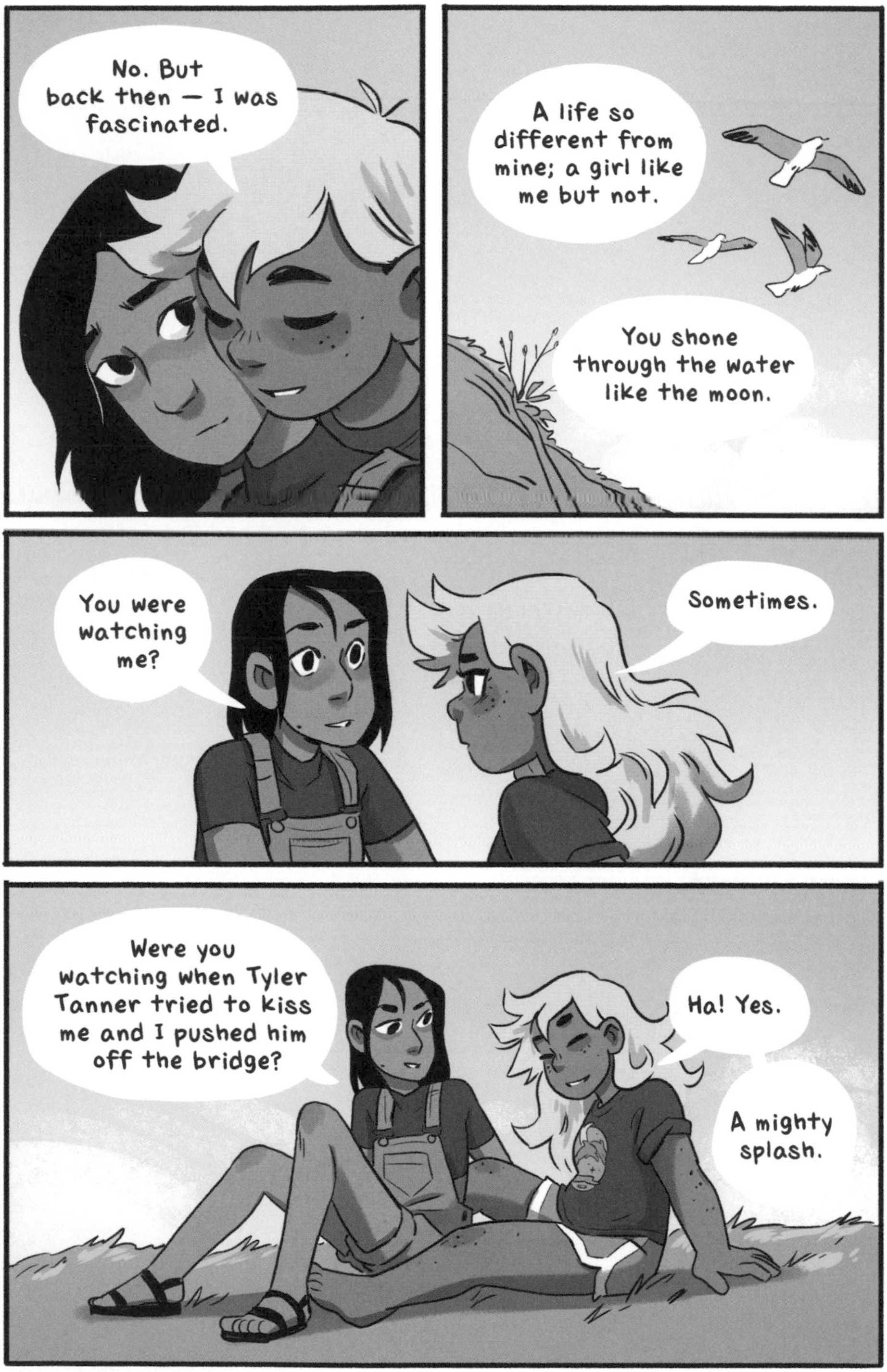
No. But back then — I was fascinated.
A life so different from mine; a girl like me but not.
You shone through the water like the moon.
You were watching me?
Sometimes.
Were you watching when Tyler Tanner tried to kiss me and I pushed him off the bridge?
Ha! Yes.
A mighty splash.

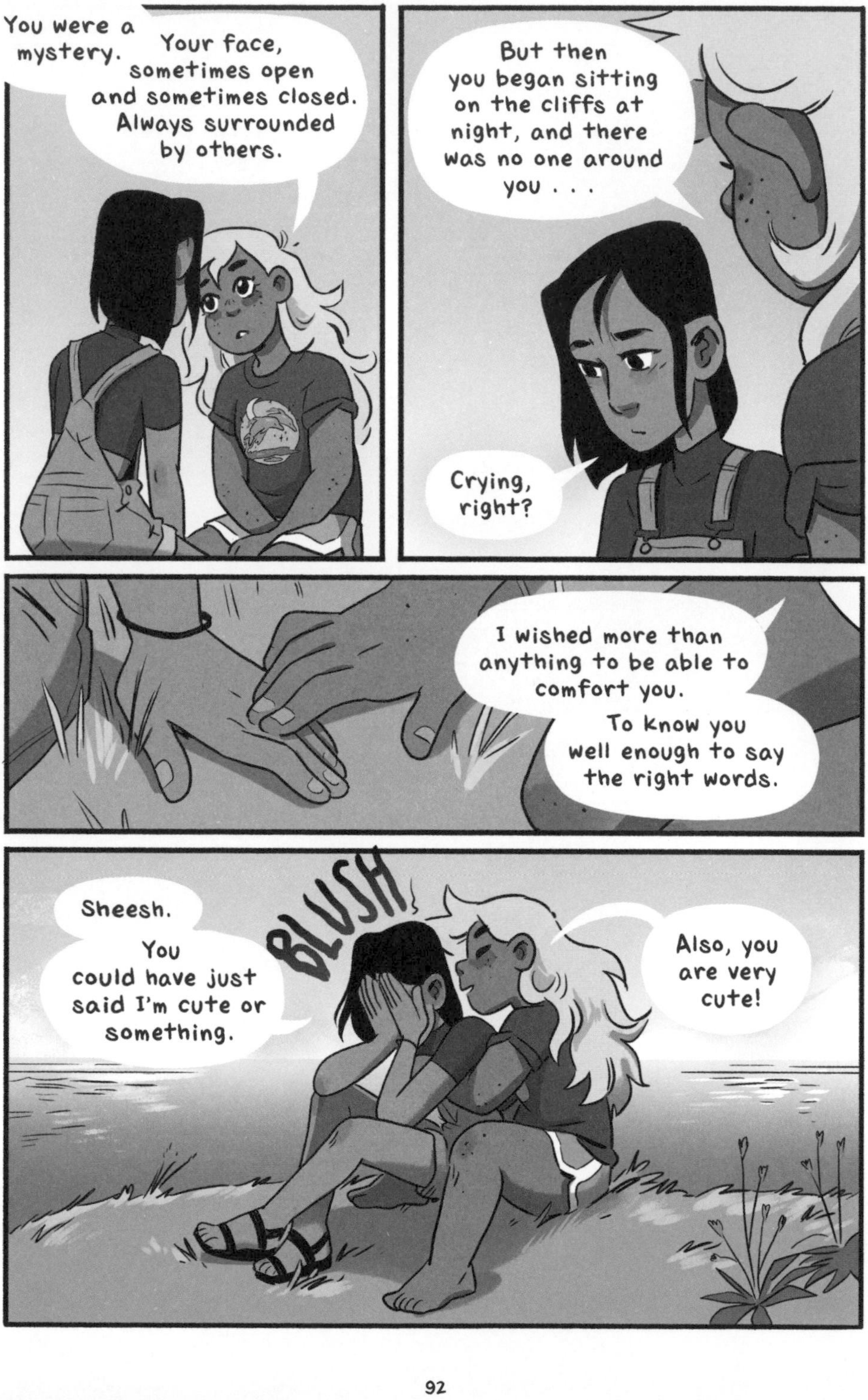
You were a mystery.
Your face, sometimes open and sometimes closed. Always surrounded by others.
But then you began sitting on the cliffs at night, and there was no one around you . . .
Crying, right?
I wished more than anything to be able to comfort you.
To know you well enough to say the right words.
Sheesh.
BLUSH
You could have just said I'm cute or something.
Also, you are very cute!

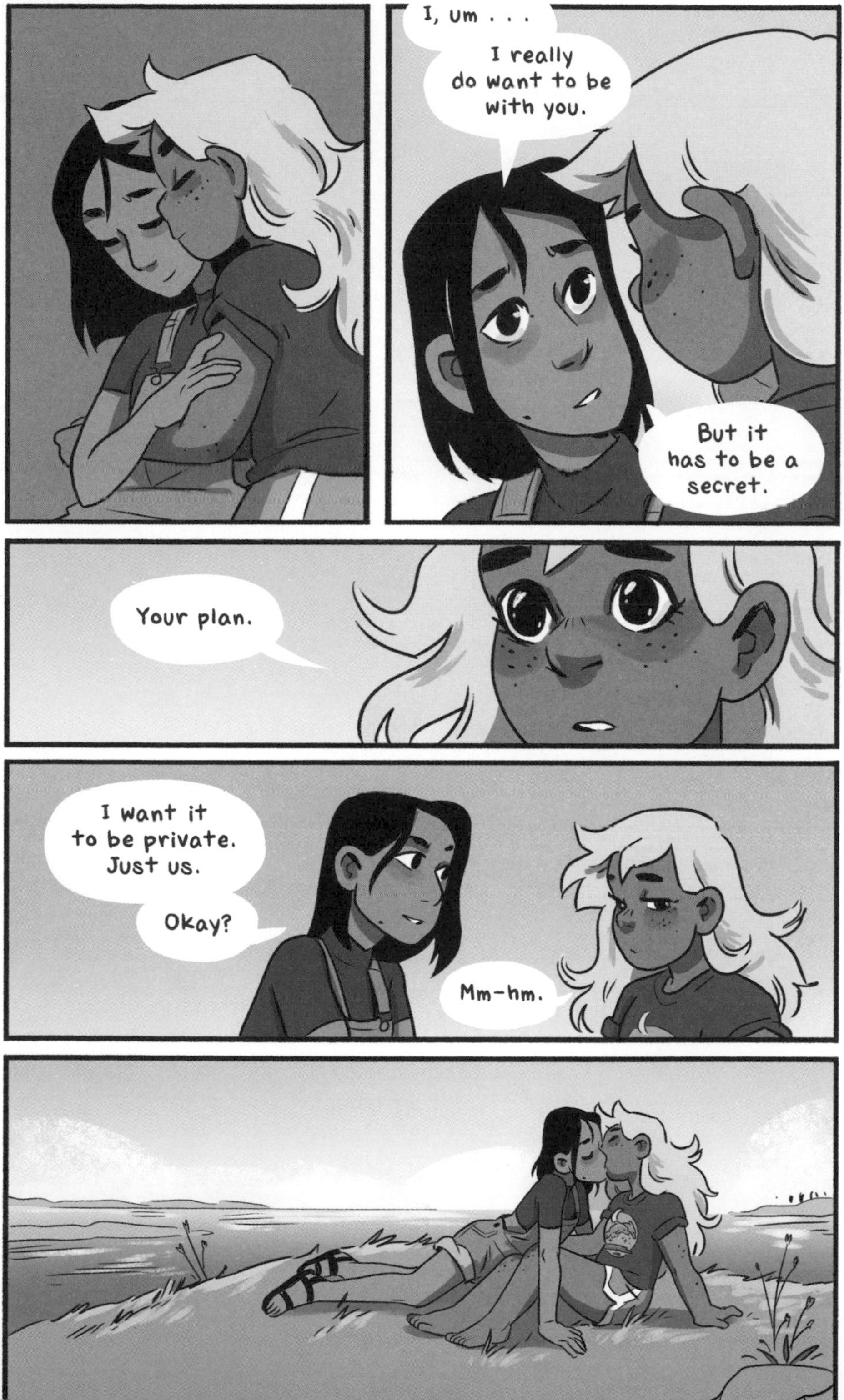
I, um . . .
I really do want to be with you.
But it has to be a secret.
Your plan.
I want it to be private. Just us.
Okay?
Mm-hm.

Race you back!

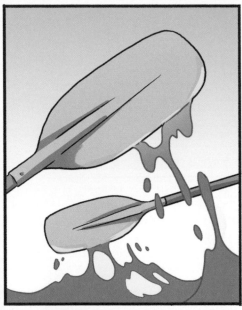

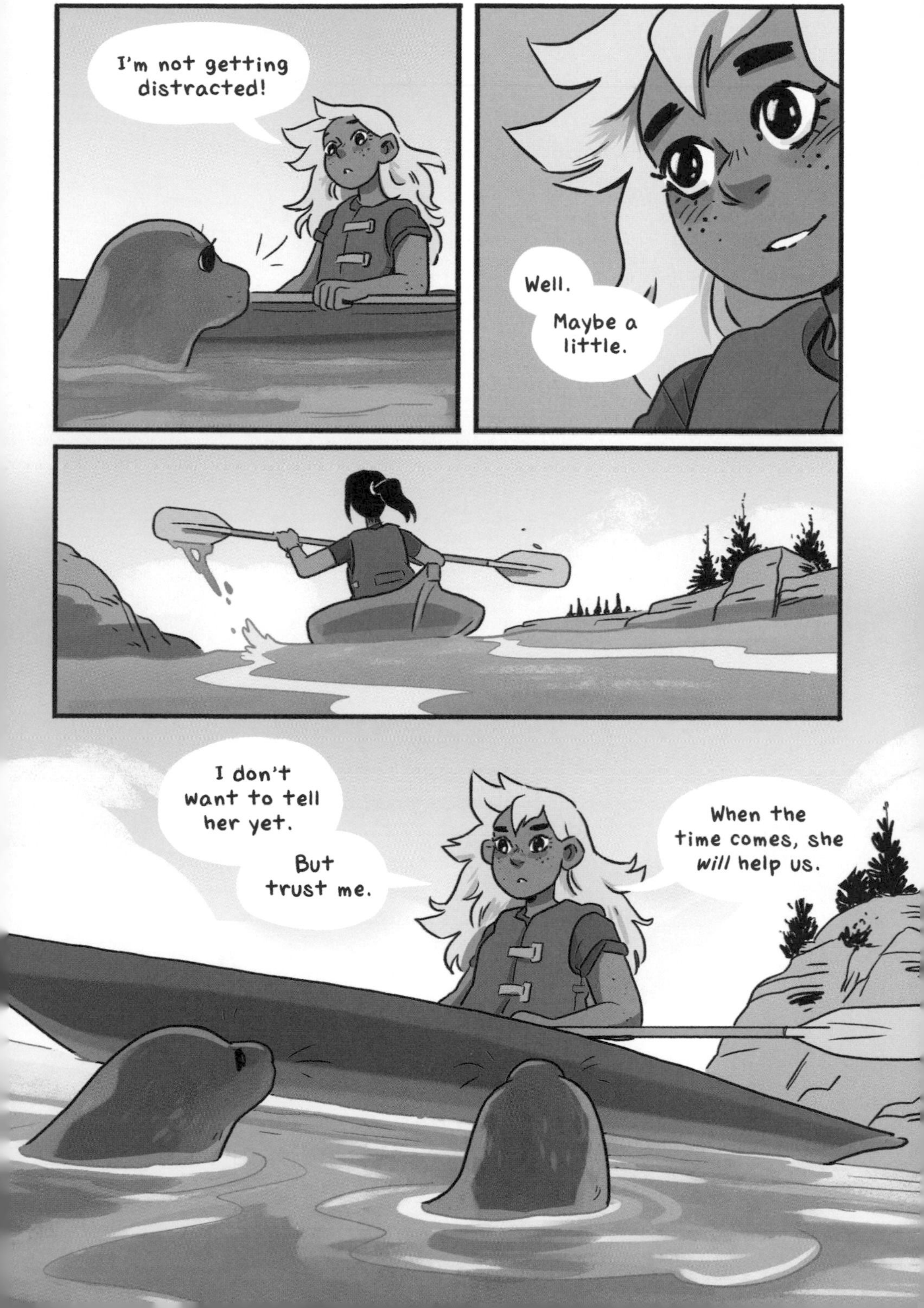
I'm not getting distracted!
Well.
Maybe a little.
I don't want to tell her yet.
But trust me.
When the time comes, she *will* help us.

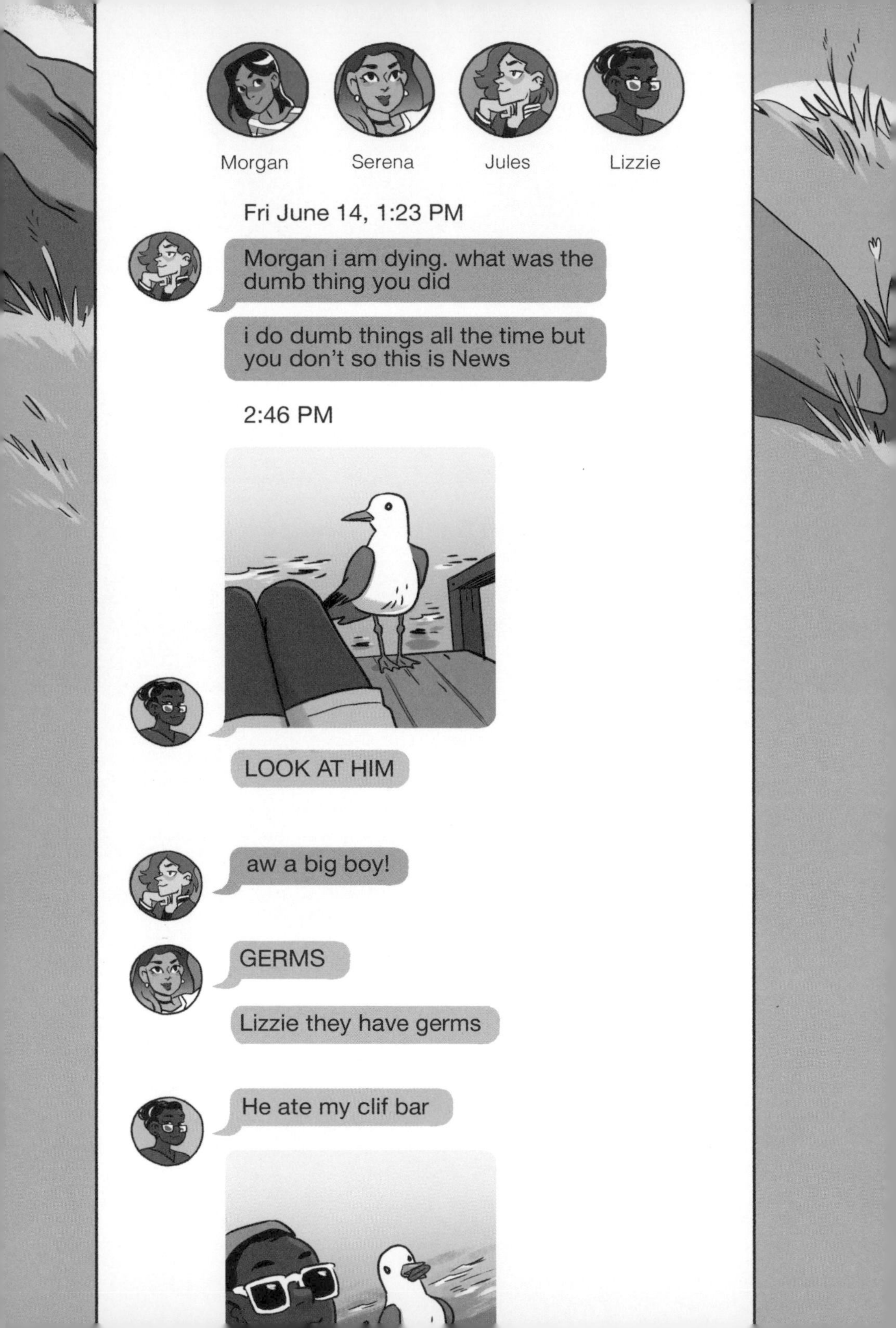
Morgan
Serena
Jules
Lizzie
Fri June 14, 1:23 PM
Morgan i am dying. what was the dumb thing you did
i do dumb things all the time but you don't so this is News
2:46 PM
LOOK AT HIM
aw a big boy!
GERMS
Lizzie they have germs
He ate my clif bar

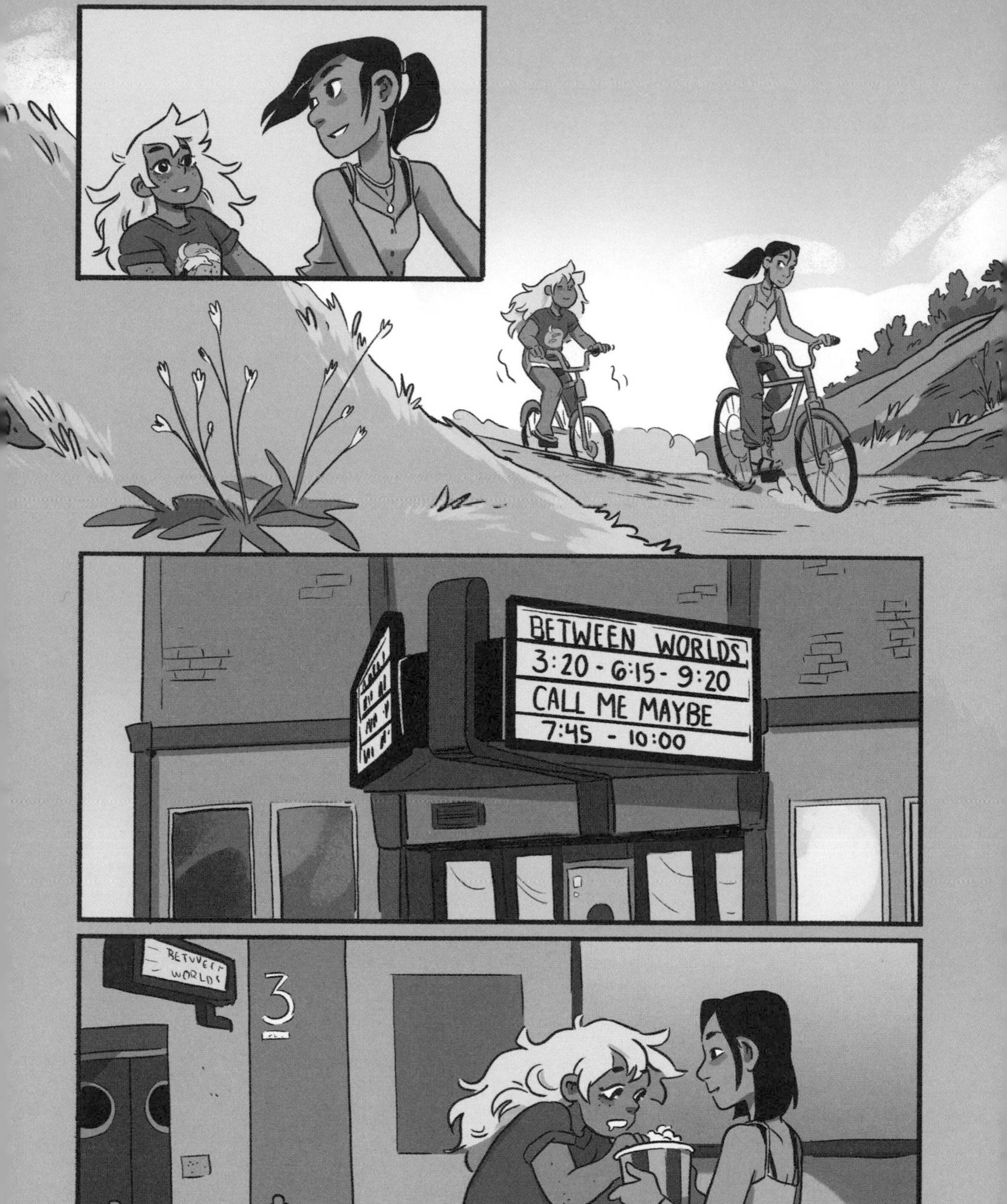
BETWEEN WORLDS
3:20 - 6:15 - 9:20
CALL ME MAYBE
7:45 - 10:00
3

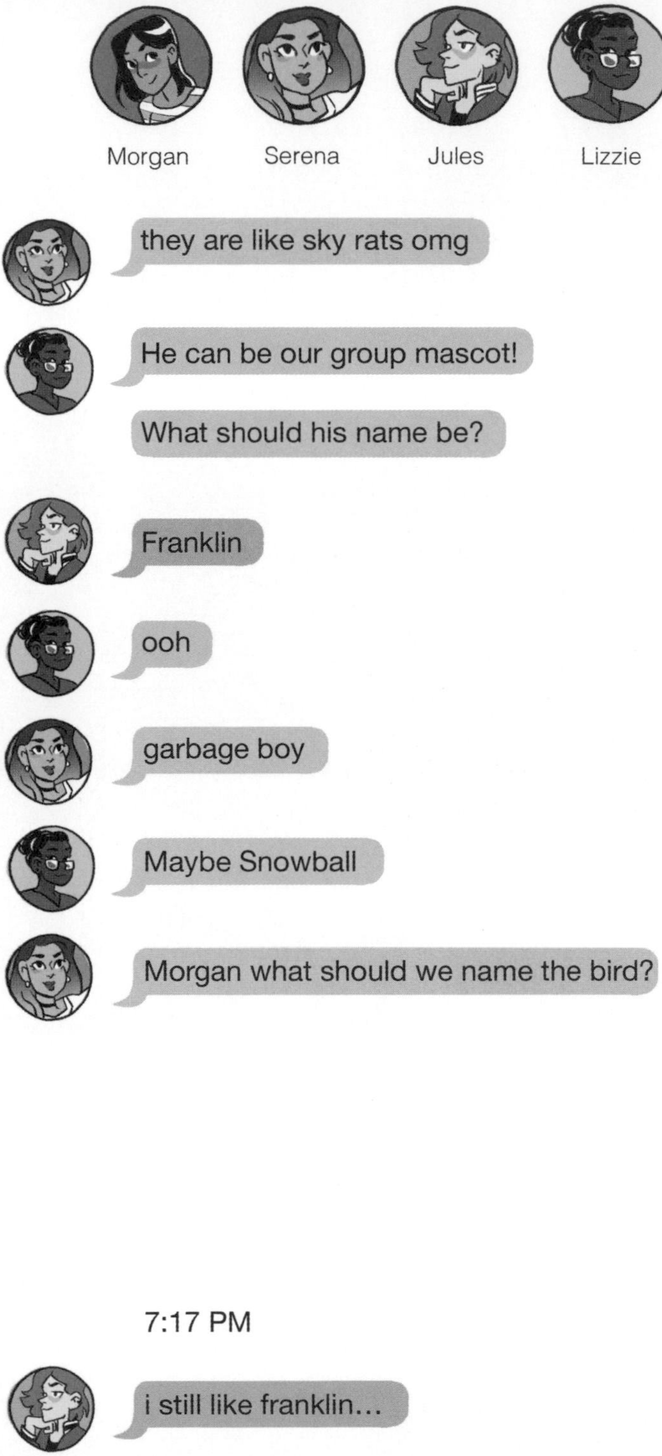
Morgan
Serena
Jules
Lizzie
they are like sky rats omg
He can be our group mascot!
What should his name be?
Franklin
ooh
garbage boy
Maybe Snowball
Morgan what should we name the bird?
7:17 PM
i still like franklin...

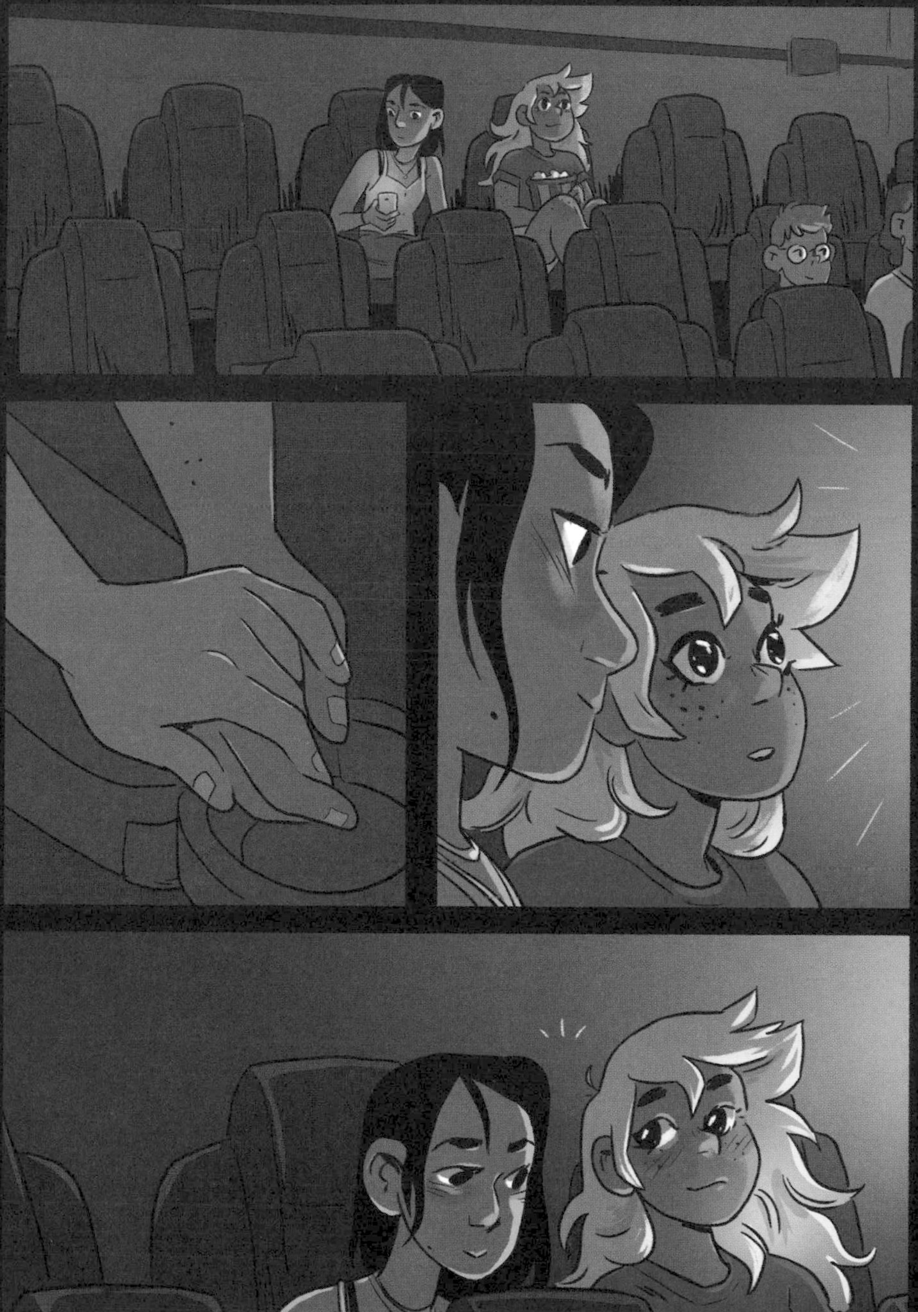

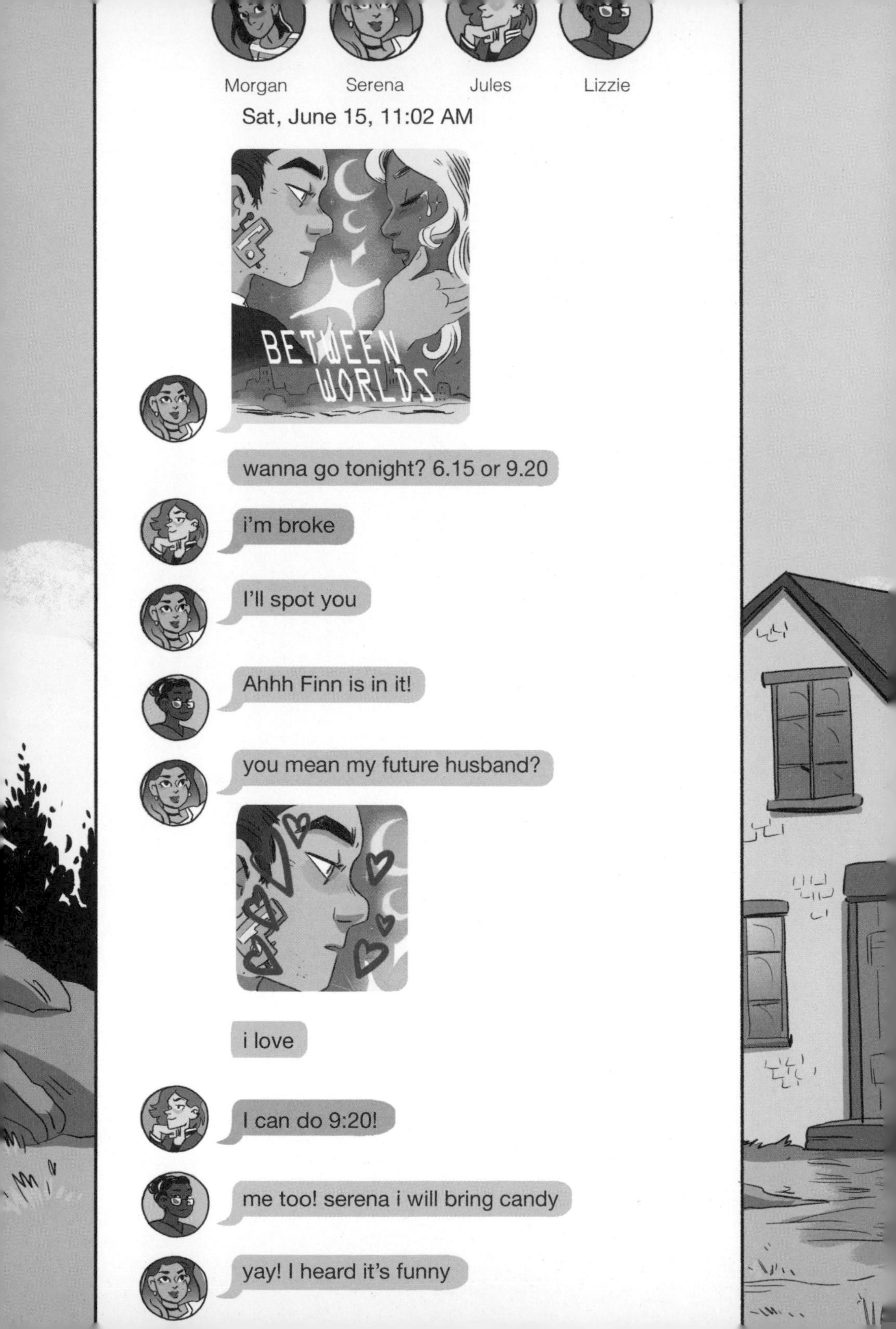
Morgan
Serena
Jules
Lizzie
Sat, June 15, 11:02 AM
BETWEEN WORLDS
wanna go tonight? 6.15 or 9.20
i'm broke
I'll spot you
Ahhh Finn is in it!
you mean my future husband?
i love
I can do 9:20!
me too! serena i will bring candy
yay! I heard it's funny

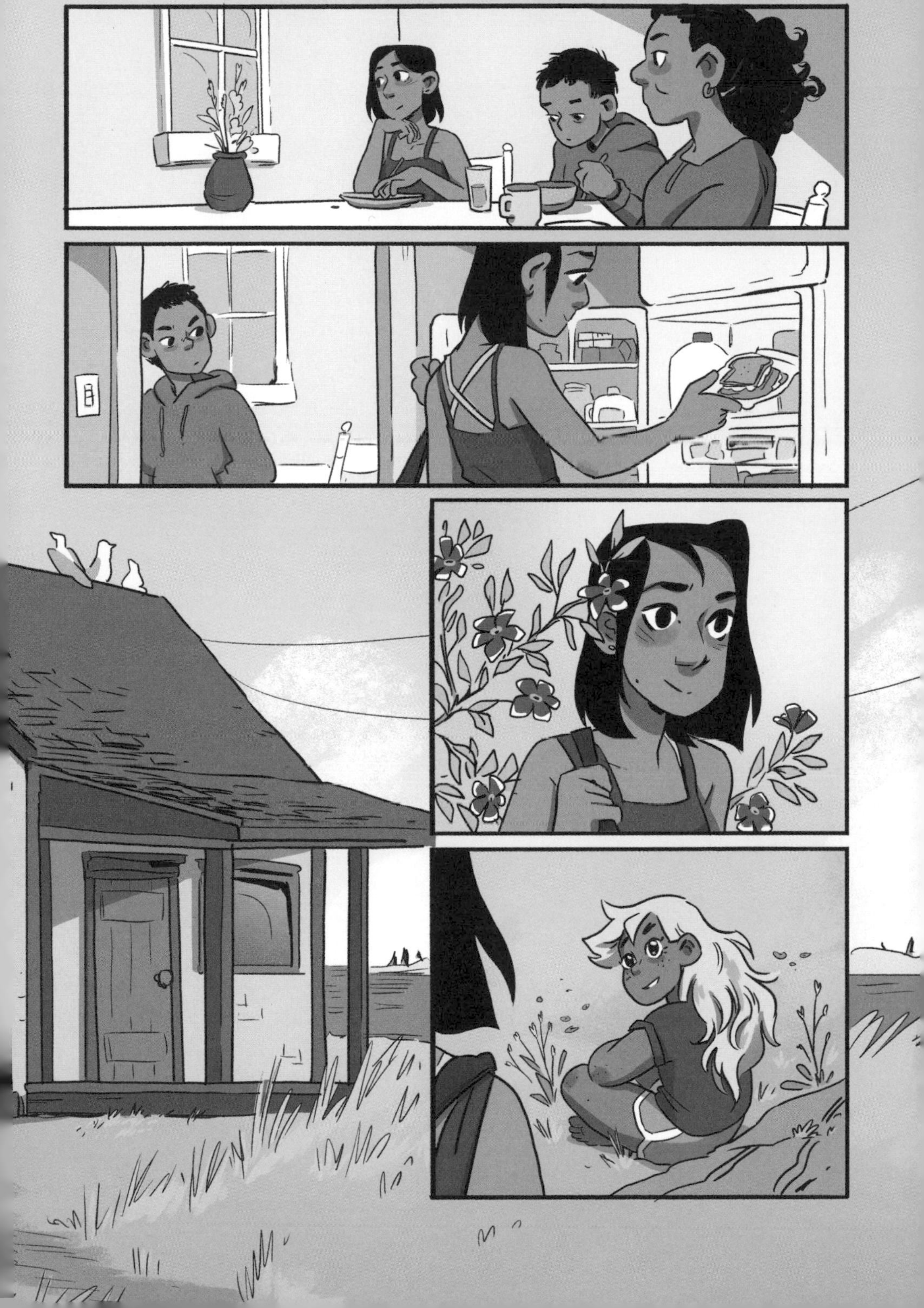

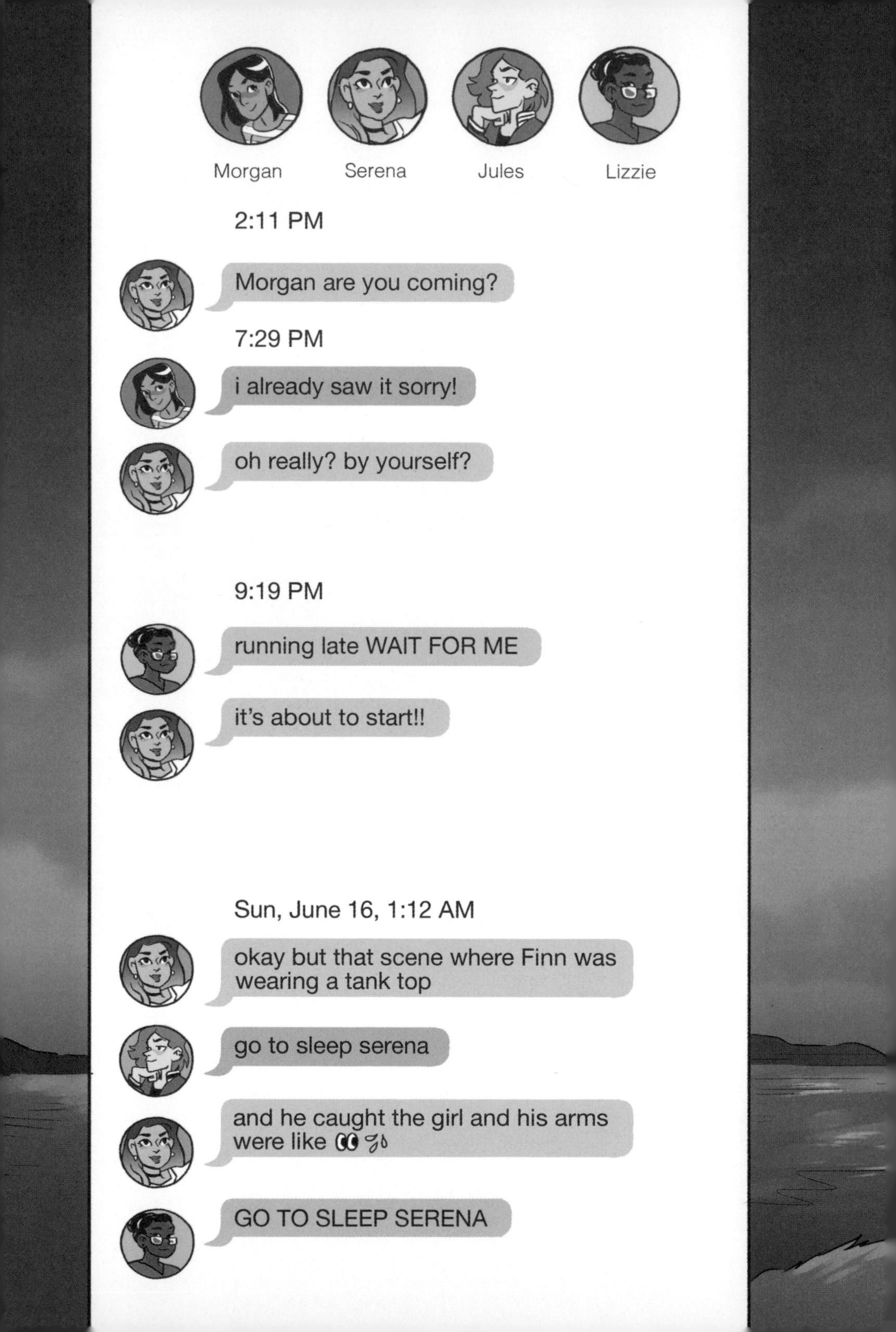

Morgan
Serena
Jules
Lizzie
2:11 PM
Morgan are you coming?
7:29 PM
i already saw it sorry!
oh really? by yourself?
9:19 PM
running late WAIT FOR ME
it's about to start!!
Sun, June 16, 1:12 AM
okay but that scene where Finn was wearing a tank top
go to sleep serena
and he caught the girl and his arms were like 👀 💪
GO TO SLEEP SERENA

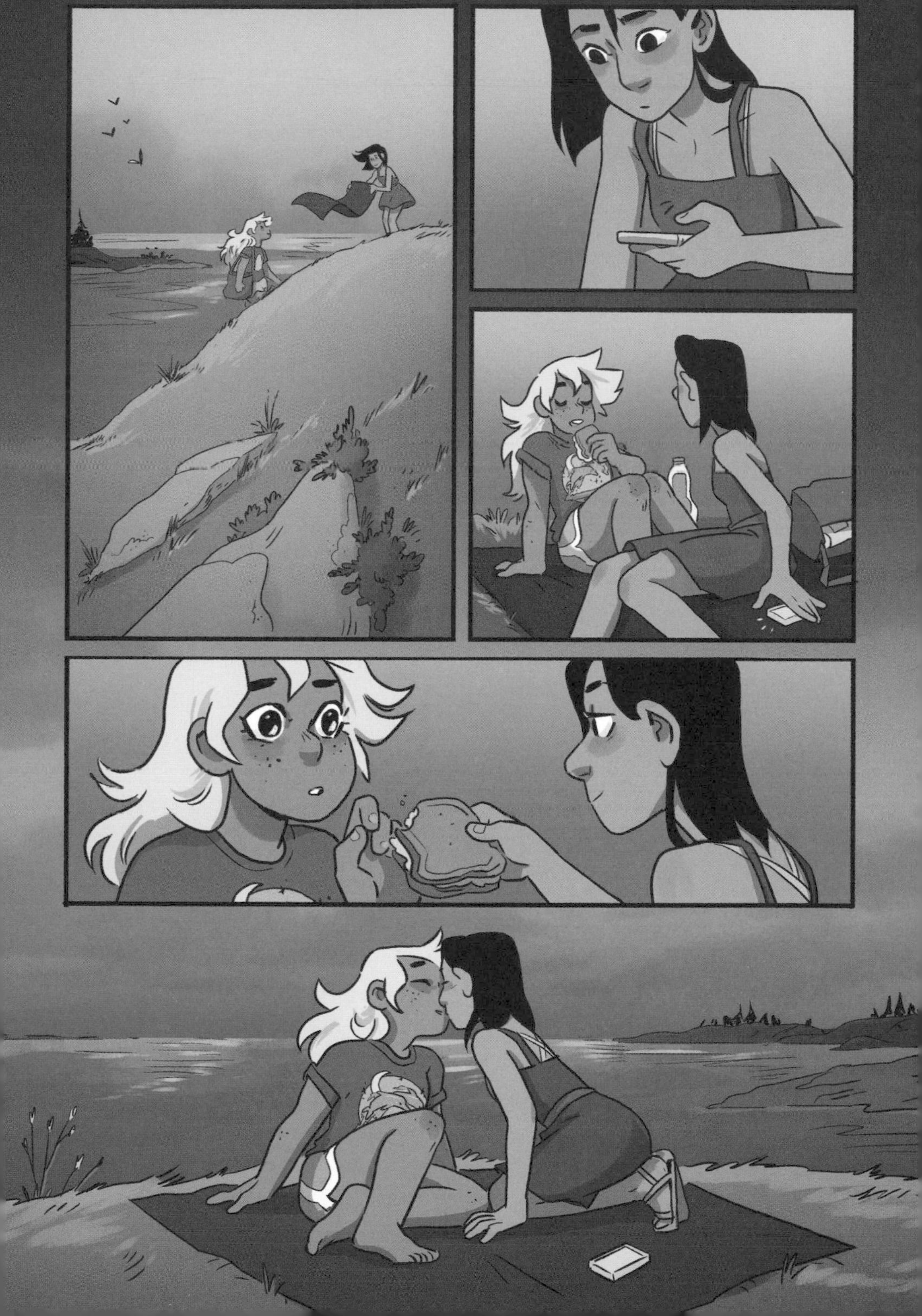

Morgan   Serena   Jules   Lizzie

Mon, June 17, 3:42 PM

 help me pick

 Aw they're both cute!

 red! I like the top

WAIT i thought you were broke!!

 i am but also i need to look hot

 I like red too

and to make tyler jealous

 oh no...not Tyler

 You guys get together ev
don't you want a change?

 ouch

and, no. familiarity is comforting

going with the black, thanks ladies

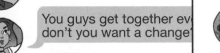

Morgan   Mom

Mon, June 17, 6:24 PM

 Hon you home for dinner?
-Mom

 Tues, June 18, 12:15 PM

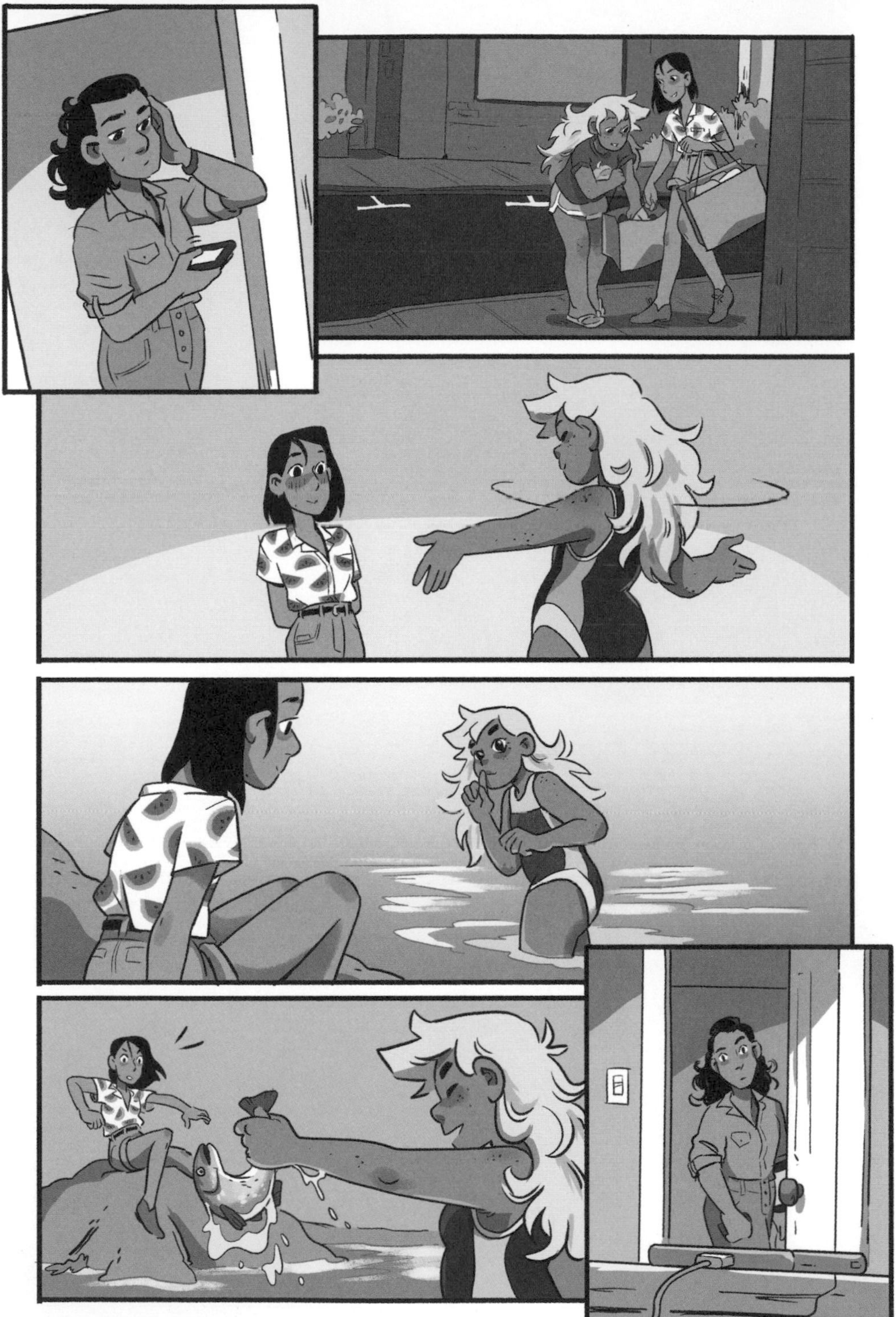

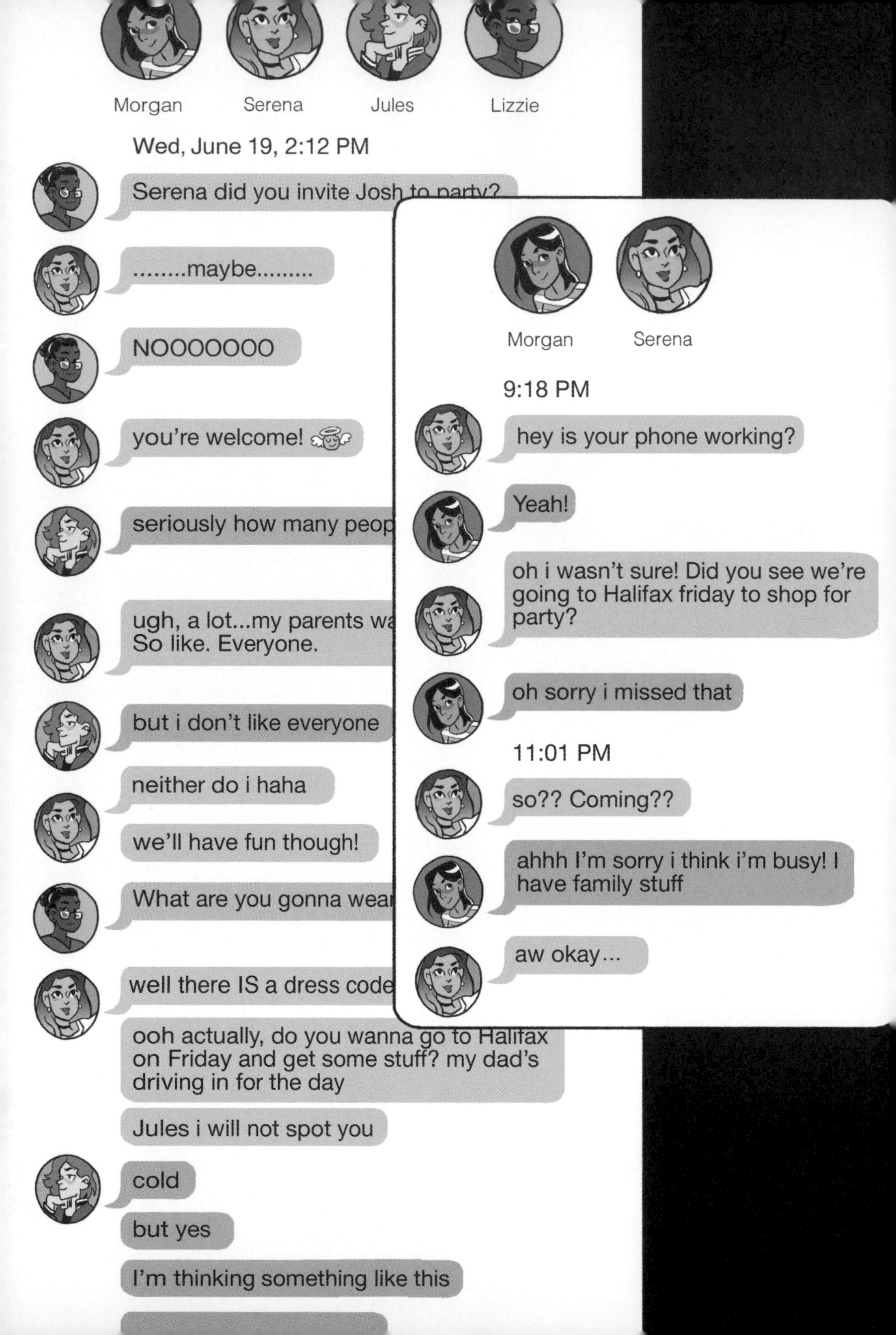

Morgan   Serena   Jules   Lizzie

Wed, June 19, 2:12 PM

 Serena did you invite Josh to party?

 ....maybe.........

 NOOOOOOO

 you're welcome! 😇

 seriously how many peop

 ugh, a lot...my parents wa
So like. Everyone.

 but i don't like everyone

 neither do i haha

 we'll have fun though!

 What are you gonna wear

 well there IS a dress code

ooh actually, do you wanna go to Halifax
on Friday and get some stuff? my dad's
driving in for the day

Jules i will not spot you

 cold

but yes

 I'm thinking something like this

Morgan   Serena

9:18 PM

 hey is your phone working?

 Yeah!

oh i wasn't sure! Did you see we're
going to Halifax friday to shop for
party?

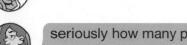 oh sorry i missed that

11:01 PM

 so?? Coming??

ahhh I'm sorry i think i'm busy! I
have family stuff

 aw okay...

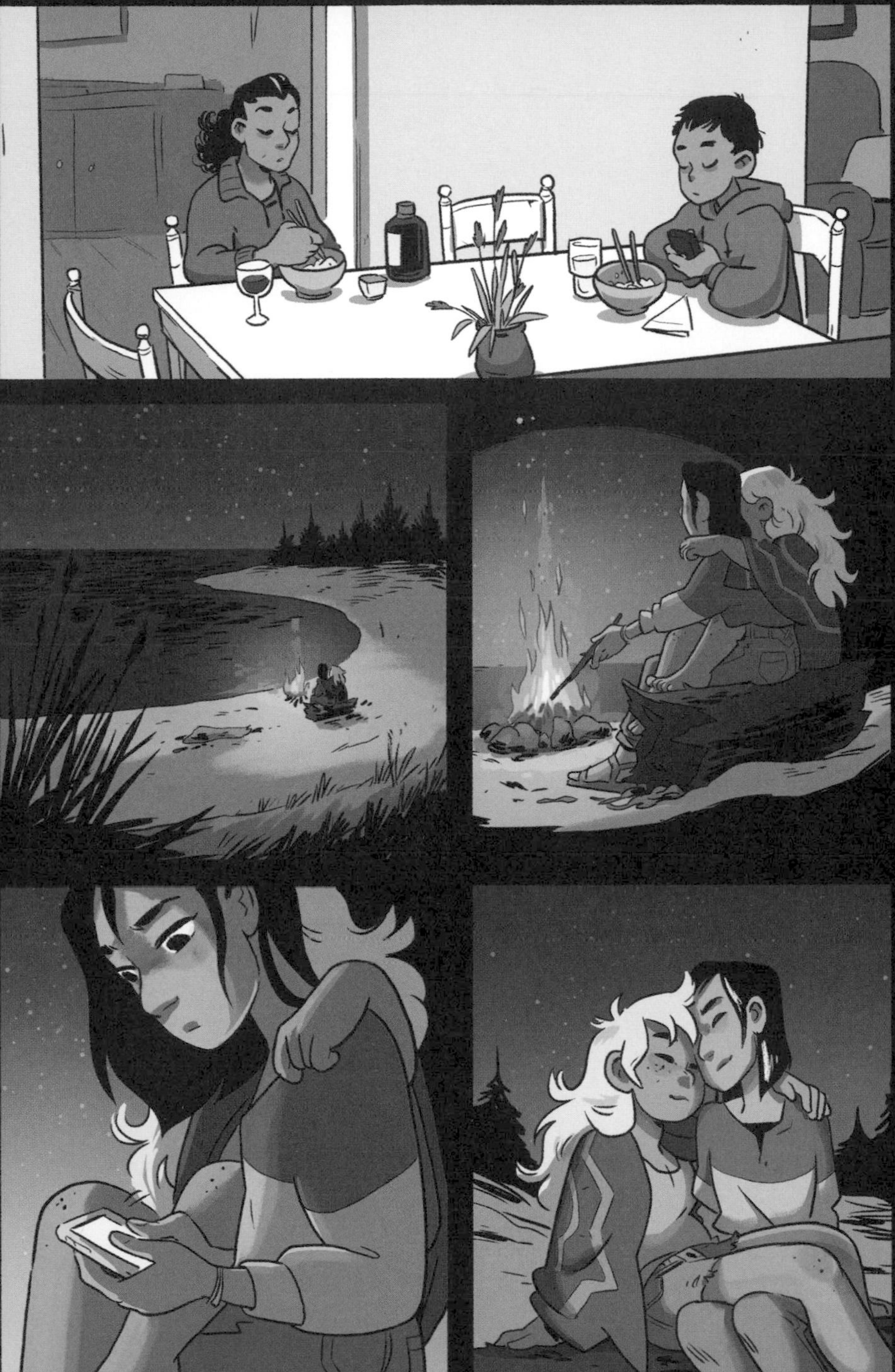

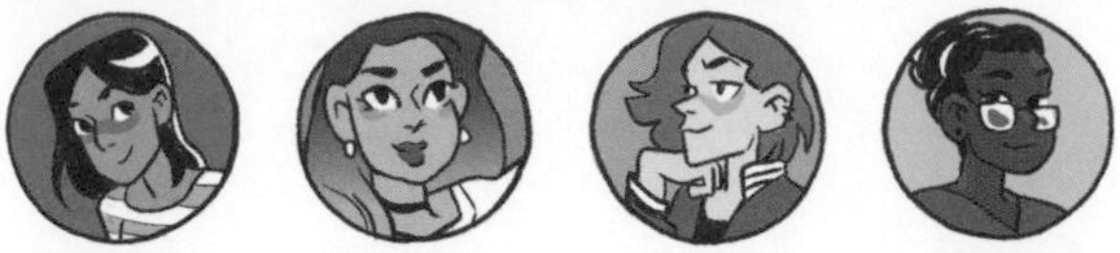

Morgan Serena Jules Lizzie

Fri, June 21, 3:59 PM

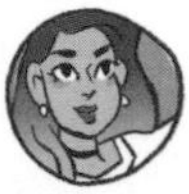

MISS YOU MORGAN

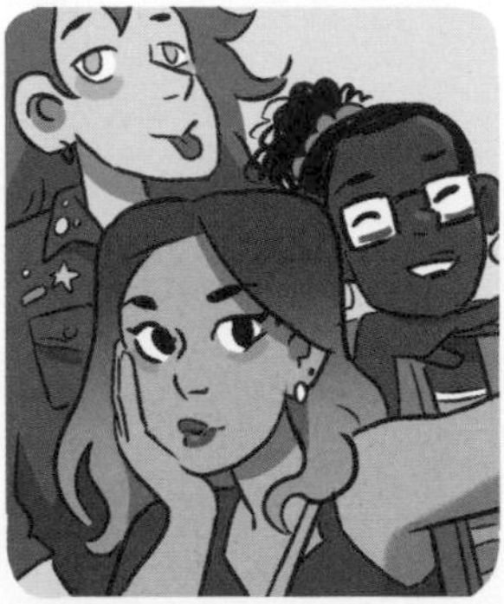

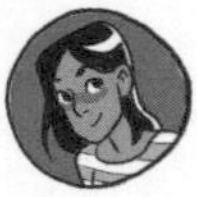

love you guys ✧♥✧

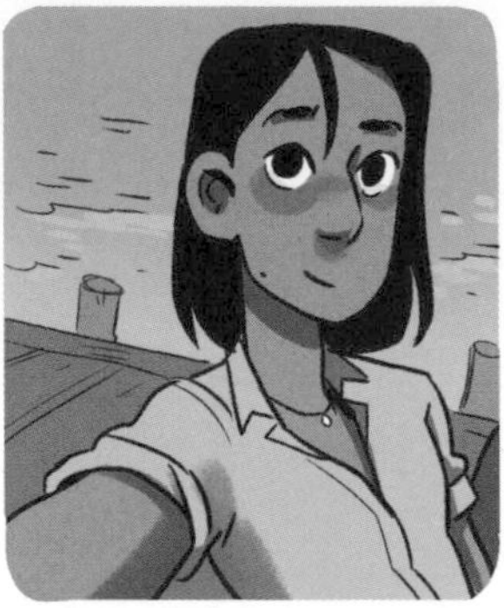

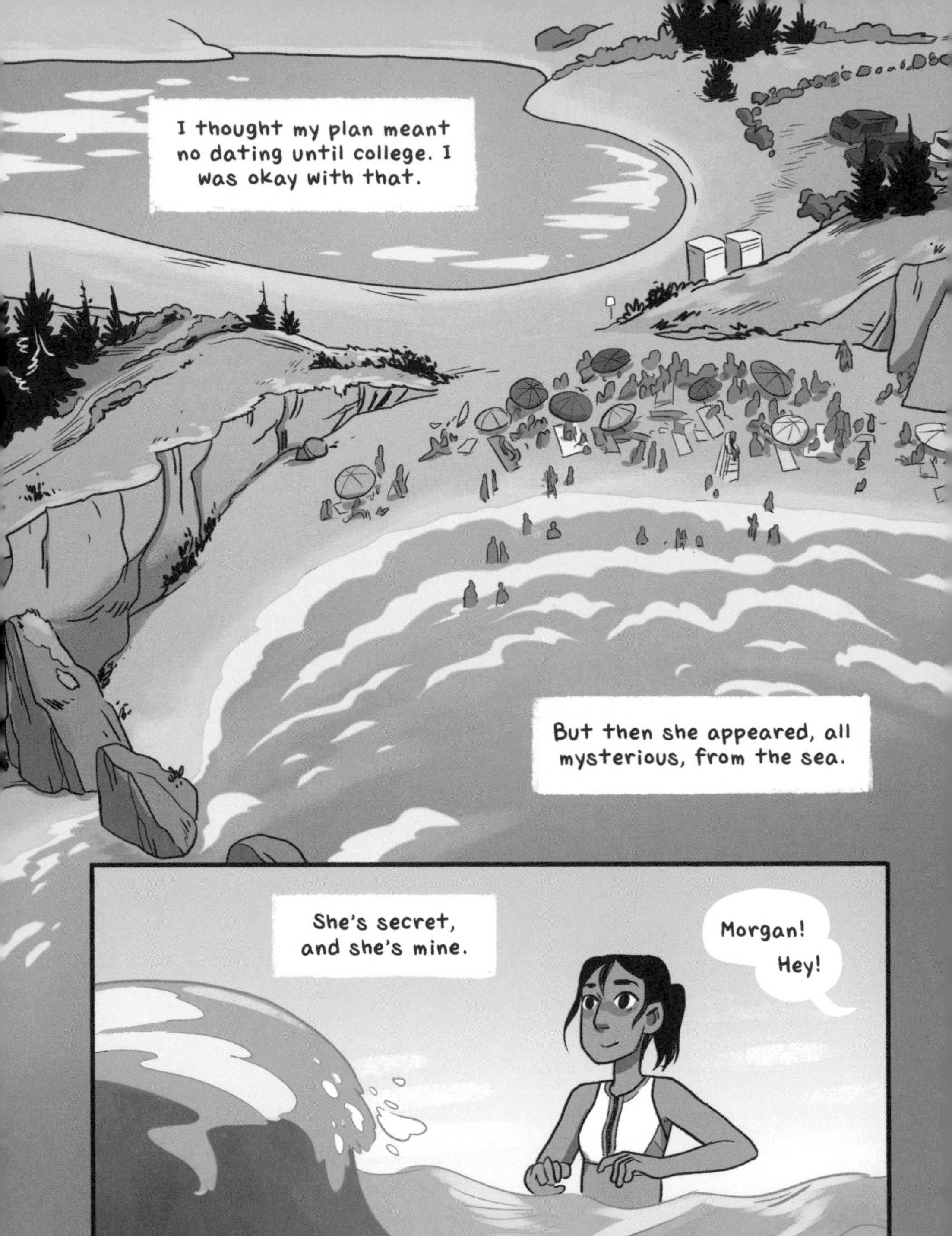
I thought my plan meant no dating until college. I was okay with that.
But then she appeared, all mysterious, from the sea.
She's secret, and she's mine.
Morgan! Hey!

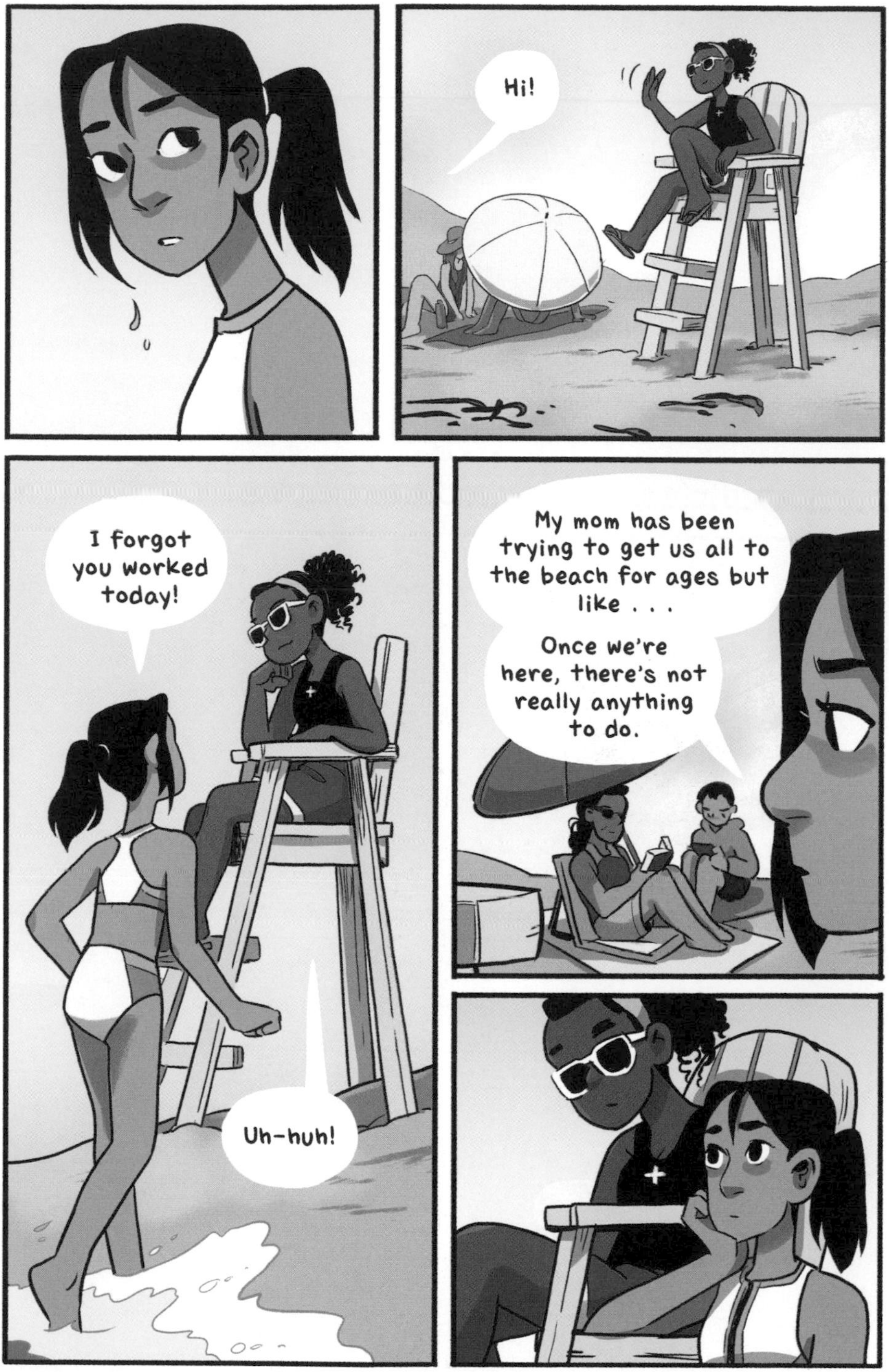
Hi!
I forgot you worked today!
Uh-huh!
My mom has been trying to get us all to the beach for ages but like . . .
Once we're here, there's not really anything to do.

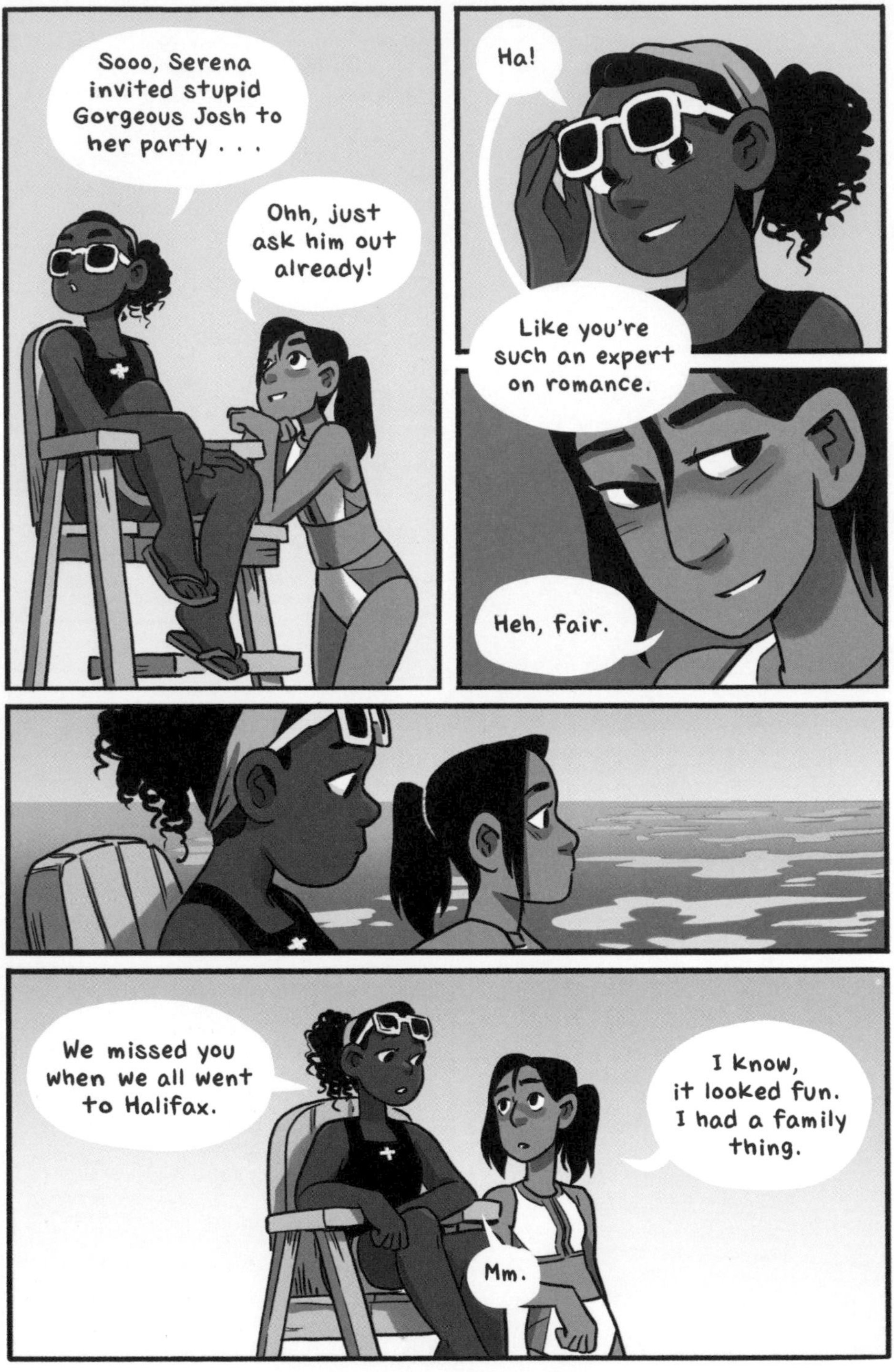
Sooo, Serena invited stupid Gorgeous Josh to her party . . .
Ohh, just ask him out already!
Ha!
Like you're such an expert on romance.
Heh, fair.
We missed you when we all went to Halifax.
I know, it looked fun. I had a family thing.
Mm.

You're not, like, mad at Serena, are you?

What?

Of course not.

Yeah, no, I didn't think so.

She was worried that something was up, though.

No, I've just been busy.

Oh no.

Don't look now, but that dolphin girl is here.

Dolphin girl —

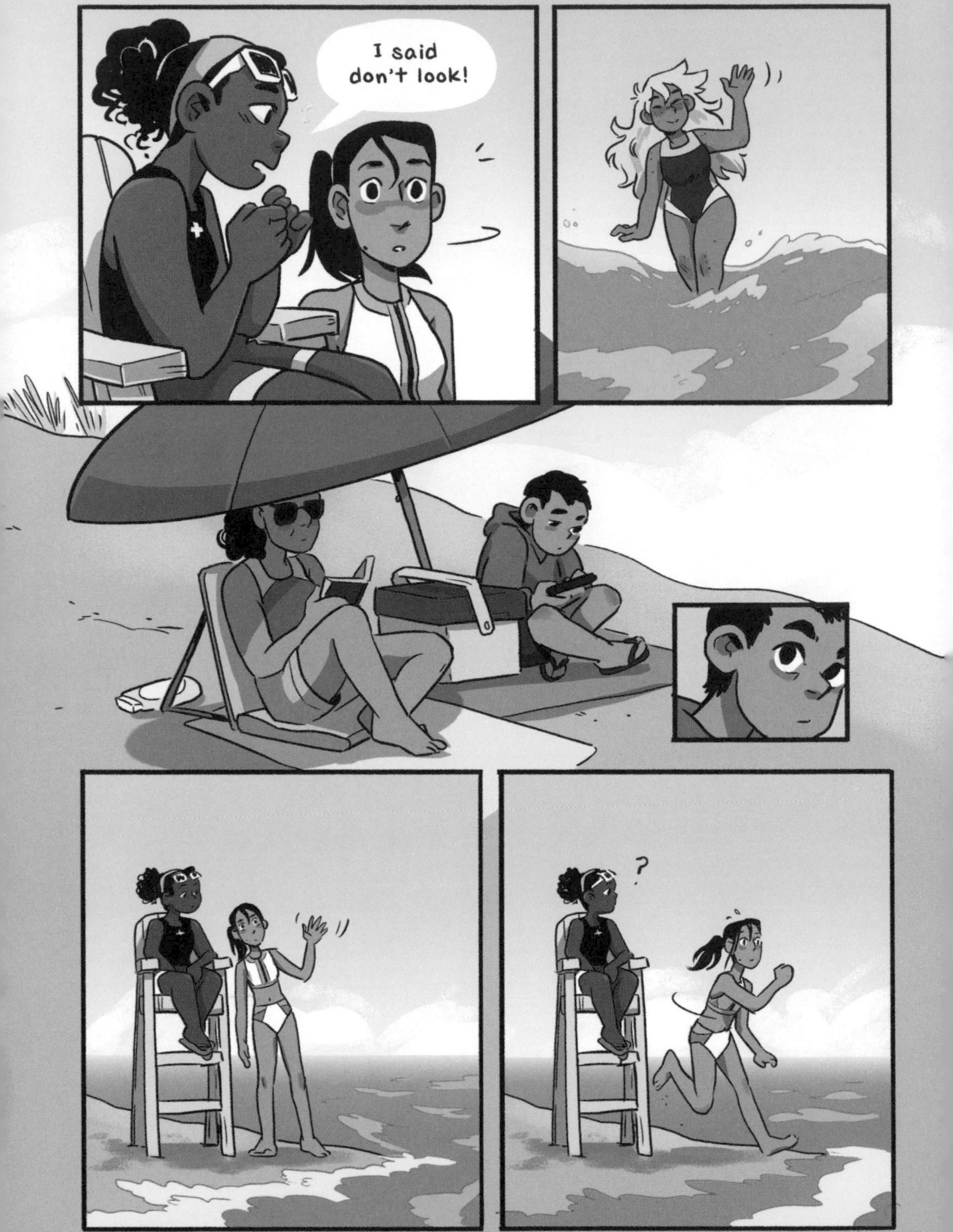
I said
don't look!
?

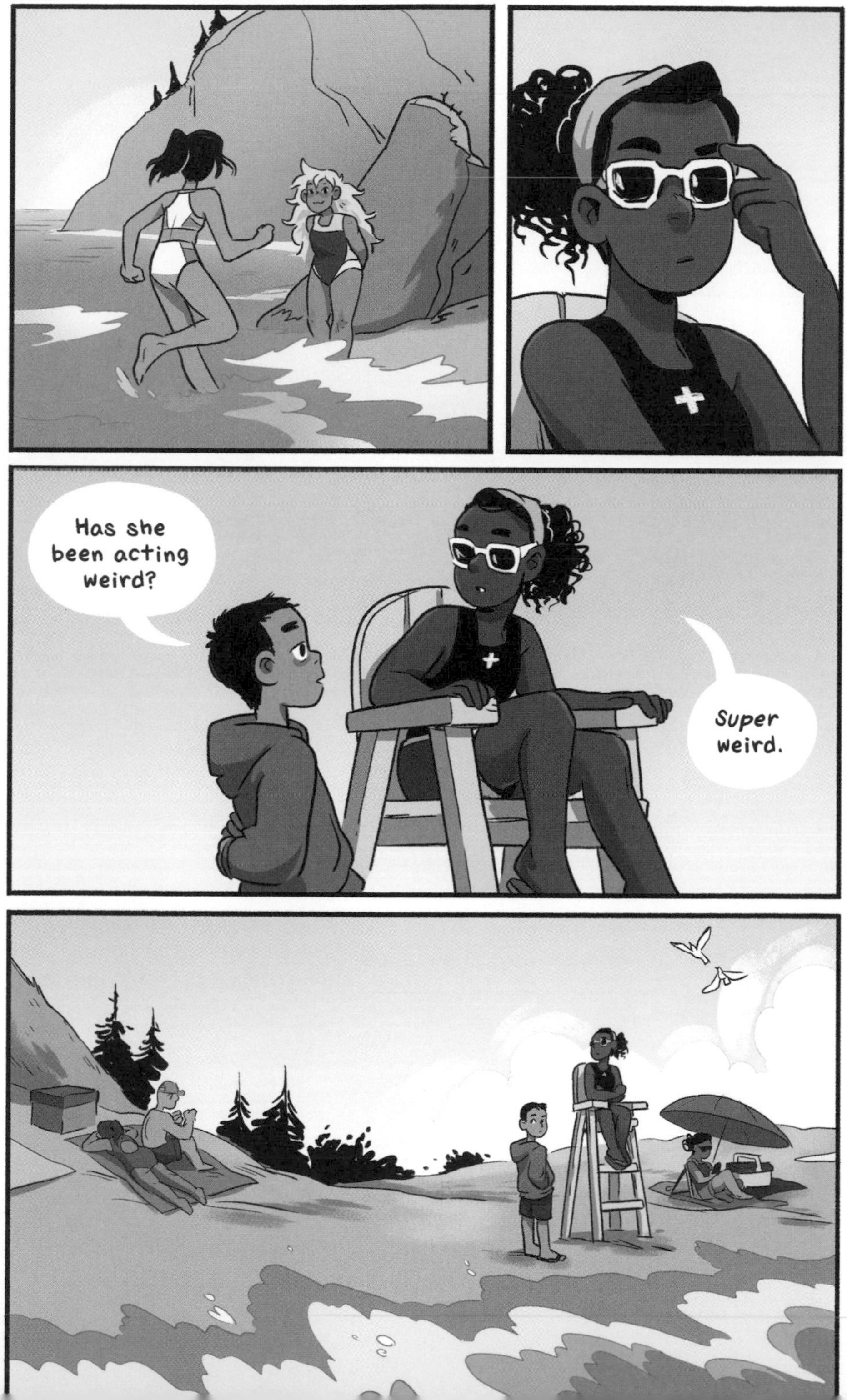
Has she been acting weird?
Super weird.

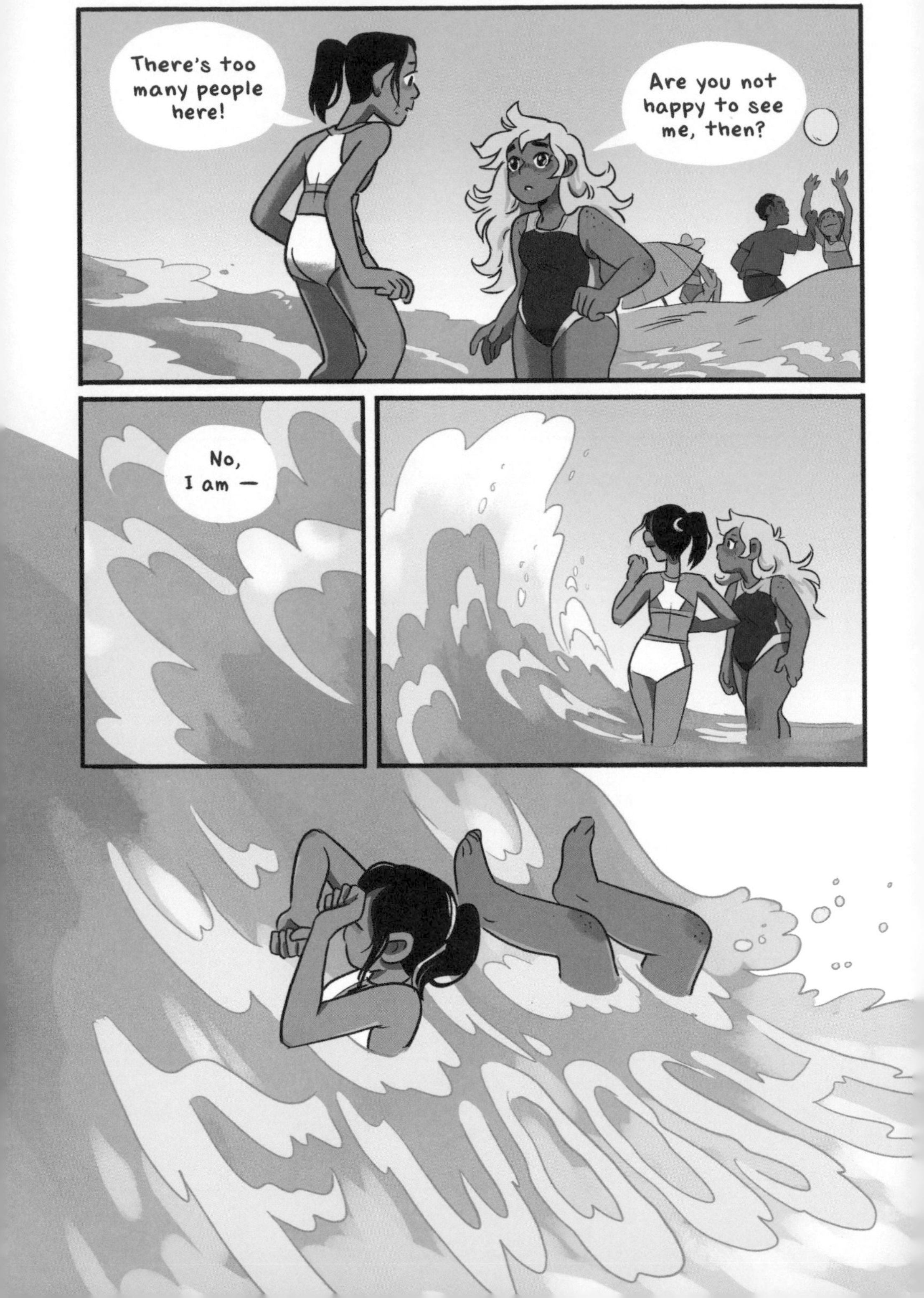
There's too many people here!
Are you not happy to see me, then?
No, I am —

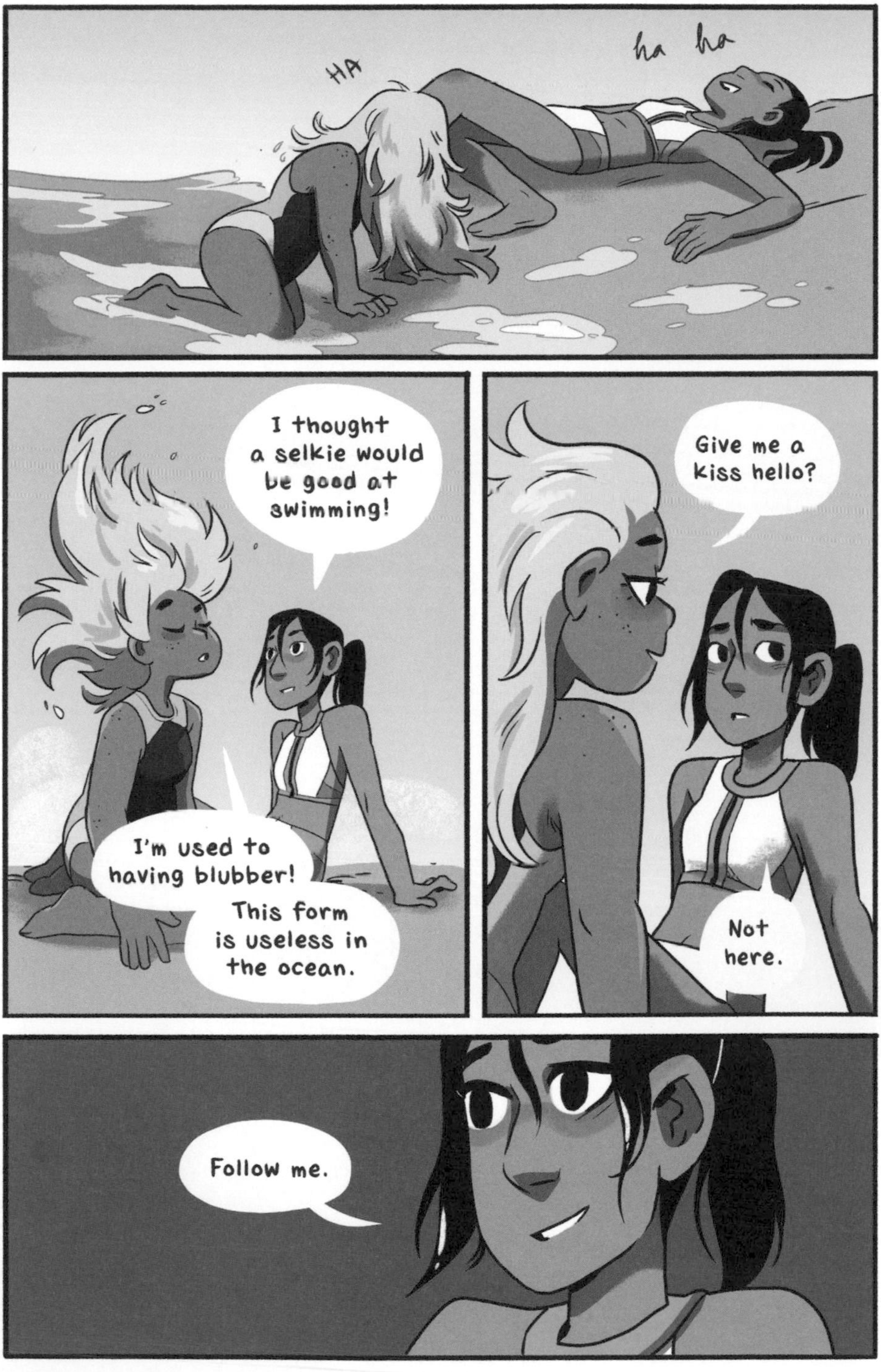
HA
ha ha
I thought a selkie would be good at swimming!
I'm used to having blubber!
This form is useless in the ocean.
Give me a kiss hello?
Not here.
Follow me.

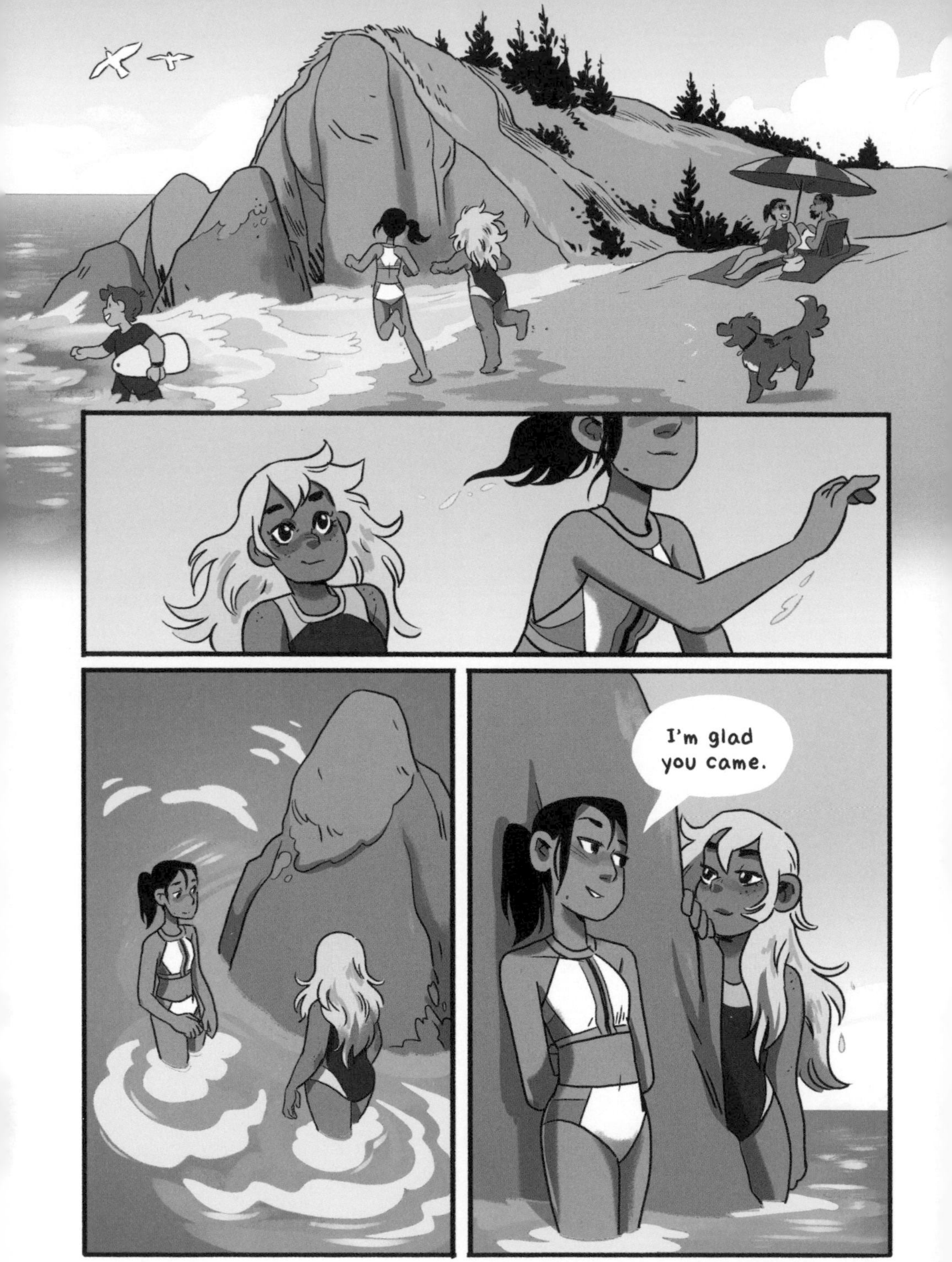
I'm glad you came.

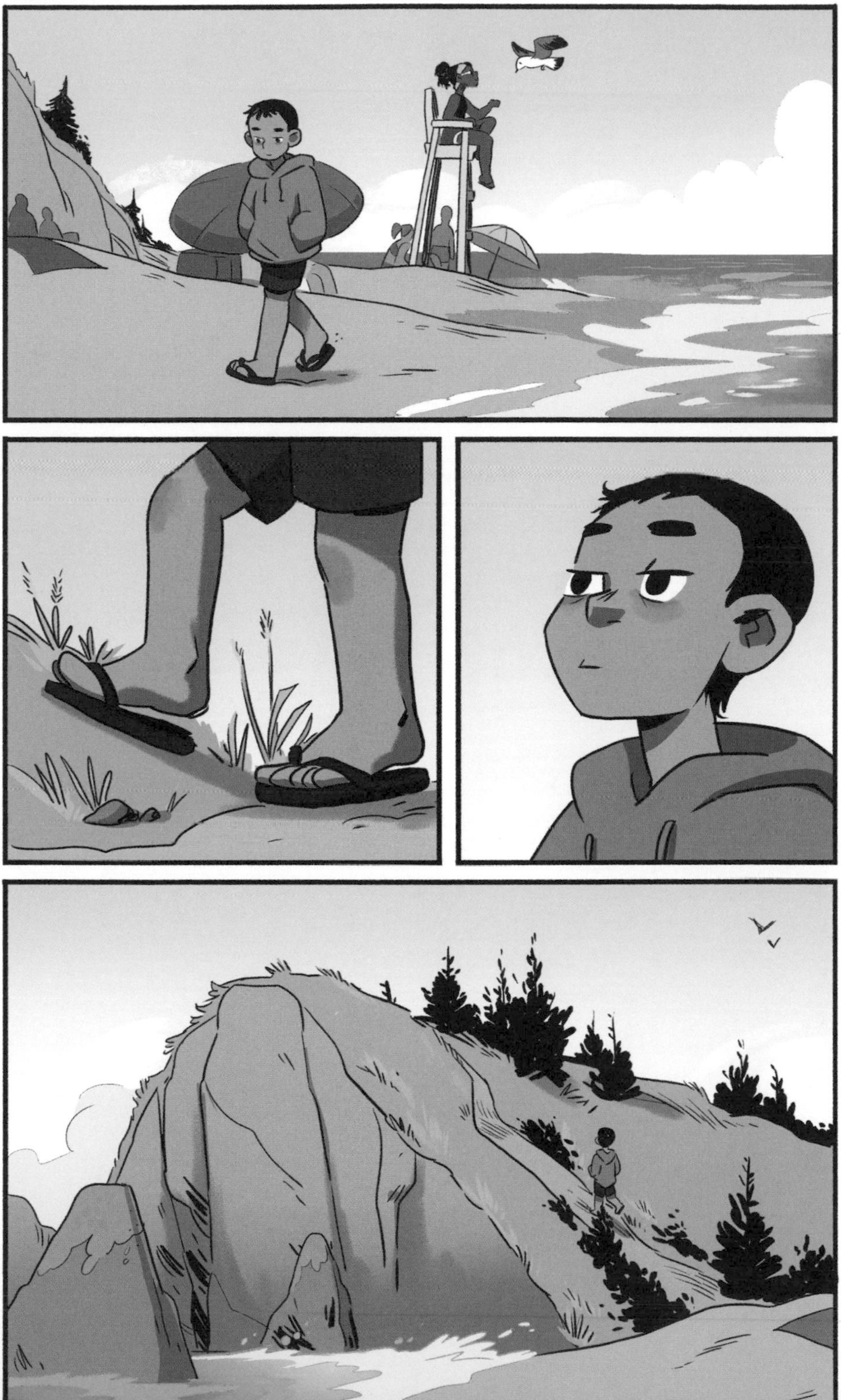

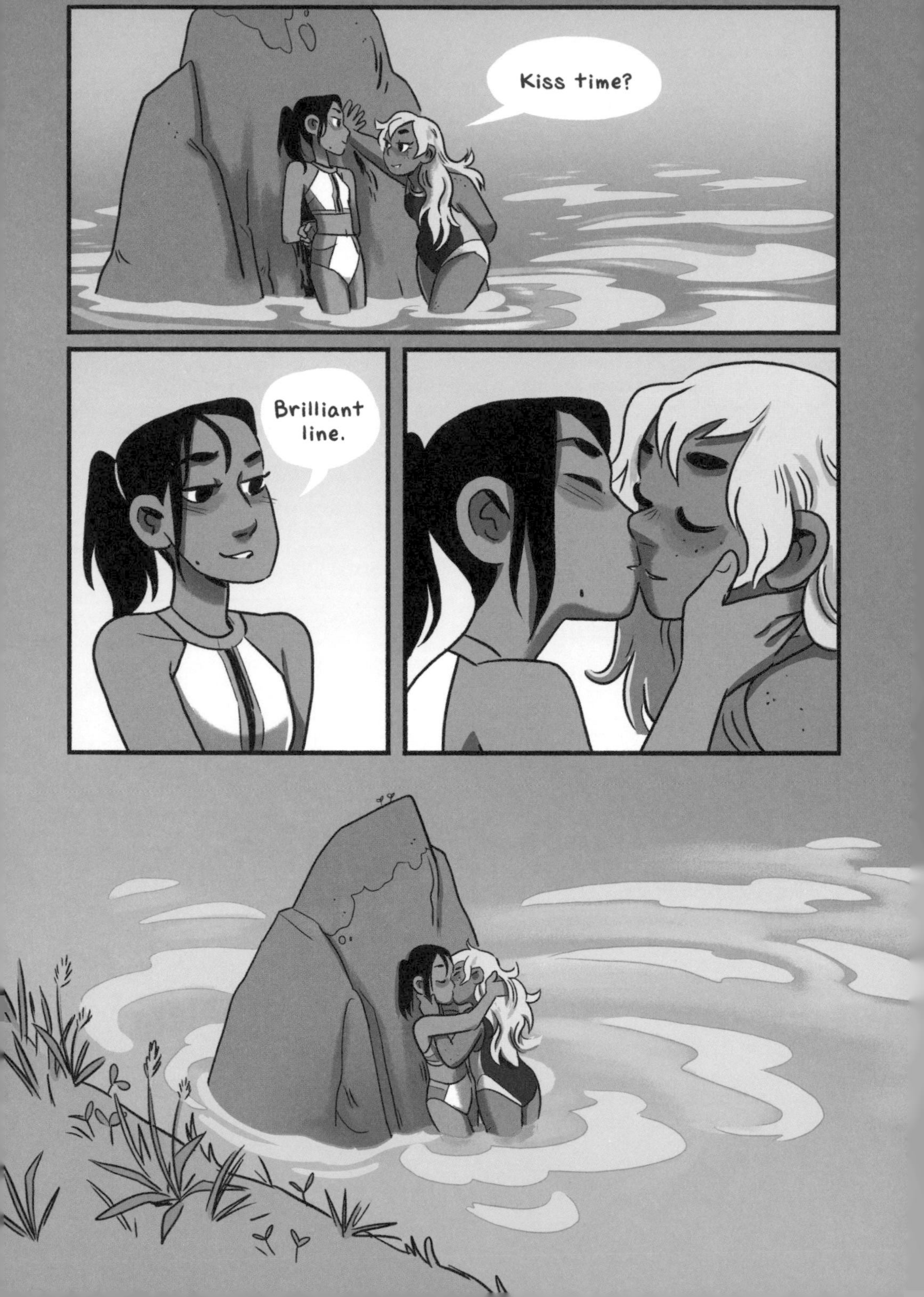
Kiss time?
Brilliant line.

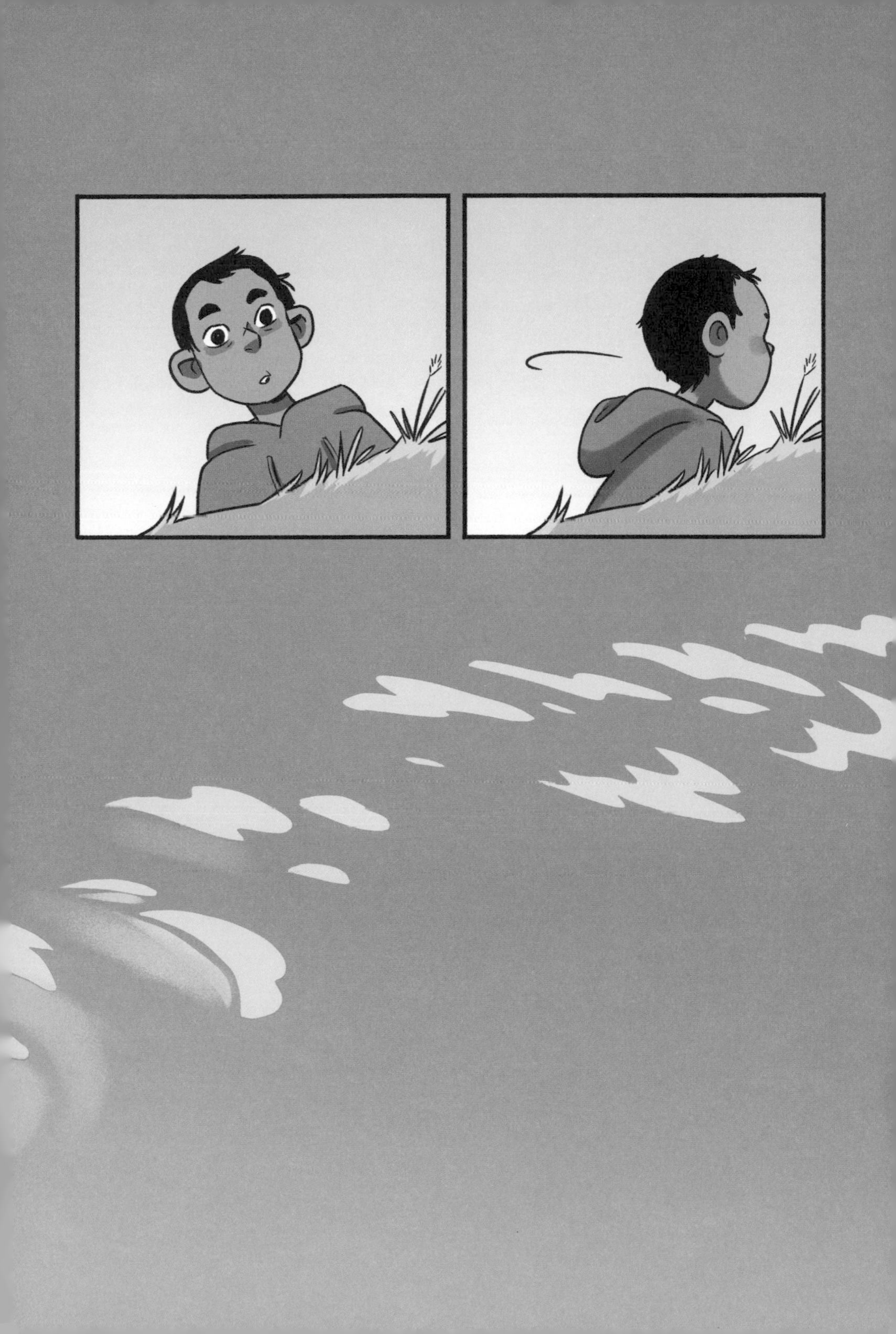

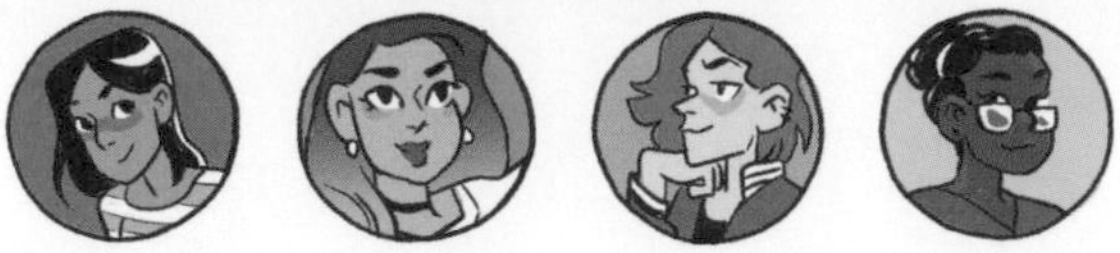

Morgan Serena Jules Lizzie

Sun, June 23, 6:57 PM

my mom is washing the dishes but she's like

CLANGING them because she is mad my dad parked on her flowers

riveting

i know...I'll try to get a video

Aiden does that every time he does dishes... he is in a permanent state of mad

Aw poor baby Aiden

NO

he's cute!

NOOO

NOT LIKE THAT

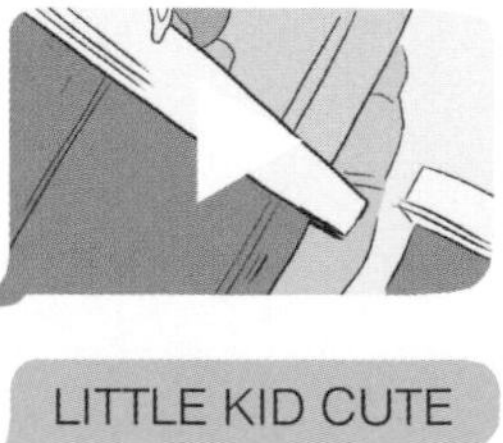

LITTLE KID CUTE

Liz......

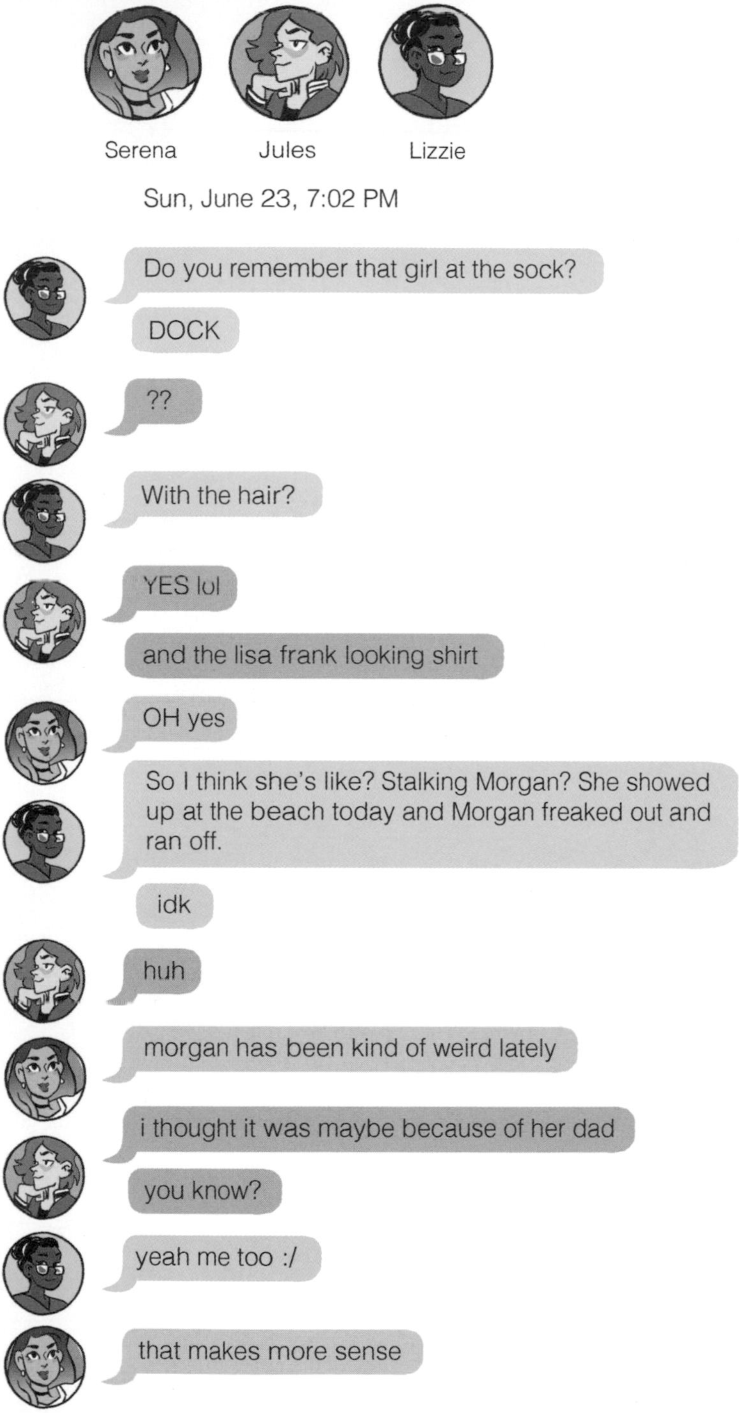
Serena
Jules
Lizzie
Sun, June 23, 7:02 PM
Do you remember that girl at the sock?
DOCK
??
With the hair?
YES lol
and the lisa frank looking shirt
OH yes
So I think she's like? Stalking Morgan? She showed up at the beach today and Morgan freaked out and ran off.
idk
huh
morgan has been kind of weird lately
i thought it was maybe because of her dad
you know?
yeah me too :/
that makes more sense

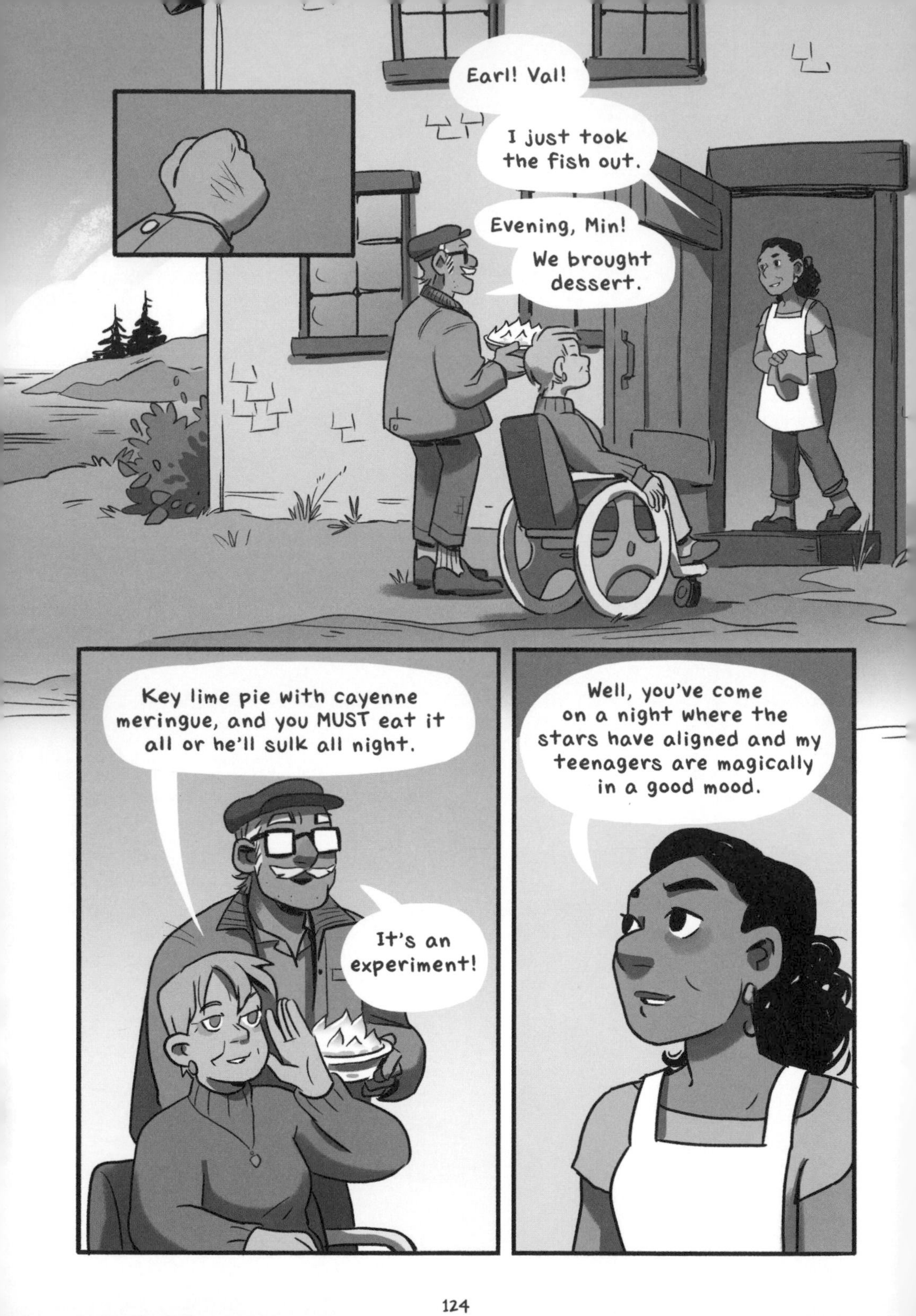

Earl! Val!
I just took the fish out.
Evening, Min!
We brought dessert.
Key lime pie with cayenne meringue, and you MUST eat it all or he'll sulk all night.
It's an experiment!
Well, you've come on a night where the stars have aligned and my teenagers are magically in a good mood.

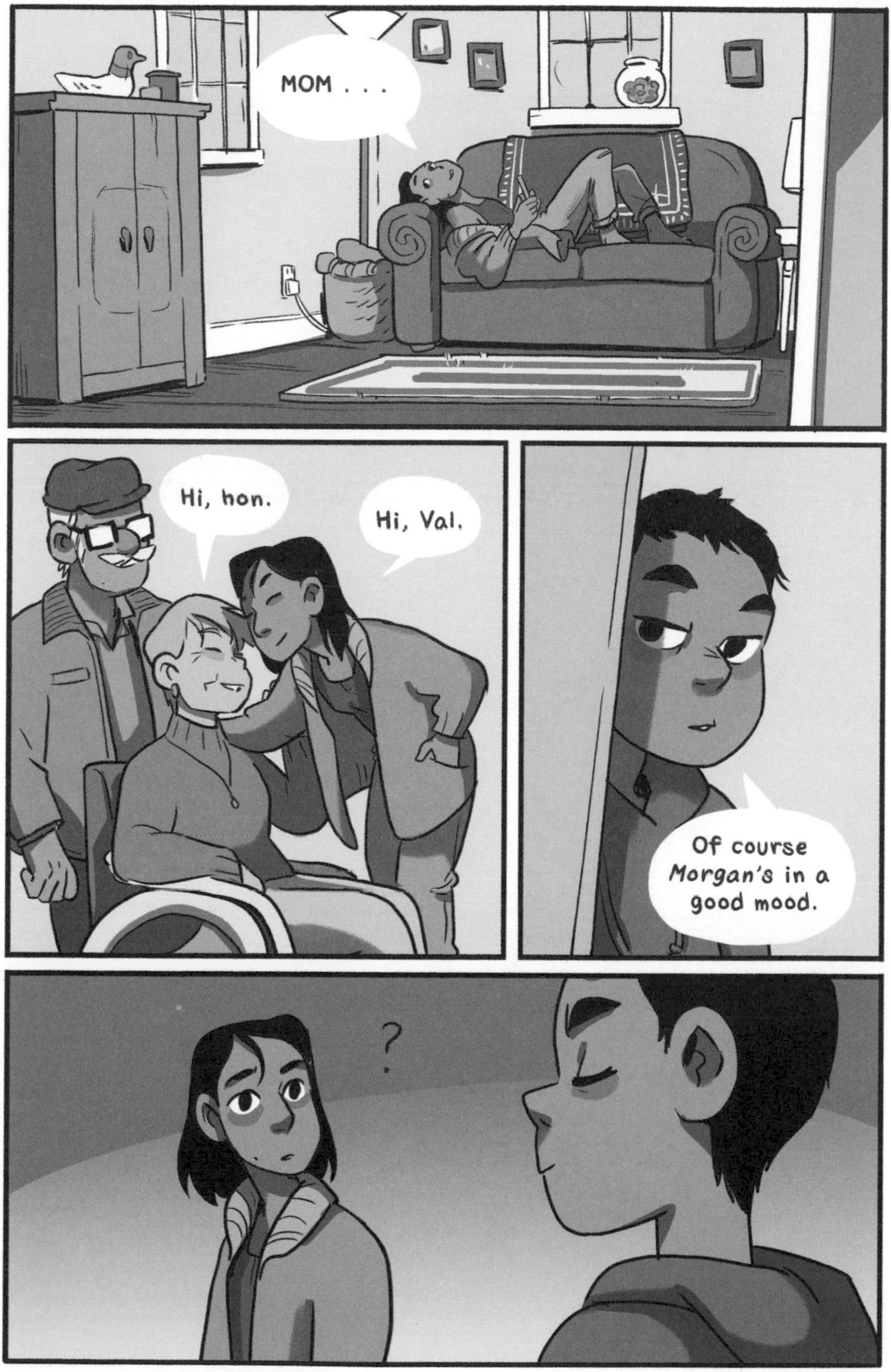
MOM . . .
Hi, hon.
Hi, Val.
Of course Morgan's in a good mood.
?

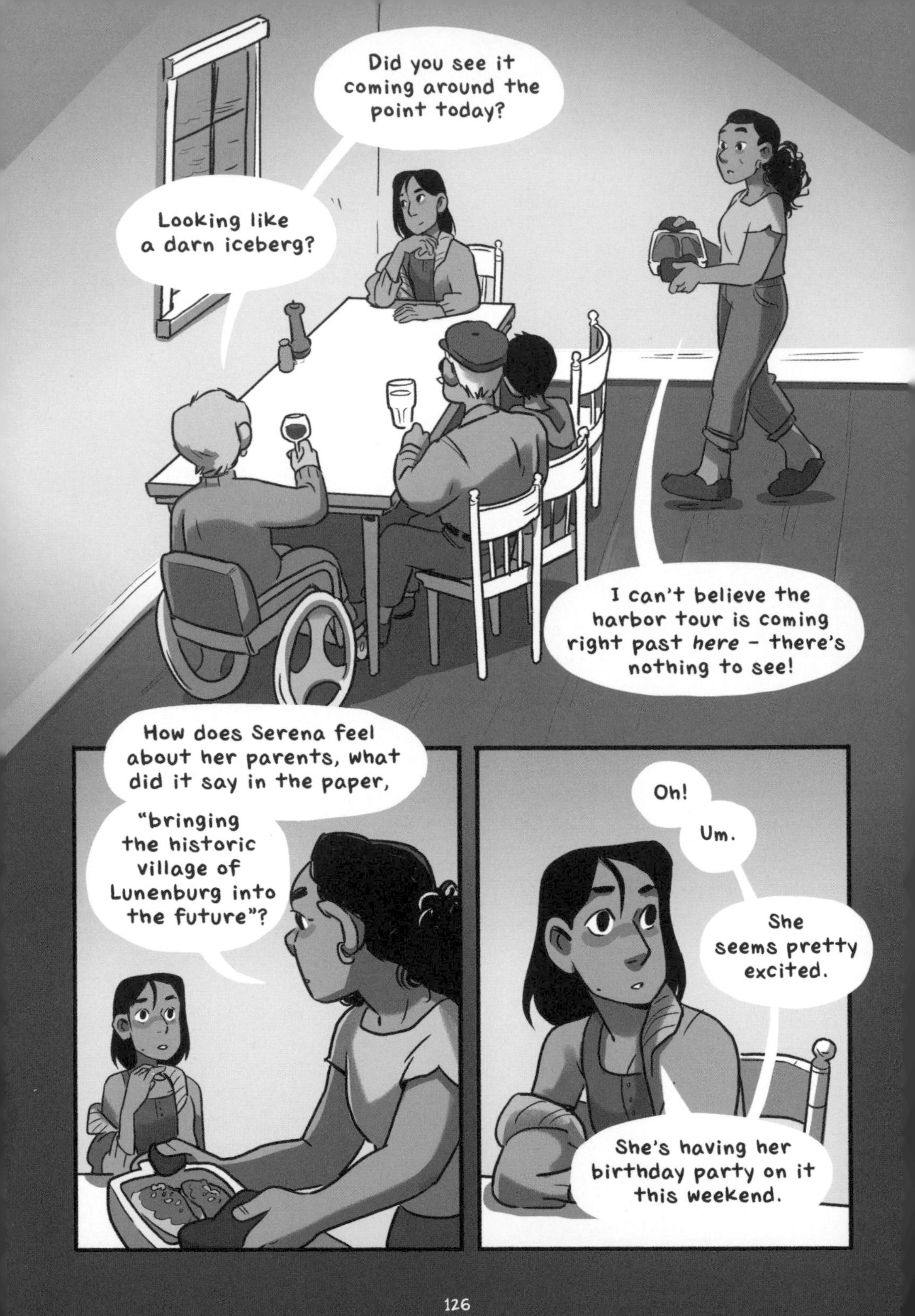
Did you see it coming around the point today?
Looking like a darn iceberg?
I can't believe the harbor tour is coming right past *here* - there's nothing to see!
How does Serena feel about her parents, what did it say in the paper,
"bringing the historic village of Lunenburg into the future"?
Oh!
Um.
She seems pretty excited.
She's having her birthday party on it this weekend.

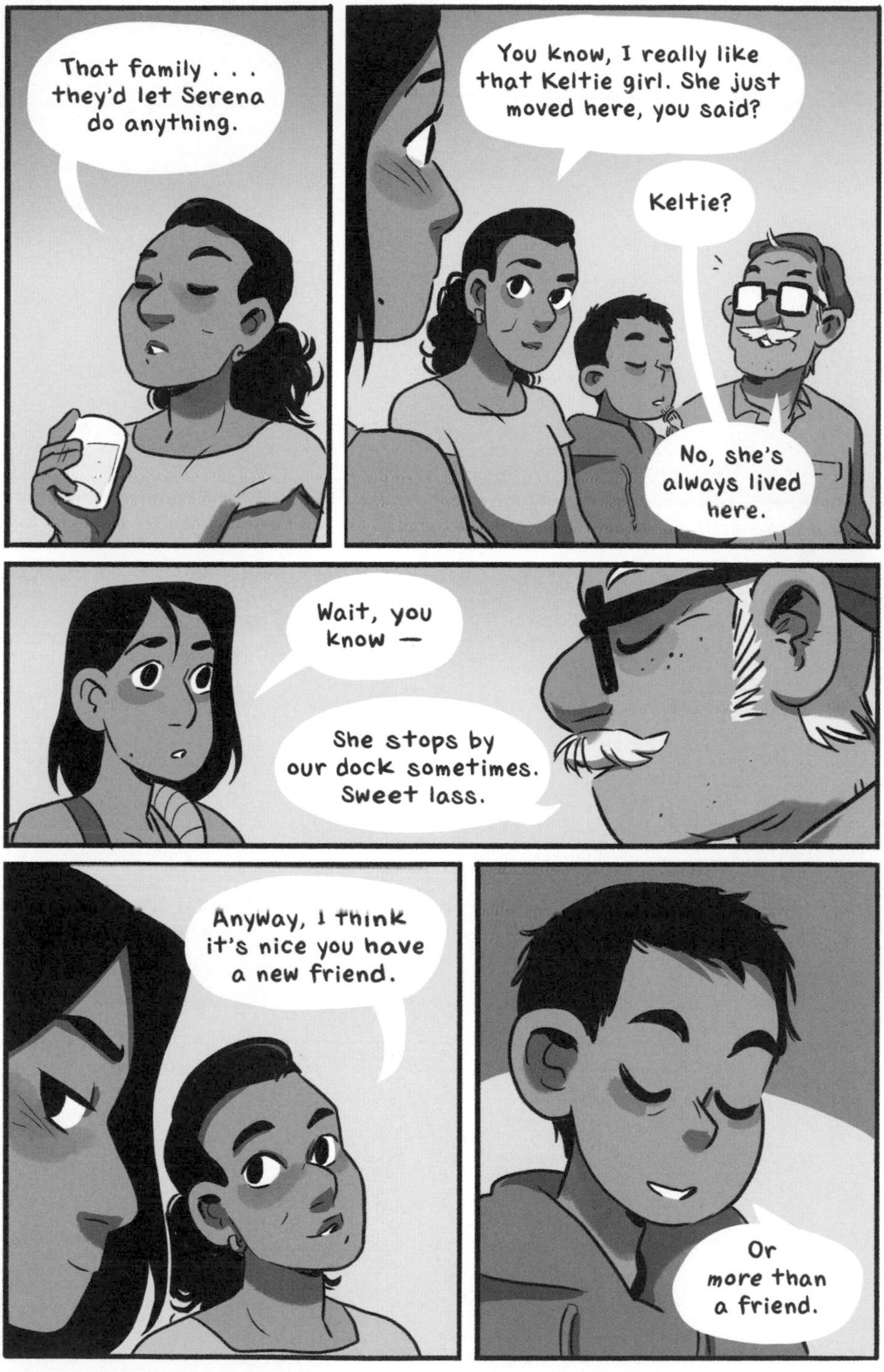
That family . . . they'd let Serena do anything.
You know, I really like that Keltie girl. She just moved here, you said?
Keltie?
No, she's always lived here.
Wait, you know —
She stops by our dock sometimes. Sweet lass.
Anyway, I think it's nice you have a new friend.
Or more than a friend.

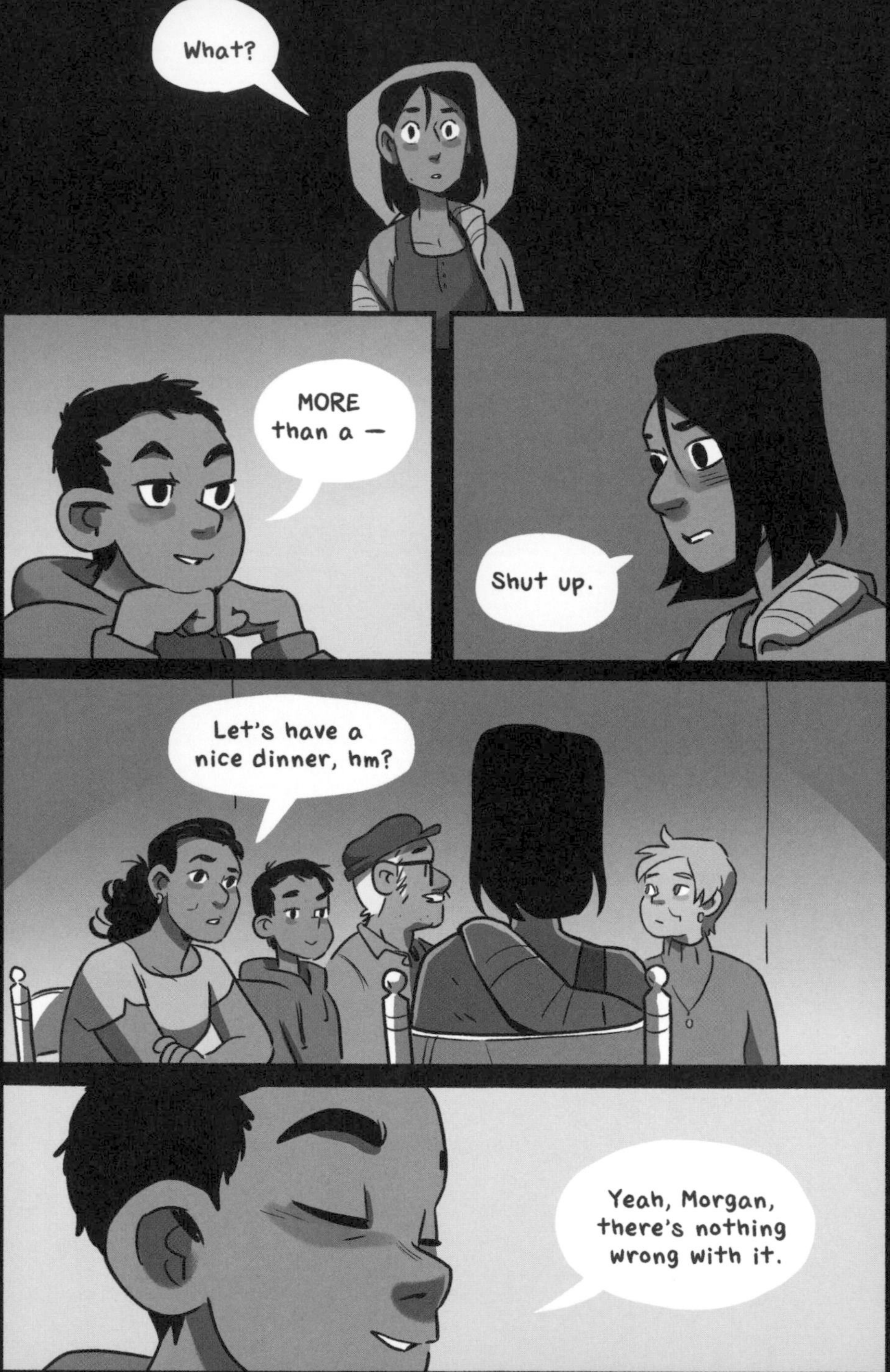
What?
MORE than a —
Shut up.
Let's have a nice dinner, hm?
Yeah, Morgan, there's nothing wrong with it.

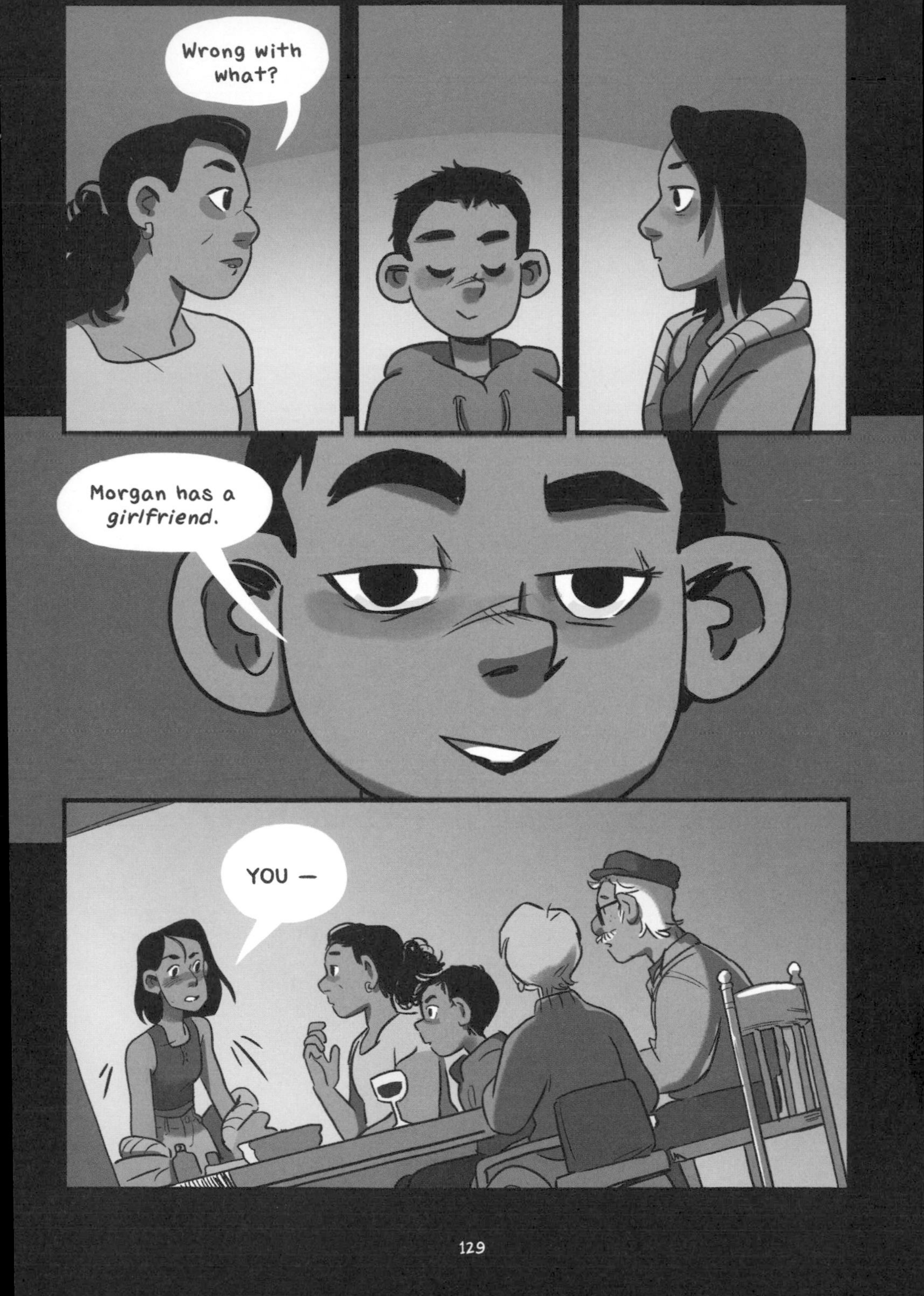
Wrong with what?
Morgan has a girlfriend.
YOU —

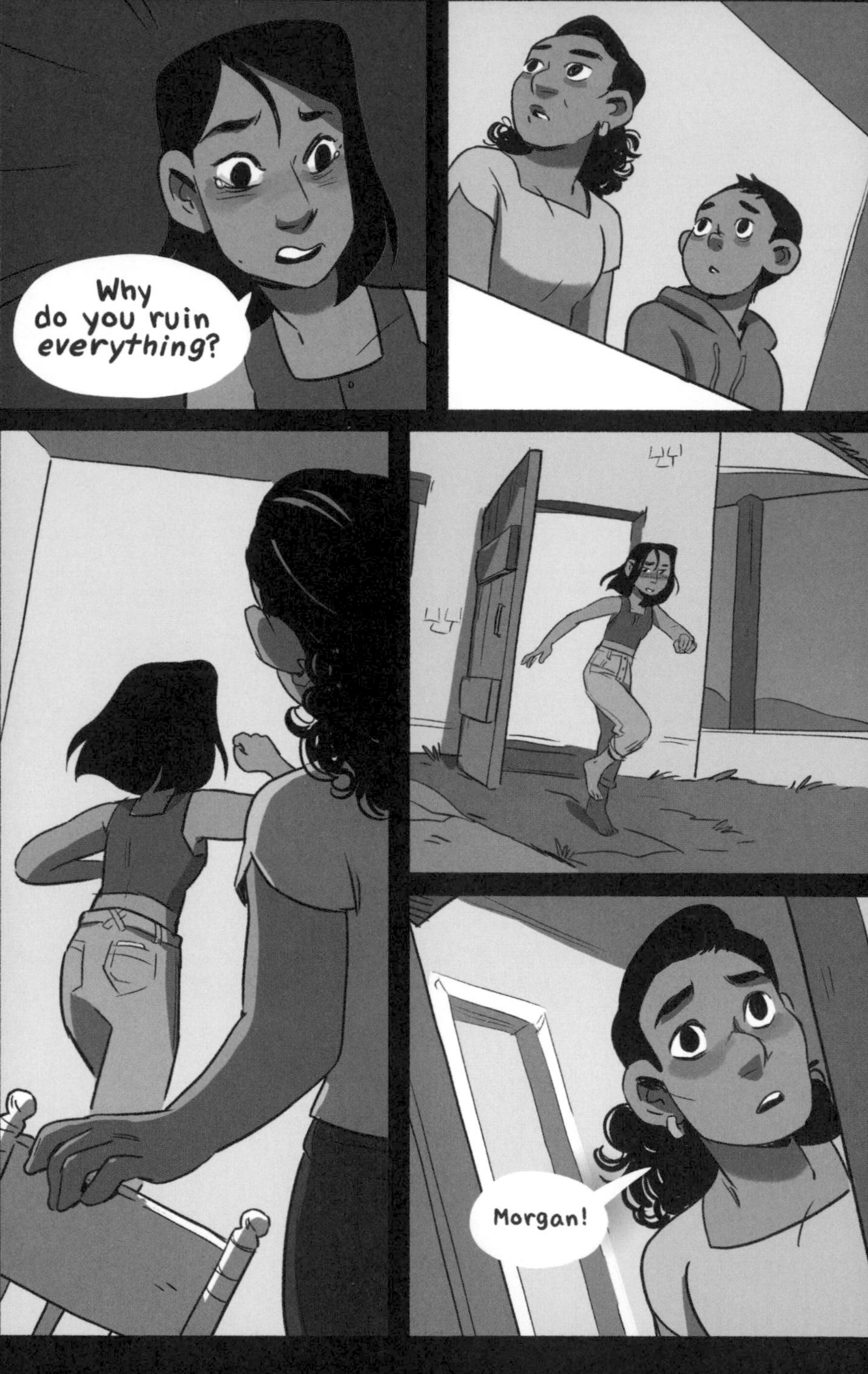
Why do you ruin everything?
Morgan!

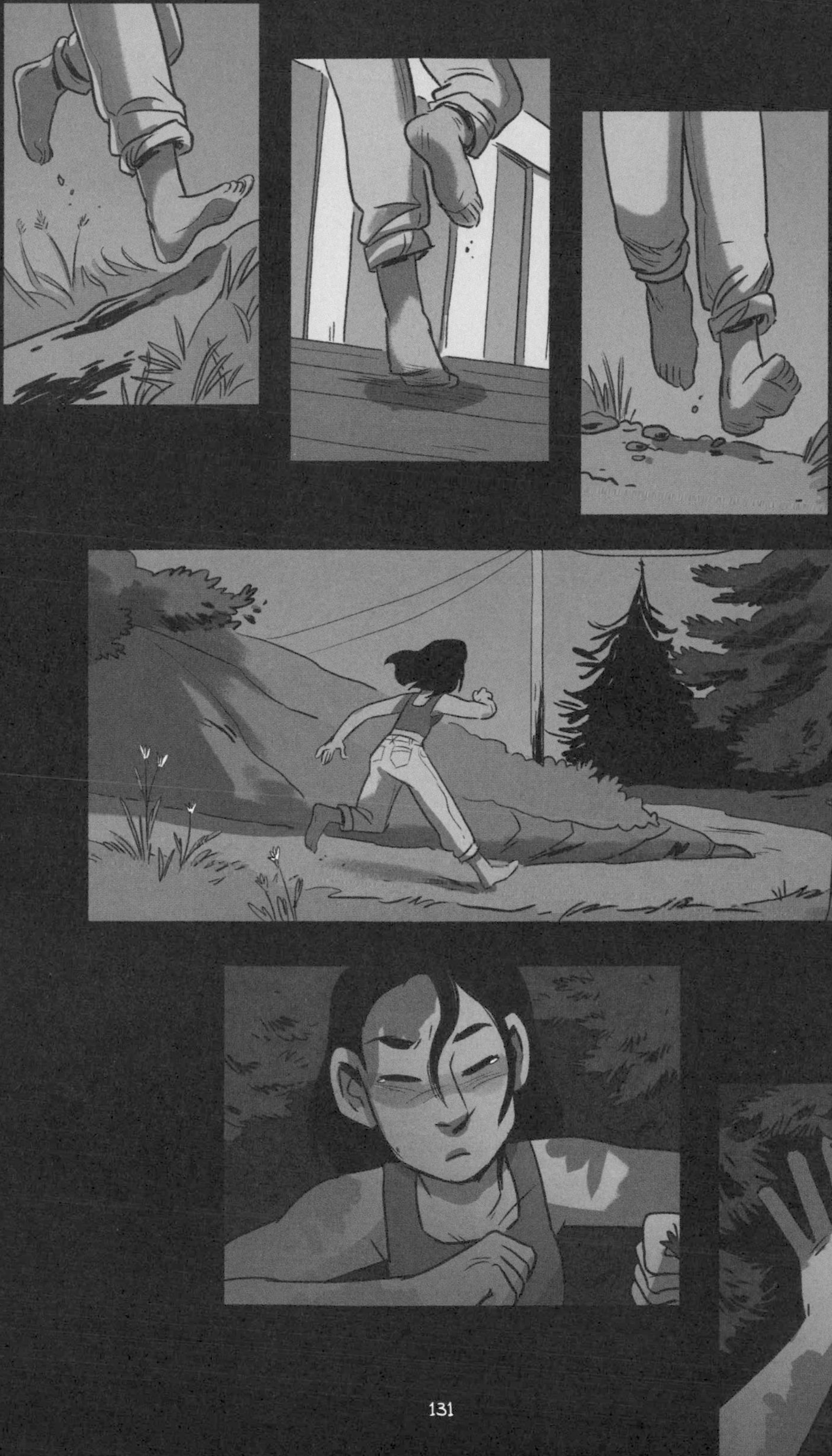

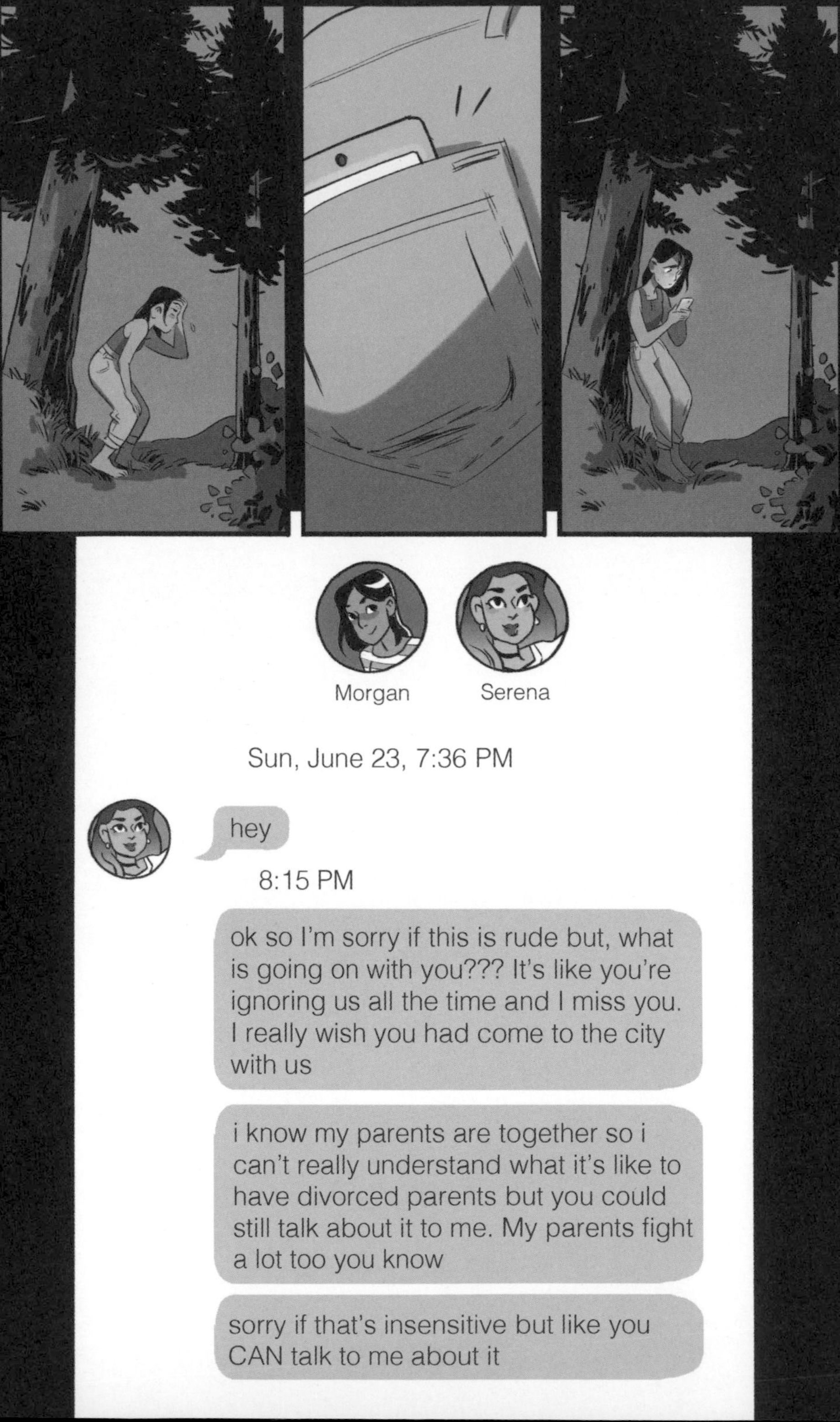

Morgan
Serena
Sun, June 23, 7:36 PM
hey
8:15 PM
ok so I'm sorry if this is rude but, what is going on with you??? It's like you're ignoring us all the time and I miss you. I really wish you had come to the city with us
i know my parents are together so i can't really understand what it's like to have divorced parents but you could still talk about it to me. My parents fight a lot too you know
sorry if that's insensitive but like you CAN talk to me about it

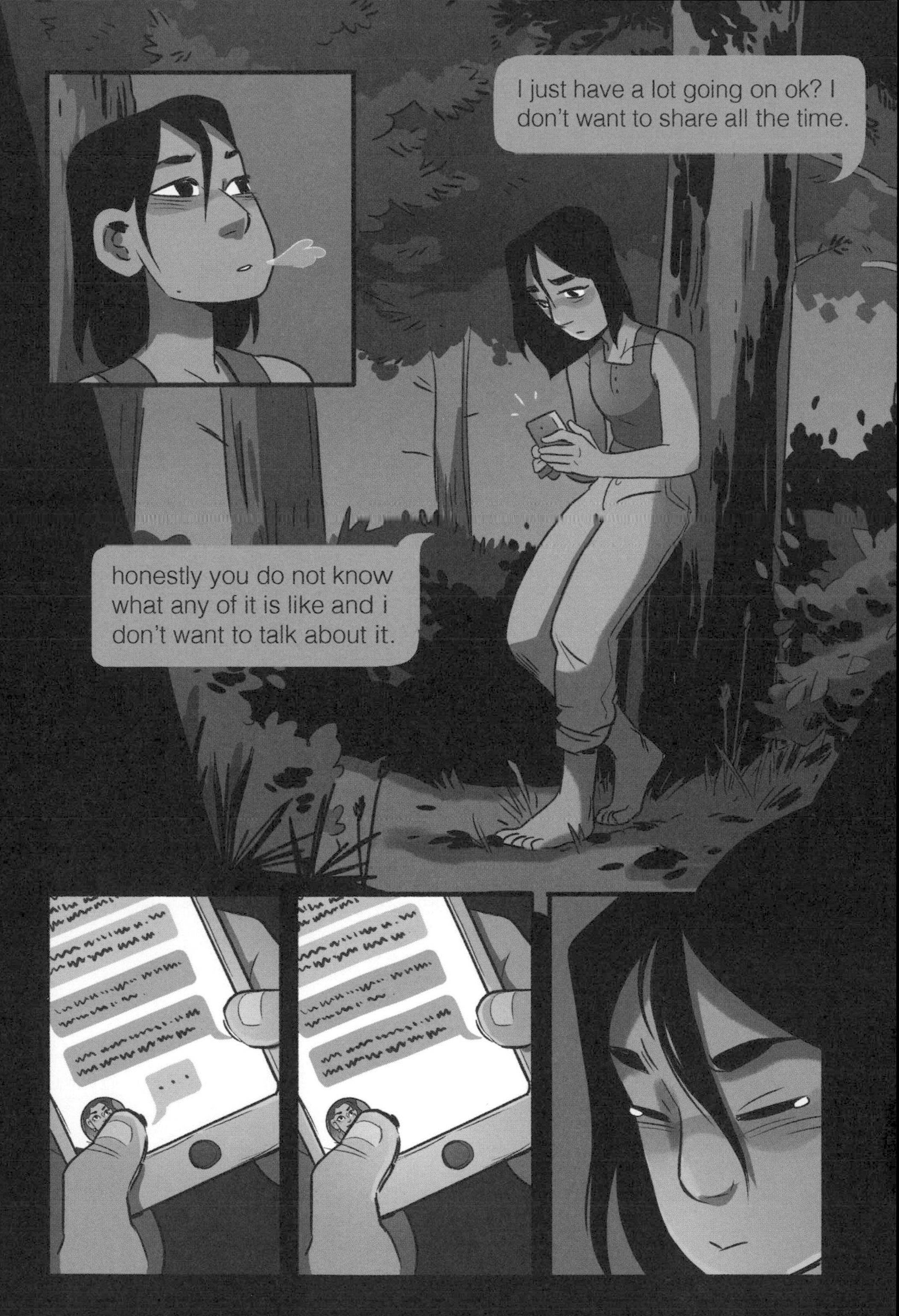
I just have a lot going on ok? I don't want to share all the time.
honestly you do not know what any of it is like and i don't want to talk about it.

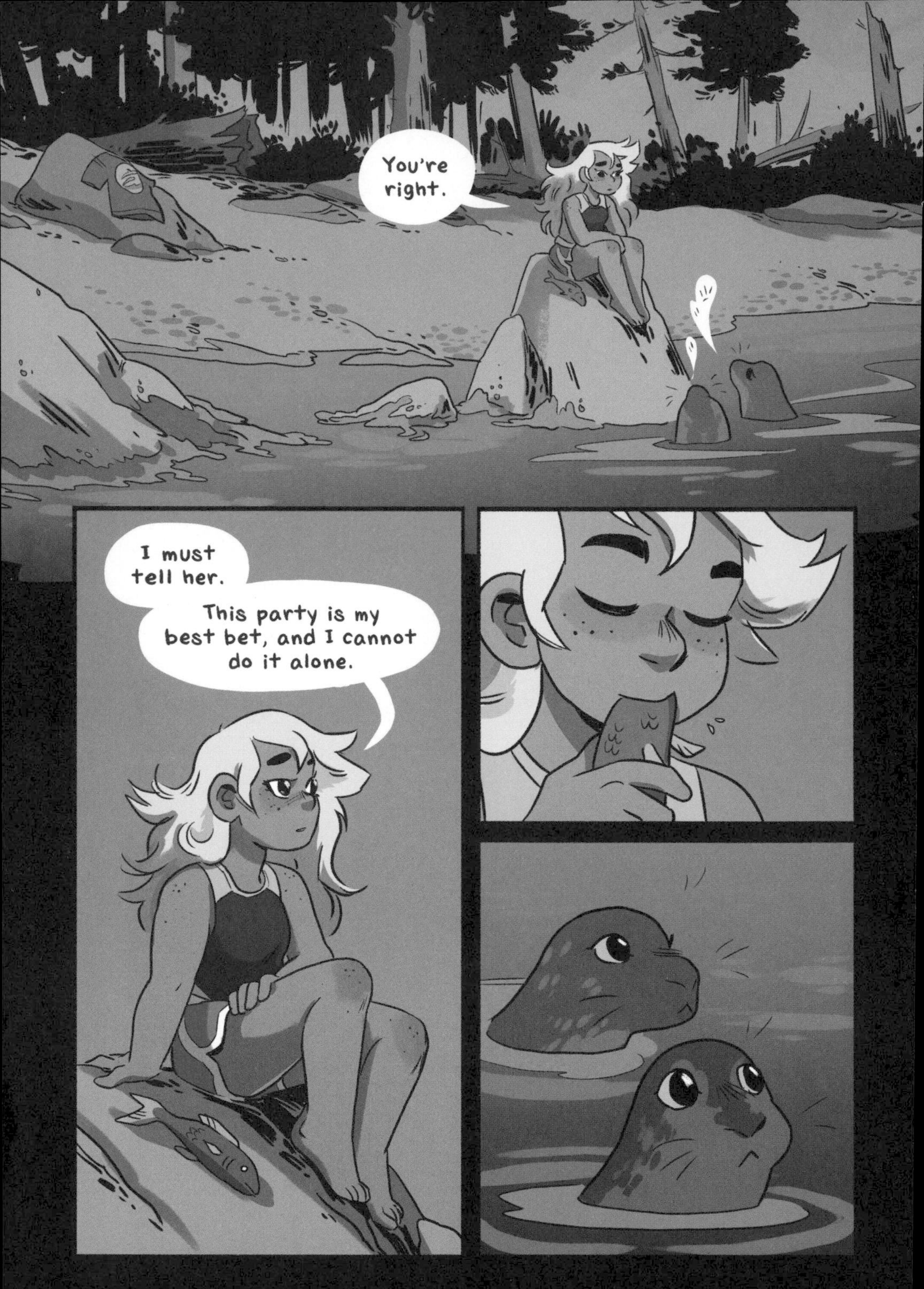

You're right.
I must tell her.
This party is my best bet, and I cannot do it alone.

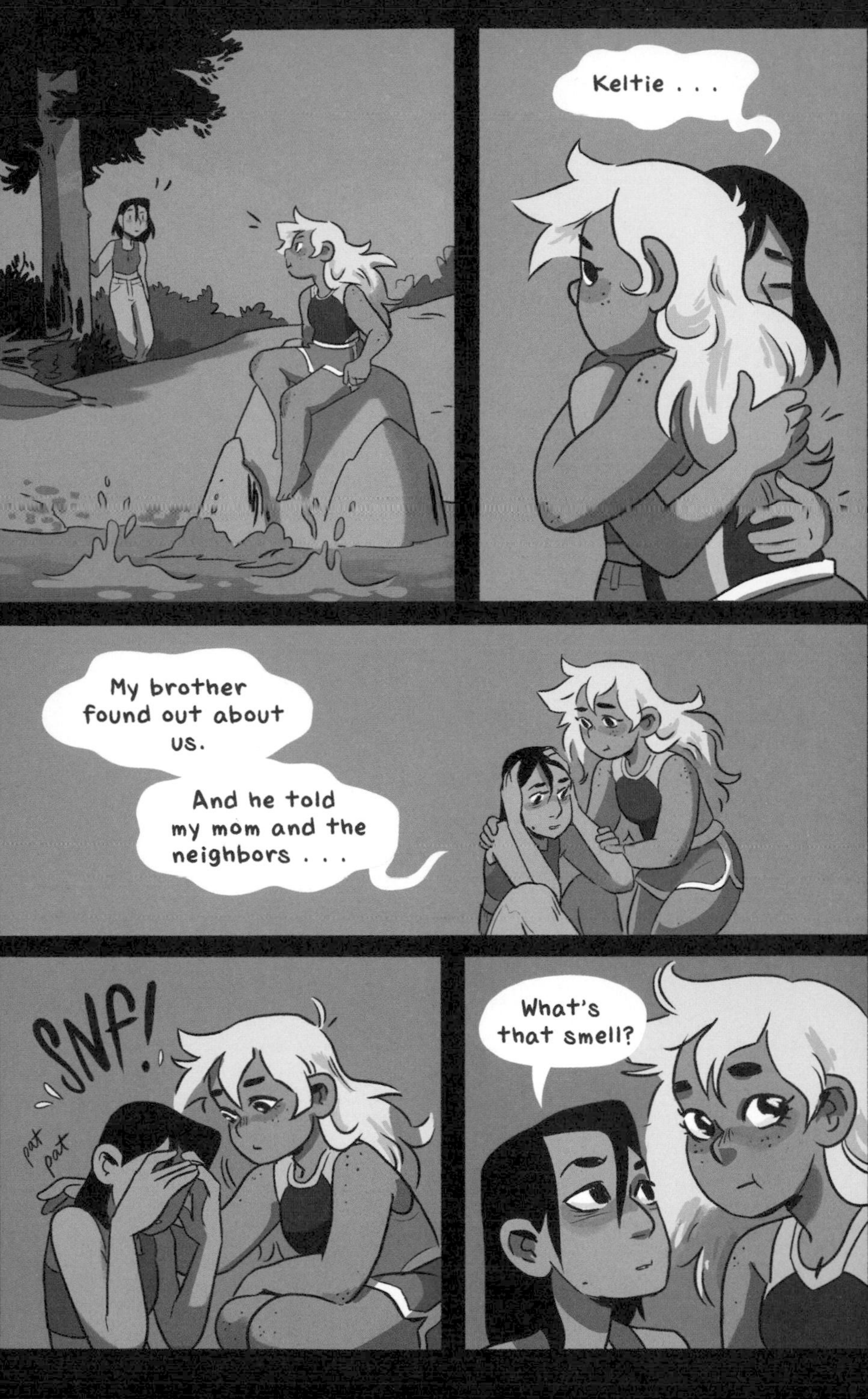
Keltie . . .
My brother found out about us.
And he told my mom and the neighbors . . .
SNF!
pat pat
What's that smell?

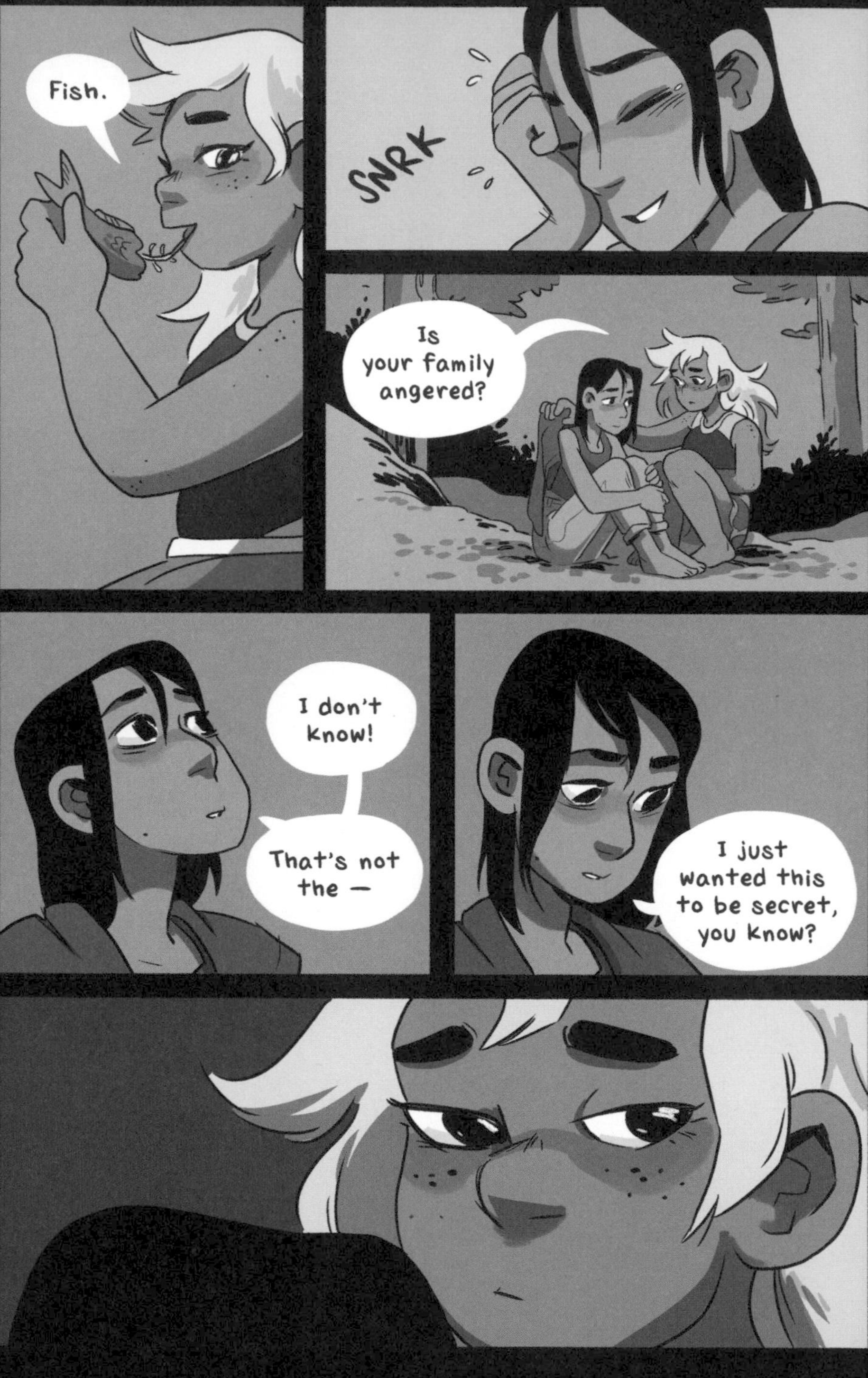
Fish.
SNRK
Is your family angered?
I don't know!
That's not the —
I just wanted this to be secret, you know?

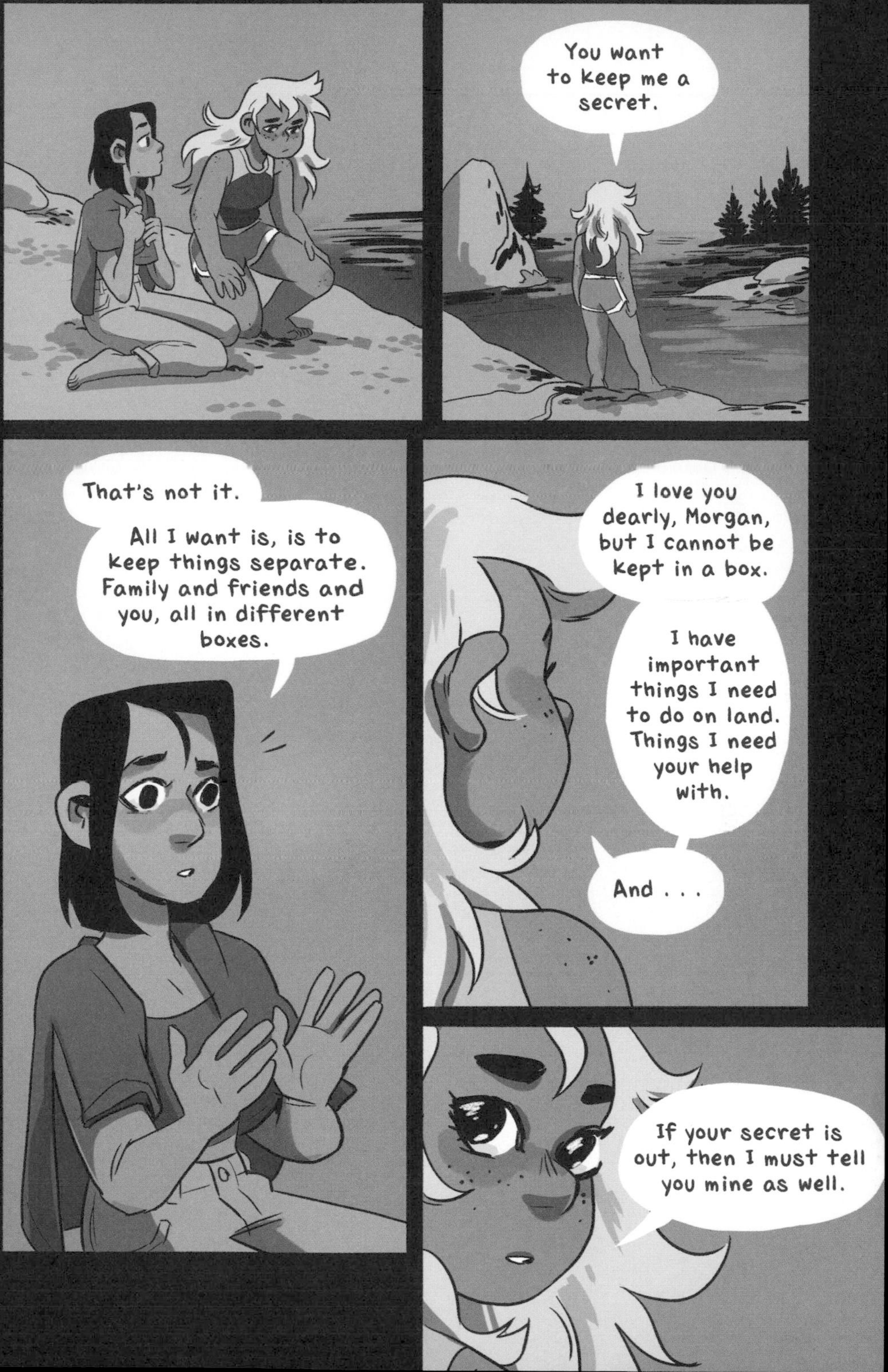

You want to keep me a secret.
That's not it.
All I want is, is to keep things separate. Family and friends and you, all in different boxes.
I love you dearly, Morgan, but I cannot be kept in a box.
I have important things I need to do on land. Things I need your help with.
And . . .
If your secret is out, then I must tell you mine as well.

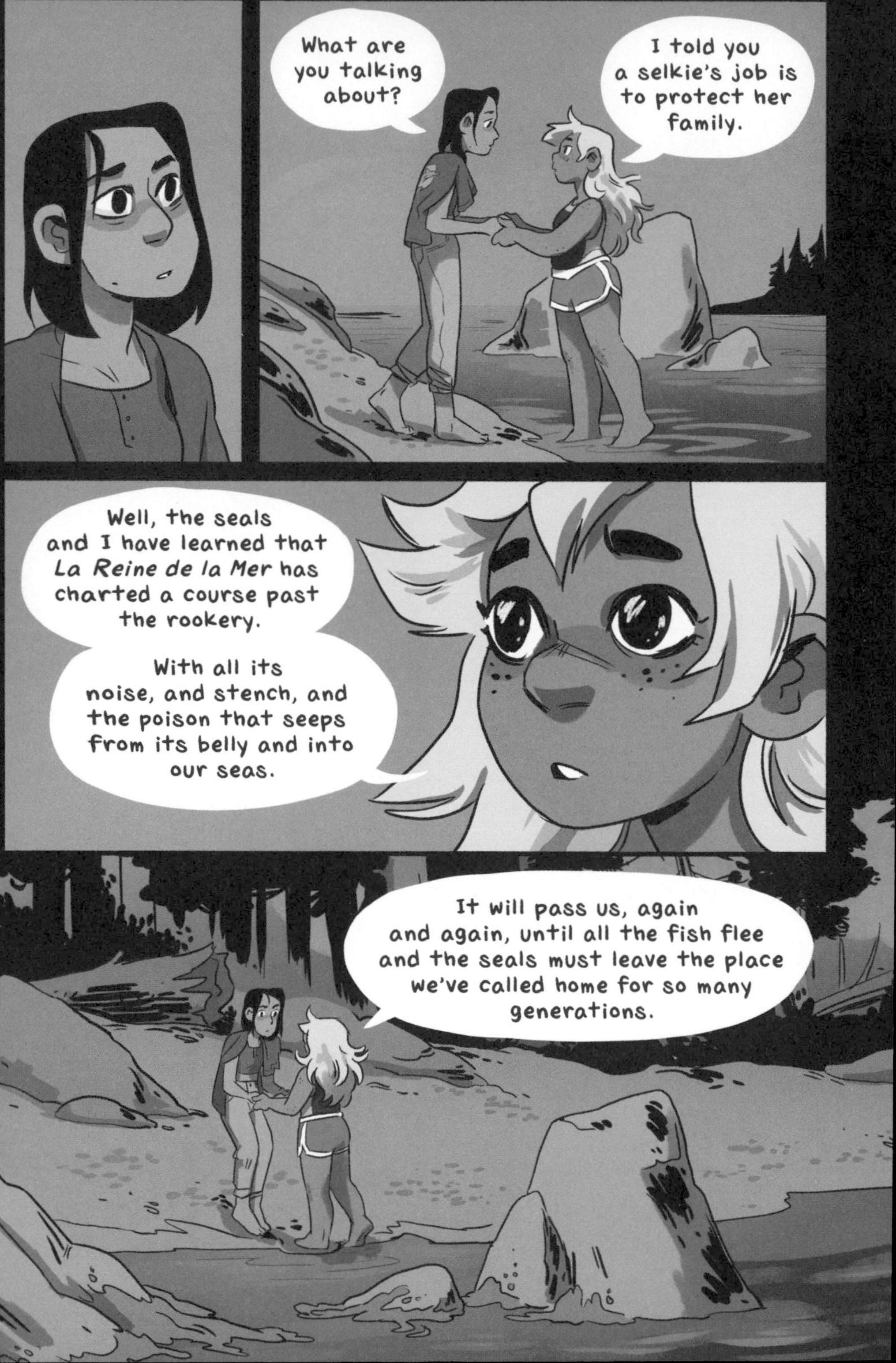
What are you talking about?
I told you a selkie's job is to protect her family.
Well, the seals and I have learned that *La Reine de la Mer* has charted a course past the rookery.
With all its noise, and stench, and the poison that seeps from its belly and into our seas.
It will pass us, again and again, until all the fish flee and the seals must leave the place we've called home for so many generations.

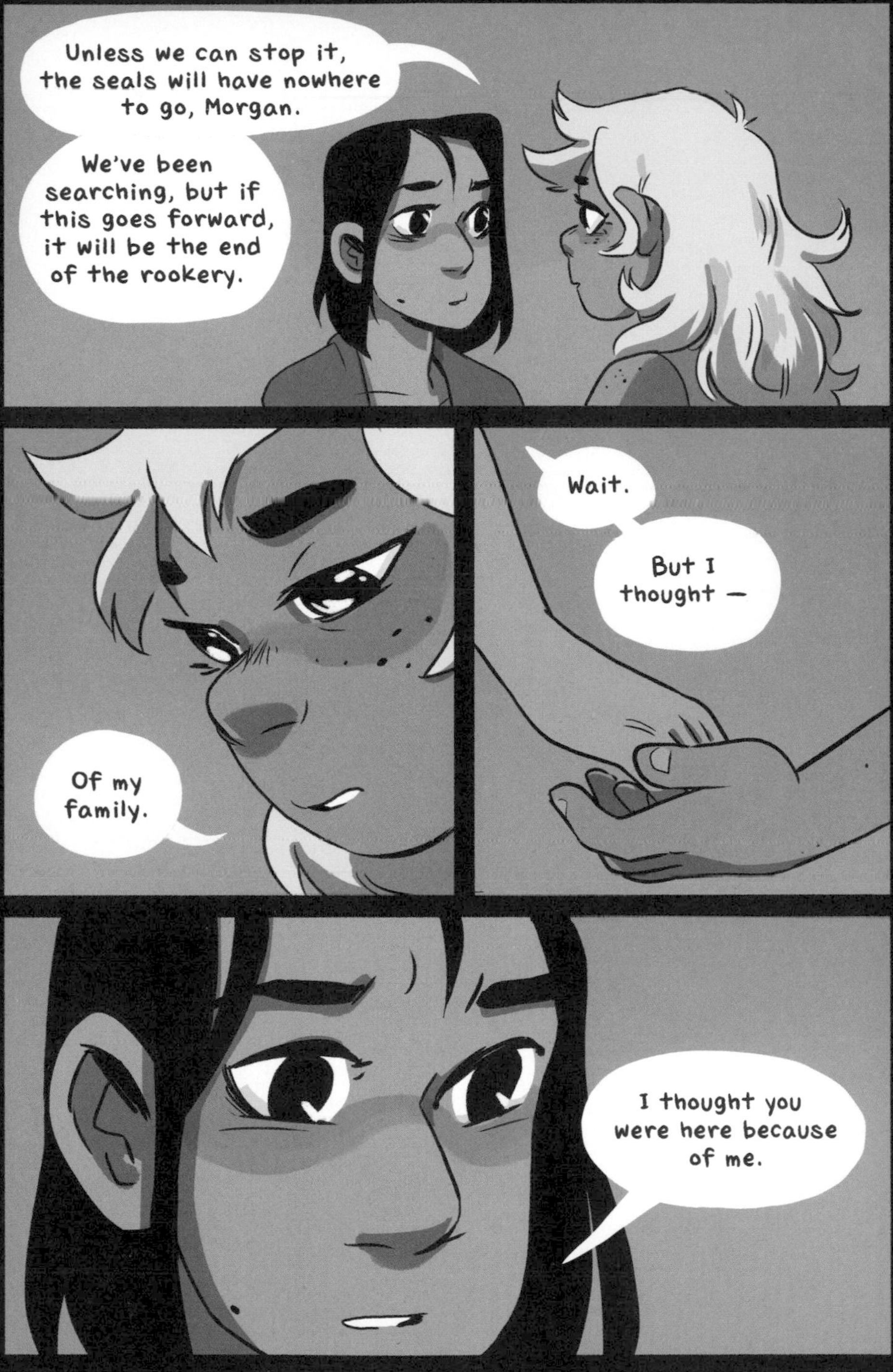
Unless we can stop it, the seals will have nowhere to go, Morgan.
We've been searching, but if this goes forward, it will be the end of the rookery.
Of my family.
Wait.
But I thought —
I thought you were here because of me.

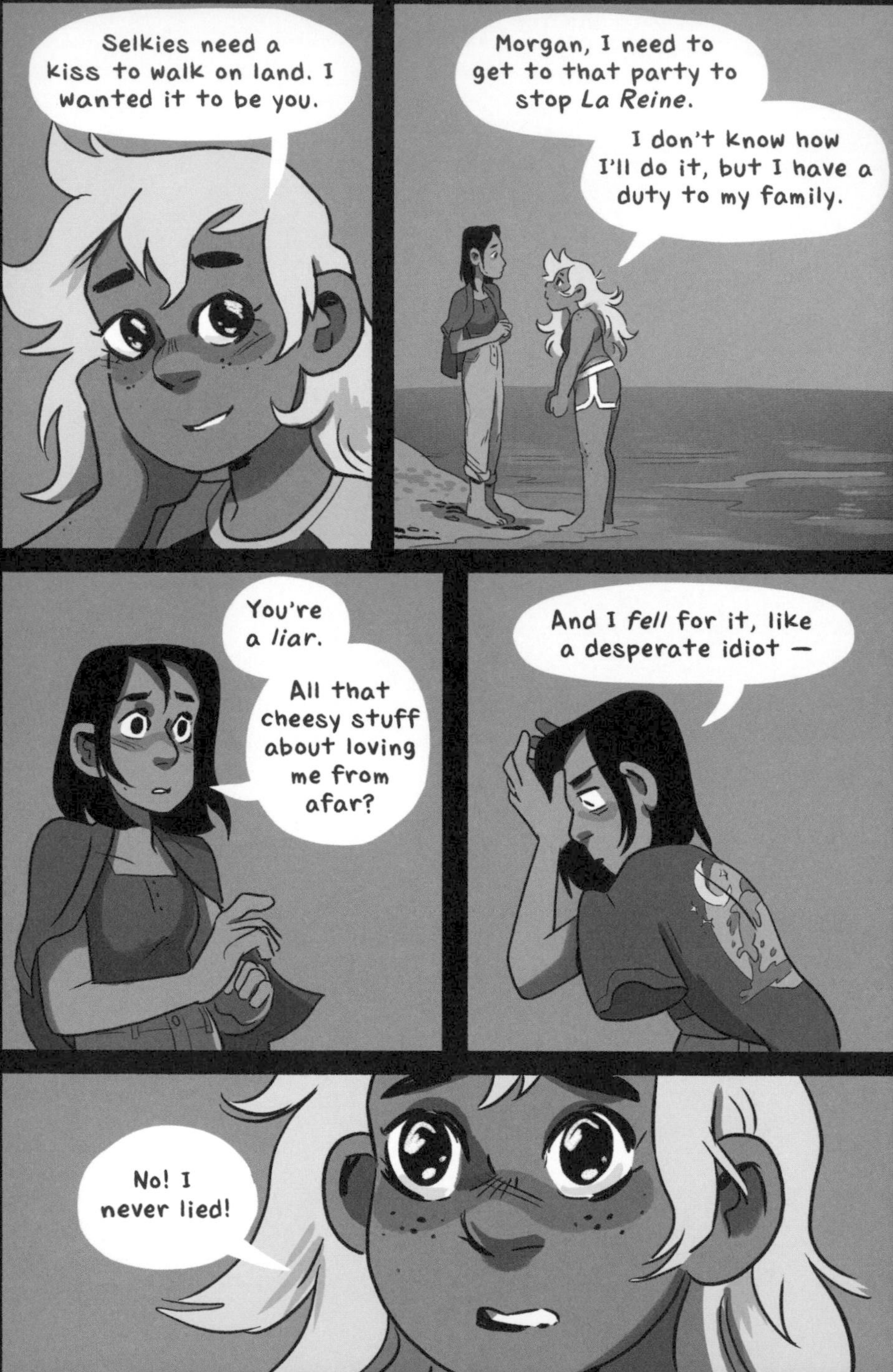
Selkies need a kiss to walk on land. I wanted it to be you.
Morgan, I need to get to that party to stop *La Reine*.
I don't know how I'll do it, but I have a duty to my family.
You're a *liar*.
All that cheesy stuff about loving me from afar?
And I *fell* for it, like a desperate idiot —
No! I never lied!

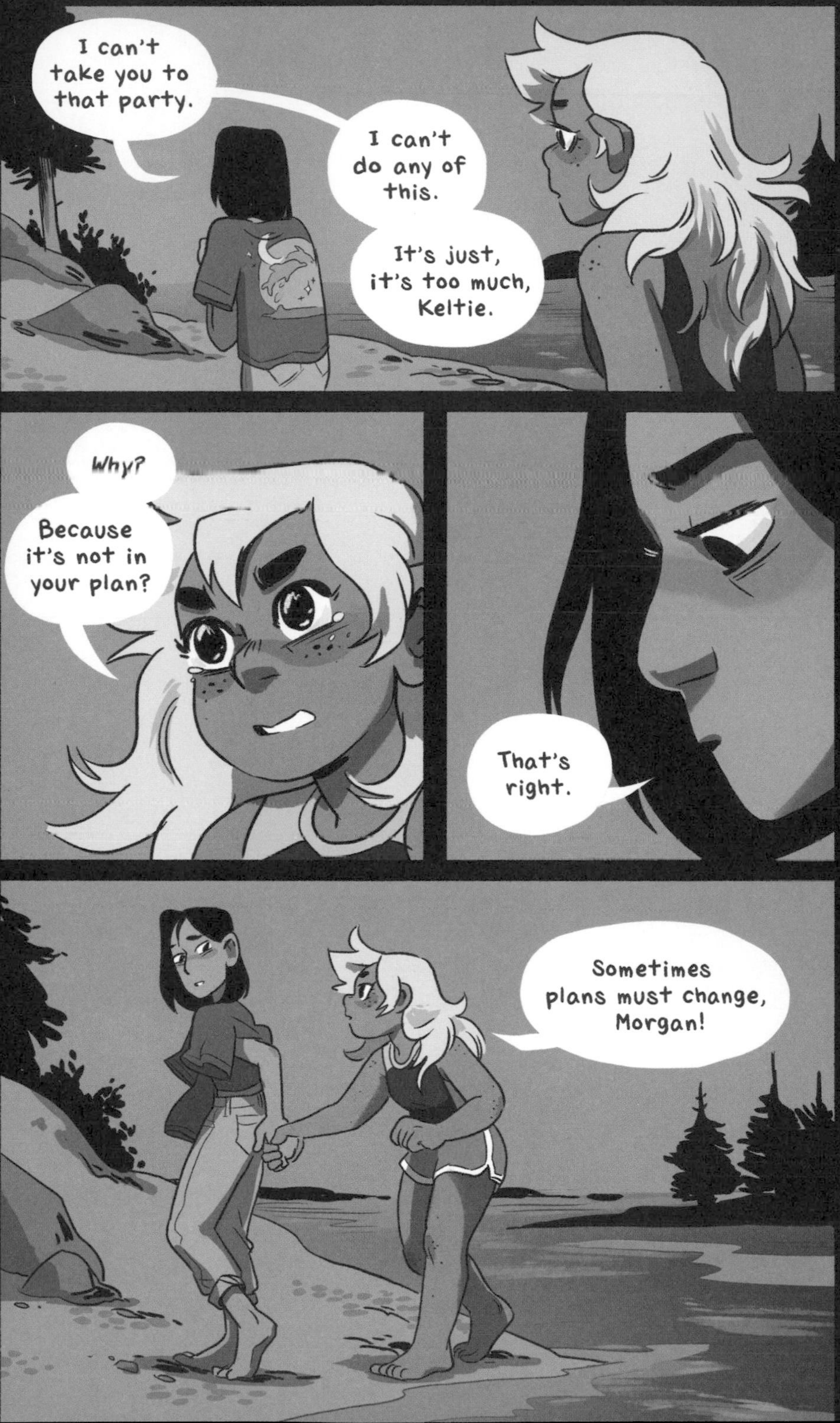
I can't take you to that party.
I can't do any of this.
It's just, it's too much, Keltie.
Why?
Because it's not in your plan?
That's right.
Sometimes plans must change, Morgan!

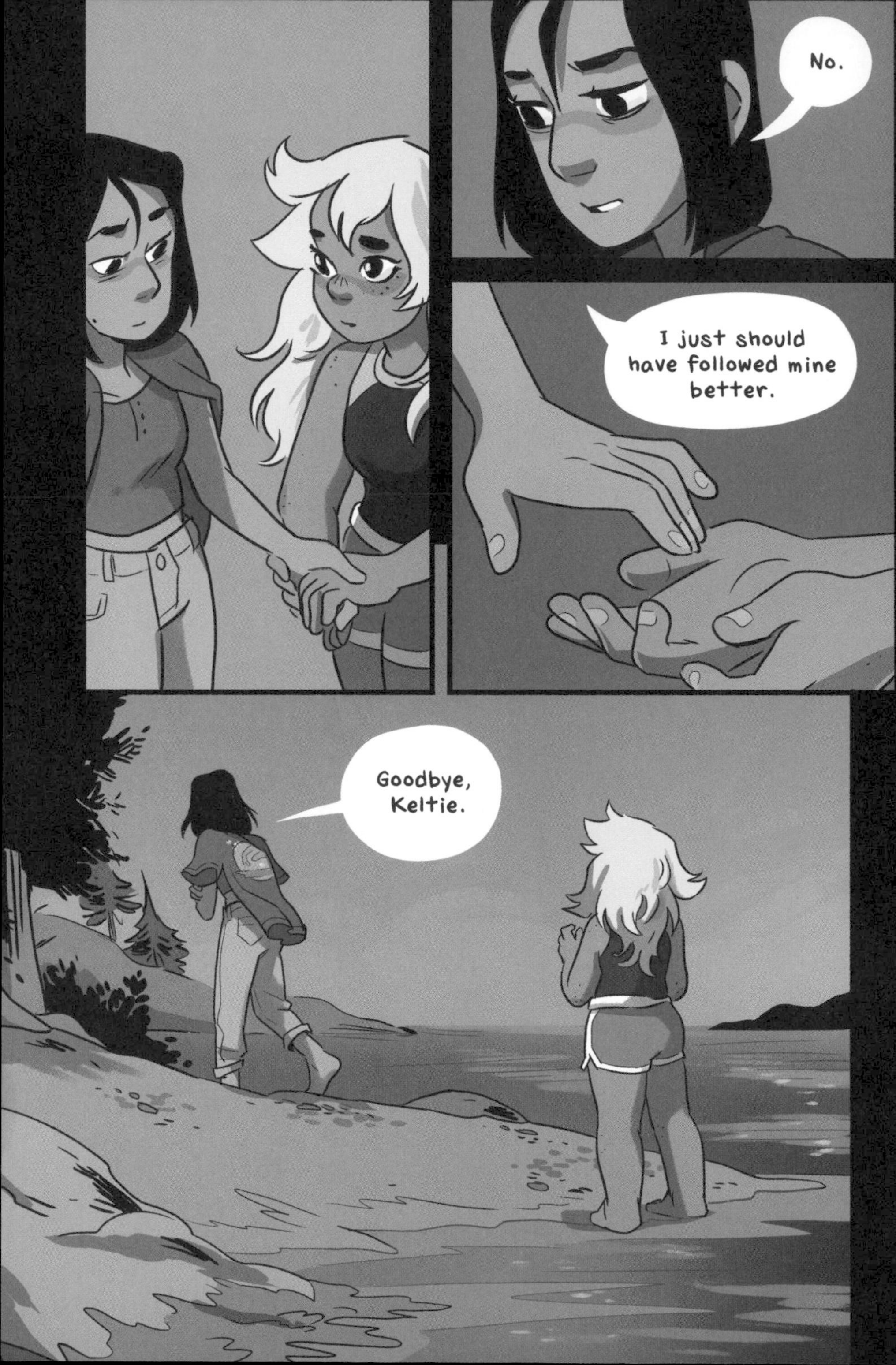
No.
I just should have followed mine better.
Goodbye, Keltie.

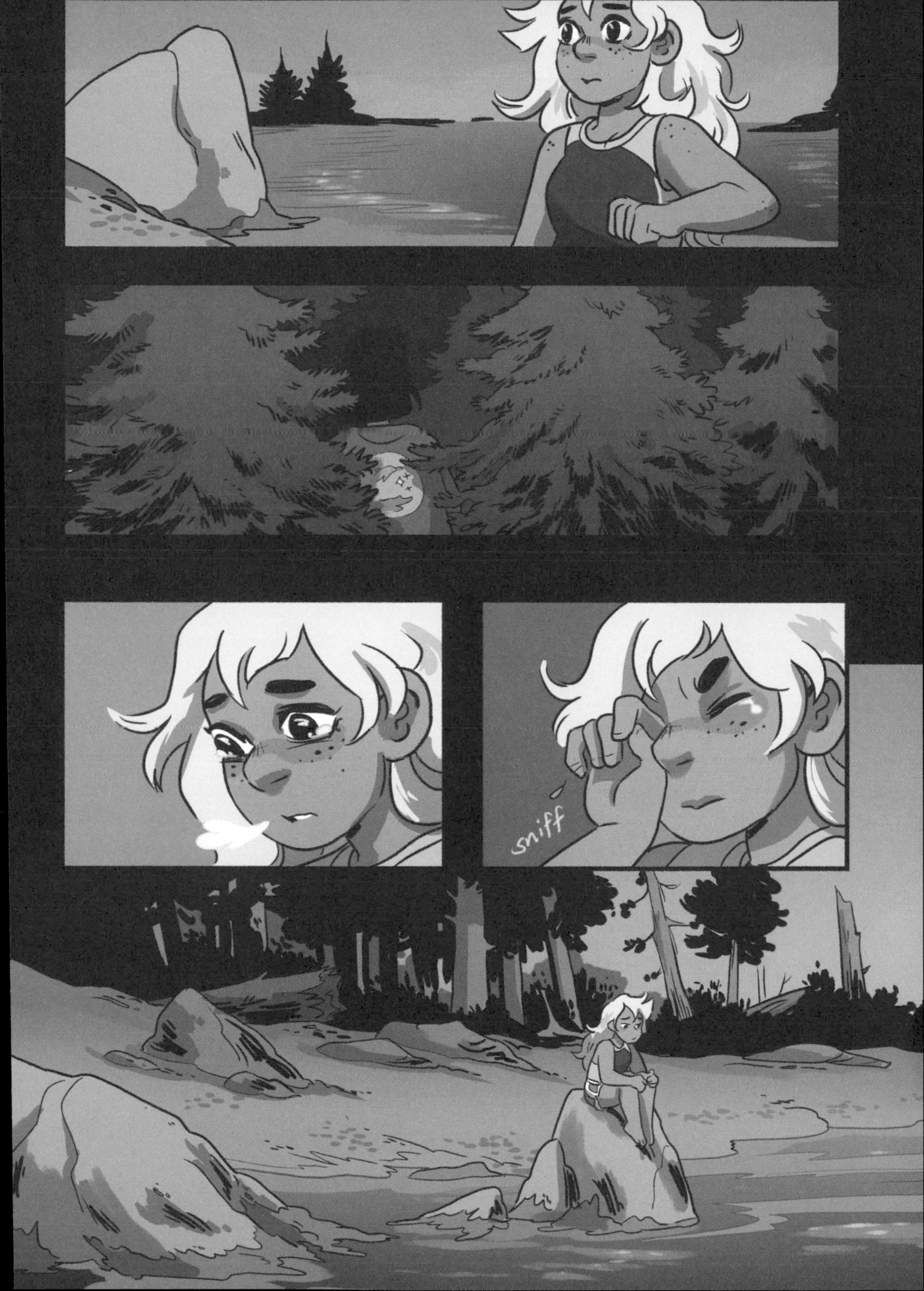
sniff

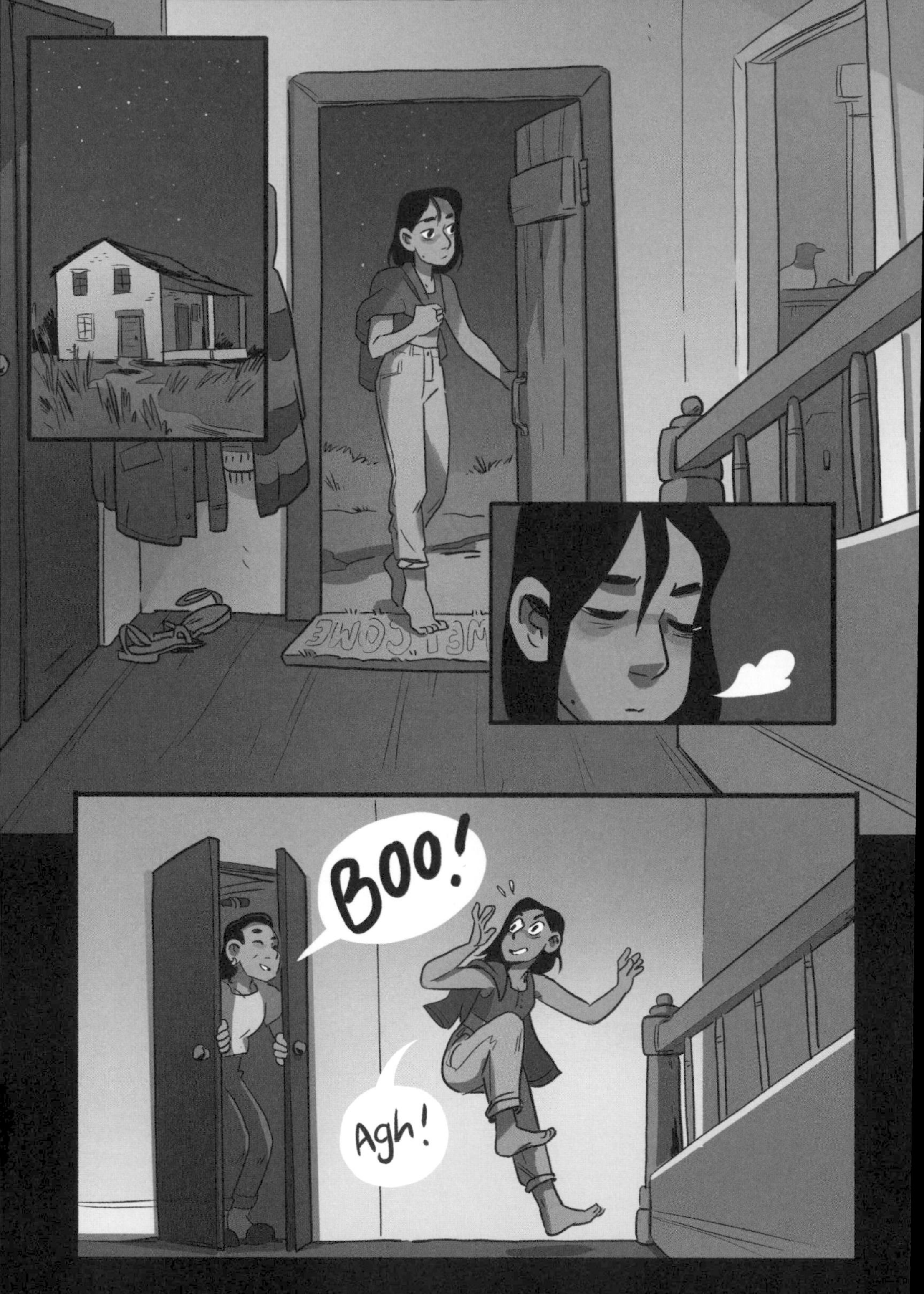
WELCOME
BOO!
Agh!

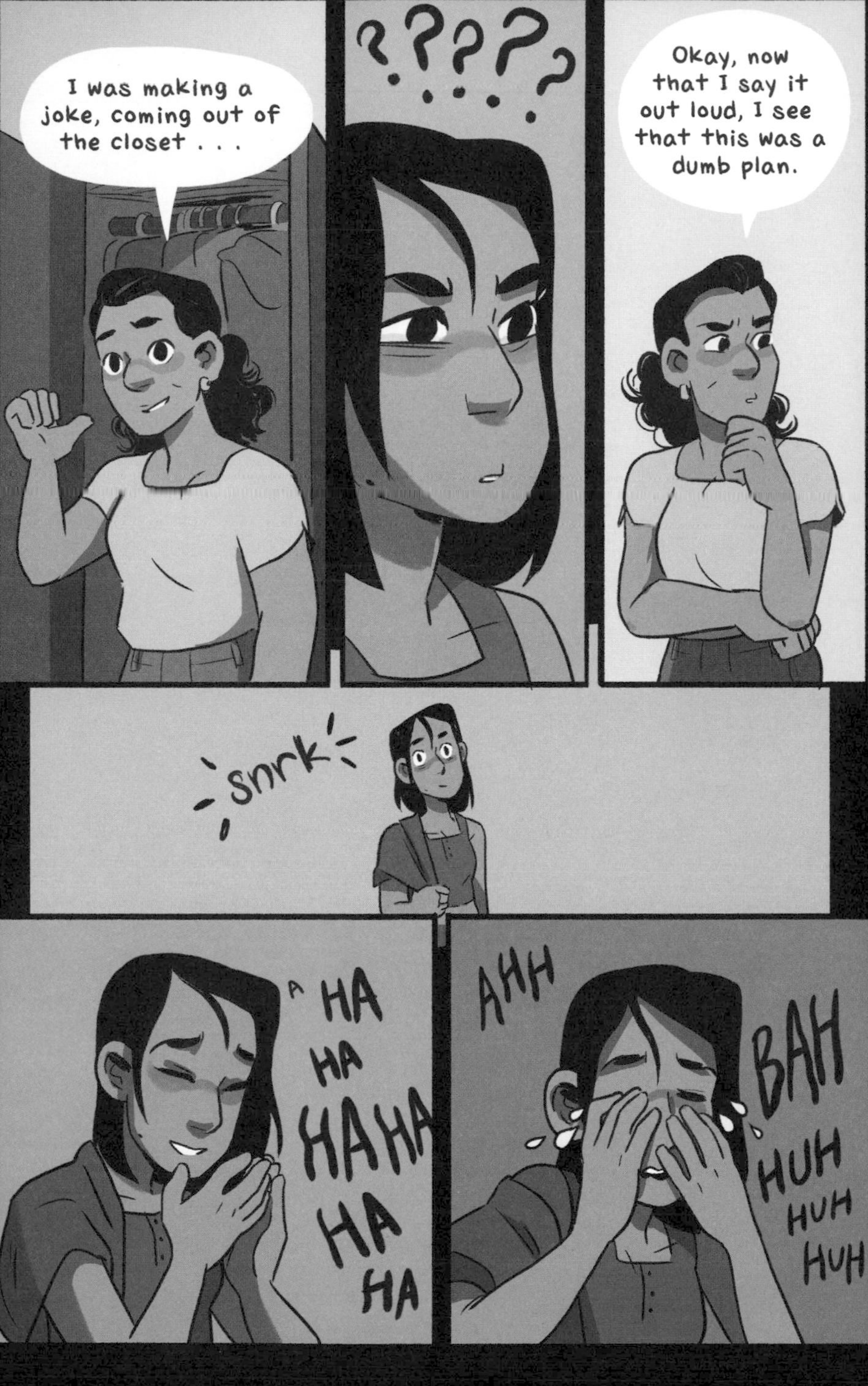
I was making a joke, coming out of the closet . . .
???????
Okay, now that I say it out loud, I see that this was a dumb plan.
snrk
A HA HA HAHA HA HA
AHH
BAH HUH HUH HUH

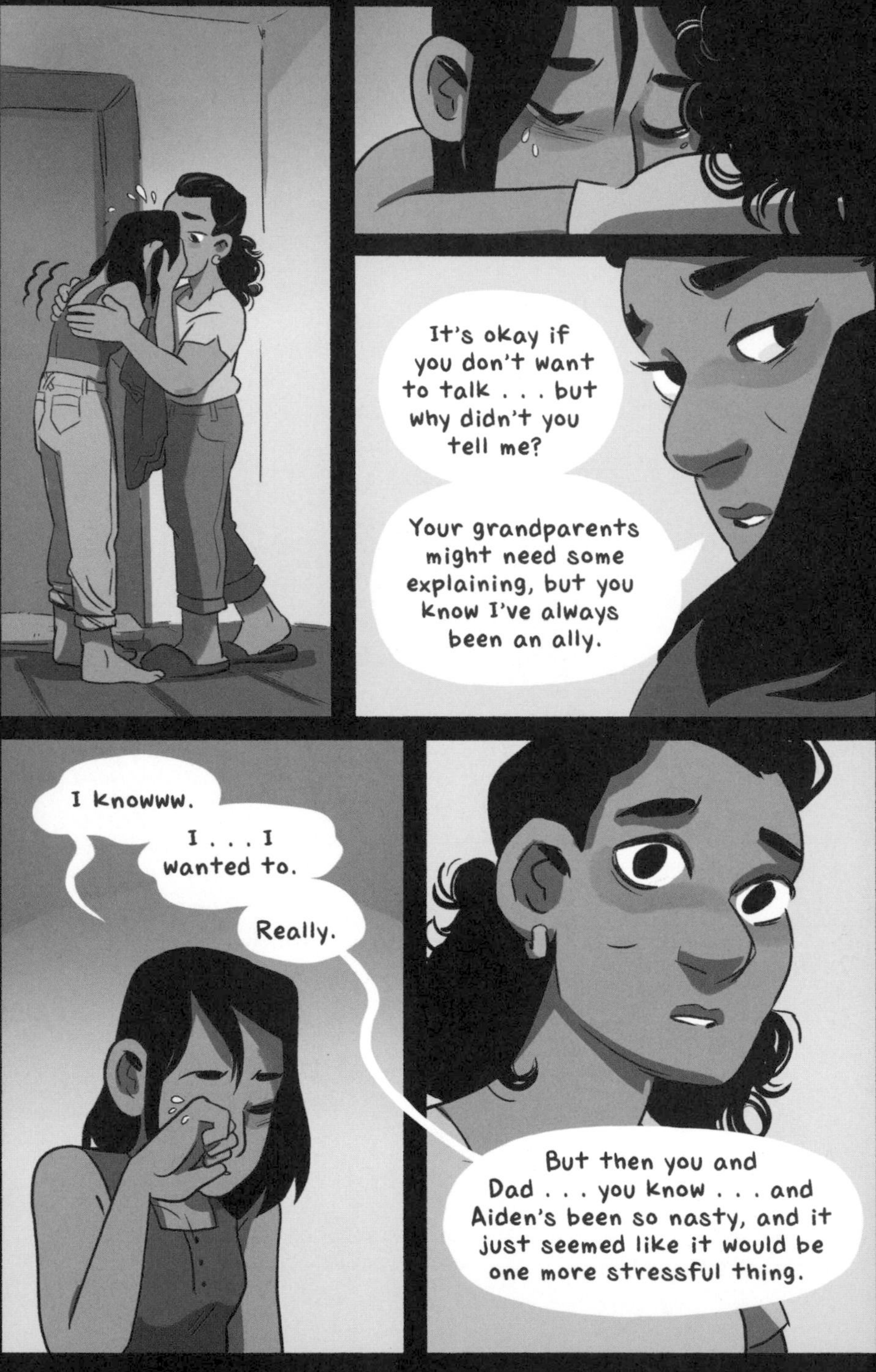
It's okay if you don't want to talk . . . but why didn't you tell me?
Your grandparents might need some explaining, but you know I've always been an ally.
I knowww.
I . . . I wanted to.
Really.
But then you and Dad . . . you know . . . and Aiden's been so nasty, and it just seemed like it would be one more stressful thing.

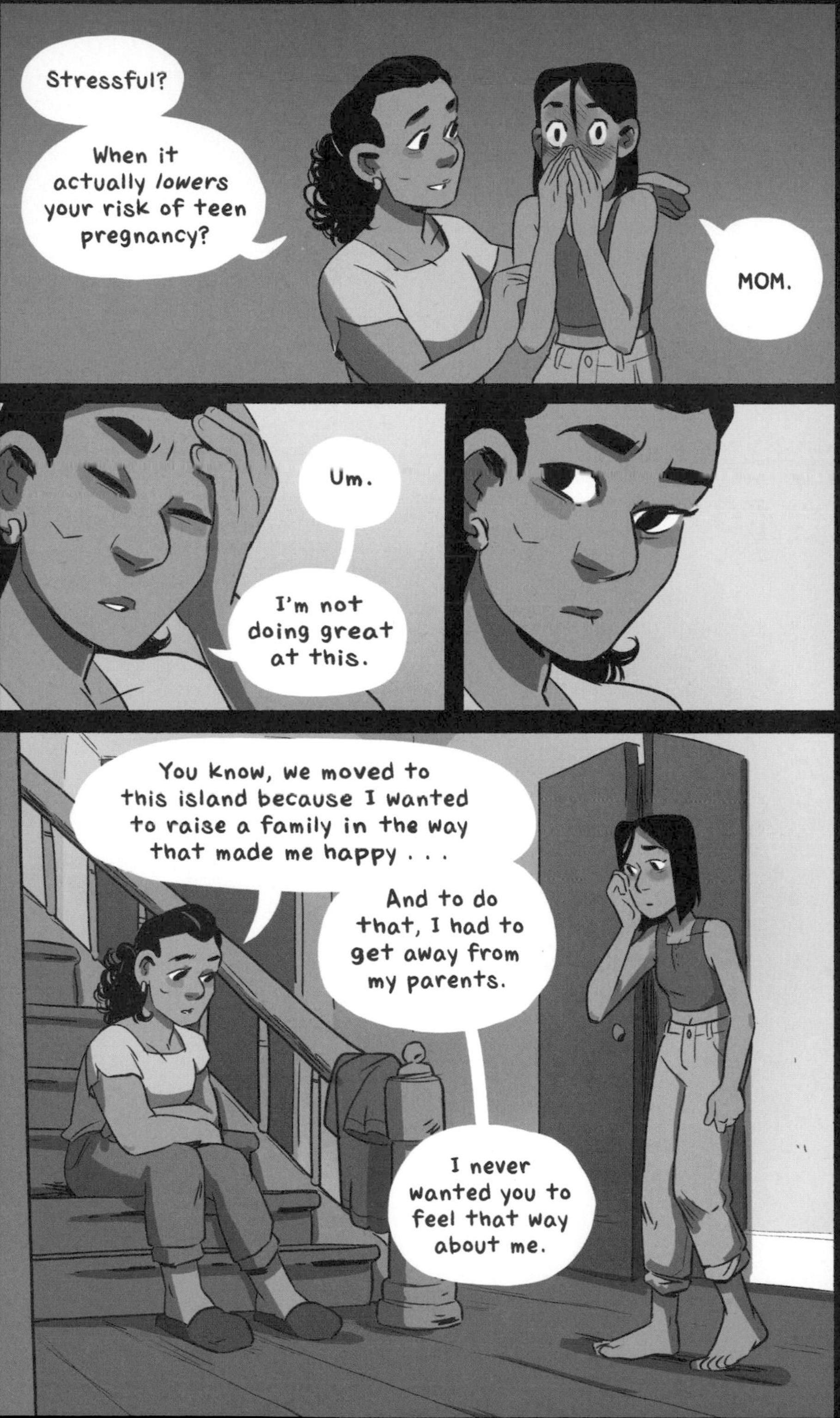
Stressful?
When it actually *lowers* your risk of teen pregnancy?
MOM.
Um.
I'm not doing great at this.
You know, we moved to this island because I wanted to raise a family in the way that made me happy . . .
And to do that, I had to get away from my parents.
I never wanted you to feel that way about me.

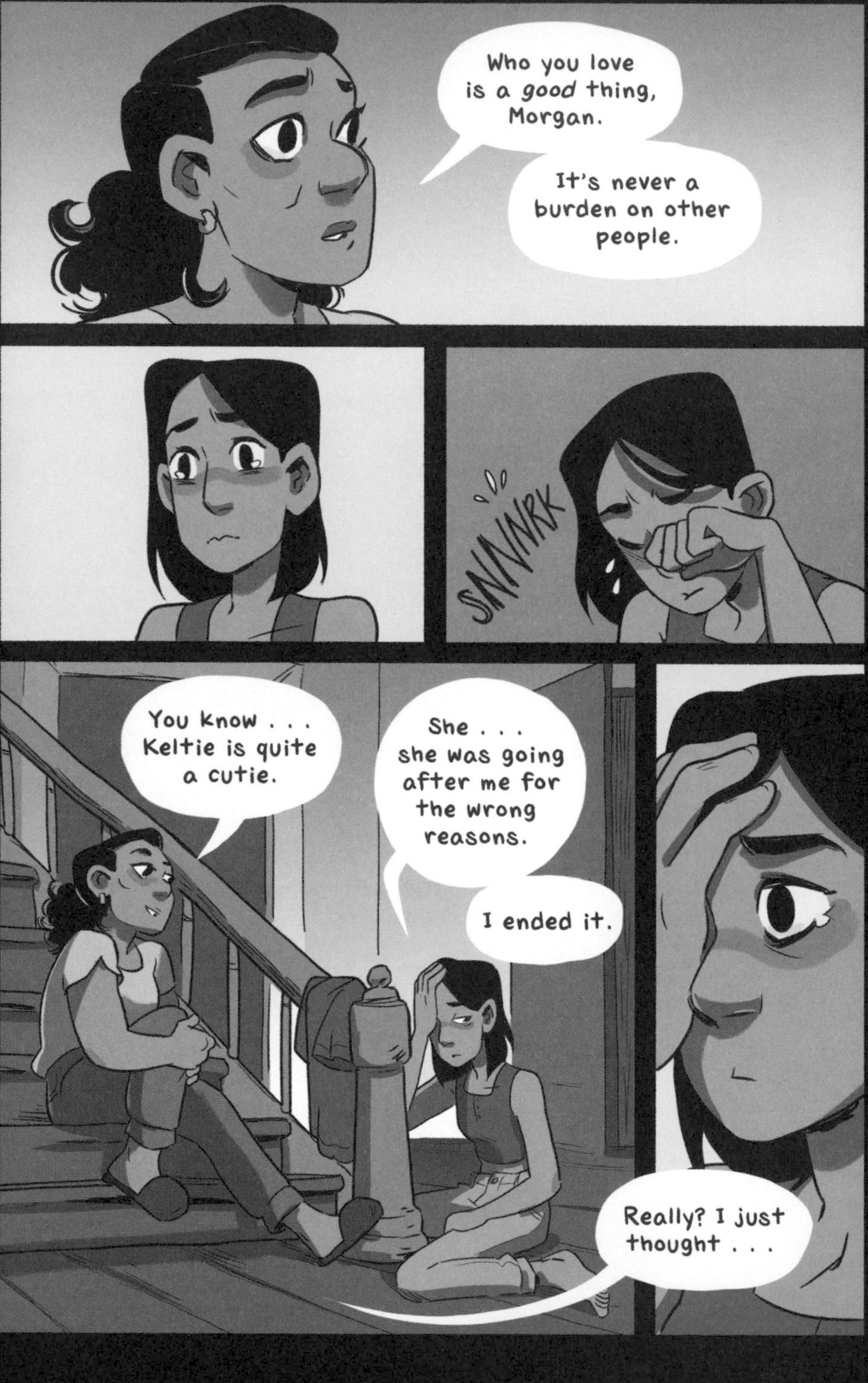
Who you love is a *good* thing, Morgan.
It's never a burden on other people.
SNIVVRK
You know . . . Keltie is quite a cutie.
She . . . she was going after me for the wrong reasons.
I ended it.
Really? I just thought . . .

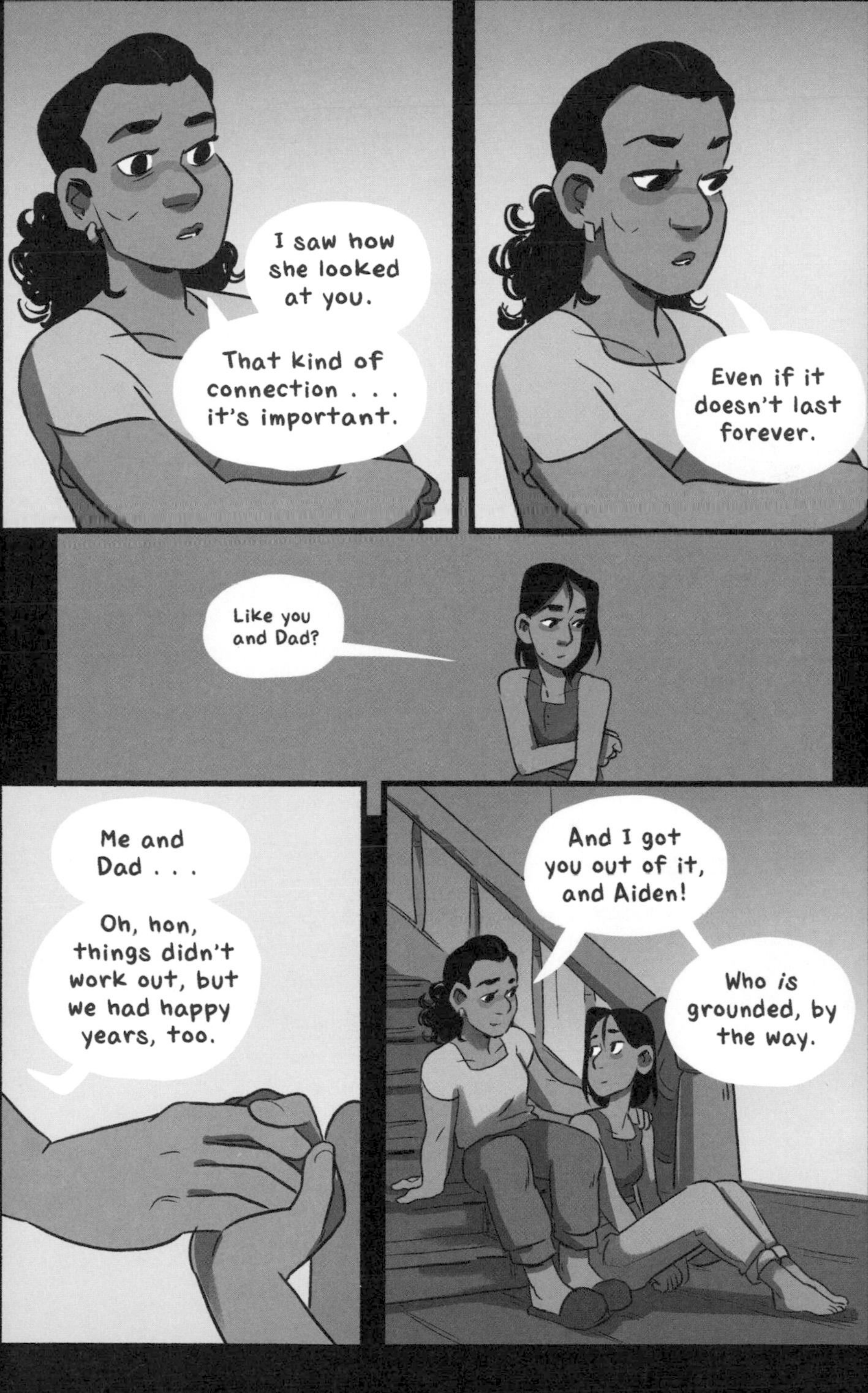

I saw how she looked at you.
That kind of connection . . . it's important.
Even if it doesn't last forever.
Like you and Dad?
Me and Dad . . .
Oh, hon, things didn't work out, but we had happy years, too.
And I got you out of it, and Aiden!
Who *is* grounded, by the way.

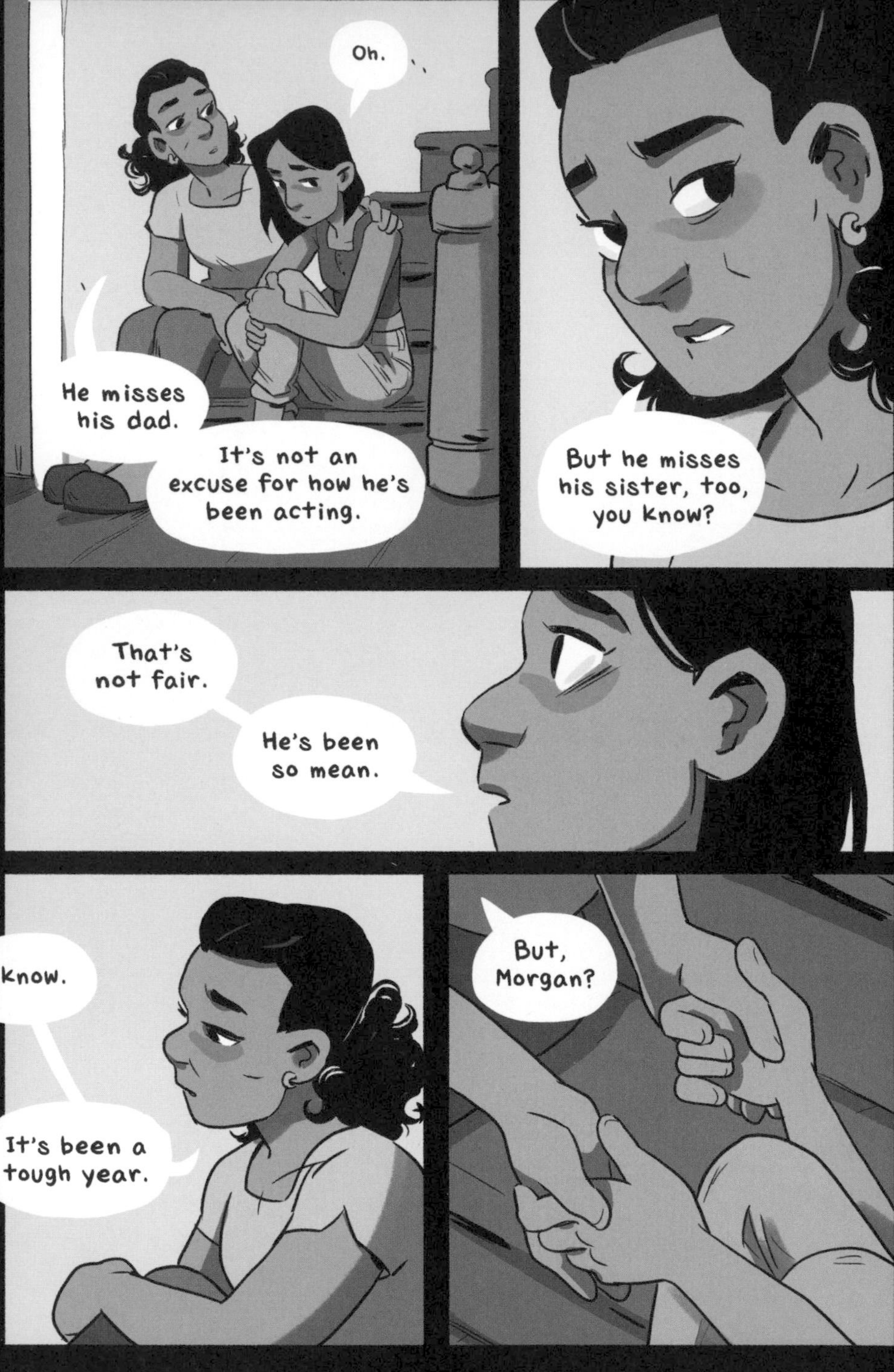
Oh. . .
He misses his dad.
It's not an excuse for how he's been acting.
But he misses his sister, too, you know?
That's not fair.
He's been so mean.
I know.
It's been a tough year.
But, Morgan?

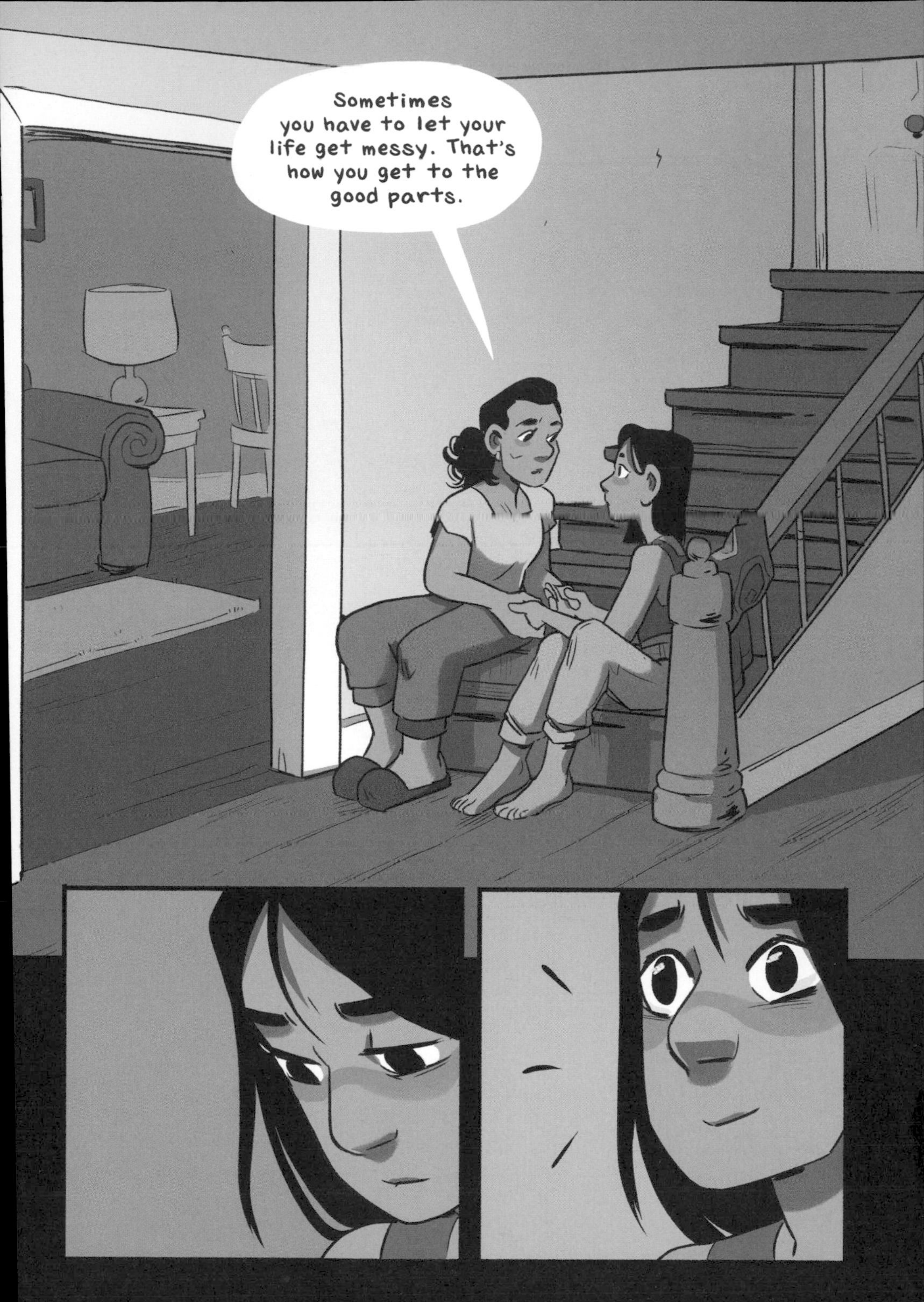
Sometimes you have to let your life get messy. That's how you get to the good parts.

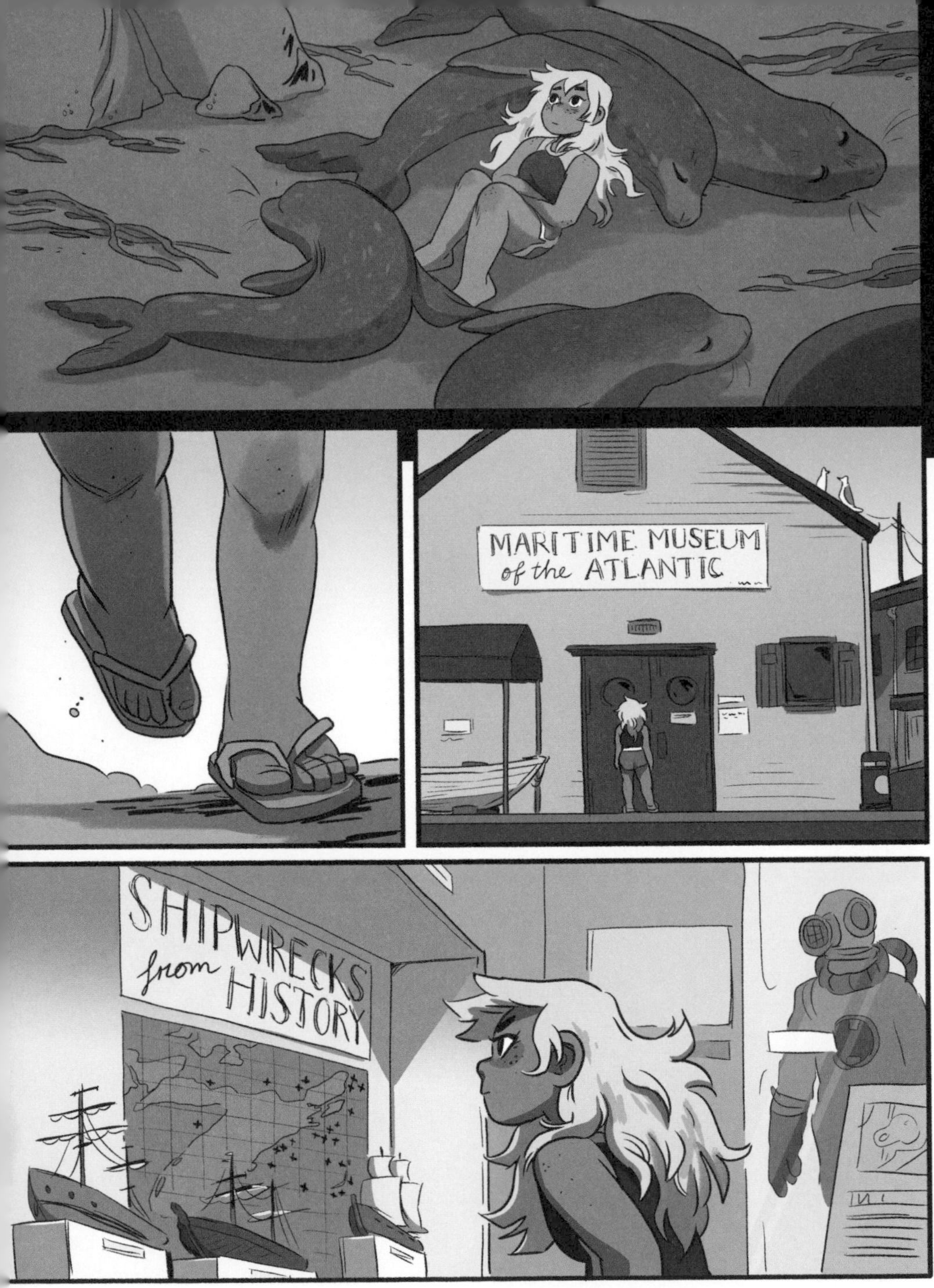
MARITIME MUSEUM
of the ATLANTIC
SHIPWRECKS
from HISTORY

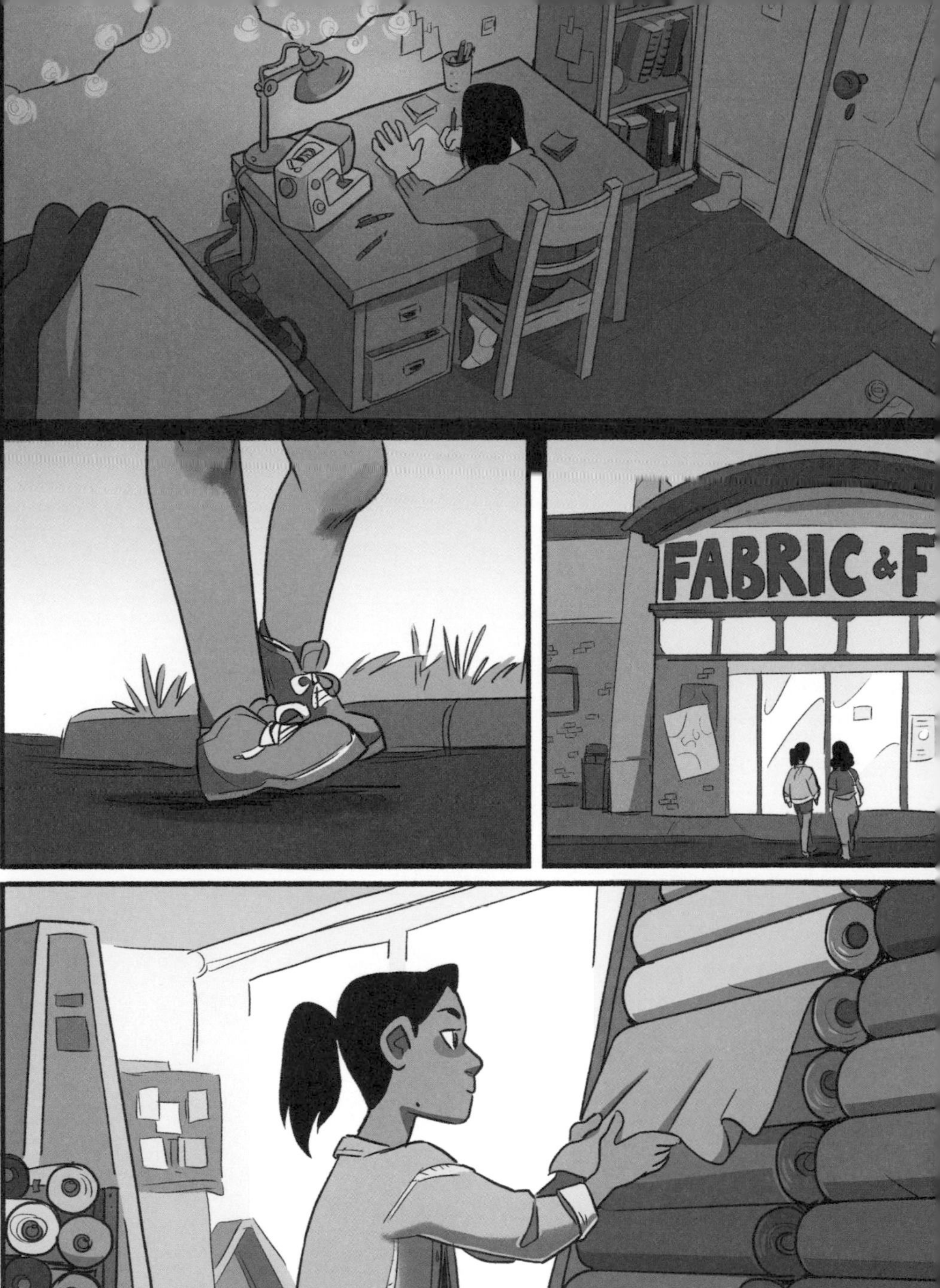
FABRIC & F

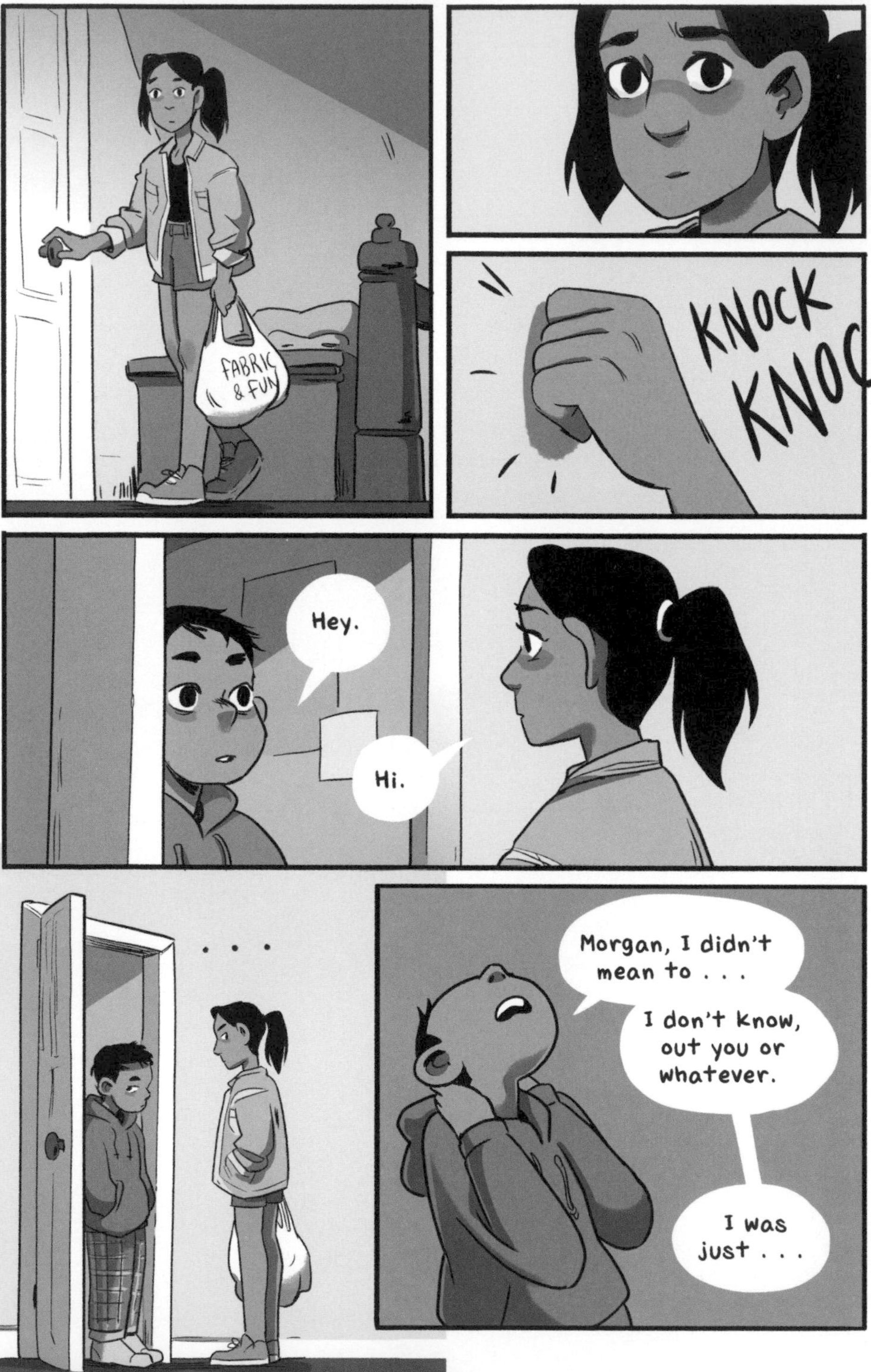
FABRIC & FUN
KNOCK
KNOCK
Hey.
Hi.
. . .
Morgan, I didn't mean to . . .
I don't know, out you or whatever.
I was just . . .

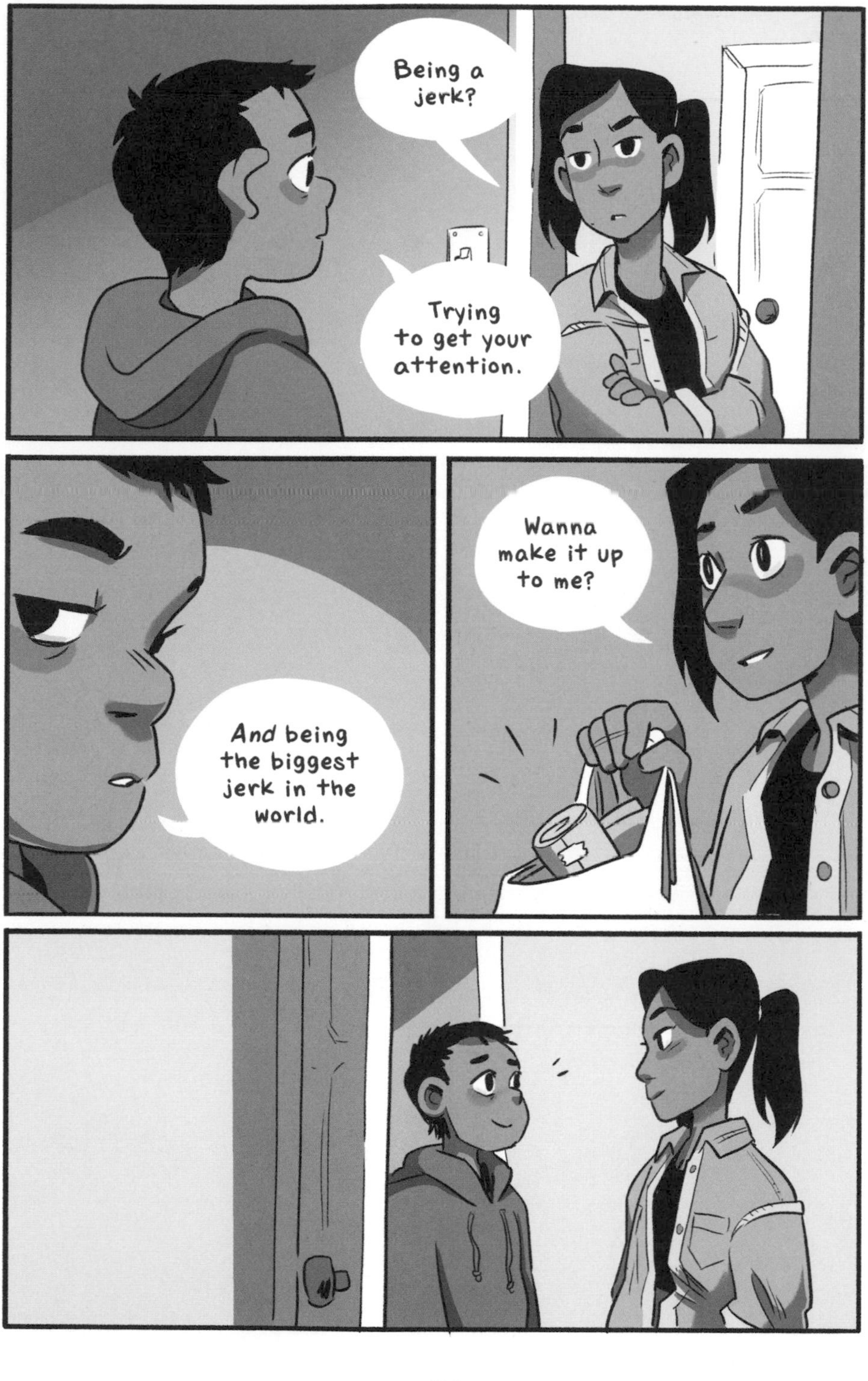
Being a jerk?
Trying to get your attention.
And being the biggest jerk in the world.
Wanna make it up to me?

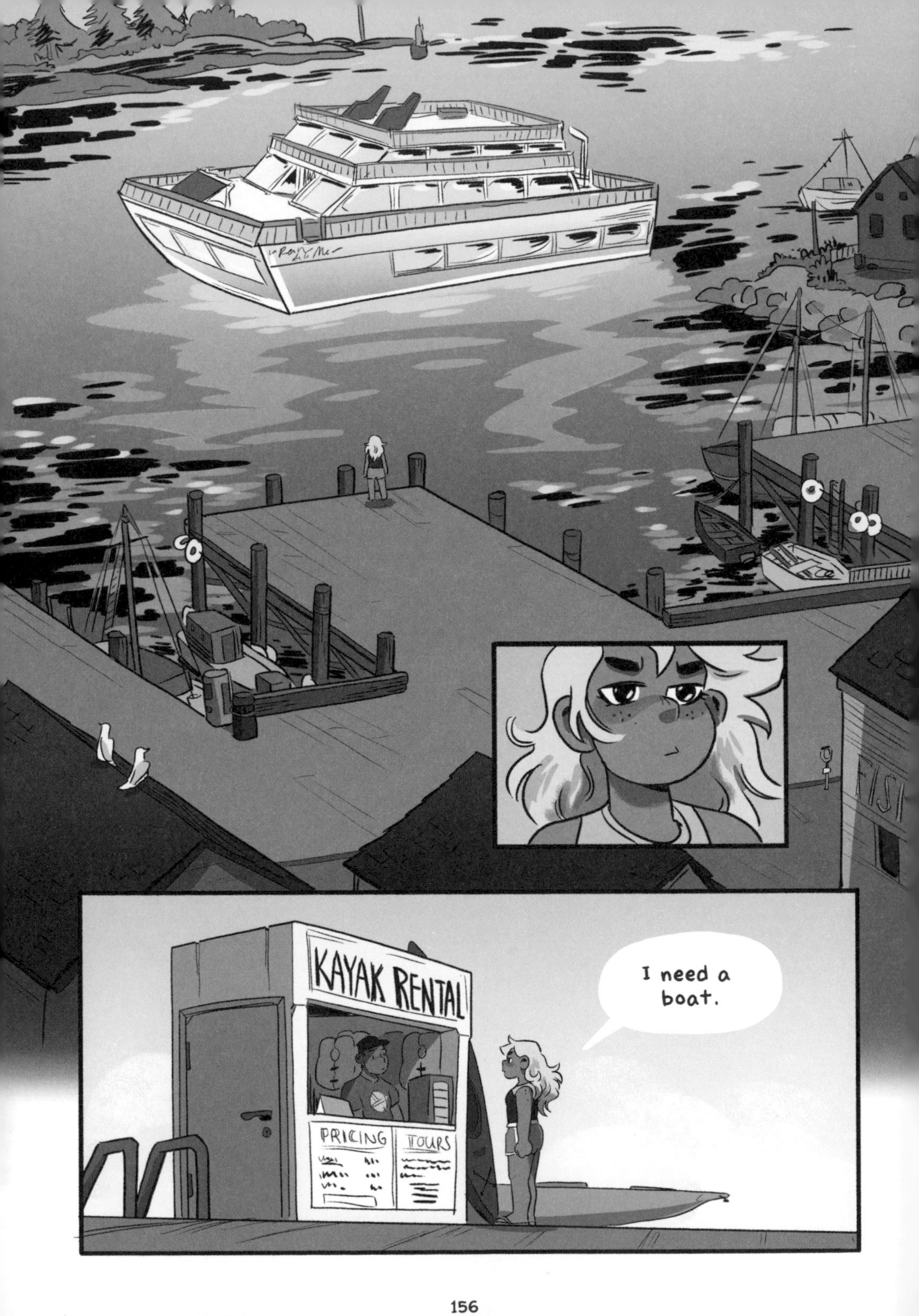
KAYAK RENTAL
PRICING
TOURS
I need a boat.

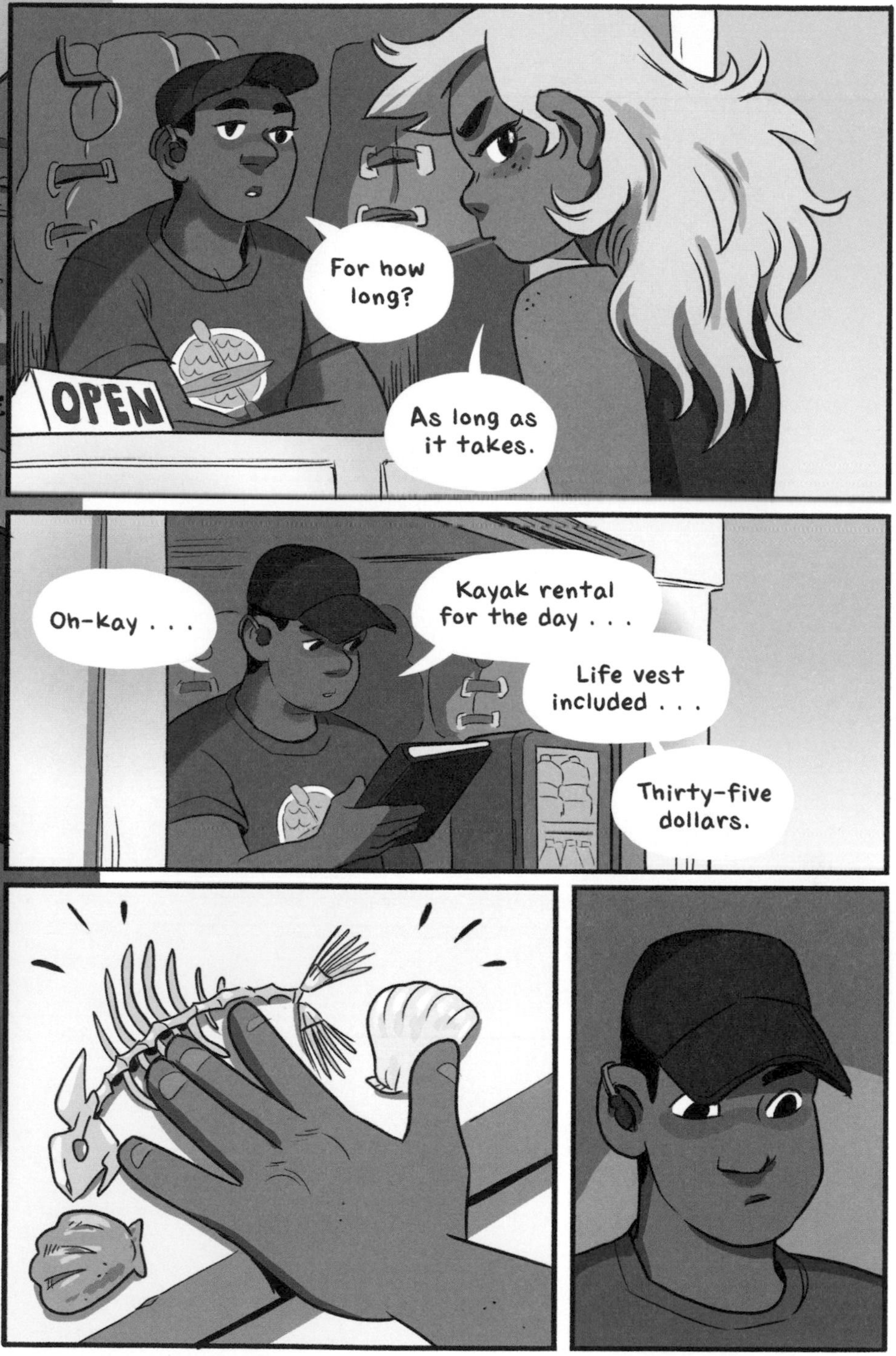
For how long?
As long as it takes.
Oh-kay . . .
Kayak rental for the day . . .
Life vest included . . .
Thirty-five dollars.
OPEN

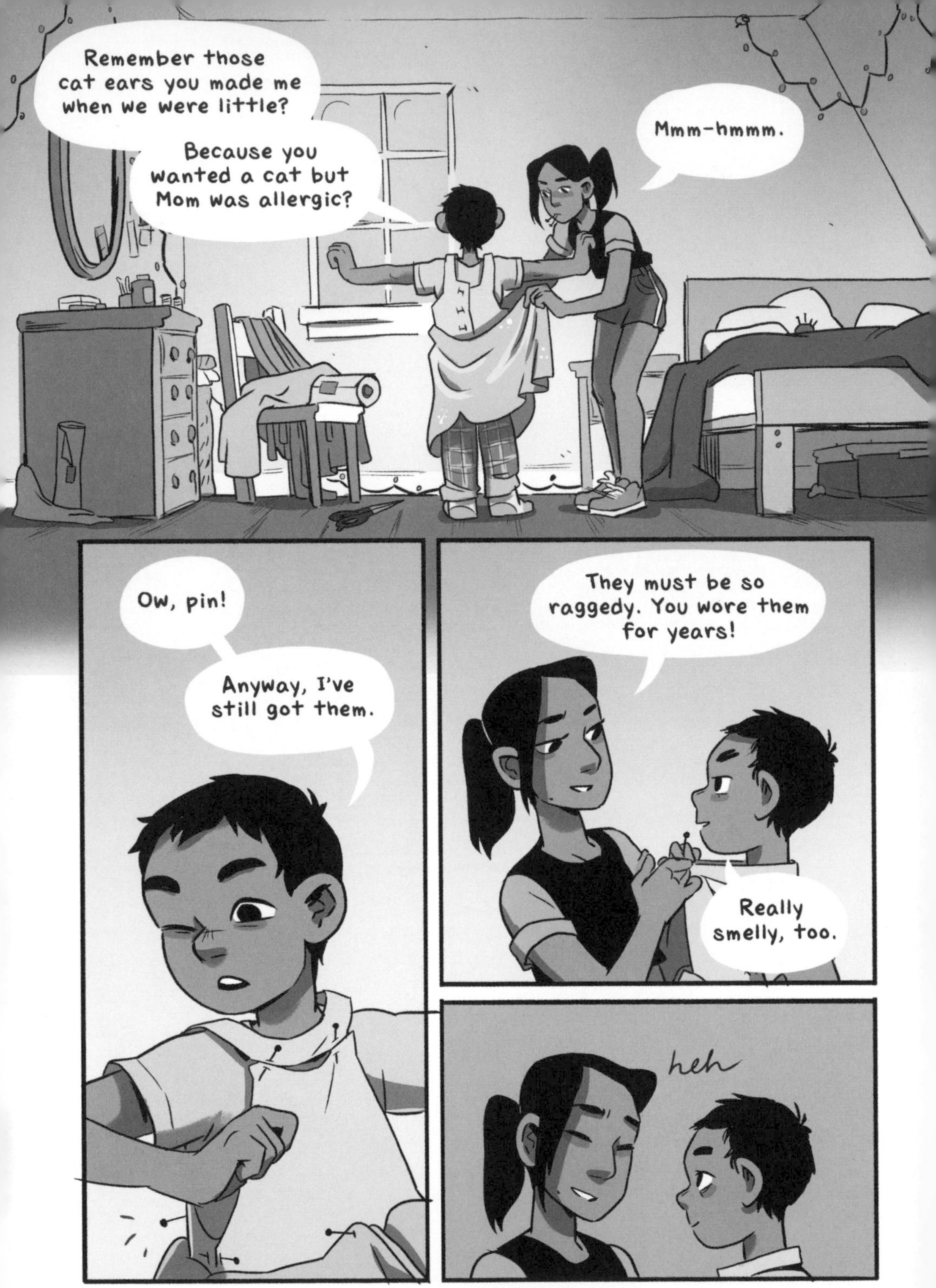

Remember those cat ears you made me when we were little?
Because you wanted a cat but Mom was allergic?
Mmm-hmmm.
Ow, pin!
Anyway, I've still got them.
They must be so raggedy. You wore them for years!
Really smelly, too.
heh

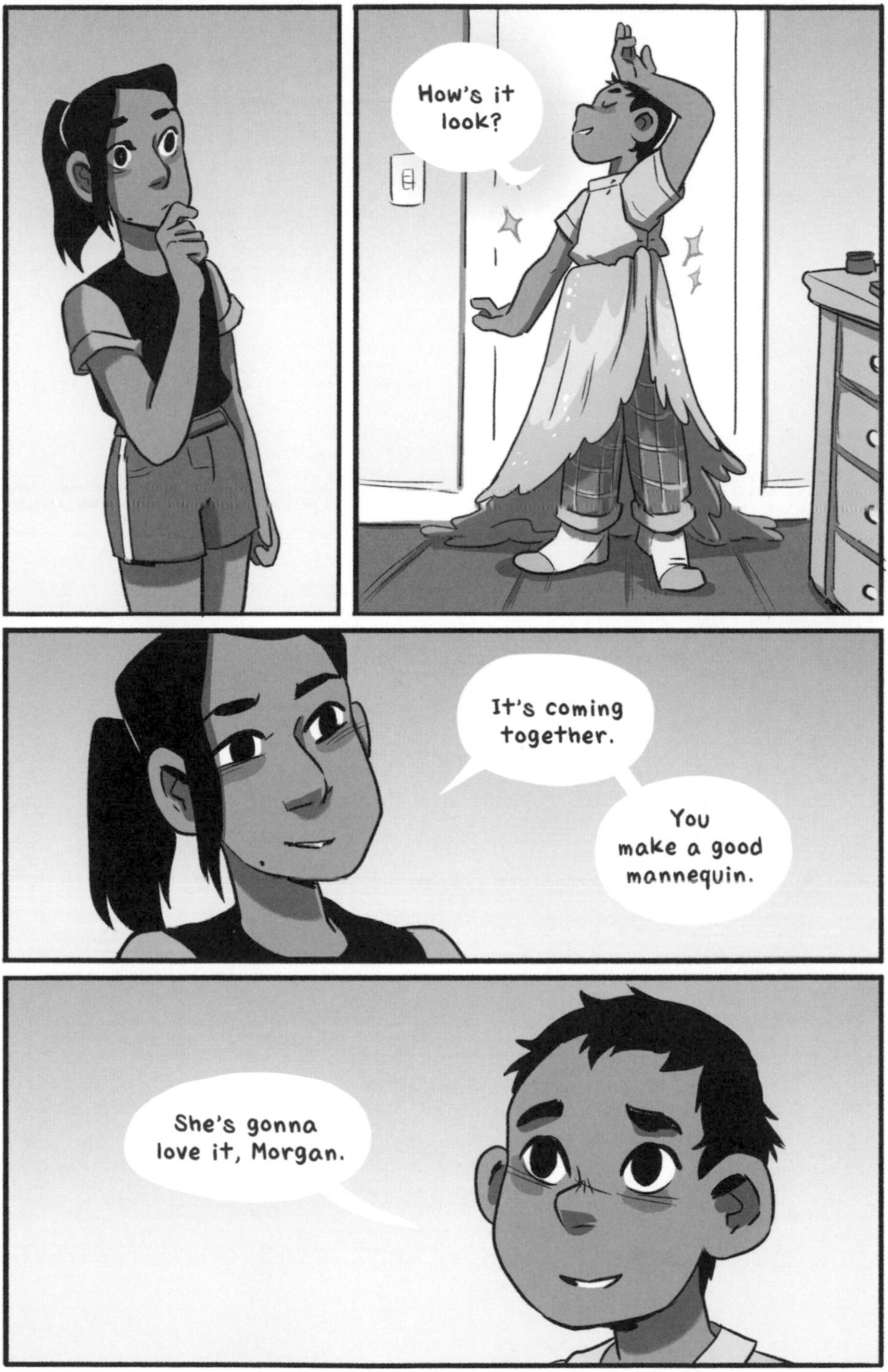
How's it look?
It's coming together.
You make a good mannequin.
She's gonna love it, Morgan.

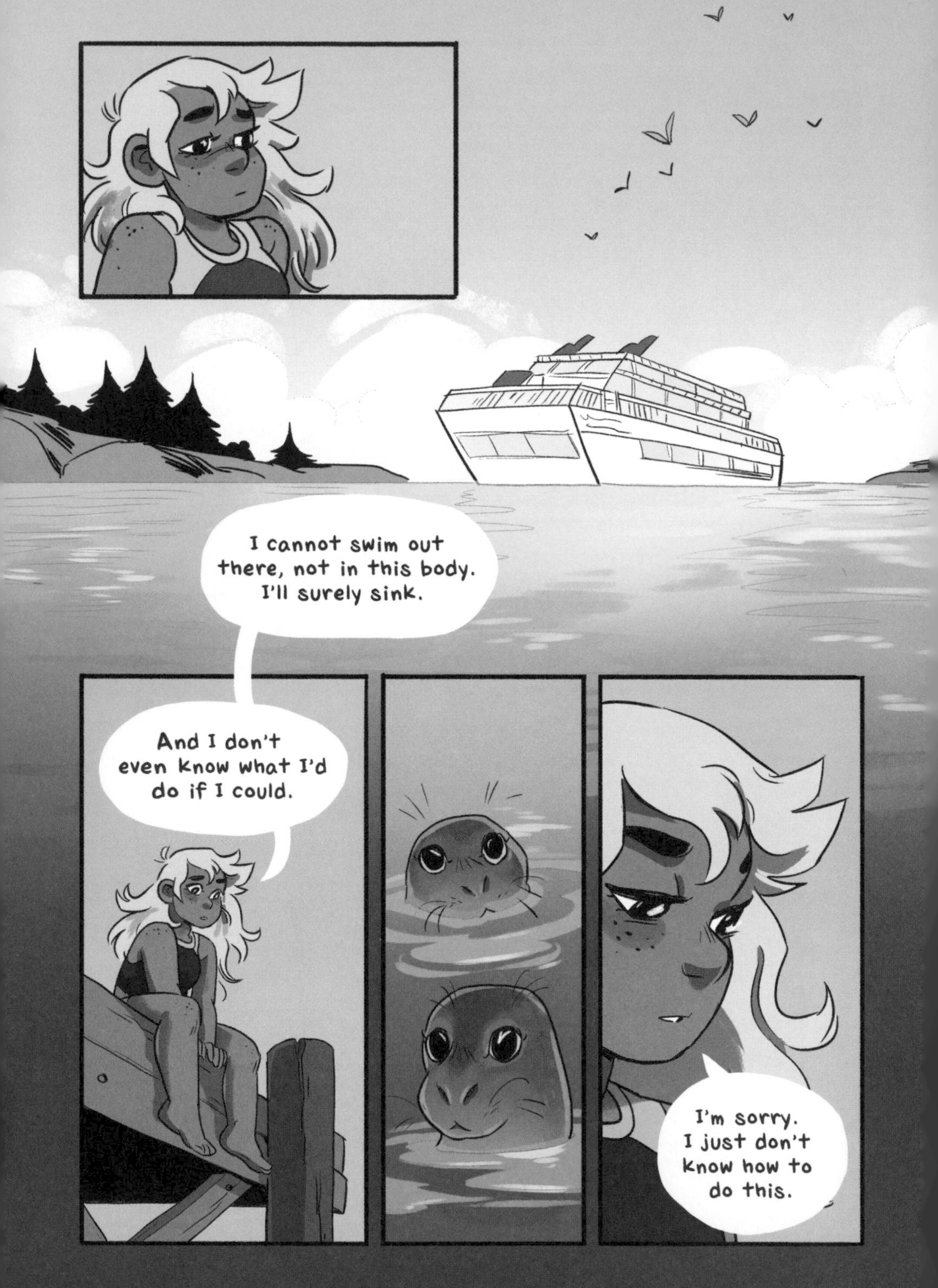
I cannot swim out there, not in this body. I'll surely sink.
And I don't even know what I'd do if I could.
I'm sorry. I just don't know how to do this.

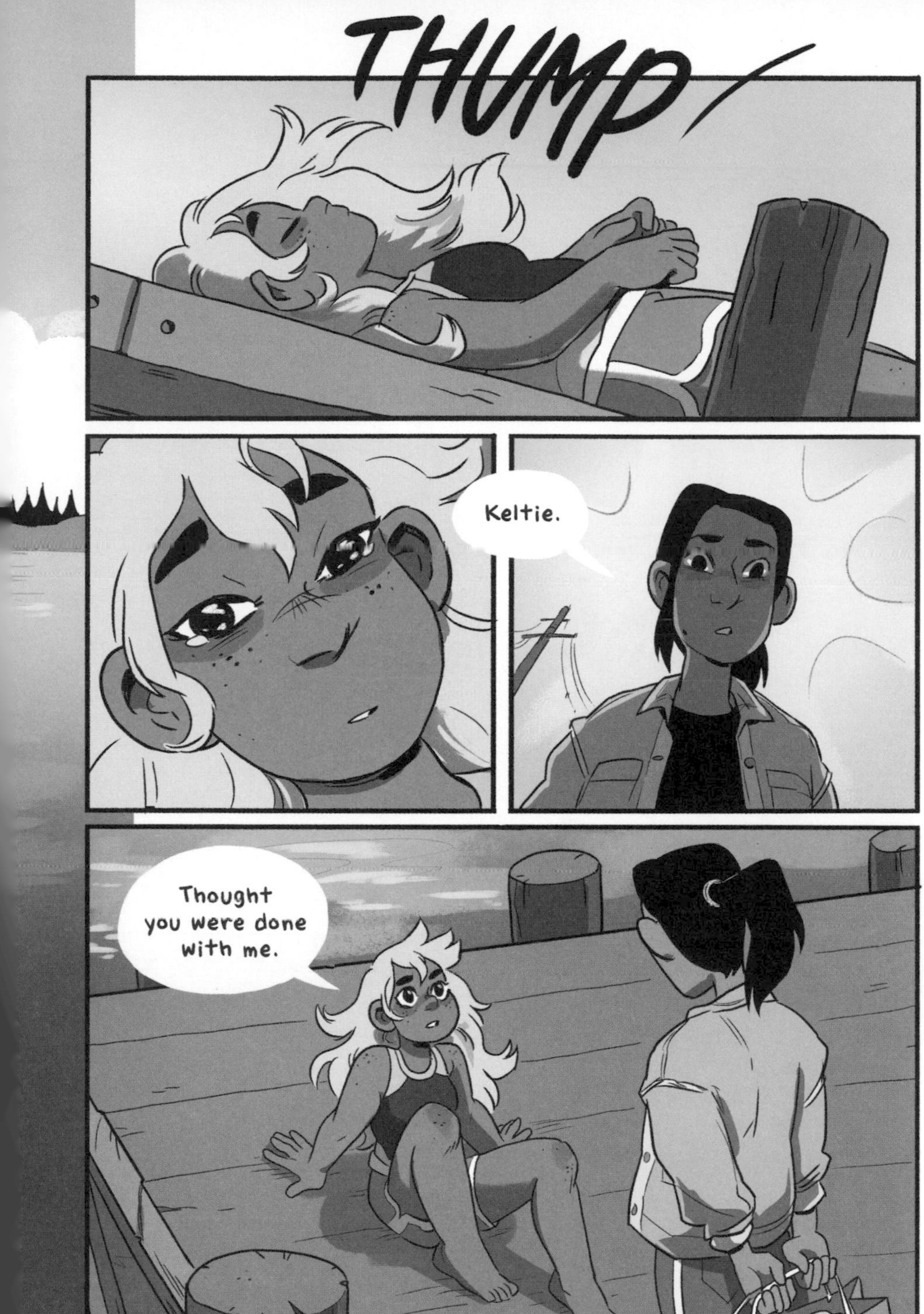
THUMP
Keltie.
Thought you were done with me.

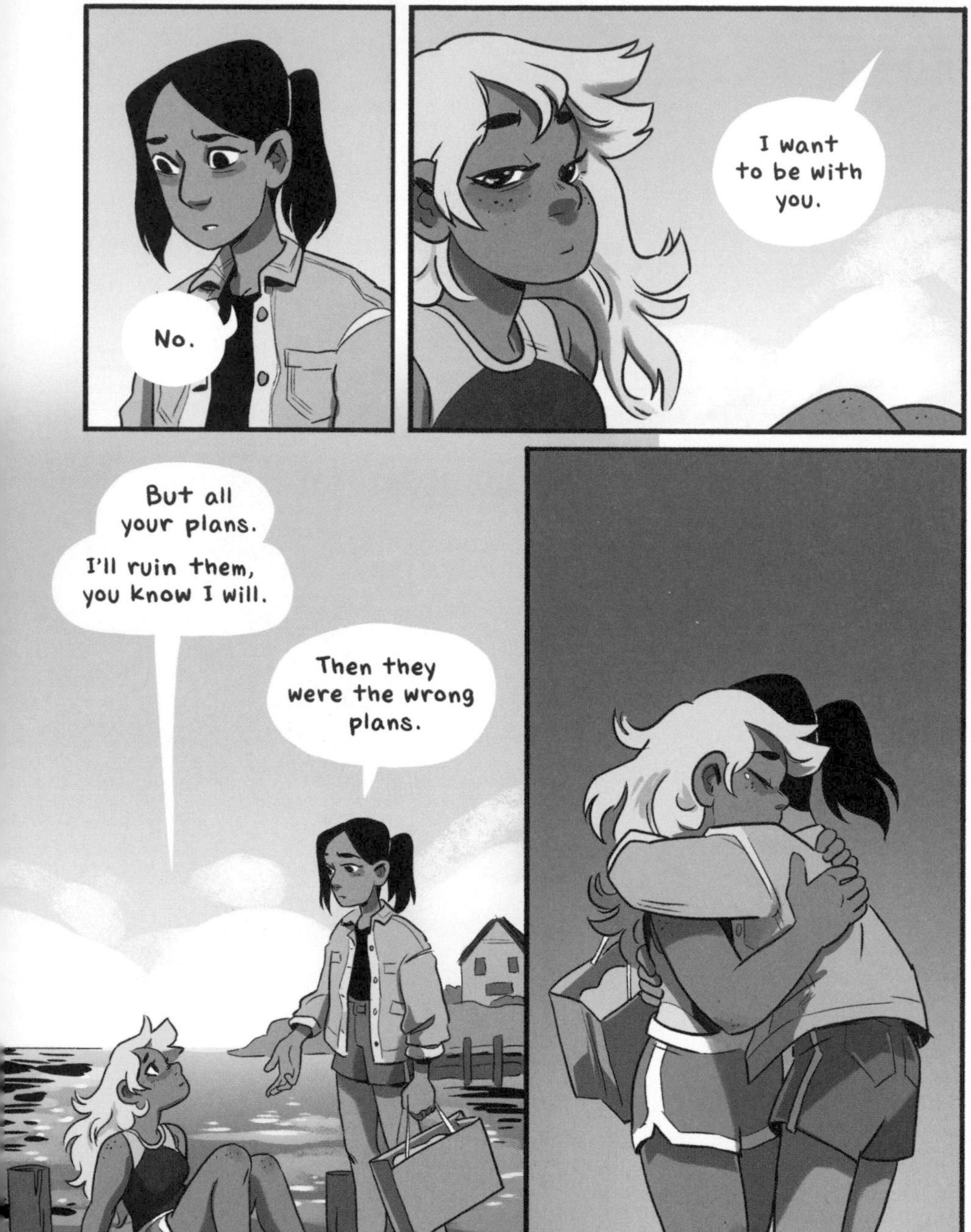
No.
I want to be with you.
But all your plans.
I'll ruin them, you know I will.
Then they were the wrong plans.

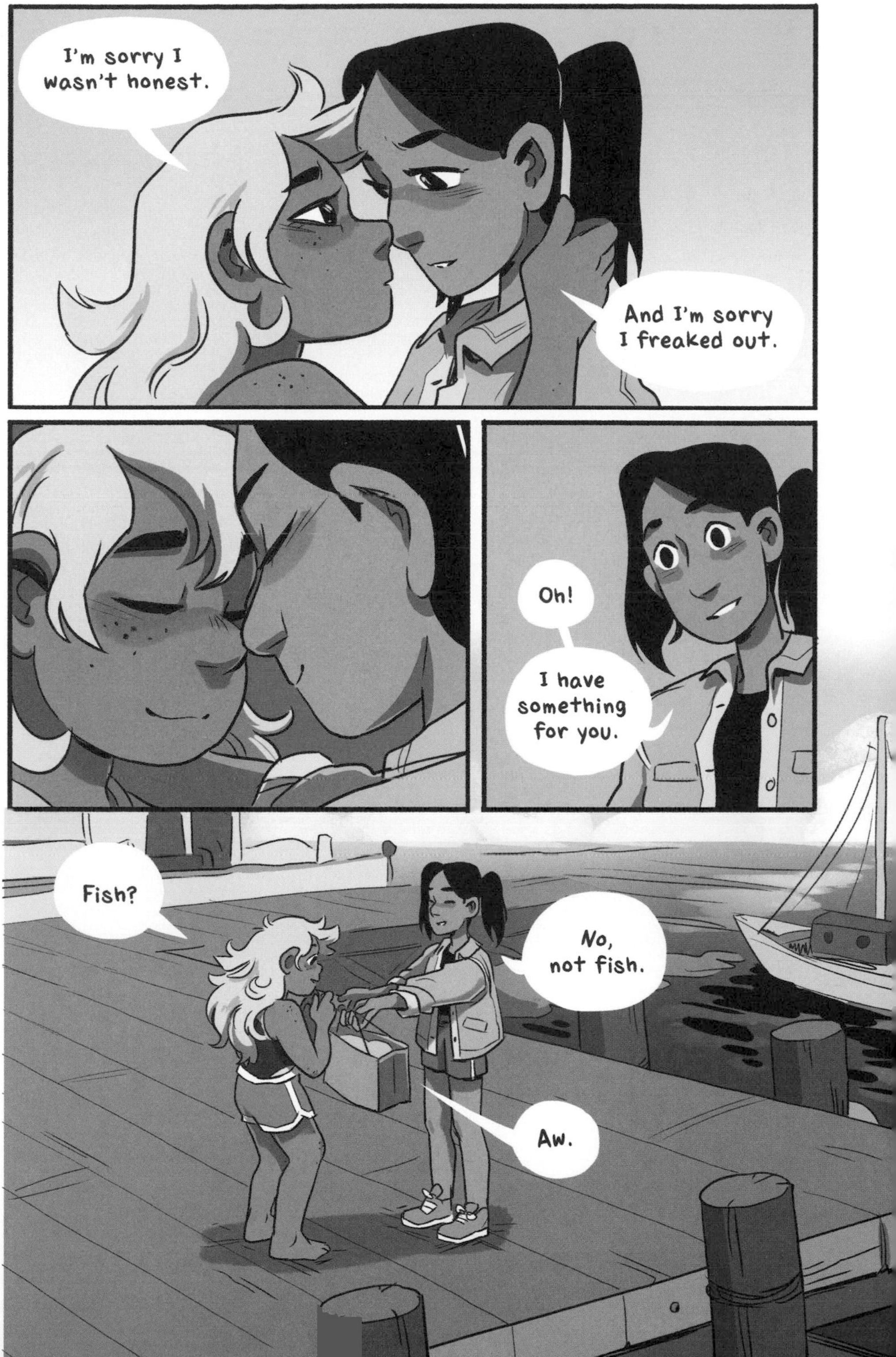
I'm sorry I wasn't honest.
And I'm sorry I freaked out.
Oh!
I have something for you.
Fish?
No, not fish.
Aw.

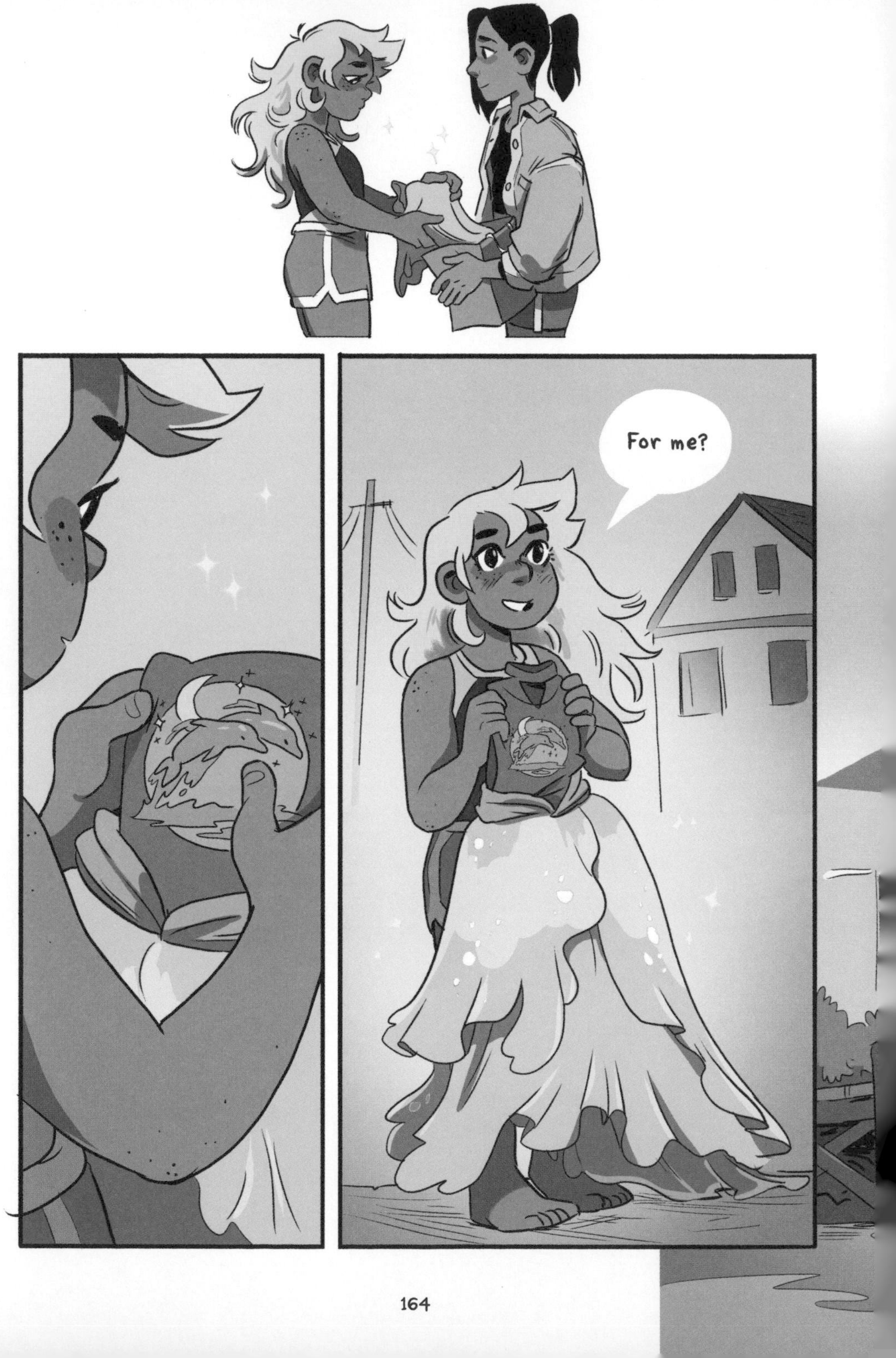
For me?

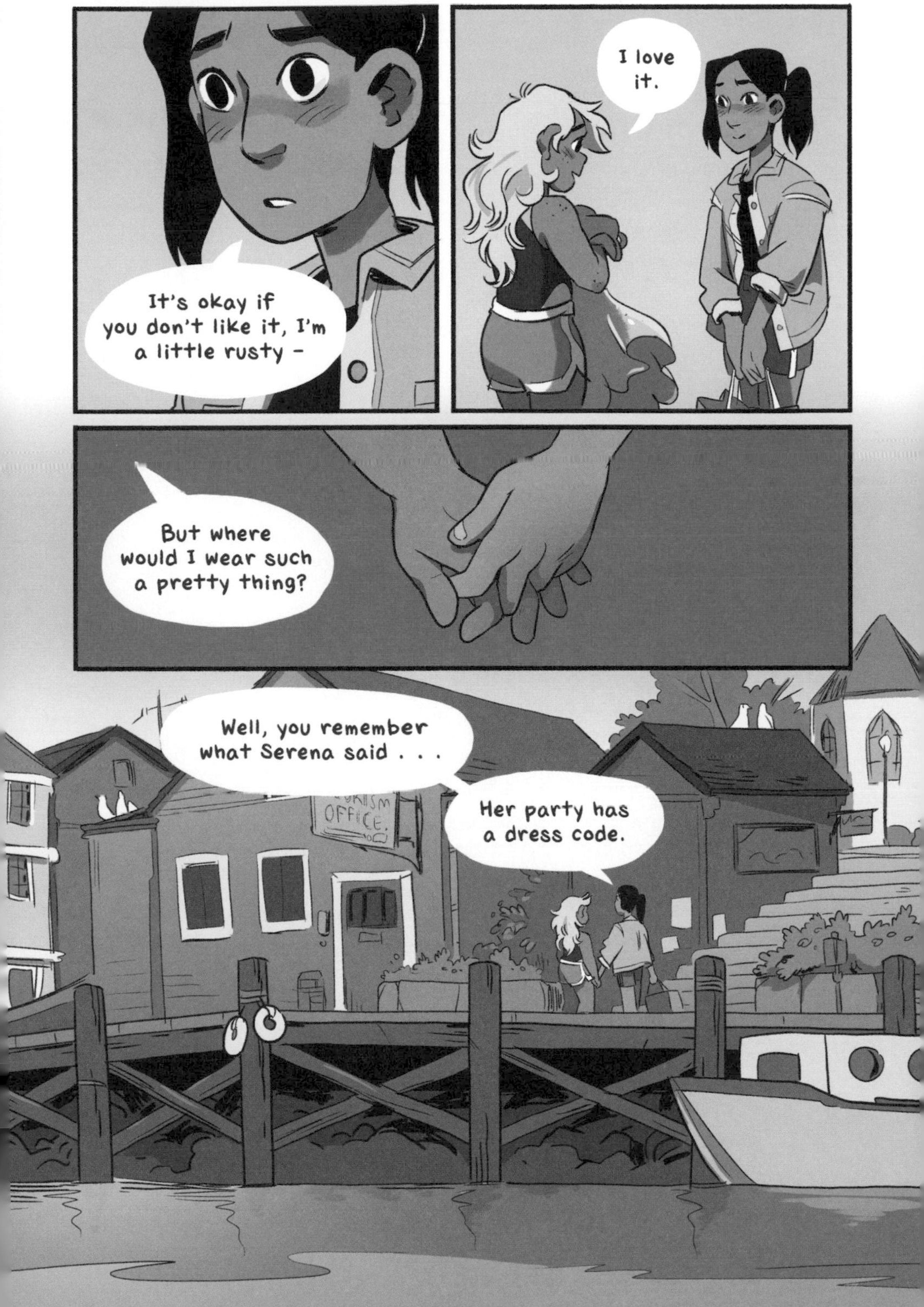
It's okay if you don't like it, I'm a little rusty –
I love it.
But where would I wear such a pretty thing?
Well, you remember what Serena said . . .
Her party has a dress code.
OFFICE

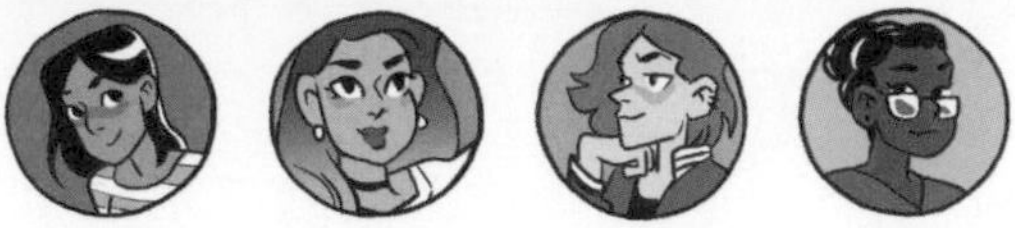

Morgan Serena Jules Lizzie

Fri, June 28, 2:12 PM

Jules: look who i saw

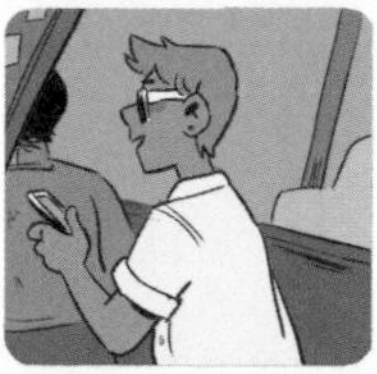

Lizzie: GOREGOUS JOSH NO

Did he see you taking his picture??

Jules: yeah i told him it was for your murder wall

Lizzie: I HATE YOU

what should I wear tomorrow

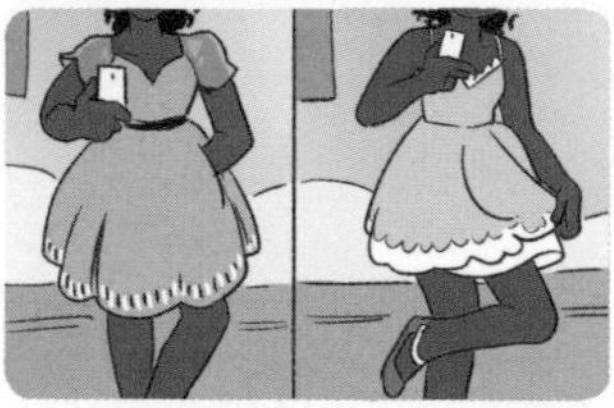

Jules: Liz they look...very similar.........

Lizzie: No the second one is like a lot sexier!

Jules: if you say so

Serena: second one!

but wear those wedges you have

Lizzie: That would be TOO sexy

Serena: don't be afraid of your own power

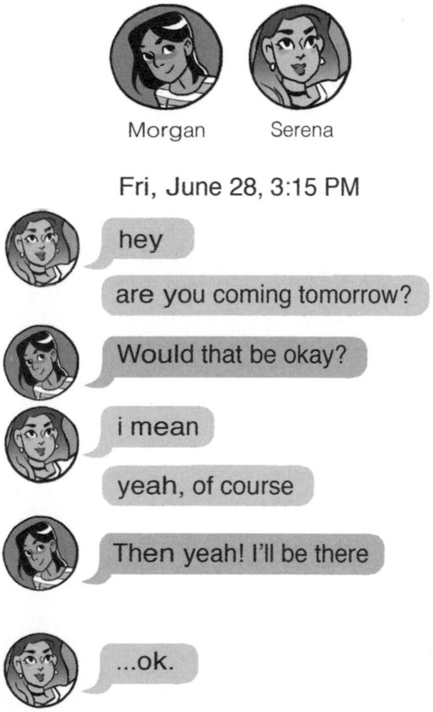
Morgan
Serena
Fri, June 28, 3:15 PM
hey
are you coming tomorrow?
Would that be okay?
i mean
yeah, of course
Then yeah! I'll be there
...ok.

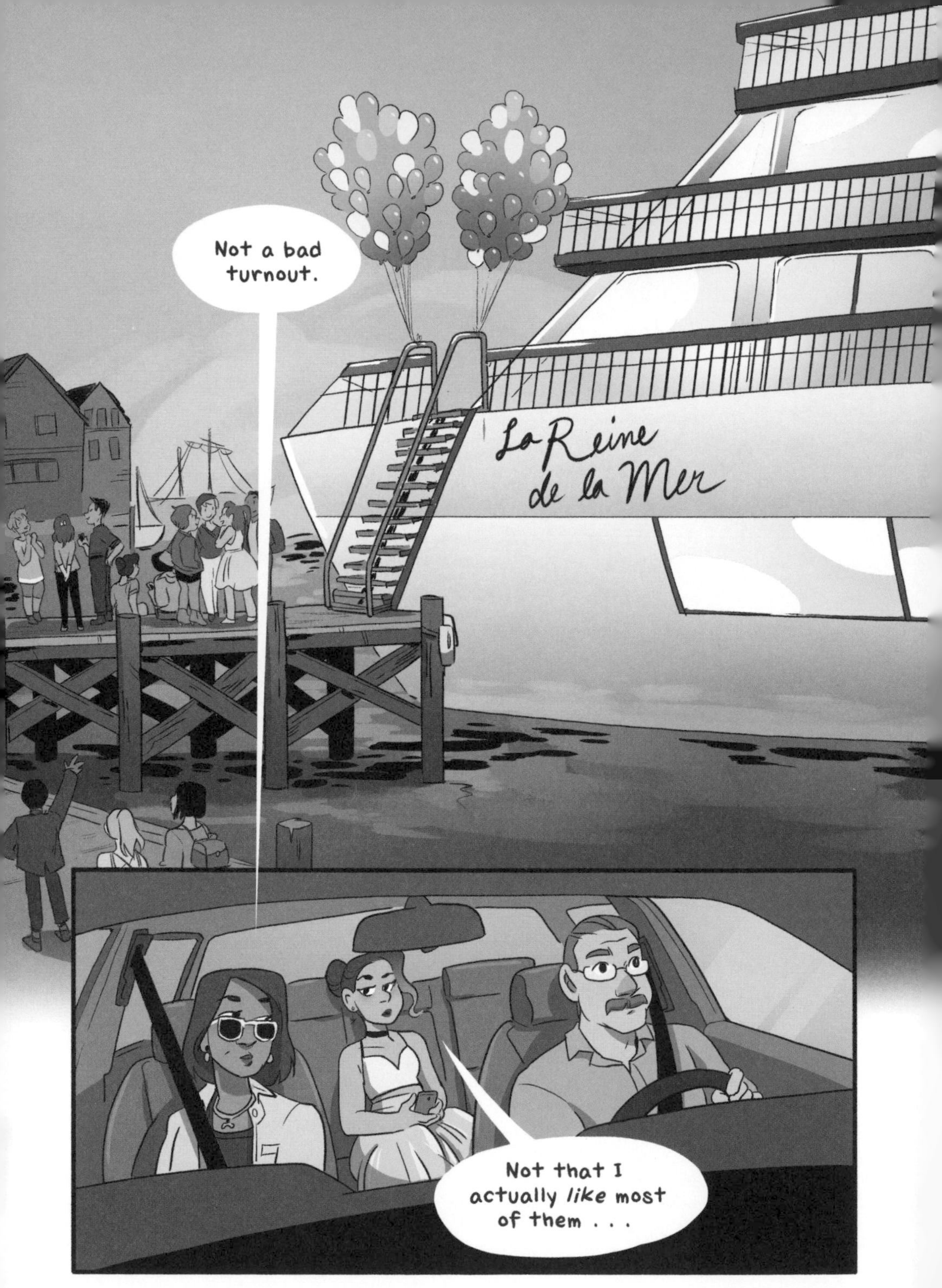
Not a bad turnout.
La Reine de la Mer
Not that I actually *like* most of them . . .

Oh, poor baby, your horrible parents are throwing you a huge birthday party.

With balloons and everything, lucky me!

It's a good advertising opportunity.

And of course we love you and want you to have a good time.

I know, Mom.

Have fun, sweetie. And don't forget to let everyone know —

Fifteen percent off harbor tours and rentals for everyone who books before July first?

That's right.

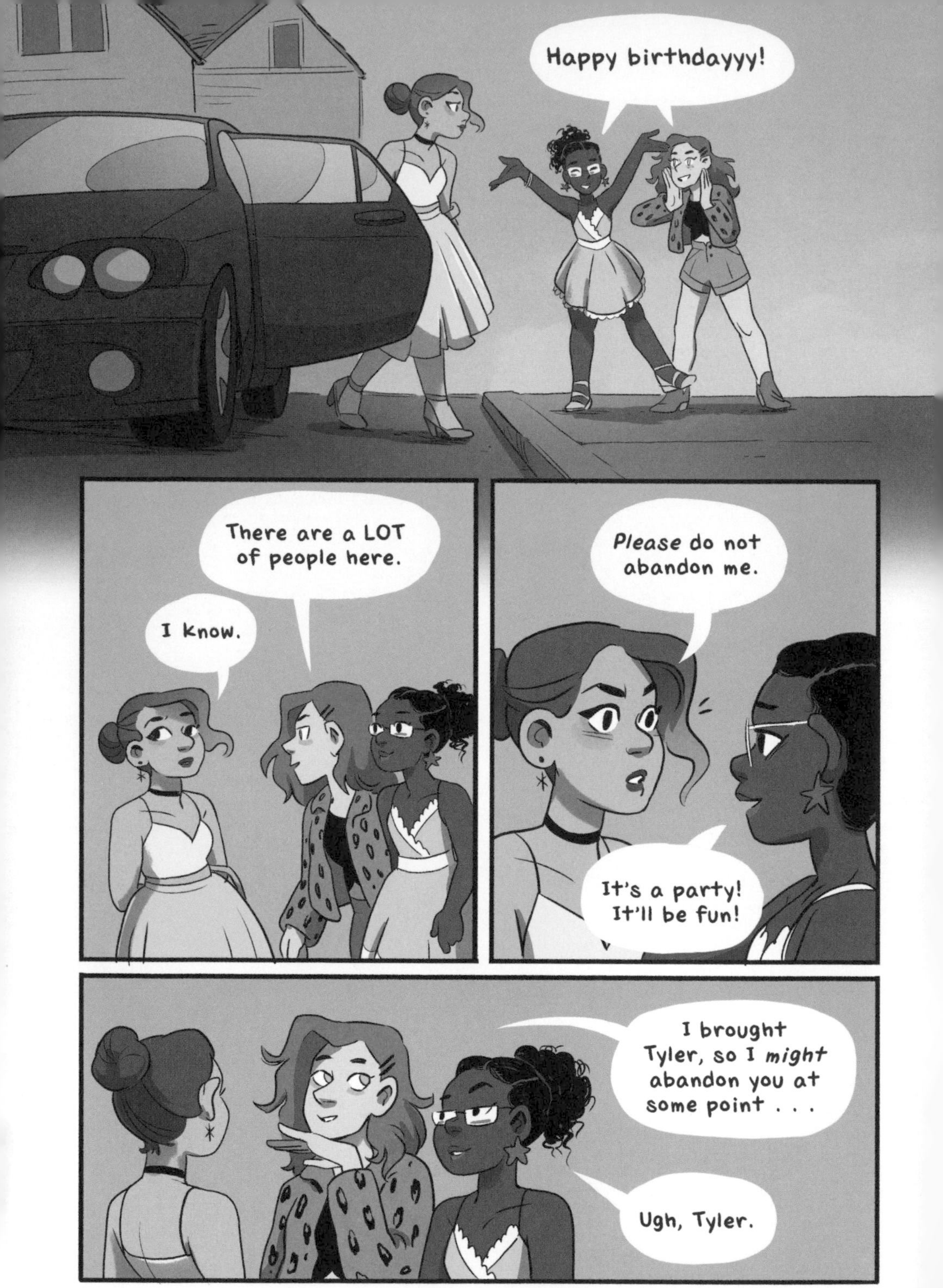
Happy birthdayyy!
There are a LOT of people here.
I know.
Please do not abandon me.
It's a party! It'll be fun!
I brought Tyler, so I *might* abandon you at some point . . .
Ugh, Tyler.

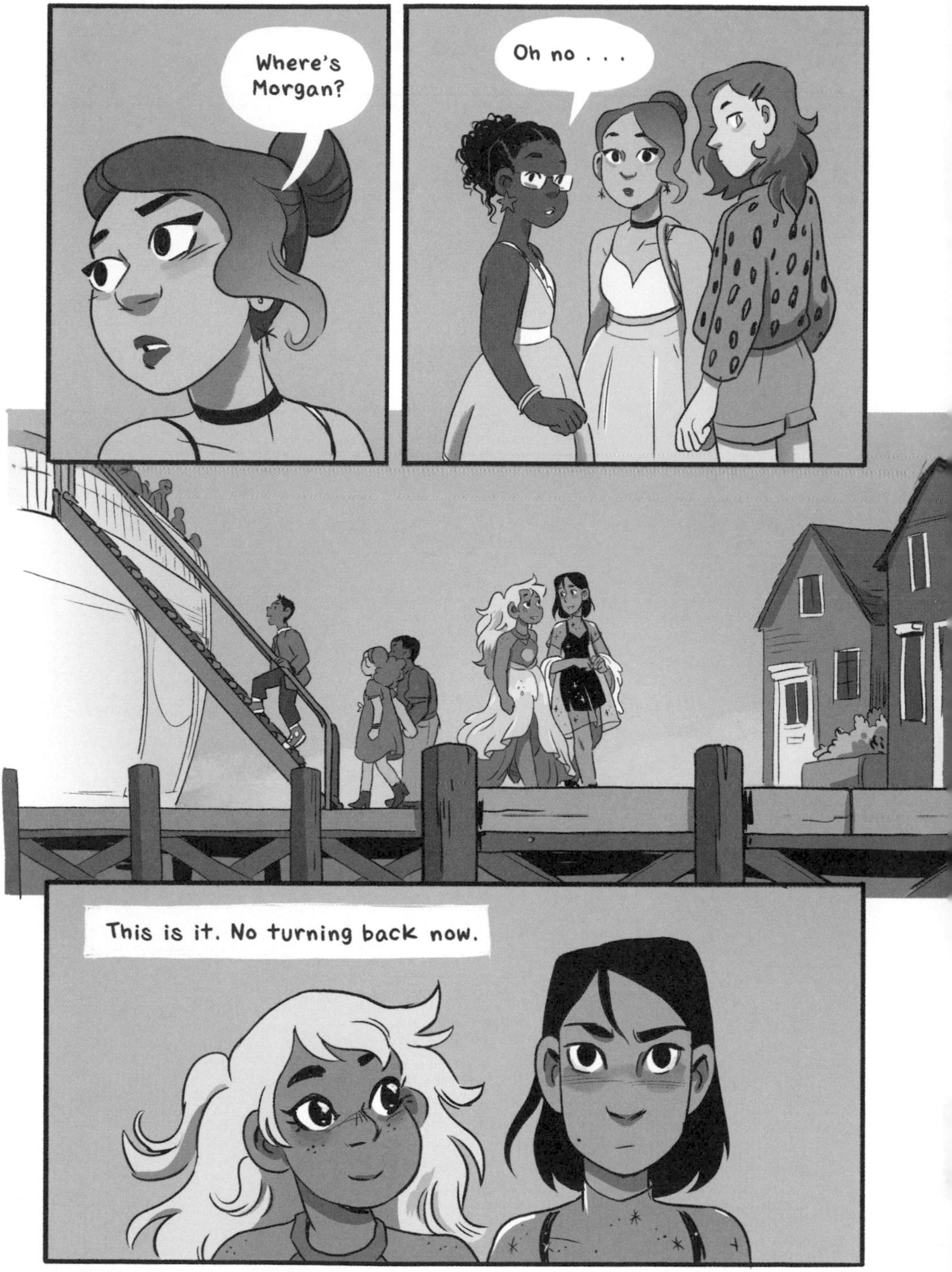

Where's Morgan?
Oh no . . .
This is it. No turning back now.

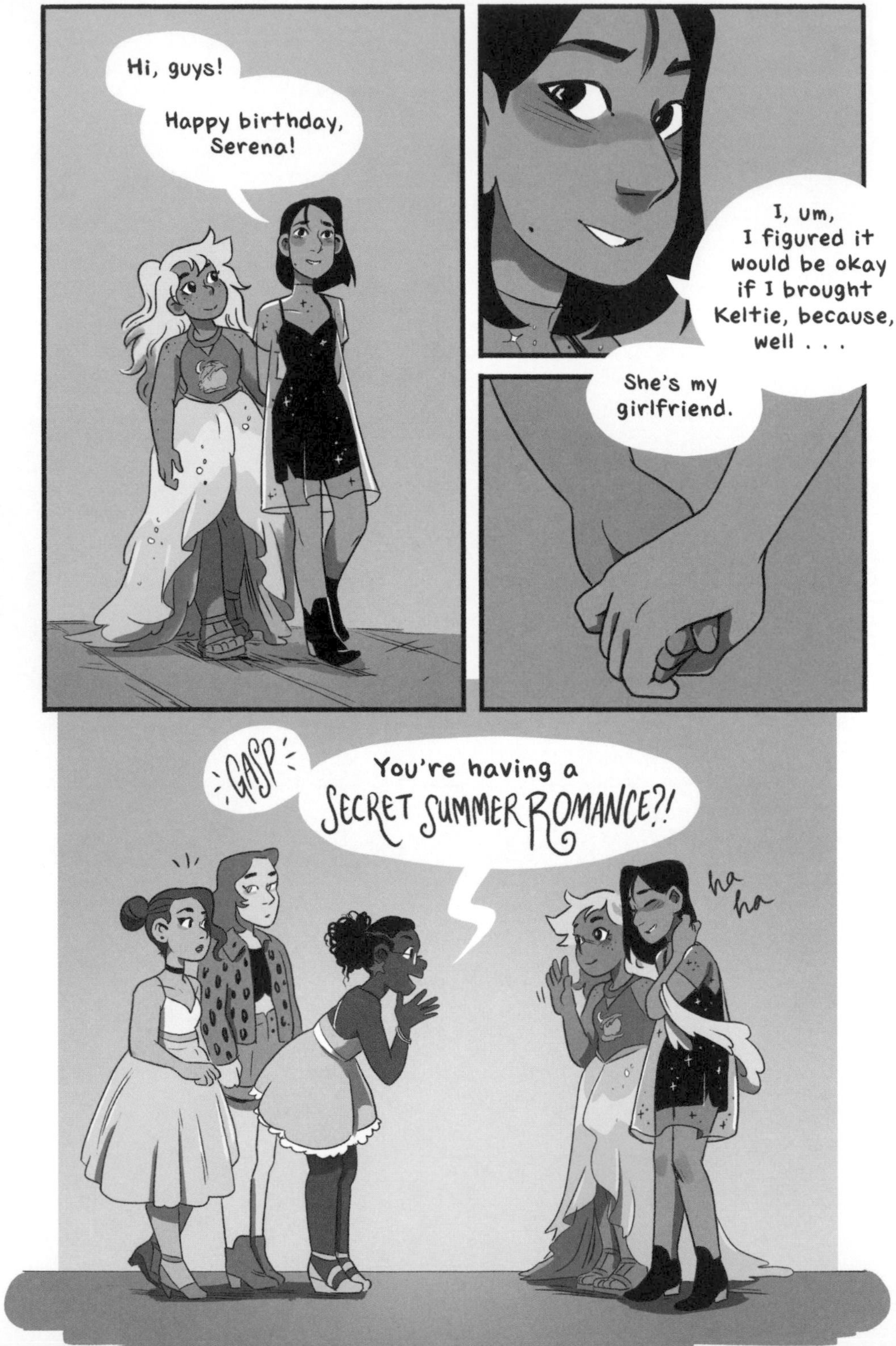
Hi, guys!
Happy birthday, Serena!
I, um, I figured it would be okay if I brought Keltie, because, well . . .
She's my girlfriend.
GASP
You're having a SECRET SUMMER ROMANCE?!
ha ha

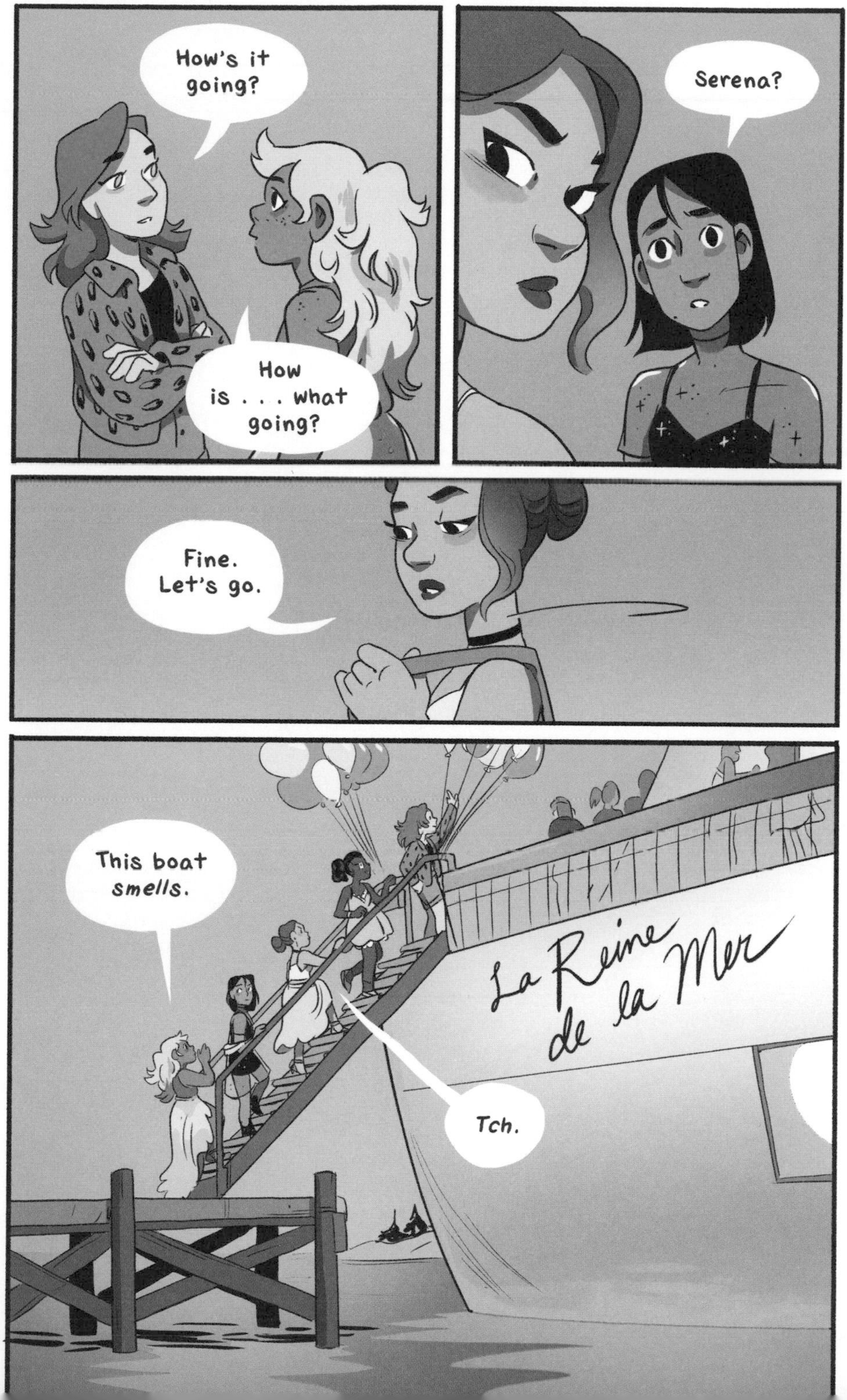
How's it going?
How is . . . what going?
Serena?
Fine. Let's go.
This boat smells.
Tch.
La Reine de la Mer

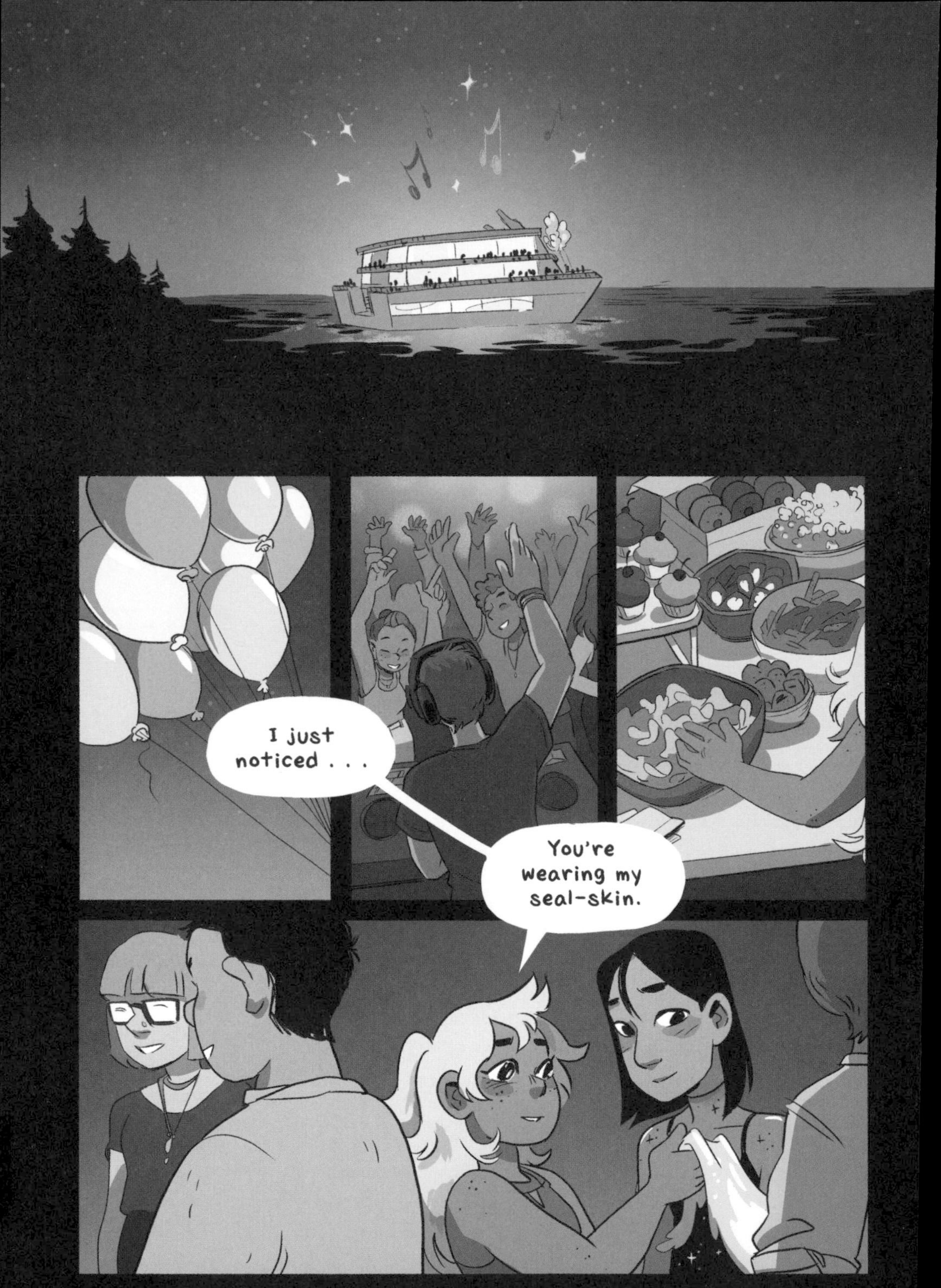
I just noticed . . .
You're wearing my seal-skin.

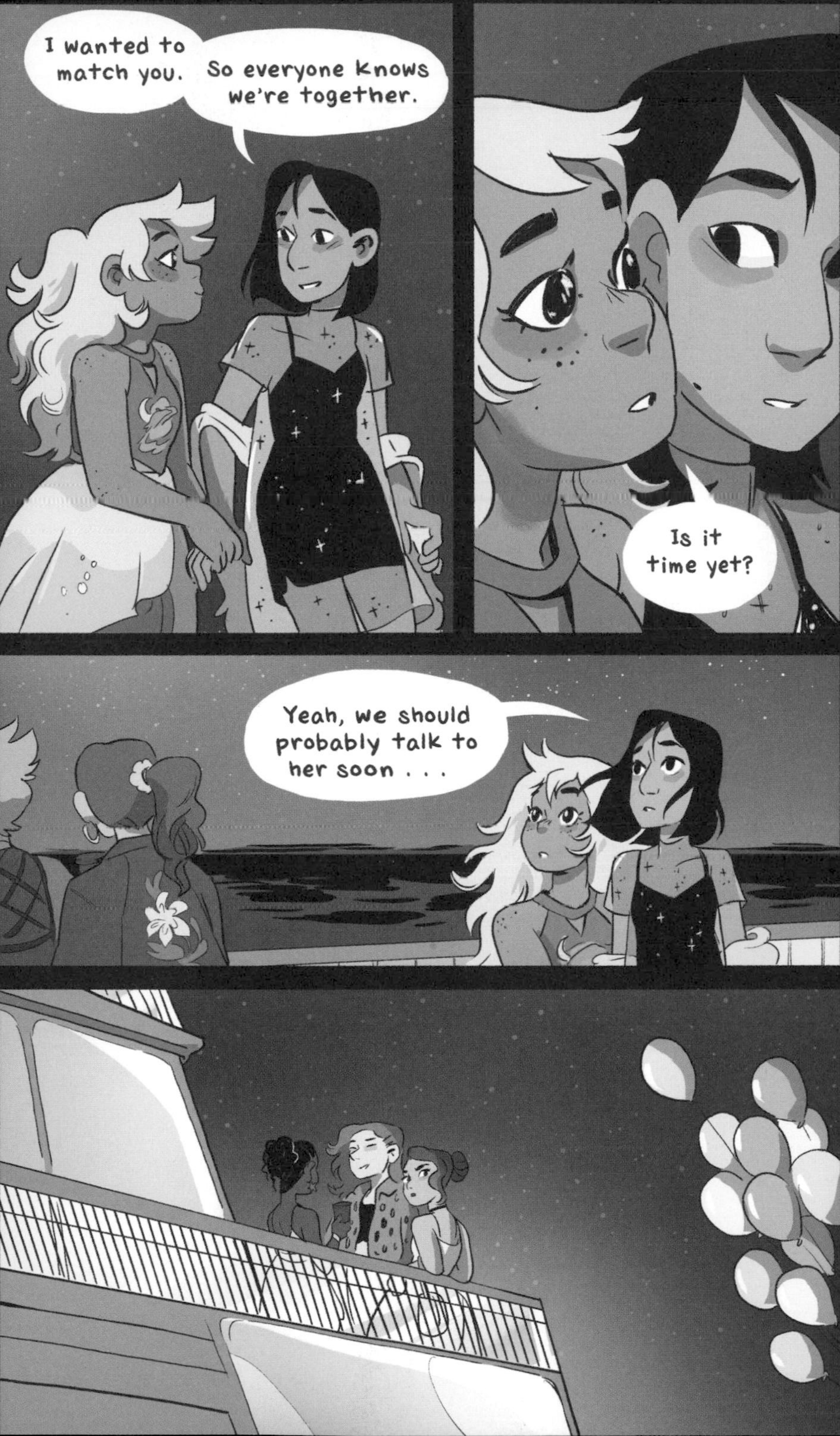
I wanted to match you.
So everyone knows we're together.
Is it time yet?
Yeah, we should probably talk to her soon . . .

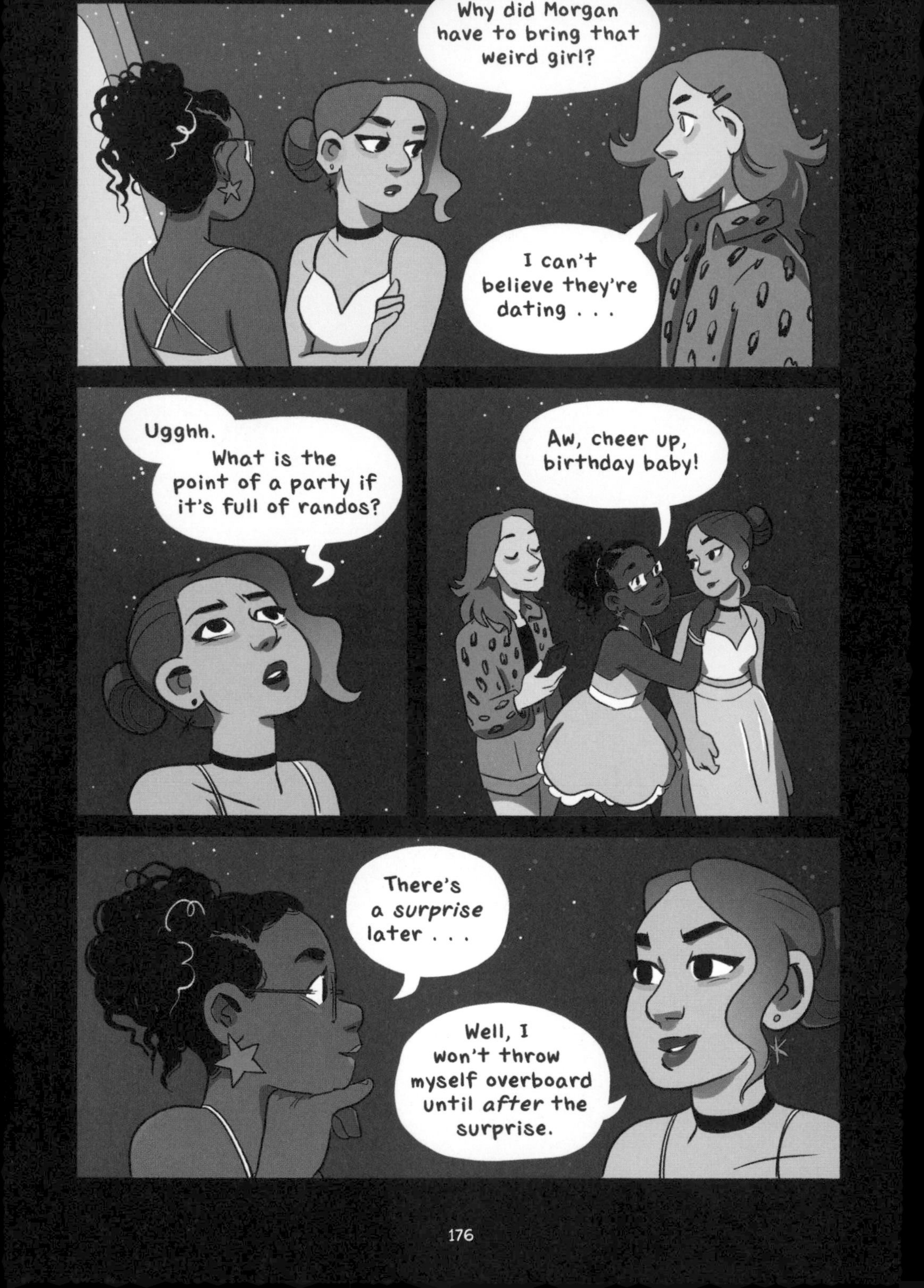
Why did Morgan have to bring that weird girl?
I can't believe they're dating . . .
Ugghh. What is the point of a party if it's full of randos?
Aw, cheer up, birthday baby!
There's a *surprise* later . . .
Well, I won't throw myself overboard until *after* the surprise.

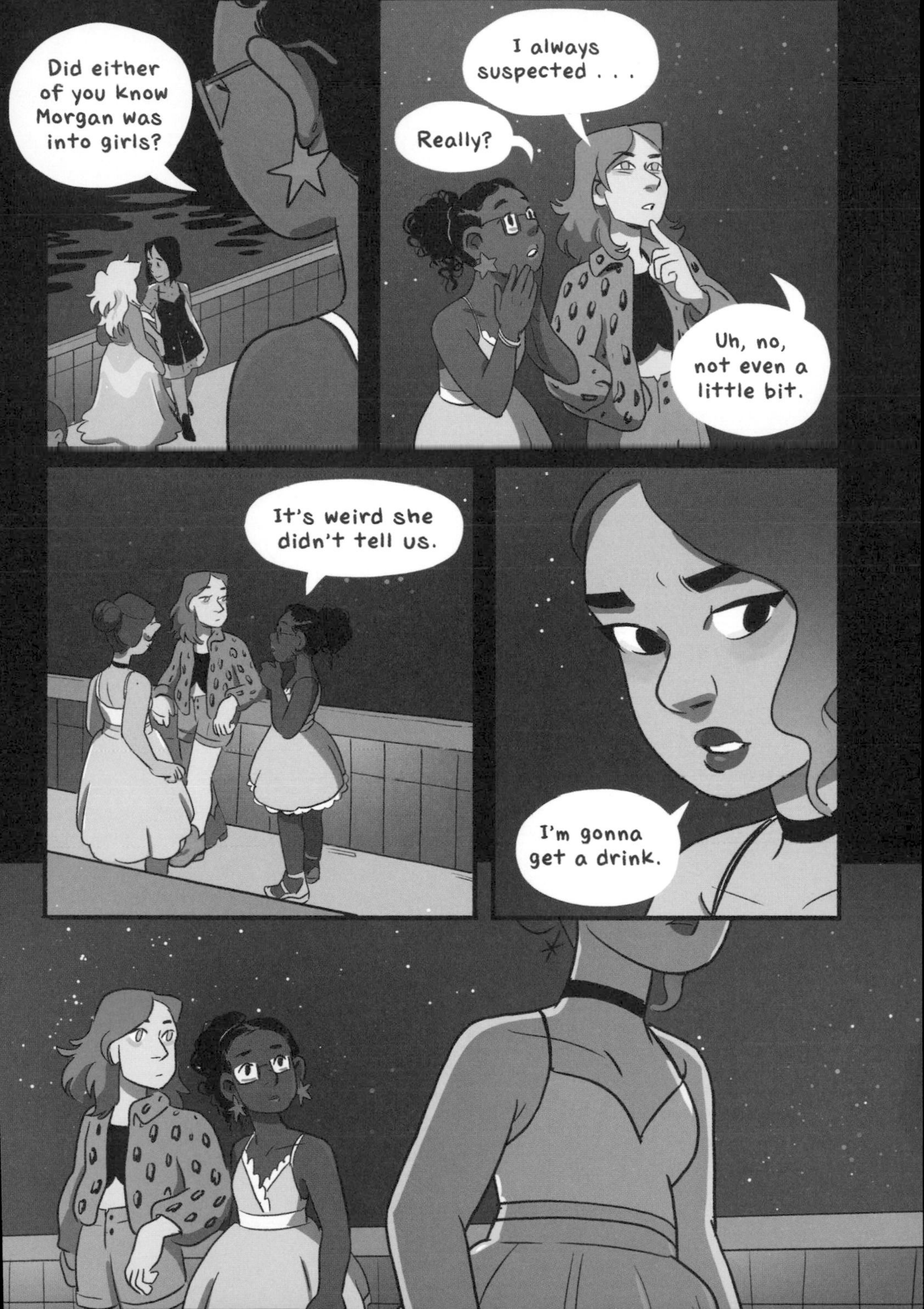
Did either of you know Morgan was into girls?
I always suspected . . .
Really?
Uh, no, not even a little bit.
It's weird she didn't tell us.
I'm gonna get a drink.

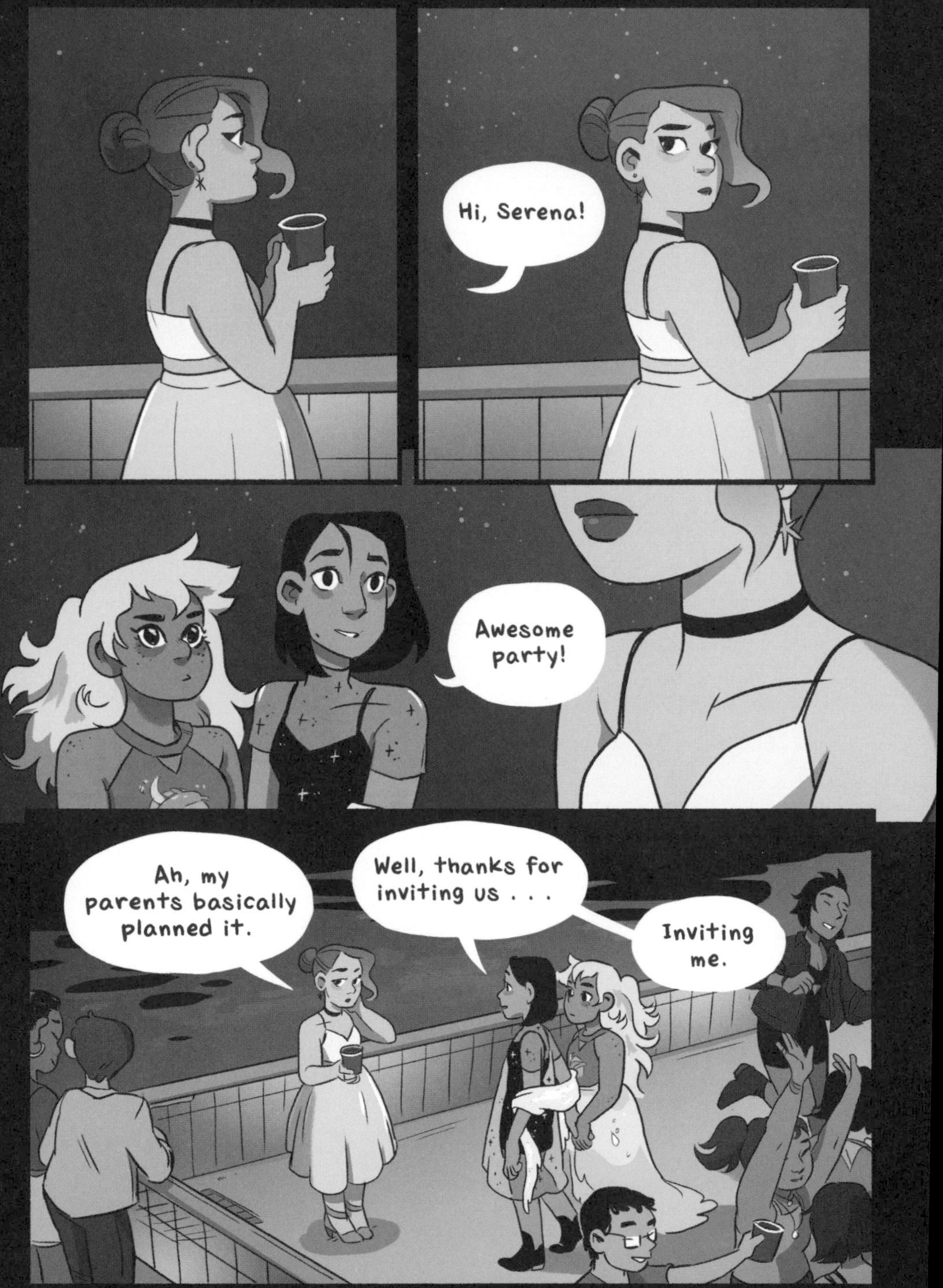
Hi, Serena!
Awesome party!
Ah, my parents basically planned it.
Well, thanks for inviting us . . .
Inviting me.

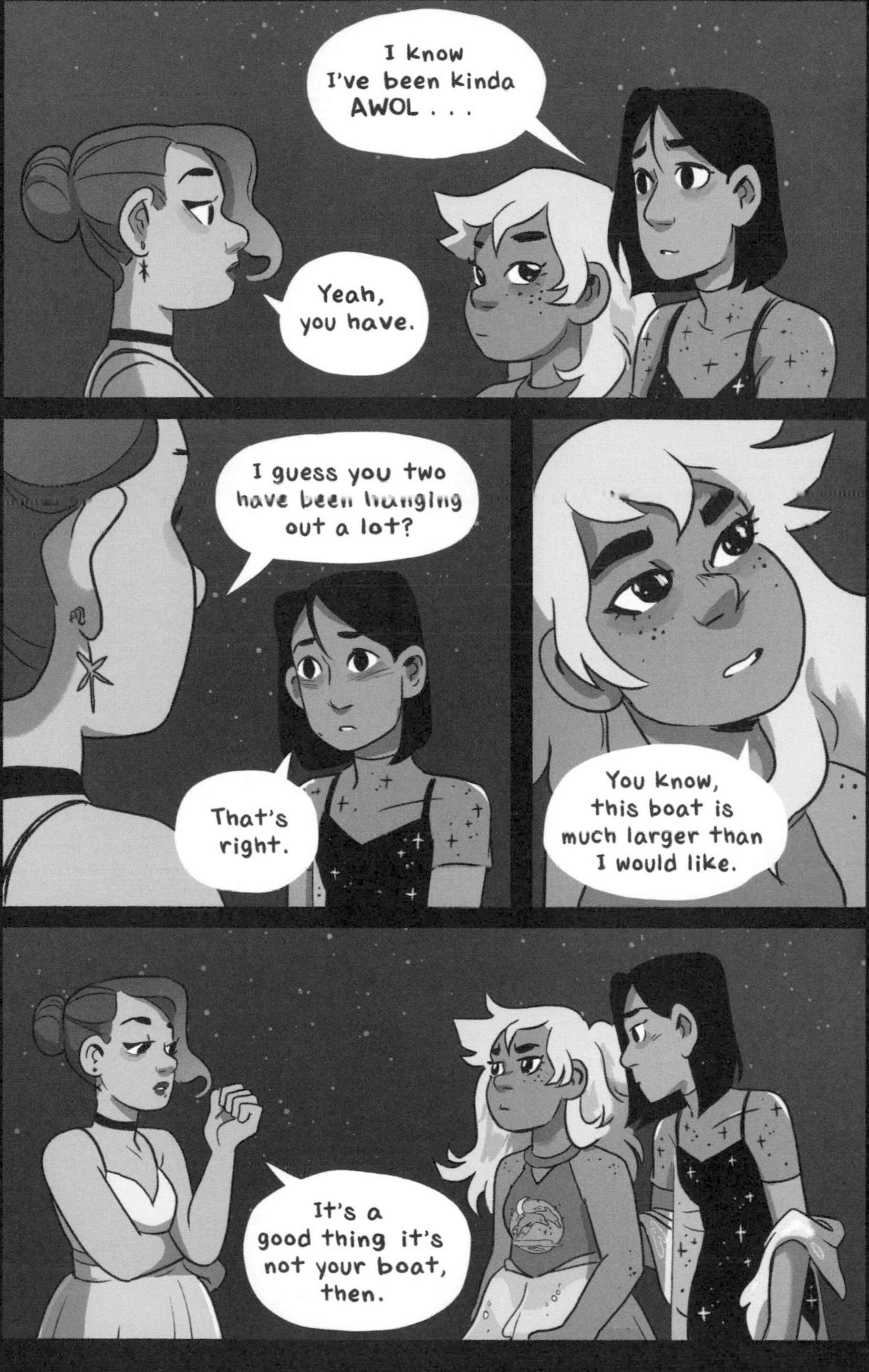
I know I've been kinda AWOL . . .
Yeah, you have.
I guess you two have been hanging out a lot?
That's right.
You know, this boat is much larger than I would like.
It's a good thing it's not your boat, then.

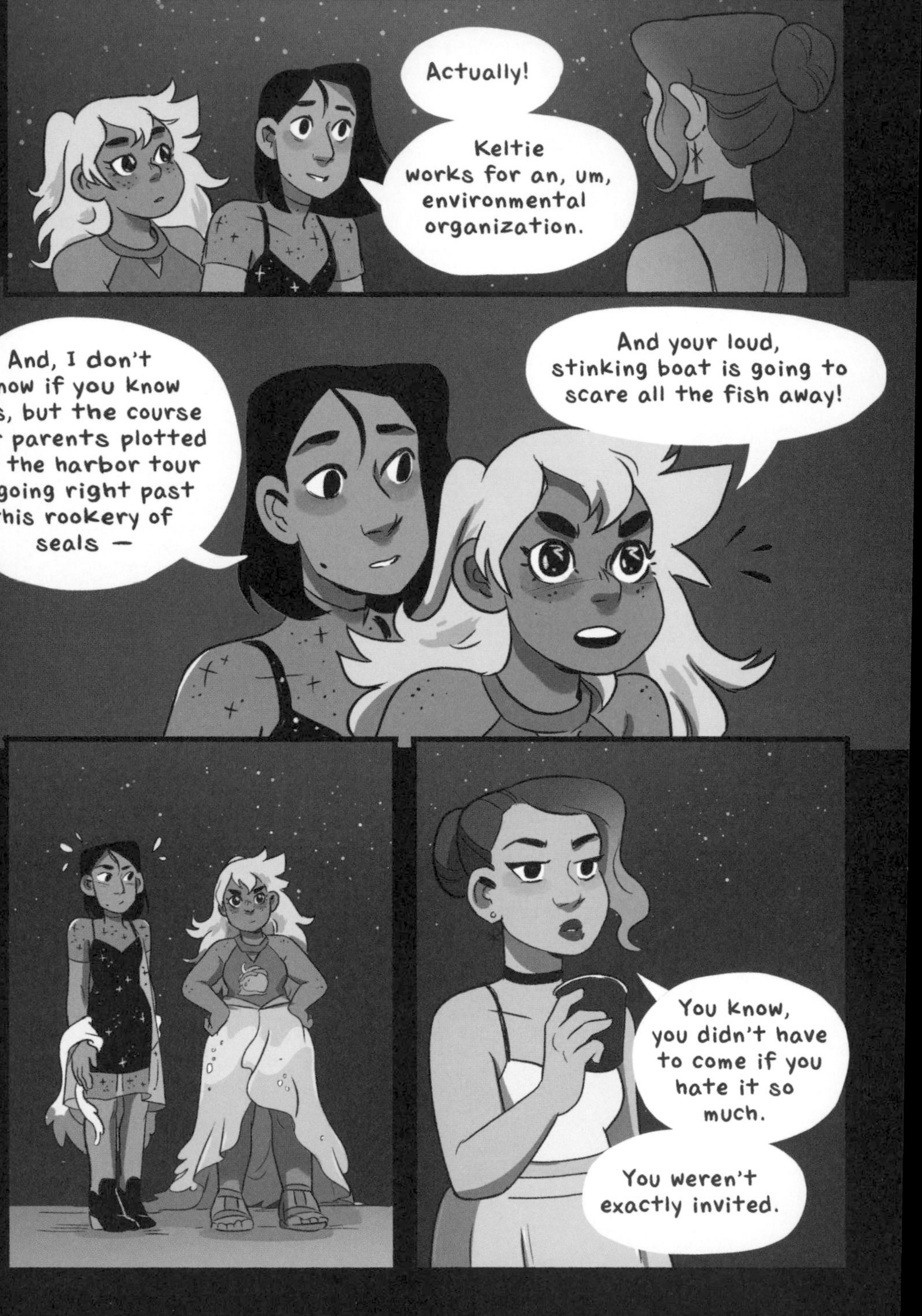
Actually!
Keltie works for an, um, environmental organization.
And, I don't know if you know this, but the course your parents plotted for the harbor tour is going right past this rookery of seals —
And your loud, stinking boat is going to scare all the fish away!
You know, you didn't have to come if you hate it so much.
You weren't exactly invited.

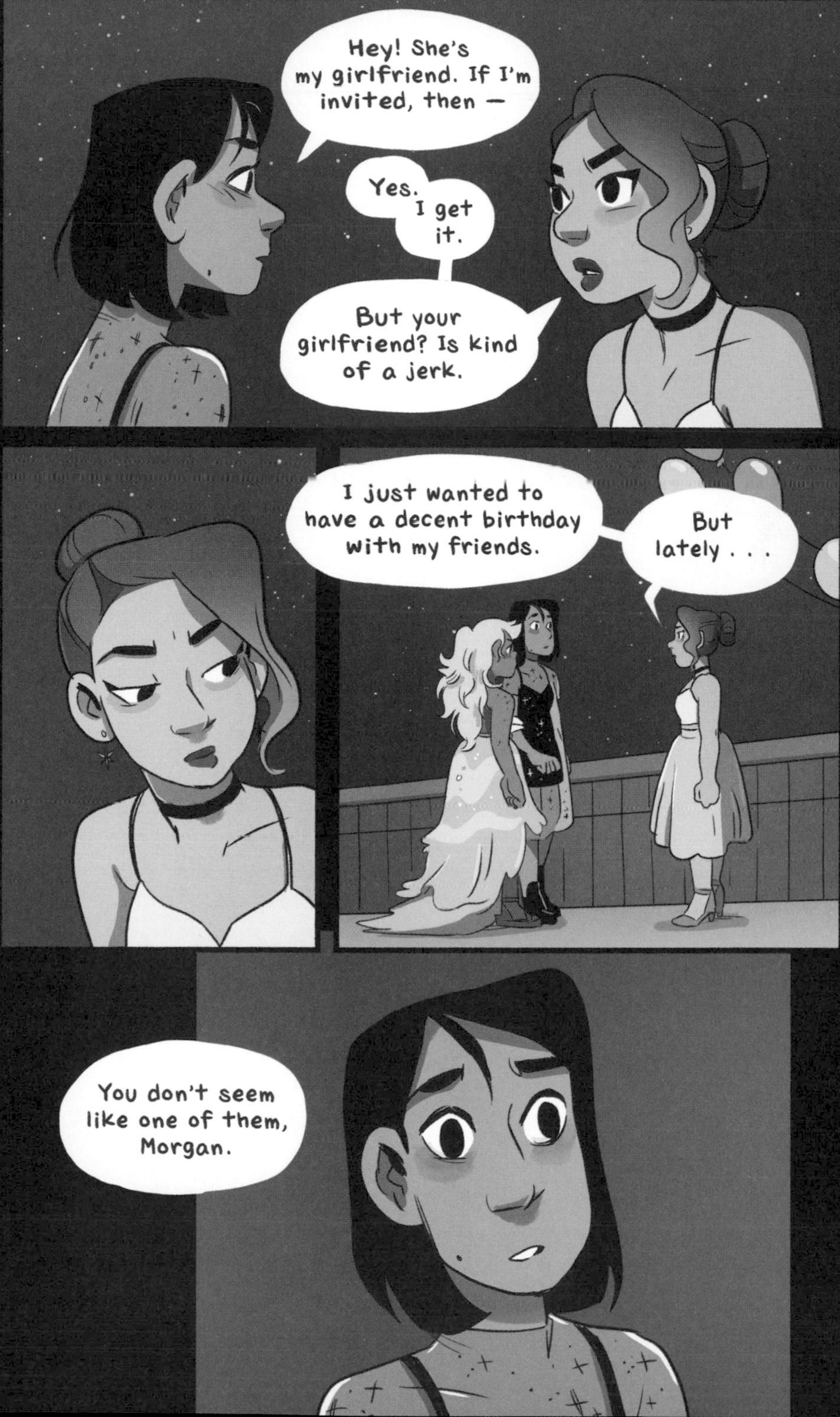
Hey! She's my girlfriend. If I'm invited, then —
Yes. I get it.
But your girlfriend? Is kind of a jerk.
I just wanted to have a decent birthday with my friends.
But lately . . .
You don't seem like one of them, Morgan.

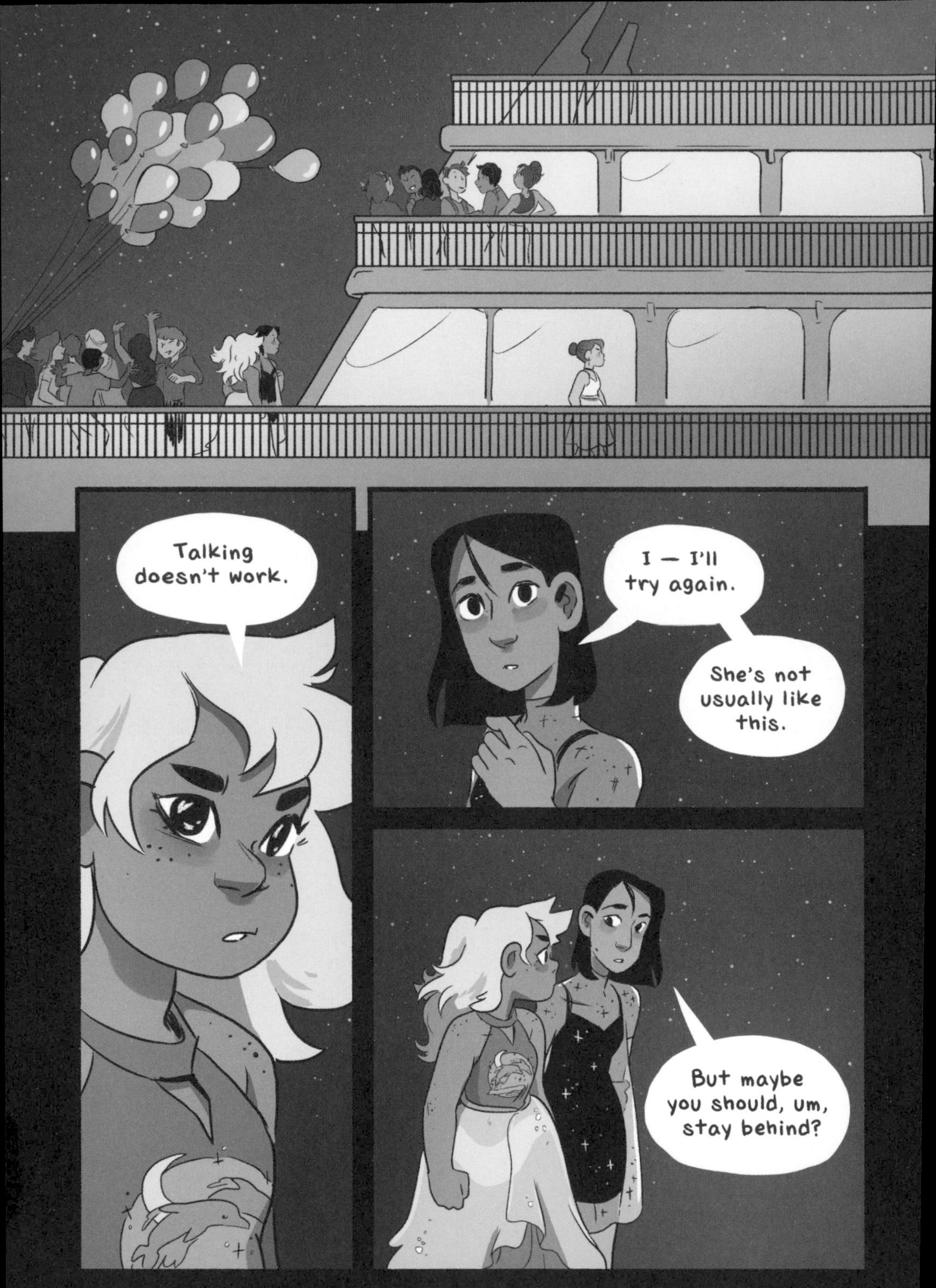
Talking doesn't work.
I — I'll try again.
She's not usually like this.
But maybe you should, um, stay behind?

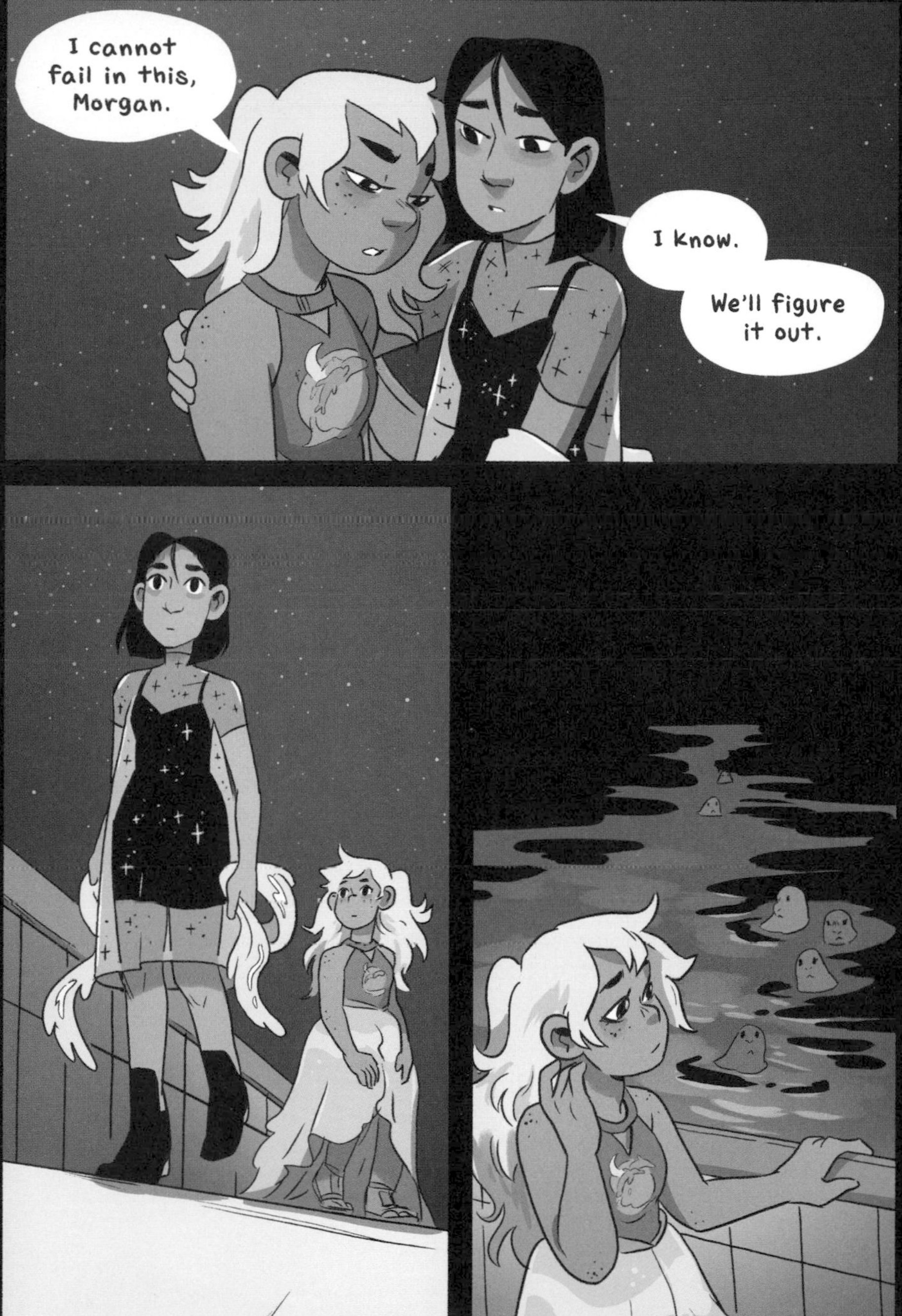
I cannot fail in this, Morgan.
I know.
We'll figure it out.

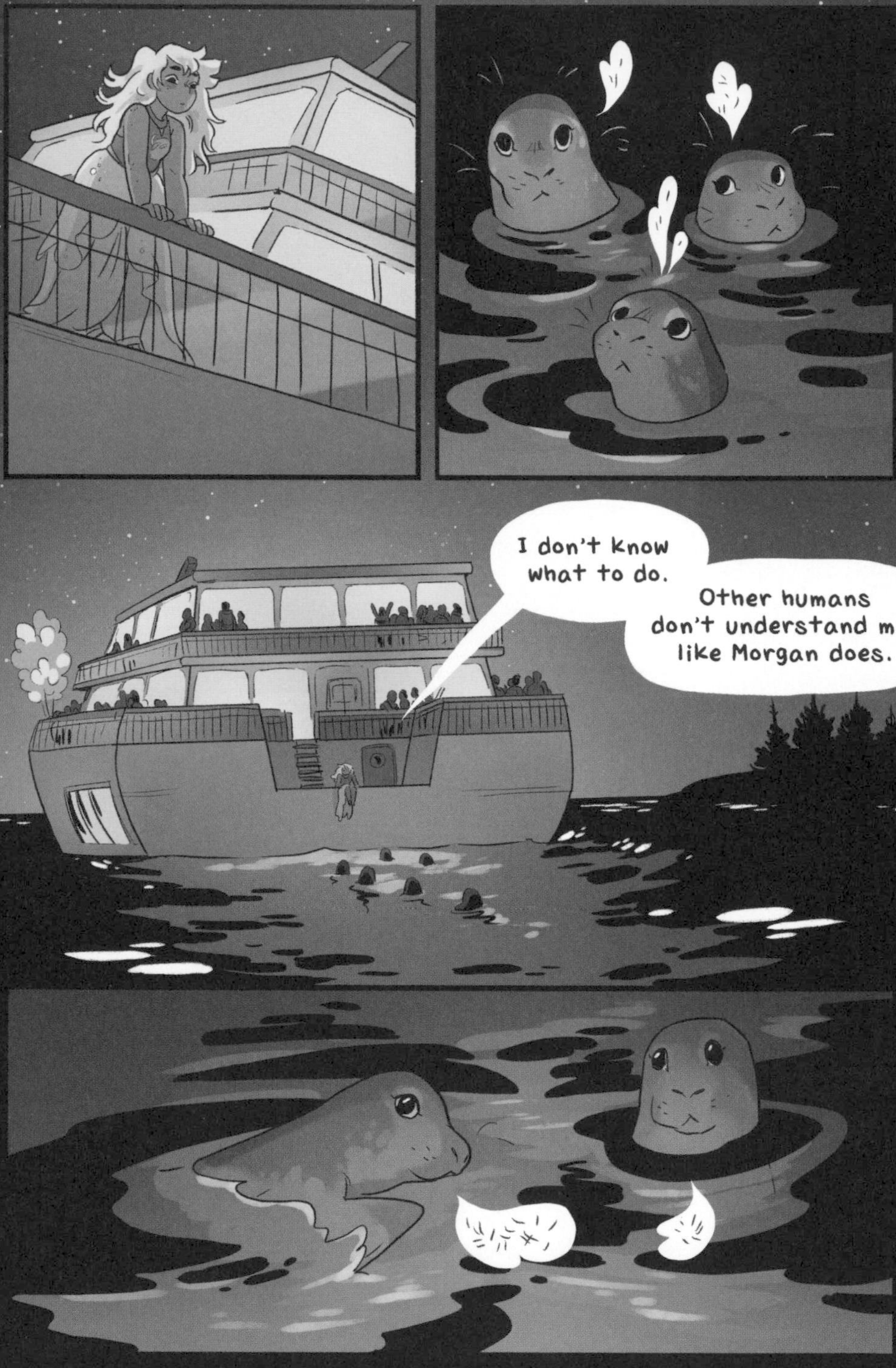

I don't know what to do.
Other humans don't understand me like Morgan does.

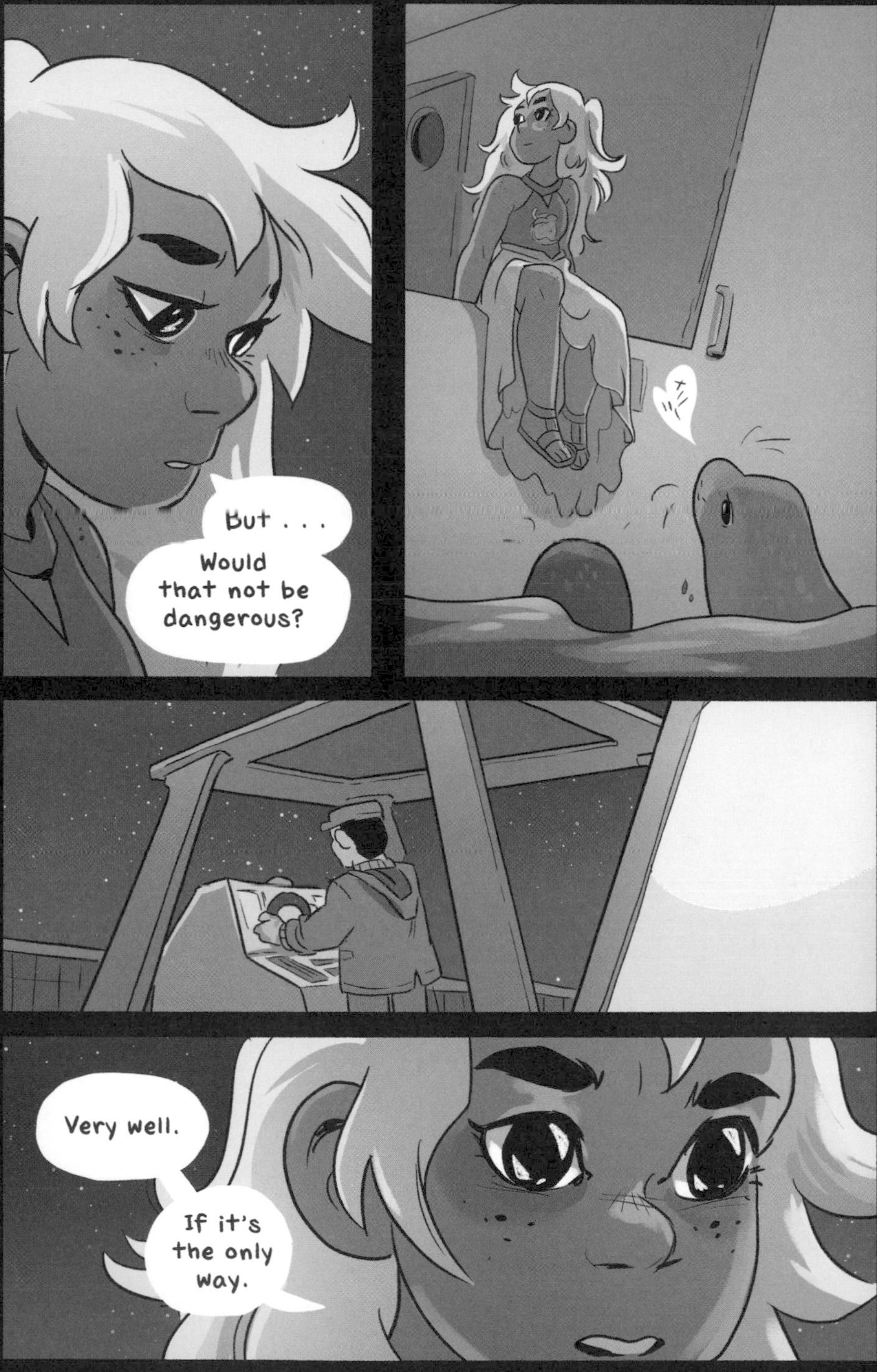

But . . .
Would that not be dangerous?
Very well.
If it's the only way.

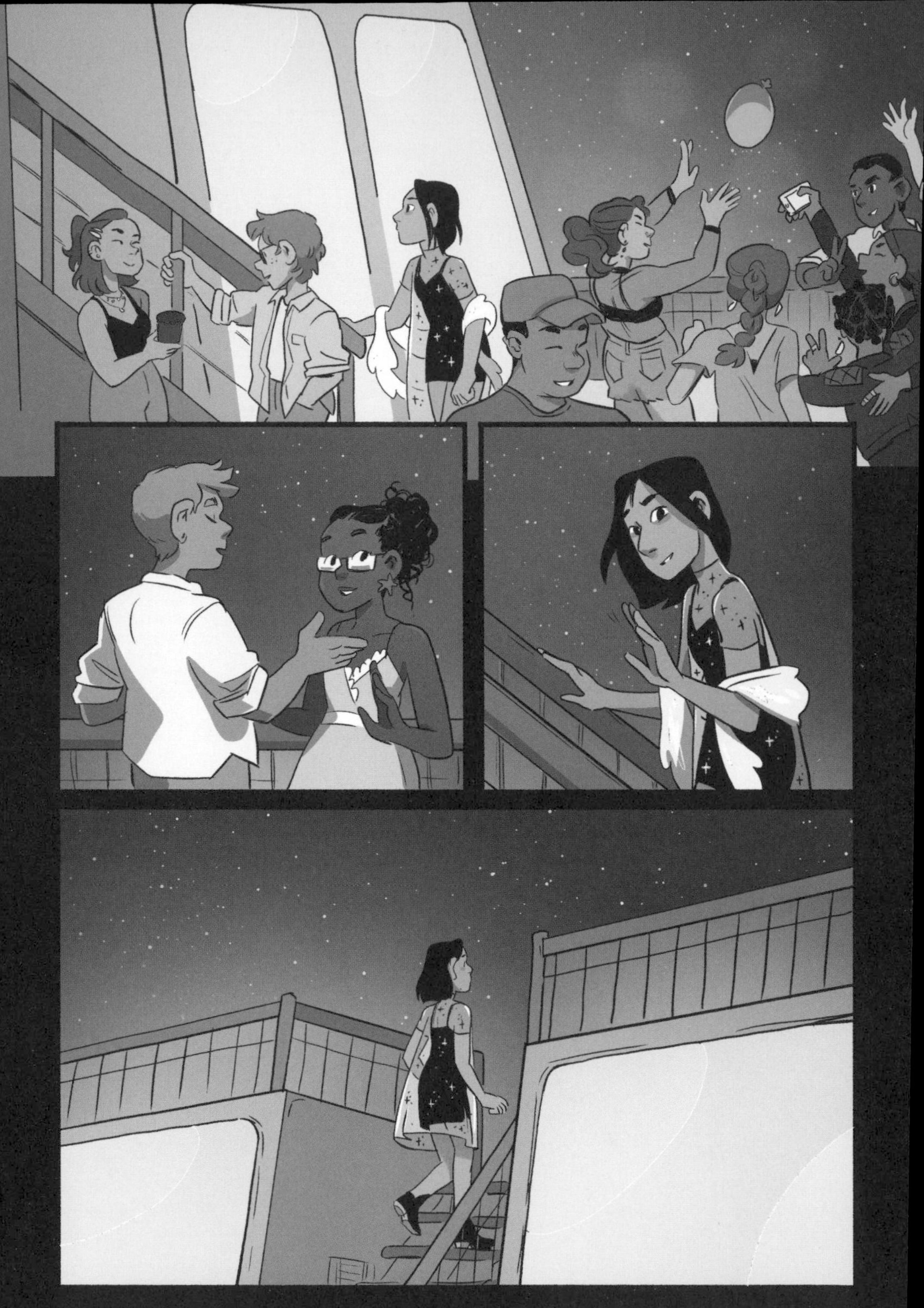

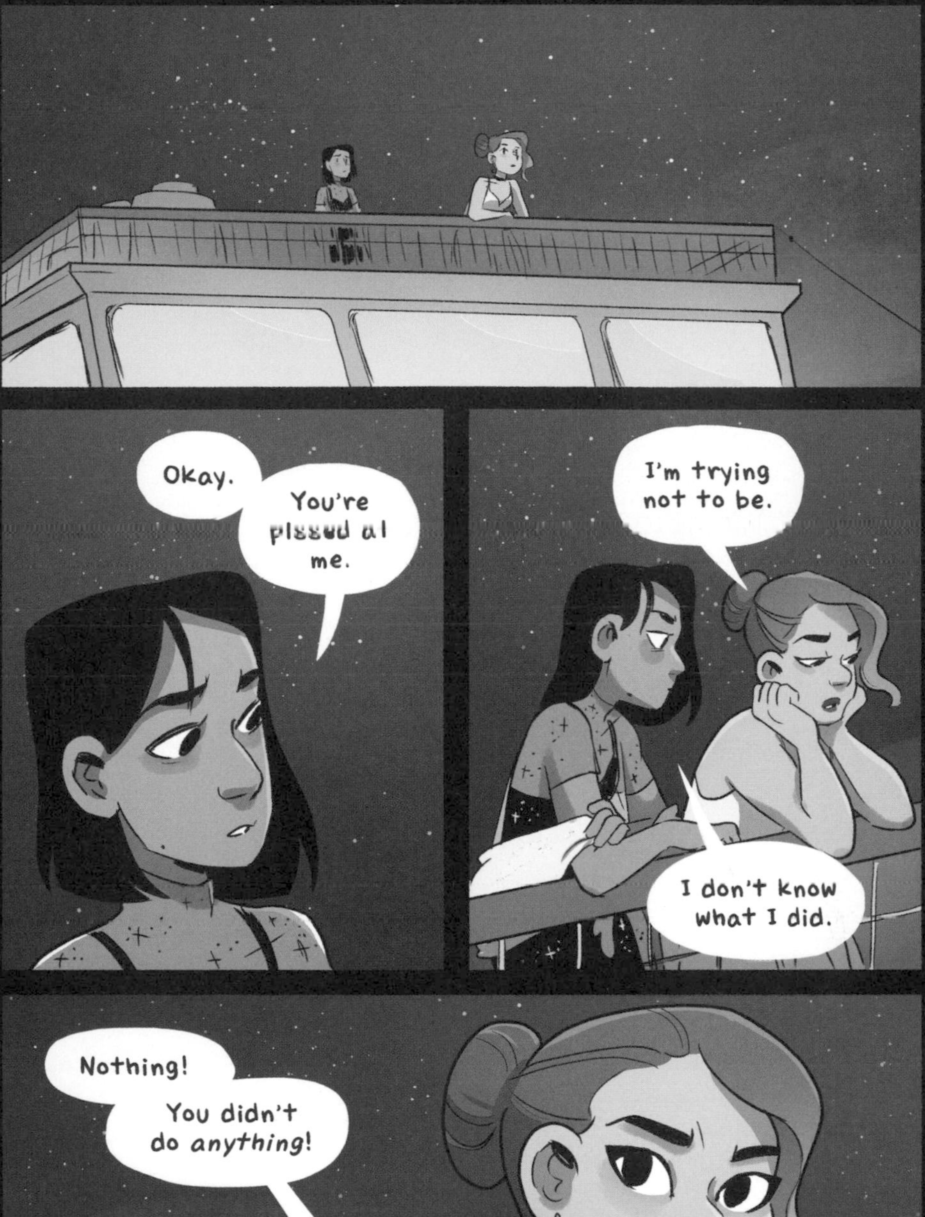
Okay.
You're pissed at me.
I'm trying not to be.
I don't know what I did.
Nothing!
You didn't do *anything*!
That's the point!

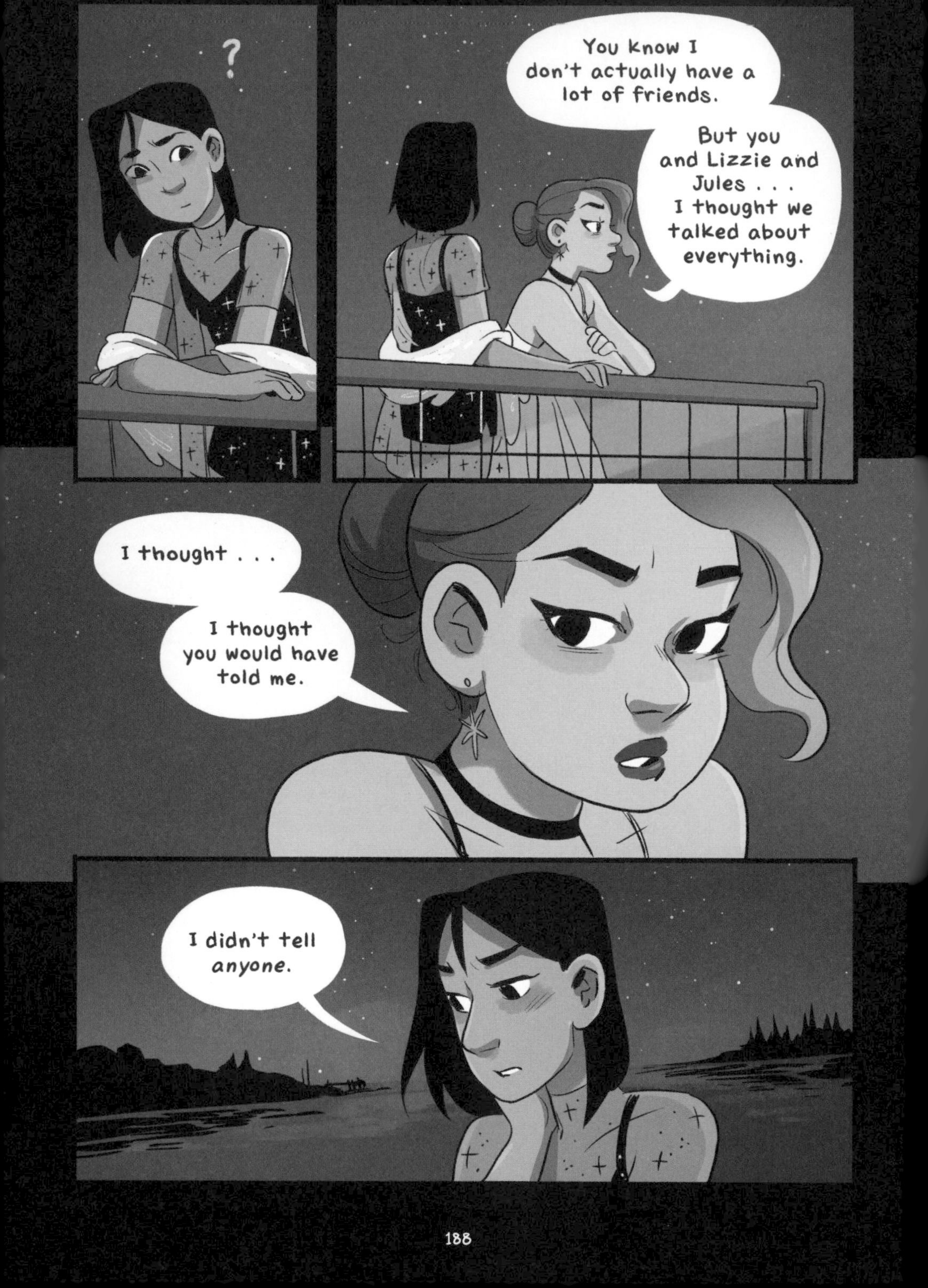
?
You know I don't actually have a lot of friends.
But you and Lizzie and Jules . . . I thought we talked about everything.
I thought . . .
I thought you would have told me.
I didn't tell *anyone*.

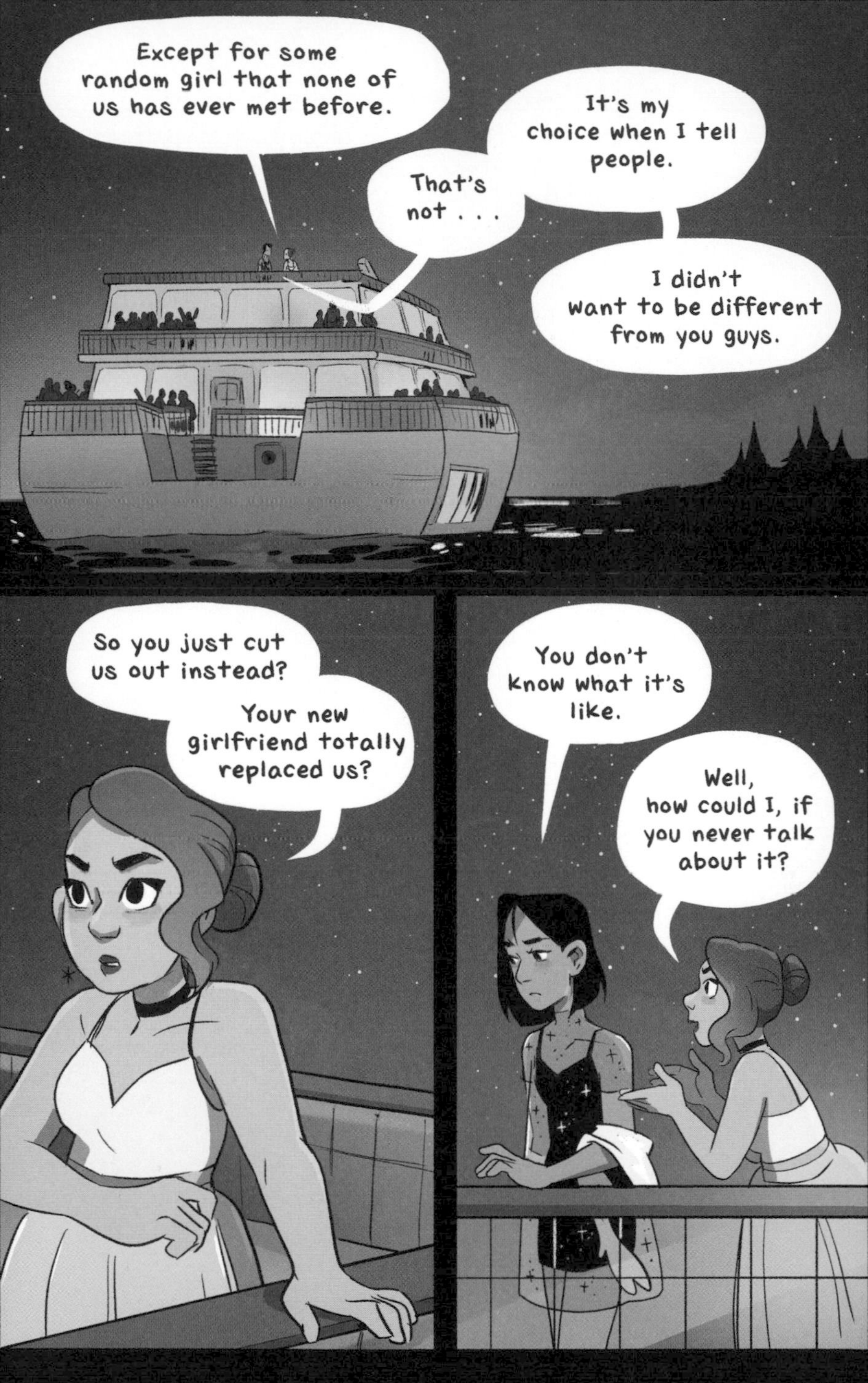
Except for some random girl that none of us has ever met before.
That's not . . .
It's my choice when I tell people.
I didn't want to be different from you guys.
So you just cut us out instead?
Your new girlfriend totally replaced us?
You don't know what it's like.
Well, how could I, if you never talk about it?

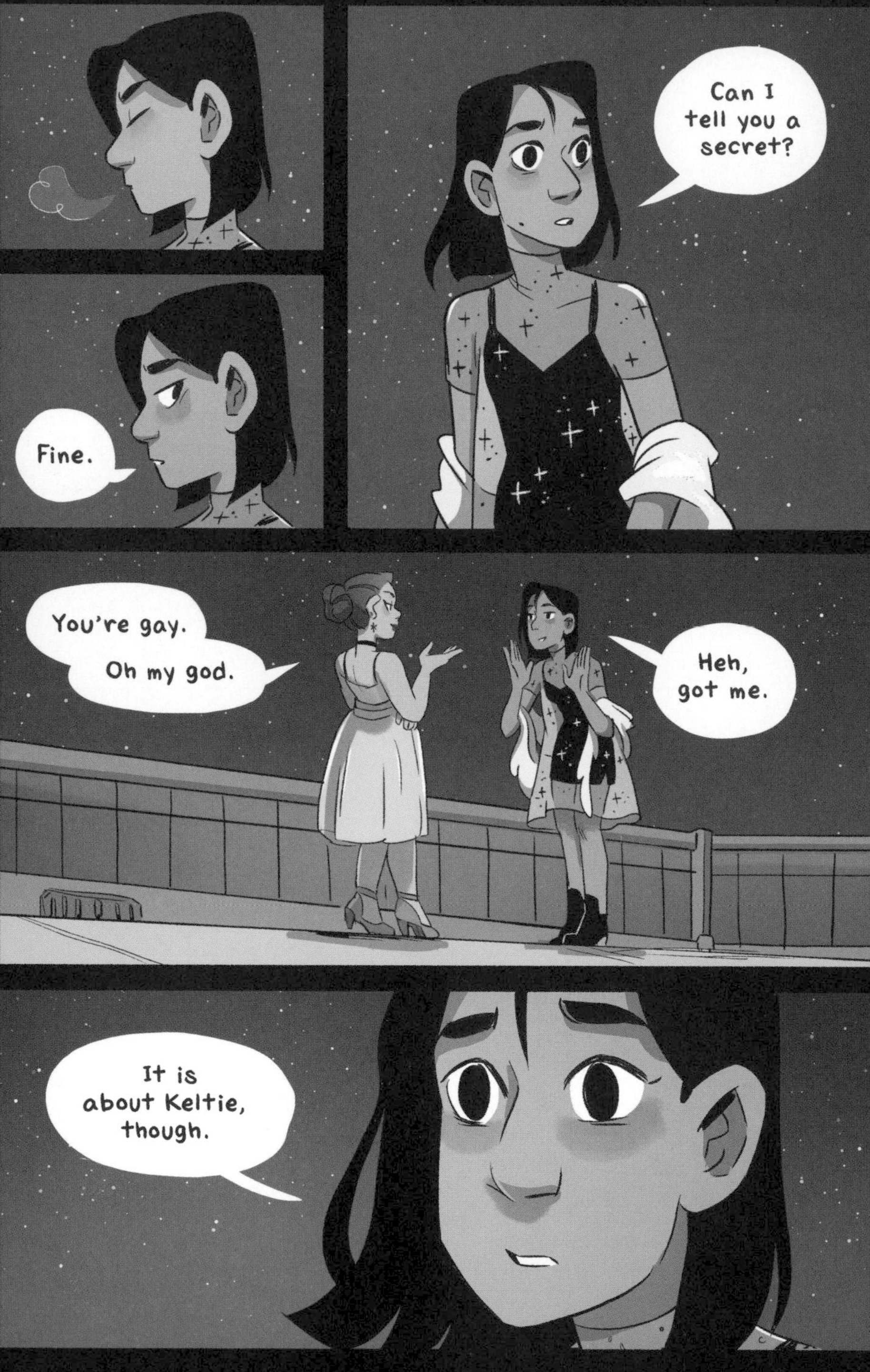
Can I tell you a secret?
Fine.
You're gay.
Oh my god.
Heh, got me.
It is about Keltie, though.

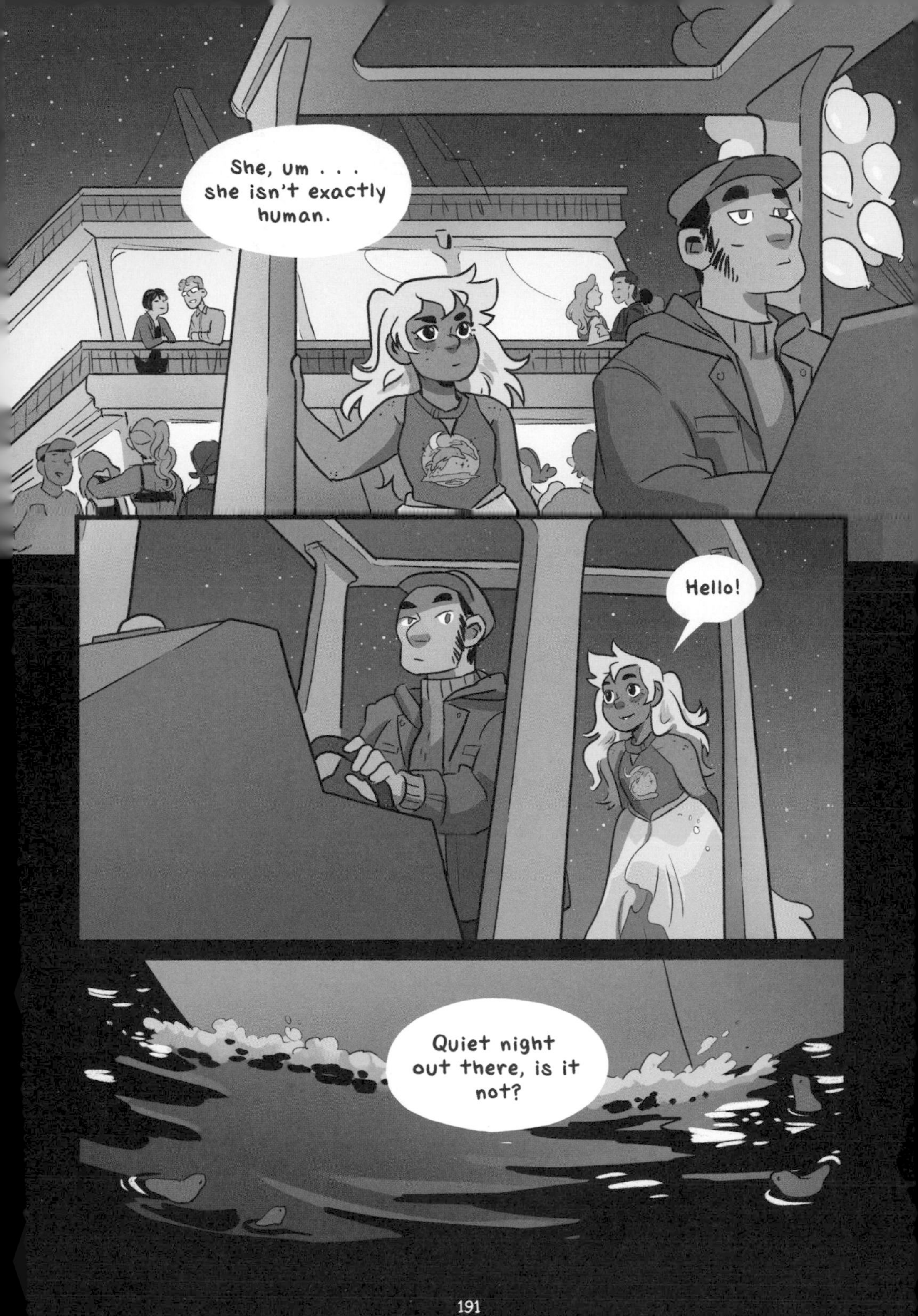
She, um . . . she isn't exactly human.
Hello!
Quiet night out there, is it not?

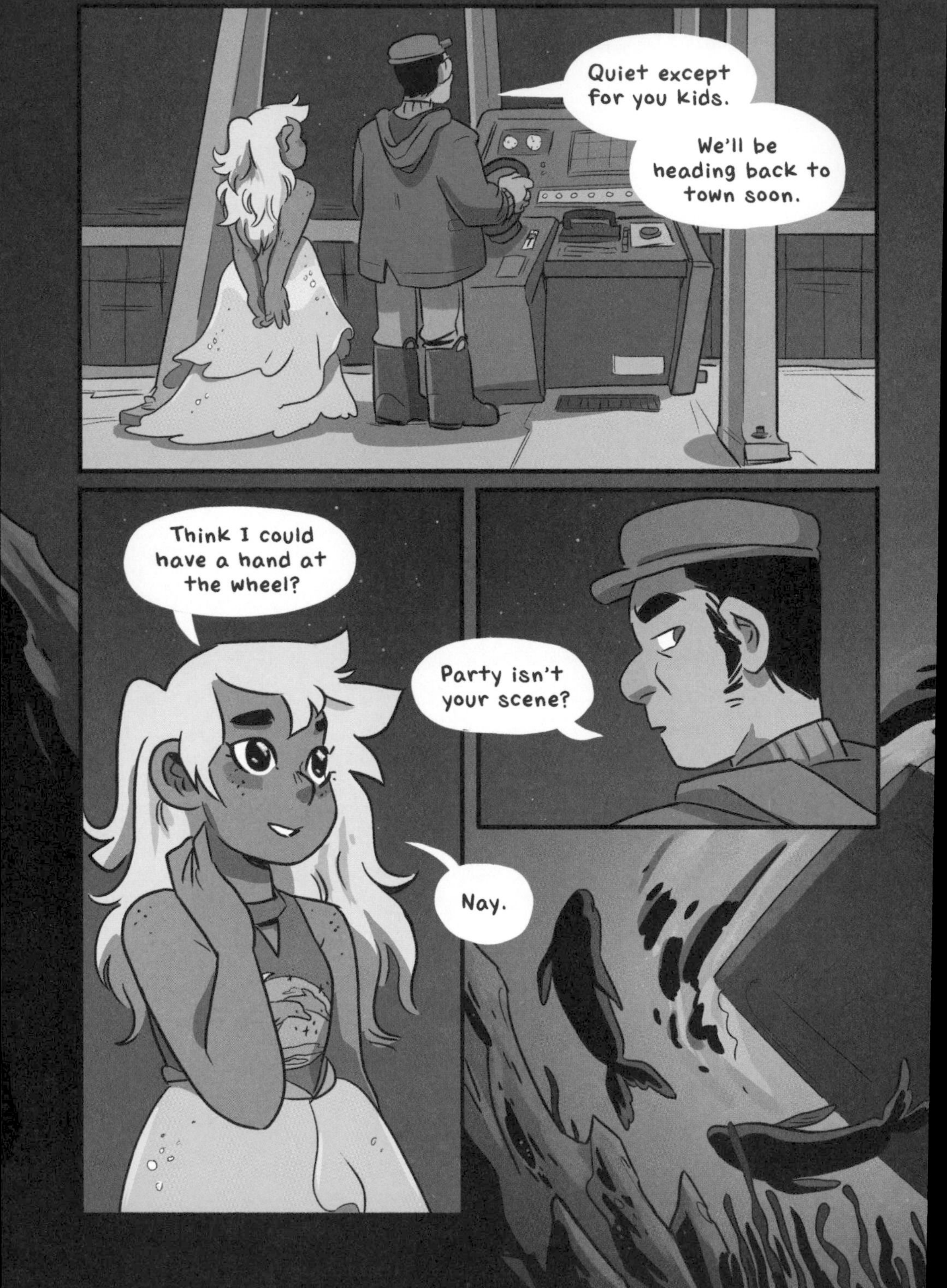
Quiet except for you kids.
We'll be heading back to town soon.
Think I could have a hand at the wheel?
Party isn't your scene?
Nay.

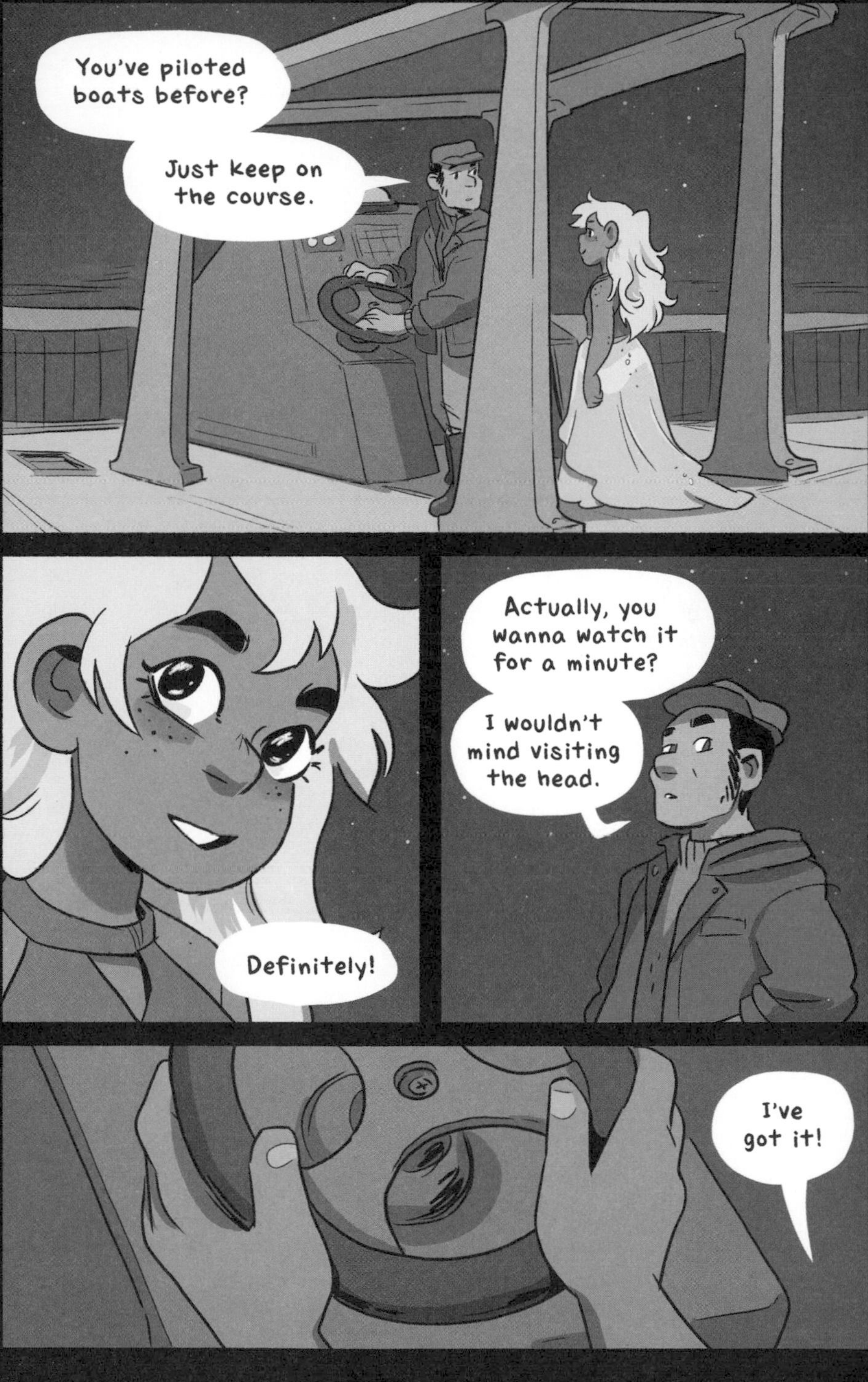
You've piloted boats before?
Just keep on the course.
Actually, you wanna watch it for a minute?
I wouldn't mind visiting the head.
Definitely!
I've got it!

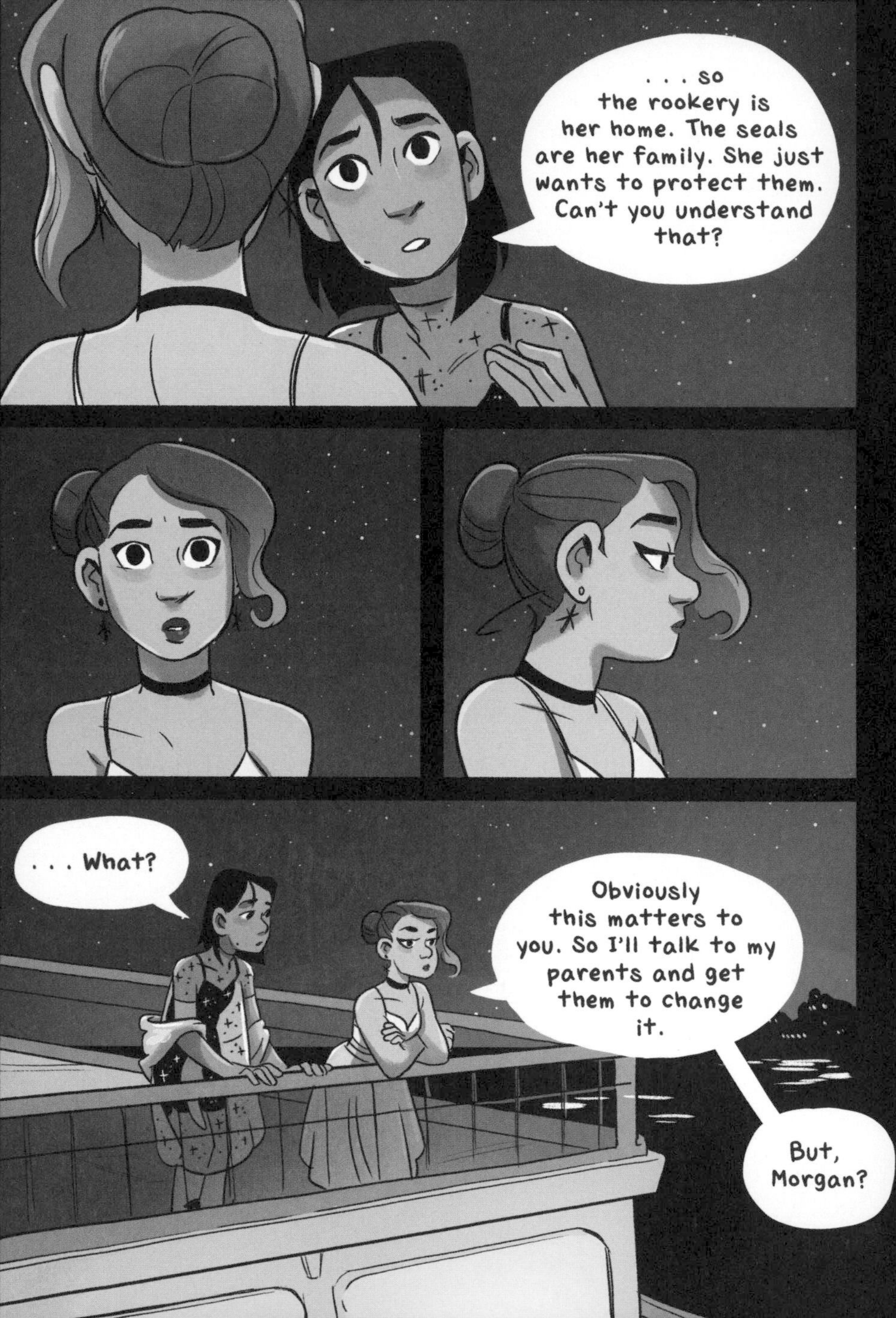
. . . so the rookery is her home. The seals are her family. She just wants to protect them. Can't you understand that?
. . . What?
Obviously this matters to you. So I'll talk to my parents and get them to change it.
But, Morgan?

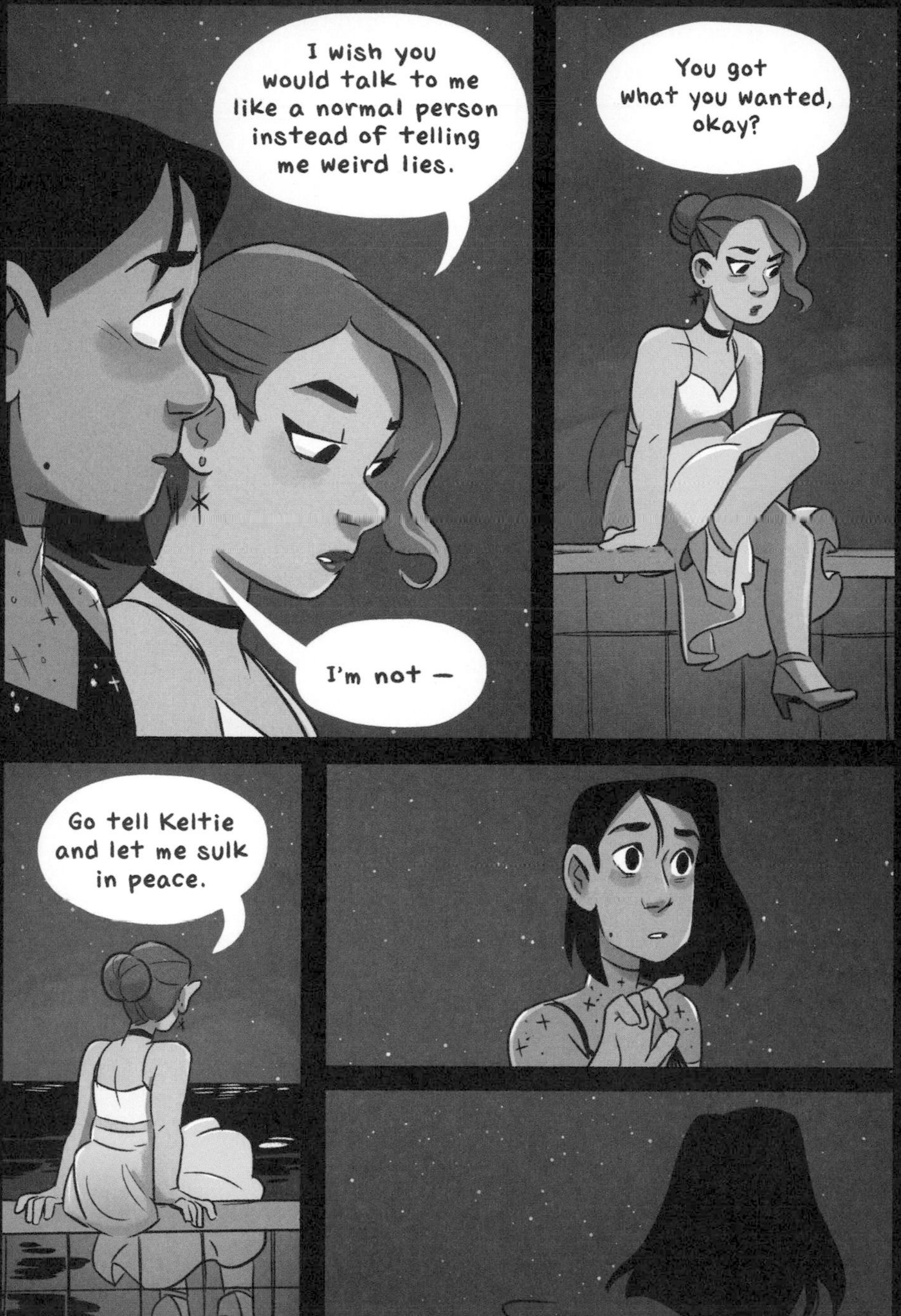
I wish you would talk to me like a normal person instead of telling me weird lies.
I'm not —
You got what you wanted, okay?
Go tell Keltie and let me sulk in peace.

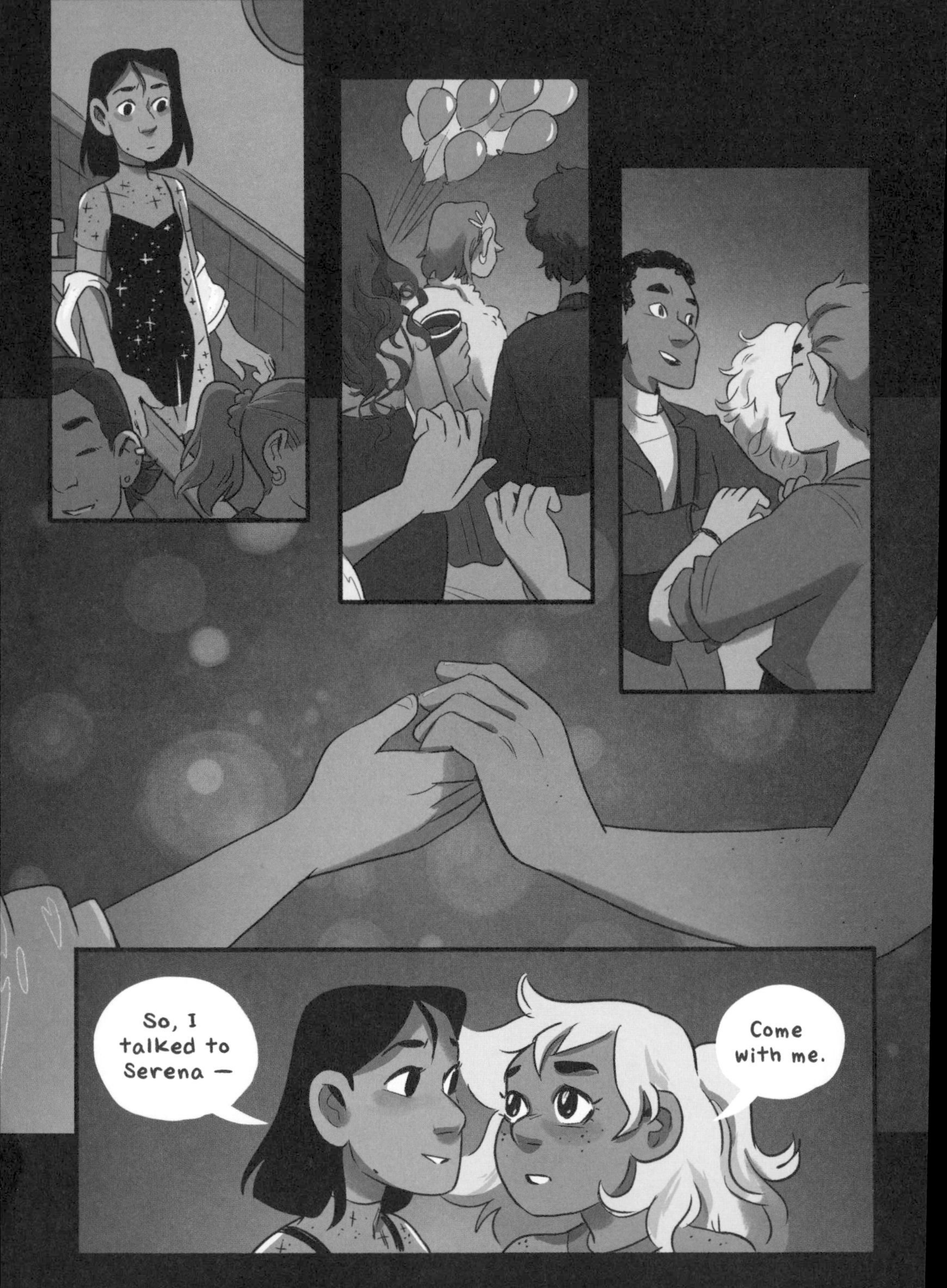
So, I talked to Serena —
Come with me.

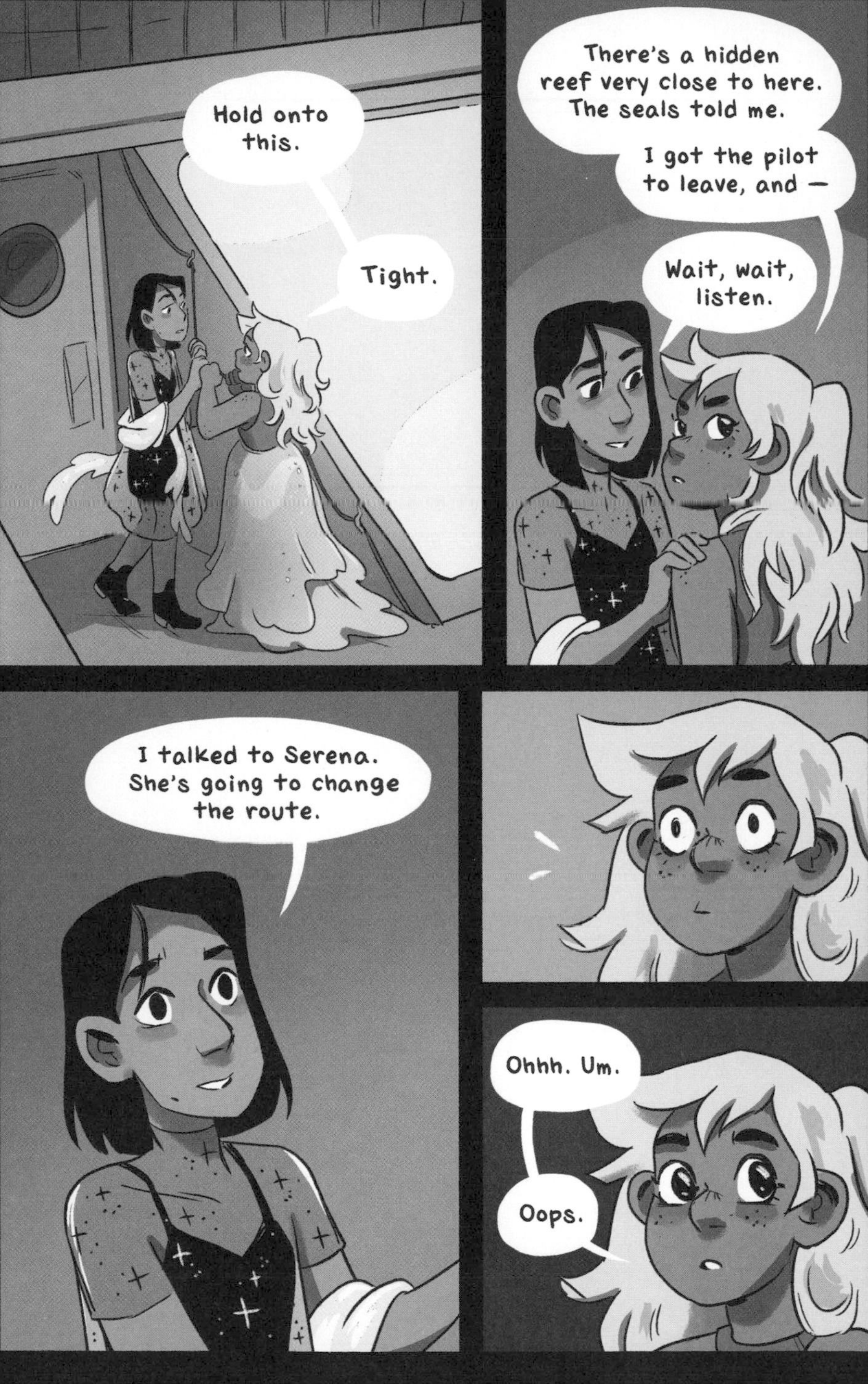
Hold onto this.
Tight.
There's a hidden reef very close to here. The seals told me.
I got the pilot to leave, and —
Wait, wait, listen.
I talked to Serena. She's going to change the route.
Ohhh. Um.
Oops.

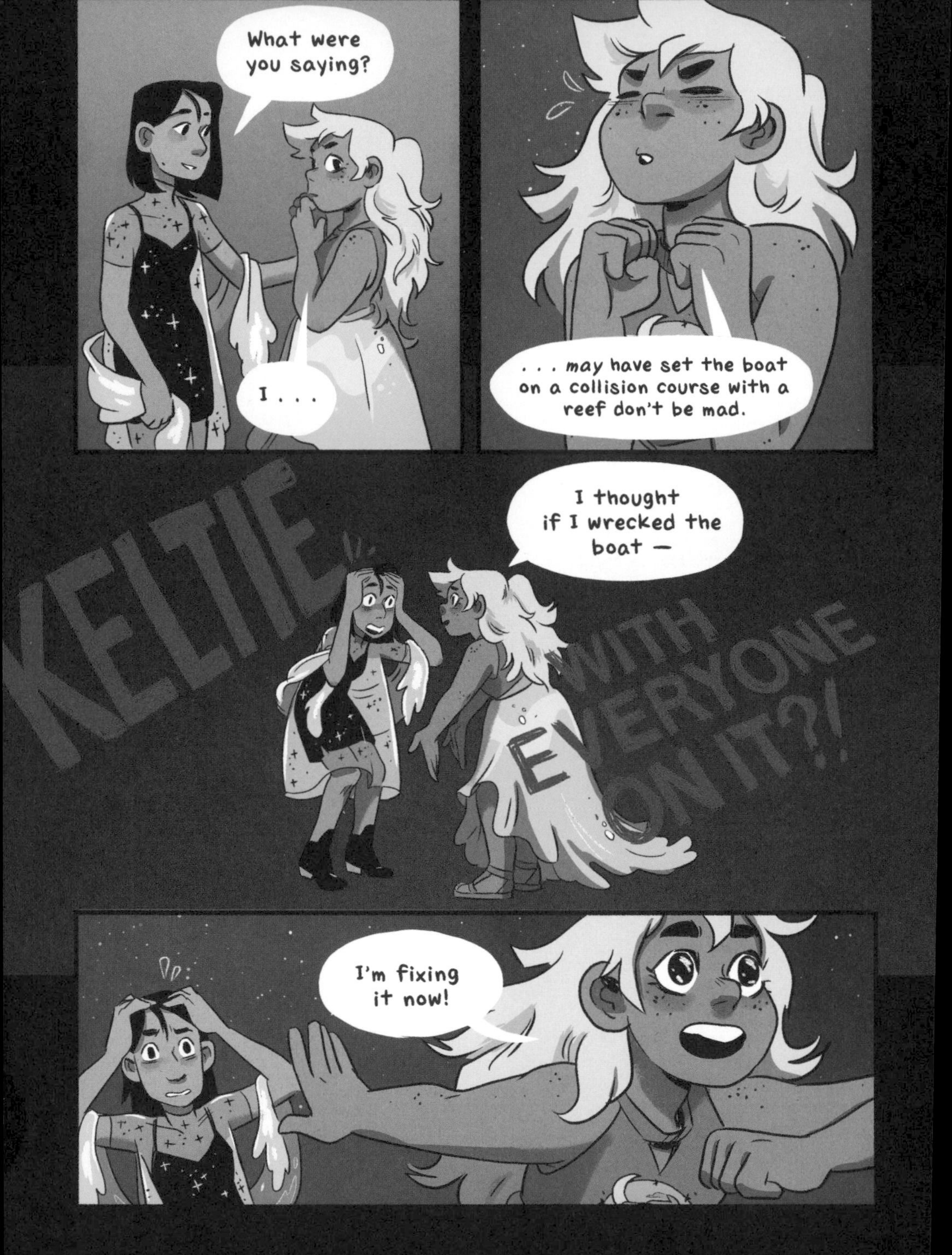
What were you saying?
I . . .
. . . may have set the boat on a collision course with a reef don't be mad.
KELTIE
I thought if I wrecked the boat —
WITH EVERYONE ON IT?!
I'm fixing it now!

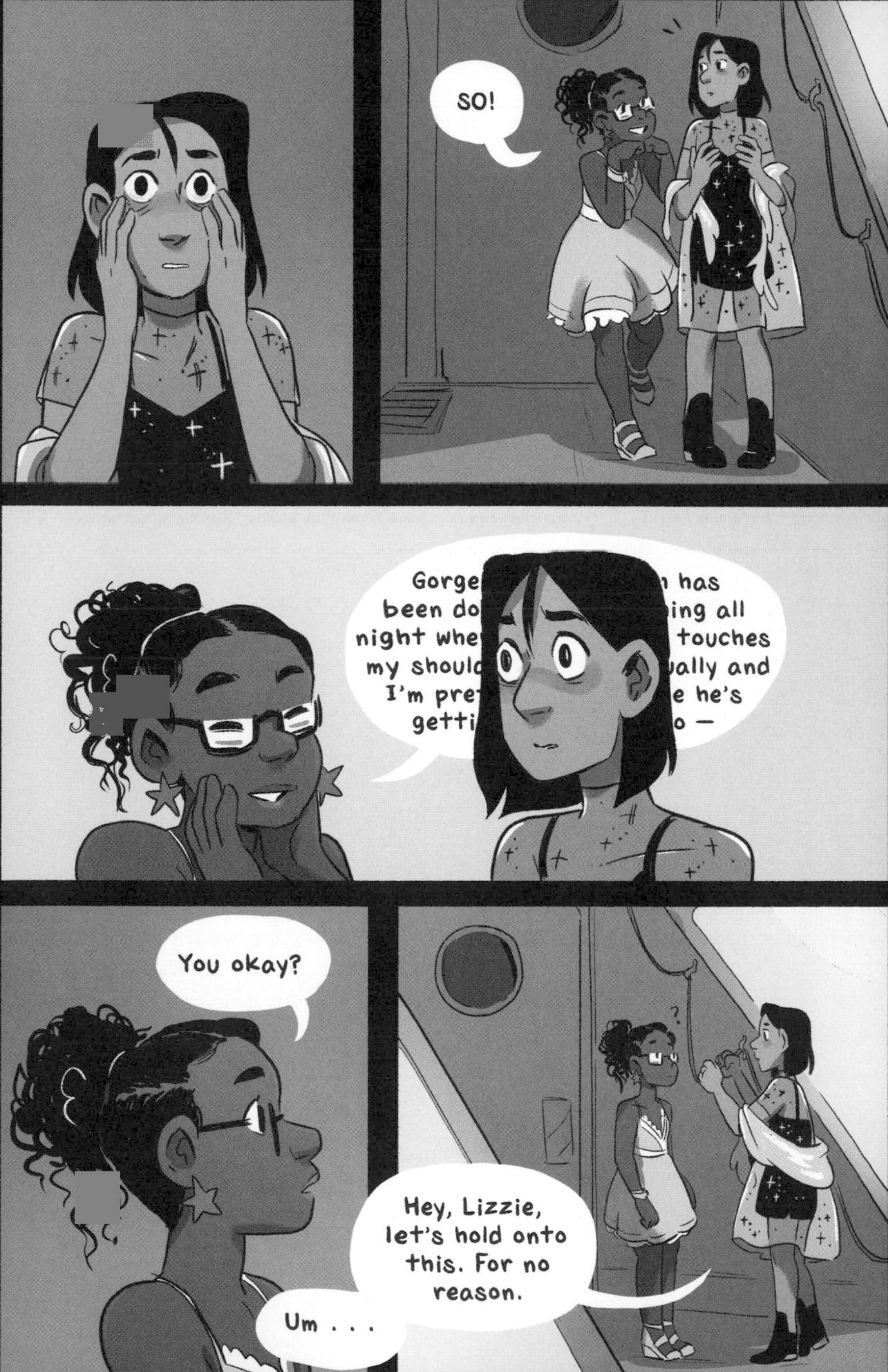
SO!
Gorge has
been do ing all
night whe touches
my should ually and
I'm pre e he's
getti o —
You okay?
Hey, Lizzie, let's hold onto this. For no reason.
Um . . .

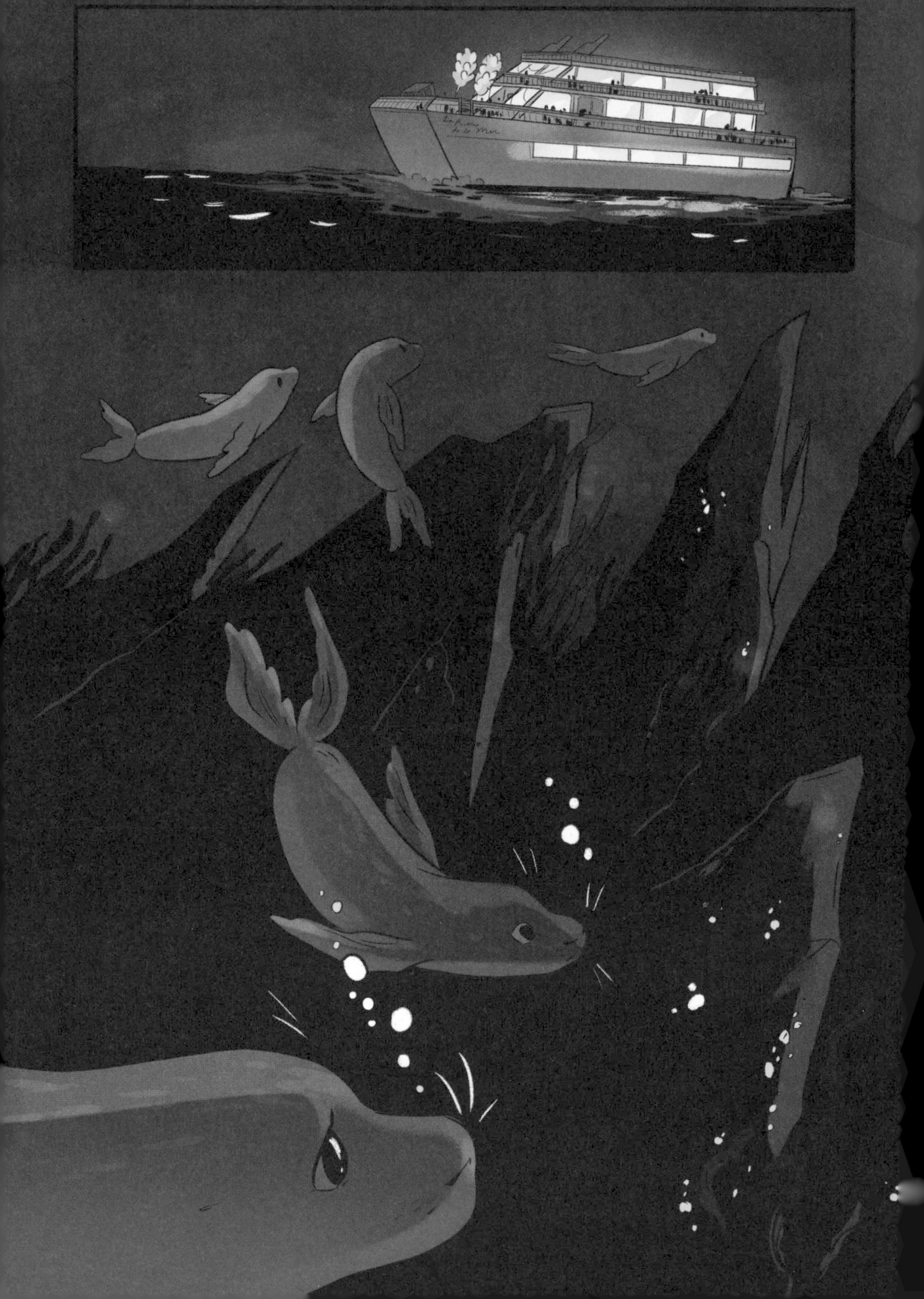

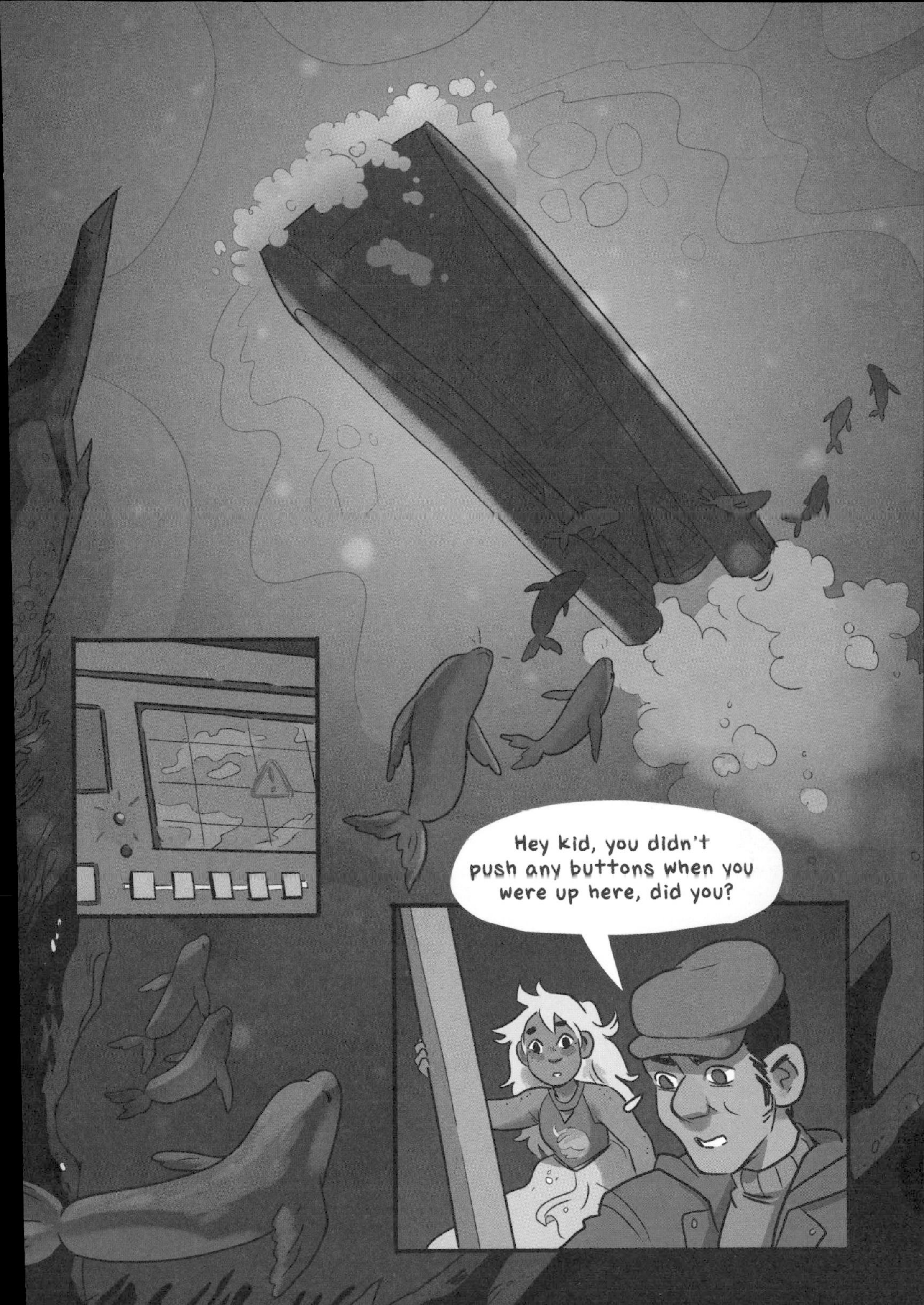
Hey kid, you didn't push any buttons when you were up here, did you?

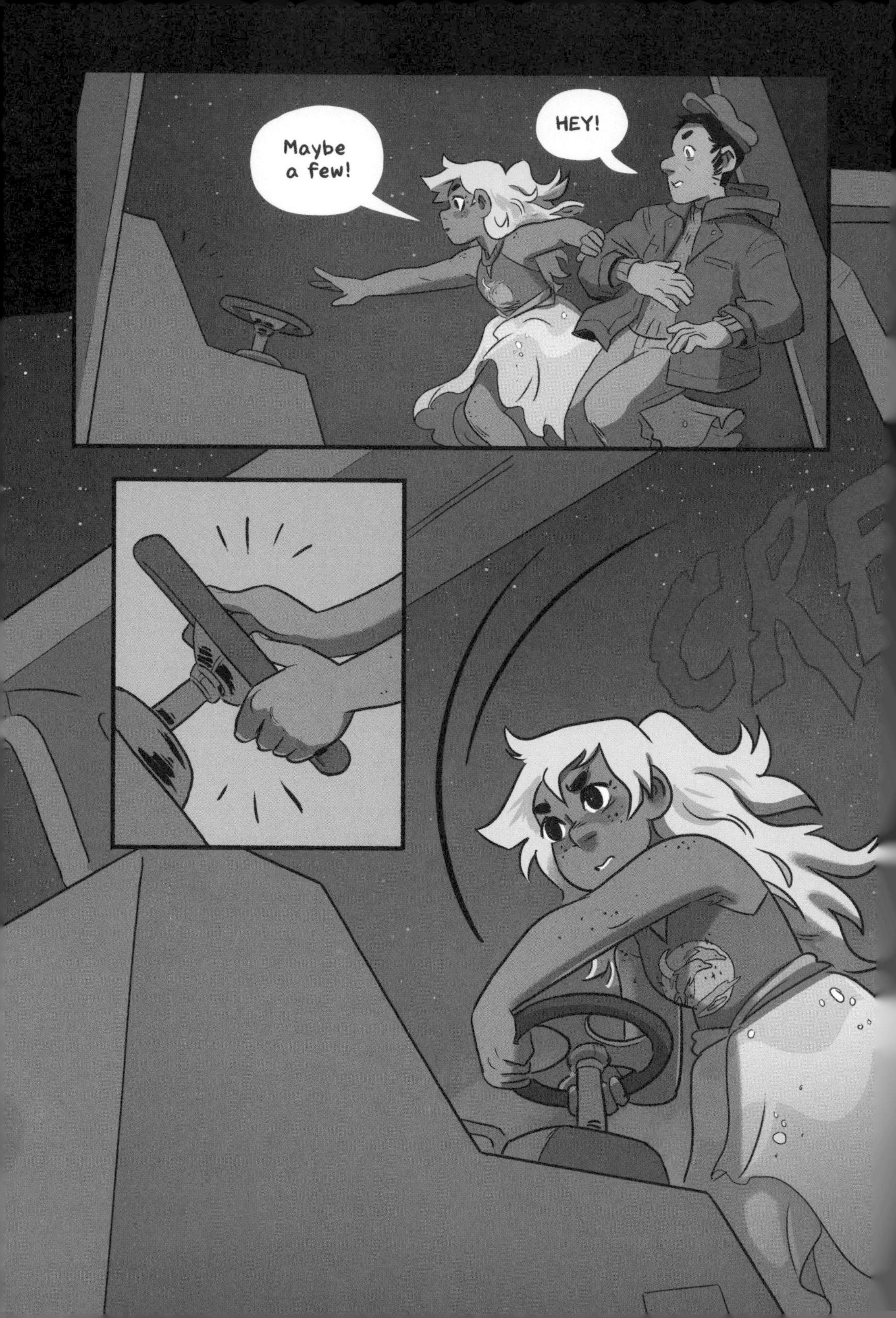
Maybe a few!
HEY!

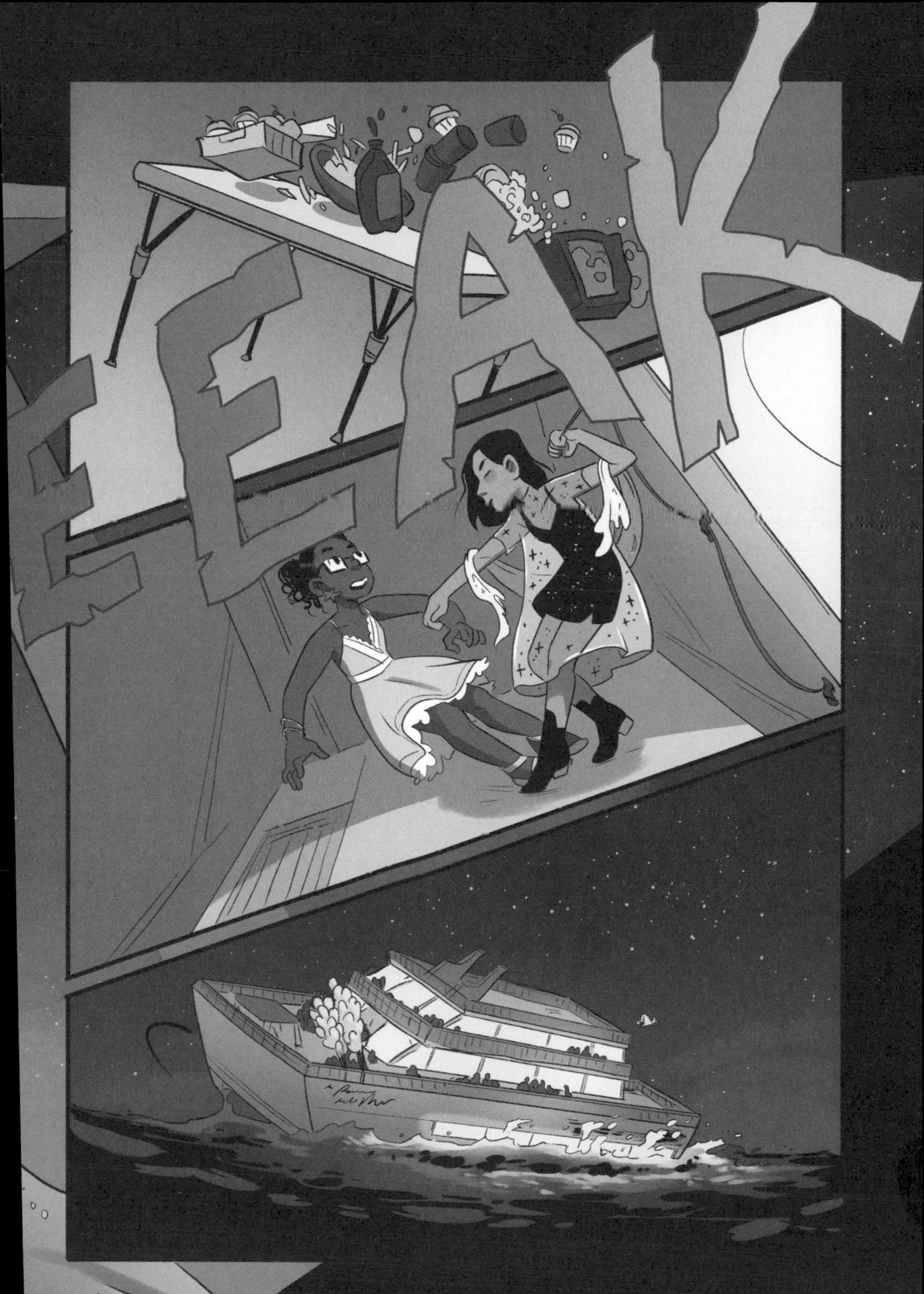
EEAK

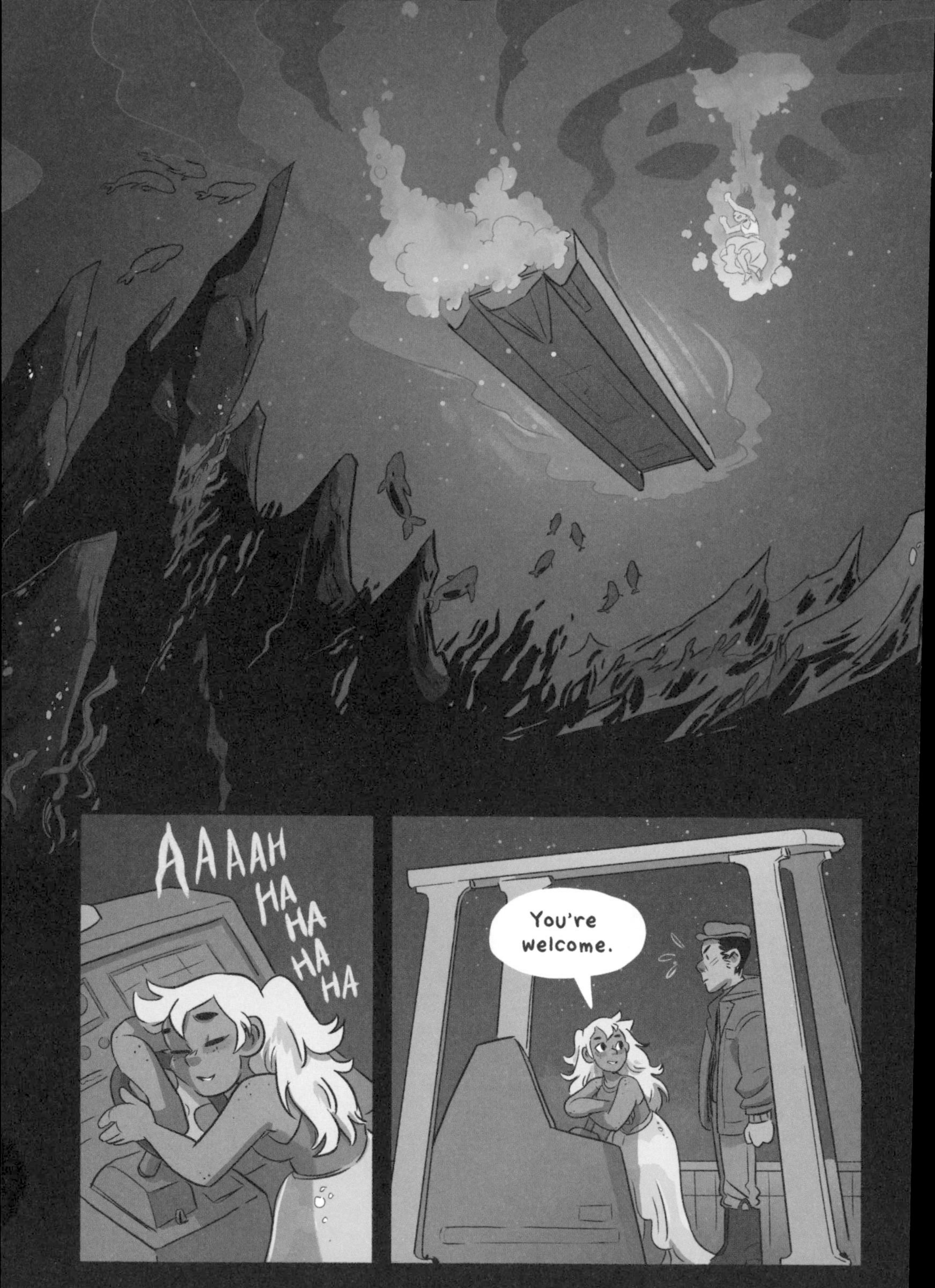
AAAAH
HA
HA
HA
HA
You're welcome.

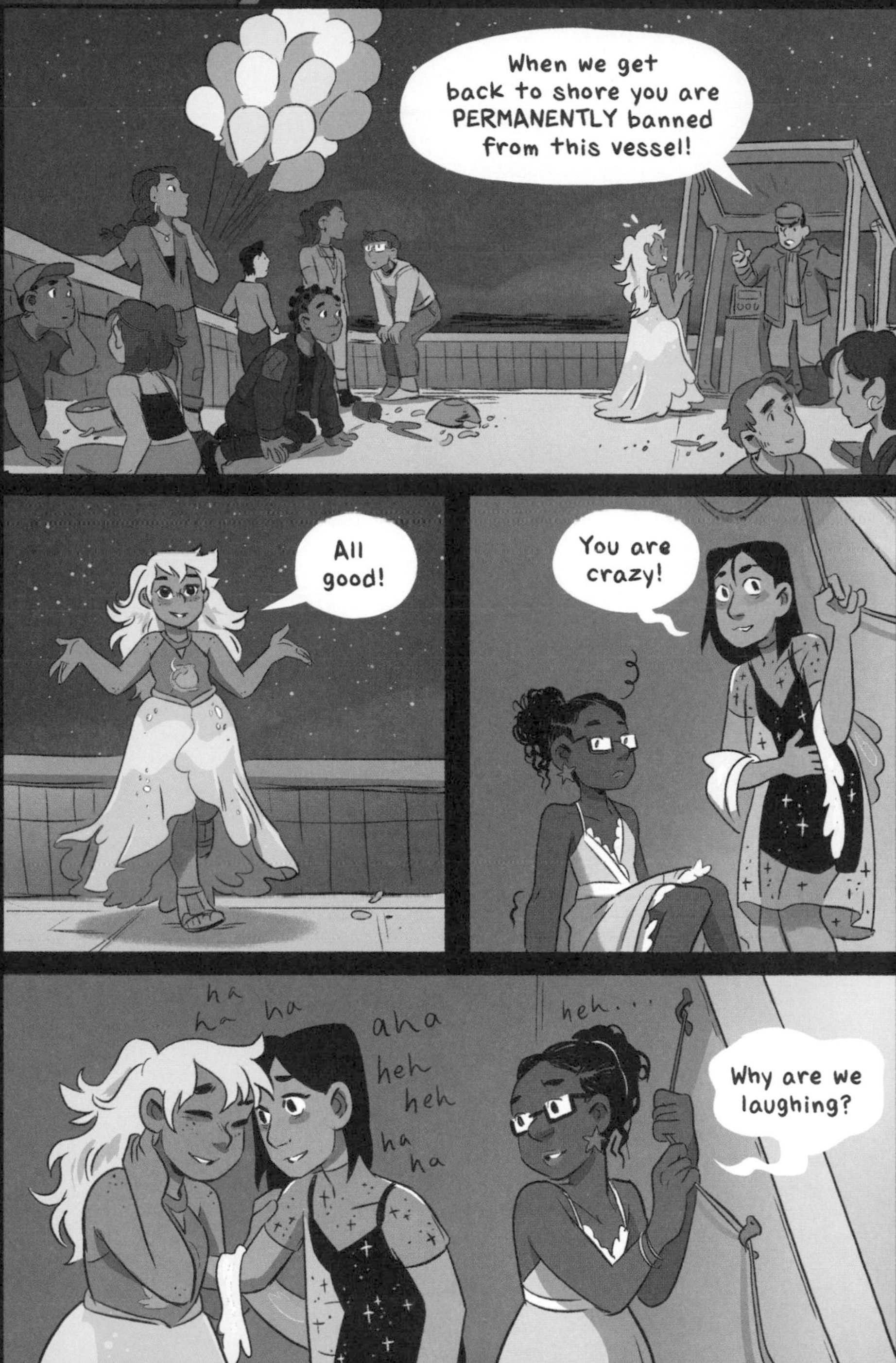
When we get back to shore you are PERMANENTLY banned from this vessel!
All good!
You are crazy!
ha ha ha
aha heh heh ha ha
heh...
Why are we laughing?

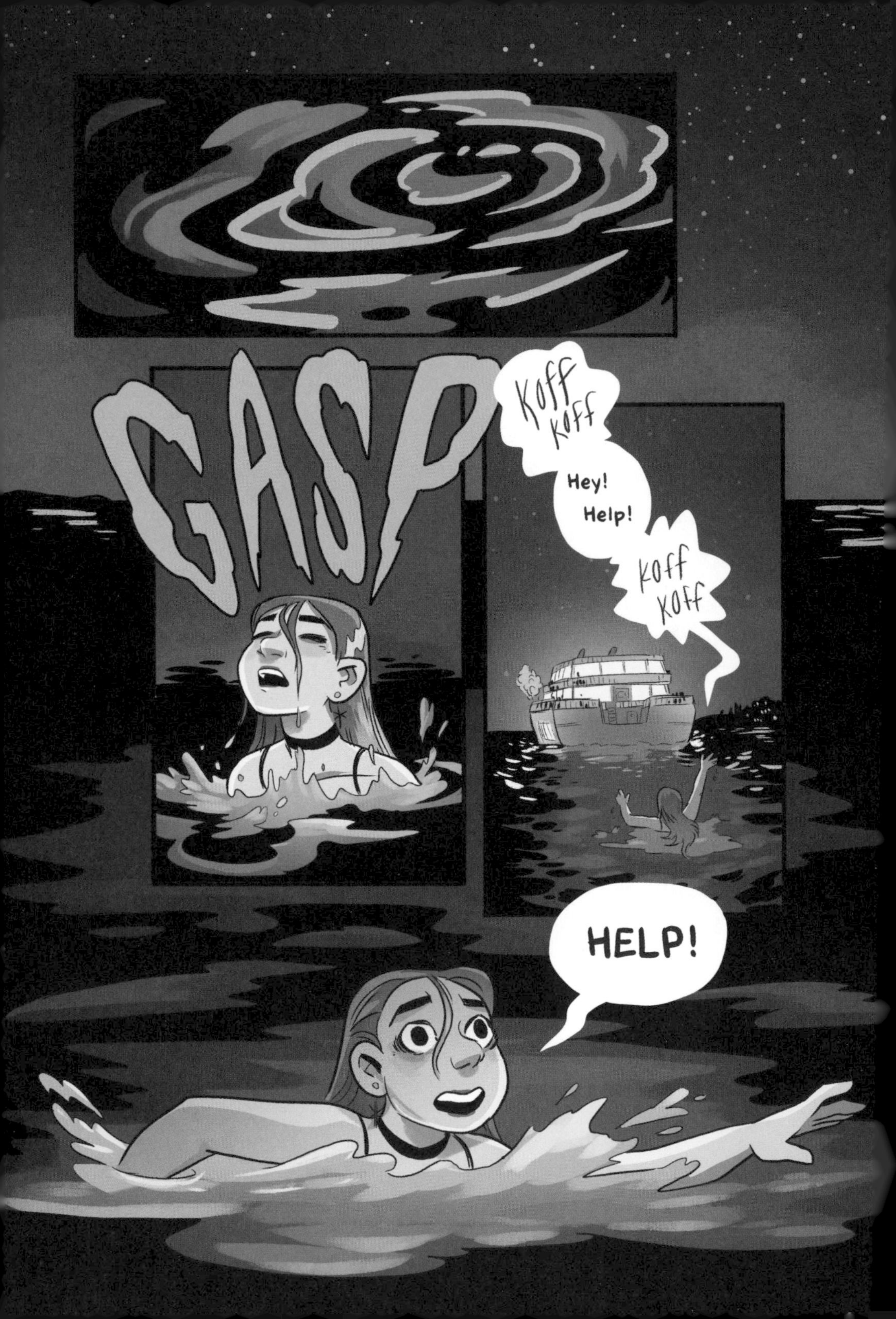
GASP
KOFF KOFF
Hey! Help!
KOFF KOFF
HELP!

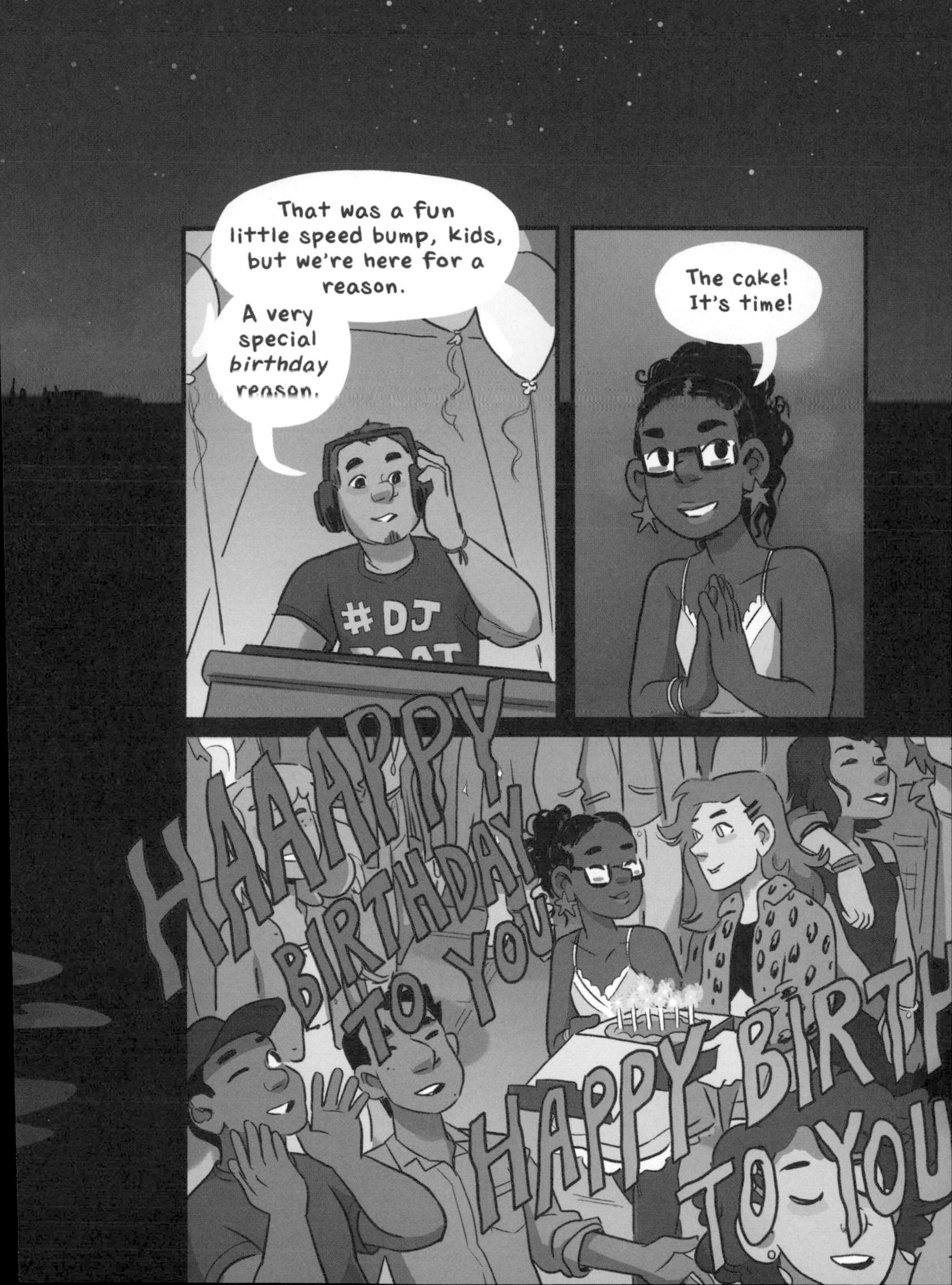
That was a fun little speed bump, kids, but we're here for a reason.
A very special *birthday* reason.
The cake! It's time!
#DJ
HAAAPPY BIRTHDAY TO YOU
HAPPY BIRTH
TO YOU

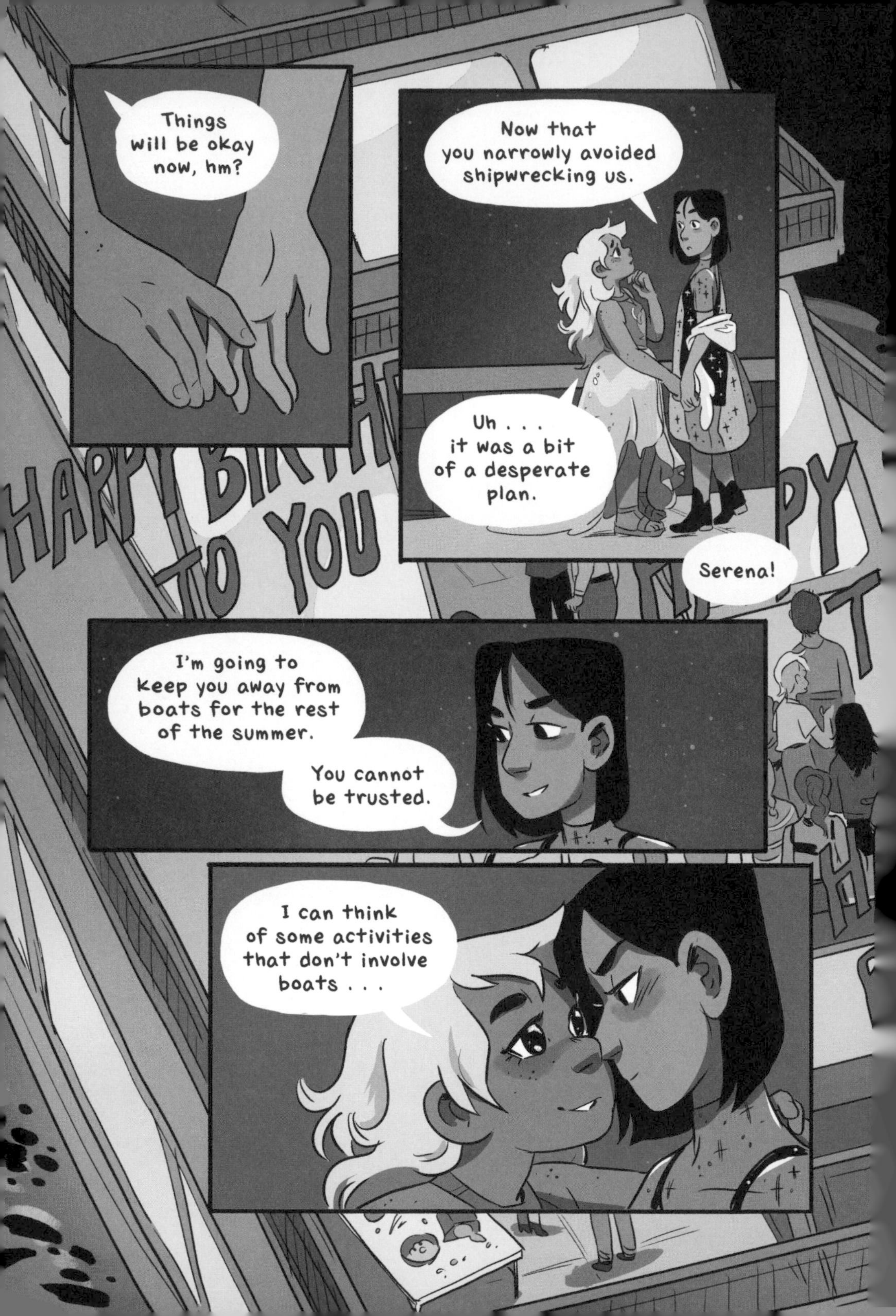
Things will be okay now, hm?
Now that you narrowly avoided shipwrecking us.
Uh . . . it was a bit of a desperate plan.
HAPPY BIRTHDAY TO YOU
Serena!
I'm going to keep you away from boats for the rest of the summer.
You cannot be trusted.
I can think of some activities that don't involve boats . . .

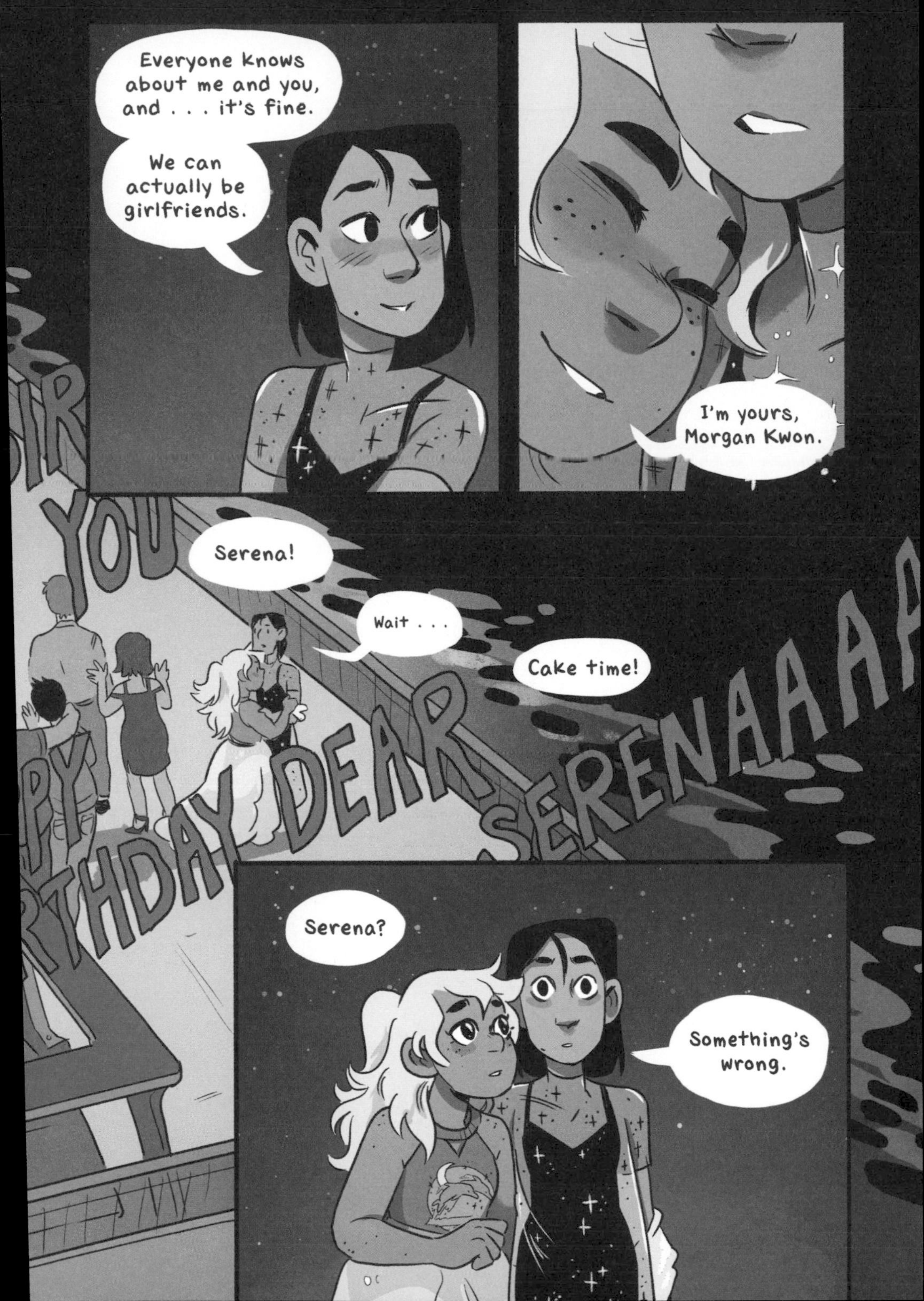
Everyone knows about me and you, and . . . it's fine.
We can actually be girlfriends.
I'm yours, Morgan Kwon.
YOU
Serena!
Wait . . .
Cake time!
DEAR
SERENAAAA
THDAY
Serena?
Something's wrong.

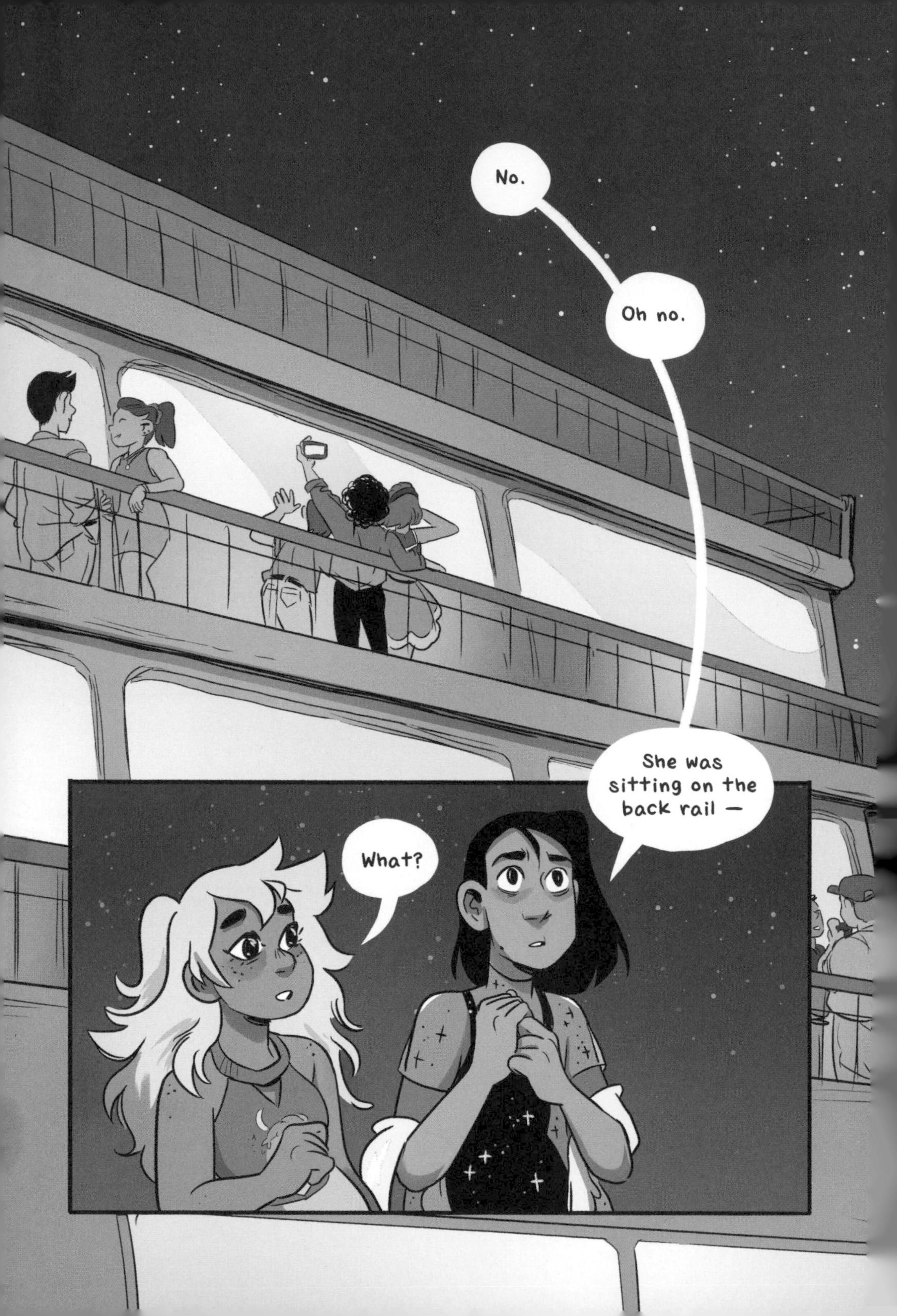
No.
Oh no.
She was sitting on the back rail —
What?

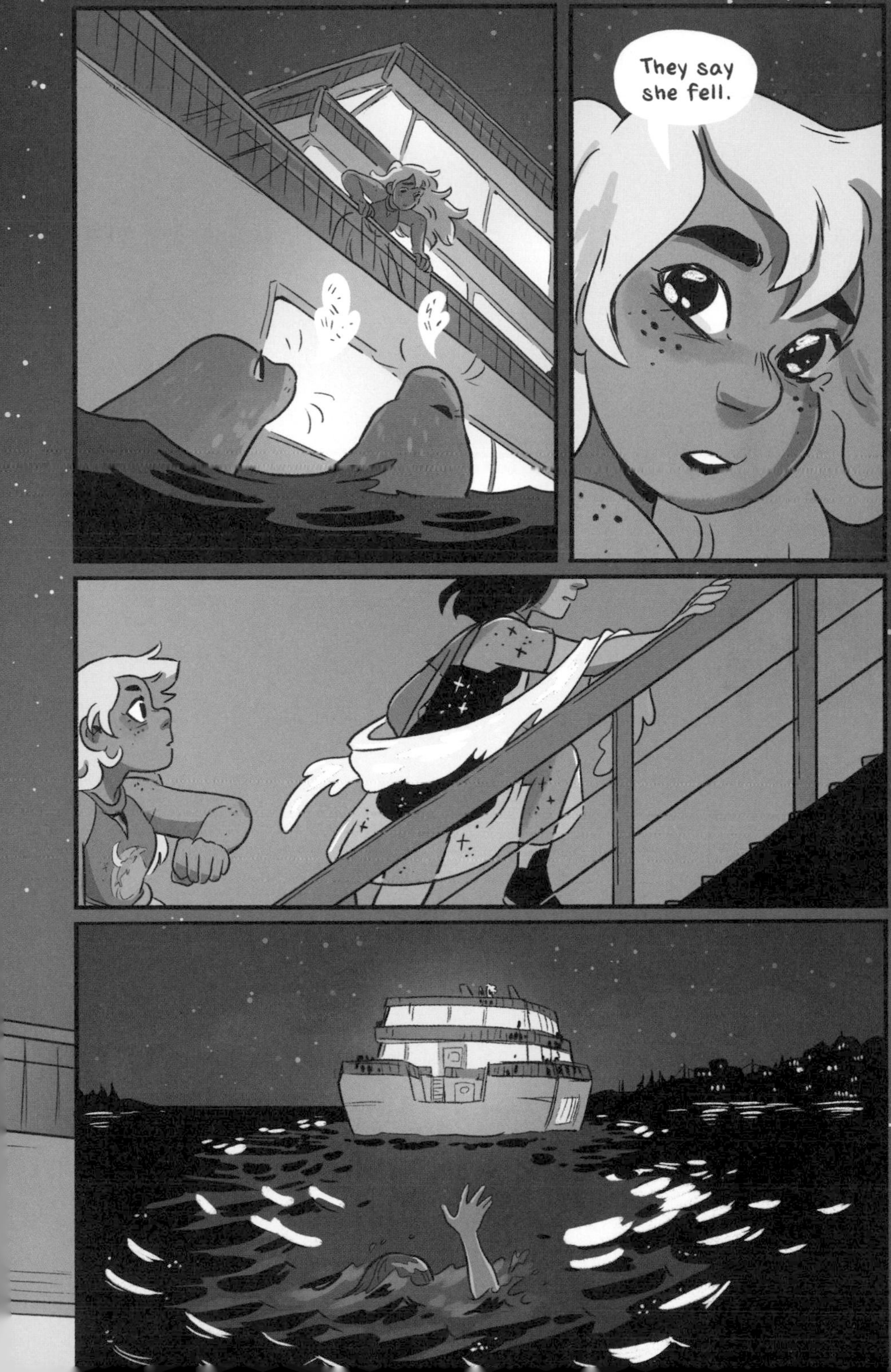
They say she fell.

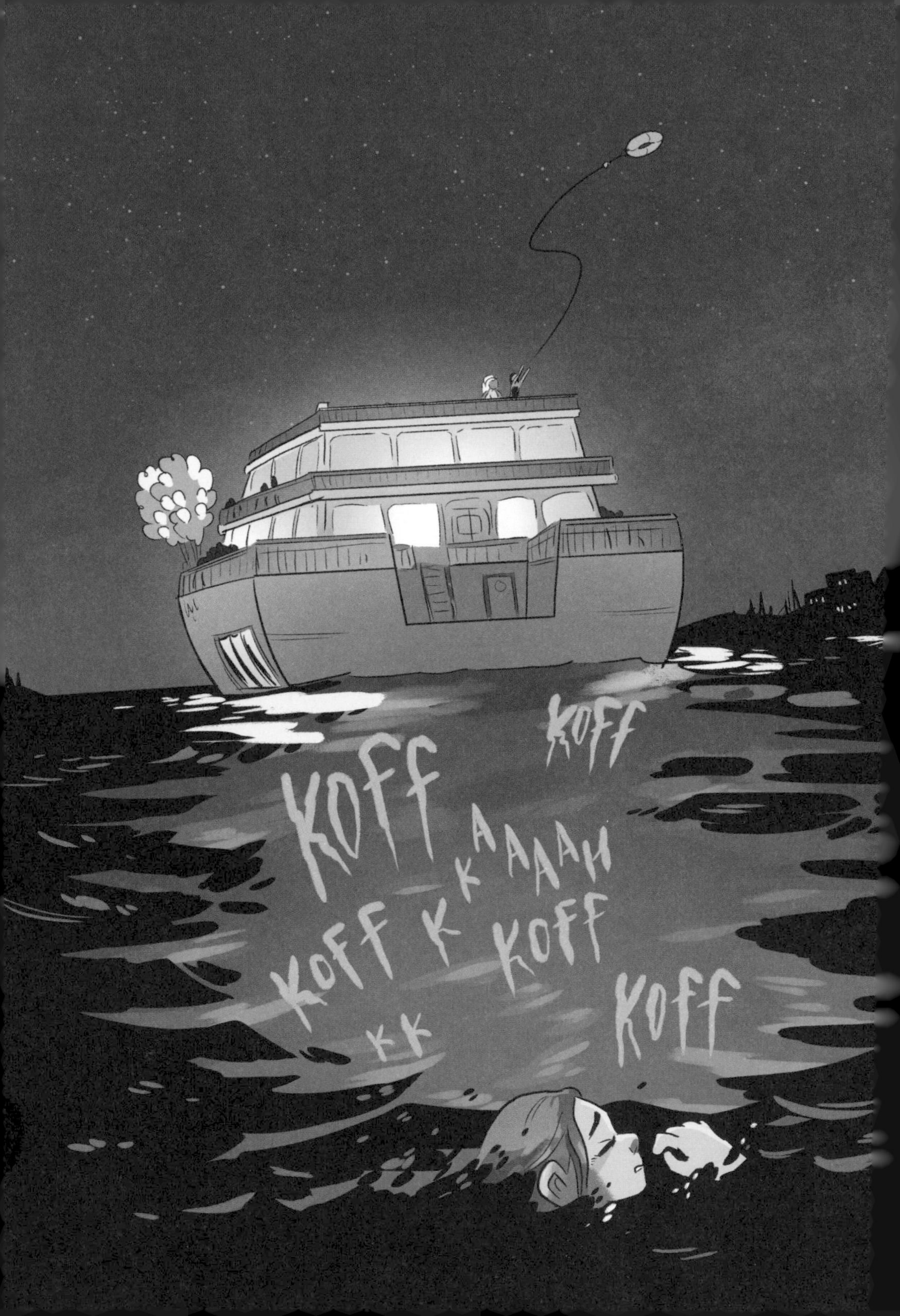
KOFF
KOFF
AAAAH
KOFF K K KOFF
KK
KOFF

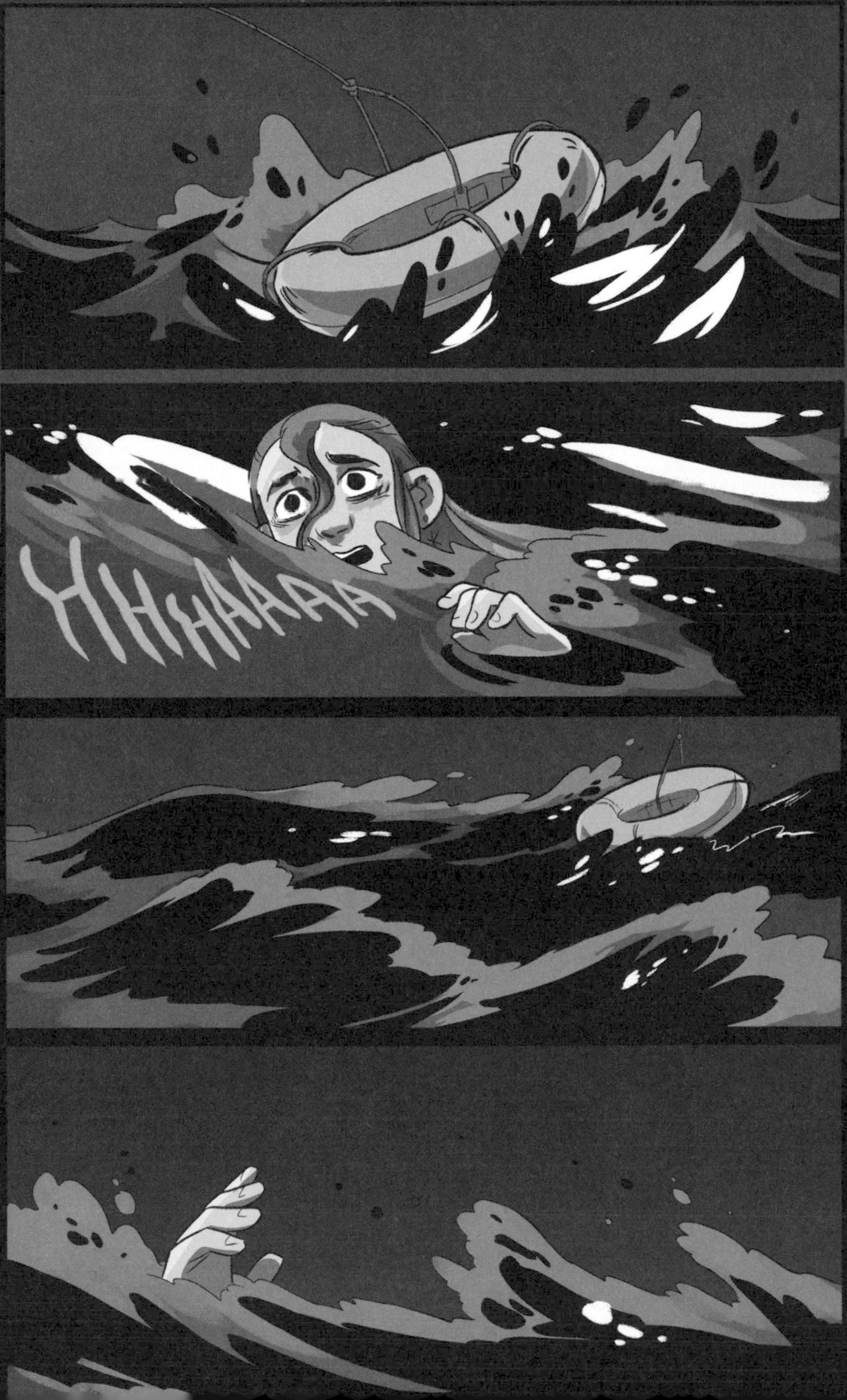
HHAAAAA

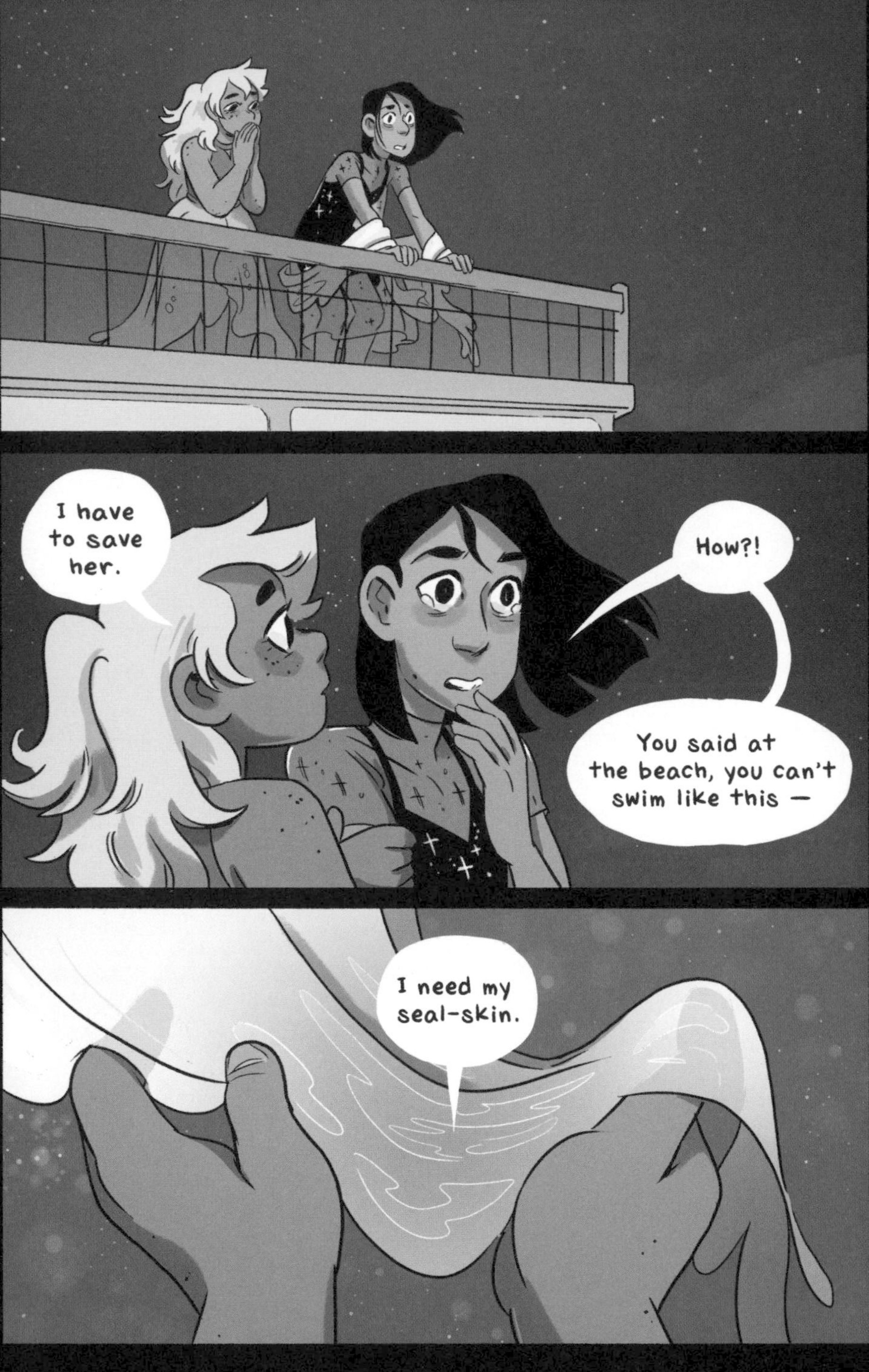
I have to save her.
How?!
You said at the beach, you can't swim like this —
I need my seal-skin.

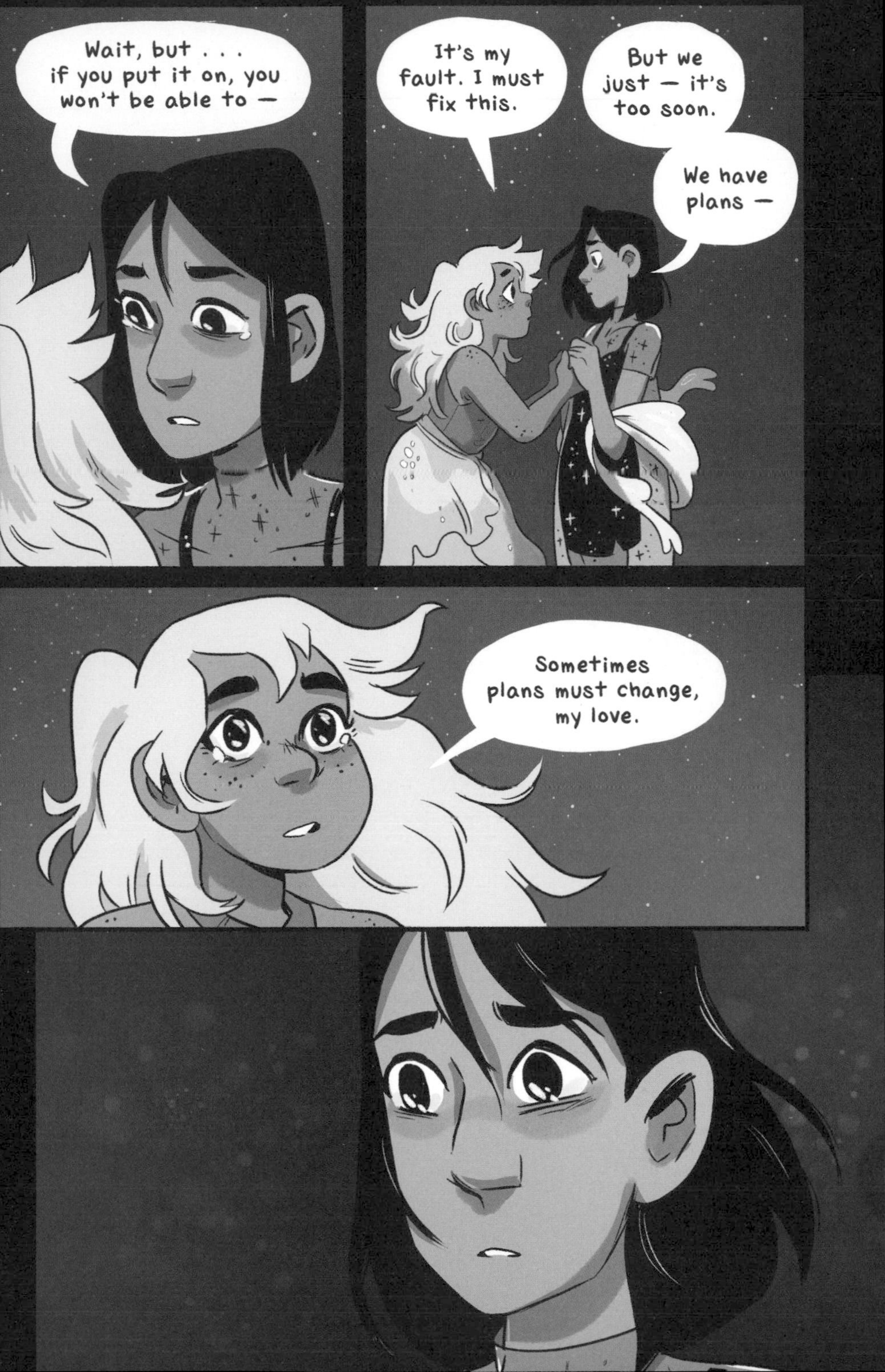
Wait, but . . . if you put it on, you won't be able to —
It's my fault. I must fix this.
But we just — it's too soon.
We have plans —
Sometimes plans must change, my love.

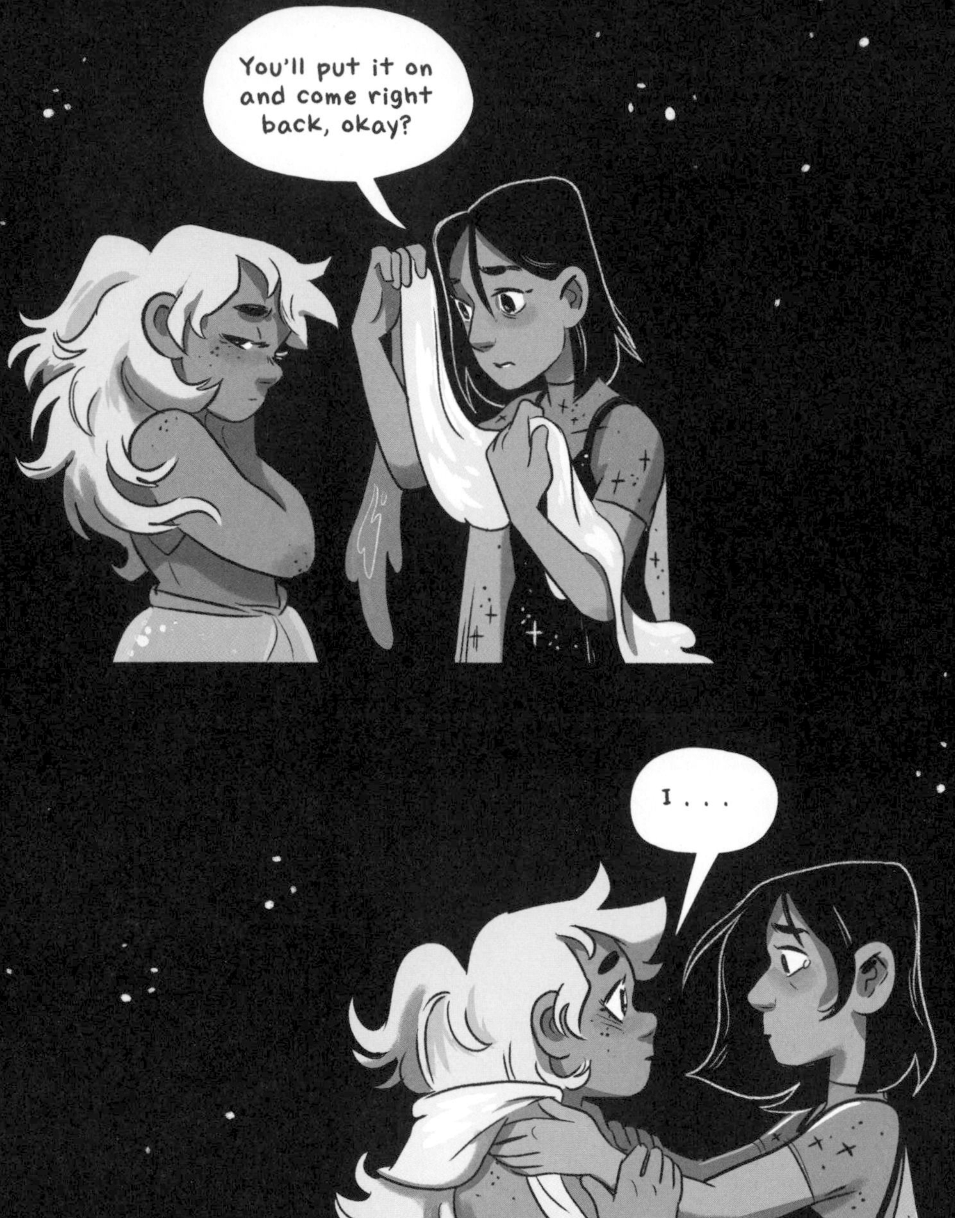
You'll put it on and come right back, okay?
I . . .

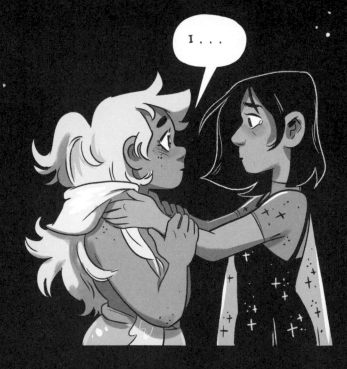

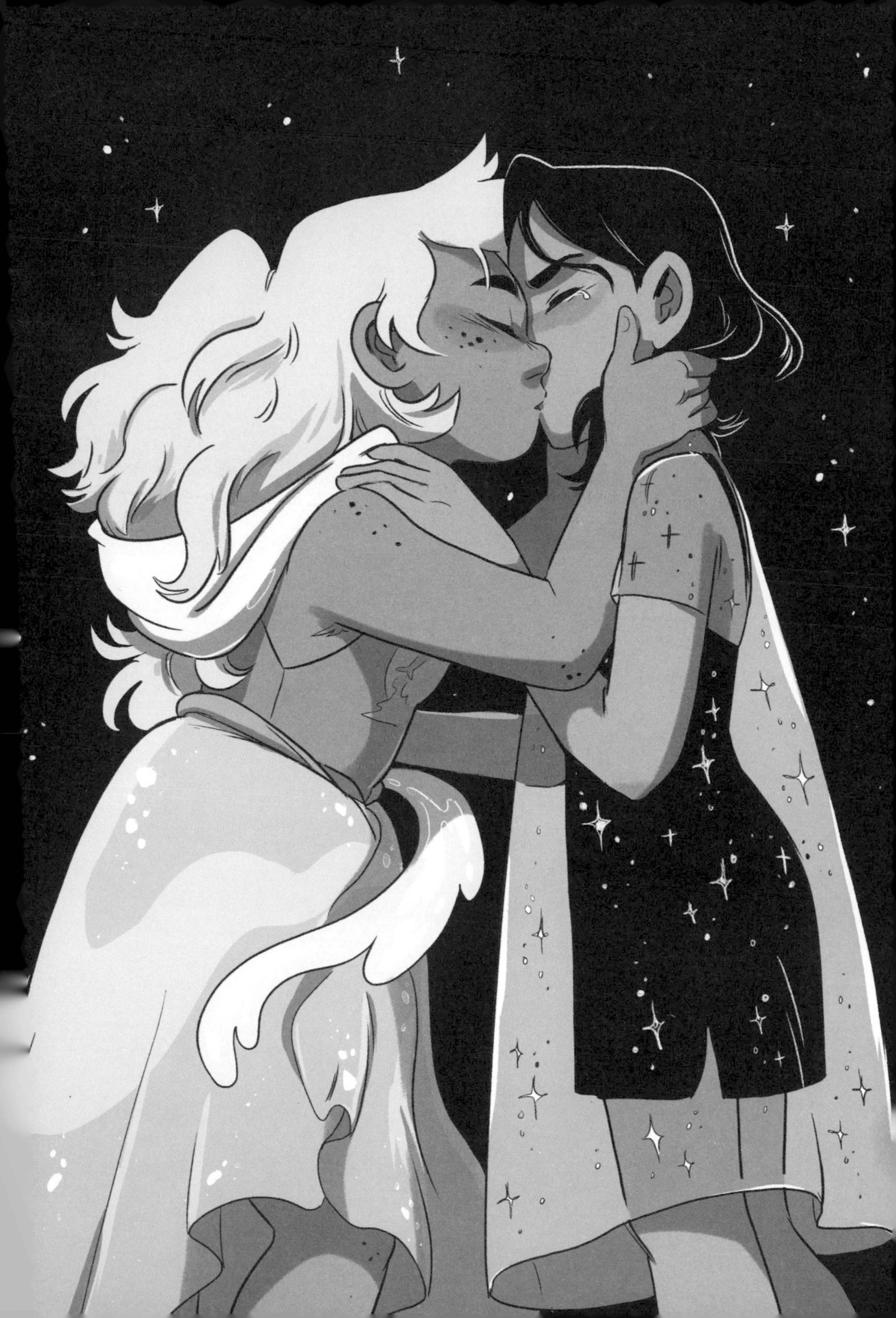

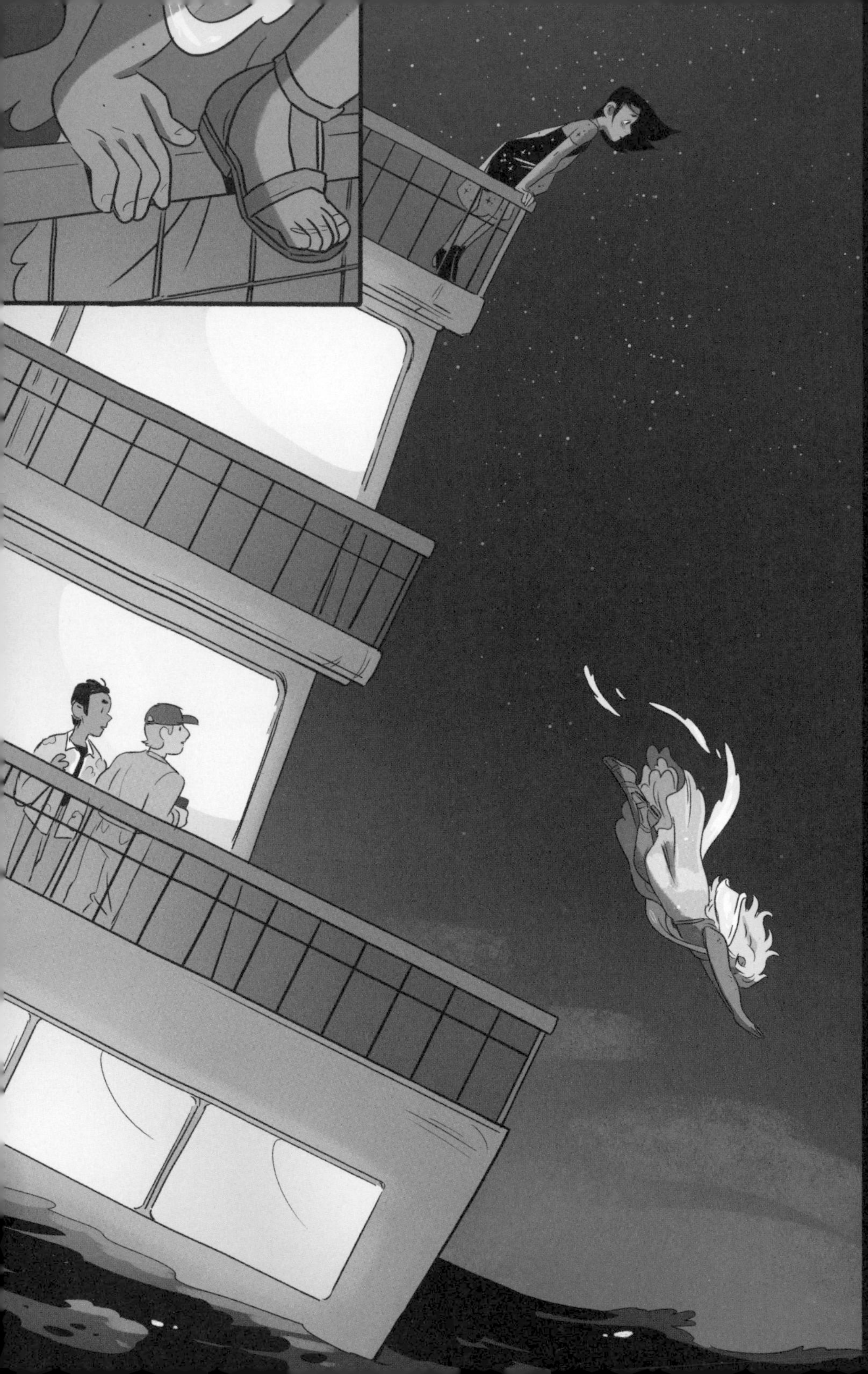

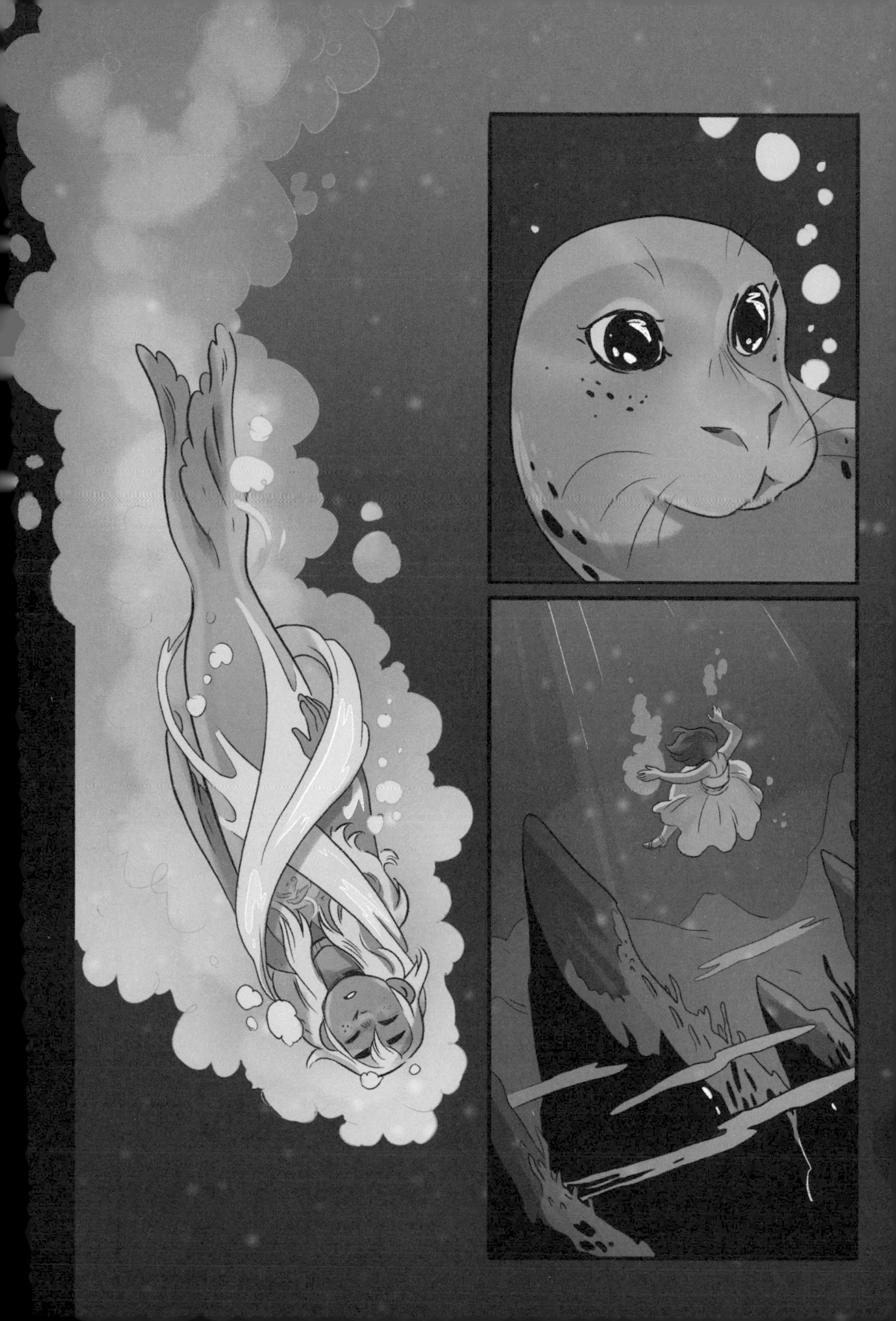

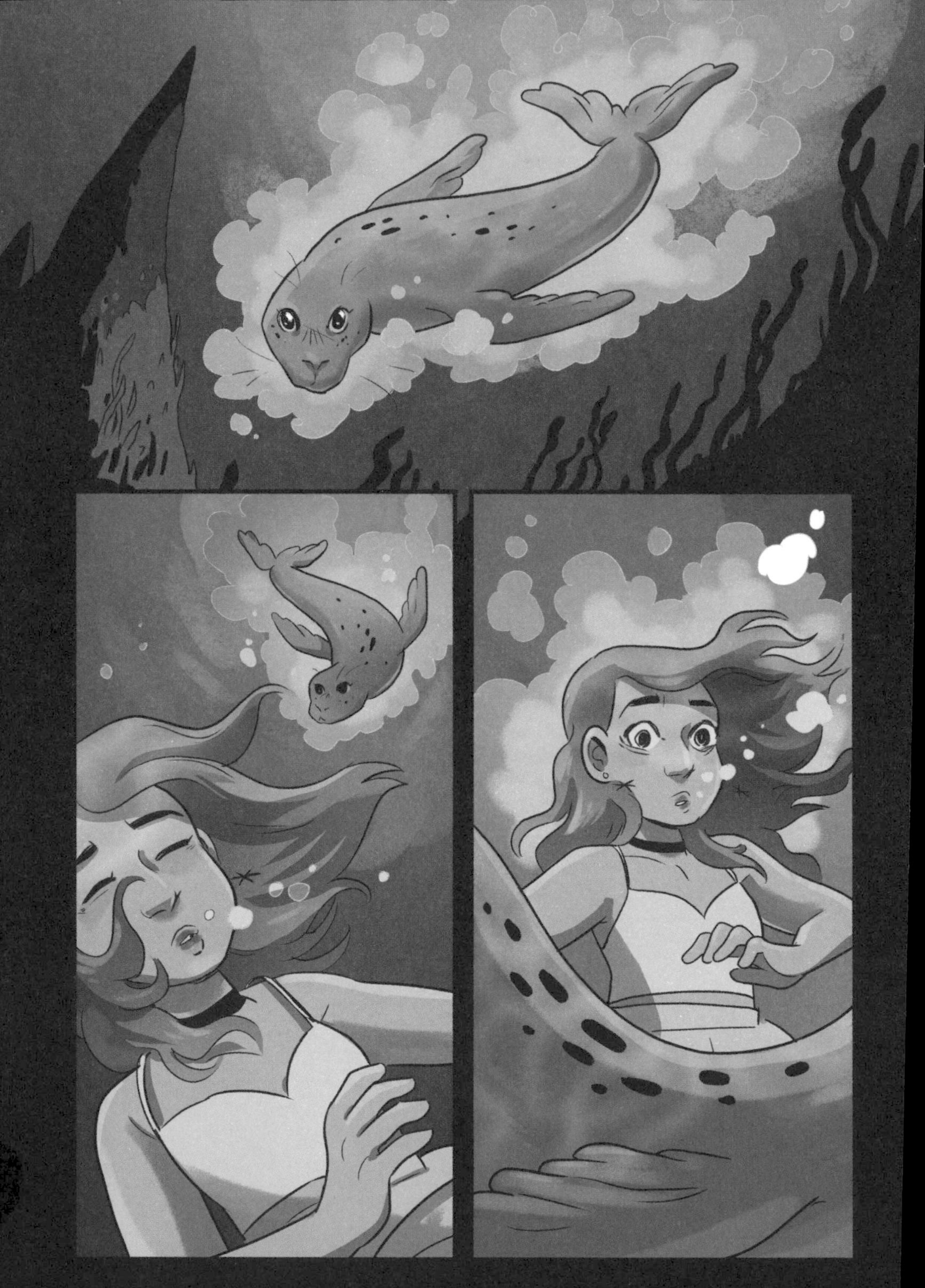

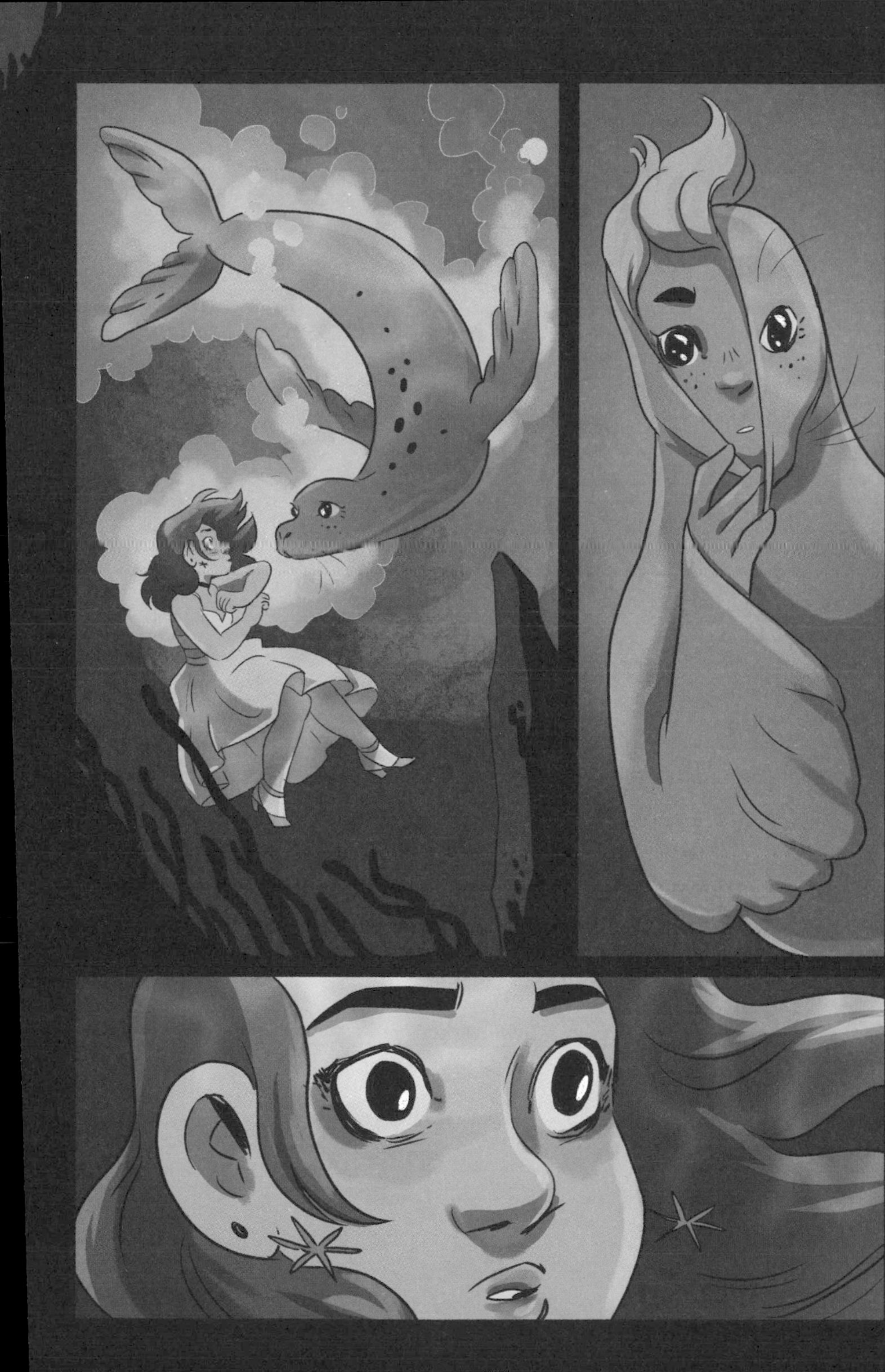

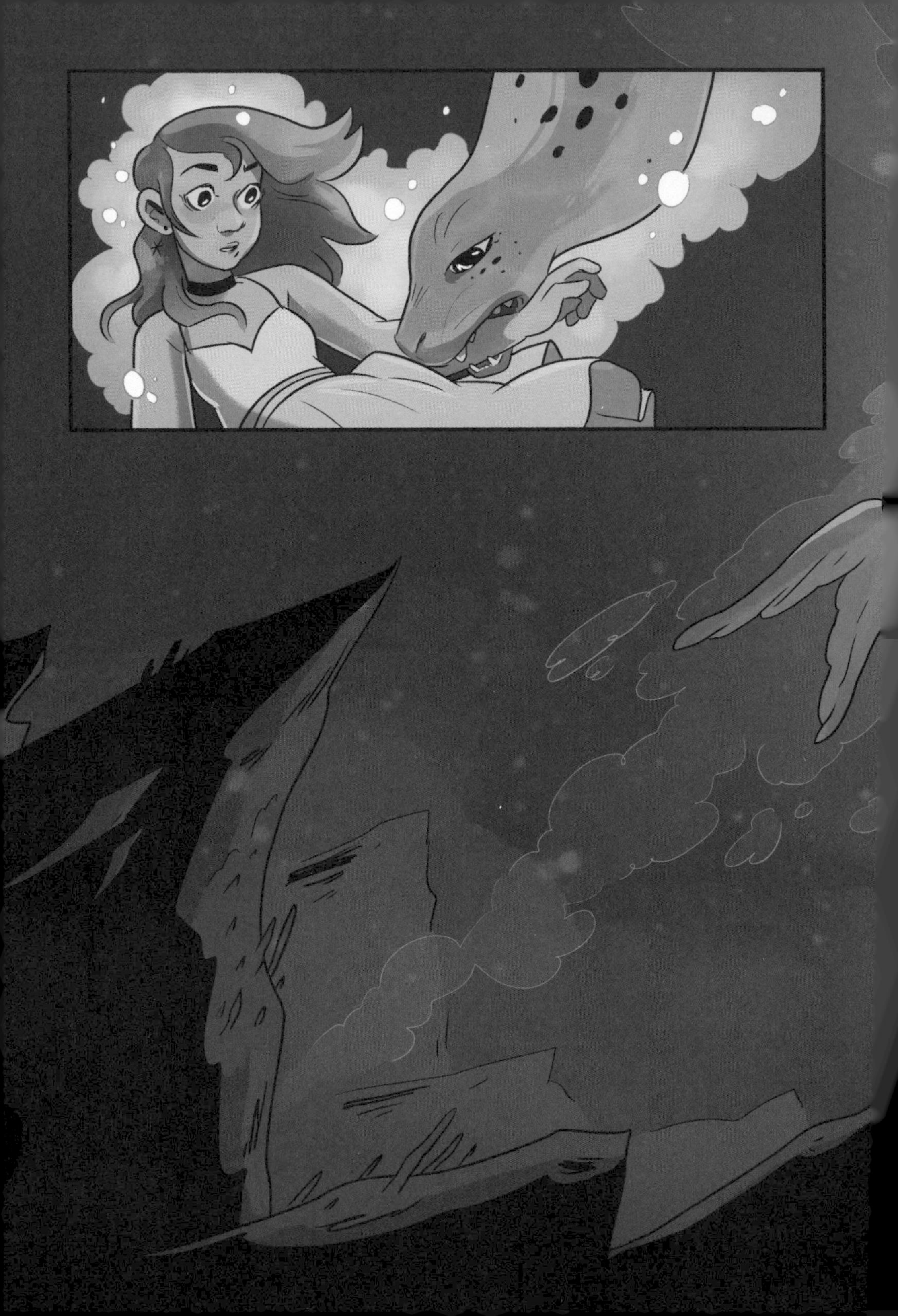

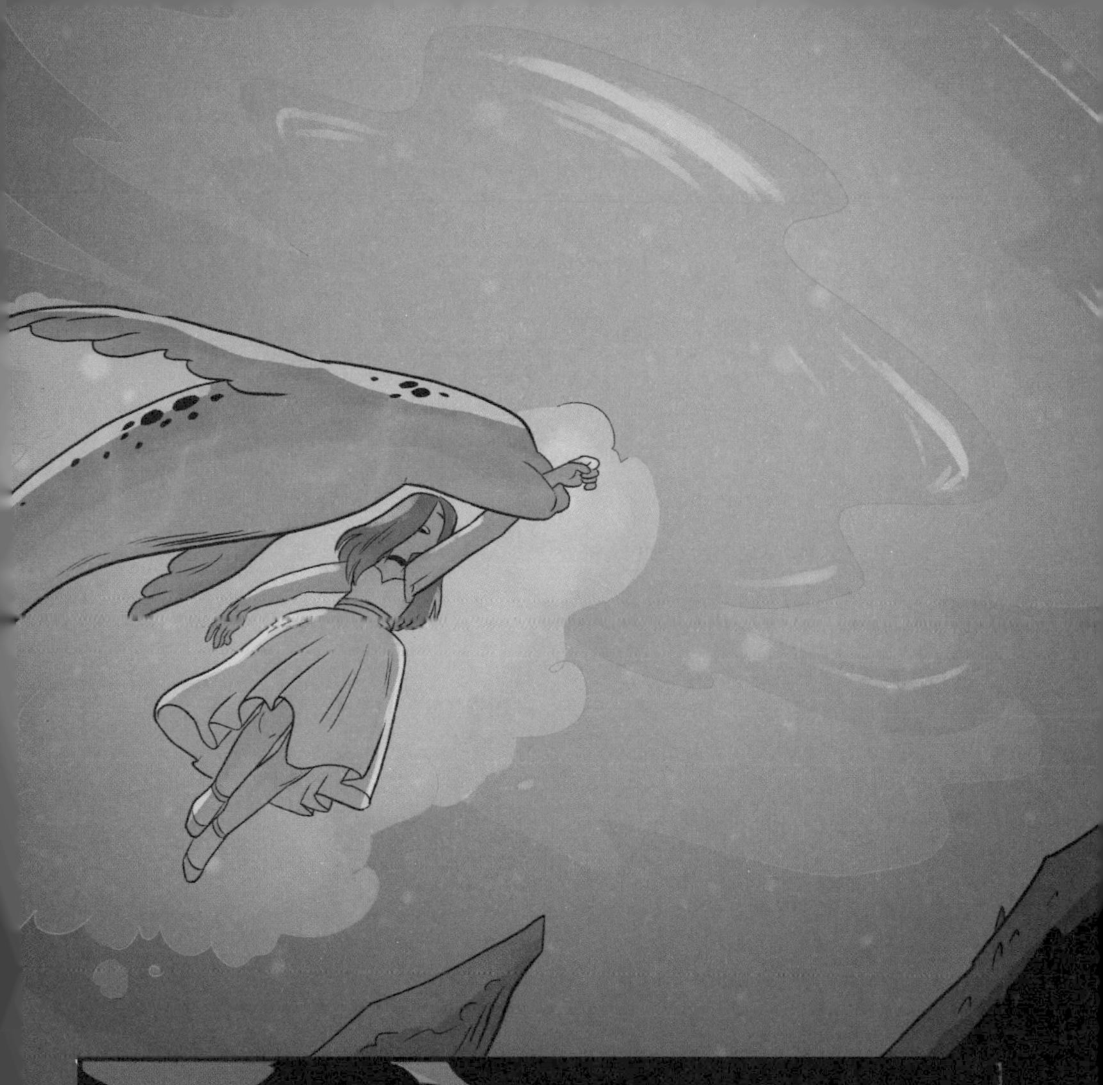
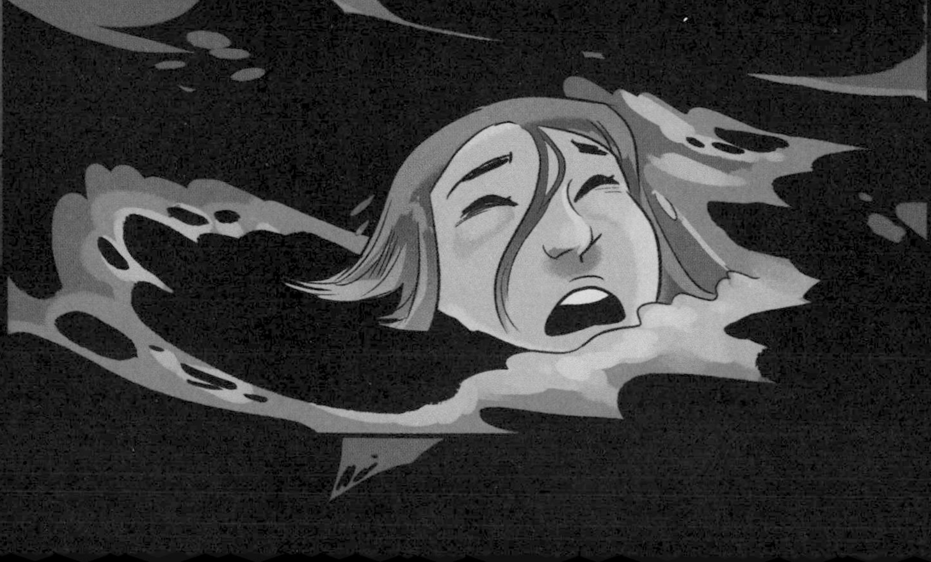

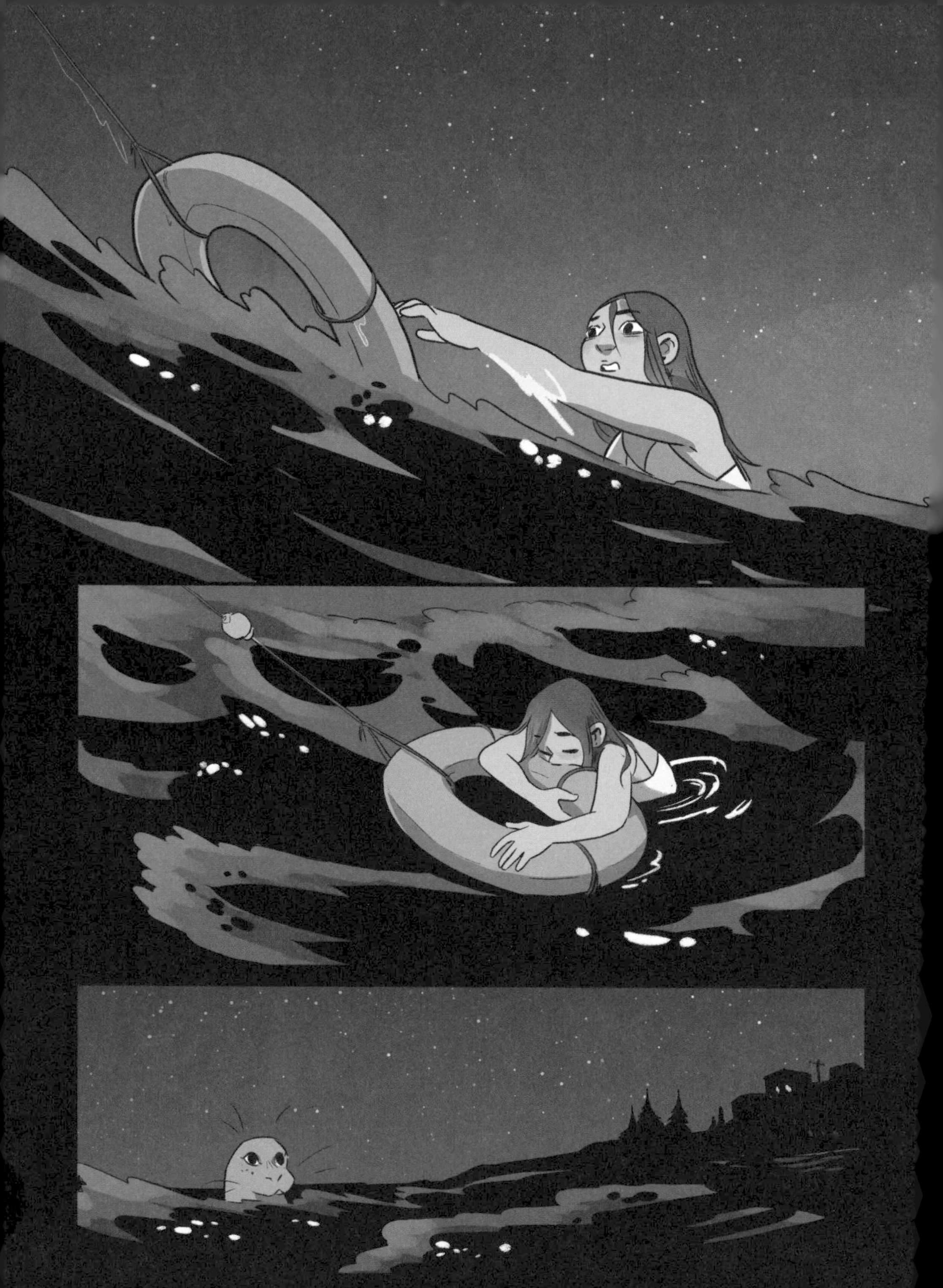

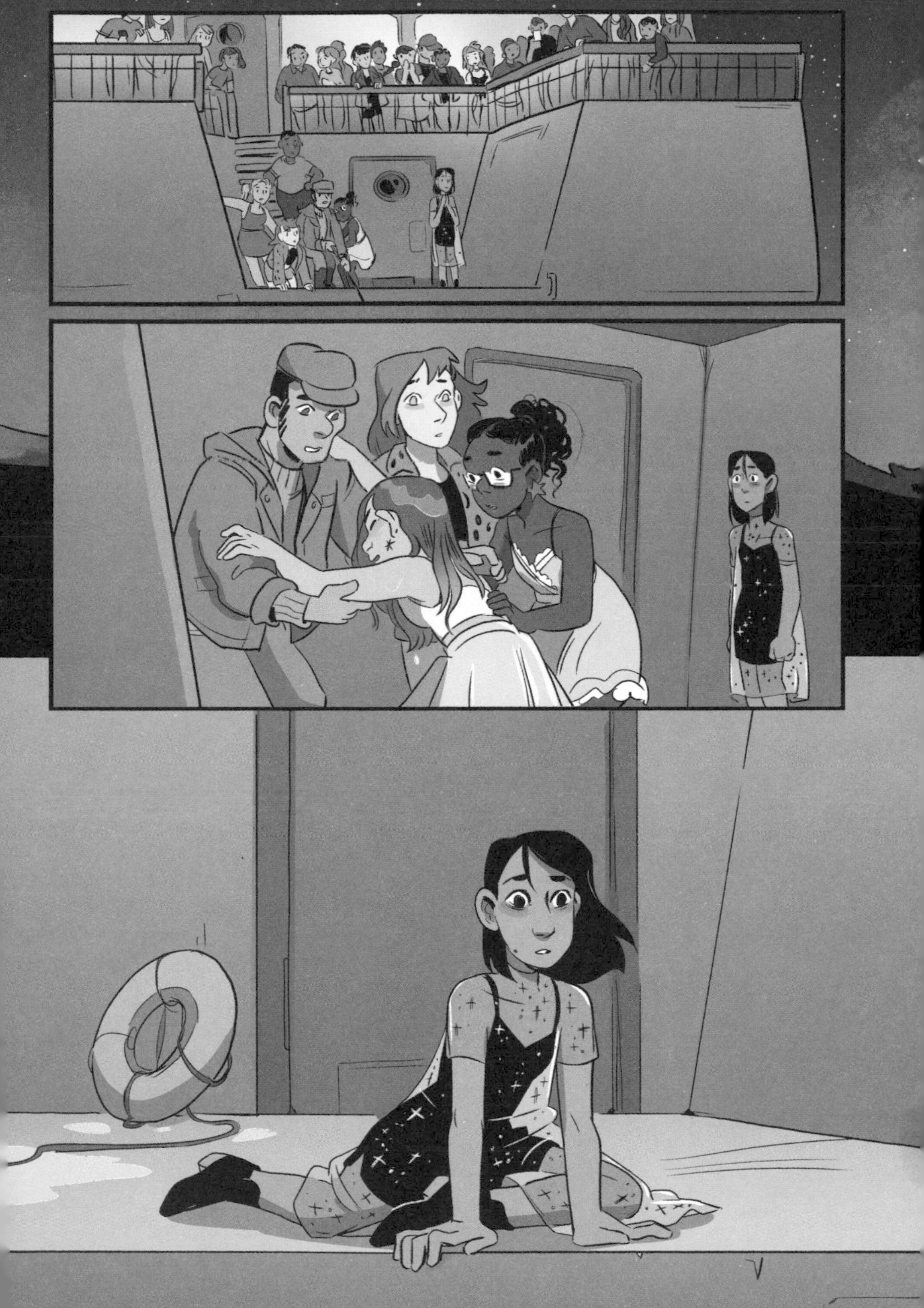

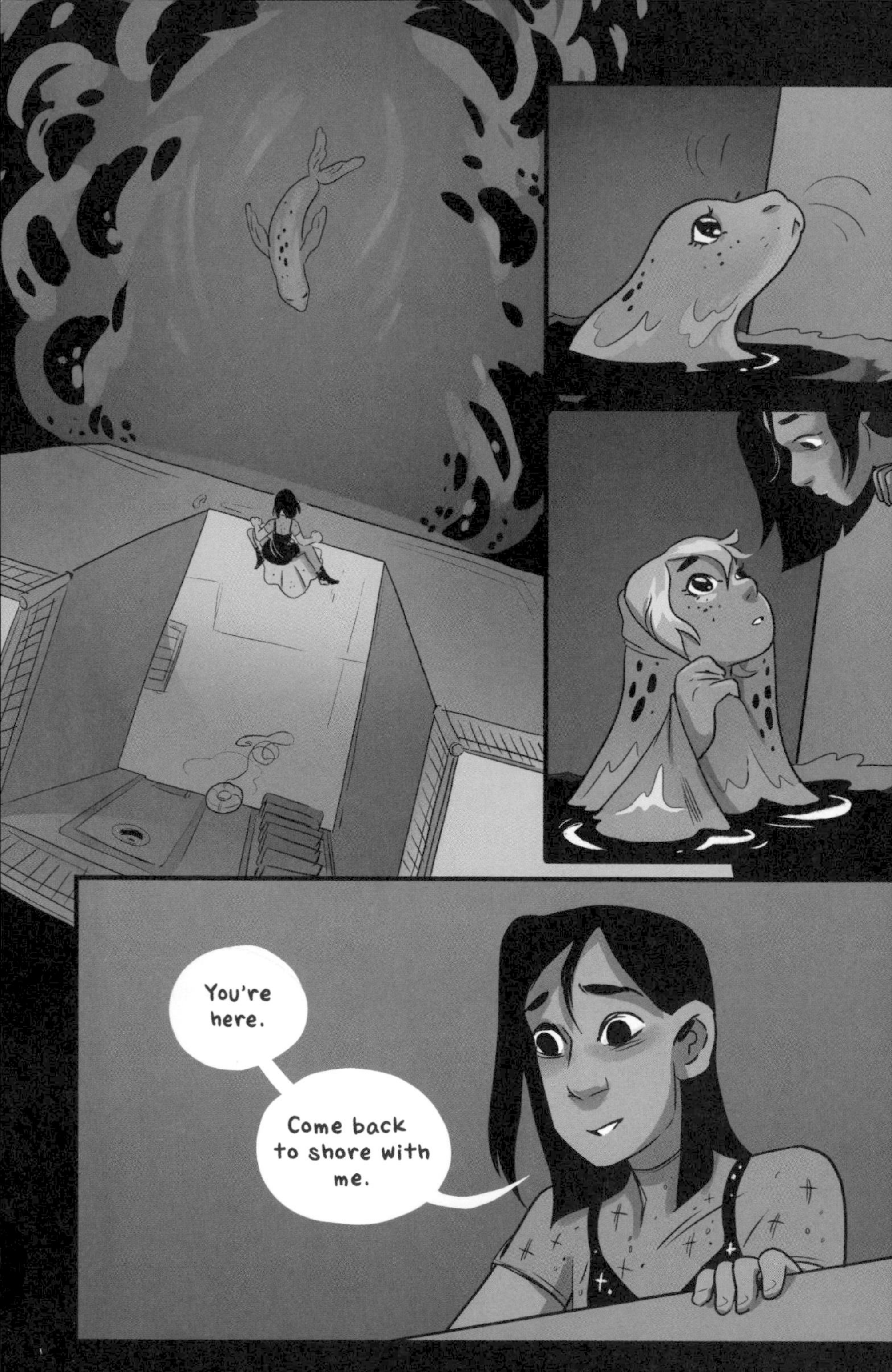
You're here.
Come back to shore with me.

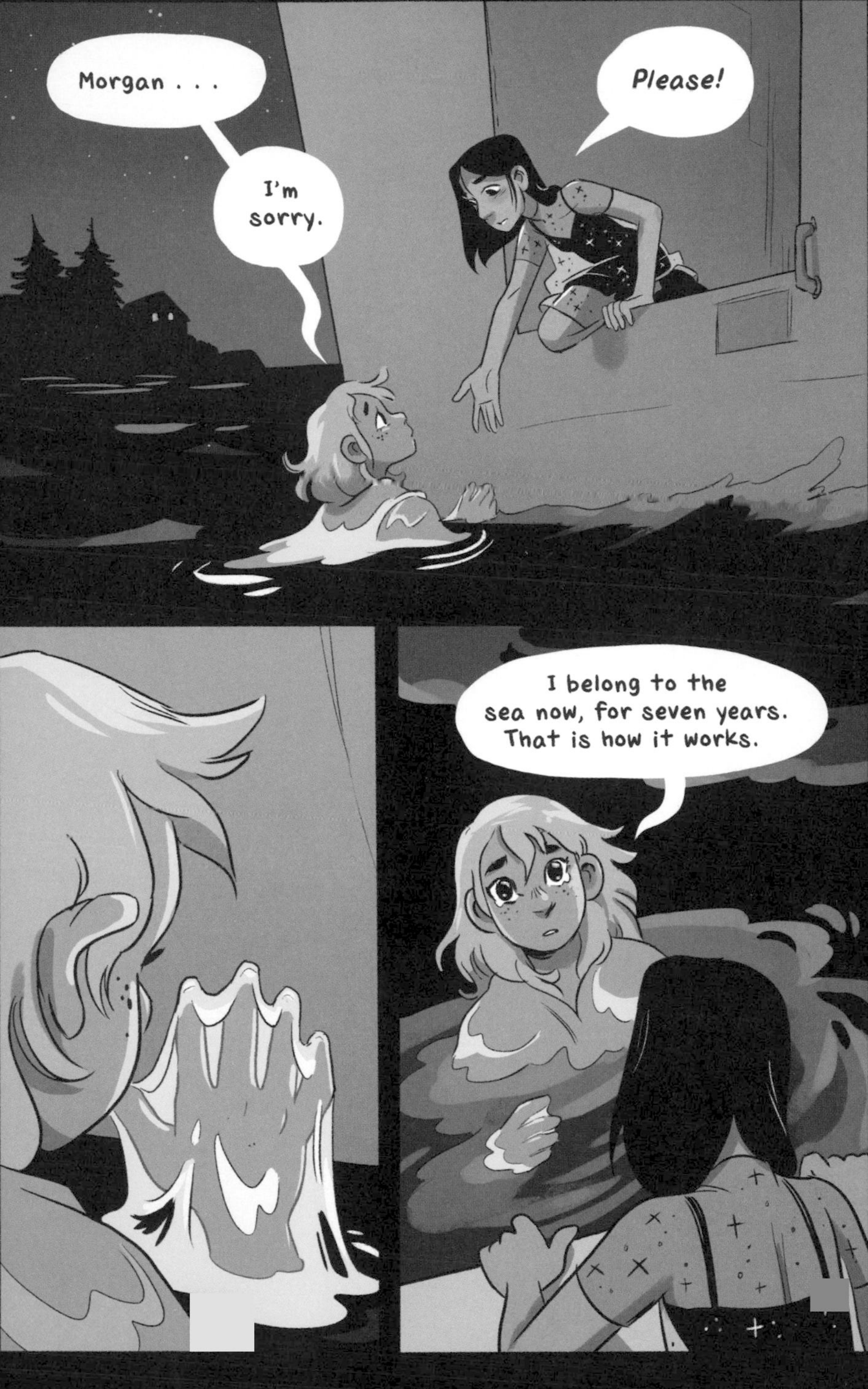
Morgan . . .
I'm sorry.
Please!
I belong to the sea now, for seven years. That is how it works.

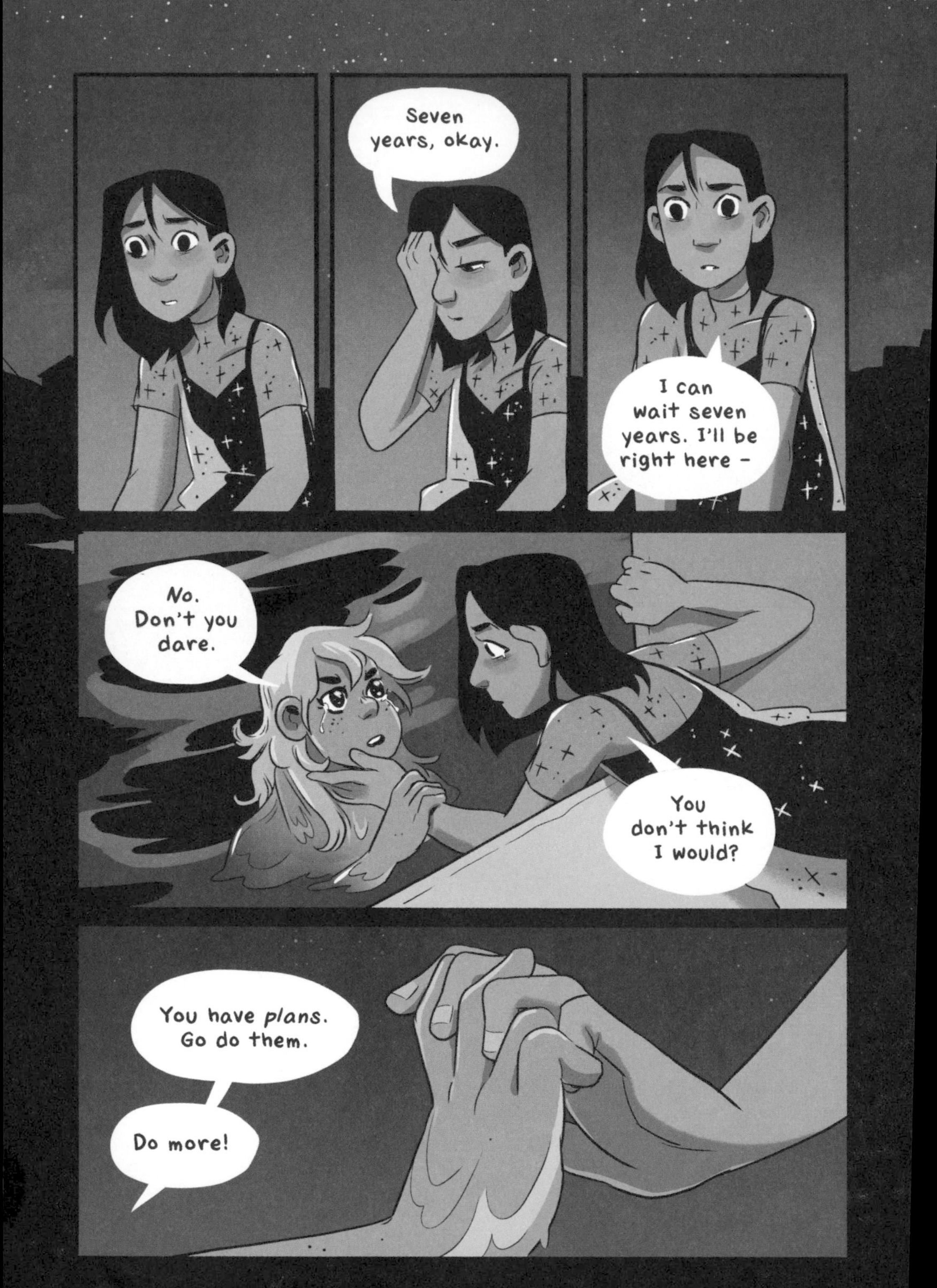
Seven years, okay.
I can wait seven years. I'll be right here -
No. Don't you dare.
You don't think I would?
You have *plans*. Go do them.
Do more!

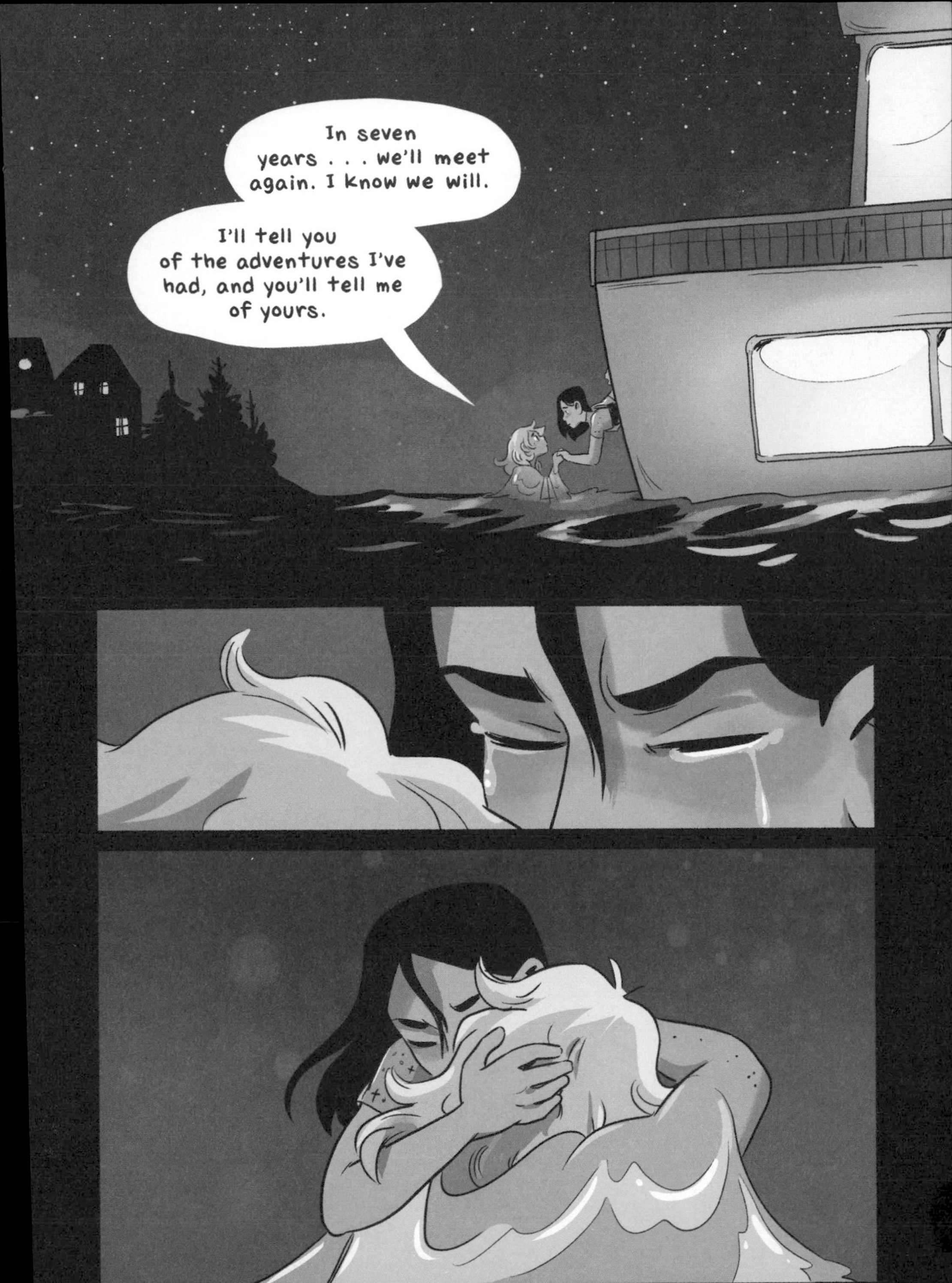
In seven years . . . we'll meet again. I know we will.
I'll tell you of the adventures I've had, and you'll tell me of yours.

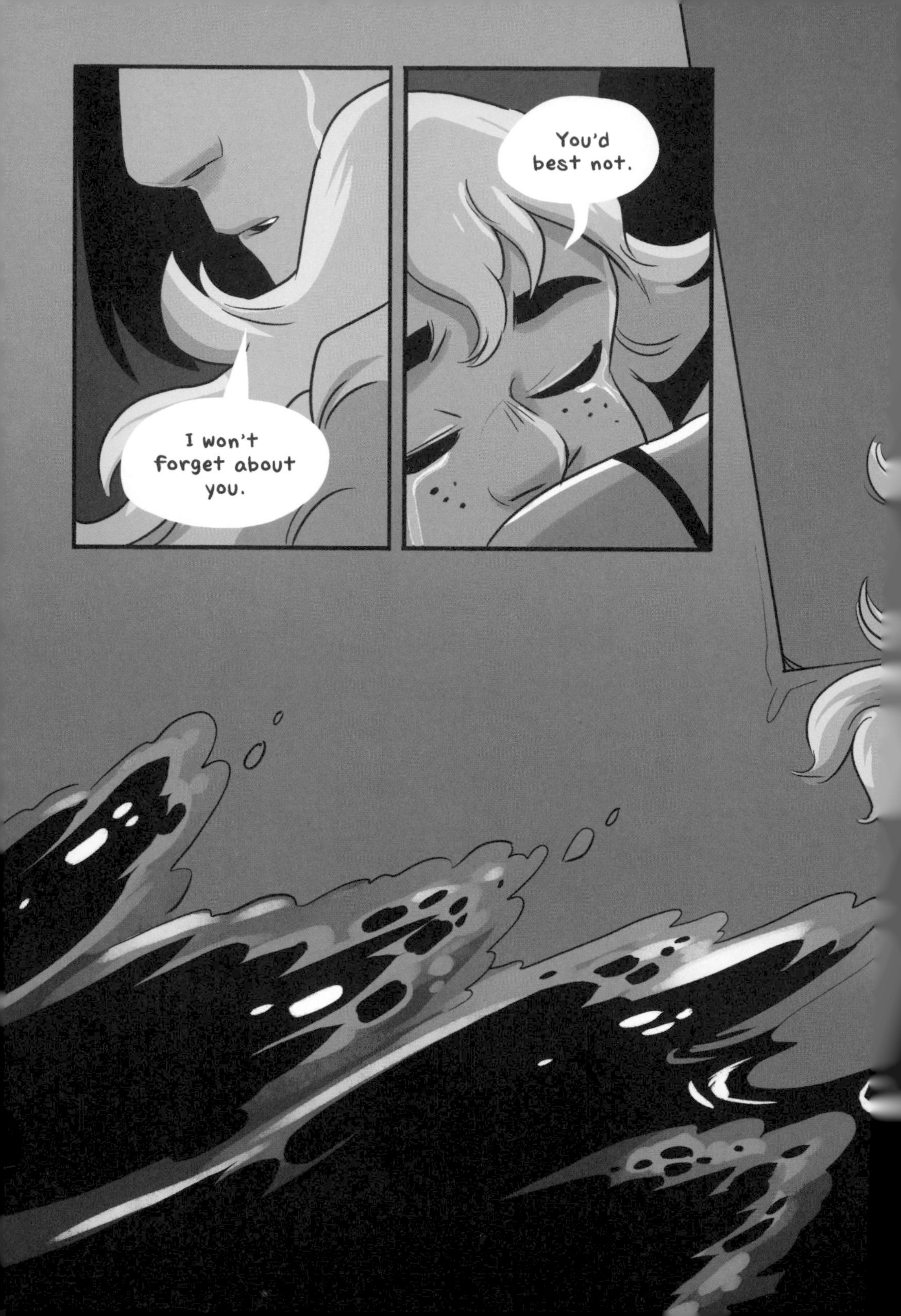
I won't forget about you.
You'd best not.

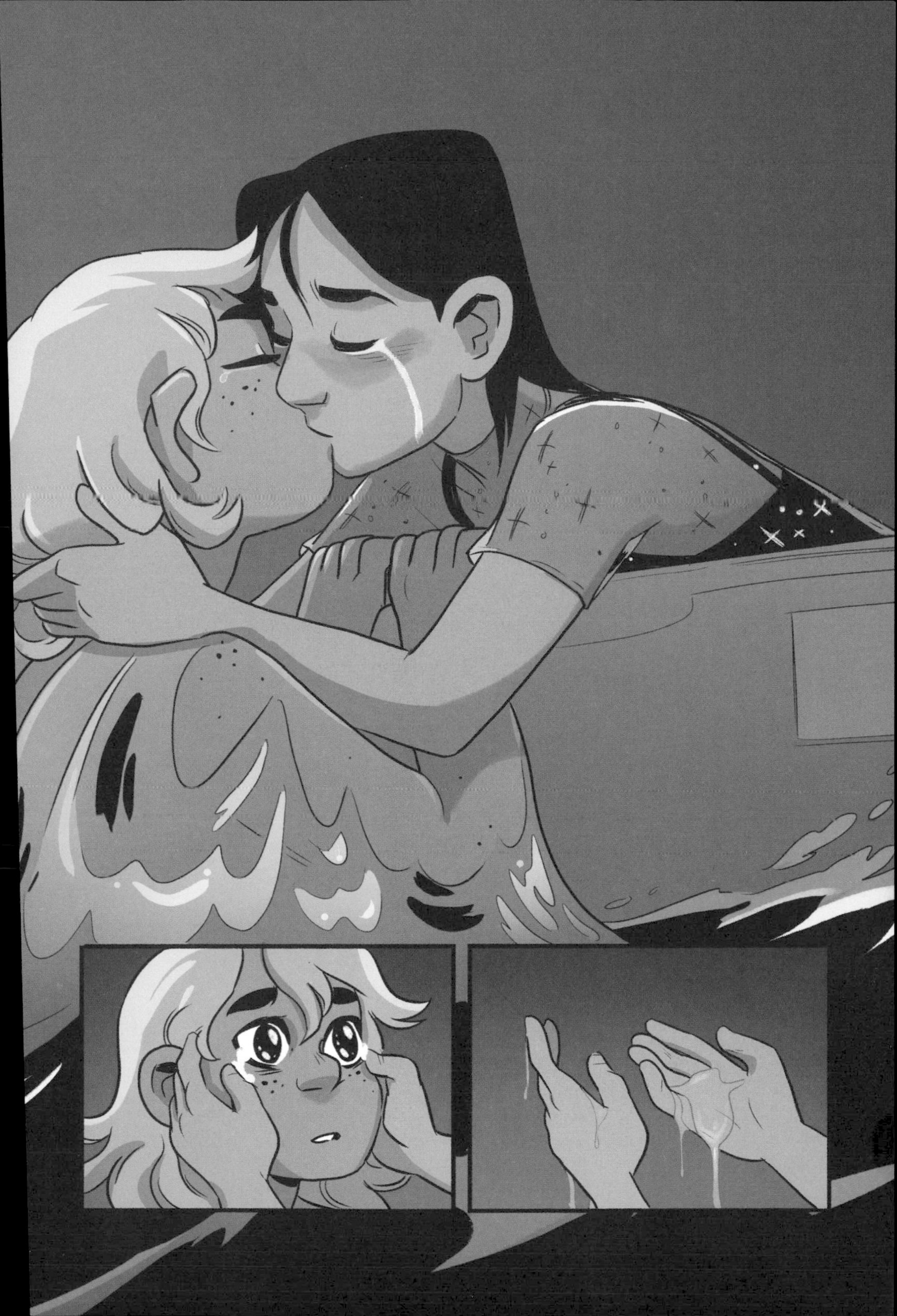

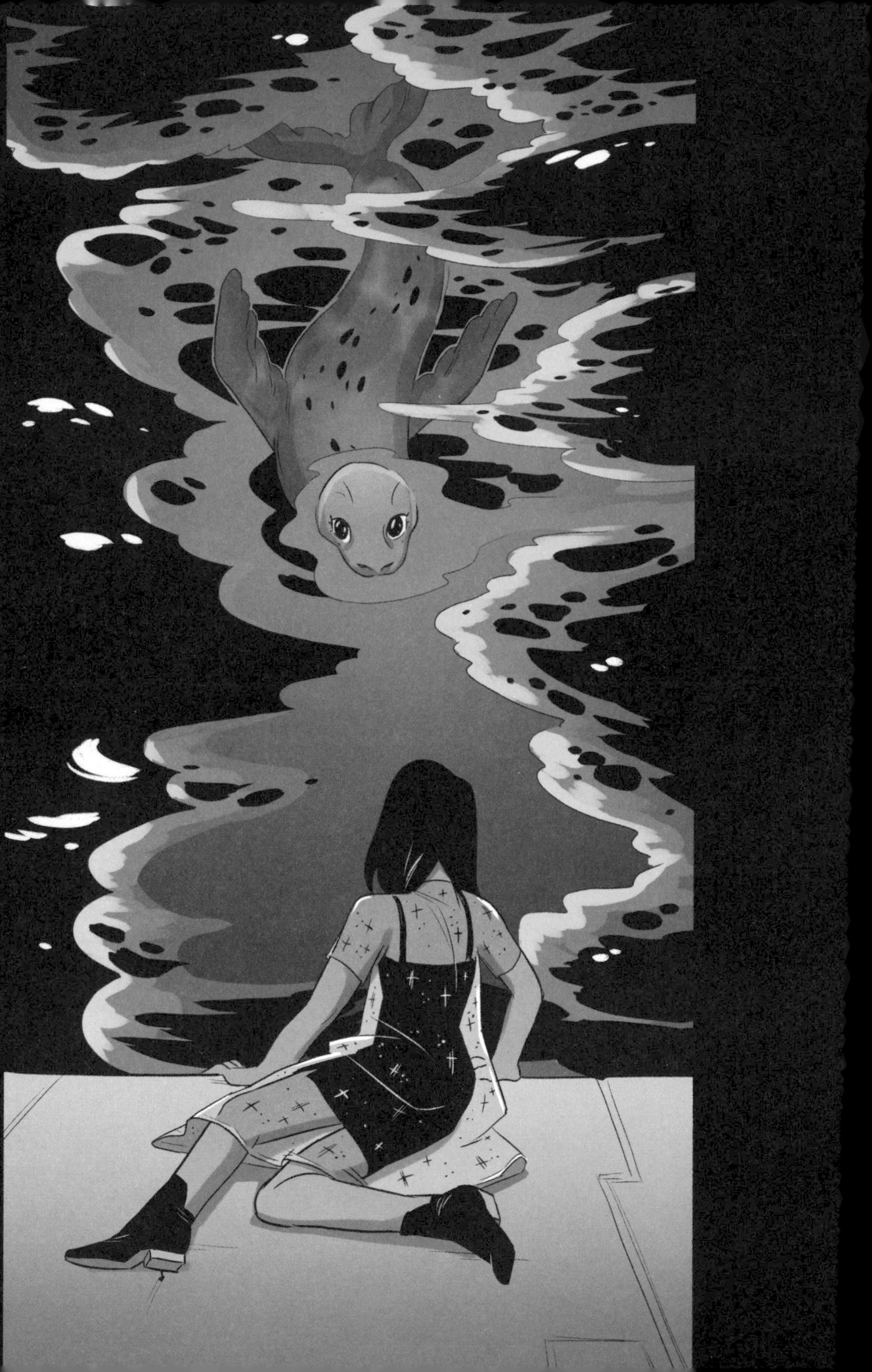

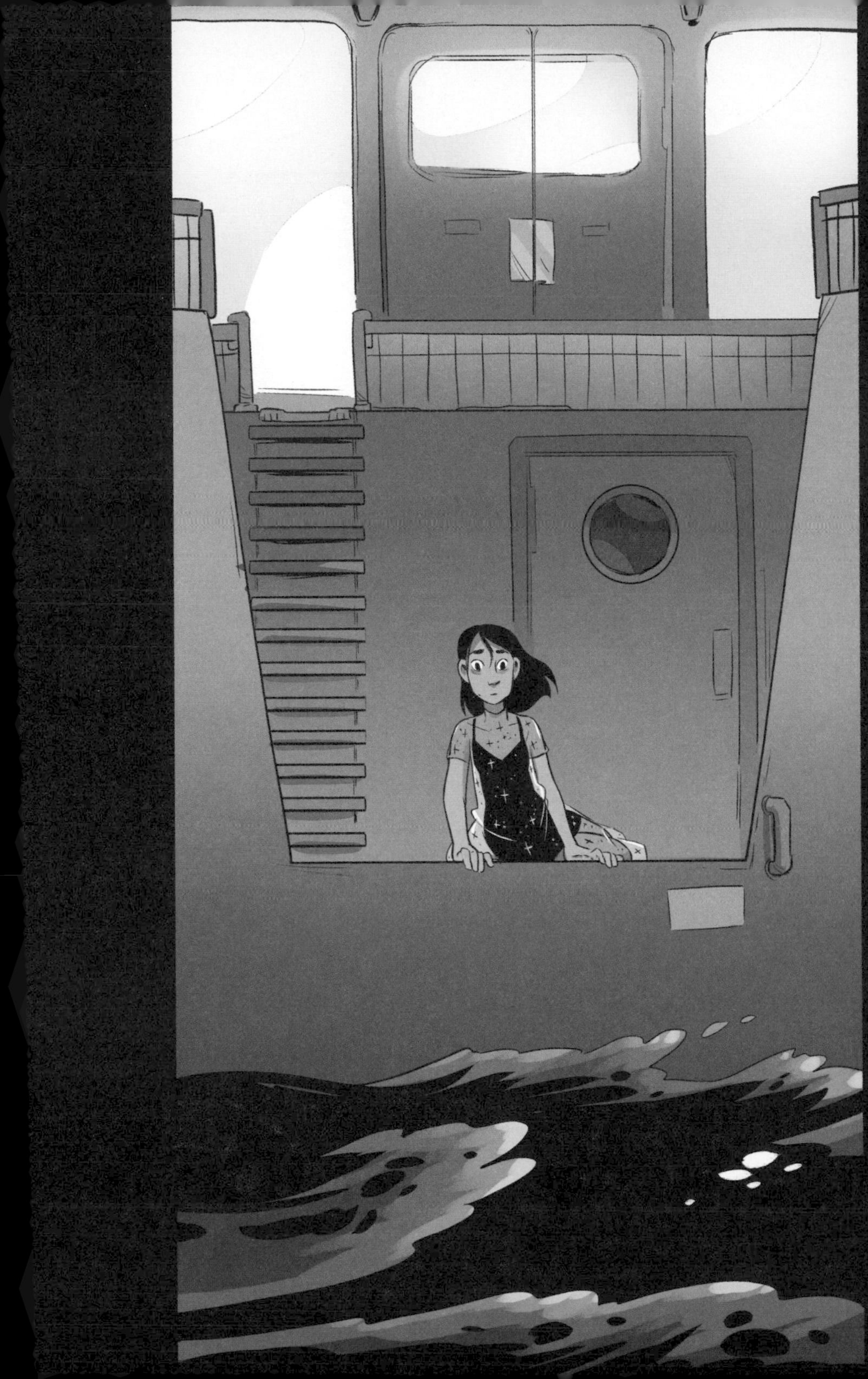

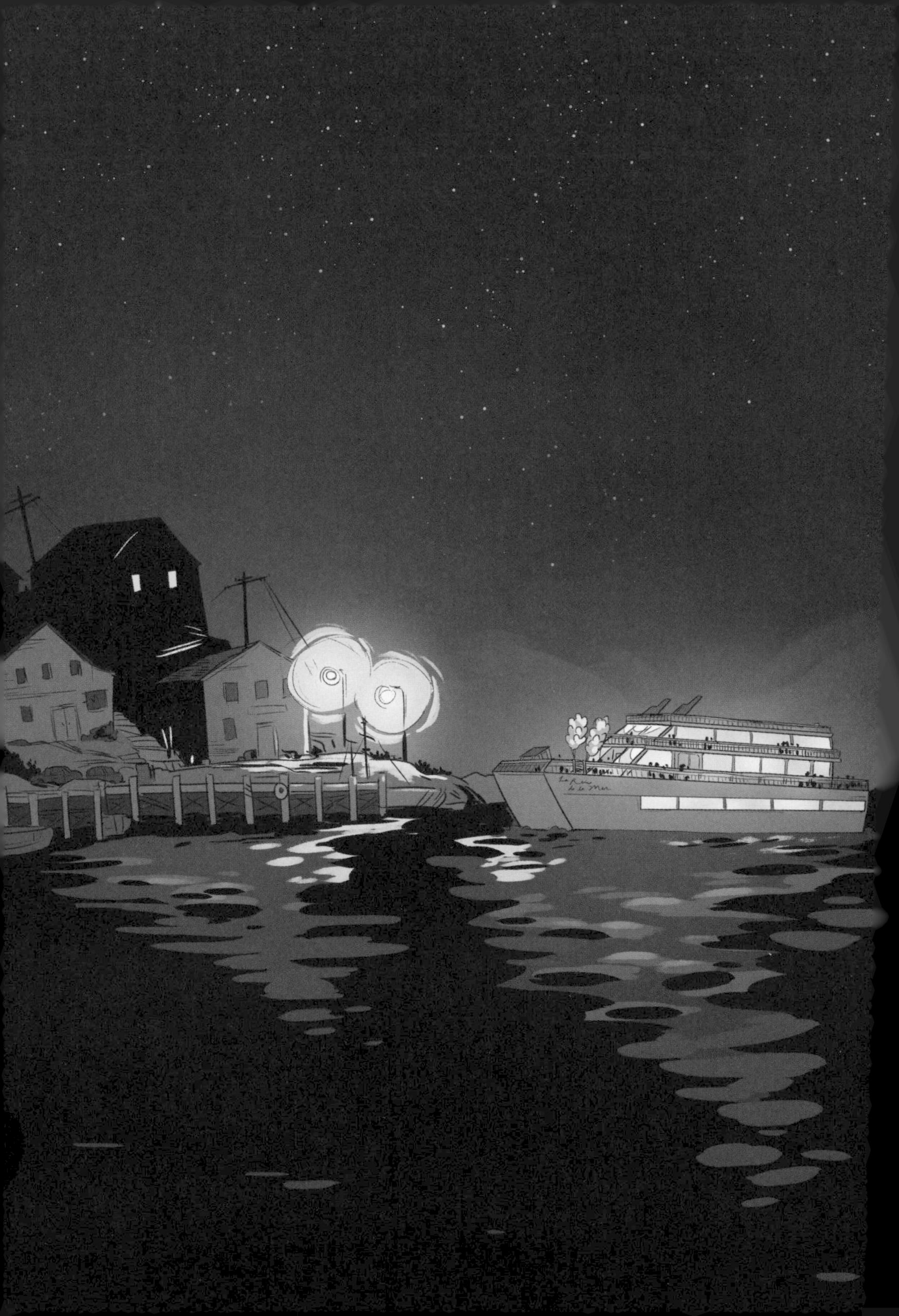

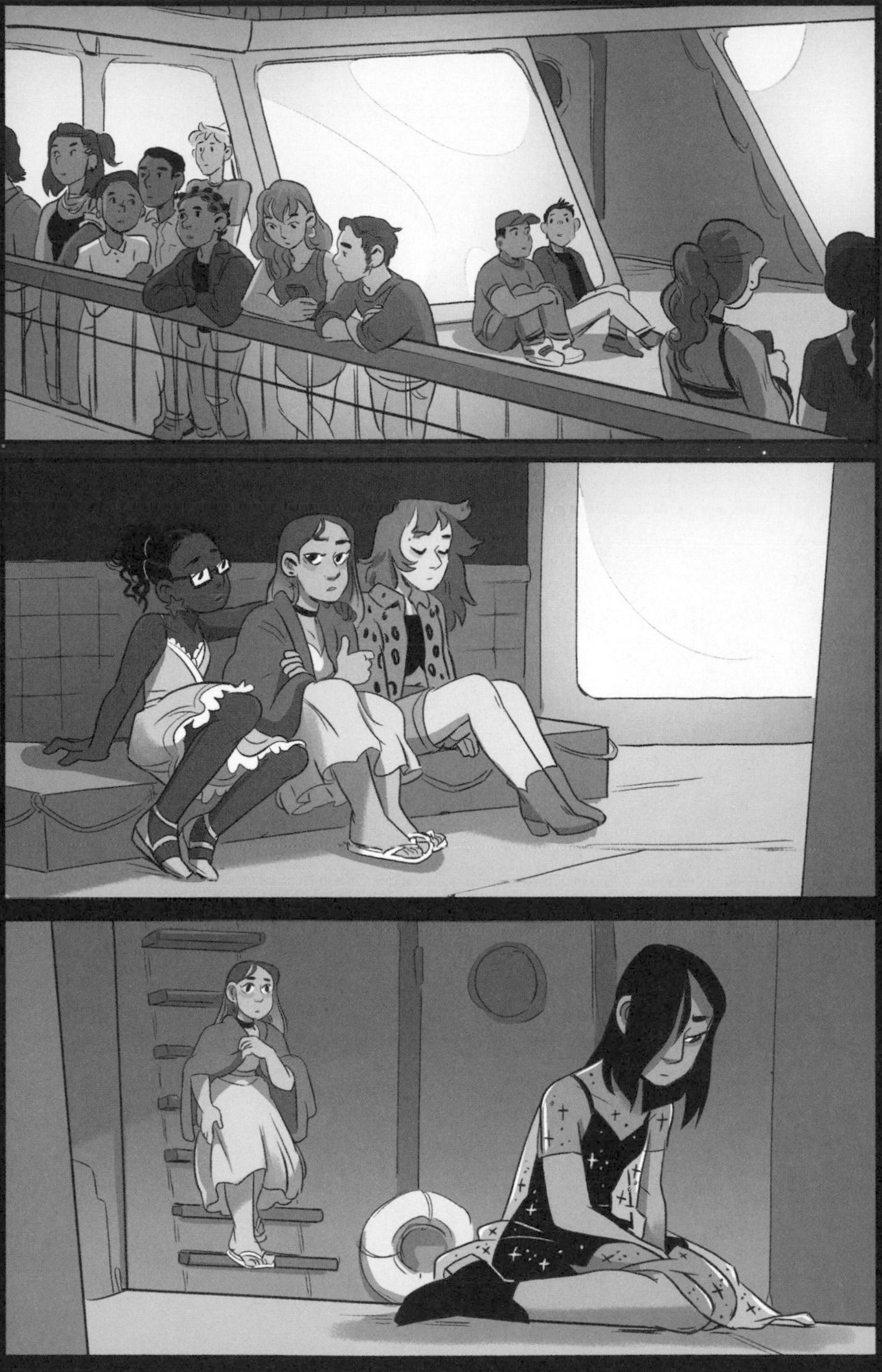

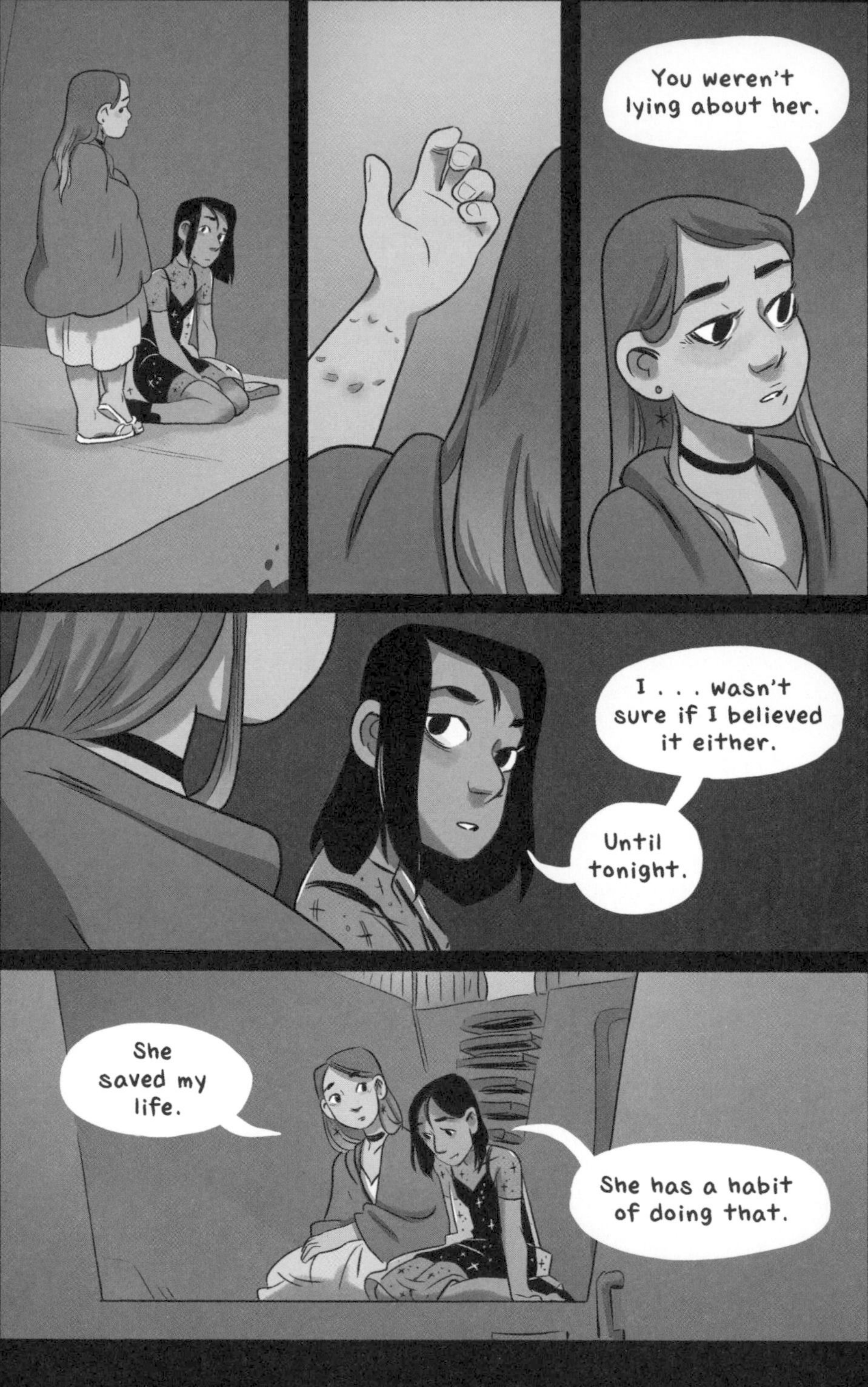
You weren't lying about her.
I . . . wasn't sure if I believed it either.
Until tonight.
She saved my life.
She has a habit of doing that.

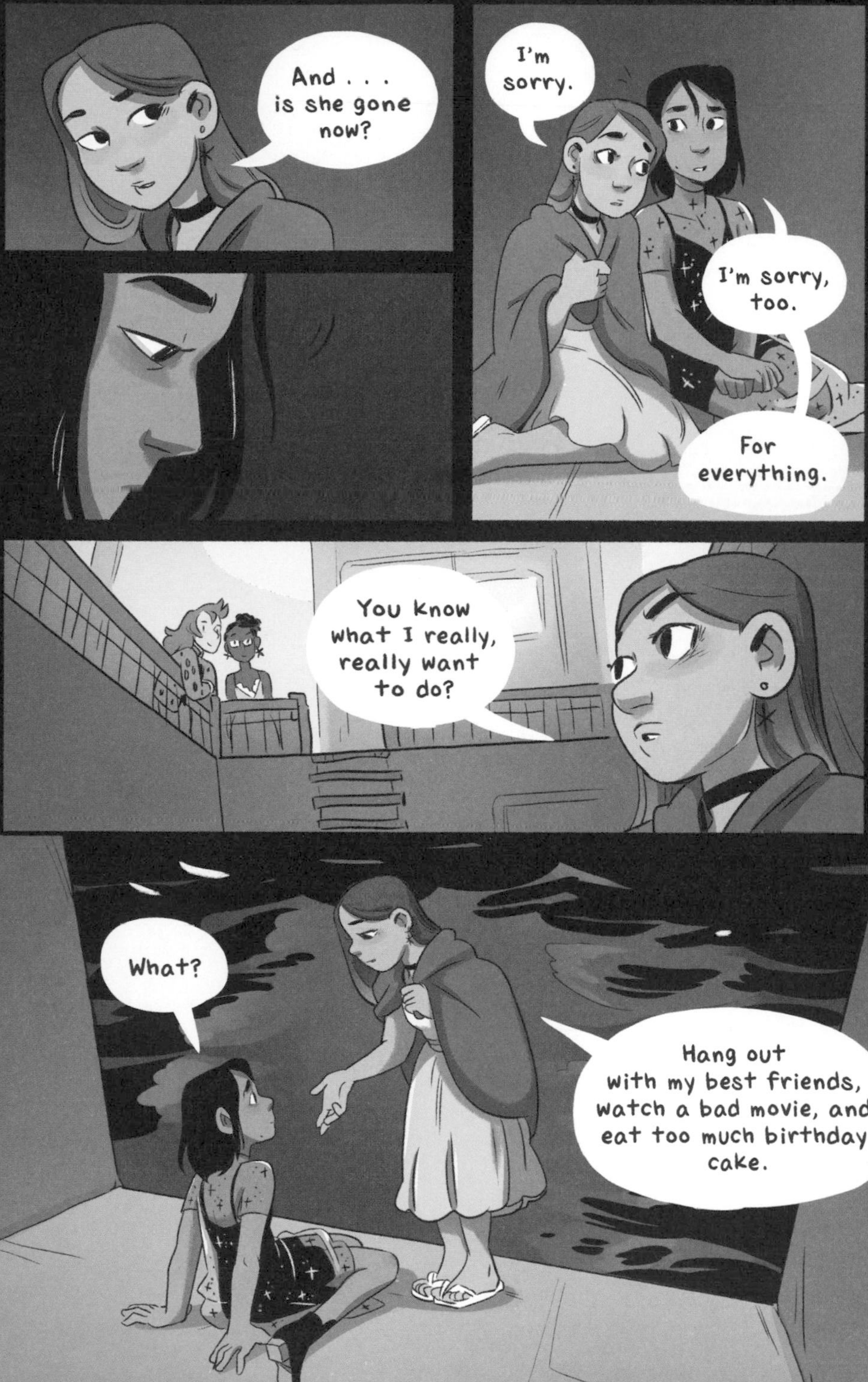

And . . . is she gone now?
I'm sorry.
I'm sorry, too.
For everything.
You know what I really, really want to do?
What?
Hang out with my best friends, watch a bad movie, and eat too much birthday cake.

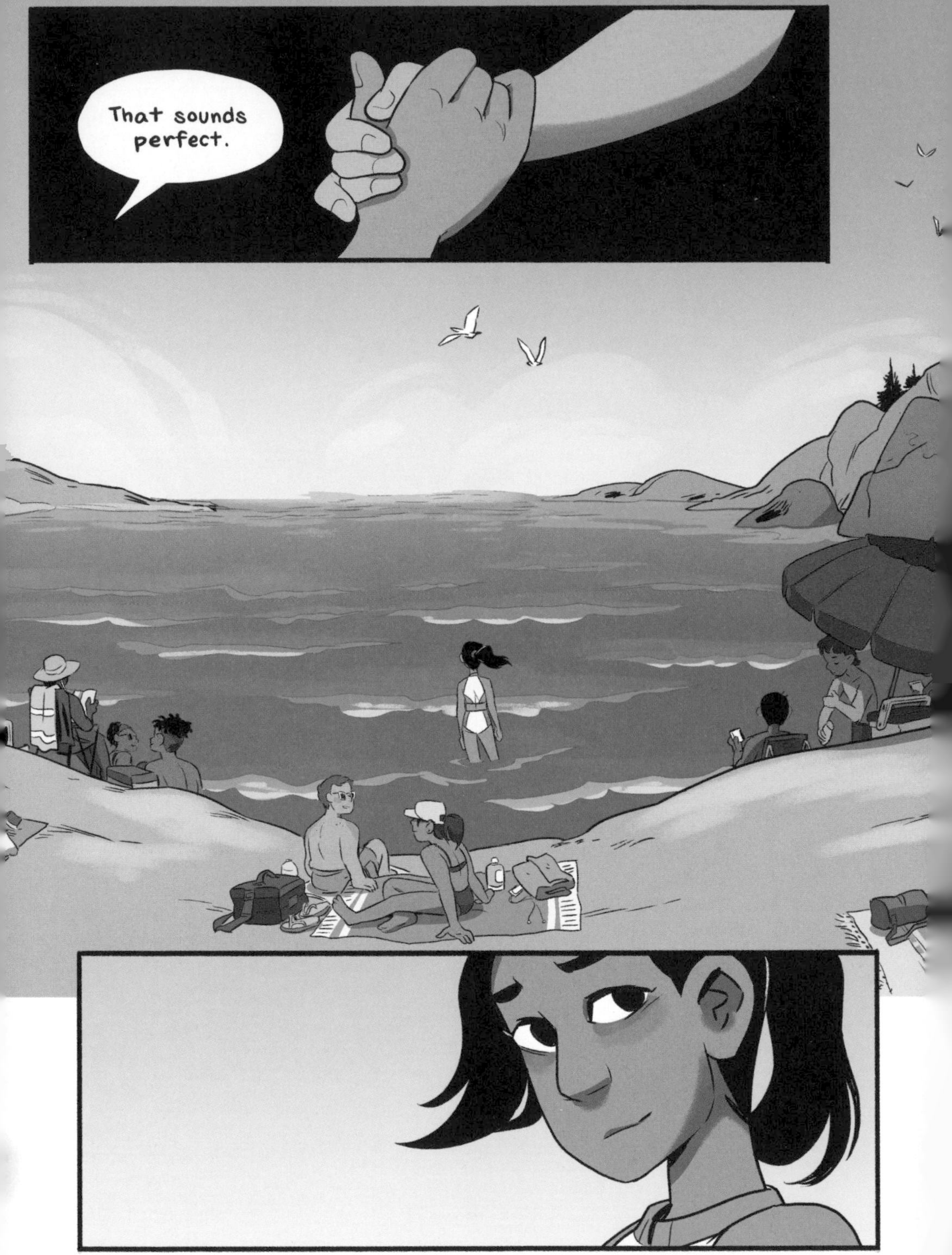
That sounds perfect.

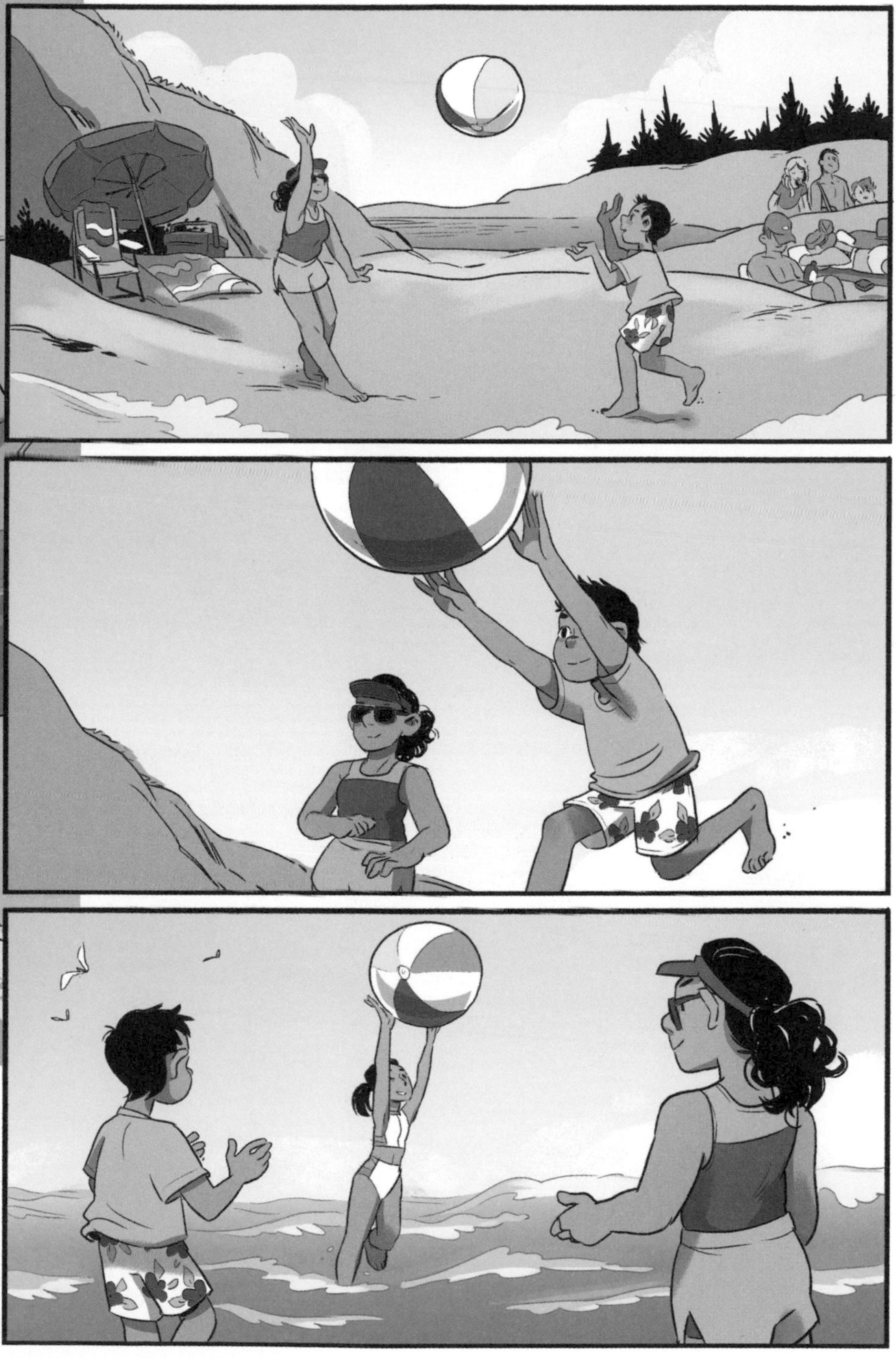

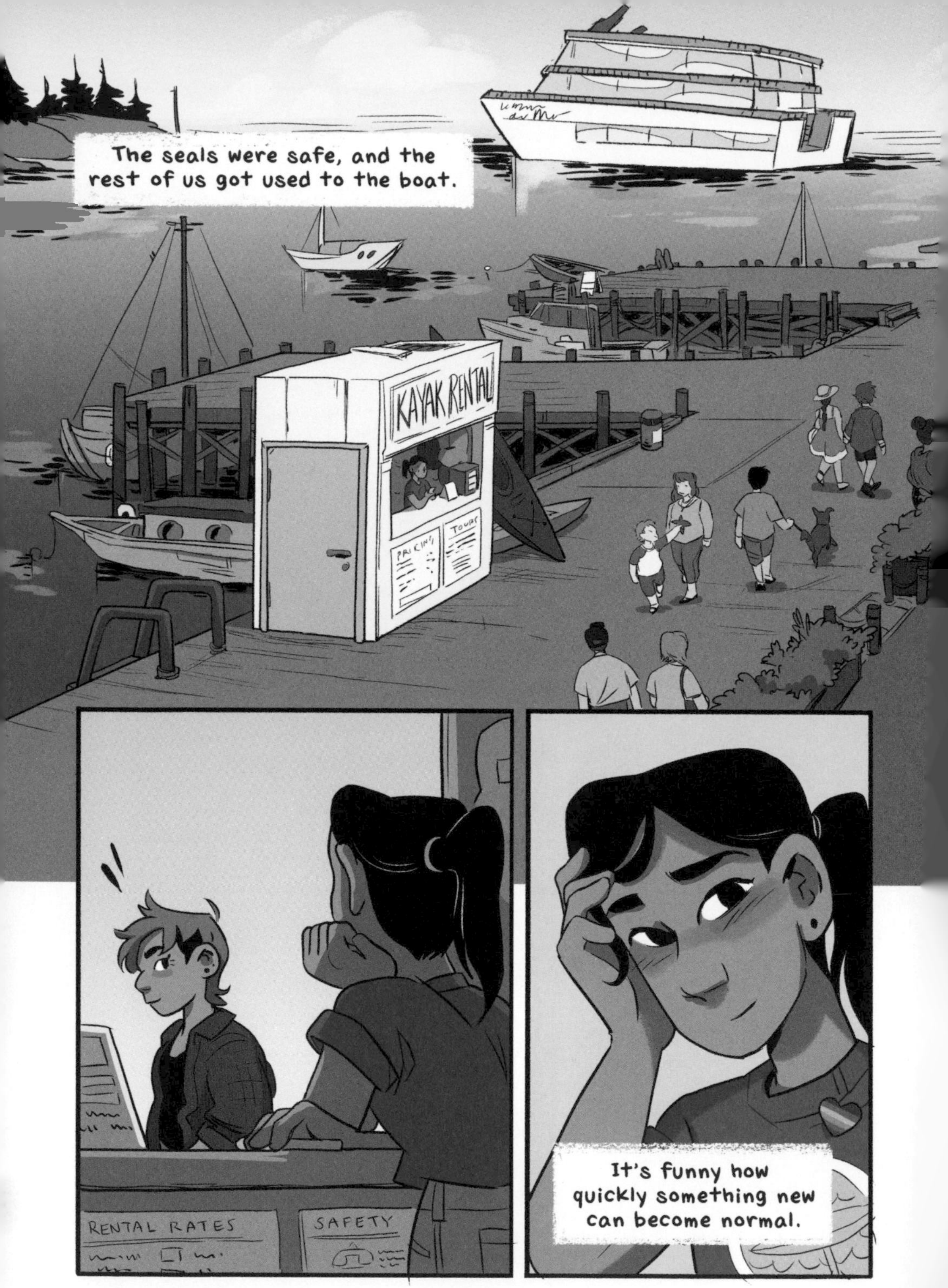
The seals were safe, and the rest of us got used to the boat.
KAYAK RENTAL
TOURS
RENTAL RATES
SAFETY
It's funny how quickly something new can become normal.

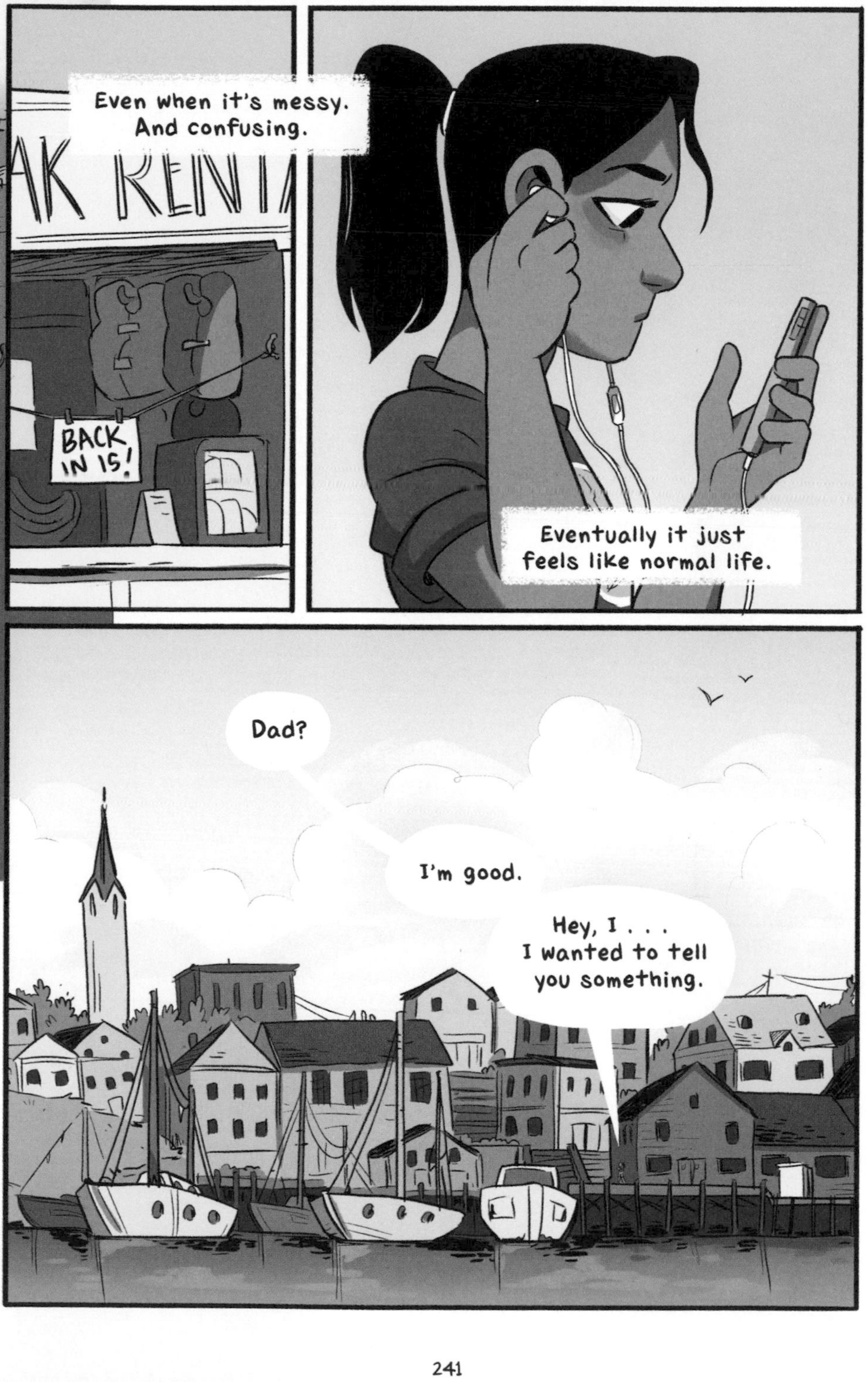
Even when it's messy.
And confusing.
AK RENT
BACK IN 15!
Eventually it just feels like normal life.
Dad?
I'm good.
Hey, I . . . I wanted to tell you something.

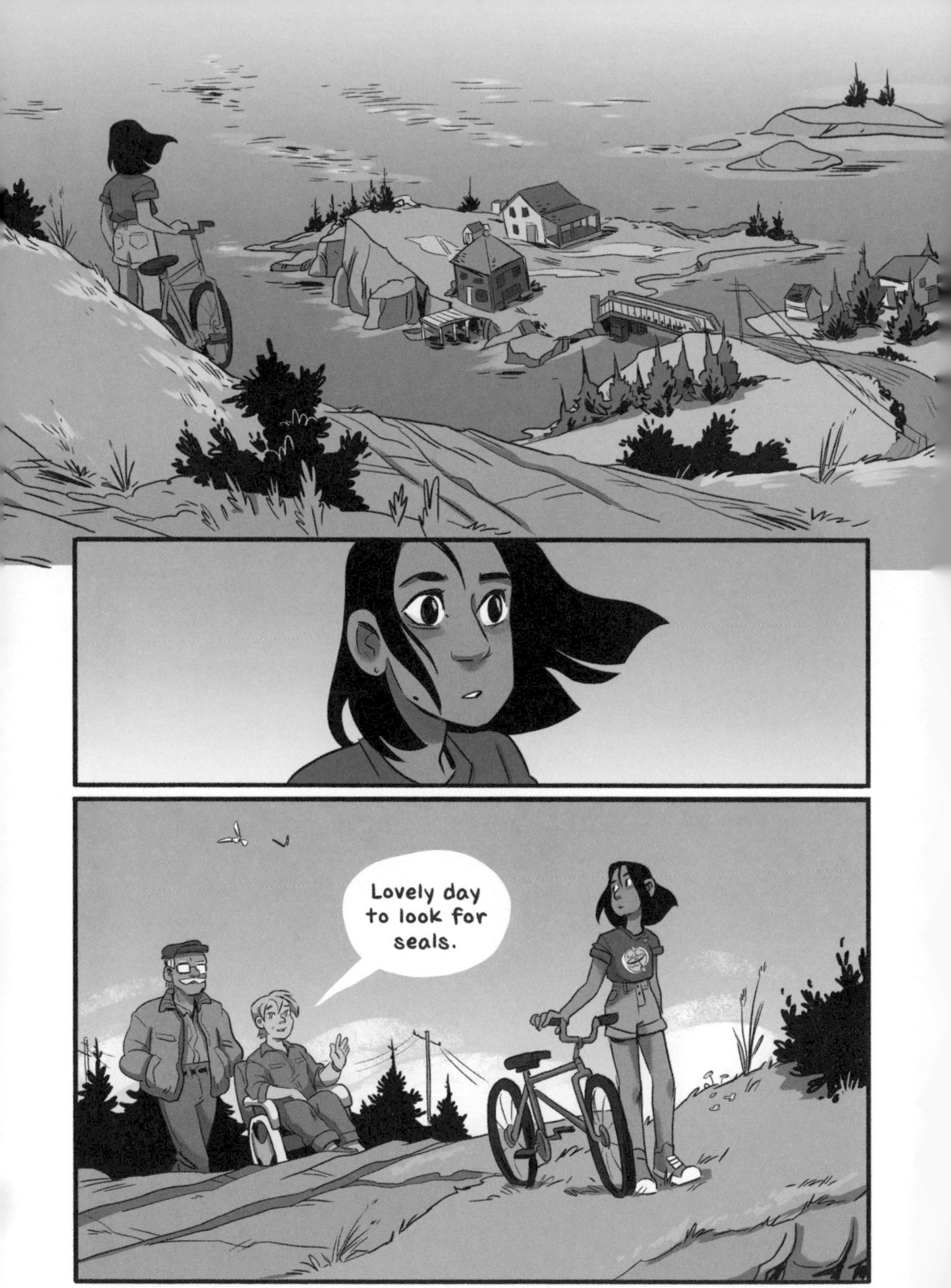
Lovely day to look for seals.

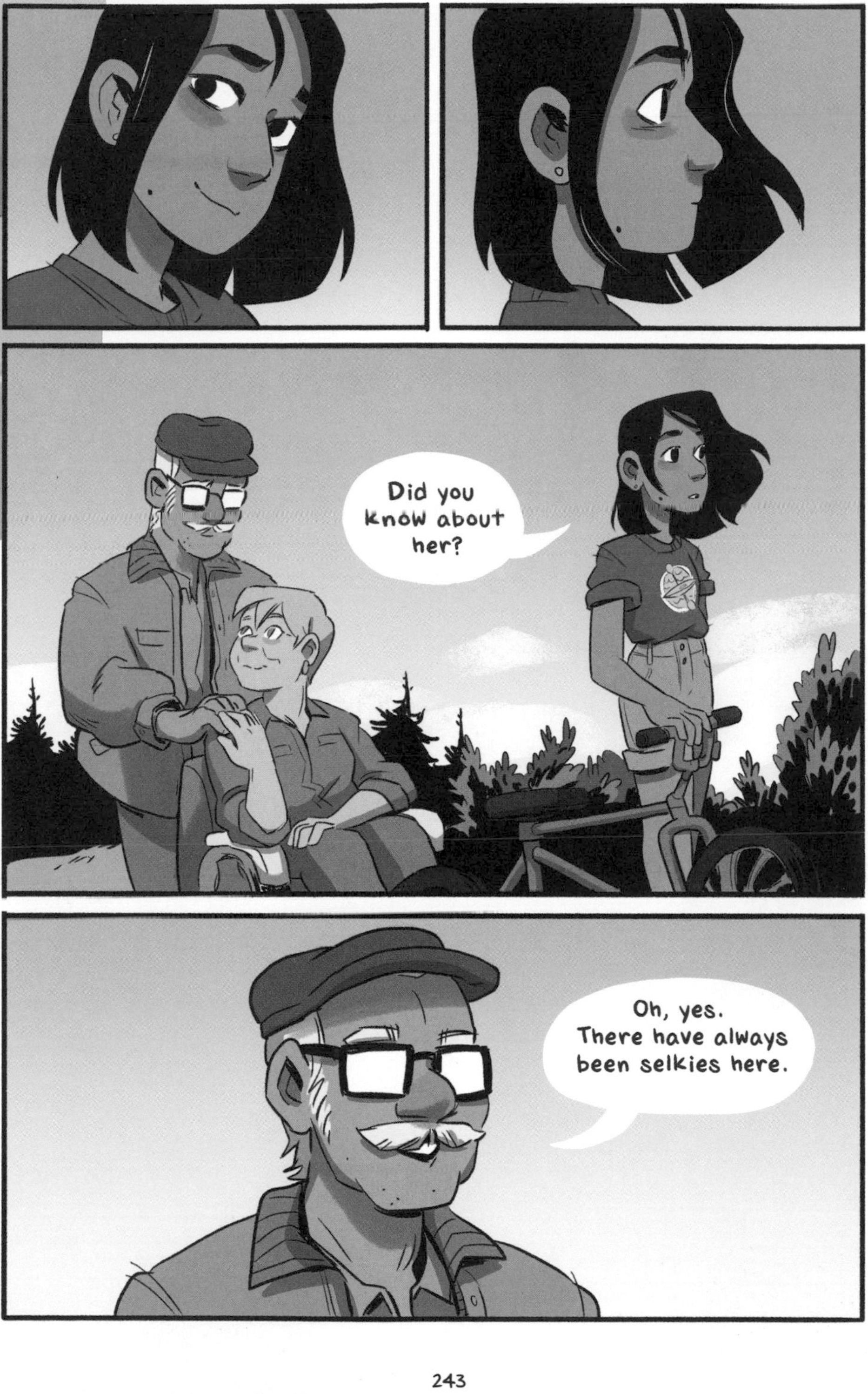
Did you know about her?
Oh, yes. There have always been selkies here.

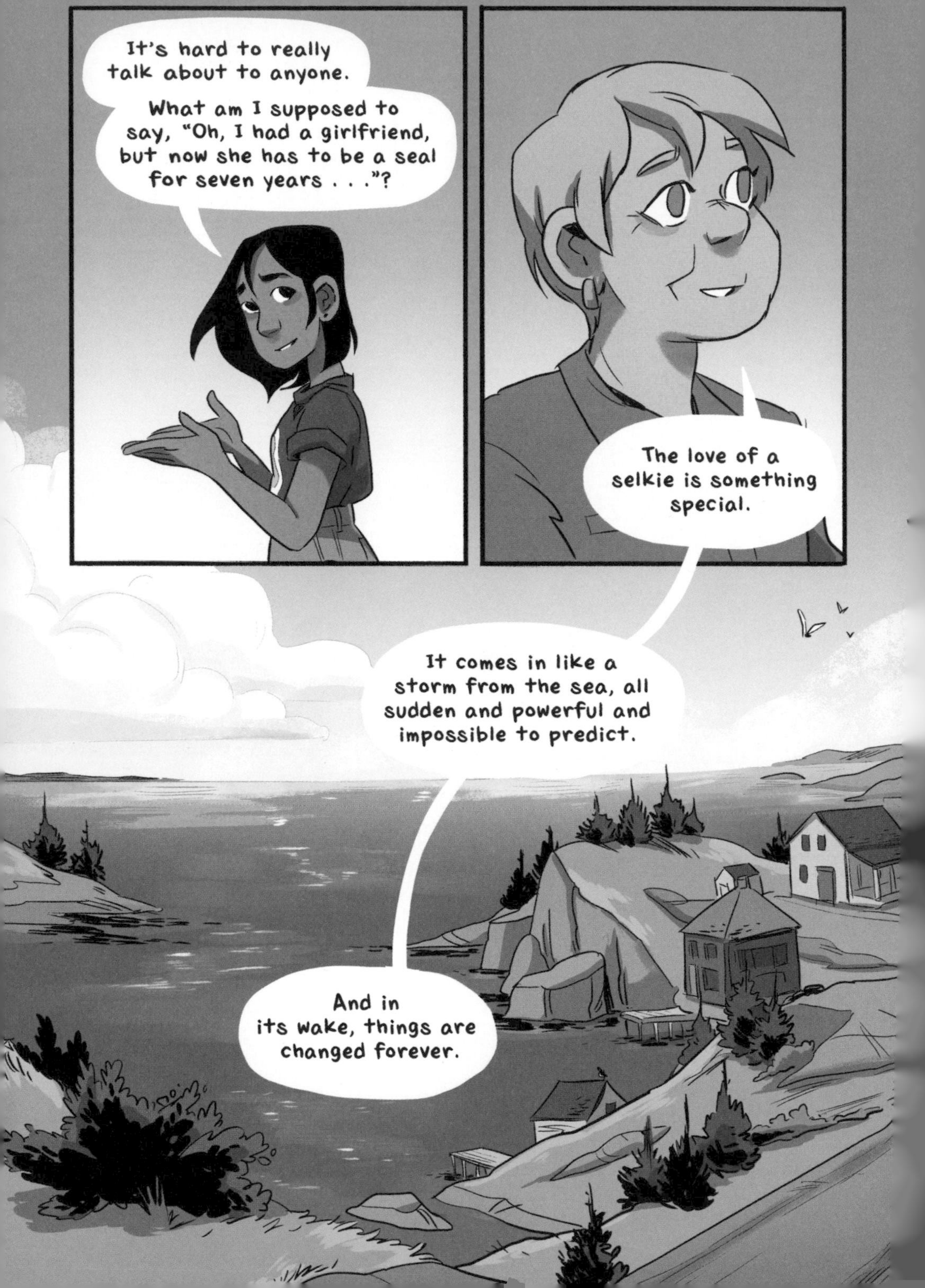
It's hard to really talk about to anyone.
What am I supposed to say, "Oh, I had a girlfriend, but now she has to be a seal for seven years . . ."?
The love of a selkie is something special.
It comes in like a storm from the sea, all sudden and powerful and impossible to predict.
And in its wake, things are changed forever.

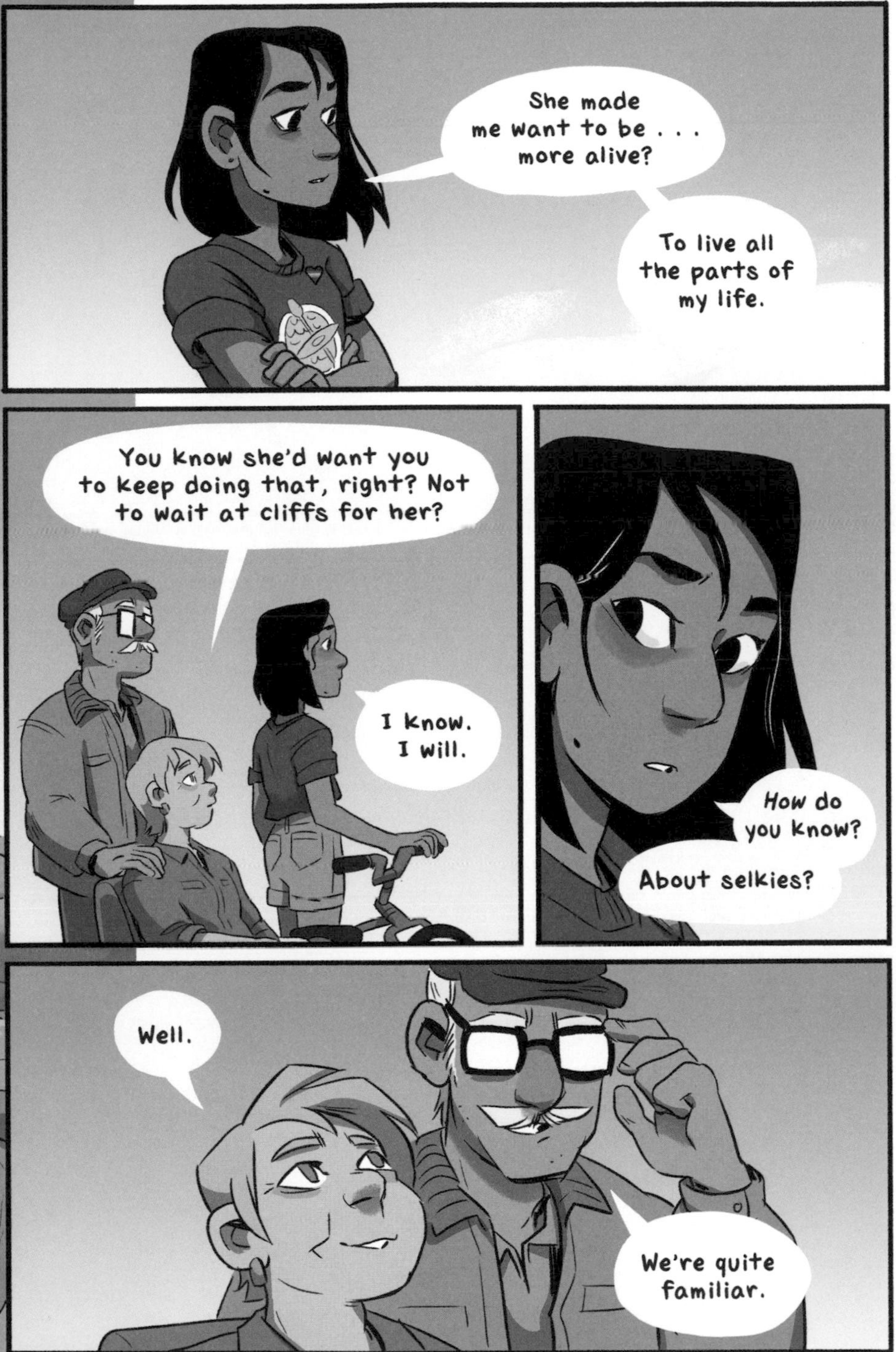
She made me want to be . . . more alive?
To live all the parts of my life.
You know she'd want you to keep doing that, right? Not to wait at cliffs for her?
I know. I will.
How do you know?
About selkies?
Well.
We're quite familiar.

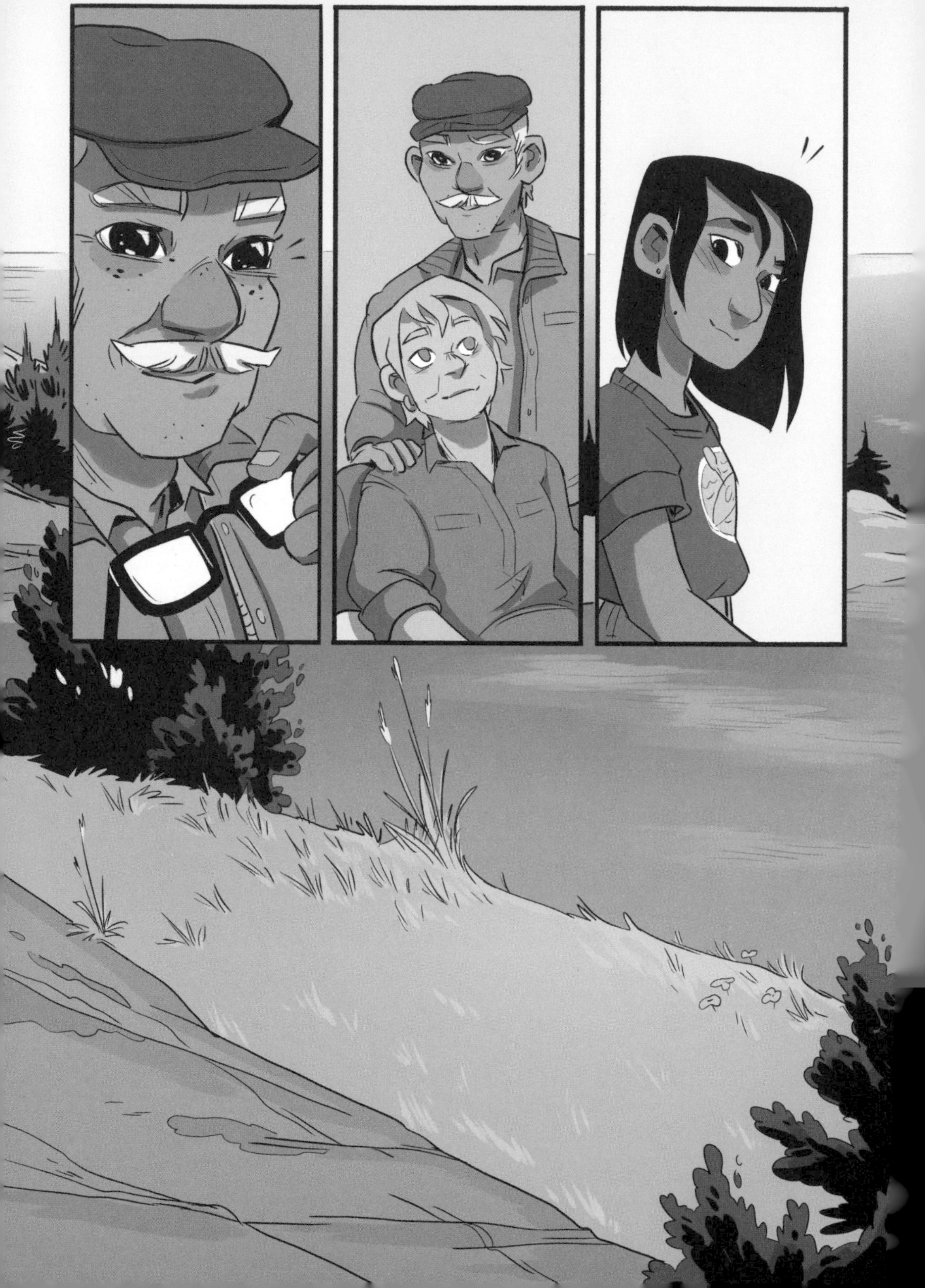

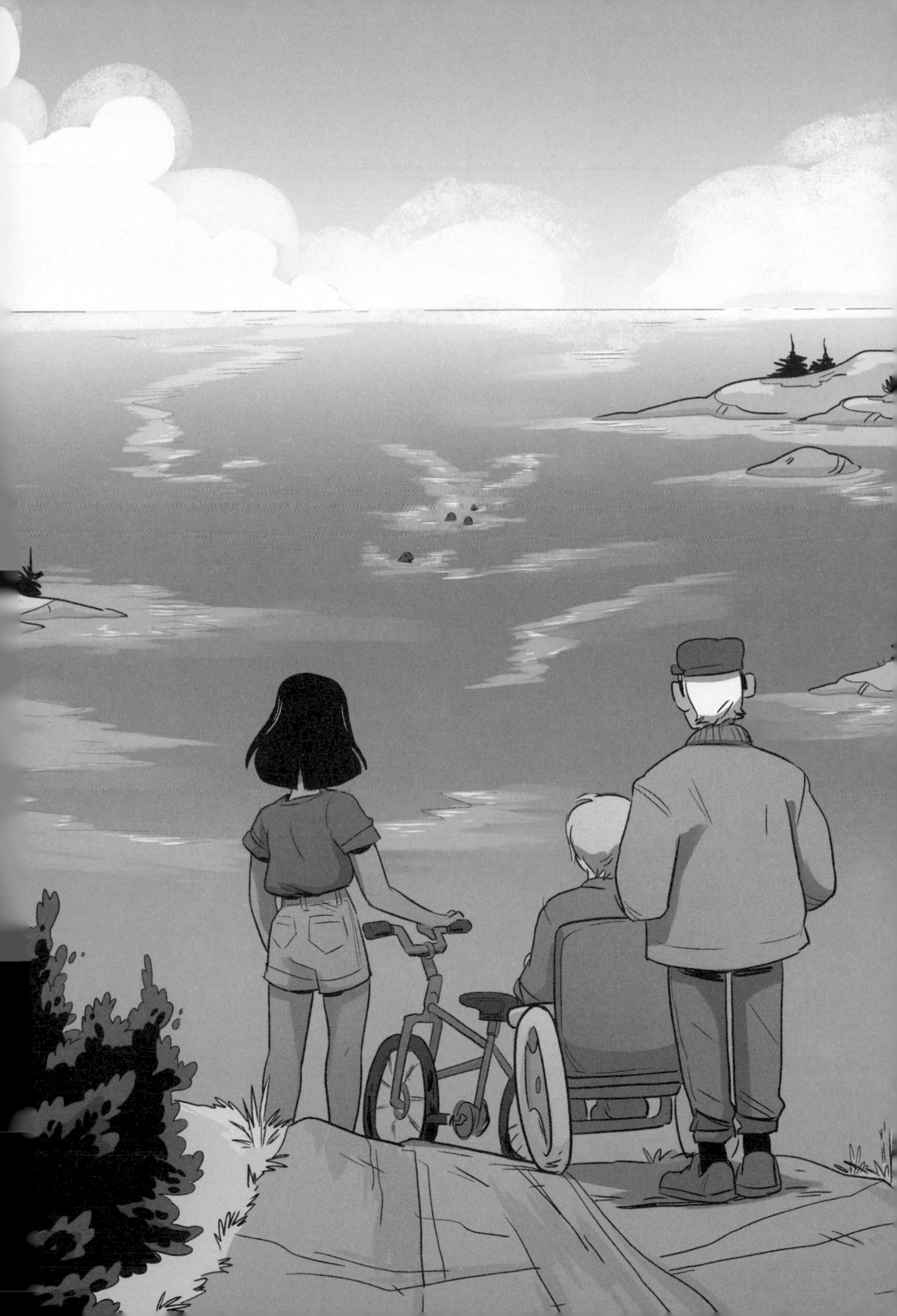

EXTRAS

These images are from my original pitch for the book. The character designs changed in subtle ways as I got used to drawing them, but the basic concepts stayed the same!

Morgan

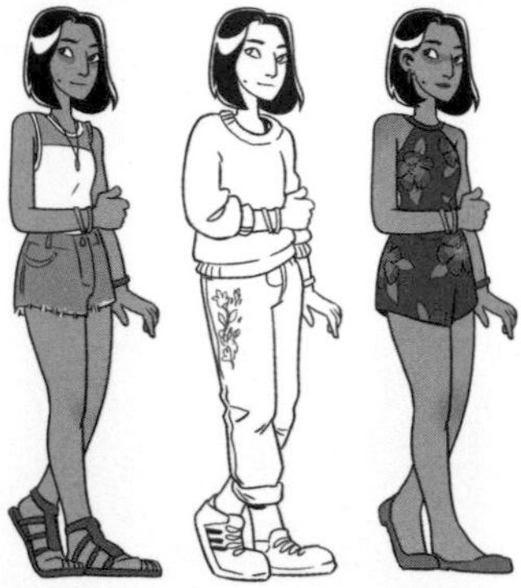

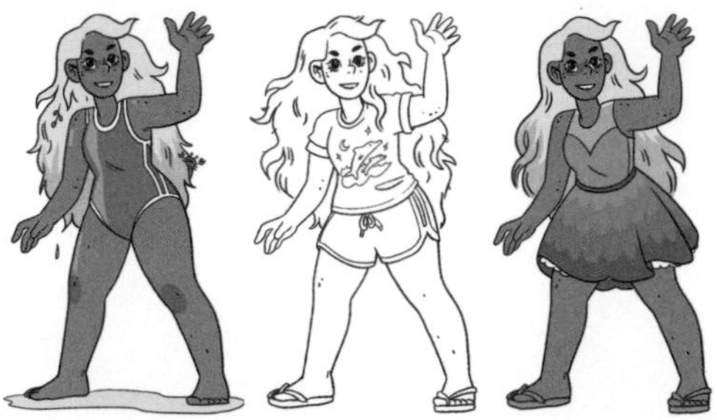

Keltie

When designing Keltie's human form, I went for a surfer girl look—tangled, sun-bleached hair, and a tan from being outside all the time. Her freckles are reminiscent of patterns on seals. Unlike Morgan, she expresses her big feelings in her face and body language.

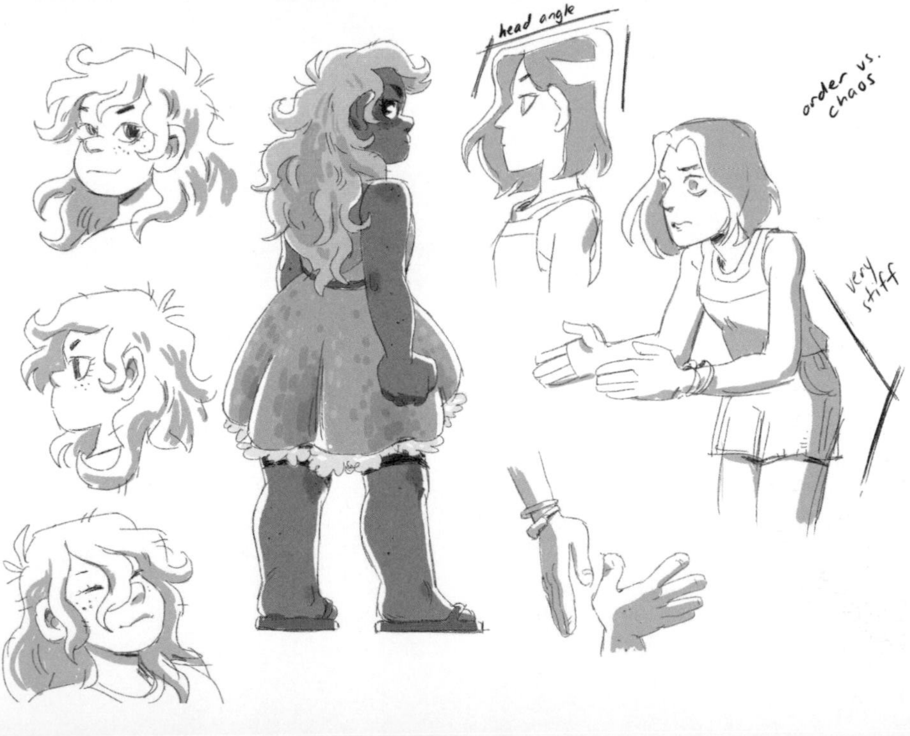
head angle
order vs. chaos
very stiff

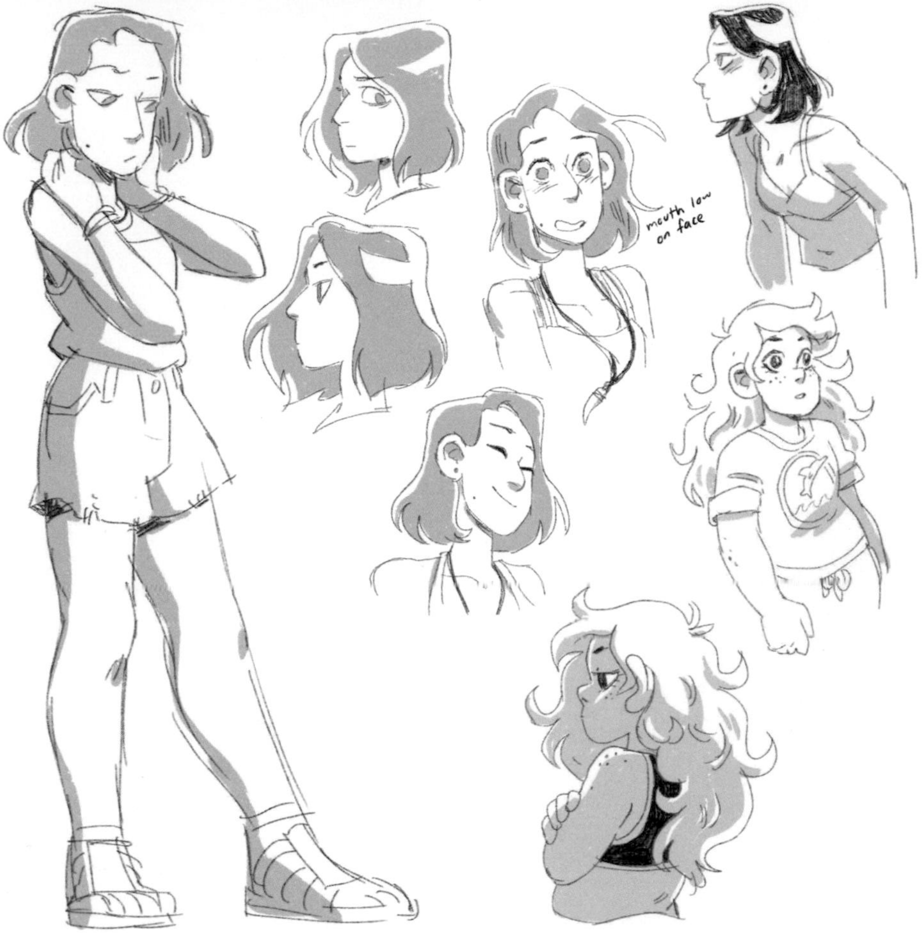
mouth low on face

Morgan is a contrast to Keltie — she's very put together, very neat and precise, someone who cares about being in control of situations. Something I really loved exploring was Morgan's body language — the way she holds herself when she's around her friends and family is very different than when she's around Keltie.

In one draft of the script Keltie gave Morgan a seal-tooth necklace rather than her seal-skin, but a seal-skin is a classic part of selkie mythology, so I decided to rewrite it.

In another draft, Keltie has never heard music before, and Morgan teaches her to dance when they pass a street busker. I had to cut the scene eventually, but the sketches are nice!

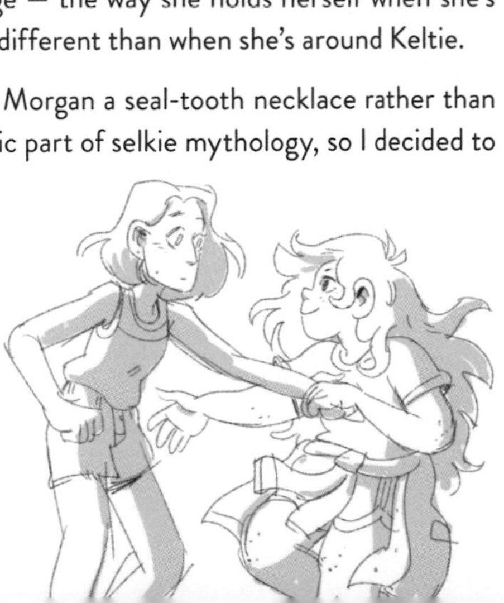

Playing around with different fashions for Keltie, including a few that she doesn't end up wearing. I think Keltie doesn't really understand the concept of clothes, but she's trying!

Contrary to Keltie, Morgan cares about clothes a LOT. It was fun looking up different outfits for her (thank you, Pinterest) and figuring out her low-key, carefully curated sense of style.

I like to doodle on my iPad as I watch reality TV in the evening (shout out to *Project Runway Junior* for inspiring Morgan's interest in fashion design). This was one of the first times that I felt like I really "got" the character designs and their personalities.

These are more iPad sketches that helped me design the character's clothes in the party scene. Morgan's dress was hard to figure out — it's more out there than what she usually wears, but by the party she's feeling more confident in herself!

A few alternate covers and color schemes.

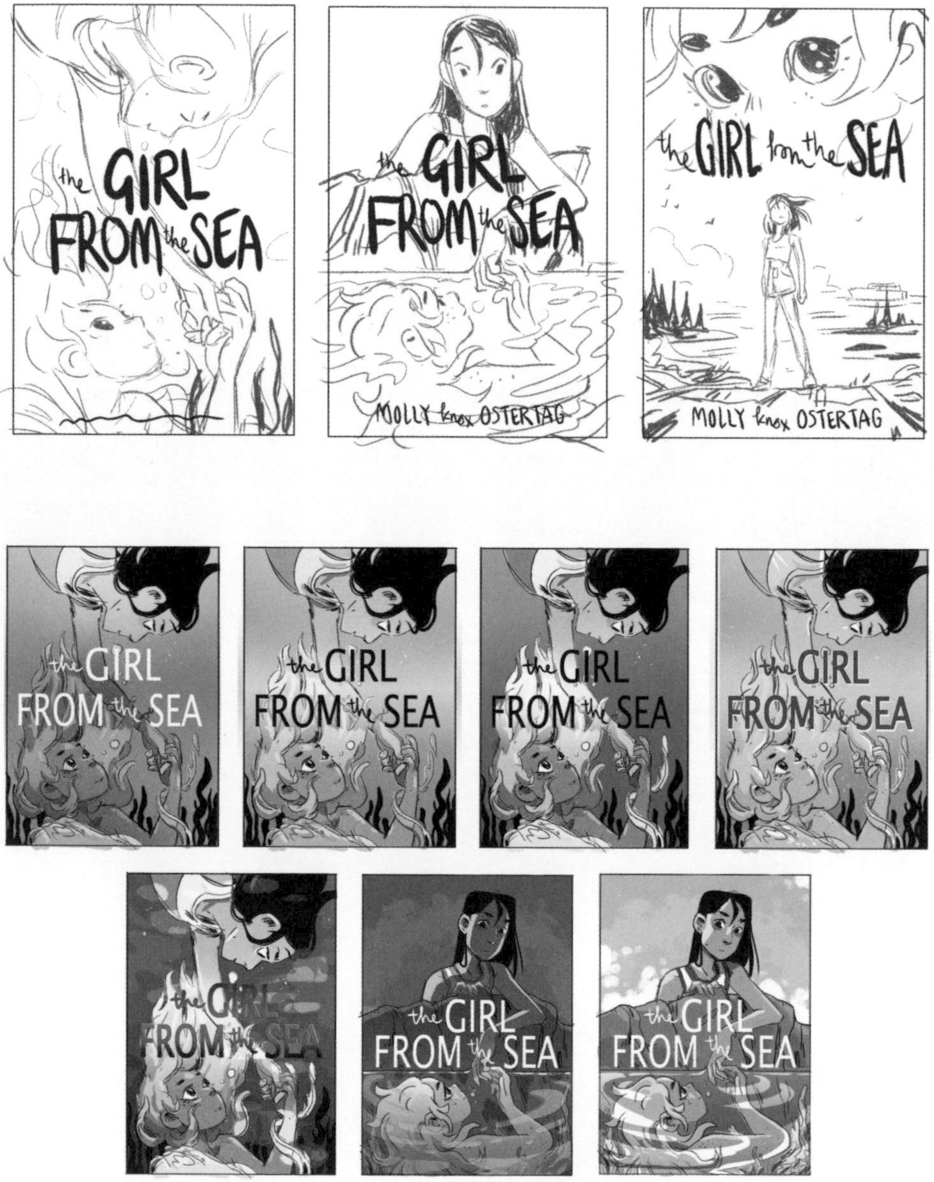
the GIRL FROM the SEA
the GIRL FROM the SEA
MOLLY knox OSTERTAG
the GIRL from the SEA
MOLLY knox OSTERTAG
the GIRL FROM the SEA
the GIRL FROM the SEA
the GIRL FROM the SEA
the GIRL FROM the SEA
the GIRL FROM the SEA
the GIRL FROM the SEA
the GIRL FROM the SEA

ACKNOWLEDGMENTS

This book is very close to my heart, and it's exciting and vulnerable to have it out in the world. I'd like to thank my agent, Jen Linnan, and my long-time editor, Amanda Maciel, for believing in this story and shepherding it through many, many drafts. Phil Falco and Shivana Sookdeo made it look beautiful, and Maarta Laiho brought a sense of life and place that literally made me cry the first time I saw the colored pages.

My wife talked through story points, encouraged me when I was anxious, and was the first person to read it. This is a story about queer romance and transformation and finding oneself through loving someone else, so in many ways it is a story about the two of us. Thank you for all of it, my love.

Wilneff Island is where I spent every summer as a kid. My parents made a home out of a tiny fishing shack on an island without plumbing or the internet, and it was perfect. Thank you for kayaks, and stories about talking seals, and letting me run wild and barefoot across the island all summer long. It will always be the most beautiful place I know.

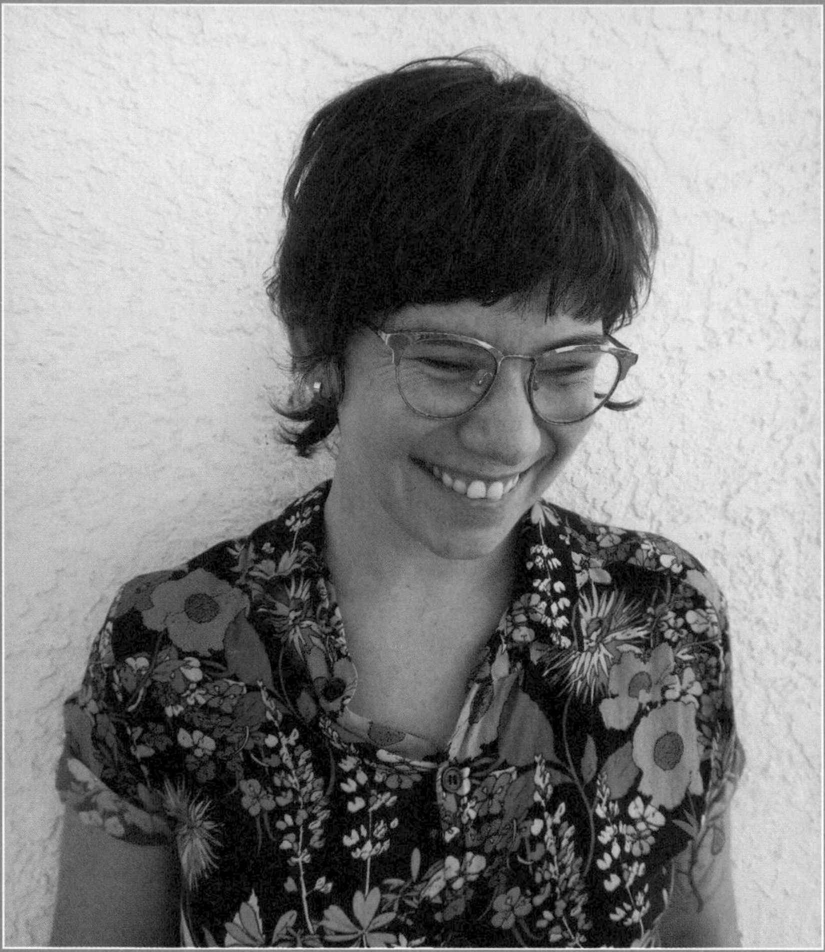

Photo by Noelle Stevenson

MOLLY KNOX OSTERTAG

is the *New York Times* bestselling author and illustrator of the acclaimed Witch Boy trilogy: *The Witch Boy*, *The Hidden Witch*, and *The Midwinter Witch*, as well as a writer for animation. A graduate of the School of Visual Arts, Molly was featured in the *Forbes* 30 Under 30: Media list in 2020. She lives in Los Angeles with her wife, two cats, and a very cuddly dog. You can visit her online at mollyostertag.com.